DEVIANT KNIGHT

KNIGHT'S RIDGE EMPIRE #4

TRACY LORRAINE

Claimed by Theo

EMMIE

The sound of a single gunshot pierces the air and my heart jumps into my throat as I watch one of my only friends stand over the man she just took to the ground.

Pride for my girl swells in my chest, but then I look down at Joker, blood oozing from his chest.

I have no idea what he's done, but there's obviously a very good reason that my friend is still staring down at him with a fierce expression on her face and her gun still trained on his head.

My heart thunders in my chest as memories of the time I've spent with Joker in the last few weeks flicker through my mind.

I wouldn't call him a friend, really, but he's been nothing but nice to me since I turned up at my pop's compound and demanded that I was allowed inside. Him and Xander being the youngest members—or prospects—of my pop's club means we had a little more in common than with the other grumpy, old bikers.

I want to stop her, but I know I can't. This is bigger than my opinion of the guy bleeding out on the floor. It's beyond what I understand about the relationship between the Royal Reapers MC and the Cirillo Crime Family.

My heart thunders as reasons why Stella would have a gun pointed at Joker flicker through my mind.

Surely he wasn't the one trying to kill her?

Surely not.

He was so sweet. Caring. The way he talked about his family, how desperately he wanted to make his dad proud of him.

Why would he want to hurt Stella?

But before I can figure any of that out, her gun fires again.

"No," I scream, seeing the bullet hole in his head and his body fall limp against the dirty floorboards of the clubhouse.

But no one hears me. No one even turns to look at me.

Dropping my head into my hands, I squeeze my eyes closed.

That didn't just happen. It can't have done. I'm dreaming. I must be.

"Open your eyes," a deep, rough, yet familiar voice says.

I don't trust that voice, but still, it doesn't stop me from complying.

My eyelids flicker open and suddenly, I'm not watching someone I thought I knew dying on the floor. I'm the one on the floor with a gun trained on them. Only, it's not Stella holding the weapon, but *him*.

Theo Cirillo.

Son of the boss. Ruthless, devious, heartless. And the bane of my fucking life.

My entire body trembles as his dark, empty eyes narrow on me.

He's waiting for me to fight, to beg and plead with him not to do it.

But why would I?

If he wants me dead, he'll kill me.

And really, what do I have to live for?

"Go on, arsehole. Do it," I taunt. "If you're man enough."

A loud bang forces me to sit up as my heart beats so fucking hard it makes my head spin. My body trembles, and I'm covered in a sheen of cold sweat.

"Oh my God," I mutter to myself, dropping my head into my hands. "It was just a dream." Just a fucking dream.

So why does it feel like he was here? Like he was watching me?

There's another bang, and after a few seconds

and a glance at the clock, I realise that it's just Dad back from work.

"Fuck my life," I mutter, throwing the covers off and padding down to the bathroom, hoping that splashing my face with cold water will wash away the lingering fear that dream dragged up.

I shouldn't be scared.

I'm *not* scared.

At least, that's what I continue to tell myself.

I pee without putting the light on before ripping the door open again and coming face to face with a shadow in the darkness.

A terrified shriek rips from my lips before light floods the hallway and burns my eyes. They instantly water, but I blink, forcing them to focus.

"What's wrong?" Dad asks, ducking down so he's eye level with me.

"N-nothing. I was just still half asleep," I lie. "I wasn't expecting to find anyone loitering out here."

"I wasn't—whatever. You should go back to bed."

I nod at him, although I already know that I'm not going to be going back to sleep anytime soon.

Closing my bedroom door, I lean back on it and tip my head to the ceiling.

I'm fucking exhausted.

Almost every single night since *that* night, I've had the exact same nightmare. Each time there's something a little different, but every single time it concludes with Theo putting an end to the bullshit tension that's between us.

It's stupid.

I mean, I know he hates me. He's made that more than obvious in the weeks since I started at Knight's Ridge and somehow managed to find my way into his life. But I'm not sure he'd ever waste the time or energy to actually kill me.

Pushing from the door, I stalk back over to my bed and pull the covers around me while my eyes continue to adjust to the darkness once more.

It's December, it's arctic outside, yet still, the curtains billow in the wind from my open window. Something that drives my dad insane.

"If you want to get a job and pay the gas bill, then feel free."

I laugh, hearing his voice in my head as clearly as if he'd just said it.

Tugging the sheets up to my chin, I lie on my side, watching the movement of the curtains and the different shapes that appear on the wall from the streetlights outside.

Eventually, the lingering fear from my dream begins to fade, and finally, I drift back off into a peaceful sleep.

Although, when my alarm blares the next morning, I don't feel anywhere near rested.

With heavy limbs, I dress for school, pulling on the fucking awful uniform complete with pleated skirt and tie, and drag my hair back into a low ponytail. I don't have the time or patience to do anything else with it.

My makeup, however... I spend plenty of time on that, perfecting my dark, brooding, resting bitch face.

With a spray of my favourite perfume, I double-check my face, making sure my heavy winged liner is on point, and tap my fingertip to my lip to make sure the deep red has dried before throwing my bag over my shoulder and swiping my leather jacket from the chair.

"Morning, Em," Piper, Dad's fiancée, sings when I join her in the kitchen.

Like most mornings, Dad is nowhere to be seen after working long into the night before scaring the ever-loving shit out of me.

"Excited for your last few days at school?" she asks, kickstarting the coffee machine beside her.

"Yep, can't wait," I deadpan. "You know how much I love that place."

She chuckles at me. "Three weeks off can't come soon enough then."

Three weeks of no school, and more importantly, no Theo Cirillo. I have no fucking clue what his game plan is, but recently he seems to be popping up even more than usual.

If he liked me, I might think he was doing it on purpose. But we all know that can't possibly be the case.

He's just... driving me fucking crazy.

"You all sorted for next week?" I ask, although I already know she is.

Dad and Piper might have only been planning their Christmas wedding for a few weeks, but everything is already in place. And thankfully, their plans involve us all leaving London for five days.

I can't fucking wait.

"You know it. I'm picking up our dresses after school. I've got my hair and nails appointment tomorrow night. I can still add you if you want—"

"No, I'm okay," I say, for what I'm sure is the millionth time.

I like Piper. No, I love Piper. She's given my dad everything he's been missing all these years, made him smile in a way I don't ever remember seeing before. For that, I will forever be grateful for her.

Plus, she also helped open my eyes to the side of my family that Dad has tried to keep me away from for the past seventeen years.

If it weren't for Piper, then I might not have discovered just the kind of men my pop and uncle are.

I've always known they were scary, and a few years ago I overheard Mum telling someone about their 'club'. I thought it was a joke until I Googled the Royal Reapers and discovered just how scary the men I'm related to really are.

The fact that my dad was ever involved in that kind of life shocked the hell out of me. He might be a tattooed, bike-loving, hulk of a man. But part of a motorcycle club? I had no fucking idea they even existed outside of Netflix and films.

My internet searches and the gossip I heard when people discovered my surname should have been enough, but after my uncle made the dumb-arse decision to abduct Piper a couple of months ago to settle some old bullshit feud with a club that doesn't even exist anymore... Well, I was more curious than ever about the life my dad had been brought up in, and the lives some of my relatives still live.

Piper eyes my chipped black nails but wisely keeps her opinions to herself.

She's going to get me in a proper dress next week, and fucking heels. She must be aware that she's already pushing her luck.

"I'll redo them, I promise," I assure her. I also plan to re-dye my dark hair just for the occasion.

"It's going to be perfect," she tells me, her eyes going all sappy as she thinks about tying the knot with my dad.

"It will."

The thought of getting dressed up in a white gown and committing my life to another isn't something I've ever thought about for myself. It's just a bullshit piece of paper that people seem to think means something. As if spending a ton of money to feed a lot of other people, most of whom you don't actually want to spend time with, ensures a happy and successful relationship.

I laugh to myself and roll my eyes so hard it hurts.

"What was that?" Piper asks, dropping some bread into the toaster.

Okay, so maybe it wasn't to myself.

"Nothing. Just remembered that I need to be in early to hand something in," I mutter, lying through my teeth.

"Do you have time for breakfast?" she asks, her brows pulling together.

Watching her slide into her stepmother role makes my heart ache.

Not because I don't want her to—I'm more than happy having her in my life. What hurts is watching her being a better mother to me than my own has been in seventeen years.

Pain slices through my chest as I think of that woman.

Shaking my head, I lock those thoughts down. Nothing good can come of thinking about *her* or how she abandoned me.

"I'll be late tonight, I've got training," I say, thinking of the kickboxing class both Dad and Piper believe I've signed up to. "Have a good day."

"Please don't get a black eye before the wedding," Piper calls, but I'm long gone, shoving my feet into my boots and grabbing my bike keys.

Without looking back, I make my way down

the back garden to the shed at the bottom where Dad and I keep our bikes.

I can't help but smile when I see my baby.

That's exactly how she looks parked next to his beast of a bike. A baby.

After opening up the double doors, I wheel my girl out, lock the shed back up and throw my leg over.

Riding her in my school skirt in this weather isn't exactly ideal, but the sun is shining and quite frankly, I don't care.

Pulling my helmet on, I secure the strap under my chin and kick the starter.

She's nowhere near as powerful as Dad's, but a thrill still shoots through me as the engine rumbles to life between my legs.

I've known I wanted a bike from as early as I can remember. While everyone around me was dreaming of the day they turn seventeen to get their car licences, I just wanted this. I did my first test on my sixteenth birthday, but Dad refused to buy me a bike, claiming that my school grades weren't good enough to deserve it.

I argued that if I went to a decent school, my results wouldn't be so dire. Well, just look where that got me. In this shitty uniform, attending one of London's most prestigious private schools and surrounded by the fucking mafia.

I can't help but laugh at the irony. Dad spent

his life trying to protect me from the Reapers and landed me straight into something worse.

He knows, of course.

He's not an idiot.

Probably how he managed to sweet-talk me into that place when I'm far from Knight's Ridge material.

I failed almost all my exams thanks to the shocking education provided to me by the drowning staff at Lovell Academy on my old estate.

I can only assume that he was expecting me to make zero friends at this place and stay well away from the conceited wankers who think they run the fucking school.

Unfortunately for me, the two friends I have managed to make are connected to them.

Stella, the only girl I've ever met who gets me without even having to talk has fucking shacked up with one of them, and Calli, my most unlikely of friends, is also a fucking mafia princess, her older brother being one of the aforementioned pricks.

They both think it's highly amusing that I can also claim my princess title, although mine belongs to the Royal Reapers MC.

It suits me more. The bikes, the leather, the black. But hell, I'm so far from a princess it's not even funny.

Calli is the princess. She's the girly one who does what the men in her life say, or at least she did before she became friends with me and Stella.

Now, every time I see her, she's breaking more and more rules. Rebelling against the shackles she's been bound to her whole life.

It's hella amusing to watch. Especially when it's around Nico, her older brother, as we wait for that vein in his temple to burst.

I'm just waiting for the day she announces she's screwed one of his mates just to piss him off and get rid of that pesky V-card. That's a sure-fire way to make him blow.

I'm still a distance from school when I spot a familiar car in my mirror.

"You've got to be fucking joking," I mutter to myself, glaring at his reflection as if he can see my response to his presence.

I purposely slow down, smiling to myself as I hog the lane, refusing to move over to let him past.

Smug satisfaction floods my veins, knowing that it's going to piss him the fuck off.

He rides my arse the whole way to Knight's Ridge. Even when he could have overtaken me, he never bothered—much to the delight of the drivers behind him who were beeping their horns in irritation.

The whole thing just amused me more.

By the time I turned into the school entrance and looked back, I had a long train of pissed-off rich bastards who wanted to show off by revving their pretentious V8s.

I shake my head as I pull into the space I've

claimed as mine. How Dad ever thought I'd fit in here is laughable.

I understand what he's trying to achieve. He's trying to right a few wrongs of my mother's making. But still.

I stare up at the building that houses most of the sixth form and let out a long sigh.

"Didn't want to move out of our way, bitch?" some girl barks in my direction. When I glance over my shoulder, I find an imitation Barbie standing beside her fire-engine red BMW. She really should have just gone all out and got a fucking pink one.

"Bite me," I hiss, flipping her off.

She blanches at my reaction. Clearly, she hasn't come across my brand of bitch yet.

Turning my back on her, I lock up my bike—not that it's really necessary around all this wealth, but it makes me feel better knowing that my girl is protected.

Pulling my hair tie out, I ruffle my fingers through the lengths before dragging it all into a messy bun on the top of my head with not even a mirror in sight, a move that I'm sure the Barbie princess behind me will be horrified with.

I've barely taken five steps from my bike when his voice cuts through the air. My entire body tenses as the deep rumble flows through me, and like always, I chastise myself for having any kind of reaction to him.

Spinning around, I continue walking backward as I glare pure hate at him.

Although, I'm pretty sure my expression falters a little when I get to see just how fucking hot he looks.

Dickhead.

His hair has been freshly cut, the sides shaved close to his head and the top longer, flopping over his brow. My fingers twitch to reach up and brush it back from his eyes. But obviously, I lock that little urge down. I have zero desire to touch him in private let alone out in public. The scruff on his face is a little longer than usual, and fuck, it makes him look even more dangerous.

"What's wrong, Miss Daisy? Didn't you enjoy riding my arse?"

His jaw tics as he glares back at me.

"What? Cat got your tongue, Cirillo?" Ripping my eyes from his, I glance at his Maserati. The one I accidentally drove into a rather large wall not so long ago. Whoops. Is there really any wonder he hates me? I've never driven a car, and the first wheel I get behind is his bazillion pound Maserati.

His fault. He gave me the keys and told me to leave that burning building as fast as I could. What did he expect? Running was hardly the fastest option.

"Your car's looking better than the last time I saw it," I comment. It's been in the garage for weeks.

"Yeah, no thanks to you," he mutters, closing the space between us now that I've slowed to a stop for fear of falling on my arse.

"Did you actually want something? Or did you just want to look at my pretty face?"

"Hardly," he scoffs, storming straight past me as if he wasn't the one who called my name across the car park only a minute ago.

"I'll take that as a no then. I hope you have a great day too."

He walks off, and just as I think he's not going to react, he looks back over his shoulder. His dark, deadly eyes hold mine for a beat before they drop to my legs.

Rolling my eyes at him, I hitch my bag up higher on my shoulder and take off in the same direction, *not* staring at his arse in his fitted trousers as he marches toward the entrance.

2

THEO

"What's wro— Ohh," Stella sings as I storm toward where she and Seb are sitting in the common room.

Both of them are on laptops, probably still desperately trying to catch up on all the shit they missed over the past couple of months.

"What did you do?" Seb asks, his eyes following someone else across the room. It doesn't take a genius to work out who.

"Why do you immediately assume that I did something?"

They both focus back on me, raising matching brows.

"You two spend too much fucking time together," I hiss, taking off in the direction of the coffee machine.

I only make it two steps before I realise that *she* beat me to it.

Sensing me approaching, she glances back.

"Just can't stay away, can you?"

"Keep dreaming, Ramsey."

I close the space between us, crowding her against the machine as it prepares her coffee.

It's dangerous. One day she's going to whip a knife out and sink it right into my chest, I'm sure, but I can't deny my desire to make her squirm.

She tries so hard to appear unaffected by me. And to others, it might look like she's not. But I know differently. I see it. Her dark chocolate eyes almost turn black when I'm close. The corner of her right one twitches and she breathes that little bit harder.

It's fucking addictive to watch.

Unlike usual, though, her eyes break from mine at my words.

"Wait," I say, possibly jumping to conclusions but running with it anyway. "You did, didn't you?"

"I did what?" she hisses, turning her attention back to her almost full mug.

"Dream of me."

"Fucking hell," she breathes, reaching for her mug and taking it from the little stand. "You really do think a lot of yourself, don't you?" But as she says the words, it's impossible to miss the slight reddening of her cheeks.

Oh yeah, I hit the nail right on the head.

"So do you, if your reaction is anything to go by. Wanna tell me about it, sweetheart?"

"Don't fucking *sweetheart* me. The only dreams I've ever had of you involve me holding a gun to your fucking head."

"Kinky, I like it."

"Jesus. It's too early for this shit. Move, unless you want to wear this."

"I'm sure I could handle it."

Her eyes roll so far back in her head I can't help but wonder how much it hurts before I take a step back, allowing her to flee—although as she moves, all I really achieve is getting a noseful of her scent.

A shot of desire hits me like a fucking lighting strike.

Reaching for a mug, I start the machine once more and wait not so patiently for it, a series of curious eyes drilling into my back.

That's only confirmed when I turn around and discover just how big my audience is.

Ignoring Stella's glare, I turn back to Seb and make my way over.

"What?" I ask when he just studies me with amusement.

"Oh, nothing, bro. Nothing at all."

"What are you working on?" I ask in a pitiful attempt to distract him.

"An English lit assignment. But that's not important." He slams the lid of his laptop down, keeping his attention fully on me. "What I really want to know is why you're stalking your little biker bitch more than usual."

"I'm not stalking her."

"Oh?"

"So you didn't just happen to be in the library late on Tuesday night when she was also in there?"

"Firstly, how the fuck do you know where I was Tuesday night? And secondly, it was a fucking coincidence that she was working there too," I argue.

"She wasn't involved, Theo. How much evidence do you need to get over it?" he asks, reminding me of the reason I started gunning for Emmie.

The second I realised who she was connected to, alarm bells started ringing. I should have figured out there was more to her sudden appearance here than met the eye. No one from the Lovell Estate just suddenly gets a place at Knight's Ridge.

Seb might be right, she might not be lying about not being involved with what Joker was planning, but add what Dad told me recently, and I don't believe she's entirely innocent for a second.

"Whatever you say," I concede, not wanting to get into another debate about Emmie's innocence in trying to kill his girl.

"It's over. Let's just leave it in the past where it belongs."

"Is it, though?" I ask, thinking of the man we've still got detained, trying to get the answers that Toby deserves.

"As far as Emmie is concerned, yeah. Just let her get on with life."

"She's still spending time at the Reapers compound," I point out.

"So? It's her grandfather's club. Why wouldn't she spend time there?"

"I just don't like it," I say, crossing my arms over my chest and resting back in my chair. The urge to turn around and look at her is almost too much to deny, but I force it down.

I've got a fucking job to do, and it doesn't include showing my hand too early.

If I want to get the answers I need, then I need... I need her to trust me.

I almost laugh out loud at that thought.

What the fuck was my father thinking when he put this fucking plan into action?

He's not a stupid man. Far fucking from it. So why he thought I was the one for this job, I have no fucking clue. Well, actually, I know damn well why he did it, but that's beside the point.

He took fucking liberties by doing what he did behind my back. I might be going along with it for the good of the Family, but if he thinks I'm happy about it, then he's got another think coming. The second this is sorted, he's going to get me out of it as simply as he seemed to get me into it.

"We're heading to homeroom," Stella says, stepping up behind Seb and looping her arms around his shoulders, dropping a kiss to the side of his neck.

"Okay, baby," he damn near purrs like the whipped motherfucker he is.

I never thought I'd see Seb willingly hand his balls over to a woman, but we've all had front row seats as he's let Stella walk all over him. Fucker doesn't even seem to care, either. Mind you, from the amount of fucking sex he's getting, I can kinda understand why. The pair of them fuck like rabbits. Not having to listen to them go at it every fucking hour is probably one of the only good things about my coach house going up in flames.

We might still live in the same building, but thankfully, I don't hear a peep from them in the flat downstairs.

I'd have got my own back if I could have found a girl who even stirred an ounce of interest in me.

For some reason, all the faceless, nameless women of my past didn't hold the same appeal.

I blame Seb and the way he and Stella are together. Even when they hated each other, there was just something... something deeper than I've ever felt.

Damn it, they've fucking broken me despite the fact that I've spent almost all of the last few weeks with a raging boner and the bluest balls on the planet.

Listening to their moans and calls for God have been all kinds of torture, and I can't deny that I need to shift some of the tension pulling my muscles tight. The hours I've spent in the gym and with my own hand only get me so far.

Maybe getting my dick wet will even make *her* a little easier to deal with.

"Come on," Seb says, clapping me on the shoulder. "It's time to move. You can lose yourself in your dirty fantasies about fucking Emmie over her bike in class instead."

"W-what?" I ask, barely registering his words. "That wasn't... I wasn't... fuck you, man. Fuck. You."

He's still laughing as he joins Alex, Nico and Toby, who are loitering by the entrance, having only just showed their faces.

"Morning, ladies," Alex sings happily. "What's got his knickers in a twist?" he asks, eyeing me suspiciously.

"Not being able to get in Emmie's. Standard," Seb happily announces, a little too loudly.

"You fucked her the night she gave you a black eye though, right?" Nico asks, clutching at straws. "I always knew she'd like it rough."

Ignoring them, I barge past, my shoulder colliding with his as I make my way out into the corridor.

"Theo, wait," a feminine voice calls as I make my way down the hall.

Fighting a groan, I turn to look at Sloane as she all but runs to catch up with me.

She either doesn't notice that I quite clearly don't want to talk to her, or she just flat-out ignores it, because she launches into a clearly practised speech about the economics project we've been paired up to do.

The deadline for it isn't until the new year, and I had every intention of just doing it over the holidays and handing it in without any drama.

I don't have the patience for Sloane, Teagan, and Lylah and their bitchy drama, and I already know that I'll somehow find myself in the middle of it if we have to start working together.

"So I was thinking we could meet between Christmas and New Year. I could come to your new place, you could show me around."

Her words blur to nothing as we keep walking, and it's not until a familiar stare makes my skin prickle with awareness that I pay attention to my surroundings.

Looking up, I find Emmie standing in the doorway to the girls' toilets, glaring at Sloane. I swear, I can see all the ways she wants to hurt the girl by my side in her gaze.

Interesting, seeing as she's usually planning my slow and painful death in her head.

Without thinking, I reach out and wrap my arm around Sloane, gripping her hip and pulling her into my side as we continue walking.

"Yeah," I find myself saying as we pass the

bathroom. "That sounds like a good plan. I can't wait to show you my new place."

I catch Emmie's eyes narrowing before she disappears from my vision.

Unfortunately, by the time we've rounded the corner, Sloane is more than comfortable with her own arm locked around my waist. And as much as I want to rip her from my side, I can't make a scene.

"This is me," I say, slowing beside the classroom I start all my mornings in.

I come to a stop, ready to duck into the room and leave her behind, but her fingers grip my jacket and I have no choice but to turn back to her.

"This was nice," she says, staring up at me with sappy eyes and an easy smile on her lips.

Easy. Yeah. That's one way to describe her.

"Yeah. Lovely. You're going to be late. Your tutor room is upstairs, right?"

She leans into me, clearly happy that I'm aware of her schedule.

Her hand slips inside my jacket, resting against my abs.

"We should talk more at lunch... about our project."

I don't need to look up from Sloane's light blue eyes to know that Emmie is passing us. The loud stomp from her non-uniform biker boots is a dead giveaway, plus the fact that her tutor room is right beside mine... It was inevitable.

Knowing that she's been hanging out in the

library during lunch for the past two weeks, I find myself telling Sloane to meet me in there.

"It'll be nice to spend some time together again. I've missed you, Theo."

Her hand slips up to my chest before she wraps it around the back of my neck.

Heat burns the side of my face and I turn to the source right as Sloane's lips land on my cheek, narrowly missing my own.

Emmie's face is twisted in disgust before she disappears inside her classroom.

"I'll see you later," I say coolly, dismissing Sloane.

It might be an abrupt end to our short time together, but I already know it won't be anywhere near enough to stop her from getting carried away with herself.

Sloane, Teagan, all of them, all they want is a chance with us. It's pathetic. And admittedly, it's partly our fault. When we were younger and a little more naïve than we are now, we loved the attention they provided us. The benefits that came with putting up with their constant whining and bitching sure made up for it.

Ducking into the room before she has a chance to have a second attempt at that kiss, I fall into my seat, Alex and Seb immediately dropping on either side of me.

Their eyes drill into each side of my head, but I keep my eyes focused on the front of the room, on the projector screen that's already illuminated with our form tutor's first class of the day.

She's a statistics teacher, and as they wait me out, I silently work out the answers to the questions she's got on the board, ready for her year twelves.

"You're going to say nothing about that?" Alex finally says, waving his hand toward the door.

"Nothing to say."

"Riiight. Sure there's not."

Slouching down in the chair, I continue working my way down the sums as our tutor appears and begins our day the same as she does every morning.

The ping of my phone pauses the conversation I'm having with my mum after leaving football practice and Knight's Ridge behind for the day.

I might have moved out, but that doesn't mean I don't take advantage of any meal she offers me.

Plus, as much as they annoy me, hanging out with my little brother and sisters isn't always hell. Not that I'm going to tell them that.

Alex: Might want to get your fat arse to Mickey's.

Theo: To watch you get knocked out again? I'm there.

Alex: Nah, Nico is going down tonight. I can feel it.

Theo: So… why do I need to be there?

Alex: Wait…

So I do, staring at the screen, waiting for something to happen. And when it does, it was so far from what I was expecting that I almost fall backward off my stool.

"You okay?" Rhea asks from beside me where I've been helping her with her maths homework. Quickly, I lock my screen before the nosey little shit notices what caused that kind of reaction within me.

"Y-yeah. I actually need to head out," I say, glancing over at Mum with an apology in my eyes, knowing that she's already had to change tonight's dinner plans with me turning up unannounced.

But as ever, she looks totally unfazed.

"Is everything okay?" she asks softly, understanding written all over her face.

She probably thinks I've just been summoned by Dad or Uncle Evan, not that an image of a sweaty girl with her hands wrapped fighting a big bad biker just landed on my phone.

"Yeah, everything's great. I'm so sorry."

"I'll plate it up for you when it's ready. If you have time, swing by later and get it."

"I will do. Thank you, Mum."

"Anytime, sweetie. You know that."

I'm halfway across the kitchen when my annoying little sister pipes up.

"You know he's going because of a girl, right?"

"Rhe," I growl.

The most innocent smile lights up her face. Conniving little witch. "What?" she asks, her voice cracking as if she's actually scared of me. "That was a picture of Emmie on your phone, was it not?"

My fists curl and my teeth grind.

"Something we should know?" Mum asks, looking a little too excited.

"No, and I'm not going to see her, just because..." They both stare at me with expectant, excited looks on their faces. "Because I'm not. Excuse me."

I duck out of the room but not before I hear Mum call, "We both love Emmie. She's so sweet."

I scoff as I pull the front door open. "Sweet my fucking arse."

I march toward my car and hate that every time I now look at it, I see her. I can picture her sitting in the driver's seat, her slim fingers wrapped around the wheel, as she drove my poor girl into a fucking wall.

I almost didn't bother picking her up when the garage called to say she was ready. I almost just told them to sell it, knowing exactly what would happen the next time I saw her, and I was fucking right.

I swear to fucking God, the whole interior smelled like her too when I dropped into the seat.

It was my own fault, I knew that, but in my panic, while the building began to burn around us, the only thing I could think about was getting her out, getting her to safety.

Fuck knows why I cared. But at that moment, I did. Too fucking much.

Irritated with myself, I jab my finger against the start button and back out of the driveway, ignoring the black, charred ground where my old home used to be. I guess I should be glad that's gone, because just like my car, she was everywhere inside there, too.

My penthouse is safe. Clear of her face and cutting comments. It's exactly how I intend on keeping it. Well, as long as Dad allows it.

My grip on the wheel tightens until my knuckles turn white.

Mickey's might actually be exactly what I need.

3

EMMIE

"**H**arder," Xander barks.

My chest heaves as I stand before him, taking orders like a little bitch. Although, if I'm going to take orders from anyone, then I'm happy for it to be him, because, man, he is fucking fine.

After fight night, I thought he'd laugh me out of the compound when I asked if he'd train me. I'd heard rumours around the clubhouse that he was a hotshot in The Circuit, but seeing as my pops and uncle had flat-out banned any of their brothers from inviting me to a fight, I was yet to see him in action.

The second I did, I knew I would do whatever it took to get myself in a ring with him. To fight, of course. Although, I'd be hard-pressed to say no to any other kind of training he might be up for.

Shame he friend-zoned me from the moment he discovered who I was related to.

Apparently, fucking your prez's granddaughter comes with a life sentence, and Xander is taking that threat seriously, goddamn it.

Pulling my arm back, I try again, slamming my fists into the foam pad things he holds up for me.

My entire body is covered in a sheen of sweat and I bounce on the balls of my feet, throwing punch after punch, imagining the red thing before me is Theo's face. Images of him flirting with Sloane in the library at lunch fill my mind. She was lapping up his attention, running her hand up his arm, brushing his hair back from his brow just like I'd imagined doing myself in the car park this morning.

Damn it.

"One more. Give it to me."

"Argh," I scream. Putting my entire weight behind it, I launch myself at Xander.

"Yes, Emmie," he praises. "You'll be taking my space in the ring in no time," he says, dropping the pads and grabbing the bottles of water beside us. But before his fingers even reach them, a round of applause sounds out from behind me.

Spinning around, I come face to face with two guys who make me groan out loud.

"Looking good, Princess Emmie," Nico says as both he and Alex take a leisurely stroll around my body.

"What the fuck are you doing here?"

Alex chuckles, finally finding my eyes once more.

"I think the bigger question is what are you doing here, shorty?"

"What the fuck does it look like?" I hiss, holding my hands out to my sides, and as if I've given them permission to perv on me, their eyes drop once more, taking in my sports bra and shorts.

Great.

"Thanks," I mutter to Xander when the bottle of water he was getting for me hits my fingers.

"Did you guys need anything?" he sneers at Nico and Alex over my shoulder. "We're in the middle of something."

Raising his arm, Nico scrubs his hand down his face.

"We gotta go talk to Mick. Please continue."

The smug as fuck look on his face should really have clued me in to what he was going to do, but as they walk off toward the office at the back of the boxing gym where all the guys train, my only reaction is to breathe a sigh of relief. A mistake, I realise not thirty minutes later.

"Oh, give me fucking strength," I mutter as I watch a familiar figure stalk in front of the floor-to-ceiling windows of one-way glass that looks out over the car park.

Xander uses my moment of distraction to his benefit, and only a second later, my feet disappear from beneath me and all the breath rips from my lungs as my back collides with the soft mat.

He straddles me, pinning my arms above my head. I'm not entirely sure it's an official move, but it sure gets the attention of our new spectator.

"See what happens when you get distracted." Xander winks, although the annoying fuck makes no move to get off me.

I thrash beneath him, but his hold only gets tighter.

The entire left side of my body burns with *his* stare, but I refuse to look over, to acknowledge that he's even here.

"You're transparent as fuck, you know that?"

"Fuck you, X. You've no idea what you're talking about."

The opportunist fuck leans forward and runs his nose up my cheek.

"What the—"

"You wanna drive him crazy, Princess Em?"

"You want my knee in your balls?"

He chuckles, his grip on my hips and wrists tightening to ensure I can't fight back.

"You think I didn't see him slip into the room Cruz hid you in the night your mate blew Joker's brains out? Or," he asks, just to add salt to the wound, "the way he looks at you?"

"Like he wants to kill me? Yeah, I get that a lot from him."

He chuckles again, the deep rumble along with his manly scent starting to mess with my head.

I've had plenty of thoughts of being beneath Xander, sure. But in none of my fantasies were we were discussing Theo fucking Cirillo. Although I must admit, I'd quite happily let him watch.

Heat rushes through me at the thought.

Christ. What is wrong with me?

"I think you might have made your point," I hiss at Xander, who seems more than happy pinning me to the mat.

"Oh yeah, do that again. His eyes almost popped out."

"Jesus. Guys and their pissing contests," I mutter, thrashing one more time, and thankfully this time, he rolls off me. "Thank you," I breathe, pushing myself up to sit and wiping the sweat off my brow with the back of my hand.

I look up just in time to see Theo slip into the same room that I assume both Nico and Alex are in.

"You gonna tell me what went down with Joker yet?" he asks for what must be the millionth time since that night.

"Nope. Not my story to tell," I say, although, to be fair, I don't know enough of the details to be able to share the whole story even if I wanted to.

Things since that night have been weird.

I finally felt like I might have found my place in the world with Stella and Calli, and then I discover that the entire time, or for the past few weeks at least, they all had suspicions that I might have been involved in the hits on Stella.

She might have assured me that she never once suspected me, and that she adamantly told the guys—Theo—that he was barking up the wrong tree, but it still hurt. Hell, it still stings a little.

Add that to the guilt over the fact that Joker *was* using me to get to Stella, well... yeah, safe to say, things have been awkward.

I've never had what I'd consider real friends before. There were a few people I hung out with from my old school, but I never found my ride or die kind of friend there. I thought I had here, and now I'm almost back where I started, not fitting in again.

And if I'm honest, I miss them.

"Wanna talk about it?" Xander offers, dropping down beside me and leaning back against the ropes.

"I didn't think you were interested in teenage girl drama," I spit, repeating just a few of his words from one night when I got a little more than tipsy at the clubhouse and came on to him.

I cringe at my memory of that night. Although not as much as when I recall his words about not screwing teenagers.

Xander is twenty-one. It's not like he's old and was talking to a child. That rejection hurt more than it should. I swallow it down, attempting to forget about it, like I'm sure he has.

Glancing over at him, I find his brows pinched, regret etched into each crease.

"I was drunk that night, Em. I didn't mean it quite like it came out."

"Sure you didn't," I mutter, looking away once more, tipping my head back to stare at the ceiling.

"I want to be your friend, Em. I just... I can't give you any more than that," he says quietly, and I swear I hear pain in his voice.

I nod, taking a sip of water.

"Sounds good to me."

"And anyway, I'm pretty sure I don't stand a chance."

"W-what are you—"

I glance at him as he nods in the direction of the office, and sure as shit, Theo's paying zero attention to whatever is happening inside the room and is instead standing at the window, watching us.

"O-oh no. There is nothing going on there," I argue.

"Yet," Xander helpfully adds. "There's nothing going on there *yet*."

My lips part to argue, but when I finally manage to drag my eyes away from Theo's angry ones as he glares at me, I find that Xander is ducking out of the ring.

"Good practice today, Em. Few more sessions

and you'll be able to take any of those motherfuckers down."

That's the plan, I think to myself.

"X," I call before he gets too far away. "Does he know we can see him?"

"Probably not. Mickey has that fancy glass that can be switched to one way. You're at an advantage right now, so make the most of it."

"Get the fuck back in here then," I demand. "I suddenly feel like doing another couple of rounds."

He laughs, and for a second, I expect him to turn me down, but then he pushes his light hair back from his brow and rejoins me in the ring— only he ups the ante this time by dragging his sweaty shirt over his head and fighting me shirtless.

It pains me not to shoot a wicked smile in Theo's direction, especially when I do glance over Xander's shoulder and find his face hard with anger, his eyes searing through Xander's back as if he can see through him to me.

"Come on, Princess Emmie. You can take him," Alex says a while later while Xander and I are still going.

My body aches and my stomach grumbles with its need for food, but my desire to torture Theo is stronger.

"We're done," I finally say, now that Alex and Nico have emerged from the office, although Theo has vanished.

"You know what you should do?" Nico offers.

"Don't tell me, it involves fewer clothes," I mutter, catching a cloth that Xander throws at me, using it to wipe my face.

"Well... that wasn't what I was going to say, but now you mention— Ow," he complains when Xander walks behind him and slaps him upside the head.

"You wanna fucking start something?" Nico asks, turning around and squaring up to him.

Xander just flips him off and disappears to the other side of the gym, clearly not thinking that Nico is any kind of threat.

"You and Stella," Alex says thoughtfully.

"Yes," Nico adds. "*That's* what I was thinking."

"She'd have me tapping out in seconds," I admit.

I haven't actually seen her fight, but I know that she'd show me up in a heartbeat.

She's been training her whole life. I've barely just started.

"I'm more than happy to find out. Bet Seb would be too."

"I'm not fighting Stella just to feed your sick fantasies."

Grabbing my bottle, I climb out of the ring.

"Well, as fun as this was, I'm gonna—" I thumb over my shoulder and turn my back on them before they can come up with any more perverted ideas.

I push through the door to the ladies' locker room with a heavy sigh.

Maybe asking Xander to train me here was a bad idea. I should have known they'd turn up eventually. I heard more than a few rumours around the clubhouse when the guys were talking about The Circuit to know that both Alex and Nico fight. It only stood to reason that they'd show their faces at Mickey's eventually. I guess I just naïvely hoped they'd train elsewhere and have nothing to do with that place.

Yeah, keep lying to yourself, Em.

The locker room is deserted. It's not exactly a shock, seeing as I was the only female in the entire gym.

Twisting the key in my locker, I pull out my towel and wash bag before heading for the shower, pushing thoughts of the guys, or more specifically one guy, from my head and focusing on the homework I've got to crack on with when I get home.

4

————

THEO

Leaving Mickey behind, I scan the gym, telling myself that I'm just seeing who's here and not looking for her.

I find Alex and Nico now in the ring that Emmie and Xander were in, but I see no sign of either of them.

Alex catches my eye as he gets Nico in a headlock and tilts his chin in the direction of the ladies' locker room.

Images of the two of them in there together fill my mind, and I take off before I've even thought about what I'm doing.

My fingers curl into fists as I march across the gym and push through the door.

Thankfully, I'm not immediately met by the image of Xander nailing Emmie against the wall as was just playing out in my mind, there don't seem to be any grunts and groans of pleasure coming from deeper in the room, either.

But the sound of running water does hit my ears, and my curiosity gets the better of me.

My shoes squeak against the tiles, but it's not enough to alert anyone to my arrival, and I soon discover that Emmie isn't expecting me... because when I come to a stop in the doorway that leads to the showers, I find her standing with her back to me, water sluicing down her skin and over her round arse.

This was probably a mistake.

But despite knowing that, I don't turn around and walk out unnoticed.

Instead, I lift my hands and curl my fingers around the doorframe as I watch her.

Taking a step back from the water, she reaches for her shampoo and sets about washing her long, dark hair.

All the while, I stand there like a fucking creep, watching her every move with my cock trying to punch its way out of my trousers and my need to make her turn around becoming almost too much to bear.

I should walk away before she sees me. I know I should. But despite the fact that my head knows it, my body doesn't make any attempt to move.

My first clue that she knows I'm here is that she doesn't turn to wash the bubbles from her hair. The second is her voice, which scares the shit out of me because I was lost watching the white foam race down the smooth skin of her spine and over her arse.

"Take a photo if you want. It'll last longer."

"Who said I didn't the last time?"

The last reaction I expect from her is laughter, but that's what I get.

"Of course you did. Don't tell me, you printed it, pinned it to your wall and now spend your free time throwing darts at it."

"Something like that, yeah," I mutter, knowing full well that if I did have a naked picture of her on my phone then I'd be doing something very different with it.

"So, did you actually want something?" she asks, her voice as cool as ever despite the fact that she's completely naked before me.

Releasing the doorframe, I scrub my hand over my face, willing myself to walk away, but all I find myself doing is leaning my shoulder against it and continuing to watch her.

My fucking need for this woman, despite the fact that she drives me to the edge of insanity, clearly knows no bounds. Just like my complete lack of care for her privacy.

"You should probably leave," she continues when I don't answer her question. "Xander's meeting me here in a minute. I can't imagine he'll be too impressed with an audience."

She shoots a look over her shoulder, a knowing

smirk curling at her lips when she catches the furious expression on my face.

No one ever gets to see under my mask. Okay, maybe the guys on occasion. But not a girl. Never a fucking girl.

Until this one.

"I don't have an issue with watching," I lie, folding my arms over my chest.

"Right," she mutters, combing the conditioner through the lengths of her hair before grabbing the shower gel and squeezing a blob into the palm of her hand.

"So is he coming or not? He doesn't seem to be in any rush."

She stills at my words.

Yeah, just like I thought.

"Did you actually come in here for a reason, Cirillo? Or did you just want to ruin my evening with your irritating presence?"

"I want to know what the hell you're doing here. With him." I damn near growl the last two words out as my frustration of her inserting herself into my life once again begins to get the better of me.

The girls at school, Sloane, Teagan, they're irritating as fuck, constantly following us around and waiting for us to throw them some kind of a bone.

But Emmie, she's an entirely different creature. She wants to be around me about as much as I want to be around her, yet we constantly seem to be near each other for one reason or another.

"Xander?" She damn near purrs his name. "Well, in case it wasn't obvious when you walked in," she shoots over her shoulder, "he's training me. That way, the next time you're a complete cunt to me—which is often, I might add—I can give you more than a black eye."

"Do I need to remind you that that black eye wasn't even intentional? Unless you've miraculously recovered your memory, something tells me that you still don't remember what happened that night."

She huffs in irritation, her shoulders bunching as she washes herself.

Yeah. Thought not.

"It doesn't matter. Next time, intentional or not, I'll make sure it hurts more."

She rinses out her hair, allowing the bubbles from her body to pool at her feet.

Turning the water off, she holds her arm out behind her. "Pass me my towel."

"Because you asked so nicely?" I ask, quirking a brow at her.

"Don't be a child, Theodore."

My jaw tics at her use of my full name.

I've only ever been called that by my parents when I'm in trouble, or when Rhea wants to piss me off.

Glancing around, I find a towel hanging on the hook a little down from me.

"This one?" I ask, lifting it from the rail.

"Yes," she hisses as I hold it out. The only problem is that she's on the other side of the room and has no chance of reaching it.

"You remember what I said about the next time you're a cunt?" she mutters, twisting her hair and wringing out the excess water.

"I'm confident it'll be worth it."

She lets out a long huff of frustration before she throws her shoulders back and turns around.

Holy fucking cunt.

Despite my attempt to slam my mask back into place, my chin damn near hits the floor as my eyes drop to her body.

"Why the shock? You were the one who took my wet underwear off that night, were you not?" she asks, tilting her head to the side in an attempt to be cute as she closes the space between us. Her perky, perfectly-sized tits bouncing a little, her hips swaying with each step, and the confidence on her face even without her usual armour of dark makeup damn near brings me to my knees.

"Why? Would you have preferred it were one of my brothers?" I hold her eyes, but fuck, it's hard. Pun intended.

"You mean, would I want anyone other than you touching me? Yes, yes I would. Now, would you excuse me? I'd like to get dressed."

Like the gentleman that I'm most certainly not, I move aside to allow her to pass—only, she doesn't make it that far before my fingers wrap around her throat and I haul her back against me.

"I don't know what you're playing at, but I'd advise you to stop."

"Me?" she asks with a laugh. "I'm not the one who jumped the second his mate messaged to say I was here. Be careful, Theo. You're starting to look a little desperate."

A bitter laugh falls from my lips.

"Hardly."

"Oh, that's right. That whore, Sloane, probably blew your tiny cock at the back of the library."

A growl rumbles up my throat, my fingers squeezing her, my fingertips digging in against her racing pulse.

"My daddy is getting married next week," she tells me randomly, damn near giving me whiplash. "You leave a visible mark on my body, he'll fucking shoot you. Boss's kid or not."

"Ah, Daddy Ramsey," I mutter. "Tell me, *Princess*," I sneer. "Does he know you're playing with the big boys yet?"

"I'm not scared of my dad, Theo." Even without looking at her, I know she's lying through her teeth. "And," she adds, "I'm not fucking scared of you, either."

Before I know I've moved, I flip us, pressing her

back against the wall and glaring down into her dark eyes.

My chest heaves with a mixture of desire and frustration which only gets stronger and more unbearable as I hold her stare.

"No?" I ask, my grip on her throat unrelenting. "You should be." Leaning in, I brush my lips against the shell of her ear, making a violent shudder rip through her body. "Do you have any idea what I'm capable of? Any clue to the pain I can cause you?"

She shrugs as if we're talking about nothing more serious than the fucking weather.

"You're scary, I get that, Theodore. You've been trained your whole life to intimidate, torture, and maim. What the fuck ever. I'm not one of your victims. I've done nothing to you, so I suggest you just walk away and turn your misplaced anger on some cunt who deserves it."

I pull back, my head spinning with confusion and pride over her words.

My eyes hold hers, searching to find the truth that I know is lingering in their depths.

"I already told you, I had nothing to do with Joker. If I did," she swallows regretfully, "I'd have fucking told you. Well... maybe not you, but Stella."

I'm still glaring death down at her when the door crashes open beside me.

"Bro, are you done fucking Em— oooh, nope. Still trying to get it up, huh?" Alex asks as I twist to the side to block her from his view. A move I instantly fucking regret when she notices and smiles up at me like she just won gold.

"Fuck. Off," I spit, not even bothering to look back at him. "How'd you even know I was in here, anyway?"

"Dude, please. I'm not a fucking idiot. Where else would you be?"

My teeth grind and I finally release Emmie's throat to turn to look at my dickhead friend.

"Get out, we're in the middle of something."

"Or join in," Emmie offers, slipping from her hiding place between me and the wall.

Alex's face lights up like it's fucking Christmas already, and my heart damn near drops into my feet.

"Emmie," I growl, turning back to her. I expect to find her standing there naked for Alex to ogle.

"What, Theodore? I thought you liked playing games with your friends."

She clutches the towel that she must have ripped from my hand to her chest. It covers all the important parts, sure, but she's still giving Alex way too much of a visual.

"What's going— Oh, sweet. Orgy in the locker room, I'm so in," Nico announces happily, making my blood boil in my veins.

Jesus fucking Christ, give me strength.

"Get the fuck out, both of you," I bark, taking a step closer to Emmie.

"We got your back, bro. Performance anxiety isn't a joke," Alex says, and I don't need to look to know he's fighting a laugh. "Happens to the best of u— wait, nope. Never happened to me. Enjoy his flaccid cock, Emmie."

Grabbing a bottle of something from the side, I launch it at Alex's head.

Stupid fuck doesn't see it coming, and it connects with his temple with an audible thud.

"Motherfucker," he growls.

"Get out before I fucking make you," I say coldly.

They might be happy to rib me, but equally, they know when to quit. And thankfully, they're more than able to read that that time is right the fuck now.

"That wasn't fucking necessary," Alex mutters, rubbing what I assume is a massive egg on the side of his head from the force of that hit.

They both back out of the room, leaving the two of us alone once more.

"You can fuck off, too. In case you missed the clues, I don't want you anywhere fucking near me."

"Oh, so your nipples aren't hard and you're not wet for me?"

"I'm cold, arsehole. And no, dry as the fucking Sahara. Happens every time I'm around your ugly face."

I can't help but smile.

"You're a really shitty liar, you know that, Hellcat?"

"Hellcat, really? That's the best you can come up with?"

She rolls her eyes but quickly realises her mistake when her back collides with the lockers, my forearms pressed on either side of her head.

Her chest heaves, defying her words from only a few minutes ago about how affected by me she is.

"What do you want from me?" she asks, her voice a little smaller than it has been since I walked in on her.

My eyes bounce between hers, searching for the answers I've been sent for.

"What are you hiding, Hellcat?"

"You want my secrets, *Boss*?"

My jaw tics as I continue staring at her.

"You'll have to break me first."

Pushing from the lockers, I take a step back.

"Don't challenge me, Ramsey. You should know by now that I never lose."

"Newsflash, wanker, nor do I."

Pulling the towel from her body, she holds it out to her side before letting it drop.

"Don't rush. It'll be the last time you see it."

It fucking pains me, but I rip my eyes away from her body, lifting my hand to push my hair back from my brow.

"Keep lying, Hellcat. I dare you."

With that threat issued once more, I spin on my

heels and walk away from her, the image of her porcelain skin and rosy pink nipples firmly locked away in my wank bank for later.

"That was quick. Did you even get it—"

Alex's words are cut off when my fist collides with his jaw and sends him stumbling back.

"Shut. The. Fuck. Up."

Nico watches with his mouth gaping open as I barge through both of them and blow out of the gym without looking back, stretching out my fingers.

EMMIE

"**F**uck," I breathe, falling back against the lockers and tipping my head up to the ceiling, willing my body to calm the fuck down.

I've never reacted to any boy the way I do to Theo fucking Cirillo.

Sure, I've had my fair share of questionable hookups in my not-so-recent past, but almost all of them were drunken or high mistakes to pass some time.

Never have I ever stood in front of a guy and had to talk myself down from climbing him like a fucking tree.

But hell, he makes it hard work not to just say fuck it and go for it.

There's a small part of me, the little whore that lives inside my cunt, mostly, that thinks I should just throw caution to the wind and jump him. Fuck out all this hate and tension that crackles between us every time we're near. But then the bigger, more rational part of me pipes up, and I remember that I'll probably have to bathe in bleach after he's come anywhere near me.

His rep around Knight's Ridge might not be as bad as Alex and Nico's, or even Seb's for that matter—pre-Stella, obviously—but fuck. I know for a fact that he's touched enough of those fake Barbie dolls to know he doesn't actually want me.

It's just me and my lack of action since moving here that leads me down the wrong road.

So what, he's pretty? Scratch that. Smoking fucking hot and exactly my type.

He's a class-A bellend.

Ignoring the towel that I dropped to the floor, I drag my clothes from my locker and tug on a pair of leggings and an oversized hoodie to hide in.

I run a brush through my wet hair. but I bother even attempting to dry it. I my shoulder and call it a day.

"Haven't I already suffered enoug to myself when I step from the locke find tweedledee and tweedledum waiti "You're missing your third musketeer I t not bothering to stop.

"Yeah, he left in dramatic fashion. mutters, rubbing at a red mark on his chin.

My eyes widen with realisation as he ste beside me.

"Did he hit you?"

"Don't think he took too kindly to our interruption."

"I wonder why?" I mutter, rolling my eyes again. It seems my eyes are almost always skyward when I'm around these pricks.

"You get him all twisted up, shorty."

"Ugh, don't start with that," I complain, assuming that they can only have got it from Xander.

"It suits."

"I'm short, yeah. I get it. Did you actually want something? Matching bruise on the other side?" I offer.

"Not really, just to say to keep pushing him. I want to see him finally crack."

"And to think, I thought you were friends and valued all his working body parts."

"Cute. I think we all know that when you two collide, it won't be to break bones."

"I can assure you, there will be plenty of blood."

"Fuck yeah," Nico says, suddenly joining the conversation. "I knew you were kinky, shorty."

"Whatever. Have you finished? I need to—"

"Emmie," someone else calls as I point toward the exit, and when I look up, I find Mickey, the owner, marching my way.

Turning my back on Alex and Nico, I happily walk toward him.

"Is everything okay?" I ask. I always feel a little weird, being here, because as of yet, I haven't seen another woman. I know they've got a women's locker room, but I can't help but wonder if Mickey is a bit of a sexist pig who doesn't want any females around.

"I hear you're looking for a job," he says, shocking the shit out of me.

"Er..." I glance over his shoulder and see Xander smiling at me.

Of course.

"Y-yeah, I am."

"Okay great. I need some female presence around this place. I'm sure you've noticed we're usually lacking a softer touch."

"I'm not sure many would describe me as soft," I tell him, much to Mickey's amusement.

"You know what I mean. I just need someone to man the reception, do a few jobs here and there. Nothing too strenuous."

"It sounds perfect, but I need out of school hours."

"Perfect, Tara was a student," he says, talking as if I should have a freaking clue who Tara was. "Just one rule."

"Okay, shoot."

"No fucking my fighters."

I choke on my own breath at his warning.

"Um... s-sure. That won't be an issue."

"That includes Xander."

I can't help but laugh, although it sounds bitter when it hits my ears. "No worries there. I've been severely friend-zoned."

"Good. You're too good, and young, for an arsehole like him." Mickey winks, telling me that his words are far from the truth. I've seen the way Mickey talks to Xander, like he's the son he never had. It's sweet. In an illegal fight circuit/gang kind of way.

I mutter some kind of agreement that I don't really feel.

"So you're in?"

"I'm in. But—" I quickly add. "I'm away next week."

"No worries, kid. We're closed. Start in the new year?"

"Sounds perfect."

"Put your shit in there," he says, handing me his phone. "I'll send you the details. I'll pay you well as long as you prove yourself to be trustworthy, but being a Ramsey, I'm sure there will be no issue there."

"You got it." I salute him and step away. "Thank you. I really appreciate it."

"Anytime, kid. I didn't really see you waiting tables or serving coffee."

"You got me there."

Alex and Nico are nowhere to be seen as I make my way out of the gym, but something tells me they heard all of that. They've probably already informed Theo as well.

Dickheads.

Pulling my helmet on, I throw my leg over my bike and make my way home, my muscles aching from the extra effort I put in with Xander to put on a good show for Theo.

Ugh. What is wrong with me?

Piper is home by the time I get back. She's sitting at the breakfast bar in the kitchen, surrounded by craft shit.

Her eyes light up when she sees me and my heart sinks.

I really, really don't want to spend my evening doing this, but the way her lips curl into a smile as she starts to get ideas stops me from arguing.

"Have you eaten?" I ask, dropping both my school and gym bag to the floor.

"Nope, not yet. I was waiting for you."

Dragging my phone from my jacket pocket, I unlock it and read the message from Calli once again trying to convince me that I want to go to the Knight's Ridge Christmas party tomorrow night.

Closing it down without answering, I open my food app.

"Thai?"

"Sounds good to me," Piper agrees.

"What happened to your pre-wedding diet?"

She winces a little before confessing, "My dress

is a little big. I think I might have gone a bit mad on the rabbit food."

"Told you," I say, remembering the number of times both Dad and I chastised her over her crash diet over the past few weeks.

"I know, I know. I'm a bad role model."

"Dude, have you met my actual mother?" I sass, rolling through the app to find my favourite dishes. "Oh wait, no. No, you haven't." My tone is full of the bitterness and resentment I feel every time I so much as think about my mother.

Useless bitch.

She spent my entire life forcing me to live in hell, also known as the Lovell Estate. She refused to give my dad custody of me despite the fact that he could clearly provide me with a much better life than she could.

We lived in a shitty high-rise flat block with drug dealers and hookers on every corner, and stabbings on almost a daily basis. She jumped from bullshit job to bullshit job, making no effort to ever better herself while she preferred to fill her body with more poison than food.

Piper's concerned stare burns into me, but I don't look up. I refuse to see the pity that I know will be lingering in her eyes.

She understands. To a point.

Her childhood wasn't all sunshine and roses. Her parents were murdered in cold blood while they slept by none other than my pops.

I shake my head.

Fucking hell, I'm surrounded by some fucked-up kids.

Piper, Stella, Seb, Toby. All their childhoods make mine look like a day at the fucking funfair in comparison.

"You want your usual?"

"You know it."

I select our favourite dishes and then pull open the fridge, grabbing us a couple of cans of Coke before sliding on to the seat beside her.

"So what are we doing, then?" I ask, staring down at the cards which are covered in what I know are my dad's sketches.

I run my fingertip over his artwork. He's so fucking talented, it makes my eyes hurt and my stomach knot with jealousy.

For as long as I can remember, he's been my idol, my hero, and I've always wanted to be just like him.

I might have grown up a little since I first thought he literally hung the moon, and I discovered some of his indiscretions, mainly his involvement with the Reapers—granted, he was a kid without a lot of choice in the matter—but I still idolise him. And his talent with a pen, a tattoo machine, hell, anything that makes a freaking mark, is one thing that I wish I possessed.

Art is in my blood. Creating is one of the only

things in the world that makes sense to me, but I'll never be as good as him.

"We're girlifying these."

"Girlifying?"

"Yeah, you know our theme is leather and lace. This," she says, pointing at Dad's black penmanship, "is the leather. We need to add the lace." She pulls over a reel of actual lace and a huge pot of diamantes.

"I'm going to regret this, aren't I?"

"You love it. One day I'll even let you drag me into helping with all yours."

I rear back in shock. "I-I'm good, thanks. I'm not getting married."

"That sounds very final," she says, although there's no judgement in her tone.

"Yup. No offence, but I don't really want to have to rely on anyone else. Ever."

"Understandable," she says, happily cutting a length of lace for her place name. "Just... never say never, Em. You don't know what—or who—is around the corner. Your dad and I should be proof that anything can happen."

"Your story is that of a twisted fairy tale," I tell her. "Two rival gang kids fall in love, and they're banished from seeing each other until they randomly reconnect years later." She laughs at me as I recall the basics of their past. I'm under no illusion that there was a truckload of pain and heartache along the way, too. One of the many reasons I'll never lose myself to a man.

I've spent almost all my life relying on a woman who walked away from me without looking back. There's no way I'm ever giving anyone else the power to hurt me like she has.

Knowing she no longer cares is hard, but I had no choice in loving her. Sadly, no matter how much she hurts me, loving her is ingrained in my soul. Any other human being, though? Nope. My heart is securely sealed in a steel lockbox, and that's exactly where it's fucking staying.

Men are good for one thing, and one thing only.

Hitting those spots even a decent vibrator can't.

I should probably mention that one of Mum's fleeting jobs was an Ann Summers rep about two years ago.

You'll never guess what I got for my fifteenth birthday.

Yeah, mother of the year... I think not.

Although, I got more pleasure out of that gift than I did almost all the others I ever received, assuming she remembered it was my birthday at all, of course.

After telling me again not to discount things in my life that aren't even an option yet, we set to work.

Our Thai was delivered about thirty minutes later, and I pushed aside the assignments I should have been working on in favour of just hanging out with Piper.

It was nice. Probably how mother/daughter time should be.

"You should get to bed," Piper says a few hours later when my eyes are starting to droop. "Your dad won't have you bunking off on the last day of the year." She winks teasingly.

"Would I?" I argue, adding an eye-roll for good measure.

I've had one day off. One. And that was after Seb's mum's funeral when we all got off-our-arses drunk. Also the night I apparently gave Theo a black eye and woke up in his bed, wearing nothing but his shirt, and had dried blood stuck to my face.

To this day, I have no fucking clue what happened.

The only thing I'm confident of is that I didn't fuck him. Thank Christ.

Although, I can't deny that immediately forgetting being that close to him does have its benefits.

"One day, Em. Then you've got three weeks off to forget all about that place."

"And the idiots that attend."

"That too," she says with a laugh. As our Student Welfare Director at Knight's Ridge, she's more than aware of the kinds of students I'm talking about.

The privileged bitches who think the world

owes them something, and the conceited pricks who think they're gods.

"Thanks for this, it's been… fun," I say, taking my plate and empty cans to the kitchen.

"Don't worry, I won't tell anyone you enjoyed yourself. Wouldn't want to ruin your image." I'm almost out of the room when she speaks again, and the words out of her mouth instantly make me groan. "Are you going to the party tomorrow night?"

"Not you as well," I mutter.

"You should go. Might help sort things out with your friends."

My chin drops, but thankfully my back is still to her so she doesn't see my reaction.

"Everything is fine with my friends."

A beat passes, and I look over my shoulder at her.

"Okay, whatever you say. I think you should go, though. Get dressed up, let your hair down. After all, you're going to spend all of next week with a bunch of boring adults." I think of Dad's friends and I can't help but smile. My pseudo uncles are anything but boring. Although they've definitely toned it down a little since finding themselves married and having kids, that's for sure.

"I think I prefer the adults," I confess.

"I'm sure you'll reconsider that after five days away."

"We'll see. Sleep well," I say, bolting from the

room before she can try to convince me to go to that damn party. Calli and Stella don't need her help on the matter.

I change out of my clothes and pull on a shirt that I really shouldn't have kept, much less use to sleep in. Then I grab my laptop and textbooks and I climb into bed to at least make a little progress.

I end up working until I pass out, slumping down on my pillows with my laptop still warming my thighs while the cool winter air from outside cools my cheeks.

6

THEO

"Sorry, son. He's busy," Galen says from his position at a computer in my father's security room.

"Well, he's going to have to un-busy himself. I need to discuss something with him. Now."

Ignoring Stella's dad, I barge through the room. Stefanos, Alex and Daemon's dad, also turns to me, but all the other soldiers working in here wisely keep their attention on the job at hand.

"Theo," Stefanos greets, although I can see the concern glittering in his eyes.

I push it all aside. I don't give a shit what Dad is in the middle of right now.

I knock once out of courtesy before pushing the door open.

There only a very small handful of men who have the balls to walk in on the boss like this, but I'm one of them. Each time, I have this lingering hope that I might be greeted by my dad and not the boss. So far, I've always been disappointed.

I think any memory of the few times my dad put his role as father above this Family are just that —a distant memory.

It makes me sad for Rhea, Atlas, and Larissa.

When I was their age, our granddad was still at the helm. But when he passed away, Dad took over and his life became work.

I get it. Running this Family, the businesses, it's a lot. Something that I'm fully prepared to take over one day, but I'll be fucked if it's at the expense of the kids that have been left at home.

I'm aware that leaves me with two very obvious choices. Don't have kids. Throw myself into this life from the get-go and forget that having a family of my own is even an option. Or have them young enough that I won't have to turn my back on them when the time comes.

Dad's still relatively young. Hopefully, he's still got a few years left. But the lives we live... they're dangerous, and knowing his health is good isn't really a sign that I might have a while before that high-backed chair behind his dark desk becomes free.

Hell, it could be tomorrow for any of us that we know.

But can I be seen to not have kids? Not really.

I'm the heir to all of this. Of course I want to

hand that down to my own son. If I don't, then it'll fall to Altas.

I think of the sweet smile of my little brother, and my stomach knots painfully that soon he's going to start getting inducted to this life. He's ten. When I was his age, I was already shooting a gun with more precision than most adults, and I was only a few short years away from the first time I directed that barrel at a human body.

Granted, it was only to maim, not kill. That came about a year later. But still, memories of it used to wake me up in a cold sweat at night.

I told Dad about it the first time I woke up terrified as this mutilated monster chased me, claiming to get his revenge as he wielded a knife in my face. but he just waved it off.

"It was just a dream. It should be the monsters in real life you should be afraid of, soldier," I remember him telling me.

From that day, he upped my training, making it his sole mission for a few years to make sure I was as dangerous and as mentally fucking screwed up as possible.

He turned me from a kid who was scared of the dark to a ruthless killer to do his bidding.

I've literally followed him to hell and back on his orders. I've trusted him to know what he's doing, but this time... this time, he's gone too far.

"I told you I wasn't to be interrupted," Dad's angry voice booms as I push the door wider and step inside. "Theo," he snaps the second his eyes land on mine.

Thankfully, he's not in here with one of our underground dancers. I guess I should be grateful that it's just him and Evan.

"Had a fun afternoon?" I ask my uncle, who's damn near covered head to toe in someone's blood.

It could belong to one of a million people, but I have a suspicion I know exactly who he's beat it out of.

"You could say that," he says, pushing from the chair in front of Dad's desk and slipping into the adjoining bathroom, I assume to clean up.

Dad sits back in his chair and stares at me.

An uncomfortable silence stretches out between us as I hold his deadly glare.

He might well have turned me into the soldier he wanted me to be, to ensure I wasn't scared of anyone. Sadly, that includes him.

"I'm not doing this," I say eventually when he makes it very clear that he's not going to start.

"It wasn't a suggestion, Theodore. It's a job. A job you're going to take seriously."

"But why? You're going to need to give me more."

He shakes his head, clearly unimpressed with my lack of obedience.

I almost laugh to myself. I've been more than lenient with it. Most normal people would have flipped their fucking lid when they looked down at that contract like I did a couple of weeks ago. Most people would have refused there and then.

What he's asking of me... what he's done without my permission or even knowledge is way beyond the realms of fucking acceptable.

"She giving you the run around already, soldier?"

"She's a pain in the fucking arse. So how about you tell me exactly what I'm looking for and give me half a fucking clue as to what I'm up against here."

His eyes hold mine for another ten seconds before he pulls his phone from inside his jacket pocket and taps on the screen before an unfamiliar voice fills the air.

"It was Emmie," the woman pleads, clearly in pain. "P-please stop. Please don't hurt me. I-I'm sorry."

My blood runs cold at the fear in the woman's voice.

"Is that—"

Dad nods once, confirming my suspicions.

"Fucking hell," I mutter, dragging my hair back from my brow.

"There's a lot you don't know, but I shouldn't need to tell you that Emmie's sudden appearance at Knight's Ridge wasn't a coincidence."

"Just tell me that she's not my fucking sister," I demand, thinking of Toby and Stella, and how if it weren't for Galen then they'd probably have fucked like rabbits to get back at Seb and not been any the wiser of the fact that they're fucking siblings.

"She's not. I can assure you, I have no secret family hiding in the shadows, nor have I ever cheated on your mother."

"Well, I guess that's something," I mutter under my breath.

Although, if we were related it might help cull my unhealthy obsession. *Or just make it even more unhealthy.*

I shake my head at my own thoughts.

"I want to know everything she knows, everything she's done. I don't trust her," he glares death at his phone as if it's the woman he's talking about, "an inch. It's taken weeks to get here. She could have sold out Emmie from the beginning but she didn't, so I'm inclined to think she's telling the truth."

"Great."

"I won't be made a fool of by a seventeen-year-old brat, Theodore. I suggest you get me the intel I need sooner rather than later."

Scrubbing my hand down my face, I try to figure out his game plan, but as ever, my head just spins with the few facts he's trusted me with.

"Why does all of this require a... contract," I finally say, unwilling to call it anything else for fear of making it too real.

"Separate issues. The contract was a peace offering. Revenge is personal."

"Right," I sigh.

"Do whatever it takes. Live out all your dirty little fantasies—or hers. Just get me the answers."

"You want me to fuck them out of her?" I ask, my brows hitting my hairline.

He stares at me, and for a moment, I'm sure I see my father in the dark depths somewhere.

"I know you better than you think I do, Theo. I know you've been pining after her since you first saw her. Go wild. You have my full blessing."

I scoff at that. "Seems to me you've taken this a little further than your blessing, Boss," I spit.

"You can thank me later. Now, was there anything else? We were in the middle of something."

"This is a bad idea," I tell him, narrowing my eyes as I back across the room.

A knowing smile tugs at the corners of his lips. "Just don't kill her... yet."

Without another word, I slip out of his office, not feeling any better about the situation than when I walked in. If anything, the knot in my stomach only grows.

Emmie is guilty of something. Something I need to get to the bottom of. Plus, I need to figure out who the fuck she really is. I fucking knew there was more to the story than anyone was letting on. Kids from the Lovell Estate don't just enrol at Knight's Ridge.

She's got Cirillo Family blood running through her veins, I'd put fucking money on it.

But she's not your sister, a little voice pipes up.

And damn it if my cock doesn't start to swell as images of all the ways I can make her confess her sins pop into my mind.

"Only you would get away with that," Galen chuckles as I storm back through the security room.

"Sometimes he does remember that he's a father as well as a boss," I grumble, keeping my eyes focused on the exit.

"What's he got you doing this time, son?" Stefanos asks as I march past.

"You don't want to know."

I don't know what else they might say. My entire focus is on escaping.

The second I'm in my car, I rev the engine and fly out of my allocated space in the underground car park entirely too fast, considering it's almost full.

I don't drive straight home like I should. Instead, my fingers grip the wheel until they start to cramp as I navigate my way through the city streets like some dickhead boy racer.

It doesn't help, though. When I pull up outside our new building hours later, I'm as restless as ever and ideas of what Emmie might have done run around my head.

She has to be guilty. Surely the blame wouldn't have been placed on her head otherwise.

But what is she hiding?

And why does my father think any of this is a good idea?

"The contract was a peace offering."

Dad's voice is as clear as day, and a shiver races down my spine.

It can only mean one thing. And if I'm right, then Emmie's father really was onto something, trying to keep her away from the club.

She's clearly not safe there if Ram would...

Shaking my head at the utter shitshow my life is turning into, I climb out of my car and head inside with every intention of taking all of this out on the state-of-the-art gym sitting in the basement.

I t doesn't help.

I collapse into bed later that night after pushing my body to the max, punishing myself for everything I've done, all the things I'm inevitably going to do in the future.

Most of which involve *her*.

He might be right about one thing, though—he does know me better than I thought he did, because I can't get her body from earlier, her defiance, her confidence, out of my fucking head.

I crack my knuckles, my newest obsession threatening to get the better of me.

It's dangerous. If I'm caught, I have no doubt

that Emmie's father would find one of his rusty guns and blow my brains out. But it seems the fear just isn't enough when it comes to my addiction to my feisty little hellcat. Plus, it's so much easier to appreciate her when she's not barking insults at me.

Forgetting all the reasons I shouldn't, I jump back up, my muscles screaming at me with every move, but I don't stop. I can't.

I'm just that fucking screwed up.

The drive across town is quicker than usual thanks to the fact that I take the Ferrari, and the traffic is almost non-existent this time of night.

I pull up on the street over from hers so I can slip up the back alleyway between the row of houses unnoticed in the darkness, like I've done more times than I want to admit.

The first time I came here was the night after the funeral. The night after she slept in my bed. The night I carried her passed-out arse from the bottom of my parents' garden, still dripping wet from the pool and with blood trickling down her face from where she'd fallen over.

Getting her in my bed might have been how I secretly wanted the night to end, but her out cold wasn't quite how I intended it.

I might be a lot of things, and I might be devious when it comes to getting what I want, but I drew the line at fucking her that night.

Maybe I can be redeemed after all. I laugh to myself as I scale the small shed that houses both her and her father's bikes before jumping over onto the extension roof.

If this setup didn't allow me easy access to my addiction, then I might be willing to point out to Dawson just how fucking unsafe it is. Especially when she's always sleeping with the window open.

7

EMMIE

When I wake up with my alarm clock blaring, drool dried to my chin, and the early morning sun beginning to fill my room, I can barely drag my eyes open, let alone muster the strength to lift my arm to stop the irritating noise.

When the ringing finally gets the better of me, I flip over with a huff, expecting all my books and laptop to go crashing to the floor with my movement. But to my surprise, no thuds fill the now silent room.

I blink in confusion before I find my dresser across the room with my books stacked up, my laptop resting on the pile.

"Huh." My brows pull together in confusion, but I soon forget about it when my phone starts ringing. "It's too early for this shit," I mutter to myself, pulling down the fabric that had bunched up around my ribs.

I groan seeing Calli's name. I already know exactly what she's going to say.

"Morning," she sings happily the second the call connects.

I groan some kind of response that makes her laugh.

"I'm just calling to remind you to pack a bag for tonight," she pushes.

"Cal," I complain, my voice rough with sleep. "I already told you, I'm not coming."

"And I already told you that you don't have a choice." The sass in her voice makes me smile. It's something that wouldn't have been there when I first met her at the beginning of the school year. The knowledge that Stella and I have corrupted her—I mean, given her the confidence she was struggling to find while being smothered by her entire overbearing family—makes me smile wider than I'm sure I should.

She's not the only one who's changed in only a few short weeks.

I've softened from the girl who barely managed to exist on that shitty council estate, who spent her entire childhood looking over her shoulder just waiting for an attack.

I might still be on my guard, but that's only with one person. I'm pretty confident that everyone else in my life now has something better to be doing.

"I don't wanna party with the rich pricks," I complain.

"You won't be," she shoots back, taking zero offence by my comment despite being from one of the wealthiest families in Knight's Ridge. "You'll be partying with me and Stella."

"Come off it, Stella will be fucking Seb in the bathroom... if we're lucky," I add, thinking of the less than private performances they've put on since they collided.

"Nah, she's on a sex ban for the night."

"Instigated by you, I assume."

"Of course," she says, smugness filling her voice.

The fact that she thinks they'll follow those rules is amusing.

Stella and Seb are a law unto themselves.

"Cal, I really don't—"

"Please," she cuts me off, her voice suddenly small and unsure, "I really want to go this year. We don't even have to stay all that long. I just—"

"Okay," I find myself saying before I really appreciate the repercussions.

I love Calli. She's so sweet, kind. Everything I'm not. And after all the years of being locked in her castle, she deserves to let her hair down.

And who am I to stop her?

We can drink the rich pricks' drinks, maybe

mess up their house a little, and hopefully stay out of trouble.

Nico wouldn't let her get in trouble anyway, and no doubt he'll be there. Just like Theo will. Ugh. My stomach twists at just the thought of his name. Butterflies I try my best to ignore the flutter in my belly as I remember him standing before me last night, caging me in against the wall, staring at my body like he couldn't get enough.

My skin heats, my heart begins to race, and damn it all to hell if my pussy doesn't fucking clench with the need to feel him inside me.

"Yeah?" she asks excitedly.

"Yes, but—" *I need to get laid. No, not just laid, railed so fucking hard I can't remember my own name.*

"But what? Anything."

I shake my head, clearing those thoughts.

I can't. Not with Knight's Ridge kids. I'm not sure those future CEOs and bankers would have any fucking clue how to do it properly anyway.

One person would, and you know it.

"Nothing. I'm just going to need to get really drunk. Or high," I add, not really caring which.

Fuck it. Both. I'll risk the crossfade if it takes me to oblivion for just a few hours.

"That, I can do. Those rick pricks will have everything you need. Promise."

"Glad they're good for something."

"Okay, so pack a bag. I've got cheer after school,

but we're getting ready at Stella's place. I'll meet you both there after."

"I thought we were coming to yours," I say, fighting to keep my irritation inside.

"Nico's being a dick, so Stella offered for us to get ready with her and then Seb can take us."

"Okay," I force out through gritted teeth.

"Awesome. I need to go get ready. Pack something sexy though, yeah?"

I scoff. "Puh-lease, would I do anything else?" I joke, knowing full well that our ideas of sexy are very different.

Callie is very much what I'd describe as a girl, although a much less conservative one since she became friends with Stella and me.

"Just... not too much leather and shit. It's Christmas after all."

"So you'd rather me dress like what? A fairy?"

"Now that I would pay to see," she jokes.

"Yeah, yeah, laugh it up. I'll see you soon."

"Laters," she says, before hanging up on me.

Falling back against my headboard, I let out a long sigh as my phone drops into my lap.

It won't be that bad. Surely, it won't be that bad.

"I s that really necessary?" I mutter, not meaning to say the words out loud and regretting it the second Calli glances over to where Sloane is rubbing herself all over Theo like a bad rash.

"You're not going to let her win, are you?" Stella asks, turning back from sucking Seb's face off, although clearly, she was multitasking.

"Win? I wasn't aware there was a competition."

"Theo doesn't want Sloane, Em," Seb adds.

"Who gives a fuck if he does?" I snap. "They aren't the reason I don't want to go tonight." I wave my hand around the school restaurant at all the idiots we're surrounded by. "They are."

Seb rolls his eyes at my dramatics but wisely keeps his mouth shut.

"It'll be fine. And with you being gone next week, it's our only chance to hang out before New Year."

"You make it sound like I'm going for ages. It's five days. I'm sure you'll barely even notice I'm gone."

"Trust me, I'll notice at the Cirillo Christmas Eve party."

"Wow, maybe I should stay then. Wouldn't want to miss that excitement." Calli's eyes light up for the briefest moment before she realises I'm being sarcastic.

Shadows fall over us and my stomach twists,

knowing that it can only be the four extensions to Seb's side. The sudden tingling of my skin also clues me into whose eyes are currently on me. Apparently, he managed to lose his cling-on.

Four trays full of food land on the table before they join us.

"It's a family event, Calli," Theo growls, but his eyes, his warning, his hate, are fully directed at me.

"Emmie *is* my family," Calli argues.

"Because that will fly with our fathers," Nico scoffs, effectively pissing on her excitement.

"Not that it matters. She won't be here. Where exactly are you going?" Theo asks, his fake interest in my life more than obvious to everyone around the table.

"As if I'm going to tell you," I mutter under my breath.

He stares at me, his lips curling in amusement.

"I'm sure I could find out."

My brows pull at his odd words.

Why the fuck would he even want to know? He should be jumping for joy that he gets five days without my poisonous stare burning into his face.

"Feel free. Turn up if you want. Join our party. Just remember who I'm going to be with," I warn. Although, I hardly think he'd show any kind of fear over my dad and his friends, even if Titch is an ex-Circuit fighter. Champion fighter, I should add.

Theo motherfucking Cirillo doesn't seem to be scared of jackshit. Which is annoying.

I'm desperate to find his weakness.

Anything. Just a tiny little chink in his armour that I can use for my own amusement and entertainment.

Everyone has them.

Seb has Stella.

Hell, even Toby now has Stella.

Nico has Calli. That and his reputation, just like Alex.

But Theo... Nothing seems to faze him, and it's annoying as fuck.

Something will make that cunt crumble. I just need to find what it is.

I think of his brother and sisters the night his coach house burned to the ground. Is it them?

I never got to see how he was with them the night of the fire. Selene, his mum, had got them back to bed before he arrived, but I remember all too well the looks of love and adoration that covered his siblings' faces when they spoke of their big brother.

The image of sitting with them on the sofa, comforting them as his coach house burned beyond the window morphs with the one of him viciously kicking me out.

It was almost as if getting rid of me from his family home, from watching his own home burn was more important than anything else.

I mean, I get it. He thought I was involved. If

the situation were reversed, I wouldn't have wanted him there either. But shit.

How could he seriously think that after sitting with my arms around his shell-shocked siblings, after I dragged Stella across the grass and farther away from the fireball she'd been thrown across the driveway by, that I could have been a part of that?

Stella's my girl. Just like he has his boys. I'd never—NEVER—knowingly let anything happen to her.

If I had any idea what Joker was playing at...

A violent shiver runs down my spine at the thought.

He seemed like such a good guy. But then again, just like I thought earlier, everyone has their weakness, and someone clearly found his.

"Is everything okay?" Stella asks quietly when she realises I'm staring at her.

"Y-yeah. Sorry. Got lost in my own head there," I confess, feeling my cheeks heat a little.

"It's okay, you know. All of that is over." I nod as she smiles at me. But just like all the other times she's tried to reassure me, guilt still twists up my insides painfully.

I should have known. I should have seen something. Helped. Anything.

Instead, I unknowingly allowed him to track my phone and help his little stalking mission.

He knew I was with her alone that night. He also knew that I'd left the building.

If Stella had hesitated for even a few more seconds while she ran back inside… well… she wouldn't be sitting here beside me now.

"I know," I lie, her face growing more and more concerned by the second. "It's just gonna take me a while to get over it."

"You're not the only one," she whispers, only making me feel even more guilty.

I've distanced myself from both Stella and Calli since that night. This is one of only a handful of lunches when I've caved and followed them to the restaurant to eat instead of making my excuses, and I hate that I haven't actually asked her how she is. How she's dealing with what she did that night.

Stella might be fierce and the baddest bitch I know, but she's also got a heart of gold, and I'm not naïve enough to think that taking Joker's life hasn't left a stain on her soul.

I smile back at her, suddenly seeing a darkness in her eyes that she keeps hidden from everyone else.

"We can talk tonight," I promise her, reaching for her hand and giving it a squeeze. "I'm sorry I've been distant."

"You have nothing to apologise for, Em. Let's just… start over, yeah? Get wasted and dance the night away like none of that ever happened."

"Sounds good to me."

The rest of lunch passes like normal. The guys chat about football, work, and other bullshit I'm not the slightest bit interested in while I attempt to drown them out, ignoring Theo's hate-filled stare while chatting to my girls. It doesn't work, though. I have no idea what he's trying to achieve, but all it does is piss me the fuck off.

Halting Calli mid-sentence, I turn to Theo and meet his glare.

"Do I have something on my face or what?" I snap, my lips pursing in frustration.

The corner of his mouth twitches in accomplishment, and I instantly know that I just fell into his trap.

"What?" I hiss when he fails to say anything.

Pressing his palms to the table, his eyes continue to hold mine as he rises.

"I need to go and talk to Coach. I'll catch you all later."

And with that, he picks up his tray and marches away from the table.

"What the fuck is his problem?" I mutter.

The guys all smirk as if they're well aware of Theo's issue, while Stella and Calli just look at me with sympathetic smiles.

"Sloane clearly ain't sucking his cock well enough," I hiss, shooting a look as the girl in question walks back into the restaurant and swiftly spins on her heels to follow him like the pathetic little puppy she is.

Someone scoffs, but I'm too focused on the pair

leaving the huge room to pay attention to who it was.

"Yeah, that must be the issue. Ow, what was that for?"

When I look back after the two of them have disappeared around the corner with Theo's arm locked around her body, his hand possessively on her hip, I find Seb rubbing a sore spot on the side of his head while Stella glowers at him.

"I haven't slept with her," he sighs.

"Oh really? I thought you'd done anyone who has a pussy around here," she snarks.

"Sloane has only ever had eyes for Theo. I left that one to him, just like he happily left Teagan for me."

"How nice of you both," I mutter.

"We were young, dumb and horny," Seb says, like it excuses their obvious lack of taste.

"So what's changed?" Stella deadpans before squealing when Seb jabs his fingers into her ribs, making her giggle and try to fight him off.

We all know she's faking it, because she's proved more than once that she can take all these boys to the floor if she wants to.

"You don't need to worry about Sloane, Em," Alex says in a weirdly serious tone.

My entire body tenses. "You think I'm worried about her? Puh-lease. She's nothing more than a skank trying to fit into a world she knows nothing about."

Both Alex and Nico stare at me as if the words that just passed my lips came out in another language.

"What?" I ask, but whatever they might have wanted to say is cut off when Toby joins us.

"Dude, put my sister down. Makes me wanna puke," he scoffs, although there's a smile on his face and a twinkle in his eye.

When I glance over, I find Stella and Seb locked in a heated kiss once more.

"Didn't stop you having a go," Alex happily points out.

"You're never going to forget about that, are you?"

"Mate, you wanted to bang your sister. Of course not."

Toby's hand lifts and he runs it over the back of his neck awkwardly.

"If I'd have known then—"

"Leave him alone," Stella instructs. "It could have easily been one of you instead." She pins them both with a look, but the pair of idiots just grin back at her.

"Kinky," Alex mutters.

"Jesus."

"On that note, I'm gonna—" I nod toward the exit.

"Go see if she's on her knees for him yet?"

"That could have really hurt," Alex sulks as he

just about catches the knife before it collides with his head.

"I thought you played with the big boys, Deimos," Stella jokes.

"Okay, I'm out. I'll see you after?" I say to Stella.

"Yeah, meet me in the car park after class. We'll head to ours to get ready and order food."

"Sounds good," I say, forcing a smile on my face as I think about what comes after all that.

Briefly, I wonder if I'll be able to find a way to get out of the party and go home instead, but then I see the excitement in Stella's eyes and my stomach sinks. I'm the world's shittiest friend.

With a pained smile, I back away from their table and make my way over to the giant doors that provide my escape.

I stop to let someone else inside when I get there and make the mistake of looking over my shoulder.

The six of them are lost in a new conversation, probably an important one they couldn't have in my presence.

My heart sinks.

The connection Stella and I share might be stronger than with any other friend I've had, but I'm achingly aware that I don't belong in their world.

She's one of them.

Part of their family.

I'm on the outside, with the wrong blood running through my veins.

I'm always going to be the outsider, and it's only made worse by the fact that their leader wants me as far away from them all as possible.

With a sigh, I take a step forward, leaving them to it and making my way to the bathroom to wallow in self-pity.

I hate it.

I've felt a lot of things in my life, mostly anger. But this pity party I seem to be unable to drag myself out of right now is one of the worst.

I've always been alone. That's something I'm more than used to. But to be a part of something and then be pushed to the sidelines—even if it is only in my own head—well, it fucking hurts.

I push open the door to the bathroom and immediately come face to face with three people I could really do without being anywhere near.

Teagan and Lylah turn their annoyingly beautiful resting bitch faces my way, and I swear they actually roll their eyes as if my mere presence is boring them.

"Excuse me," I say, holding my head high.

There's no way I'll ever cower to these bitches.

I'm almost at the cubicle when Sloane's voice pierces the air.

"He doesn't want you, you know that, right?"

My spine straightens and my fists curl. The image of ploughing one into her perfectly symmetrical face flashes through my mind. I bet she wouldn't look so irritatingly put together with blood gushing from her nose.

I've got a million responses on my tongue, but in my need to not get into another fight at school, especially days before Dad's wedding, I bite down on the inside of my lips, physically stopping any cutting responses from spilling free.

I lock myself into the cubicle, but I can't relax. Something tells me that comment was only the beginning.

"So you've seen his new penthouse," Teagan starts before my arse has even hit the toilet.

"Oh. My. God. Yes!" Sloane gushes. "It's amazing. And," she adds. I can tell whatever is coming next is purely for my benefit, "I'm the only one to be invited in, other than the guys."

I roll my eyes so hard it hurts. It's no secret how selective Theo has been in inviting people into his new place. I'm not sure if that's because the old one burned to the ground, or just because he was fed up with constantly having everyone and their wife inside, but he's done a full one-eighty, keeping everyone but his inner circle—and Sloane the slut, it seems—out.

Since I made my excuses to avoid attending Stella's Thanksgiving a few weeks ago, not feeling ready to face them all after the night at the Reapers compound, I've dodged any other invites to their new place. But I've overheard enough times just how antisocial Theo has become since getting his own place that no one else has access to. It makes me wonder which version of Theo is the real one. The one who allowed everyone to socialise in his house, or the recluse.

Something tells me it's the latter. Although he never seemed that bothered by everyone always loitering in his coach house.

"I'm going to spend the weekend with him. Hang out at his penthouse. Clothing, not necessary, if you know what I mean."

I manage to catch my groan of irritation before it erupts.

Yes, Sloane. The entire fucking school knows what you mean.

"Man, I'm jealous as fuck." I think that's Lylah, but to be fair, it could be either of them.

"It's their fault, you know. Since *they* started here, they barely look at us."

It doesn't take a genius to work out who *they* are.

"I don't even get what they see in them. Neither of them is even that pretty. And fighting... ugh. That's never attractive for a girl."

Flushing the toilet, I drown out their words as I right my uniform and pull my mask into place. I walk out with my shoulders back and my head held high.

"Oh, whoops," Teagan shrieks in faux horror. "We forgot you were in there."

"Sure you did," I state, holding her eyes as I make my way to the basins.

Turning the tap on, I focus on what I'm doing while the three of them watch me with judgemental eyes.

"Did you want the answer to your question?"

When no one responds, I continue. I had no intention of leaving without pointing this out anyway.

"The reason *they* are different is because they don't just immediately fall on their backs and open their legs in a pathetic attempt to trap a guy who is way, *way* too good for them."

Teagan scoffs. "Not what I heard. Stella fucked Seb before she even knew who he was. She—"

Holding my dripping wet hand up, I cut her off mid-flow.

"Entirely different situation. Stella isn't a cheap whore who only wants Seb as arm candy. She *is* one of them. She belongs with them. And, more than that, she proved her place.

"Just like you three proved yours. They made use of you when you were fresh and fun. Now... now they want something a little more... challenging. And I'm sorry to tell you, your overused, easy cunts aren't it."

Grabbing a paper towel, I dry my hands, ball it up and throw it into the bin, and all the while they stare at me with gaping mouths.

"It was fun talking to you. I hope you enjoy the rest of your day."

I almost think they're going to let me escape without getting the final word, but I'm hardly surprised when Sloane pipes up before I walk through the door.

"I'm still the one who's going to be in Theo's bed tonight."

"Good for you. Enjoy it while you can."

I let the door swing closed behind me and make my way down the hallway with a smug smile pulling at my lips. It's either that or force myself to acknowledge the jealousy that's knotting my stomach at the thought of Sloane getting that close to Theo tonight.

"What's got you so happy?" an amused, familiar voice says from behind me.

"Oh, just making enemies in the bathroom."

Calli turns around just in time to see the trio exit the toilets.

"Ah, but I can't lie, I'm disappointed. None of them are bleeding."

"Yet," I add, much to her amusement.

"True. You've got all night to break one of their noses."

"Don't tempt me," I mutter, falling into step beside her as we make our way through the building, ready for our afternoon class.

"I'll meet you at Stella's later," Calli says before we part ways, her toward history and me toward my favourite lesson of the week. Art. The one place I can escape those vapid bitches and just be me.

I nod in agreement and make my way down to my class, more than ready to put my AirPods in and drown out the world while I sketch.

8

EMMIE

"This place is insane," I say to Stella as I follow both her and Seb into their new fancy flat.

The huge floor-to-ceiling windows showcase the views of the city beyond, and the inside... well it's something I could only dream of.

It's so spacious, modern yet homely and comfortable at the same time. I have no idea how Seb managed it, but it's incredible. No wonder he gets laid at every possible moment.

Glancing over my shoulder, I find a soft smile playing on Stella's lips as she stares up at Seb like he just single-handedly hung the moon.

"Yeah," she sighs like a lovesick puppy, and I wait for the inevitable sound of lip-smacking to commence, but thankfully, it never comes.

"I'll leave you both to it," Seb says, and when I

look back once more, I watch him peck Stella on the lips and disappear down toward the bedrooms.

Silence settles between us, and the knot I've become more than used to when it comes to everything that happened with Stella returns full force.

"You want a drink?" she asks, thankfully breaking it.

"Uh... yeah, sure."

"I thought we could order takeout. Any preference? I was thinking Chinese, it's Calli's favourite."

"Chinese is good with me," I agree, trailing her into the kitchen.

She pulls the fridge open and grabs a couple of bottles of something before knocking the tops off and passing one over after I've hauled myself up on the counter.

Her eyes hold mine for a beat and they narrow in concern.

"Em, everything is fi—"

"Don't," I whisper. "Don't say it's fine. It's not."

I quickly look over my shoulder to make sure we're alone and that Seb isn't loitering, listening to me be anything less than the heartless bitch I portray myself as.

"Em?" she questions, taking a step closer, her brows pinched.

"I just... I almost got you killed, Stella. And I

had no idea. I was literally leading him to your door."

"You didn't know," she argues.

"But I should have." I blow out a long sigh and drop my head. "I ignored all my dad's requests and stepped foot into a world he warned me about. I might be okay, but look what happened."

"You couldn't have known. None of us could. If anyone suspected that Jonas had a secret family, a son who quite clearly wanted to impress him, then maybe all of this would have been over a long time ago. Hell, maybe it wouldn't have even started."

I shake my head, unable to believe it all.

Jonas, the man who everyone thought was Toby's cunt of a father, ended up not being his father at all. Just a fucking psycho hell-bent on ensuring his legacy within the Family.

"If anything, this is our fault. Theo thought for a while that the Reapers were involved. If we'd have said something instead of letting him run around throwing accusations, then you might have had a reason to be a little more alert."

"He really thought it was me."

She doesn't respond, but her eyes soften.

"He knows it wasn't now."

"Does he?" I ask, thinking back to our interaction only last night at Mickey's.

He still hates me, possibly even more than he ever did when he thought I was involved with this shit with Stella.

"Of course. Theo's just..." She trails off, seemingly as unable to figure him out as I am. "I dunno. Stubborn." She shrugs.

"I was going to say psychopath, but I guess stubborn works too."

She throws her head back and laughs before muttering, "You have no idea."

The demand for her to explain what she means by that burns on the tip of my tongue, but I manage to swallow it down.

The last thing I want is for tonight to turn into one long-arse conversation about how fucked up Theo and the rest of the guys are.

"So what are we ordering?"

Thankfully, my question distracts her and she grabs her phone, pulls up the menu and hands it to me.

"Pick whatever dishes you want. Seb can eat whatever we can't."

"Sounds good to me."

I select my favourite dishes as well as Calli's before handing it back for her to add to.

"So any idea what's happening tonight?" I ask once the order is placed.

"Just a Christmas party with the conceited fucks of Knight's Ridge."

"Exactly as I feared."

"The benefits of partying with kids who have more money than sense... more alcohol and drugs than you can imagine."

"I think I'm going to need it."

"I'm not carrying your drunk ass out of that place," Stella sulks with a smirk.

"Was I asking you to?" I sass.

"Oh, maybe Theo will rescue you again, give you another opportunity to give him a black eye."

"I don't need him to give me an opportunity. And we all know he deserves it. Oh," I say, suddenly remembering my less than delightful encounter with the Witches of the Ridge earlier in the toilets and recounting it.

"Ugh, you'd have thought they'd have learned their lesson by now. Dumb bitches," Stella mutters, draining her drink. "How're things with your dad?" she asks, changing the subject.

"Yeah, good. He's too focused on next week to notice what I'm doing."

"I can't believe he hasn't figured out that you've been hanging out with your grandad and uncle."

"I'm on borrowed time, I know. I need to talk to him."

"Maybe while you're away. It might give him time to cool down so he doesn't immediately do something stupid."

"It'll be fine," I assure her, although my heart picks up speed and my palms begin to sweat just thinking of confessing that I've been doing the one thing he adamantly asked me not to when I moved in with him, let alone after what went down with Piper, Cruz and Pops.

She gives me a sceptical look but thankfully changes the subject, and I allow myself to forget everything that happened recently and just enjoy hanging out with my friend.

It's nice. No. More than nice.

It's exactly what I didn't know I needed.

Calli arrives not long later with both her bags and the takeout we ordered after she intercepted the delivery guy in the car park.

"Where's Seb?" she asks when she sits at the dining table beside me and fills her plate with a spoonful of every dish we ordered.

"Hiding down there," I say, pointing down the hall.

"You've banished him?" Calli asks Stella.

"Banished? No. I just don't think he was up for girl time."

"Why isn't he with the guys?"

"No idea. Said he had some shit to do."

Callie shrugs, unconcerned about what Seb's actually doing, and begins stuffing her face.

"I'm sorry, the party is where?" I ask, pinning Calli with a death stare.

She's sitting at the dressing table while Stella curls her hair.

"Um..." She hesitates nervously. "I thought I told you."

"No. No, you didn't. I would remember if you'd told me it was at fucking Sloane's house. Jesus, Cal." I reach for the bottle sitting on the bedside table and swallow a couple of shots.

In a huff, I fall back onto Stella and Seb's bed.

"Okay, so I didn't because I knew you wouldn't come, and I wanted you to. *We* wanted you to."

Stella also looks over at me, a hopeful smile playing on her lips.

"We're just gonna go and get wasted. Show them assholes how to really party."

"But—"

"We don't even need to see them. Or the person she'll most probably be hanging off."

Of course all the guys are going.

Calli turns around completely when I don't respond.

"Please, Em. This is our Christmas with you."

"Speaking of..." Stella says excitedly, racing toward one of the many wardrobe doors that line one wall of her ginormous bedroom. "Gifts," she exclaims, pulling two identical boxes out. Only one is wrapped in pink and gold paper and the other is black and gold.

I'm hardly surprised when she hands the black one to me and the pink to Calli.

"You really thought this out, huh?" I ask, rubbing the black bow on the top between my fingers.

"Yep," she agrees happily, clearly proud of whatever is inside the boxes.

I swallow nervously. "I... um... haven't—"

"Stop," Stella says, holding her hand up. "I don't give to receive."

"That's not what Seb says," Calli squeals excitedly, her eyes sparkling with happiness and vodka.

I can't help but snort a laugh, the shots we did together not so long ago more than having an effect.

"We need to find you a boy tonight, Miss Cirillo."

She grimaces at my comment. "I'm not giving my V-card to anyone who'll be at tonight's party."

My lips part to argue, but I quickly find I have nothing to say because I agree, I don't want anyone at the party touching me with a barge pole either.

"Exactly," she says with a smile.

"Okay, fine. Maybe not tonight, but we will find you a guy."

"Not that I don't agree, but any chance you could open those?" Stella asks, nodding toward the two presents sitting in mine and Calli's laps as she bounces on the balls of her feet.

"Yeah, sorry."

We both rip into the paper to discover a fancy black wooden box inside.

"What have you done, Stel?" Calli asks, getting suspicious.

"Just something I think every princess needs."

My eyes roll but open the box.

"Oh my God, Stella," I squeal looking down at a brand new, gleaming, black knife.

"Stella," Calli also squeals, staring down at her new accessory. "It's fucking purple."

Stella lifts one shoulder, an accomplished grin pulling at her lips. "You like them?"

"I love it. Thank you so much."

"Just promise me something," she says, a little too seriously for my liking.

"Hmm…"

"Don't use it to kill Theo. She says the words so seriously it almost makes me laugh—until I imagine holding it up against his throat and for once, experience him being on the losing team. That makes my mouth water. My fingers pluck the heavy weapon from the box and wrap them around the handle, imagining how it might feel to threaten him. To make him bleed.

"I'll promise not to kill him. Can't promise anything else."

"You can hardly talk, Stel. We know all about your kinky knife shit," Calli pipes up, twisting her knife this way and that, watching it reflect the spotlights from above.

"Meh, have all the fun you want. I'm sure Emmie's hot daddy will tidy up the mess later." She flashes us her inner thigh that's more than exposed in her short dress as a shadow falls over the room from the doorway.

"Still lusting over a man you can't have, baby?" Seb's deep voice booms through the room.

"He wouldn't want me with your initials on my thigh."

"That was the point," he states, holding her stare.

The chemistry between them, even across the room, is burning fucking hot, and it only serves to remind me just how long it's been since I've been with a guy. I think of my most recent ex. He certainly knew how to make me scream.

As much as I might like to claim that my vibrator collection is all I need, I can admit— especially when I'm halfway to being drunk—that sometimes you just need a sweaty roll around the sheets with a halfway talented guy.

My temperature spikes as I watch them both eye fuck each other, and a real screwed-up part of my brain kinda wishes they'd just go for it— wouldn't be the first time in our company. Surely a little live porn is better than nothing at all. Right?

Realising that I'm imagining my best friend screwing her fella, I shake my head, forcing the thoughts from my mind.

I should go back home, find Archer and make use of everything I know he can give me.

Maybe I could sneak out of this damn party and...

"Emmie," Stella shouts, dragging me from my own head, and when I look up, I find her waving at me.

"Sorry. I'm here."

Her shoulders shake with a laugh.

"Ready to go?"

I stare at her for a beat, seriously considering telling her no. But then I remember both her and Calli telling me how much they wanted us to party together.

The last time we did was Halloween, and that couldn't have ended worse. Since then, shit has been too fucked up to let go and enjoy ourselves, and I'd be lying if I said I didn't want that.

My lips part to agree, but then a deep voice rumbles from somewhere else in the flat and my stomach sinks.

"Sorry," Stella mouths.

Forcing a smile onto my lips, I push to stand, smoothing my skirt down.

"There's a thigh strap in that box if you feel the need to go armed."

"Huh," I say, rolling the idea around my head.

"Em, you can't—" Calli starts, but she soon realises she's not quick enough because I slip the strap into place and tuck my sheathed knife into it.

My skirt is so short that no one will miss the fact I came... prepared. I smile to myself as I picture the horrified expression on Sloane's perfect face.

Maybe she'll take my words a little more seriously. Maybe not.

Taking a step forward, I take in my reflection. I hold my head a little higher at the image that stares back at me.

Oh hell yeah. Sloane and her little bitches can kiss my motherfucking arse.

With a flounce, I spin around, swipe the bottle we've been pouring shots from and tip it to my deep purple lips, swallowing what's left and revelling in the burn down my throat.

"Okay, I'm ready."

I grab my jacket from the bed and place my bag over my shoulder before marching out of the room with three sets of eyes burning into my back.

9

THEO

I can think of better ways of spending my Friday night than having to deal with Sloane pawing over me like she owns my arse.

We've got people locked in Dad's secret torture chamber. I'd rather be listening to them scream.

Or even better...

I could be listening to her scr—

My thoughts are forgotten when footsteps move my way.

I know she's here. Her bike was parked under the shelter I made sure was installed a few weeks ago.

Resting back on Seb's sofa, I widen my legs, my fists curling on my thighs as I wait.

I have no idea how I know it's her. But I do.

She's never been one to shy away, and I just know she's walking out here with her head held high to prove a point.

It's the reason I shouted for them to hurry the fuck up.

I knew she'd hear the words for what they were.

A challenge.

An invitation.

Her biker boots appear first. As usual, the laces are loose. It's annoying as fuck, but I doubt that me telling her so will make her change her ways. She seems to go out of her way to piss me off at every turn, so it'll just be more ammunition for her.

Her legs are covered in floral lace tights and my eyes track all the way up until they widen at the switchblade tucked into a strap around her thigh.

The sight makes my chest tighten.

The things I could do to her with that blade.

The guys ripped Seb for branding Stella the way he did. But fuck, did I fucking understand it.

My fists tighten, my short nails digging into my palms as I continue up, over her almost obscenely short, pleated black and white tartan skirt, to her black vest which shows the perfect tease of the kind of underwear she's got on beneath. There are straps criss-crossing over her chest, the lace of the cups sitting well above the neck of her top.

Her hair is down, but she's done something to make it huge, and her makeup, like normal, is dark. So fucking dark.

I bite down on the insides of my cheeks as I imagine just how fucking beautiful she'd look with it streaming down her cheeks as she choked on my cock.

Fuck.

I need to get a fucking grip where this girl is concerned.

She's a liar. A traitor.

She's my fucking—

I slam my thoughts down. They're too fucked up to even begin to process, which is why I've mostly been living in denial since Dad dropped the bomb.

"Did you want to take a picture?" she sasses, her voice cutting through my thoughts and dragging my focus back to her. "You can make use of it later when you go to bed alone."

Fighting to keep my expression neutral, almost bored, I run my eyes down the length of her body.

"Nah, I'm good. I've got better."

Lifting her hand, she ruffles her hair. It's a nervous move, something I noticed on the first day I met her.

"Sure you have. Tell me, why aren't you currently being bossed around by your little pet?"

I know exactly what—or whom—she's talking about, but that's not how I play it.

"I'm sorry?" I ask, sitting forward, my brows pinching together.

She studies me for a beat, obviously trying to figure out if I'm playing her or not.

"I'm surprised she let you out of her sight. She sure is... possessive."

I have no idea what Sloane has been spouting off at school, but I can imagine.

Sloane might act dumb at times, but just like everyone else, she's seen the tension between the two of us. And *meddling* should be Sloane's middle name.

"Well," I say, my voice empty, not giving away just how much my body reacts to her, "I guess she doesn't want to lose me, or what I can provide her with."

Forcing my muscles to move, I uncurl my fists and crack my knuckles.

Her eyes follow my movements, watching my fingers with hungry eyes.

She thinks she plays it cool around me. That I can't see exactly what she wants, what she needs. But I can read her like a fucking open book.

A fact it seems my father has figured out too.

If only she was so open with her secrets. It might make this whole job a hell of a lot easier.

Because that's all she is.

A job.

A game.

A pawn.

"Lucky girl," she sasses with a dramatic eye-roll. "But I guess some just have to settle."

I don't get to come up with a cutting response

because Seb, Stella and Calli appear over her shoulder.

"Ah, good. You're not close enough to slit his throat yet," Seb deadpans.

Emmie mutters something under her breath which I swear is something about never getting that close to me.

Clearly, she's forgotten last night already.

"So are we going or what?"

Emmie looks over at Stella when she steps into Seb's side.

She looks hot in her little black dress, and when Seb turns to look at her, a very familiar look fills his eyes.

"Yes, before they start going at it," I say, knowing exactly what Seb's feeling right now. But unlike him, I'm not about three seconds from acting on it.

Pushing from the sofa, I turn my back on the four of them, allowing me to rearrange myself without witnesses as I head toward the door.

"You're so fucking transparent, bro," Seb shouts behind me.

Flipping him off, I storm through the door.

The lift is still waiting on this floor, so only a second after I hit the button, the doors open.

Sadly, though, they don't get a chance to close, locking me inside the small space alone because Seb's hand darts out to stop them.

He shakes his head, smiling at me as he steps

inside, Emmie, Stella and Calli following closely behind.

The second they're inside, the door closes, locking me in with Emmie standing right in front of me.

She's added her leather jacket to complete her outfit, but it does little to dampen my desire.

I shove my hands in my pockets as nothing more than a way to stop myself from reaching for her. Although, all I manage to achieve is to make the bulge of my hard-on that much more obvious.

"You're so fucked," Seb mouths to me over Stella's shoulder.

I shake my head in denial, but there's no way he believes me.

There are only a couple of people who know me. The real me. And Seb is one of them.

We've been brothers for as long as I can remember. He sees through my mask, my pretence. He knows that while others might see the brutal, ruthless monster my father has created, underneath, I'm still the same Theo I was before my training.

Dragging his amused eyes from me, he focuses on his girl while mine inevitably find Emmie.

Even from behind, I can tell how fast her chest is heaving. And apparently, I'm not the only one. Calli frowns at her before saying, "You okay, Em?"

"Y-yeah, of course. Why wouldn't I be?"

Calli studies her for a little longer before deciding to let it go.

"No reason."

It seems like an eternity while I'm surrounded by her scent, her curves in touching distance as she quite clearly freaks out about something, but eventually, the car comes to a stop and the doors open.

Seb, Stella and Calli immediately move forward, but right as Emmie takes a step, my hand darts out to grab her arm.

"Wait," I demand, pulling her back into my body.

Her scent gets stronger, and I swallow harshly as I fight to remember why I stopped her in the first place.

Leaning down, she shudders when my breath rushes over her skin.

I can't help but smile.

"Em, what are you—"

Stella's concerned face appears before us and I reach out, jamming my finger into the close door button, effectively shutting her out.

"What are you doing?" Emmie asks, although her voice lacks its usual biting tone.

"You're scared. Why?" I ask, my lips brushing against the shell of her ear.

A tiny whimper rips from her and feeds some twisted need deep inside me at having her at my mercy.

Her body stiffens.

"I'm not scared of you," she spits, having found her sass once more.

"But you're scared of something," I point out.

"Bullshit. I'm not scared of any—"

Her back collides with the wall, her hips pushed forward because of the handrail.

"Liar," I hiss, slamming my hands beside her head.

She stares up at me, her dark eyes spearing hate right at me.

"So you keep saying," she says flatly. "Better start working harder to dig up my dirty secrets, huh?"

She moves to duck under my arm, but I'm faster.

My fingers dig into her chin as I drag her back in front of me.

It has to hurt—I'm not exactly being gentle—but she doesn't so much as flinch.

"I will break you," I warn.

"I'm looking forward to seeing you try."

I hold her eyes, but it's damn near painful not to glance down at her lips. And fuck, if temptation doesn't become too much.

"Go on, I dare you," she seethes, using my line.

"Nah, you're all good. Why have bitter and frigid when I can have sweet and easy." It's a low blow, I know that, and I almost feel bad as her chin drops and her eyes soften with hurt for the briefest moment.

It's good to know there is a heart under all that steel armour, I guess.

"I'm not—" she starts to argue but quickly slams her lips shut. "You know what, for the likes of you, I am. You should be so fucking lucky to get anywhere near me."

"I'm pretty close now, Hellcat."

"Because I'm letting you. Something I'll ensure your easy little friend will be more than aware of."

"She wouldn't believe—"

In a move that shocks the shit out of me, she reaches up on her tiptoes and presses her lips to my neck.

"What the—" I blurt out as what I can only describe as a fucking electric shock rocks through my body, zeroing right in on my cock, which is once again straining to be set free.

She pulls back, looking at the mark she left behind with accomplishment written all over her face.

Lifting my hand, I press my fingers to my tingling skin.

"Come on, Cirillo. It's time to party."

This time when she makes her move to escape, I let her.

She presses the button to open the door, and I just manage to find my wits to say something before she steps out to join our confused, concerned and amused audience when they appear.

"Do not test me tonight, Ramsey. You won't like the outcome."

"Bite me, dickhead."

And fuck if my mouth doesn't water at the thought of doing just that. I bet her pale skin would look beautiful with my teeth marks and a little blood covering it.

She flips me off over her shoulder and storms past our amused friends.

"What just happened?" Calli asks innocently, looking between me and Emmie's quickly retreating back.

"Probably easier not to even attempt to understand what's going on there, Cal," Stella helpfully points out.

"She's not wrong. I have no fucking clue," I state, quickly following Emmie's trail.

I find her loitering in the car park, looking between mine and Seb's cars.

"Get any thoughts of driving out of your head right the fuck now," I tell her.

"You're never going to let that go, are you?"

"You smashed up my car. Do you have any idea how much it costs?"

She waves her hand as if it's nothing, which I know for a fact isn't the case. She's not grown up with the wealth we have thanks to the Family. I know she's intimidated by it. It's why she's been running around town trying to get a job. It's why Mickey offered her one.

"You driving us to this fucking shitshow or what?"

"Get in," I mutter, unlocking the car and dropping into the driver's seat.

Thankfully, she doesn't decide to join me in the front. I'm not sure I'd be able to cope with that proximity all the way across town to Sloane's place. Instead, she rips open the back door, a little too forcefully for my liking, and drops inside.

Seb joins me two seconds later, obviously deciding it's safer to put some distance between him and Stella whilst in my car.

Wise fucking move.

It's bad enough that they fucked in and on my Ferrari. I don't need any of their bodily fluids in my Maserati too, especially after it's only just been fully valeted.

"What?" I snap when I find him staring at me with a smug as fuck grin playing on his face.

"Oh, nothing, mate. Nothing at all. Just enjoying the show."

"You're a cunt," I mutter as female voices fill the space around us.

"Takes one to know one. Now drive. I wanna get my girl nice and drunk and out on the dancefloor."

"Should have just stayed home, save everyone else's eyes."

"She wouldn't fucking allow it," he sulks.

"Lucky us." I press my finger into the start button and delight in the feeling of my girl coming to life beneath me.

"I'm gonna get my licence," Emmie states behind me. "I am driving this thing again. Maybe even the Ferrari."

She's baiting me, I know she is. But damn it, it works.

"Over my dead body," I growl, flooring the accelerator and flying out of the car park.

Everyone other than me laughs.

Fuckers.

The journey is painful at best while Seb continues to rib me, only encouraging Emmie to get even deeper under my skin than she already is.

And it doesn't fucking help that I can see damn near all the way up to her cunt because she's sitting in the middle seat of the back of my car.

Any sane guy would have readjusted the mirror so he couldn't see.

I've never claimed to have retained much of my sanity.

Safe to say that by the time we pull up in Sloane's already packed driveway, I'm fucking hard as nails and my entire body is strung as tight as a fucking bow.

"Wow, her house is small, huh?" Emmie comments, leaning over Calli to get a look at Sloane's family estate.

It's got nothing on the Cirillo one, but it's still on the impressive side.

"Don't tell me, this is all funded by crime too?"

"No, actually," Seb answers for me. "Sloane's family business is legit. Her father, grandad and all those who came before have always had their fingers on the newest technology and invested in all the right places."

"Great," she mutters, sounding bored out of her skull. "As long as that means they've got plenty of decent alcohol inside, I'm all in."

"Didn't think you wanted to come," Stella pokes.

"We're here now, and I'm more than ready to get away from that prick," she says, nodding toward me, "and get wasted. If I'm really lucky, not every guy inside is a pig-headed, entitled dickhead who thinks the world owes him something."

"Wow, don't hold back, Em," Seb mutters before getting out and opening the door for the girls.

"Have I ever sugar-coated, Sebastian?"

Emmie takes off toward the open front door without bothering to wait for any of us.

"Well, she's in a good mood," Stella mutters. "What exactly did you say to her in the elevator?" Her eyes hold mine for a beat before dropping to my neck. "Because we all know what she did." Her eyes sparkle with excitement.

"She can try to mark her territory all she likes. It won't make an ounce of difference."

"If by that you mean that Sloane is such a whore she won't care about having another girl's lipstick stain on your neck, then, no, it won't. But if you mean—"

"Seb, rein your girl in. I don't need this shit."

Seb just laughs. "I thought you knew by now that Stella's a law unto herself. I have no chance of controlling shit."

"Never thought I'd say this, but I think I like you both better when you're fucking. At least you're not giving me shit."

"Nah, just a raging hard-on," Stella shouts, helpfully ensuring it's loud enough so that everyone loitering out here hears, their eyes dropping to my crotch in amusement.

"Did you bring your Vaseline?" Seb's voice booms before I step into the house and get swallowed by the music pounding from the speakers that have been set up in what's usually the Thompsons' formal dining room. But for tonight, everything has been cleared out in favour of a DJ.

I walk through the gyrating bodies on the makeshift dancefloor and head toward the kitchen where I assume the rest of the guys already are. And if I'm really unlucky, it'll be where Sloane's waiting for me, too.

I quickly discover I'm right, because not two seconds after stepping over the threshold into the kitchen does she appear through the mass of bodies and bound over to me.

Her dress is small and... cute, I guess. It's not really my thing. It's more something Alex or Nico would go for. I like my girls a little... darker.

"You came," she exclaims, her voice high-pitched and slurred.

Her arms rest over my shoulders, her fingers immediately brushing over the short hair at the nape of my neck.

Her touch sends a shiver down my spine, and not a good one.

"Where else would I be?" I ask, giving her entirely the wrong idea.

I might not have a choice about attending this thing, but rest assured, spending the night with Sloane is not the reason.

We have boys here tonight, just like we do at every Knight's Ridge party, distributing, working, and I'll be fucked if I'm not here to keep an eye on them.

We've had enough things go to shit recently. I'm not risking one of them offering goods up to the wrong people and having the cops turn up at the door.

She tenses against me, her fingers stilling, and I know why. She's found Emmie's lipstick.

I could have wiped it off, I'm more than aware of that fact, but something stopped me. A fucked up, twisted part of me likes it.

And more than that, I fucking love Sloane's reaction.

"What's this?"

"What?" I ask innocently. "Did you think the party started here?"

She gasps, her face falling for a beat before she recovers.

I have no idea why she's so hurt. I've barely touched her in months. I thought she'd moved on to one of the rugby team players. From what I heard, she got caught banging him in the locker room by their coach not so long ago. But the second we were paired up for that damn assignment, it was like no time had passed between the last time I had her on her knees for me.

My cock aches at the thought of her throat, only it's not her face, not her light eyes that stare up at me as she gags on my length.

Pressing the length of her body to mine, I see the moment she registers how hard I am against her stomach.

"Hmm..." she hums, her lips brushing across my cheek. "Seems to me that your pre-party was just a tease." She slips her hand between our bodies and grasps me through my trousers. "Want me to take the edge off?"

My lips part to respond while my body wars with itself. My head screams no, already knowing that she's not the one I want, while my painfully hard cock begs for it. It's been weeks since it's seen any action other than my own fucking hand.

The guys might joke about my lack of company recently, but they're only speaking the truth. It seems to have become my norm since Emmie unknowingly strolled into my life.

I thought it was just a phase, that I'd find someone else after a while who would grab my interest and get my dick hard. But it hasn't happened.

Hell, it's only got worse. And that contract sure doesn't fucking help. Although it's just another reason why I can't go after what I really want.

I need to think with my head, get the job done and move on, instead of thinking with my lonely dick.

"Cirillo, about fucking time, man," Alex barks, thankfully saving me from making a decision I'd probably regret.

"It was our fault," Stella says, joining us with Seb on one side and Calli on the other.

"Probably?" Alex asks with a laugh. "Drinks?" he offers.

"Why else are we here?" Stella asks, glancing around the room before her eyes lock on Sloane. "It's certainly not for the outstanding company."

Sloane scoffs, although she isn't so offended that she releases her grip on me.

"Are you going to let her get away with talking to me like that?"

My brows almost hit my hairline.

"I ain't saying shit to Stella. You're more than capable of fighting your own battles."

She's about to slink off to sulk when someone else joins us in the kitchen, her eyes immediately locking on mine before they drop to Sloane's.

Emmie might think that she keeps her expression neutral at seeing us together. But I see deeper than most, I'm sure. I see the slight widening of her eyes, the way her pupils darken in anger and the way her lips purse. If I could see down to her hips, I'm sure I'd find her fingers curled into tiny fists as she imagines slamming them into Sloane's perfectly straight nose.

Her appearance means that when Sloane releases me, I wrap my fingers around her hip and pin her in place.

Dropping my lips to her ear, I say, "I didn't think you liked losing."

She shudders, and I know without looking that her expression tells everyone just how badly she wants me.

Am I an arsehole?

Hell, yeah. But I can't help it.

Getting under Emmie's skin has become something of an obsession.

10

EMMIE

"Hey, can I get you another?"

Turning around to find the owner of the deep, unfamiliar voice who just offered to get me a refill, I'm pleasantly surprised when I find a guy who isn't wearing a polo and chinos, which seems to be the dress code here tonight. Apart from Theo and his boys, who stand out like a sore thumb in their dark trousers and shirts.

"Uh... yeah, that would be great. Thank you..."

"Ben," he says, giving me a smile that makes a deep dimple pop in his cheek.

He's cute, long-ish sandy blond hair, blue eyes, freshly shaven. Pretty much Theo's complete opposite. Not really my type, but I've had enough vodka that I don't really give a shit right now.

He's hot, and that's all I need.

"Thanks, Ben," I say in what I hope is my most seductive voice.

"Pleasure's all mine…" His words confirm that he most definitely fits in with the Knight's Ridge crowd rather than the brand of dicks from my past, but I push it aside. He doesn't scream wealthy and pretentious, and that's enough for me right now.

"Emmie."

"Pretty," he murmurs, running his eyes appreciatively down the length of my body. He pauses when he spots my switchblade, but he doesn't seem turned off.

"Vodka and Coke. Make it a double. Or a triple," I say with a shrug.

"I'll see what I can do, babe." He winks and ducks out of the room, leaving me alone once more.

With my eyes on the dancing crowd before me, I hop up on the dresser at my back and watch as the bodies bump and grind. Seb and Stella are unsurprisingly in the middle, hands and mouths everywhere. Alex is also getting his freak on with some girl I recognise from one of my classes.

Nico is on the edge of the crowd, chatting to Toby and a couple of other girls, but thankfully, Theo and his hoebag are nowhere in sight.

My stomach knots as I consider what that might mean.

Has she dragged him up to her bedroom and…

A violent shudder rips through me as I picture

his hands over her body, whispering the dirty things he wants to do to her in her ear.

My skin still hums from the car ride here. I knew he was watching me in the mirror—my skin burned with need every time his stare landed on me. If it weren't for Stella and Calli sitting on either side of me, I might have been even more brazen than just discreetly widening my legs, giving him just a few more inches to eat up.

It was dangerous—I was more than aware that he spent more time with his eyes on my body than he did with them on the road.

But there are worse ways to go. At least I'd have died knowing I was driving him to the brink of insanity.

"You're in luck," Ben says when he returns with two cups in hand. "My cousin was in the kitchen, let me use the bottle of Grey Goose she'd stashed for her nearest and dearest."

"Sweet. Thank you," I say with a smile, taking my drink from him and allowing our fingers to brush. There's no body-jolting spark, but there's not nothing, which I take as a good sign.

I don't really care about the quality of the vodka. I only want it to serve one purpose: get me wasted and make me forget about *him* and the way he makes me feel every time we're anywhere near each other. But as I take a sip, I can't help but appreciate how much nicer it is.

"Good?" Ben asks, his eyes locked on my lips as I lick up the excess liquid.

"Really good."

"You can thank me later." He winks once again, suggesting that he's teasing... but when his eyes drop to my lips once more, I can't help but wonder if he is or if he's just planned out our entire evening in his head.

"So you don't go to Knight's Ridge, right?"

"No," he says, having a sip of his own drink and taking a step forward so we don't have to shout quite so loudly at each other, but instead of standing to my side like any normal stranger, he gently nudges my knees apart with his free hand and steps between them, placing his palm against the wood of the unit beside me, lowering his body so we're at eye level. "Thank fuck, have you seen the state of their football team?"

"Not really," I confess, although I'm achingly aware of who's on it.

Knowing that this guy is quite clearly Theo's rival should raise some red flags. I mean, it does. But not enough to make me stop or put any space between us.

The image of him whispering in Sloane's ear in the kitchen not so long ago assaults me and I go all in with this guy, whoever he is, wrapping my leg around the back of his thigh and forcing him closer.

"So who do you play for, then?"

In all honesty, I couldn't give a rat's arse about his team, or the game in general. But if my suspicions are correct, I'm sure one of the members of our team will alert the boss. And I kinda can't wait to see his reaction.

Excitement bubbles up inside me. I love watching him lose control. It doesn't happen very often. But the couple of times it has... Damn. I'm not sure I've ever been so turned on in my life.

"All Hallows," he says, as if that's meant to mean something to me. As if I'm meant to be... impressed? "It's in Oxford," he adds.

"Right. Cool."

Reaching up, he tucks my hair behind my ear, his warm knuckles brushing over my cheek.

"You're not like all the others, are you?"

"I should really fucking hope not."

He chuckles, not allowing me to get a read on whether I've just impressed or offended him. Not that I really give a shit.

"Clearly I've been in the wrong city," he murmurs. "Dance with me?"

Downing my drink, which is a total waste for how much it probably cost, I wince at the burn. He took my words seriously, because it's strong. Stronger than any I made myself.

He really is a man on a mission.

Well, luckily for him, so am I.

Wrapping his hands around my waist, he

effortlessly lifts me from the dresser and drags me back toward the dancing crowd.

Ducking down, his lips brush my ear, his hot breath tickling over my skin.

"And to think I wasn't going to come tonight."

"I'm glad you did," I breathe, leaning into him as he pulls me into his body, hips moving in time to the music.

This boy can dance. That much is immediately obvious.

"Me too. Tell me you're single."

I can't help but laugh at the hope and slight desperation in his voice. "Painfully so."

"Well," he says, rolling his hips against me, "maybe I can be of assistance."

"What makes you think I'm *that* kind of girl, Ben?"

"I don't. I'm just trying my luck."

"Trying to win one over on the Knight's Ridge team, more like," I tease.

He tenses, giving me all the answer I need.

"It's cool," I shout when the music suddenly gets louder as the song changes. "I'd be lying if I said my intentions with you were entirely innocent."

"Where have you been all my life?" he kids, taking my hand and making me twirl away from him. More than a few eyes fall on us as we dance, and as each song passes my head becomes increasingly fuzzy.

It's pretty much everything I hoped it would be.

Stella shoots me a knowing look, along with an appreciative glance over my dance partner. She nods, a cheeky smile playing on her face, but then she tilts her chin, gesturing to a place—or I should say a person—behind me.

I don't need her to tell me. I know he's there.

I felt it the moment he stepped into the room.

All the hairs on the back of my neck lifted and my temperature picked up a few extra degrees, which is really saying something seeing as it's like a freaking sauna in here.

"I need to pee," I tell Ben.

"I'll take you. I know where the secret ones are."

I hold his stare for a beat, feeling less than in control of myself. But, grateful that I'm not going to stand in a long queue, I happily accept his offer and take his hand.

My legs are like jelly as I make my way across the room, everything—other than the death glare I'm receiving from Theo—a blur.

He's standing in the only doorway to get out of the room, so we have no choice but to try and squeeze around him to go wherever it is that we're going.

I'm hardly surprised when his hand wraps around my upper arm, but when I look over, I don't find his eyes burning into me, but into Ben.

"Emmie," he warns, still not bothering to look at me, "I warned you," he growls, low enough that only I hear.

"And I told you to get fucked. Excuse us. We've got somewhere... better to be."

To my shock, he releases my arm when I take a step forward, but we don't get to escape before his voice hits me again.

"I'm fucking watching you, Thompson." Theo's voice is cold and deadly. It hits me right in the clit.

Stupid fucking vodka.

Thompson.

That name really should mean something, I know it should, but I'm struggling to get a grasp on any kind of rational thought. Well, anything other than the, "Fuck you, Cirillo. You don't fucking own me," I snarl at Theo as we continue out of the room.

"What the fuck was that?" Ben asks, looking back at a seething mafia psychopath.

"*That* was a jumped-up, conceited, bellend of epic proportions, dickhead."

"R-right," he states. "I can't disagree, but I'd also rather not die tonight."

"He won't kill you tonight."

"No, he'll fucking torture me for two weeks for touching you before allowing me the pleasure."

"He's not that bad," I agree, although it's weak at best.

"Emmie," he says, leading us up a hidden set of

stairs that seem to magically appear at the back of the house where no one else is. "You're far from stupid, so don't act like it. I was drawn to you because you're not like all the other girls here. You're not a dumb airhead, so don't even try it."

My lips part to respond to that, but no words come out. Well, not ones in relation to what he said, anyway.

"How do you know where you're going?" I ask my brows pulling together as we get to the top of the stairs.

His hand rests at the small of my back as he leads me toward a closed door.

His quiet chuckle is all I need for everything to slot into place.

Twirling toward him, the world around me spins, and I have no choice but to reach out for the wall to steady myself.

"Who's your cousin?" I demand, although I already know the answer.

"Sloane. Hence the vodka."

"Damn it," I hiss quietly, although not quietly enough it seems, when his brow furrows.

"My cousin doesn't have a say in who I spend time with."

"Ah, so you're aware of how she feels about me, then."

My knees threaten to give out, and I stumble a little.

"Are you okay?" he asks, reaching for me.

"Y-yeah. I just need to…" I thumb toward the door just behind me, hoping like hell it's a bathroom, because I need a moment.

"Go for it. I'll wait out here."

I pause for a second, looking back at him.

"What?" he asks.

"You're a good guy, huh?"

He shrugs, a slight blush hitting his cheeks. "Give me a chance and you might get to find out."

I walk into the bathroom, more confused than ever. I thought he was using me to piss Theo off. Maybe he is. But I'm not sure if that's all it is.

Guilt hits me, because I was fully intending on using him. But knowing that he's being a gentleman and taking care of me right now… well, it makes me feel like the shittiest human on the planet.

I lower my arse to the toilet after fighting with my irritating but sexy bodysuit thing and undoing the poppers. Why I thought this was a good idea to wear on a night where I wanted to get off-my-head drunk, fuck only knows.

I'm still wrestling with the bloody thing some ungodly amount of time later when a knock on the door startles me.

"Emmie, you okay in there?"

"Shit," I hiss, wobbling on my one leg, the other propped up on the toilet as I attempt to do the poppers back up. "Y-yeah. I'll be right there. Underwear malfunction," I say, quieter.

"Okay. Do you need... er... help?"

I run the idea through my head for all of half a second. "No, no. I'm good."

Finally, I get the damn thing done up, make quick work of washing my hands, and pull the door open.

I find Ben standing with his hands deep in his jeans' pockets and almost lose my fight not to roll my eyes at him.

"You good?" he asks, pushing from the wall, concern etched into his face.

A shadow at the end of the hall catches my eye as a coldness washes over me, but I push it aside. I'm too drunk to take it seriously.

I nod. "Get me another drink, yeah? That good shit your cousin would probably hate to know I'm drinking."

"You got it, babe."

His hand finds its home at the small of my back and we walk back down the stairs once more to rejoin the party.

A couple of people give us curious glances, seeing as the back of the house we just emerged from seems to be out of bounds, but I guess those rules don't apply to family.

My steps falter the second we turn into the kitchen when we walk straight into Theo and Sloane.

"Cous, give us two more of those vodkas."

Sloane holds Ben's eyes for a beat before she turns her glare on me.

"Sorry, *cous,* I don't give the good shit to skanks."

I scoff. "That's rich. Give me the cheap shit. Anything that will make me forget I'm currently anywhere near you," I seethe.

She pauses for a second before nodding in agreement.

"I've got just the thing."

Removing herself from Theo, she makes her way to the counter to pour our drinks.

"Ignore her. She's never played well with others."

"Why am I not surprised."

I turn into Ben's body, achingly aware of Theo's attention, but I pointedly ignore him.

"You sure you should have more?" Ben asks, once again brushing my cheek with his knuckle and tucking my hair back.

He might have said he didn't want to be on the end of Theo's wrath, but he doesn't seem to be all that bothered about flaunting me in front of him right now.

"Trust me, I could drink you under the table. I've had years of practice."

"Fair enough. I admire a woman who knows her limits."

I'm still holding his eyes when Sloane appears once more.

"I'm not sure what your last slave died of, Bennett, but this is the last drink I'm making you and your skank tonight."

Taking the cup from her, I raise it in salute, seriously tempted to throw it in her face but more than aware that it would be a waste.

"I hope the night brings you everything you've been dreaming of," I say insincerely before downing the drink in one.

A threatening growl rumbles up her throat when I pass my empty glass back to her and thank her.

With a flounce, she spins away from me, flicking her long hair over her shoulder and bouncing up to Theo, who barely reacts to her. He's too busy glaring death at me.

"We should go dance again," I suggest, running my palms up Ben's chest and looping my hands around his neck. I can barely reach him, he's so freaking tall, but the burning stare that's heating my skin spurs me on.

I'm playing with fire, I know I am. But I can't stop.

I crave the fucking burn like a junkie.

"Sure, can't argue with that."

His hand finds mine behind his neck, and he twists our fingers together and pulls me from the kitchen.

The vodka hits me upside the head long before we've even left the room, and I sway behind him, my head spinning and my stomach churning as if I just downed it on an empty belly.

But the second Ben pulls me to a stop on the edge of the dancefloor, I push it all aside in favour of mindlessly moving with him and forgetting all the bullshit.

It works for a while, but one violent turn of my stomach and I know my night is about to come to a swift end.

11

THEO

"Emmie, wait," Ben calls after her as she bolts from the room as if the hounds of hell are on her tail.

My entire body stiffens, and before I know what I'm doing, I've shoved Sloane away from me.

From her squeal of shock, I wouldn't be surprised to find that I'd knocked her clean off her feet.

I follow them to the back of the house and up the same stairs from earlier this evening.

Watching her leave with him fucking pained me. I followed them up, ready to make a point about just who Emmie belongs to.

I don't give a fuck who he is. No one—and I mean no one—takes what belongs to me.

"Get the fuck out of my way," I demand, twisting my fingers in the back of his t-shirt and dragging him back down the stairs.

"What the—"

He glances over his shoulder, his eyes colliding with mine, and a resigned look covers his face.

"Leave her the fuck alone," I growl, dragging him farther backward, forcing him to lose his footing and tumble down the stairs he'd climbed.

"Motherfucker," he grunts as he hits each step.

It's far from the first time we've clashed. It's just usually on the pitch, and never over a girl.

My fucking girl.

I fly at the door and push the handle, but it doesn't budge.

"Emmie?" I boom, pounding my fist down on the door. "Emmie, open the fucking door," I shout, my heart beginning to race.

The way she ran from the room... something isn't right.

"Emmie."

"She's drunk," Ben says, finally making it back up the stairs. "She's probably just puking."

Turning my head slowly, I hold his concerned stare.

"Did I say I needed your fucking help?" I seethe quietly.

"Fuck you, Cirillo. Emmie's cool. I want to make sure she's okay."

"You," I spit, turning to face him. "You fucking did this. What did you give her?"

He pales at my accusation. "What? I didn't— I

wouldn't... She was throwing back vodka like it was going out of fashion. That's not my fault."

I pull my arm back, ready to shut him the fuck up, when a loud thud sounds from behind the locked door.

"Emmie," I breathe.

Uncurling my fist, I give the dick a forceful shove to get him out of my way before I run full force at the door, my shoulder colliding with the solid wood.

"Emmie?" I shout, but when no response comes, I try again.

Thankfully, the lock gives on my second attempt and I fly into the bathroom, unable to catch myself before I crash into the basin. My ribs smart as I slam into the ceramic, but the sight of the slumped figure on the floor ensures I don't feel any of it.

"Emmie," I cry, dropping to my knees beside her and brushing her hair from her face.

She's out cold, her skin covered in a sheen of sweat, her chest heaving as her heart gallops in her chest.

A shadow falls over us from the doorway.

"Want to tell me again that you didn't give her anything?" I bark, grabbing some toilet paper to clean her up. She might have got to the toilet before she puked, but that didn't stop her getting it over herself.

"It's going to be okay," I whisper so only she can hear.

"I didn't. I fucking swear to you."

When I look up, I see the truth in his eyes, but it does little to calm my already out of control temper.

"Your cousin needs to watch her fucking back," I seethe, assuming that this can only have come from her. "For her own good, she might want to go home with you, whenever you fuck off."

"No, she wouldn't."

"No?" I ask. "Who else made Emmie a drink tonight?"

His lips part to argue, but he knows as well as I do that it was Sloane.

"Keep her out of my goddamn way or I'll strangle the fucking life out of her with my bare hands."

He holds my eyes and nods once.

"Do you need me to—"

"Just leave. You've done enough."

He swallows harshly, and I'm expecting him to refuse when he finally takes a step back.

It's not until his footsteps pound down the stairs that I finally speak once more.

"Em, can you hear me?" I ask, my voice cool and calm despite the riot of panic and anger that's raging inside of me.

I should call Stella and Calli to come look after her and go and deal with Sloane.

Emmie won't want me looking after her, won't want me seeing her weak and vulnerable—again, although last time was of her own doing. But despite knowing all that, leaving her right now, even in the care of her friends is not what's going to happen.

"I'm going to get you out of here, okay?" I ask her, already knowing that she can't respond.

Slipping one arm beneath her knees and another under her back, I lift her from the floor.

I don't see her bag or coat with her, and I'm sure as fuck not going to go marching back into the party with her like this to find it.

Tucking her closer to my body, I make my way back down the stairs, but instead of heading toward the party, I turn right, toward one of the many ways out of this house.

I'm not exactly proud of it, but I've snuck in and out of this place more times than I can count over the years. I know it almost as well as I do my parents' estate.

Emmie murmurs something in my arms when the bitter winter air hits us and she unconsciously snuggles closer into my body.

Damn it. I shouldn't fucking like it so much.

"Come on, you beautiful little liar. You think you can refrain from vomiting in my car on the way home?" I know she's not going to answer me, but I ask the question anyway.

If she were awake, something tells me that she'd

make sure she was sick just to put her mark on the inside of my car like she did on the exterior.

Juggling her in my arms, I manage to unlock the door and pull it open without dropping her to the ground.

I second guess myself as I begin to lower her to the passenger seat. Maybe I should have laid her out in the back.

"Fuck it," I mutter, reaching over her passed-out body to plug the safety belt in. "Please, please, do not puke," I beg, glancing down to the spotless mat at her feet. "I'll get us home as quick as I can, okay?"

She groans once more, her head lolling to the side, making me question once more if I should have laid her down.

Quickly closing the door, I race around the bonnet and drop in beside her.

With one more glance at her, I jam my finger into the start button and set off, blowing out of Sloane's huge driveway with a spray of gravel clattering the cars behind me.

Pulling up my contacts on the screen, I find Seb and hit call.

"Yo, bro. What's popping?"

"You're wasted," I point out.

"Uh... yeah. Question is, why aren't you?"

"Seb," I warn.

"Oh yeah, 'cos you've got a massive stick up your arse and are in complete denial about who you want to be grinding it up on the dancefloor with. If you—"

"I've got Emmie," I blurt out, cutting off his incessant, drunken rambling.

"Wait… what? You fucking caved to her?"

"No, arsehole. Her drink was spiked. She's passed out in my passenger seat."

"Shit," he hisses, suddenly sounding sober.

The loud music in the background begins to fade as I assume he moves to a quieter room.

"What do you need us to do?" I can't help but shake my head at his immediate use of the term *us*.

He and Stella are sickening at times, but I couldn't be happier that he's found her. He deserves some joy after all the shit he's been through.

"Nothing. I'm just going to take her home and let her sleep it off."

"Home?" he asks curiously.

"Just let Stella and Calli know that she's safe."

"You think they'll belie—"

"And find her bag and coat."

"Fine," he says on a sigh, "but if you hurt her or make this worse in any way, I won't do a thing to hold Stella back."

"Pfft, like you could anyway," I scoff.

"Whatever, just… don't do anything fucking stupid," he warns.

"Sure," I agree, pressing my thumb to the

phone button on my steering wheel and cutting him off.

We're only a few minutes from home, and only the sound of Emmie's increased breathing fills the car.

"We're almost there, Hellcat. You gonna be okay?"

I don't expect a response, so when a very weak, "Yeah," falls from her lips I damn near crash the car when I twist to look at her.

"Fuck," I bark, righting the steering wheel before we mount the curb and kill the drunk guy who's weaving around on the pavement.

"Theo." My name is so quiet, and when nothing else follows I start to think that I imagined it. But then she says it again. "Theo?"

"Yeah, Hellcat."

I gasp when the heat of her hand lands on my thigh.

Her fingers squeeze lightly, and by the time I've schooled my reaction to her touch and look over, she seems to be out cold again.

"Em?"

Nothing.

Dropping my hand from the wheel, I wrap my fingers around her tiny hand and beg my heart to stop racing.

12

EMMIE

I turn over, sink into the mattress and nuzzle the soft yet firm pillow beneath my cheek.

It's amaz— It's not mine.

Hazy memories from the night before mix with the putrid taste in my mouth and the throbbing of my brain, which only seems to increase with every second that passes.

Go back to sleep, I beg my body. But it's too late, because my brain is too alert.

I bolt up in bed, ripping my eyelids open, peeling the dried makeup apart. My head spins and my stomach turns to the point I press my palm to it and bend my knee, getting ready to run.

But run where?

I have no fucking idea where I am.

The last person I remember being with was the guy I was dancing with.

Fuck. What did I do last night?

I rack my brain for any kind of memory as to how the evening ended, but before I manage to drag anything up, movement in the corner makes my heart jump into my throat and my eyes shoot over.

"Holy fuck," I breathe, another wave of nausea washing over me.

Theo is sitting in a dark grey, high-backed, wing-armchair. It looks like a fucking throne, and if I weren't currently suffering the hangover from hell then I might just laugh at him.

He's still wearing his black trousers and shirt from the night before, only it's now unbuttoned, exposing his toned chest and abs. Something my eyes can't resist as they drop to eat up the expanse of rippling muscles.

I might have seen him in nothing but a pair of swim shorts the night of our impromptu pool party, but being here right now in a room alone with him —or at least I assume we're alone—it feels that much more intimate.

Dragging my eyes back up before my lingering stare starts making his over-inflated ego bigger than it already is, I find his exhausted dark green eyes. It takes me a second to register what's different about him, but the moment I realise that I'm looking at an entirely different version of the boy I love to hate, panic ripples through me.

I can handle angry, cold-hearted Theo. I have

no idea who this person is who's staring at me with genuine concern in his eyes.

Swallowing down my unease, I fall back on my usual coping mechanism. Sarcasm and spiteful words.

"Why are you looking at me like that?" I spit, my lip curling in disgust.

"Me?" he asks, sitting forward and pointing at himself as an incredulous expression passes over his face. "Why am I sitting here watching you?" He pushes from the chair, running his fingers through his already messy hair. "Fucking hell, Emmie," he mutters, anger deepening his voice, his face pulling tight into a grimace, a look I'm much more familiar with. "Do you remember anything of last night?" he booms, his voice echoing around the room, making me wince and my head pound even harder.

"N-no," I squeak in a quiet voice, which makes me sound about as weak as I feel right now.

Flicking the covers off me, I slide to the end of the bed as he stands with every muscle in his body pulled tight in the doorway.

His eyes drop to what I'm wearing, and I do the same.

"You undressed me?" I ask, although it's fucking pointless. I'm wearing his shirt, and I'm pretty sure that I was completely incapable of anything when I left that party last night.

Sucking his bottom lip into his mouth, he drags

it through his teeth, clearly fighting whatever it is he wants to do or say.

In the end, he goes with nothing and turns his back on me, leaving the room.

All the air I didn't know I was holding comes rushing out of my lungs as the room suddenly becomes cold and lonely without his presence.

Damn it, Theo.

Why did it have to be him to come to my rescue?

Why?

He's hardly a white freaking knight, so why even try? Why not just leave me to drown in my own vomit? I'm sure that's where last night would have gone if he didn't bring me back here.

For the first time since I opened my eyes, I look around the bedroom I'm currently inside.

Holy shit.

Did he bring me back to his penthouse?

The sound of something breaking somewhere else in the flat makes me flinch, but I refuse to feel bad about it. I didn't ask him to bring me here and watch over me like some fucking mother hen.

Pushing from the bed, I sigh when my feet sink into what I swear has to be the world's softest and thickest carpet.

It's black, just like almost everything else in this room. I feel weirdly comfortable here, surrounded by the kind of darkness I'm used to, but I stuff that thought down as quickly as it appears. I'm too hungover to deal with those kinds of fucked-up thoughts.

I should be feeling all kinds of out of place. Theo clearly has more money than I'm ever likely to see in a lifetime. His home should not be a place I feel relaxed in any way.

Glancing at the bedside table, I find a glass of water and a packet of painkillers.

Refusing to feel anything about the kind gesture, I robotically pop a couple of pills from the packet and throw them back, downing the entire glass of water in one.

It swirls about uncomfortably in my empty stomach, making me regret it instantly.

Walking on unsteady legs, I head toward a slightly open door in the hope I might find a bathroom behind it.

As I push the door open, my breath catches in my throat at the sight before me.

"Ho-ly fuuuck," I breathe, stepping farther into the most insane bathroom I've ever seen.

It's black. Literally. Everything is black.

I guess I shouldn't really be surprised. It mirrors his soul, after all.

My eyes are still shooting around the room, taking it all in as I push the door closed behind me.

If the pain in my head weren't so bad, I'd be convinced this was a dream.

Hiking up the white shirt Theo dressed me in, I can't help but notice that I'm the only light thing in the room as I lower my arse to the first black toilet I've ever sat on in my life.

I find a new toothbrush resting on the side of the basin with some toothpaste beside it.

It's the only thing that isn't hidden behind a cupboard, so I can only assume he's left it for me.

With a frown wrinkling my brow, I grab them both and set about freshening my mouth up.

As the vile taste in my mouth vanishes, it seems to allow the aches that are assaulting my body to get worse with every second I stand there.

What the hell happened last night?

I've had enough raging hangovers in my time to know that this is beyond the average.

Placing the toothbrush back down, I rest my palms on the edge of the counter and roll my aching neck.

I shouldn't hurt this much, especially after the insane bed he let me sleep in.

My eyes find the shower, and they widen at the sight of all the jets.

Oh, hell yes.

I shed Theo's shirt and let it pool untidily on the floor, smiling like a naughty little child because the mess will irritate the hell out of him. It doesn't matter that he won't see it. It makes my chest puff with defiance.

It takes me longer than I'd like to get the shower on, but I quickly discover that it was worth it when water erupts from all directions.

TRACY LORRAINE

Stepping into it, I groan loudly as the jets immediately begin to massage my sore muscles.

Okay, this *is heaven.*

I close my eyes, tip my head back and just indulge in the unexpected treat.

I don't hear a thing over the roar of the water, but that doesn't mean I don't feel the exact moment he pushes the door open and steps inside.

A violent shiver runs down my spine, and damn it if my nipples don't pebble or my thighs don't clench.

His mere presence shouldn't affect me as strongly as it does, especially when I'm practically half-dead from whatever I unknowingly took last night, because that's the only explanation for how I feel altogether.

This isn't just vodka.

It makes me wonder what happened to the guy —Ben. If he spiked my drink, I can only assume that he's already worm food.

After the way he reacted to Theo last night, I wouldn't have thought he'd have been so desperate to pull a stunt like that, but then again, I have no idea who he really is. He could have been playing me from the moment he walked over, and in my need to punish Theo and forget my reality, I was like putty in his hand.

Jesus.

All of this was my fault.

I knew going last night was a bad idea. I should

154

have just stayed home and continued my pity party for one.

When he doesn't move or say anything for the longest fucking time, my curiosity gets the better of me and I lower my head and drag my eyes open.

He's standing right in the doorway with his hands deep in his trouser pockets, his shirt still open and a hard, tortured expression on his face.

His eyelids are heavy as he watches me. His jaw tics, and there's a muscle in his temple that pulsates.

He's holding himself back, that much is obvious.

I guess it's just what from, that's the question. Fucking me or killing me.

Call me fucking twisted, but I really want to know which way he's leaning.

One side of my lip curls into a smirk.

"Either join me or fuck off. The staring is just creepy."

My voice is flat, completely belying how I'm really feeling at issuing him that kind of ultimatum.

I know he's going to choose the latter, and I'm also aware that it makes me a self-punishing masochist. But I can't help myself. And who knows, maybe seeing him walk away from me after such a blatant offer will help sever whatever this fucked-up shit is between us.

He hesitates, the line between his brows

deepening before his eyes take another leisurely stroll around my body.

My skin prickles as if he's actually touching me, and my clit aches for some attention.

But just as I think he might take me up on the offer, or I might up the stakes by making a start on myself, he spins on his heels and marches from the room.

Disappointment floods me and I fall back against the cold, marble-covered wall behind me as all the air rushes from my lungs.

I knew it was going to happen. It really shouldn't hurt quite so bad.

Lifting my hands to my hair, I run my fingers through the sopping lengths and look around for some shampoo.

Just like the rest of the room, there's nothing on display.

"Weird fucking prick," I mutter to myself as I attempt to wring the water out and turn to stop the shower.

I'll have to have another when I get home.

My hand just touches the dial when the warmth of a body burns the bare skin of my back.

I still, overwhelmed by shock that he came back. I'm so stunned that I don't even think to fight when his fingers wrap around my wrists and pull them both behind my back.

I very quickly regather my wits when he starts

wrapping something around them, binding them together tightly.

"What are you doing?" It's meant to come out harshly, but damn it, my voice sounds needy and desperate.

A dark laugh falls from his lips as his burning fingers grip the back of my neck, pressing me against the cold wall. My nipples pebble as the shower dial digs into my stomach.

"Don't make me fucking regret this, Hellcat," he groans before the fingers of his other hand brush down my spine.

"Oh God," I moan, unable to keep it in.

It's been so long since anyone has touched me like this that I'm already on the verge of combusting from the anticipation alone.

"You want this?" he breathes, his fingers moving over my arse.

My hips roll in my need, and the second his foot hits my ankle I follow orders and widen my stance, giving him the access I desperately need him to have.

His touch is so light, so gentle, nothing like I expected from him.

My entire body trembles, a demand for him to touch me properly dancing on the tip of my tongue, but I bite it back. Something tells me he wouldn't take too kindly to me attempting to throw my weight around. Although that might also be exactly—

"Holy fuck, yes," I scream when his restraint finally snaps and he forces two fingers inside me.

"Jesus," he grunts as if he's in physical pain.

I know why. No one's stretched my cunt out for a very long time. I bet I'm as tight as a fucking nun down there.

His fingers push in further, and it's not exactly a challenge for him, seeing as I'm fucking dripping.

If being full of his fingers didn't feel so head-spinningly good, then I might be a little embarrassed at showing him so blatantly just how badly I need this—him.

"So fucking wet for me, Hellcat. You've been imagining this, haven't you?"

He pulls his digits almost all the way out of me, pushing them up to circle my clit and cover me in my own juices.

"N-no," I argue, even though we both know I'm lying through my teeth. He literally has the evidence of my dishonesty all over his fingers.

"You like lying to me, don't you?"

His fingers circle me in the most delicious way that his words don't even register.

"Yes," I cry when he dips them back inside me again.

My knees tremble and my pussy clamps down on him.

I'm so freaking close already. It's fucking embarrassing.

"I don't fucking think so," he grunts, forcefully

pulling me back and slamming me into the other wall so I'm facing him.

The dark hunger in his eyes makes my breath catch, but that reaction is nothing compared to the shock that races through me the second I drop my eyes and see him.

All. Of. Him.

"Holy—"

I don't need to look up from the impressive girth of his cock that's proudly bobbing in front of him to know he's got a fucking smirk on his face.

No wonder he lets the guys' ribbing go over his head.

"You were right," he states, his voice giving nothing away. Thankfully, though, he's lost his armour, and that weapon he's currently rocking is telling me everything I need to know right now.

He needs this as much as I do.

He's been fucking dreaming about this as much as I have. I'd put money on it... if I had any.

His words confuse me enough that I'm able to drag my eyes away from what is arguably the best part about this prick, and I find his face once more.

His usually well-trimmed stubble is a little longer than I'm used to seeing, and his hair is slicked back from standing under the torrent of water as he fingered me.

My pussy clenches around nothing, my body begging to feel him again.

"Was I?" I ask, my eyes narrowing in

frustration. I don't want to have a fucking heart to heart right now.

"Yeah. If I'd have fucked you that night, you definitely would have known about it the next morning."

Usually, I'd have some cutting remark about his overinflated ego compensating for the size of his cock.

Evidently, that is not fucking true.

I'm not sure if I'm disappointed or just desperate.

Okay, fine. I'm just desperate.

"Big words for a guy who's just standing there like he doesn't know what to do with me." I tilt my head to the side and stare at him impassively.

A lopsided, almost cute smile plays on his lips. "Is that what you think? That I don't know what I'm doing?"

I shrug, because the evidence speaks for itself.

We're both standing here naked, both clearly desperate for what could come next, yet he's the one who hit pause.

I hold his eyes for a beat before dropping down his body to his cock once more, and my mouth waters with my need to know how he tastes.

Bitter and salty, probably.

Unable to stop myself, my knees bend and I prepare to hit the tiled floor beneath me to force him into action. Only, right as I start to descend, his hot, unforgiving fingers wrap around my throat, dragging me back up and pinning me to the wall.

"You're not in charge here, Hellcat."

"No? Because it looks like you're dropping the ball, Cirillo." He swallows, his Adam's apple bobbing with the move. "Give me what I need, or I'll do it myself. You can even watch if you like."

His eyes flash with desire, but he quickly locks it down.

"Your wrists are bound. I'd like to see you try."

"I can be creative. I don't need a man to—" His fingers tighten while his other hand cups my pussy, one digit slipping inside. "Fuck."

"You were saying?"

His eyes hold mine, daring me to argue with him.

I can't. There's no way in hell that I could get myself off half as well as I suspect he can, and fuck, he knows it too.

Cocky, arrogant dick.

I spread my legs as he slides two fingers deep inside me, curling them until he finds the spot that makes me hiss in a shocked breath and forces my eyes to close.

"Look at me," he demands. "I want you to watch me as you come. I want you to know who's doing it."

Like I could imagine anyone else.

"Good." Amusement and achievement dances in his burning green eyes.

Fuck. Did I say that out loud?

My back arches against the wall as he presses his thumb to my clit, working me faster, harder and making my release approach quicker than I want it to.

My arms ache as I tug at my restraints, desperate to reach for him, to dig my nails into his corded forearm as he pumps me hard.

"Theo, fuck," I cry, both loving and hating that he manages to make me call out his name.

His face is pulled tight with determination as he pushes me closer to release.

My chest heaves, my skin damp with sweat as the water continues to rain down beside us, splashing my legs as it hits the floor.

"You gonna come for me, Hellcat?" Theo asks, his voice deep and rough with need.

"Oh God, please."

"Fuck," he grunts. Hearing you beg is the fucking sweetest kind of torture, Em."

"Oh, Christ. Fuck. Fuck," I start falling into the most intense... wait. "What?" I squeal as my brain begins to function once more. "No," I spit. "Not. Finished."

The smile he gives me would make the devil himself quiver in fright.

His hand releases my throat, allowing me to drag in a deep lungful of air, but the relief is short-lived because his fingers twist in my hair and I'm forced to my knees.

I fall forward, unable to catch myself with my hands bound, but he thankfully—painfully—holds me upright.

My teeth grind as I stare up at him, his huge dick right in my face.

"You're a fucking cunt," I spit, holding his stare so he knows how fucking sincere I'm being.

His only response is to smile before his eyes drop to my lips.

"Care to use that mouth for something more... useful, Hellcat?"

"That's brave of you after that stunt. I might be inclined to bite it of—"

He makes the most of my parted lips and thrusts his cock into my mouth.

My lips stretch around his width as he pushes all the way inside. Not expecting the intrusion, I gag the second he hits the back of my throat.

"Come on, Hellcat. We both know you can handle cock better than that."

While he's still got his fingers buried in my hair, holding tight enough to pinch, the other hand moves toward my face, his knuckles gently brushing down my cheek.

The two actions are so at odds that it makes my head spin and I almost forget his comment.

How? How could he possibly know how good I am at this?

He pulls back, allowing me to suck in a deep breath.

"I'm not a whore," I hiss.

"Did I say you were?" he asks almost innocently.

But I'm learning all too quickly that there's nothing fucking innocent about Theo Cirillo. I'm beginning to discover that I've only scratched the surface of his depravity.

Thankfully, the situation is entirely mutual, because this, right now?

I'm all fucking over it.

Parting my lips, I allow him to feed his length back in, a little gentler this time.

I relax my throat, already knowing that he's not going to be polite and be satisfied with just the tip.

His teeth grind, making his jaw pop when I take him in my throat.

This isn't my first rodeo where deep throating is concerned. But fuck, I've never had something of that size this freaking deep.

My eyes burn and my lungs scream for air as he holds himself still for a beat too long.

This time when he caresses my cheek, he collects up the tear that drops.

Releasing me once more, he lifts his thumb to his mouth, licking the drop of water off it.

"I hate yo—"

Not allowing me to finish my insult, he takes complete control of both our movements, fucking my mouth and throat like a man possessed.

He doesn't say a word, doesn't make a fucking sound as he uses me.

My shoulders ache, my body burns red fucking hot, and my pussy clenches, desperate to rediscover my lost release as he races toward his.

As much as I might want to rip it away from him at the very last minute like he did to me, I know I'm not going to get the chance.

His hold on me is too tight.

I'm nothing more than his rag doll right now, just along for the ride until he decides what to do next.

His cock swells even bigger beneath my lips, the taste of him already beginning to coat my tongue before the first violent jerk of his release hits him.

He pulls out, allowing the first rope of cum to fill my mouth before he shoots the rest over my face and on my tits.

His eyes trace every drop as his chest heaves, his hand still slowly stroking his length.

I sit there, my own breathing ragged, tears streaked down my cheeks and my lips puffy from his punishing thrusts.

Time seems to stand still as we stare at each other.

I have no idea what to expect, but it certainly isn't what happens next.

His hands grasp my upper arms and he places

me on my feet, spinning me so my back's to him and cutting off our connection.

Coldness rips through me as I stare at the black and white marble wall before me.

"What are you—"

"Shut up," he snaps, and unlike usual, I find my lips slamming shut at his harsh request.

Leaning around me, he presses his hand to the wall, and like magic, a door opens, revealing an array of fancy products.

Pulling a bottle out, he pops the top and squirts whatever it is into his hand.

My gasp of shock rips through the bathroom as his hands find my hair and the scent of floral shampoo hits my nose.

A blue blob of liquid hits my breast and I stare at it.

"Why's it blue?" I ask, my confusion making me forget his previous demand.

"It's for brunettes," he informs me, his fingers massaging my head in the most delicious way.

The tension in my body from the night before begins to ebb away with every stroke of his fingertips.

He works in silence until a thought hits me.

"This is Sloane's, isn't it?"

He pauses and sucks in a breath that damn near empties the room of air.

Then in a flash, his fingers are gone and he's pulling at whatever he bound my wrists with.

Relief floods me, but it only lasts a few seconds because the moment I turn and look at him, I know exactly what's coming next.

And I don't even try to stop him as he storms, dripping wet, out of the bathroom.

13

EMMIE

I stand there under the powerful water jets for the longest time, just staring at the door, waiting—hoping—that he'll come back and finish whatever that was the respectable way. But he never does.

By the time I move, all the weird blue shampoo has been washed down the drain.

Unable to cut the water off until I've put some conditioner through, I reach into the hidden cupboard and pull the other bottle out.

I stare at it, as if the answer to why Theo suddenly freaked out and left after my legit question will appear on the label.

I should have been the one walking out after realizing that he's using his fuck toy's products on me.

No wonder her hair is always so shiny and

perfect. These bottles probably cost more than my dad earns in a month.

Knowing that, I squeeze out a more-than-generous amount into my palm before coating the ends of my hair in it.

I'm still standing under the water, rinsing it out when a door slams somewhere in the flat.

In a rush, I turn the water off and grab one of the very precisely folded towels to cover up with.

I might want him to barge back in here and finish me off, but I don't want to look like I was waiting.

I'm stepping out of the bathroom when a voice calls through the flat, although it's not the one I was expecting.

"Emmie?"

Two seconds later, Stella's silver hair pokes around the bedroom door.

Her expression drops the second her eyes lock on me standing there, dripping in water and wearing only a towel.

"What did he do?" she asks.

My lips part to reply, but a motherfucking lump of emotion suddenly appears in my throat, stopping me from saying anything.

I swallow roughly in the hope of forcing it down but it goes nowhere. Instead, my eyes burn with tears.

No.

That motherfucker isn't going to make me cry. He's not.

"Em?"

"I'm okay," I force out, walking farther into the room in the hope of finding some clothes. "Shit," I hiss when I find nothing. "I don't have any—"

"Clothes," she says softly, lifting the overnight bag I left at her place. She's also got my bag and leather jacket from last night.

"Thank you," I say quietly.

"Want me to give you a minute?" she offers.

Shaking my head, I take the bag from her and turn my back as I tug out the sweats and hoodie I'd packed for this morning.

"Where did he go?"

"I'm not sure. He just knocked and told me to come up here to you."

"Well, that was... considerate of him." I roll my eyes so hard it hurts.

"What did he do?" she asks again.

"Oh, you know. Took me up on my offer of a shower, ripped my orgasm from me at the last minute then got his own and stormed out."

She doesn't recover from her shock quickly enough. Her chin is still hanging open when I turn back to her.

"He fucked you?" she asks.

I scoff. "No," I damn near sulk. Fucking wish he had. I might be feeling less... frustrated right now.

I bite down on my bottom lip as I imagine how it might feel with him stretching me open with that massive—

"So what did—"

"Do we have to?" I ask with a wince.

"N-no. Not if you don't want to. I'm just... he's spent all this time not touching you and then—"

"He touched me and stormed out. He's a fucking joke. I don't even know why I'm here. Why insist on looking after me if he's just going to bail?"

"Do you remember what happened last night?" Stella asks as I follow her out of Theo's bedroom, although not before I dump my towel on the floor and mess up the bed he must have made while I was in the shower. It's petty and means nothing in the grand scheme of things, but hell if it doesn't make me feel better.

"Holy shit," I mutter as the hallway opens up in the most incredible living room space. "It's..."

"Black?" Stella asks with a laugh. "It's funny, because I thought it would have been Daemon's apartment that looked like it belongs to the devil, but his is somewhat normal. This, though... this is..."

"Incredible," I breathe, looking around at everything.

I researched black interiors before I painted my bedroom at Mum's place, and then Dad's, and I was blown away by some of the houses. But this...

what Theo's done is way beyond anything I remember seeing online.

"It's just like a bigger version of your bedroom."

"Uh... I'm not sure the two could be compared."

"Maybe you should show him yours," she suggests with a wink.

"Oh yeah, that's not going to be happening. Current situation aside, can you imagine my dad's reaction if he found him in there? Not just any boy, oh no, the son of a legit mafia boss."

"Could be a member of the MC. Can you imagine if it were Xander? Older and part of the club you should be nowhere near."

"I need coffee," I mutter, putting an end to this pointless conversation.

It doesn't matter what boy I end up with. None will ever be good enough for my dad, I'm sure. And I really don't need to worry about it being Theo because... ugh... just no.

"Wanna go grab breakfast?"

"I really, really do. Where's Cal?"

"Down with Seb. Let's go get her and have a girls' day."

"I am not going to a fucking spa," I argue.

"We'll see." She winks, and I groan as if it pains me to even consider it.

I blame it on the hangover, but much to my horror, Stella and Calli dragged me to Calli's mum's spa and forced me to kick back and relax as some softly spoken woman slapped some sweet-smelling shit on my face, and another fixed my nails after looking at my chipped black polish and dodgy cuticles with disdain written all over her face.

But I can't deny that when I finally walk back into my house later that afternoon, I don't feel a million times better than I did when I woke up, or even when I first looked at Stella.

"Hello?" I shout into the quiet house, but I get no response. Instead, I do find a note on the side.

Em,

Gone out to dinner before I go to work. You know what to do. Be good.

Dad

Happy that I'm not going to get the third degree about last night from either Dad or Piper, I kick off my boots, dump my bags on the stairs and make my way through to the kitchen for a drink.

I spend the night curled up in my bed, watching some serial killer series on Netflix. It's great. It gives me plenty of ideas for how I could end Sloane for her dumb-arse fucking idea to spike my drink last night.

I was all for storming over to her place and having it out with her the second Stella told me the truth about the night before, but apparently, Theo already warned her against it.

I wasn't exactly thrilled with the idea of following his lordship's rules, but also, I didn't really have the energy to go up against the conniving bitch.

I'm happy to let her stew for a bit.

She has to know we'll retaliate. Unless she's even dumber than I think she is and doesn't realise we know that it's her. I wouldn't put it past her.

I'm almost asleep with my TV still playing and lighting up my dark room when my phone dings in my bag and wakes me up.

I dig it out and open the message Stella sent to our group chat.

I barely crack a smile at the meme she's sent, but that's not because it's not funny, but because there's another message waiting for me—one from someone I didn't expect to hear from again today.

I hesitate with my thumb hovering above his message, debating whether I should even open it.

He'll see that I've read it, and then I'll ignore him.

I don't know why that thought makes my stomach clench, but it does nonetheless.

"Fuck it," I mutter, hitting the screen before I can change my mind.

His Lordship: Don't even think about finishing what I started earlier.

My eyes open so wide as I read those words that I'm surprised they don't pop right out of my head.

My thumbs begin flying across the screen before I've even realised I'm typing.

Emmie: I don't take orders from entitled douchebags, so go fuck yourself. You're not getting anything else out of me.

I sit there with my heart racing, staring at the screen, waiting to see if he's going to read it. And if he is, if he'll respond.

My breath catches in my throat only thirty seconds later when *read* appears beneath my message.

"Oh fuck," I breathe, knowing that I've poked the beast.

The little dots telling me that he's typing start bouncing and butterflies erupt in my belly.

His Lordship: We'll see. I know you're still thinking about how my fingers felt inside you…

"Shit," I hiss as my face heats.

Damn it. He's right. And just the thought

makes my entire body burn red hot to feel that delicious stretch from his skilled fingers.

His Lordship: You're thinking about it right now, aren't you?

Emmie: No. I've already found someone else to finish the job, and he was way better than you could ever have been.

His Lordship: Bullshit. You've been with Stella and Calli all day. Unless there's something I don't know about my cousin, no one else has touched you. And nor will they. Including you.

Emmie: Have you always been this much of a dick?

He starts typing a response, but I'm not done.

Emmie: I'm going now, got things to be doing…

I add two winking faces on either side of an aubergine emoji and hit send.

His Lordship: Your cunt is mine, Hellcat. No one touches it but me.

"Pfft," I scoff.

Emmie: Then maybe you should have treated it with a little more respect earlier. You're getting nowhere near me again. You ruined your one and only chance.

His Lordship: I know where you live.

Emmie: Ooooh, I'm so scared.

My eye-roll emoji doesn't really emphasise just how hard I rolled my eyes at his threat.

His Lordship: I'll take that as my invitation. Do. Not. Touch.

"Fucking dickhead," I mutter to myself before making a decision I already know I'm going to regret. But fuck it. I refuse to let him think he's won.

Pushing my knickers and sleep shorts over my hips, I rummage around in my bedside table for my biggest vibrator and get to work, snapping a couple of photos at different angles.

For some reason I don't really want to acknowledge, I never turn my little friend on, and I don't get myself off despite the fact that I'm still desperate for it.

I already know my vibrator is going to pale in comparison to what I was on the brink of getting earlier, so I don't lower myself to a subpar orgasm just out of defiance.

Goddamn you, Theo Cirillo.

I flick through the images I took, select the best one, and send it to Theo before putting my phone on aeroplane mode, righting my clothing and snuggling down into bed, more than ready to pass out and sleep off the lingering effects from the night before.

small whimper rips from my victim's throat as I tighten my grip on the pliers I've got around his little finger.

At this point, I'm amazed he's still got any to play with.

His face is a pattern of cuts and bruises. His clothing is dirty and covered in both dried and fresh blood.

But the pain on his face settles something inside me that *she* woke up.

The second she accused me of using Sloane's shit on her, my very loose grip on my sanity snapped and I either walked out, or she was the one who ended up screaming, her nails clawing at me as I fucked her so hard she'd never feel the same again.

But I couldn't.

I shouldn't have even let it get as far as I did.

The second I heard the shower running, I

should have stayed where I was with my hands curled around the kitchen counter and my head bowed.

I shouldn't have even brought her home.

It was a mistake. All of it.

And now I'm going to pay for it, because I want her.

More than ever.

And I can't have her.

The pliers clatter against the concrete floor as I throw them across the room when his pathetic whimpers of pain no longer do it for me.

Instead, I pull my arm back and slam my fist into his already broken nose.

Blood sprays, covering both of us, but I don't stop.

Not until the cunt passes out from a particularly hard blow to his temple.

"I think you can probably stop now," a familiar, equally angry voice comes from behind me as I stand with my chest heaving, staring down at the pathetic excuse for a man.

I always knew he was a controlling cunt. But the truth... That's far worse than I ever could have imagined.

I tried to ignore my need for this.

After getting Stella to make sure Emmie was okay, I hit the gym. Hard.

But I should have known it would only chase my demons away for so long. The second I stepped back inside my flat, all I could smell was her. All I could see was her.

I put myself through the most agonising shower, wishing that she was there with me, pulled on some fresh clothes and left as fast as I could.

And, I found myself back down here. Deep in Dad's torture chamber, staring at a man who very nearly ripped through the people I care about.

"Yeah, I know," I mutter, cracking my knuckles as I continue staring at his slumped form. "Sorry," I say, finally turning around to look at my spectator. "Did I steal your thunder?"

Toby shrugs, glancing back at the man who claimed to be his father all these years, only to be hurting everyone he loves at the same time.

"Nah, as long as he's getting punished, I'm good."

Bloodlust shines bright in his eyes, making me wonder if he's telling the truth.

"He said anything else?"

I shake my head.

Our prisoner seems to be holding his secrets pretty tight to his chest. It's the only reason he's still alive—because we know there's more.

Almost everything we know so far is down to the DNA tests we carried out.

The relief on Toby's face, although laced with fury when he discovered that this cunt never had a hand—or cock—in making him, was one I'll never forget.

He might have lost something in that moment, but he gained so much more. I mean, in this life, who doesn't want a kick-arse sister like Stella?

I know the whole thing has messed with his head more than he's admitting to. I can see in the depths of his light blue eyes every time I look into them. It's in his stance every time he stands over the man behind me, hoping that whatever pain he's causing will be enough to finally reveal all.

At this point, I'm pretty sure we've got all the main information out of him.

Jealousy. All of it boils down to his inability to control his jealousy that Maria never really gave him her heart. She always belonged to Galen. Although, if we were to dig even deeper, I wouldn't be surprised if it had started years before that. They trained together. They grew up together. Galen claims that they were like us. Tight, close. A team. But I suspect there's more to that, at least from Jonas's perspective.

Toby stares at the man who claimed to be his father all these years, the cunt who controlled his and his mother's lives, spits on his passed-out form and then turns to leave.

I follow him down the hall. His shoulders are pulled tight with tension as his feet pound on the cold, grey concrete floor.

He continues forward when I stop at another door.

This place doesn't just hold that snake, but any

enemies Dad and the others deem worthy enough to keep alive.

I turn to the metal door, my fingers itching to slide the little panel aside and look at her.

I've known that she's been here for a long time. Longer than I should. But the others don't know.

Guilt rips through me for all the secrets I'm keeping, all the lies I tell for my old man despite the questions I have over whether he deserves my loyalty over my boys or not.

Dad might be the boss, but one day, that'll be me. And I'll be nothing if I don't have my boys right beside me.

It's too early in the game to make them question my decisions.

I pinch the small handle and move the screen, but I only get halfway across when Toby must notice that I'm no longer behind him.

"Theo?" he calls, his hard voice echoing down the concrete enclosed space.

"Coming," I say calmly, finally alerting the woman inside the cell to my presence.

Her tired, empty eyes find mine, and we both gasp in shock.

She because she's got a visitor. Me because of how familiar those dark depths are.

Fuck. Wrong move, Cirillo.

I slam the little panel shut as quickly as I opened it and turn away from the door.

But as much as I hate having reality slammed in

my face like that, it helps. It makes me remember that this is a job. It's not my reality.

Walking into my bathroom to find her naked in my shower isn't my reality. It's an illusion that I don't need to fall too deep into, because something tells me clawing my way out is going to be fucking impossible.

Turning my back on the door and the women curled into the corner of the dank room, I head toward the exit of the basement to catch up with Toby.

"Everything okay?" he asks, clearly suspicious as fuck as to what made me pause.

"Yeah, great."

His eyes drop to the blood that's covering me as we unlock the door and climb the stairs.

It's dark when we finally emerge from the building, making me wonder just how long I was down there with Jonas.

"You going somewhere?" Toby asks with curiosity, eyeing the blood that's covering me as we walk toward our cars.

"Um..." My answer should be yes. I should go back upstairs and wash it all off. I'm more than aware of that, but it doesn't stop me craving going somewhere else—the same place I've spent entirely too much time over the past few weeks.

How I've not been discovered yet, fuck only knows.

"Yeah. When are you moving in?" I ask,

knowing that he's crashing with Nico in his basement. I understand why. He doesn't feel like he fits anywhere since the truth came out, but putting up with Nico's arse for a long period of time can't be all that much fun. The guy's a fucking man whore of epic proportions, and I can't imagine he's calmed his ways just because he has a housemate.

"After Christmas, hopefully. The building work is meant to be done this week. I'll move in without furniture if I have to," he confesses, confirming my previous thoughts.

The offer for him to crash with me is right on the tip of my tongue, but I force it down.

My new place is a new start for me. And that includes not having to be a hotel for everyone.

I just want to close myself in and... secretly obsess over a girl I shouldn't even be thinking about.

"Awesome. It'll be great."

"Yeah," he agrees, but there's a weight to it that I don't have the ability to help him relieve.

"Stella will be stoked to have you close." Thankfully, the mention of his sister puts a smile on his face. It's about the only thing that does these days, unless he's unleashing his inner demon and torturing the man who did his best to ruin his life over the past nineteen years.

I always wondered if Toby was too soft for this life. He's always been the nice one, the thoughtful one out of us. But I'm quickly learning that the monster is there. It's just buried deeper than it is in the rest of us.

"The flats are soundproof, right?" he asks with a smirk, knowing that his new place shares a wall with his sister and Seb.

I chuckle. "Sure are. You can fuck all the girls you like, and she'll be none the wiser."

He shakes his head, a smile playing on his lips.

"Good to know," he says, unlocking his car and dropping into the driver's seat.

I do the same once he's pulled out, but after starting the engine and turning the heat on, I know I won't be heading home.

Instead, I just slump back in the seat and blow out a long, pained breath.

The second I close my eyes, all I see is her.

Water running in rivulets down her mouthwatering body. Her nipples, rosy and peaked, just begging for my mouth. The smooth apex of her thighs so fucking tempting, the perfect tease for what's hiding between them.

The noises she made when I was knuckles deep inside her echo through my mind, and my cock continues to harden.

Tugging at my trousers, I make some space for my erection as my need to take the edge off gets the better of me.

I squeeze my length, a groan ripping my up throat as the memories of her on her knees before me, her mouth full of my cock, her lips stretching around me, fill my mind.

I knew she'd look fucking perfect staring up at me with wide eyes, tears and makeup streaked down her hollow cheeks as she sucked me, but fuck... It was so much more than I ever could have dreamed up.

Perfect doesn't even begin to describe the feeling of her taking all of me in her mouth until she choked.

My phone vibrates in my pocket, cutting off my dirty trip down memory lane, and I can't help but smile when I see her name lighting up my screen.

It's as if she knew.

I shake my head as I read her reply to the warning message I sent hours ago.

I wasn't expecting a response, although, I must admit, I wanted one.

I shouldn't have left her like I did earlier, but I did, and it's too late to do anything about it now.

We shoot a couple of teasing messages back and forth, none of which do anything for my aching hard-on, but it's not until her final message... *that* photo... that any good intentions I had of heading back inside and trying to push aside my obsessive need for this girl shatter in favour of indulging my addiction.

My body might be in a hurry, but I don't rush to get to her.

I sit for a little longer in the car park, shoot off a

couple of emails and dig out some intel for Evan on the Italians he tasked me to monitor before I make a tortuously slow journey across town.

There's no way she knows what's coming. So far, my midnight visits have gone unnoticed thanks to the fact the girl sleeps like the fucking dead, but something tells me everything is going to change tonight.

15

EMMIE

My back arches, my shoulders pulling tight as Theo thrusts into me from behind, tugging on my bound wrists to get me in the exact position he wants me in as his giant cock stretches me wide open.

"Yes," I cry as he thrusts forward, filling me so that the pain and pleasure collide in the most dizzying sensation.

Water continues to rain down on my back, and my cheek is crushed against the marble wall. I move away every time he pulls out and crash into it again when he fills me.

It's going to leave a more-than-obvious bruise, but right now, I couldn't care less.

I just need more.

More of him.

More of his dick.

More mindless pleasure.

I race toward my orgasm all too quickly, and just like I fear, he won't let me have this one either.

He pulls out and my body shivers with the sudden onslaught of coldness without his burning touch.

My mind stirs to life as I mindlessly reach for the duvet, vaguely aware that it was real coldness that woke me.

I fight to remain in the deliciousness of that dream, even if I know it was a figment of my imagination, because it was better than reality.

My fingers connect with something, but I quickly discover that it's not the cool softness of my sheets, but the warmth of a... person.

I sit up, my eyes flying open and my heart jumping into my throat.

My lips part, ready to scream, but the second my gaze locks on the figure perched on the edge of my bed, a burning hot palm crashes against my mouth cutting me off before anything escapes my throat.

He pushes against my face and I fall back to my mattress, my eyes still wide and locked on his haunting ones.

A noise fills the room, a buzzing sound, and my brows pinch as I try to place it. But the second I do, all the breath races from my lungs, hitting his hand that's still clamped over my face.

He looms over me like a devil of the night.

"Do not make a noise," he whispers. His voice

is low, deep, rough, and it hits me right between the legs.

I nod, unable to do anything else, continuing to hold his stare.

"Good girl."

A strange warmth floods my body at his praise, and once he's convinced I'm telling the truth, he releases me.

Sucking in a deep breath, I watch him hook his fingers into my shorts and knickers and drag them down my legs.

My mouth waters for the release that he's ripped away from me twice now. I don't care that one of them was a dream. It sure felt real enough in the moment.

The buzzing continues, and when I glance to the side, I find the drawer of my bedside table open and the vibrator I used for that photo earlier missing. Well, not missing just—fuck.

He pushes my thighs wide and presses the tip of the toy to my clit.

It's so powerful that my hips jump from the bed.

"Hellcat," he growls, his hand wrapping around my hip and pinning me in place.

"Oh God," I gasp as he presses it against me once more.

"Were you dreaming about me?"

"No."

His hand leaves my hip in favour of teasing my entrance.

"You're lying. You're soaked. It's for me, isn't it?"

"Never," I cry, a little too loudly. "What the fuck?" I shriek, although it doesn't come out because the motherfucker just stuffed my own knickers into my mouth.

My hand lifts to tug them out but he catches my wrist.

"Hold the headboard, Hellcat. And do as you're told."

"Or what?" I hiss around the fabric.

I have no idea if he makes out the words or not until he responds.

"Try me. I dare you."

Deciding that I want my orgasm too badly this time, I reach behind me and wrap my fingers around the bars of my headboard.

He nods before focusing his attention back on my pussy.

My vibrator leaves my clit, dropping lower, and he pushes it inside me.

I moan around the lace in my mouth and roll my hips.

It feels good. But it's not what I really want.

I want him. Damn it. Him and his massive fucking cock.

But I know better than to break his rules right now if I want a happy ending.

This little shit isn't leaving until he's got me off this time.

I fucking deserve it for putting up with his irritating arse.

"This looks good on you," he says, wrapping his fingers around the fabric bunched around my middle.

I don't need to look down to know what I'm wearing. It's become my favourite sleep shirt. One I hoped no one would discover.

I moan as he pushes it up, exposing my bare breasts beneath.

"But this looks better."

My back arches, offering myself up to him, but other than stare hungrily at my body, he doesn't touch me.

Damn him.

"Please," I beg, despite the fact that I know he can't understand me.

Dragging the vibrator from my body, he moves it back up.

He builds me higher and higher, alternating between fucking me with it and teasing my clit.

I writhe and moan desperately for the release he keeps me on the edge of.

My grip on the bars behind me becomes so tight my fingers cramp into position.

I want to reach for him, demand he let me fall. Anything. But I don't, too afraid that he'll walk away as quickly as he did earlier without giving me what I need.

Again and again, he brings me right to the edge, watching my body for my tells to know when to pull back.

"Fucking hell," I scream, thrashing about in frustration.

"You want to come, Hellcat?" he growls, his voice even deeper than before, making me burn even hotter.

Ripping my eyes from his, I drop them down his body, but it's too dark to see anything, to see if he's as turned on by this as I hope he is.

Fuck, I wish he were naked.

He must decide that I can't take much more, because the next time he drags the vibrator from me and presses it against my clit, his fingers find my entrance.

He thrusts two deep inside me, curling them exactly as he did in the shower earlier, making lights flash behind my eyes.

"FUUUCK," I scream as he rubs at me, finally pushing me over the edge.

My body explodes into a million pieces as my orgasm finally slams into me.

It goes on and on, sweat covering my body as I convulse and ride out every single second of it.

When it finally subsides and I rip my eyes open, I find him still staring down at me with such intensity in his depths that it makes my breath catch.

He works me for another second, ensuring that I've ridden out every ounce of pleasure before dragging his fingers from my body.

He holds them up between us. They glisten in the stream of light coming from the moon, and I wince at just how wet they are.

Turning my vibrator off, he throws it to the bed and reaches up to tug my knickers from my mouth.

"Oh my God," I gasp, hungrily sucking in deep lungfuls of air.

Although my relief is soon cut short when he shoves his fingers past my lips.

"Clean them," he demands, his dark green eyes catching in the moonlight, his hair falling forward, making my fingers twitch to reach for it.

But I don't move. I can't while I'm locked in that dangerous stare.

My tongue does as he demands and I lap at his fingers, tasting my release on him.

His pupils dilate as he stares down at me.

"Fuck," he grunts, but he never moves. He stands there like a statue looming over me.

After the longest time, he finally stands up, his eyes ghosting down the length of my exposed body.

"Do not let go," he warns, shoving his sweats down over his arse and letting his giant erection free.

My mouth waters to taste him again, but I do as I'm told and stay put as he wraps his fingers around himself and starts stroking.

"Holy shit, that's hot," I breathe, although I slam my lips shut when I realise I said it out loud.

I really don't want to give him the satisfaction of thinking I like any inch of him.

His eyes find mine once more as he works himself harder, almost violently.

Getting me off must have got him halfway to his release, because it's only a couple of minutes before he's blowing his load over my tits as a low, sexy growl rumbles in the back of his throat.

Hot jets of cum burn into my skin, making my body ache for another release.

The second he's done, he tucks himself away and presses his knee to the edge of my bed, lowering a little to inspect the mess he's made on my chest.

Dipping his finger into one of the pools of sticky spunk, he begins writing something. Something that I soon discover is his name.

Fuck.

He's claiming me in the most primal way, and fuck if it doesn't make my cunt wet for him all over again.

"No one touches you, Hellcat. Not even your own fingers. I'll know if you do."

I want to ask how, but all words vanish the second his eyes find mine.

Instead, I just nod like a fucking puppet who's happy to follow his instruction.

"Good girl."

Before I know what's happening, he's standing in front of the window, ready to climb out.

Scrambling to sit up, I flick the switch on my lamp, filling the room with soft white light.

I gasp when I take him in, or more so the blood that's covering him.

"Theo, what—"

"See you soon, Hellcat," he says, cutting off my concern over the fact that he's fucking covered in blood.

"Wait," I cry out, a thought slamming into me.

He turns back and looks at me through my open window.

His brow quirks impatiently.

"This isn't the first time you've been here in the middle of the night, is it?"

The smirk he gives me is all the answer I need.

Motherfucker.

"Good afternoon, sunshine," Dad sings when I shuffle through the kitchen sometime before midday the next morning.

I grunt some kind of inaudible reply as I make my way over to the coffee machine, turning my back on both him and Piper, who are sitting at the island.

"Friday night's party that good, huh?"

My entire body tenses.

"Something like that," I mutter, reaching for a mug and placing it on the little stand.

"Emmie," Dad warns. "You're meant to be—"

"A teenager?" I ask, cutting him off.

"Behaving," he corrects.

"Did you have to pick me up from the police station or the hospital?" I ask, resting my back against the side and raising a brow at him.

"There's plenty of trouble you can get in without ending up in either of them."

Don't I fucking know it.

"I've got it, Dad. You don't need to worry."

He stares at me with a blank expression.

"Look, no bruises," I gesture to my mostly covered body. "And," I hold my hands up for Piper to see, "I even got my nails fixed."

She nods, a smile playing on her lips.

"They look great."

"You two want another coffee?" I ask as a peace offering.

"Sure." Dad pushes both of their mugs toward me, and once mine has finished, I put a new pod in and make them each a new one of their favourite. "Do you have plans for the day?"

"Uh…" I hesitate. I do have plans, but not ones I can tell him.

The guilt punch to the chest I'm becoming all too used to threatens to knock the wind out of me as I prepare to lie once more.

"Just heading to the gym, then meeting the girls."

"The gym you've got a job at?" he asks.

"That's the one." I knew telling Piper the other night would make it back pretty swiftly.

I'd told her the truth… mostly. I just couldn't tell her the actual name of the gym, because Mickey's Place would ring more than a few alarm bells. So I was forced to tell her it was the new place that's opened up on the other side of town. Somewhere they're both unlikely to visit, giving me a little bit of breathing space.

"I know I was the one who said about getting a job, but I don't want it to take focus away from school, kiddo."

"It won't, Dad. Plus, I need something other than school. Somewhere with *normal* people."

"Are you suggesting your friends aren't normal?" Dad asks, amusement crinkling his eyes.

"You've met them. What would you say?"

"Fair enough," he mutters, taking his fresh coffee from me when I hand it over. "We're leaving at one o'clock tomorrow and not a second later."

"I know, Dad. You've told me about a million times. I'm not going to screw this up for you."

"I know. I'm just..."

"Impatient?" I ask with a knowing look when he glances at Piper with this soft, completely head-over-heels in love look on his face. It's nice to see, if not totally fucking bizarre.

All my life my father has been this larger-than-life, terrifying, inked, rough-around-the-edges kind of guy. The second I learned about his MC past and who that side of my family really were, it made total sense.

He had the bike and the dangerous look down pat. I can only imagine how brutal he'd have been if he stayed in that life.

But he gave it up... for me.

I let out a sigh as he reaches out and tucks a lock of Piper's hair behind her ear.

He screwed my mum when he was depressed over the fact that he thought Piper was dead—and at the hand of my pops, no less.

I wasn't even meant to exist. And Mum certainly wasn't in any place to be a mother. She never even grew into the role.

I'm amazed she didn't abandon me sooner. I can only assume it was the child benefit and the money from Dad that kept her in the hellhole that is the Lovell Estate with me.

Although that doesn't explain where she is now. She could have had another two years of money if she'd stuck around.

Assuming I could have stuck it at Lovell Academy to attempt some A-levels. I barely hung around long enough to get any GCSEs.

"Yeah," Dad murmurs, reminding me that we were in the middle of a conversation. "You could say that. Feels like I've waited my entire life for this."

He leans forward, peppering kisses along Piper's jaw.

"Ugh, you two are sickening," I mutter, placing Piper's coffee down and grabbing mine, more than ready to make my escape.

To be fair to them, they mostly keep PDAs around the house to a minimum, which I appreciate. But seeing them together, as long as it's

PG-13, doesn't bother me like I thought it would. Mostly, I'm just happy for them. And maybe, just maybe a little bit jealous.

I was aware of the fact, but seeing Dad so affectionate with Piper makes it even more glaringly obvious that that isn't how any of my interactions with Theo have been.

Sure, he's covered me in his jizz twice now. But he hasn't even got close to kissing me. Hell, he won't even let me touch him.

Twisted fuck.

Neither of them says anything as I leave the room. I soon realise why when I look back and find them lost in their kiss.

My chest constricts at the sight.

Damn it.

The second I step back into my room, all I see, all I smell, is him.

My phone taunts me from my bedside table, but I ignore it.

I don't want to know if he's sent anything after his late-night visit.

After pausing, staring at it and wishing I was psychic for longer than I should, I grab my clothes for the day and head to the bathroom, more than ready to wash his scent and touch from me. It seems completely counterintuitive to shower before hitting the gym, but there's no way I'm leaving this house with his scent in my nose.

No way in hell.

Tomorrow we're leaving town for five days.

I'll be able to put him and school behind me as if neither exists.

─────

I spend two hours taking all my frustrations and anger out on Xander, and then another couple of the guys come over to get involved. Apparently, taking on the prez's granddaughter is a thing they all want to be a part of. And I'm more than happy to indulge them as each of them has a different technique and varying skills that they're more than willing to teach me.

By the time I'm showered once more and dressed in normal clothes, I feel like I can take on the world. Or maybe Theo, at least.

Although the thought of fighting him off after he's climbed through my window doesn't seem like a good idea. Maybe I can just kick his arse if he tries a stunt like he did in the shower yesterday morning again. He fucking well deserves it for that.

"I thought I was going to have to come and get you," a deep, rumbling, familiar voice says when I finally make my way out of the locker room.

Being inside that silent room after the last time was pure torture. The whole time I was in the shower, I was looking over my shoulder, listening for any kind of clue that he might just appear.

I hate that I'm a little disappointed that he never did.

I shake the ridiculous thoughts from my head as I make my way over to my uncle.

"How's it going, kid?"

"Yeah, not bad," I say. "You good?"

"Always." He winks, taking my bag from me and wrapping his arm around my shoulder.

"Killed anyone today?" I ask as casually as if I'm asking about the weather.

"Not yet, but it's still early. Only been awake an hour."

"Good night, huh?"

"Sure was, kid. But your ears are way too young and innocent for details."

"I highly doubt that, Cruz. Try me."

He looks down at me and laughs.

"Because I'm not already dicing with death spending time with you. I don't need to corrupt you any more than you already are."

"Pfft. You're aware of the estate I grew up on, right? I've seen people shooting up and fucking in public all my life. Not much can shock me now—even your questionable morals, apparently."

"Your mum's a bitch. Sorry."

"Agreed. Now are you going to feed me or what?"

He laughs, coming to a stop beside his bike which is parked next to mine and making it look like a toy.

He throws my gym bag over his body to save me from carrying it and climbs on.

"Usual place?"

"You know it."

The rumble of his engine vibrates through me as I get on my own much-less-powerful bike and turn the engine.

"Let's go then," Cruz barks, flipping his helmet down as I pull mine on and taking off across the car park.

I trail him across the city and squeal in delight as we weave in and out of the traffic, exactly like Dad refuses to do when we're out together.

He insists on being a sensible parent, setting a good example. Problem is, I know exactly how he likes to ride his bike when he's alone, and hell, I crave that adrenaline hit as much as he does. Even if my bike only does about three miles an hour in comparison.

It won't be long until I can play with the big boys. Excitement zips through my veins as we damn near jump a set of lights before Cruz pulls his beast to a stop outside our favourite place.

He drags his helmet off and runs fingers through his hair, more than aware of the three women standing outside the shop next door to the place we're going.

They might be fully grown adults, but it doesn't stop them whispering and ogling him like they're horny teenagers. I get it. Cruz was gifted with some dangerously good looks. Just like my dad, not that I like to admit that very often.

"No hooking up when you're hanging with your niece," I remind him when he leisurely checks each of them out. Knowing him, he's probably imagining having them all at the same time.

He might be a looker, but he's also a massive fucking man whore.

"I know the rules, baby girl."

"Ugh, really?" I ask, shuddering at the name Dad calls Piper when he thinks I'm not listening. Cruz only does it to get a rise out of me, and it works every damn time.

Cruz laughs as he presses his hand to my lower back and pushes me forward. The move is purely for the women, I'm not stupid, but damn, it works. They all swoon so hard I'm worried we might have to go and pick the three of them up.

"You're so in there," I say as we walk through the door and get blasted by hot air from the heater above it.

Rubbing my hands together, I allow Cruz to push me toward a booth at the back. The scent of sugar and chocolate makes my mouth water and my stomach growl.

I stuffed a cereal bar in my mouth as I left the house earlier, but that's all I've had since stopping for burgers with Calli and Stella after the spa last night.

"I thought women were banned on our dates," Cruz sulks behind me.

"They are. Mostly for my entertainment. Anyway, something tells me you're not lacking for action if the dark circles around your eyes are anything to go by."

"Maybe I was out with the guys." The mischief in his eyes tells me that he was *not*, in fact, out with the guys.

"Sure. You having the usual?" I ask when I spot one of the regular waitresses heading our way.

"Good afternoon," she says happily, her eyes lingering on Cruz a beat too long as they usually do.

"Lacey, how's it going?" he drawls, making her cheeks heat.

"Ignore him," I say, kicking him in the shin under the table. "We'll have our usual please, Lace."

"You got it, sweetheart." She smiles at me before racing across the small seating area to place our order.

"I can't take you anywhere."

He shrugs and stretches his big arse body out on the bench.

"Got you something, kiddo," he says, pulling a box from the inside of his jacket.

"Cruz," I complain, remembering the conversation we had not so long ago about Christmas presents.

He just shrugs. "Open it."

He slides a black box across the table.

My curiosity stops me from arguing and I pull the top off and lift the little piece of foam protecting the contents.

"Oh my God. Cruz!" I half squeal, half laugh as I stare down at a dog tag with the Reapers emblem engraved on it. "Does Pops know you've given me this?"

He shakes his head. "Thought it was time," he says as if it's nothing.

This tag... owning one of these is as life-changing for anyone who's a part of the Reapers as having their ink on your skin.

Lifting my eyes from the gift, I hold his for a beat.

"I know shit's been weird this year, kid." He shifts awkwardly and rests his elbows on the table, wrapping his hand around his clenched fist. "All that shit with Piper and—"

"It's okay," I say in a rush. I mean, it's not really. He abducted Piper and threatened to kill her, and got my dad shot in the meantime.

It was a shitshow. It still is, with Dad refusing to have anything to do with Cruz or Pops. I understand why, fuck do I.

But unlike him, I've also made the effort to talk to Cruz about it. And I mean really talk. Hearing his reasons for it all from his own mouth helped me to see things a little differently.

I'm not sure I'll ever truly forgive him for it. But I understand, and I refuse to lose another family member I actually like because of bad judgement and dodgy morals.

Cruz lets out a sigh. "How are they? Looking forward to next week?"

I smile, thinking about how happy Dad and Piper are.

"Yeah, they're buzzing. It's pretty cute."

"Don't let D hear you call him that."

I laugh, but it's filled with sadness.

"He's different. Happy. I hope you get to see it one day."

Cruz keeps his face impassive, but I see the pain in his eyes. Eyes that are so similar to Dad's.

"Yeah, maybe. Gotta admit, kinda wish I could see him saying 'I do'. Never thought it would happen."

"You and me both. I'll send you some pictures though, promise."

"Damn right you will. I wanna see my beautiful niece in a dress for once."

"Ugh, don't you start," I complain.

"And don't think I haven't noticed these," he says, pointing to my nails.

"It's for Piper," I argue, dropping my hands to my lap.

She never told me that she didn't want me to have black nails for the wedding, but I saw her eyes every time she looked at them, so yesterday, I did something very, very out of character. When the woman in the spa asked what colour I wanted, I pointed to a very pale pink and swallowed nervously.

"It's cute. I like it."

"It's... yeah. It's probably not going to stick," I say.

"I've got something else," he admits, pulling an envelope from his pocket. "Could you... could you give this to your dad for me, maybe?"

"You know you should just give it to him yourself," I point out. "It might mean more if you made the effort."

"I know, but I don't think he needs to bust his knuckles on my face days before he ties the knot to the woman who's owned his heart all his damn life."

"Careful, Cruz. That almost sounds romantic."

He snorts a laugh.

"I just want him... them... to be happy. You know that."

"I do. But I don't think it would hurt telling them yourself."

"I have. It's just... in there."

I take the ivory envelope from him and slide it into my handbag beside me.

"Can you give it to him the night before?"

"Whatever you want," I agree, my eyes widening in delight when Lacey makes her way over with a trayful of goodness.

She passes plates of our favourite salted caramel and vanilla ice cream waffles toward us before giving us both a giant mug of hot chocolate with all the trimmings.

It's more sugar than I should probably eat in a month, but fuck it.

Grabbing my spoon, I dive in as Cruz thanks Lacey, making her giggle like a schoolgirl.

"I can't wait for a woman to knock you on your arse, old man," I mutter around a mouthful of waffle once she's out of earshot.

"One, I'm not old." I raise a brow at him. "We can't all be seventeen, brat. And two, no woman is knocking me anywhere. Love is for dreamers."

"Dad's a dreamer?"

"Hell yeah. He spent almost all his adult life dreaming about a girl he thought was dead."

"Love sick fool," I say with a laugh.

"See. You get me."

"I do. Let the fun times roll, eh?"

He stares at me, his lips parting to say something before he changes his mind.

"Spit it out, old man."

Narrowing his eyes, he leans forward and whispers, "You better not be having more fun than me, kid."

Sitting back, I smile innocently. "I've no idea what you're talking about." He scoffs. "You know the reputation of the school I go to."

"Too fucking right. I know the boys who run it, too."

Thankfully, I manage to turn the conversation away from school and anything related to the name Cirillo and spend a couple of hours chatting about bullshit with my uncle before heading home with my new piece of jewellery safely zipped inside my bag.

I already know that Dad's going to blow his top when he finds out I've been hanging out with Cruz, let alone spending time at the compound with Pops. But finding this, what is effectively my lifetime pass to the Reapers, will tip him right over the fucking edge.

17

THEO

"No offense, but are you planning on going home anytime soon?" Seb asks from the other sofa where he and Stella are twisted together like a pretzel.

I blow out a breath and stare up at the ceiling to my flat.

Stella whispers something in Seb's ear and his eyes widen, a smile appearing on his face.

"You're so fucking right," he tells her, but his eyes hold mine, assuring I see his amusement from whatever she just said. "Sad fuck, it's only been a few hours."

"Time probably feels like it's standing still," Stella says, loud enough that I can hear her this time.

"Ah, I remember it well. When you were in America—"

"He was a cunt." I finish for him. "I know what you two are implying, and you're talking shit."

"Are we?" Stella asks, sitting up a little higher. "It's been a day and you're all fidgety and shit."

"It's got nothing to do with her."

A smile twitches at Stella's lips.

"Her?" she asks, faking confusion. "I was talking about you not working, but if this is about Em—"

"Don't," I snap. "Don't say her fucking—"

"Bro," Seb barks, pushing Stella out of the way for a beat before placing her so she's straddling his lap. "You are so fucked. You might as well just admit it. We see it all. And, we'll even keep your dirty secret from the others."

"No idea what you're talking about."

Stella laughs before it cuts off with a loud gasp from whatever Seb is doing to her that I can't see. I knew I was on borrowed time with the two of them. The quiet cuddling was too good to be true.

"It's okay to miss her," she moans, her head falling back.

"Miss her?" I scoff. "I'm enjoying the peace."

"Liar," Seb mumbles before peeling Stella's hoodie up, exposing her bra.

"Fucking hell, man. If you wanted me to leave, you could have just said."

"You don't have to leave. Watch if you want."

"Oh shit," Stella cries, "You should probably leave."

"Christ," I mutter, pushing from the sofa and taking my empty bottles to the kitchen as Stella grinds down on Seb's lap.

"I'll see you guys tomorrow."

"Yup. Your parents' party. Got it."

Seb puts his thumb up behind Stella's back and I let myself out, leaving them to their antics.

I might not want to sit there and watch them fuck, but equally, I don't really want to sit alone in the silence of my flat.

I pull my phone out of my pocket as I make my way to my own kitchen for another drink.

Nico, Alex and Toby are out somewhere. They invited us all earlier, but I wasn't really in the mood for it.

I'm still not. But... ugh.

I knock the top off a bottle of beer and throw it across the counter, watching as it bounces to a stop in the corner.

My entire body is tense, and my need to move, to do something, anything means that I end up pacing back and forth through the length of my flat.

I stand at the windows, staring out across the city, but the car lights moving below do little to ease the tension pulling my muscles tight.

I could go out, get wasted with the guys and hook up with some random chick for the night. It might even help for a bit. But I know it's not going to cut it.

There's only one thing that does.

Grabbing my tablet, I turn it on and power up the app I've become addicted to.

My heart pounds as I wait for it to load. I don't know why. I know exactly what I'm going to find, and it's going to be nothing but disappointing.

The second the image of the room appears, it looks as I feared.

Empty.

The bed is neatly made, and although there are signs of her being there, all the things she uses every day like the hairbrush that always sits on her dressing table next to her massive makeup bag has gone.

The boots that always sit by the door are no longer there.

I blow out a frustrated breath, not wanting to resort to my next move.

I resisted last night. Just barely.

My tablet taunted me from the bedside table as I laid there, staring up at the ceiling with images of the night before filling my mind.

I expected her to close her window after Saturday night, but to my surprise, when I walked up her back garden, I found it open as usual. Only this time, the sight made my cock ache until it hurt because I knew it was an invitation.

She knew about my nightly addiction, and fuck if she wasn't feeding it.

It's why going cold turkey last night was so fucking hard.

For weeks I've visited her while she's slept.

Some nights I've just watched her. Others, I've got myself off with the sound of her talking in her sleep. Then there are the couple that I really pushed my luck, painting my cum over her lips as she laid there, completely unaware of my presence let alone anything else.

Knowing that she was going to lick her lips at some point and taste me... Fuck. Even now it gets me hard as fucking steel.

Unable to stop myself, I open the next app, my need to know unbearable.

It's a different app from the one the guys and I use to keep tabs on each other. I didn't want to risk them knowing what I was doing. They already suspect too much.

It takes forever to search. The little wheel in the middle of the screen teases me for the longest time before a map appears, slowly zooming in on a location to the south of the city.

"Holy fuck," I breathe when it finally comes to a stop, giving me her exact location.

She's only an hour and a half away.

Fuck.

I shouldn't have looked.

I'd convinced myself that they'd be at the other end of the country or something. Too far away for me to be able to do anything.

I glance up at the huge silver clock that covers almost all the back wall of the living room.

Eleven pm.

If I left now...

The number of beers I've had doesn't factor at all into my decision as I storm toward my bedroom, shed the clothes I've been wearing all day and throw myself under the shower.

I'm done in only minutes, and less than a quarter of an hour later, I'm in the lift heading toward the underground garage with the keys to my Ferrari locked in my hand and my mind firmly set on my prize.

The overhead lights flicker to life when I push the door open and step inside the vast space that currently only houses mine and Daemon's vehicle collection.

My car lights up as I get closer, and before I've even thought through the process of starting her up, I'm waiting for the gates to open and pressing my foot on the accelerator toward the destination I've already plugged into the GPS.

I t only takes me an hour to get to her location, and when I'm confident I'm in the right place, I abandon my baby in a dark layby and stiffly climb out.

My tense muscles refuse to relax as I move, my heart thundering in my chest so hard my hands are shaking in my need to get to her.

Fuck. This is wrong.

All of this is fucked up beyond belief.

I shouldn't be here.

I shouldn't be fucking stalking her like a fucking loser.

I really don't think that's what Dad had in mind when he agreed to all of this. But one thing he might just have been right about was how badly I want her.

Because fuck.

My balls ache, my cock strains against the loose fabric of the sweats I'm wearing, and my nails dig into my palms with my need to feel her writhing body beneath me.

Mum's always warned me that I have an obsessive personality like my father. I didn't see it as a kid. Hell, I didn't understand it.

I don't think I ever have until this very moment.

A twig snaps beneath my foot and I look back at my car, knowing that I should get back in, drive home and pretend that none of this ever happened.

That I never set up cameras in her room one night when she was sleeping soundly. That I ensured I could track her no matter where she goes so that I can always find her, whether she's in danger or even if she's just running from a deranged psycho—me. And I certainly shouldn't have just rolled over and accepted the fate that those above us decided for us.

She should be more than a job. She *is* more than a job. I can admit that to myself. But she is a job nonetheless, and my father, the boss, expects me to deliver.

It's what he raised me for. What he trained me for.

Being a soldier, being made, embracing my heritage, focusing on my future, my legacy... that was my first real obsession. Well, after Lego and football. But even still. It has nothing on my need for her. The unfiltered, irrational, dangerous obsession I have for the woman who may or may not be lying to all of us. Who may be a threat to our empire. A woman who could bring me to my fucking knees if I'm not very, very careful around her.

A cabin comes into view through the trees. Soft outside lights illuminate it in the darkness, and as I get closer, I realise that some of that light is actually coming from inside.

My steps falter a little at the thought of everyone still being awake inside.

After stopping behind a tree to allow my app to pinpoint her location a little more precisely, I head toward the cabin, or more specifically, the open window at the very end of the huge wooden building.

My need for her far outweighs the risk of being caught, so without a second thought, I haul myself up and into the dark room to find exactly what I hoped: her sleeping form in the middle of the giant bed.

18

EMMIE

For a holiday with a bunch of adults, I'm having a surprisingly good time. Although that might just be seeing the infectious happiness on my dad's face.

Today has been everything I hoped for both of them.

It was relaxed, full of love and laughter. Dad even managed to get his friends to mostly behave. Although the fact that they're all here with their own girlfriends and wives helped to keep them in line.

It's late when I finally fall into bed, and I'm exhausted after being up early with Piper and the other women to get ready. I caved and allowed Biff to do my makeup while Danni set to work curling all our hair.

By the end of it, even I could admit that I looked like a fairly normal bridesmaid. Pretty, even.

It was weird seeing myself dressed up without the heavy black eye makeup and dark red or purple lips.

The dress we picked for me fit like a second skin, accentuating my curves and making me look like... well... a girl.

That being said, I was more than happy to shed all of it the second Piper gave me the nod.

The curtains at the window billow with a gust of ice-cold air.

The weather today was perfect for the Christmas wedding Piper planned. The hard frost this morning meant the early morning photographs were more than festive with what looked like snow covering everything, then this afternoon the sun was so bright it was hard not to squint the whole time.

I grab my phone and start scrolling through social media, looking at the photos Stella and Calli have uploaded from the annual Cirillo Christmas Eve party that I was thankfully far, far away from.

I'd like to think that Stella and Calli wouldn't have even asked me to go, given the circumstances but I have a suspicion that they'd ignore the beef between Theo and me and demand I be there, if for no other reason than their own entertainment.

I think back to the one and only time I've been inside the Cirillo mansion, the night Theo's coach house burned to the ground. I didn't want to go inside for obvious reasons. Reasons that were well-founded when he did appear. The second he saw me there in his house, I really thought the vein in his temple was going to pop.

It was a good job he wasn't half an hour earlier to see me sitting with his siblings, because I can only imagine that that really would have tipped him over the edge.

A loud muffled moan from above hits my ears and I wince, having a really good idea about what's happening upstairs.

Ugh, gross.

Both Zach and Biff's and Spike and Kas's rooms cover mine. It could be coming from either. Or both.

I shake my head, wishing I could close my ears when someone giggles.

"Jesus," I mutter, continuing to scroll, looking at all the wealth that screams from every designer piece of clothing and lavish jewellery.

Embarrassingly, I slow my scrolling when I get to a photo with Theo standing right in the middle, talking to some blonde-haired girl I don't recognise.

She looks like the most perfect Barbie doll, and I can only imagine how good they'd look together, side by side.

An uncomfortable wave of jealousy flows through my body, making my stomach knot painfully.

That's the kind of girl Theo should be with. He knows it too.

Probably why he's standing with her, moron.

I roll my eyes and force myself to keep scrolling.

It doesn't help, because the image of Theo with his hair perfectly styled, wearing his sharp black suit is burned into my eyes.

The only thing better than him looking deadly in that outfit was when he was standing before me in nothing. Okay, I'm lying. I'll take him in sweats any day, too. The way the fabric hugs his…

I shake my head once more, desperately needing those kinds of thoughts gone.

Above me, something—a bed, I'm assuming—starts banging.

"Oh, for the love of God," I mutter, my own body beginning to burn a bit hotter at the thought of what everyone else is clearly up to.

I bet even Danni, who's a bazillion months pregnant, is getting more action than me.

I stare at the curtains once more, longingly.

If we were home right now, I wonder if I'd have got a visit?

Probably not, he's too busy partying with Barbie.

It's been three days since his last night-time visit. Since he edged me over and over until it literally felt like I was going to explode if he didn't let me fall.

Well, as far as I know, it's been three days.

I know I should have closed my window after

discovering his antics on Saturday night. I went to. But the second my fingers closed around the handle it felt wrong, and I immediately backed away, leaving it open, hoping that he'd return for a repeat performance.

I sigh, the banging upstairs only getting louder.

If he did come, he didn't wake me. And I'm not sure how I feel about that.

Did he just watch me? Did he... do anything?

Was he even there?

I blow out a frustrated sigh, fed up with second-guessing myself.

It doesn't matter if he did come. He clearly didn't want me aware of his visit if he did. And that right there is the issue.

Whatever *this* thing between us is, it's hidden darkness and cloaked in secrets.

Yeah, it makes it hotter, more tempting.

But it doesn't change the fact that the two of us could never be.

For starters, we hate each other...

When a scream rips through my room, I sit up, swinging my legs from the edge of the bed and realising that I've got two options.

Lie back like a creep and get myself off to the sounds of one of my pseudo uncles banging his woman, or take the joint that Kas slipped me earlier and get the fuck out of this room, this cabin.

I can lie here wishing that Theo might slip

through that open window all night, but we all know it's never going to happen.

He's too busy in London, schmoozing all his parents' wealthy and influential guests, probably trying to decide which Barbie doll he's going to let bounce on his giant dick when the party slows down.

Fuck. Maybe he won't even limit it to one.

I've heard all the gossip at school. I might not be interested in joining in, but that doesn't mean I don't listen.

"Fuck it," I mutter, swiping the joint and a lighter from the bedside table where I placed it earlier, tugging on a pair of boots and shoving my arms through a Rebel Ink hoodie that I shamelessly stole from Titch.

Wrapping it tightly around myself, I pull the hood up and shove my phone in my pocket before swinging my leg over the window frame and dropping to the frozen ground below.

My breath comes out in white clouds as the grass and fallen leaves and twigs crunch beneath my feet.

A whole-body shiver rips through me, but I don't let it stop me and walk deeper into the undergrowth.

The moon is bright and high in the sky, allowing me enough light to navigate my way around the trees.

I come to a stop when I'm confident that I'm far

enough away from the cabin that I won't be spotted should anyone look out of the windows. Leaning back against a huge tree trunk, I bring the joint to my lips before flicking the lighter, making the space around me glow orange.

I suck in a deep hit, fighting my need to cough as my throat contracts around the smoke, but the second it fills my lungs I already feel it start to take effect.

My muscles relax as I exhale, a buzz flowing through my veins as I sag back against the tree with a lazy smile playing on my lips.

This is better than listening to whomever get their rocks off upstairs.

I can't have taken any more than four hits, my body beginning to shiver violently against the cold, my teeth chattering, when a rustling and then a crack sounds out behind me.

My heart jumps into my throat and I freeze, my body trembling but not just from the cold this time.

What the fuck was I thinking, coming out here in the dead of night?

It's just an animal.

Just a fox.

A badger.

A...

The footsteps come closer, and any high I'd got from the joint seems to vanish as my fear takes over.

I'm going to die out here. Alone. In my pyjamas.

Damn it, I don't even have underwear on.

What is it that most normal mothers tell their daughters? Make sure you always go out with clean knickers in case you end up in hospital.

Or give easy access to the psychotic rapist who's about to attack you.

Whatever it is is right on the other side of the tree now.

I glance to the side and see a puff of cold air.

Fuck.

It really is a person.

Or a bear. *In the Essex countryside… unlikely.*

Fuck. Fuck. Fuck.

I squeeze my eyes tight, not wanting to look at my killer. Not wanting to remember my final moment at the hands of whoever is about to slit my throat or…

A figure looms over me. Even with my eyes closed, I see the shadow of his body as he blocks the moonlight.

A whimper threatens to rip up my throat as I summon the courage to open my eyes and stop being such a pussy.

I wouldn't be this pathetic if I weren't already halfway stoned, I'm sure of it.

But then his scent hits me and my eyes fly open.

"What the fuck are you—"

His hand clamps down over my mouth, stopping my shrill screeching.

"Shut up, Hellcat. Unless you want daddy dearest down here," he warns.

"Me?" I hiss behind his hand. "You should be the one who—" His hand tightens, stopping me from issuing my own warning about the reason my dad and the others really don't want to find him here.

I narrow my eyes at him, silently asking the millions of questions that are on the tip of my tongue but unable to spill free.

He stares at me in the darkness, his eyes wide and dangerous, but there's an amused smirk playing on his lips.

His fingers find mine, and for the briefest moment, I think he's going to hold my hand.

A weird rush of excitement flows through my veins before reality hits and he plucks the joint from my fingertips and lifts it to his lips.

I watch, enthralled as he takes a hit, his eyes drilling into me the whole time.

My stomach clenches with desire when he slowly releases the smoke, letting it billow from his full, tempting lips.

"What are you doing out here alone, Hellcat?" he asks, his voice rough and dripping with sex.

"Trying to get myself raped and killed, obviously," I mutter sarcastically.

His lips press into a flat line and his jaw tics in frustration.

"Not. Funny," he spits, stepping closer until his heat seeps into my freezing body.

"Why are you out here alone?" he tries again.

Rolling my eyes, I steal my spliff back and take a drag, his eyes locked on my lips the entire time.

"Because," I say, blowing the smoke in his face, "the couples above me were fucking. Loudly," I add.

A smirk twitches at his lips.

"Missing me, Hellcat?" he asks, leaning in and brushing the tip of his nose along my cheek.

It's a weirdly tender move compared to what I'm used to from him.

"S-shouldn't you be at your parents' pretentious party right now?"

"Should be, yeah. But it seems that I'm here instead."

"Why?" I breathe.

He doesn't respond, he just stares into my eyes, our noses only a whisper apart, our clouded breaths mingling as our chests heave.

"Wish I knew," he finally says, but it's so quiet I wonder if he even realises that he said it out loud. "I was at their party."

"I know, I've seen photos." The second the words are out of my mouth, I realise they were a mistake.

"You been stalking me, Hellcat?"

I scoff. "That's rich. Why are you here, Theodore? What could you possibly need from me that meant you drove all this way on Christmas Eve?" His teeth grind as I say his whole name, and I can't help the wave of satisfaction that washes through me.

He steps closer still, pinning me between his hard body and the tree at my back.

"Clearly, it wasn't for your stellar personality," he mutters.

"What can I give you that any of those Barbie dolls you were walking around with tonight can't?"

His eyes flick between mine and the hoodie I'm wearing. It allows me to predict the next words that fall from his lips as he not-so-subtly avoids my question.

"Whose is this?"

"My boyfriend's," I shoot back.

"Right," he laughs. "If that is in any way true, then you've got a hell of a lot of apologies to give him."

My brows pinch as I think about the two times we've been together. I wouldn't exactly describe that as a hell of a lot, but whatever.

Stupid fuck hasn't even kissed me. Or fucked me.

If he's trying to mark his territory or whatever the hell this is, then he really should up his game.

"Like you'd care either way. Your morals are so loose they're almost non-existent."

"Oh, Hellcat," he says, dark amusement dancing in his eyes. "You have no fucking idea."

A gasp rips from my lips when he tugs the hoodie apart and hungrily stares down at my hard nipples, which are more than obvious beneath my thin tank, and he pushes his hand beneath the fabric of my pyjama bottoms.

A low growl rumbles in his throat when he discovers that I have nothing beneath them.

"You'll have me thinking you were waiting for me," he murmurs, pushing two fingers lower and plunging them inside me. "Fuck. You were, weren't you?"

I shake my head almost violently with my need to deny the truth. "No," I cry into the silence around us.

"You wanna get us caught?" he asks, his lips brushing my cheek, his hot breath flowing down my neck and making me shiver.

"Y-you shouldn't be here. Y-you should—"

"I don't think you want me to be anywhere else, Hellcat."

"Fuck," I moan when he hits that spots that makes bright lights flash behind my eyes. "B-but why?" I try again, my hips writhing, meeting his fingers thrust for thrust.

"Because…" he starts, but then he pauses and looks me dead in the eyes, "I wanted my Christmas present early."

Darkness engulfs his green depths a second

before he rips his fingers from my body, leaving me cold and empty.

My muscles ripple, desperate to feel the delicious stretch, the pressure in just the right place.

"Well, you're not going the right way about it," I hiss, but it's too late, he's already putting his plan into action. And, more than that, I already know that I'm going to let it happen.

Because honestly, I think there could be a chance that I want it even more than he does.

His fingers grip my hair, and with a painful shove, I find myself on my knees before him once more.

I've barely managed to steady myself before my hands are reaching for his waistband.

"Greedy girl," he damn near groans when I drag the zip down and tug the fabric over his hips, freeing his thick cock.

With my eyes locked on it, I wrap my fingers around the width, loving just how hard and smooth he is against my hand.

"Shit," he hisses, staring down at me with this intense look that makes my pussy flood. It quickly occurs to me that this is the first time he's allowed me to touch him, and I can only imagine he's having the same reaction as I have every time he touches me.

His fingers, even the lightest graze, burn me from the inside out.

I've never ached for a guy before like I do for him. Like I might actually die if I don't feel him stretching me open with that huge dick sometime soon.

"You gonna put that dirty mouth on me, Hellcat?" he growls when I do nothing but stare, my mouth watering with every second that passes.

I nod, but the movement is so small I doubt he sees it in the darkness.

Leaning forward, I lick up his tip, tasting the precum that's already leaking.

I groan when his taste fills my mouth.

"Gonna need more than that, tease."

Theo's fingers twitch in my hair, and I get just enough warning of what's coming next to suck in a huge breath before the head of his cock is forced past my lips. He doesn't stop until he's right in my throat, cutting off my air supply.

I hum in appreciation as his grip tightens to the point of pain and his eyes slam closed as he absorbs the sensation of my mouth, of my tongue lapping at the underside of his cock.

The second he gathers himself, his eyelids flicker open and he stares down at me, his dark eyes holding mine as I take him in my mouth.

"You suck me so good, Hellcat," he rumbles, his other thumb brushing my cheek tenderly.

My head spins with the move just like the last time he did it, but it's soon forgotten when he thrusts his hips, his cock pushing deeper in my throat.

My lungs burn, my eyes water, and drool spills over my chin as he punishes my mouth. His grip remains tight on my hair as if he's worried I'll break away. Clearly, he doesn't know me as well as he claims to, because I want this. I want him.

Fuck, do I want him.

I hum around him, sensing that he's getting close. His movements are getting less controlled, his width swelling.

"Fuck. Emmie," he groans, his eyes narrowing, but he never breaks eye contact as his release slams into him, his cock jerking violently in my mouth, cum hitting the back of my throat and covering my tongue before he pulls back.

When he's spent, he lets his cock slip free. Drool and cum run from the sides of my mouth but he lifts his thumb to my skin, collecting it up and pushing the evidence of his orgasm back inside.

"Swallow," he demands, and I do instantly. "Fuck, you look good on your knees for me, Hellcat." His thumb continues to stroke my chin appreciatively.

His eyes bounce between mine, indecision filling the darkness.

"No," I spit, "don't you dare turn your back on me before you get me off again."

He smirks, and damn if the sight of his arrogance doesn't make my clit pound with need.

"After you just sucked me so good, wouldn't dream of it, Hellcat."

Dragging me to my feet, he holds me right in front of him, his eyes locked on what I'm sure are my swollen lips.

My heart thunders in my chest as I wait for him to walk away.

As much as I don't want that, I tell myself that I won't beg. That I won't lower myself to showing just how much I need him right now.

19
___

THEO

Kiss her.

My body screams at me to move, to take her, claim her. To sate the burning need within me. To fucking consume her and ruin her for any other motherfucker.

But while my body might be fully on board with that plan, my head isn't.

My head knows all the reasons I can't, despite the fact that I came all this way. Again. That I walked away from my parents' house, the place I have a duty to be.

My phone has been blowing up since the second the guys realised I left, but I haven't responded to them.

No one, not even me, understands my need to be here. To be close to her. To touch her.

"Theo," she whispers, my thumb still resting on her bottom lip, my palm cupping her delicate jaw.

Her soft, unsure voice does things to me. Things I've never felt before and things I don't want to even try to unpack.

Desperation oozes from her, and I know without checking that she's fucking dripping wet for me.

It would be so easy to bend her over and own her completely.

But as much as I might need that, crave that, I can't.

This situation is already too fucked up. If I do that then...

"Shit," I hiss, releasing her and pushing my fingers into my hair, dragging it back until it burns.

"Go on then, you fucking pussy. Walk away," she barks, making my breath catch. "Go. I don't need you," she seethes. "I brought my vibrator with me. It does a much better jo—"

"No, you didn't," I state confidently.

Her eyes narrow.

"Yes, I—"

Dropping my hand to her throat, I push her up against the tree behind her. Her eyes widen in shock, but there's not enough to cover the desire darkening her already blown eyes.

Stoned is a good look on this little liar.

Getting right in her face, my nose grazes hers, our brows pressing together.

"Liar," I hiss. "It's still in your top drawer at home."

Her eyes widen, but that's the only reaction she gives.

"It's been three days since I got you off, and you didn't bring your trusty toy. How badly do you need it, Hellcat?"

"I've got my own fingers," she hisses, her hand lifting from her side. To start with, I think she's just going to prove a point about its existence, but I clearly completely misread her intentions because almost faster than I can process, her palm flies toward my face.

Unfortunately for her, I've been training for this shit since before I even knew what Dad was preparing me for.

A shocked squeal rips from her lips as my fingers wrap around her wrist, stopping her from making contact right at the last minute. I might have allowed her to wrap her tiny fingers around my shaft, but that's all she's getting of me. If I allow her to touch me, then all bets are going to be off.

"What the fuck?" she hisses when I pin her unforgivingly up against the tree and press the length of my body against her. My already hardening cock nestles between her arse cheeks, making it wake up again even faster than before.

"Only good girls get rewards, Hellcat," I breathe in her ear, loving how she shudders at the sensation of my breath racing over her chilled but over-sensitive skin, along with the words.

"Please," she whimpers before stilling when she realises she said it out loud.

"Hands on the tree, and do as you're told."

She nods, and I release her hand when she tries to comply.

Stepping back, I slide my hands down her sides, tucking them into the waist of her pyjama bottoms and pushing them down her legs.

In a flash, they're pooled at her ankles.

"Kick them off," I demand.

She hesitates, and I understand why. She's going to have to toe her boots off and stand on the ground barefoot. I should care, but right now, the only thing I can think about is tasting her.

I shouldn't do it. It's one step closer to fucking her. Just another addiction to add to all the others, because I know that once I get a taste, I'm never going to want to stop.

But fuck. It's Christmas, and she's so fucking horny and desperate I can already smell it.

In a rush, she sheds the clothing around her feet and stands before me with her back arched, her arse sticking out, tempting me.

Fucking tease.

She's got her cheek pressed against the trunk, looking the other way so when I raise my hand, she's none the wiser.

Until my hand cracks across her arse.

Her scream pierces the night air around us,

making an animal that was probably sleeping somewhere near scurry away in fright.

"Fuck, Theo."

My cock swells at my name on her lips and my palm twitches to go again, to see my bright red handprint across her pale skin.

"Say it again," I growl.

"Fuck?"

"Don't fucking push me, Hellcat."

My hand smacks against her arse once more.

"Argh," she cries out before giving me what I want. "Theo."

"Yes," I hiss, connecting with her arse once more.

There's no way her skin isn't glowing for me, but damn it for being too dark to really appreciate it.

I smooth the burn with my palm, gently rubbing and squeezing her round arse.

"P-please," she whimpers.

"Fuck, Em. You're soaked," I groan, pushing my fingers between her legs and finding her dripping. "Like the pain, huh?"

She cries out when she loses my touch but quickly complies when I grab her hips, forcing her to bend in half and widen her legs.

But her complaints only last so long because I drop my arse to the ground and indulge in the only thing filling my mind. I taste her.

And fuck. She's sweeter than I ever could have imagined.

Parting her with two fingers, I lap at her clit, quickly learning how she likes it when her hips start rolling and unintelligible words fall from her lips.

She's so fucking wet, her juices drip down my chin.

Reaching up, I wipe some away with the back of my hand before plunging two fingers inside her.

Her muscles ripple around me as she gushes. I lap it all up, desperate for more despite the fact that I'm fucking drowning in her right now.

Tipping my head back a little, I find her staring down at me with wide, desire-filled, dark eyes. Electricity zaps through me as our eyes connect.

"Theo," she breathes before sucking her bottom lip into her mouth, her teeth sinking into it.

"You gonna come all over my face, Hellcat?" I ask against her, allowing the vibrations of my voice to add to her pleasure.

"Yes. Yes, fuck," she cries when I push my fingers higher, rubbing more violently at her G-spot.

Her entire body trembles above me as her release races forward.

"Oh my God," she screams when it finally slams into her.

Her knees buckle, but I take her weight, not

stopping my movements as I let her ride out her pleasure, drinking down everything she gives me.

As she begins to come down, panting white clouds of breath into the air above me, I sit back. There's only one thought in my mind.

I am beyond fucked with this girl.

The moment her eyes open and lock on mine, I know exactly what's going to fall from her lips.

"Fuck me. Please." It's quickly followed by a violent shiver.

Shaking my head, I regretfully slide out from beneath her body.

"I can't, Em," I say, hating the vulnerability in my voice.

She spins, staring down at the tent in my trousers.

Taking a step forward, she reaches out a hand, but I catch it before she makes contact.

Her eyes narrow as she stills and her face hardens.

"Lovell Estate pussy not good enough for the mafia prince, is that it? Would fucking me be lowering yourself just a step too far?"

"No, that's not—"

"Or you'd just rather fuck one of those Barbie dolls you spent all evening entertaining? Am I just a bit of rough to you, a bit of fun for you to use for whatever you want and then just drop?"

Her teeth start chattering and she rips her hand out of my grasp, snatching her pyjama bottoms and boots from the ground and clutching them to her chest.

"You're freezing. Let's get you back." I take a step forward, ready to reach for her, but she darts around me.

"Fuck you, Theodore. I don't want your pity. Your judgement. Fuck. You. Ow," she cries as she attempts to storm away, stumbling in the undergrowth.

I catch her easily before she hits the ground.

"Get the fuck off me," she screams, fighting against my hold, but she's no match for my strength.

"Thrash as much as you like, Hellcat. I'm delivering you back to your bed."

"I don't need you," she hisses.

"Ain't that the fucking truth," I mutter under my breath.

Her eyes narrow on mine, flashing with the need to hurt me.

It only takes a few minutes to approach the cabin, and when I walk directly to her bedroom window she whispers, "Of course."

Lifting her inside, the warmth from the room hits me as I put her on her feet and quickly join her before she locks me out.

The side light by her bed might be dim, but it still burns my eyes. It allows me the chance to study her for the first time tonight.

She looks beautiful and freshly fucked. Her

cheeks are red from the cold, her eyes bright from the release, but they're circled with a darkness I don't like.

She hasn't been sleeping well.

Some sick and perverted part of me wonders if it's because I haven't been here.

It's stupid, because until the other night, she had no clue I'd ever been in her room.

"How did you know where I was?" she demands, opening a door and disappearing inside what I assume is a bathroom.

"I know everything," I confess, dropping into the chair at the end of her bed and getting myself comfortable while she cleans up.

The second she appears in the doorway, still bare from the waist down, she pauses and glares pure death at me.

"What the hell are you doing? You need to leave."

I don't respond, I just let my eyes track her as she crosses the room and drags a clean pair of pyjama bottoms from her suitcase, which predictably hasn't been unpacked despite the fact that she's been here two days already.

My fists curl at her lack of care and organisation, but I force it aside.

"You're cold. Get in bed."

"I'll still be cold in there." *You could join me.*

She doesn't say those final words, but I can read them in her eyes.

After a long stand-off where neither of us says anything, she must decide that she's cold enough to comply and crawls into bed, flicking the light off and plunging us into darkness.

"How many nights have you watched me sleep?" she asks, her voice rough.

"More than I should," I confess.

20

EMMIE

I sleep like the dead. Well, if the dead's slumber is full of dirty dreams of a certain green-eyed boy with a voice that just drips sex and has skills he's too much of a cunt to have been blessed with.

The second I open my eyes, I look at the chair at the bottom of the bed. The one he was still sitting in when I passed out.

I didn't intend on falling asleep with him here, but the second my head hit the pillow, my exhaustion, the weed, and the few drinks Dad had allowed me to have throughout the day hit me and I couldn't stop myself.

My tongue sneaks out, wetting my dry lips. I pause halfway, realising they taste salty, just like his... "No," I breathe, lifting my hand to touch my fingertips to my lips. "No, he wouldn't, would he?"

What the fuck am I even saying? Of course he fucking would.

I reach for my phone, opening the last conversation I had with him, and before I can think better of it, I scroll up to his dick pic.

"Damn it. You don't deserve to have a cock that pretty," I mutter in a huff.

Ripping my eyes away from it, I stare at the empty text box, my thumbs hovering over the letters.

What would I even type?

Thanks for being a total fucking creep but giving me the best head of my life?

An unamused laugh falls from my lips.

Like he needs me to tell him just how good he was to inflate his ego some more.

I sit there for the longest time, listening to people move around the cabin. The scent of bacon frying hits me and makes my stomach growl, but still, I never start typing.

When three little dots start bouncing on the screen, I damn near piss my pants.

Is he... is he also staring at our chat?

Surely not. He probably left the second I fell asleep and went and fucked one of those dim Barbie dolls. Someone who won't tarnish his rep should he accidentally get her pregnant or some shit. Someone I'm sure his father would approve of. A daughter of one of his trusted soldiers. Probably of Greek blood.

"Ugh," I groan, throwing myself back on the bed feeling ridiculous for the jealousy that knots my stomach up tight.

But that's all forgotten when my phone vibrates with an incoming message.

Sucking in a deep breath, I try to prepare for what he might have sent.

By the time I pluck up the courage to look, I've convinced myself it'll just be Calli or Stella and those bouncing dots were just my phone's way of testing my nerve after last night.

Damn, did I want him to fuck me against that tree.

Even now, all these hours later, my thighs clench with the idea of how full I'd feel, fully seated on his cock.

My breath catches when I discover I'm wrong, that he was typing me a message after all.

His Lordship: Merry Christmas, Hellcat. Check your top drawer.

My eyes narrow at his message, but I'm powerless but to follow orders.

Inside the drawer, I find a freshly-made joint.

Rolling my eyes, I'm about to reply when another message pops up.

His Lordship: I hope you slept well.

Emmie: Merry Christmas. I hope you enjoyed the rest of your party.

Reading it back, I realise it sounds even more bitter than I was intending, so I quickly send another.

Emmie: Thank you.

I just about manage to refrain from telling him that I'd take his cock over a joint as a gift any day, but I'm not asking—begging—again. The fact that I did it once was enough and mortifying.

Never in a million years did I think he'd actually refuse.

Hurt cuts through me.

He was hard and more than ready to go.

"I can't."

His words slice me open as if he were saying them now, right in front of me.

I shouldn't care. I shouldn't want to fuck him either. But damn it, I do. Badly.

Having his mouth on me last night, his fingers as deep as they'd go... All it's done is make me crave him that much more. To know how our bodies would feel writhing together, how his muscles would bunch with every move. How painful his fingers would be digging into my hips as he tried to bury himself inside me.

Damn it. I'm wet for him again and he's not even here.

His Lordship: I really enjoyed the rest of my night. Thank you for asking.

My fingers brush my lips once more, but I refuse to believe what my head, what my body, is trying to tell me.

That he went back to the party and fucked a girl with the brain cells of a gnat senseless because she's safe.

I refuse to believe anything else.

***

"**M**orning, sleepyhead," Dad says, shooting me an insanely happy smile when I finally make it to the kitchen a long time later.

The scent of breakfast cooking has long since vanished. I might have been starved, but I was in no state to grace any of these lot with my presence.

One look in the mirror and the events of the night before came slamming back into me.

My cheek was red with scratches from the rough tree, and my arse had his fingertips bruised into it along with a still rosy patch from his palm—not that they'd see that, but still, I'd know it was there.

"Merry Christmas," I say, forcing as much joy into it as possible as eight sets of eyes follow me through the room until I drop into a chair at the table.

"Merry Christmas, kiddo," Dad says, marching over and placing a sloppy kiss on my cheek.

"Ew. Not necessary," I mutter. "You're all way too happy," I state, looking at everyone.

"It's Christmas Day, why wouldn't we be happy?" Titch says, bouncing on the balls of his feet like an excited kid.

"And you all got laid last night," I scoff, making both Kas and Spike spit out the mouthful of coffee they'd both taken.

"Emmie," Dad scolds.

"What? You got married, but thankfully you were out there..." I gesture to the attached treehouse part of the cabin the newlyweds are staying in. "But those three couples..." I pin each of them with a look, "Some of them, or all of them, were going at it like rabbits last night. Right. Above. My. Head," I point out with a raised brow.

"Jealous, kid?" Titch asks, much to my dad's horror.

"Emmie, do not answer that," he growls.

"Ugh, keep your hair on, old man. I don't want to screw your old, wrinkly friends."

The looks on their faces is literally everything.

Truth is, my dad's friends are hot. And not that old. But it's too easy to rile them up.

The women all smother laughs while the guys look completely offended.

"I'll give you old, kid," Titch starts, batting Danni's hand out of the way before she can stop him, "and I'll raise you this." He lifts his shirt, flashing us a shot of his six-pack.

"Ugh, put it away," Zach complains. "Emmie isn't going to be impressed with your beer gut. This, on the other hand…"

"Okay, okay," I say, holding up my hands. "This wasn't meant to turn into a dick-measuring contest. I was just—"

"It should," Spike adds, joining in for the first time. "We all know that I'd win hands down."

"I think I might go back to bed." I know it's my fault, I poked the beasts, but ugh. I can't cope with the surge of testosterone.

"Would you like some breakfast?" Piper asks me, ignoring the guys as they start bickering like little kids.

It's not all that different from the way Theo and his friends are together. It makes me realise that really, they never grow up.

"I can make my own. You should be enjoying yourself."

She doesn't hear a word of it and sets about making a second round of breakfast just for me.

W e had a great day. Probably the best Christmas I've ever had, to be honest.

I've spent most Christmases of the past with Mum, but even the few I've had with Dad haven't been like this.

It wasn't until Piper returned to his life that I really appreciate just how sad and lonely he was. There was always something missing, a darkness in his eyes that I never knew anything about.

But the second he saw her again, it was like he came back to life.

He's an entirely different man now. The only thing that oozes from him is happiness and contentment. I love seeing it. Even if it does make me feel lonely.

I don't resent Piper at all. I love her as a stepmum; she's everything I could ever ask for. But when I moved in with Dad, I thought it was going to be the two of us. That we'd get to make up for some lost time. But he's got a new life now, and sometimes, like now, when they're all joking with their friends, I can't help but feel like I'm in the way.

I love all these guys like family, but I can't help feeling like they're not totally themselves when I'm around, thanks to Dad chastising them for their language and behaviour, which is completely unnecessary. If they had any idea of the things I've seen and experienced, they'd probably be horrified.

"You okay?" Kas asks, dropping down on the sofa beside me.

Kas is only a few years older than me. She's also had a less than conventional upbringing, from what I understand. The first time we met, I knew she got me in a way that most other people don't.

"Yeah, I'm good. Tired."

"I'm sorry we kept you up last night." Her smirk and slightly pink cheeks tell me that most of the noise I had to endure was from her and Spike. I bet her big brother was thrilled, assuming he wasn't too busy himself.

"It's fine. At least some people are getting action."

She stares at me for a beat. "Really no boys on the go then, huh?"

Titch was ribbing me earlier about school and boys, but like hell was I going to confess to what was really happening in my life.

"No. And I don't need one."

"Girl, we never *need* a guy," she says with a wink. "I'm sure you could make use of one, though."

I laugh at her, but I can't deny that she's right.

Theo refusing me last night just makes me more determined to go out and find someone who'd be willing to make me scream.

Maybe I should just go back to Lovell, find

Archer and let him work me over. I doubt he'd refuse.

The thought of someone else touching me makes my blood run cold.

Damn it.

I hate that he's got this power over me. He isn't even here, yet he's controlling my damn thoughts, my body.

It's probably exactly what he was hoping for. He is a power-hungry prick, after all.

"Let's play Monopoly," Titch booms, making everyone groan.

"You cheated last time, like fuck am I playing with you," Zach complains.

"I didn't fucking cheat. You're just a sore loser. Just because you're the boss, it doesn't mean you're the best."

"I'm gonna leave you to it, get an early night," I say, although I can admit to myself that it's a lie.

It's almost midnight, and I can't help hoping that I might get a visitor.

I've barely closed my door behind me when my phone starts ringing. My heart jumps into my throat that it could be him but when I look down, it's a video call from Stella.

Swiping my finger across the screen, I wait for the call to connect.

"Merry Christmas," both she and Calli slur.

They're utterly wasted. Their cheeks are

flushed, eyes wide and glittering. Their makeup is smudged and their smiles wide.

It makes an ache pull at my chest as I sit on the edge of my bed, keeping the room in darkness in the hope that they can't see how I really feel.

"Merry Christmas," I say back. "You guys had a good day?" I ask, although the answer is staring right back at me.

"We miss you," Calli whines. "When are you back?"

"Friday lunchtime."

"We're going out Saturday night," she states. "I wanna get drunk and crazy with both my girls."

"Okay," I say without a second thought. "Where are you now?"

"Our place," Stella says a beat before Seb and Toby appear behind her.

"Merry Christmas, Emmie," they say in unison.

I return the sentiment before asking the question that's on the tip of my tongue. "Is everyone there?"

A look passes between Stella and Calli that makes my breath catch.

One of them turns the screen around and I get to see Nico, Alex, and even Daemon sitting on their sofas.

"Uh... where's Theo?" I ask, my heart rate picking up. If he's not there, then he could be coming here.

Butterflies erupt in my belly at the thought.

"He's staying the night at his parents'. Family shit," Seb says easily.

"Oh... okay." I hate the disappointment in my voice.

It's Christmas, for fuck's sake. He should be with his family. His siblings.

I think of his brother and sisters. It was clear from just the short time I spent with them the night of the fire that they idolise their big brother.

I can just imagine him sitting on the floor of their living room, building Lego, playing cars, or whatever it is kids want these days.

Hell, they're so fucking wealthy they probably each got the latest Xbox or whatever and spent the day glued to it as they fought or raced each other.

The thought of Theo doting on the three of them brings a smile to my lips.

I haven't seen it with my own eyes, but I just know it's how his day has been.

It hits me then. The weakness I was searching for. It's them.

Although that's not exactly the kind of weakness I want. There's no way I'd use them in this twisted thing between us.

Fucking hell. What is wrong with me?

They flip the camera back around and ask me about my day, about the presents I received, and they happily tell me what they got as Alex delivers them fresh shots.

"I should let you go and enjoy yourselves," I say when it becomes clear they're missing out on whatever the guys are laughing about a while later.

"We miss you, Em," Stella says with a pout.

"You're drunk, you have no idea what you're talking about."

"I do. I miss you. Things haven't been the same since... yeah. You know I don't blame you at all, right?" she slurs.

"I do," I say past the lump that crawls up my throat.

I'd never betray her, never. But the guilt is still there nonetheless.

"Everything's cool, I promise."

She smiles at me, concern wrinkling her brow.

"Okay. We're celebrating New Year together. Okay?"

"Okay," I agree. "Enjoy your night. Make sure Seb gives you a screaming Christmas gift," I wink.

"Already done a few times over, Em," Seb shouts from somewhere, making Stella smile.

"He's not lying. He woke me with—"

"Okay, I'm going," I say in a rush. "Bye."

I jam my finger into the screen and blow out a long breath, my shoulders deflating as I do.

21

THEO

I hate the defeat in her posture as she hangs up on the call.

There is a part of me that thinks she deserves it. But there's a bigger part that doesn't believe that, that wants to comfort her.

She sits in the dark unmoving for a few seconds before I push from the chair and crawl onto the bed behind her.

Her spine straightens the second she senses me, but she doesn't turn around or try to rip me a new one when she discovers that I've been eavesdropping.

Pushing my fingers into her soft hair, I tilt her head to the side and run my nose up the smooth column of her throat.

"I thought you were at home playing with your brother and sisters," she whispers, sounding as dejected as she looks.

"They're asleep. And I can think of much better ways to spend my Christmas night than hanging out with my parents."

"Hanging out with your friends, maybe."

"Maybe." She shivers when I brush my lips over her soft skin. "You lied to them," I state, making it very clear that I listened to every word.

"Did I?" she asks, sounding a little breathless already.

"Yeah. You told Stella that everything was cool. It's not though, is it?"

My lips brush over the shell of her ear as I wait for her response.

"You still don't believe I had nothing to do with it?" Hurt fills her voice.

"It doesn't matter what I think. It's your friends you care about."

She blows out a breath. "True. I couldn't give a fuck what you think."

"Now I know you're lying," I whisper in her ear.

"It doesn't really matter, does it?" she asks.

"Why?"

"You believe what you like. You steamroll over anything you think is wrong. If you decide I really am a threat then you'll eliminate me like Joker. Like Jonas."

I startle as the image her words form fills my eyes.

Emmie on the floor with bullet holes in her body, or worse, in one of Dad's torture chambers.

I'm ruthless. I do what needs to be done to the people who wrong us. I've done it time and time again. More than I'm happy to confess to. But could I do it to her?

My blood turns cold.

I don't even need to think about it. I know the answer. And I fear that if it comes to it, my refusal could ruin everything Dad's trained me for over the years.

I swallow. Hard.

"You think I want to kill you?"

A shudder rips through her but she remains silent for a few seconds.

"I have this recurring dream that you do," she confesses quietly. "Exactly like Stella killed Joker. Only I'm in his place, and you were in hers."

"Is there a reason I'd want to kill you, Emmie?"

She shakes her head. "N-no. I swear to you, I didn't know about Joker."

"I know," I tell her. "I believe you." And I do. I see how much Stella means to her. If she knew anything wasn't right, then I truly believe she'd have alerted us to it. I also see the guilt she carries around that she didn't know and so couldn't stop it. But there's not much I can do to help with that. That's something she's going to have to come to terms with in her own time.

"Y-you do?"

Shifting so I'm on my arse, I stretch my legs out, pinning her between my thighs and wrapping one arm around her middle, holding her back against my front.

"I do. But I need to know if there's anything else, Em."

"What do you mean?" she asks, sounding confused, and I know that if I were to turn her around, I'd find a frown marring her beautiful face.

"I mean, is there anything you're hiding from me?"

"What? No, of course not. Like what?"

"Anything," I say.

She pauses, thinking. "You're still looking at the club? You think I'm involved in something else?"

"My friends, my family. They're everything to me, Hellcat. It would be naïve of me not to ask."

Her shoulders stiffen, her usual fight returning.

"You really don't think much of me, do you? I'm not lying to you. If I knew something, anything, I'd tell you. Well, maybe not you." I know she's rolling her eyes at me, and I can't help but smile. "But Stella. Calli."

"Okay," I breathe, letting my lips brush her neck once more. She relaxes again until the next word falls from my mouth. "But—"

"Jesus, Theo."

"But," I continue. "If I do discover that you're lying to me, then I will do whatever it takes to protect those I love."

"Right. Sure." She tries to remove herself from my hold, but my arm tenses around her, my fingers tightening in her hair to hold her in place.

"Don't run from me, Hellcat."

"That's exactly what I should be doing. You're a fucking psycho, Theo. You know that, right?"

My only response is to chuckle, because hell, she doesn't know the half of it.

"How did you know where I was?" she asks, just like she did the other night.

"I tracked you," I state, as if it's not obvious.

Her head dips as she looks at her phone.

"Right. Of course." Reaching over, she places it on the nightstand. "Guess I'll be getting a new one."

"If you think that would stop me from finding you, then you're really underestimating me."

"You say you believe me. I've told you there's nothing else. What do you want from me?"

"Million-dollar question right there," I say, licking a line up her neck.

"Clearly, it's not sex, or you'd have fucked me by now."

"Maybe I'm just being a gentleman."

She scoffs at my words.

"Yeah, maybe. Excuse me." She places her hands on my knees and pushes. This time, I let her go.

"You shouldn't be here. You should be at home

with your friends." The sombre look on her face makes my chest hurt.

It's Christmas Day. It should be one of the happiest days of the year.

"What if I want to be here?"

"You hate me, Theo. Why would you want to be here?" She waves me off and slips into the bathroom.

The sound of the shower turning on gets my attention and I push from the bed, following her.

She left the door open, so I can only take that as an invitation.

Resting my shoulder on the doorframe, I watch as she peels her clothes from her body and steps under the spray, completely unfazed that I'm watching her. Every inch of her.

Her hair is piled on top of her head to keep it dry, and she makes quick work of covering her mouthwatering body in bubbles and rinsing them away.

All too quickly, she reaches for a towel and wraps it around herself, hiding from me.

"Excuse me," she says, stepping up to me, her eyes locked on my chest as she waits for me to move out of her way.

"Emmie," I say, waiting for her to look up at me.

When she doesn't, I reach out and tuck my fingers under her chin, forcing her to meet my eyes.

My breath catches in my throat at the sight of her tears.

"What is it?"

She shakes her head. The movement is so subtle that if I weren't touching her then I'd never have known it had happened.

"Today. It's... it's been a long day."

My eyes narrow as if I'll be able to read the reason for her sadness in her eyes, but I can't. She's closed down.

"Talk to me," I beg quietly.

"So you can use it against me later? Hard pass, thanks. You should just leave."

She tries to slip past me, but I'm not having any of it.

Dropping my hand, I wrap my fingers around her throat and press her up against the bathroom wall.

"I'm not going anywhere," I tell her roughly before doing something I know I'm going to regret, but I need that look out of her eyes. I need to give her something else to focus on.

The bolt of electricity that shoots through me is like nothing I've ever felt before, and it makes my blood turn red hot in an instant as my lips brush against hers.

She doesn't move for a few seconds, too stunned, much like I am, but now I'm here, I'm not giving up so easily.

My lips brush against hers, begging her to respond.

When she does, my knees damn near give out with relief.

It starts soft, innocent, and it's like nothing I've ever felt before.

Her sadness and desperation seeps into me and I wish I could take it away, or at least help shoulder the weight.

I lick across her bottom lip. They part slightly, and I make the most of the opportunity. But the second my tongue collides with hers, her hands slam down on my chest and she pushes me back.

"No," she breathes, her eyes downcast once more. "I'm not doing this. I'm not letting you do this."

Before I can gather my wits, she's gone, leaving me alone in her bathroom.

When I find her, she's dragging my shirt on, the one she stole the night of Seb's mum's funeral, and discarding the towel.

"I know you want me," I say, watching as she crosses the room to the bed.

"Yeah. You've got a nice cock. The rest of you though, not so much."

"Em," I breathe.

"What? You suddenly want to fuck me? To make it all better? You're half the fucking problem," she lies.

"I don't believe you. I don't think I hold the power to make you cry."

She scoffs. "You got that fucking right. You're nothing to me, Theo. Just a power-hungry, arrogant jerk who gets his kicks stalking me and watching me sleep."

My eyes widen, but I don't know why I'm shocked at her words. They're the truth, after all. Actually, they only scratch the surface of the truth.

There's so much she doesn't know. So much that she's going to hate me for. Even more than she does now.

Kicking my shoes off, I drag my hoodie over my head—much to her horror—and crawl onto her bed. Despite my need to get close to her, I stay on top of the covers.

"You had a bad day?" I ask, resting my head on my fist, looking down at her.

She doesn't speak for the longest time, and I start to think she's not going to reply.

I'm so focused on her shallow breaths that when she does speak, it startles me.

"It's been a good day," she says, but the words don't hold any weight.

She stares at the ceiling, blinking back the tears that are threatening to spill.

I'm probably the last person she wants to cry in front of, and although it's twisted as fuck, I want her to.

Why?

269

Because I want to put her the fuck back together.

Yeah. Fucked up.

"It's just..." she continues after a long, heavy silence. "It's stupid," she sighs, dismissing whatever is bothering her.

Reaching for her hand, I twist my fingers with hers. "It's not stupid if it makes you sad," I tell her honestly.

"I... I've never had a Christmas where I haven't at least spoken to my mum," she says in a rush, as if the speed will stop me from hearing it.

But it doesn't, and my chest constricts, knowing that I'm a part of her pain right now.

"She didn't call you?" I ask, cringing at my question.

She shakes her head.

"I shouldn't care," she mutters before finally meeting my eyes. "And I really shouldn't be telling you about it."

"Who else are you going to tell?" I ask.

Her dad's probably with his new wife, and her friends are wasted at home.

A sad and bitter laugh falls from her lips.

"Fuck, I'm pathetic."

She throws her arm over her eyes, blocking the world out.

"Missing your mum isn't pathetic," I tell her.

"She's a shit mum. She doesn't deserve for me to miss her."

"Easier said than done though, huh?"

"What would you know about it? Your mum's amazing."

I suck in a quick breath at the reminder that they've met. That she's spent time with those closest to me, and for some fucking reason, they all fucking love her. After one meeting.

"Yeah," I admit. "She is, despite everything Dad's put her through."

"Oh?"

"It's nothing major or scandalous like Toby and Stella's parents. But being married to the boss comes with certain challenges."

"I can only imagine."

Can you?

"Tell me about your mum," I say, giving her hand a gentle squeeze, hoping that it's the encouragement she needs to open up.

Her lips part to respond, but before any words come out, she closes them again. She moves her arm and her eyes find mine.

"Why? Why do you care?"

I shrug. "No reason. But I'm here and willing to listen."

A deep frown forms between her brows at my response.

She doesn't trust me, and I don't blame her. But I'm willing to put in some work to change that.

"I don't know what I can tell you that you probably haven't already guessed. You know where I grew up. You must know what it's like there."

"I do," I agree.

"My life was dodging dealers, pimps and everything in between. The opposite of your privileged life.

"I've had weeks where I've survived on mouldy bread and questionably cloudy water. Mum used to go days without showing her face, even when I was too young to be left alone."

"Why didn't your dad take you away?"

"He didn't know. The thing about my mum is that she's a master at hiding what a fuck-up she is. Dad knew it was shit, but she never allowed him to see the truth."

"You could have told him."

"You think she didn't have contingencies in place?" She rolls her eyes so hard it must hurt.

"She blackmailed you?" I guess.

"Pretty much. I didn't feel like I had a choice. I've always hated her, but she's my mum, you know? It's... it's fucked up. But I didn't want to lose her, no matter how shit she made my life.

"I always hoped she'd get better. She promised me this incredible future where she'd get a good job, get us out of hell. But obviously, it was all bullshit.

"She loved it there. She could get her fix on every corner and find guys to make sure she could afford to pay all the dealers."

"She used to turn tricks while you were there?"

A bitter laugh falls from her lips.

"Of course she did."

Silence descends between us. I've got a million questions about her life before she appeared in Knight's Ridge, but I swallow them down, either too afraid to know the truth or suspecting she won't even want to answer.

And if she did, I know that it would end with me killing the woman responsible.

My main question, though... Is Emmie as untrustworthy as her mother, or is her mother throwing her under a bus?

I want to say it's the latter. But as they say, the apple never falls far from the tree.

Just look at me and my father. Two peas in a pod. He's trained me to be his perfect soldier, his perfect heir. Who's to say Cora hasn't done the exact same thing with Emmie?

Because she's not this good a liar, a little voice says.

"Did she hurt you? Did *they* ever hurt you?" I ask in the end, needing to know if there's any other motherfucker out there who needs to be taught a lesson.

"Why, what would you do about it?"

"Kill them," I spit without missing a beat.

Her eyes widen in shock, her lips opening and closing as she fails to find a response.

In the end, she just shakes her head.

"I might have been clueless for most of my childhood, but everyone around me knew who my dad was. Who my grandad was. Thankfully, no one laid a hand on me."

"Good," I say, although I can't help feeling a little disappointed. How better to get her to trust me than to kill someone who wronged her? "Where do you think she's gone?" I risk asking.

She shrugs. "Run away with her pimp? Her dealer? Dead in a ditch somewhere? Who the fuck knows? Wherever she is, she's clearly forgotten I ever existed."

"I'm sure that's not true," I whisper. Her mother hasn't forgotten her, because she's trying to pin her crimes on her.

Fuck. I really hope Emmie isn't tangled up in the middle of all this.

She can't be. She just fucking can't be.

"Theo?" she eventually says. It's been so long that I started to wonder if she'd fallen asleep.

"Yeah?"

"Can you be honest with me for once?"

"I can try."

"Why are you really here? Why have you really been creeping into my bedroom at night and watching me sleep and..." She trails off, making me wonder if she's figured out what I've been doing. Well, other than spying on her, of course.

"Because I have to," I answer honestly.

Her brows wrinkle.

"Because being anywhere else feels wrong."

"Th—"

"I'm sorry about your mum, Em. You deserve better."

Cupping her jaw, I drop my lips to hers once more to attempt that kiss again.

This time, when I part hers and lick at her tongue, she doesn't freak out. Instead, she leans into me, wrapping her hands around my back and sliding us closer together.

It's the most painful kind of hell, because I don't deserve it. Any of it.

22

EMMIE

The moment I come to life the next morning and realise that I'm not being clutched tightly like I was before I drifted off to sleep, I push my hand out, trying to find him. Only, I'm met with a cold, empty bed.

"Fuck," I breathe, rolling onto my bed, forcing down the disappointment that threatens to consume me.

I knew it was too good to be true.

If I didn't remember just how his lips felt moving against mine, then I'd say I'd dreamed it all.

But I know I didn't.

Lifting my finger to my still kiss-swollen lips, I remember every second.

The way he moved so gently against me, the words he whispered against my skin, telling me that

I deserved more than what Mum had given me, that I was worth more.

It was weird, hearing those words come from his lips. And not just because I don't think I've ever heard anyone say them to me before, but they were so at odds with everything he's ever said to me.

There's a part of me that doesn't want to believe he meant them, but then I remember the look in his sparkling green eyes and it makes my chest ache.

He meant them.

I just... I just don't understand the change.

It hit me upside the head, but I was powerless but to accept his words, his touch, his kiss.

It's why it hurts so much this morning that he's gone.

Like it was all a figment of my imagination.

I reach for my phone, and my heart tumbles in my chest the second I wake it up and find a message from him.

His Lordship: I'm sorry I had to leave. I was going to wake you to say goodbye, but you looked so beautiful in your sleep. I've got to work tonight. I don't know if I'll get there, but I want you at my flat tomorrow night when I get off.

My teeth grind at his demands, but I can't deny

that my thighs don't clench at the thought of returning to his flat. Although, reading it again, all I see is that he's not going to be here tonight. I shouldn't be disappointed but...

I blow out a long breath. What the hell is that arsehole doing to me?

I hate him. I shouldn't want him anywhere near me.

Or at least... I should hate him.

He's everything I don't like in guys. All my turn-offs rolled into one sexy, toned, dirty package.

"Argh," I complain, covering my face with my hands.

He's worming his way under my skin, and I'm scared that I might actually like it.

It takes me longer than it should to come up with a reply.

As desperate as I am to agree that I'll meet him tomorrow night, I also do not want to be that girl.

Emmie: I've already got plans.

It's a lie. I have absolutely nothing planned, although I'm sure I could if I asked Calli or Stella to do something.

His Lordship: Cancel them. It wasn't a suggestion.

Desire washes through me at his tone. It's like his deep voice growls the words in my ears and my skin pricks with goosebumps.

"Damn it, Cirillo," I mutter to myself.

Emmie: We'll see.

I put my phone down, ready to get up to see what the day will hold, but it lights up once more as I stand.

His Lordship: We will.

I don't open the message to show that I've read it just to wind him up, because I know his controlling, obsessive arse will hate it.

With a smug grin playing on my lips, I head for the bathroom, although the second I'm in the doorway, all I see is him pushing me up against the wall, trying to kiss my sadness away.

Fuck. I was pathetic last night.

Mentally, I pull up my big girl knickers and shove all my hurt and dejection over my mum down back inside the steel vault it belongs in.

I tell myself that it was just because it was Christmas. It made me all sentimental and shit. Today, in the harsh light of day, I know I'm better off without her brand of fucked-up toxic in my life. I'm better without the Lovell Estate and the jerks I was surrounded by tainting my existence.

But even knowing all that, there's still a little girl deep inside me who just wants her mum. And I fear that's never going to go away.

Or maybe I just need the closure of knowing she no longer wants me. Or that she's dead.

If I got the chance to say goodbye, in whatever form that needed to take, maybe all of this would have been easier.

Shaking my head, I strip Theo's shirt from my body and step into the shower once more, but it's nowhere near as enjoyable as when his eyes were laser-focused on my body.

"Holy fucking shit, Titch. What the hell are you doing?" I screech, clutching the towel tighter around my body. "What if I walked out there naked?"

He pales slightly but his narrowed, angry eyes never leave mine.

"I think we need to have a little chat," he states coldly.

My heart plummets, my blood running cold.

There are a couple of things that he could want to talk to me about that might put that look in his eyes, and none of them are good.

"Any chance I could be dressed for it?" I snark.

"I'll wait," he says, resting back in the chair that usually holds another, younger, sexier, bad boy.

With a huff, I grab some clothes from my case that I never bothered unpacking and stomp back into my bathroom.

My hands tremble as I dress and I chastise myself for being such a pussy.

But if Titch knows about Theo, Mickey's, the club...

My stomach churns.

Shit. He definitely knows something.

I thought I was safe at Mickey's. Titch might have spent many years training there and fighting in the Circuit, but he's left all that behind now. He's about to be a fucking father, there's no way he should be anywhere near underground MMA fights.

I just hoped that would mean that I'd be safe there.

I am safe there. The guys in there know who I am and wouldn't dream of laying a finger on me.

But Titch is the only one who'd snitch back to my dad.

Fuck.

Fuck.

I take my time getting ready, knowing that it's going to test his patience. I put my makeup on as if I were applying my armour, and when I finally reach for the door, I've got my head held high and my shoulders pulled back.

"You know what this is, right?" Titch asks before I can even see him.

When I walk into the room, I find he's got the shirt I was wearing in his hand, his finger tapping the logo on the left breast.

"The Cirillo crest. I'm not an idiot, Titch. I know exactly who I go to school with. Who my friends are."

He nods, absorbing my words.

His silence makes me more nervous than it should.

"Wanna tell me why I saw Theo Cirillo walking away from this very cabin first thing this morning when I got up for a piss?" His eyes hold mine as he says the words that make the world fall from beneath my feet.

"Um..."

"Or did you want to try to give me a good reason as to why I shouldn't tell your dad?"

My lips part, but I can't find an argument.

"It's not what it looks like," I finally say, cringing at just how cliché that sounds.

"Oh sure. You gonna try telling me that you snuck him in for a game of Monopoly?"

"No, I didn't. But I also didn't ask him here to have sex." Come to think of it, I didn't ask him to come here at all, but I'm not getting into that situation with Titch. This is bad enough.

"I wasn't born yesterday, Em. Teenage boys only sneak into girls' rooms for one thing."

Placing my hands on my hips, I give him my

best resting bitch face, which admittedly isn't hard because it's pretty much my usual face.

"Usually, I'd agree with you. But read my lips," I say, pointing to my mouth. "I didn't sleep with him. I haven't slept with him."

He holds my eyes, searching for the lie that isn't quite there.

"Then why was he here, and why did he feel the need to sneak out?"

I sigh. "You've met my dad, right?"

"Fuck, Emmie," Titch sighs, scrubbing his hand down his face.

"You could have caught the attention of any boy at that school, but it had to be him, didn't it?"

I shrug. "Trust me, it wasn't intentional." I drop down on the edge of my bed.

"Do you have any idea what you're getting in the middle of right now?"

A bitter laugh rips from my lips.

"I'm aware. More than aware. But Pops, the club, and the Cirillos are mostly on good terms."

"The club?" he asks, noticing just how casually I mentioned it.

"Yes, the fucking club. What of it?"

His fists clench as he hears all my unspoken words.

"Your father is going to kill you, Emmie."

"With all due respect, Titch, you have no idea what you're talking about or what my life is like."

"Don't I?" he asks, pushing to the edge of the chair.

"I know what I'm doing, I promise."

"You're in the middle of a fucking MC and the mafia, Em. I'm sorry, but there's no way in hell you know what you're doing right now."

"Maybe not. But it's my life. My mistakes to make, don't you think?"

"If he hurts you—"

"He won't," I say with a confidence I certainly don't feel.

"I want to trust you, Emmie. You're a smart young woman, but if you end up hurt then—"

"It won't be your fault, Titch. It will be mine."

He nods, reaching back to rub at his neck as a conflicted expression passes across his face.

"Let me help you."

"H-help me?" I ask, my brows pulling together.

"Yeah. Let me train you, show you how to defend yourself should the worst—"

"I've already got it covered. Xander's been training me," I say, knowing full well that Titch knows who he is. He fought him, beat him, a few months ago.

"Jesus fucking Christ, Em."

I scoot closer to where he's sitting, holding his eyes.

"I appreciate your concern, Titch. And I know how badly you want to go to my dad with this, but please... I'm just... I'm just trying to find who I am, where I come from. I'm just trying to understand the part of my life that he kept from me. I'm not joining the MC. I'm not going to become one of their club whores. I'm just... learning about that side of my life. Surely you can understand that."

His jaw tics as he stares back at me.

"You're playing with some very dangerous people, Emmie."

"I'm being protected by some very dangerous people," I say, spinning his words on their head. "No one will touch me. I'm a Ramsey," I state proudly.

"Fuck. Your dad is going to kill both of us."

I smile at him. "Thank you," I whisper.

"If anyone gives you any shit, if you need anything... If that little punk needs his arse kicking, you call me, yes?"

"Of course."

"And when your old man finds out about this, you keep my fucking name out of it."

"Sure thing."

He pushes to stand, nodding at me, although I can tell by the hard set of his face that he isn't happy with any of this.

"I understand needing to find yourself, Emmie. I do. But if I hear you're in any kind of trouble, I'll stand right beside your dad and do whatever is necessary to make sure you're safe."

He's at the door, his fingers wrapped around the handle when I find some words.

"Who are you really worried about here? Theo and the Cirillos, or Pops and the club?"

"Your father."

And with that, he's gone.

"Fuck," I breathe, falling back on the bed with dread churning in my stomach.

If Titch walks straight out there and tells Dad, I'm fucked. He'll never let me out of the house again and will probably board up my bedroom window.

The rest of our holiday was nice—well, as long as I forget about the concerned glances Titch shot me anytime we were in the same room. We chilled out, ate, drank, argued over board games... Pretty much like any usual family. Only the men in my life are full of swear words and covered in tattoos. Hell, so are most of the women.

I was on edge almost the whole time. Every time Dad spoke to me or Piper asked me a question, I was waiting for them to demand answers about what I've been up to recently.

But as the hours went on, I started to realise that Titch kept his word. For now, at least.

It wasn't until we were packing up the cars to leave Friday morning that either of us brought it up again.

"Thank you," I said when we found ourselves alone at the boot of his car.

"I remember what it was like, being your age and trying to find your place in life. Just don't make me regret trusting you."

"I won't," I promised, hoping like hell it was one I could keep.

He gave me a sad, concerned smile and left it there.

I was grateful. My head was already messed up after a night of barely any sleep. Between worrying about what he was going to do with my secret and my lack of a night-time visitor, I found myself tossing and turning almost until the sun came up.

I never responded to Theo's message, and he never sent another—something I'm not all that happy about, but I guess I can hardly complain.

The movement of the car eventually lulls me to sleep on the way back to the city, and when I open my eyes, I find we're slowing down in front of Dad's house.

"Home sweet home," he says, smiling at his new bride.

"You two are so happy it's sickening."

"Well, I guess it's a good thing you're not going to have to put up with us for a few days then, huh?" Dad says with a wicked glint in his eye as he practically eye fucks Piper.

If I weren't so happy for them, I might just puke all over the back seat of his car.

Excitement zaps through me as I think about Dad's wedding/Christmas present from Piper. New Year in Las Vegas. It doesn't get much better than that. Plus, I get the house to myself.

They're heading inside to repack and then heading straight to a hotel tonight ready for a flight first thing in the morning. After being surrounded by them for the past few days, I can't wait for the quiet, even if it means spending New Year without either of my parents. At least I'll have my friends. Hopefully.

Dad's already warned me about throwing a raging party, but seriously, the kids I go to school with all live in penthouses and mansions—why the hell would anyone want to party here?

"Peace and quiet," I sigh. "Can't wait."

Dad's eyes meet mine in the rearview mirror as he pulls the handbrake.

"I'll be good, I promise."

"I know," he says, a softness in his voice that's not usually there. "I'm proud of you, you know that, right?"

I smile back as my stomach knots. "Thanks, Dad."

23

THEO

I stare down at the unread message I sent Emmie this afternoon, reminding her that she's busy tonight and spelling out exactly where I wanted her when I finished my shift at the casino.

The time between Christmas and New Year is always insanely busy at the hotel, and other than spending Christmas with my parents and my nights with Emmie, I've been here.

I'm wiped. But not enough to go home alone and actually sleep.

I can't. Not without her.

I didn't mean to crash with her on Wednesday night, but lying there with her in my arms relaxed me more than I thought possible, and when her breathing was shallow and her body melted against my side, I was powerless but to close my eyes and drift off with her.

It was a risk. One that I've been paying for every second since. But I can't regret it.

I achieved what I needed to. I'm showing her that she can trust me, and that's the only way I'm going to get to the bottom of what's going on with her mother.

My gut tells me that she's got nothing to do with whatever shit Cora's pulled with Dad, but I know I'd be naïve to allow her pretty face, sinful curves and sweet cunt to sway my opinions.

I need to think with my head, not my cock.

It's what Dad expects of me.

"So," the man himself says. "How's it going with your little lady?" It's unusual for Dad to be on the floor, but he makes an exception during this time of year, more than willing to stand beside his most loyal associates and put some of his own money down on the tables.

"It's... uh..."

He raises a brow at me.

"Did she have a good holiday?"

I turn to look at him, my brows narrowing in suspicion.

"What? Don't forget who taught you all you know, boy."

"You've been watching me." The accusation tastes bitter on my tongue. I thought he trusted me. Clearly, I was wrong.

"Just keeping an eye on my asset."

"Emmie's not yours," I spit, a little too harshly.

His brows lift in shock at the tone of my voice.

"No," he agrees, his voice chilling but his face as neutral as ever, "she's yours. I'm glad you're keeping a tight lead on her."

"Whatever this shit is with her mother, Emmie's not involved."

"Know that for a fact, do you?"

My lips part, but I'm too slow to respond. He's already heard my answer loud and clear.

"You're no use to me or this Family if you don't use your head, soldier."

My teeth grind and my jaw pops in frustration.

"Get me facts. Give me something concrete that she wasn't involved, and I'll let it go."

"Want to give me some more information?" I hiss, frustrated as fuck that he's thrown me into this bullshit with the bare minimum.

He nods at someone across the room, but I don't look to see who he's greeting. I'm too invested in what he might be about to say next.

"Cora's been an associate for years. A trusted associate." I narrow my eyes at him, reading between the lines.

"She was working the Lovell Estate for you?"

He nods once.

"She's loyal." She's blood, is what he means.

"How?"

His refusal is subtle. If my eyes weren't laser-focused on him then I might miss the slight shake of his head.

"Not now. Just get me the answers I need. One of them is a snake. I need to know which."

"Probably not the one who has no fucking idea what's going on. Do you know that she thinks her mum is dead?"

"Probably for the best. She will be if I discover she's been lying to me."

My lips part to respond, but he beats me to it.

"You've got a job to do," he states, stalking across the room and running his hand down my mother's back where she talks to the other wives.

My phone vibrates in my hand and excitement shoots through my veins that she's finally responded.

Although it isn't her name that flashes up when I lift the screen, the one that stares back at me is almost as good. Almost.

I open the email and scroll down the text until I find the results I wanted.

"Bingo," I breathe, staring down at the evidence I needed. Although, I must admit that I wasn't expecting to see that surname connected to Emmie.

Dad might not have been willing to answer my question about Emmie being Cirillo Family by blood, but we've got enough connections for me to find that answer for myself.

Maybe that was his plan. He wanted to see how resourceful I could be. Clearly, he really doesn't think much of my skills.

All I needed was a little DNA from Emmie. Easy.

I'm about to pull our chat back up again to send her another reminder when a shadow falls over me.

"Evan is glaring at you from the blackjack table," Seb says, glancing between me and the phone in my hand.

"Evan can fuck off," I mutter, shooting him a sneer and ensuring he can lip-read every one of my words.

I shouldn't taunt him. But after that brief conversation with Dad, I'm more than ready to get the fuck out of here and discover whether Emmie has made the right decision about how our night is going to go.

"Who's got your panties in a twist?" Seb grunts, turning so his back is to the wall, giving him a view of the room before us.

"My panties?" I ask with a snort. "You've been spending too much time with your girl."

"Exactly as it should be. How's it going with yours?"

I rear back.

"Oh, don't look so fucking shocked. You're so gone for her it's not even funny."

"I don't even know who you're talking about."

He barks out a laugh. "You're so full of shit the entire room can smell it, Cirillo. Where'd you go Christmas night, huh?"

I swallow.

"Because I know you didn't stay at your parents', or come home, or even crash here," he says, his eyes shooting up, gesturing to the hotel.

"I went for a drive to clear my head."

"You know, if you hadn't had my back so many times over the years, I'd be offended right now. I can track your fucking phone, you lying piece of shit. Just tell me you went to her."

I glare at my best friend, begging him to shut the fuck up.

But I know him better than that.

He's also loved up as fuck, and although he'd never admit to being a romantic, I can see this sappy plan about me getting with his girl's best friend playing out in his mind.

"I—"

"Stop," he says, sensing the lie coming. "Just stop. I know exactly what you've been doing. And if you didn't want me finding out, you'd have disconnected from the tracker. Wouldn't be the first time," he grumbles. "So..."

I let out a heavy sigh. He's expecting me to tell him that I trailed her, fucked her into next week like he knows I've been dying to do since she turned up at Knight's Ridge, and that everything is going to be fine. Happily ever after, here we come. But that's not how this thing is going to play out.

"We just hung out," I confess.

His brows lift in shock.

"Don't tell me you hung out with her and then

came home to use that tub of Vaseline Alex bought you for Christmas."

"It's complicated."

"It's pretty simple. You're both perfect for each other and both insanely hot for each other. Just pull your head out of your arse, or your cock out of your trousers and fucking bang her. Make her yours."

My teeth grind in frustration.

Yeah, ain't that the fucking problem. If I bang her then...

"Shit," I hiss, pushing my hair back from my brow and casting a look around the room.

"What?" Seb asks as if I've seen some trouble about to kick off.

"N-nothing. I just—"

"Need her."

My eyes find his, but I don't see any teasing, just understanding.

"It's fucked up, man. I can't even tell you—"

"You don't have to tell me anything. Tell her, maybe." He reaches up and rubs the back of his neck. "Shit, I'm not good at this stuff. I make it up as I go along and Stella kicks my arse if I get it wrong. But... if you want her, if you think it might be something, then the only person who matters, who should know what's going on in your fucked-up head is her."

"And what if she doesn't want to hear it? What if she can't deal with—"

"This is Emmie we're talking about. We both

know that you can throw anything at her and it won't scare her away. She's not Sloane. She's not some prim and proper princess who expects to be treated like glass and is happy to live in the shadows—to a point—just to be with you. Emmie is... she's the whole package. If you want it."

"Jesus Christ, bro. You're not making this any easier to take."

"Trust me, when you figure it out, it'll be worth it."

"Fucking hell, I never thought I'd see the day you got yourself this fucking whipped."

He shrugs as if he doesn't have a care in the world.

"I gotta tell you, it's not a bad place to be."

"I can see that." And I can, because despite everything he's been through over the past few years, with Stella by his side, he's happier than I ever remember seeing him. They might be a match made in hell and have a relationship that I'm sure many would describe as toxic, but it works for them. They both smile wider when they're together. They're both stronger when they're together. It's equally as annoying as it is heart-warming.

Things are changing for all of us. And it's happening faster than I thought it would.

We're all heading toward the end of our time at Knight's Ridge, and our futures are more than just a little up in the air.

Dad wants me to join him and work full-time for the Family. But I don't. Not yet, at least. I know it's my future, my destiny or what the fuck ever. But I'm not ready yet. It's why I've got completed applications sitting on my computer at home for my chosen universities. They're all in London, and all of them will allow me to continue working part-time as I am now. Nothing has to change. I just need to get Dad to see it the same way.

He's always humoured my dreams to graduate, but I don't think he ever really took my wishes seriously. He just thought I'd change my mind when the time came and he could set me up with a hand-picked role in the Family, and we'd be set. Well, the time is coming and he doesn't seem quite so happy about the direction my future is heading in.

Apart from the woman he wants at my side— should she live that long, of course.

Ice fills my blood at the thought of what will happen to her should it turn out that she is lying to us. That she has been her mother's accomplice all this time.

"Go find her when we've finished here. Talk to her."

"I don't know if—"

"Don't be a fucking pussy, Cirillo. We all know what you want. You're only lying to yourself by pretending you don't know it too. Go find her and fucking finally take what you've been dreaming of for the past few months."

My cock jerks at the thought of her hot, tight pussy. Fuck. She's always wet for me, I can just imagine how she'd feel as I pushed into her, stretched her open.

"What's the alternative? Going home alone to your pot of Vaseline?"

"You're a fucking pain in my arse, Sebastian."

"Yeah, yeah. Heard it all before," he says with a smile, slapping me on the shoulder. "You can thank me later."

"We'll see," I mutter, nodding at one of Dad's associates who's caught my eye across the room.

I do my best at pushing thoughts of Emmie waiting for me in my flat out of my head as I work the room, greet people who've been in my life longer than I can even remember and say all the right things to our associates as Dad expects me to.

But by the time my shift finally comes to an end and I manage to slip from the casino, every single muscle in my body is pulled tight and my patience after all the bullshit ego-stroking is at an all-time low.

Jamming my finger into the lift call button, I

watch as the numbers descend from the hotel room floors above me.

Excited chatter sounds out from behind me as patrons enjoy their night and everything the hotel and casino offer them, but I block it all out.

My only focus is on what the rest of my night is going to hold.

I wait until I'm alone in the lift before I pull my phone out and open Emmie's tracking app.

I want her to be inside my flat, exactly as I told her to be.

I second-guessed myself more than once before I finally sent that request for her to be waiting for me.

It meant opening up my home to someone else. Something I've refused to do since moving in.

Even Seb doesn't have access to my flat right now.

After having everyone and their wife in my space at the coach house, I just needed some solitude. But the promise of having Emmie in my bed again meant I uploaded her prints that I took when she was sleeping one night and allowed her access to both the building and my home.

I can't say I'm not nervous about it.

If she's done as she's told then she could be snooping around my place right now. Although something tells me that she wouldn't.

She's not Sloane or Teagan. She doesn't care

about finding dirt on me, or something that can be used to get close to me.

It's in that moment that I realise that Dad's concerns earlier might be well-founded.

I trust her. And that's fucking dangerous.

My hand trembles slightly as I wait for the app to load as I descend through the building toward the underground garage where my Ferrari awaits. I knew I'd be desperate to get home, and there was only one car worthy of that job.

It's not until I step out of the lift that my phone finally locates her.

And just as I feared, her little fucking dot is nowhere near my flat.

"Motherfucker," I grunt, unlocking my car and falling into the driver's seat.

Pulling up our chat, I fire off a quick warning.

Theo: Play with fire, Miss Ramsey, and you will get fucking burned.

24

EMMIE

Throwing back the last of my drink, I slam the glass down on the table and laugh at the pathetic joke Xander just told.

"You're a fucking idiot," I blurt out, my words slurred from the number of vodkas I've had.

Cruz eyes me from the other end of the table, but I just wave him off.

I'm good. I'm in control and the vodka is just feeding the excitement bubbling in my belly from blowing that demanding arsehole off.

I smile to myself, thinking about my turned-off phone sitting in my bedroom.

Take that, fuckwit.

I can almost picture him climbing through the window I left cracked open especially for him and finding it sitting there with the note I left.

Try better next time.

I can't help myself. I blame the vodka, but I

giggle to myself as I think of the furious expression on his face as he stares down at that note.

Things might have changed between us the other night. I might have opened up and let him see some of my more vulnerable parts, but that doesn't mean I'm about to follow the second he snaps his fingers. And that's exactly why I jumped at the chance to hang out here tonight with Xander and the guys instead of waiting around in his flat like a desperate slut as he requested.

The knowledge that he'd somehow given me permission to get inside should have been enough to take him up on the offer, really. A chance to properly snoop around, knowing that he wouldn't be there to catch me.

But what exactly would I get from that?

I'm not interested in his deep and dark secrets. I can take a good guess at some of the shit he's done. And while it might terrify some girls, quite honestly, I don't really care.

What he does, what my pops and Cruz do, what my dad did... It's their lives. And who am I to criticise that?

They want to go out there and kill people, well, that's on their conscience, not mine.

"What's amusing you?" Gunner, one of Xander's mates asks. "X's joke doesn't deserve that reaction."

"Too fucking right. Private joke," I say, gesturing to my empty glass when the prospect who's running the bar tonight comes over to clear the table.

"Cruz has cut you off, Princess."

My teeth grind at that nickname.

"Cruz can get fucked," I say loud enough so he can hear me.

My uncle just smiles and shakes his head. 'One more', he mouths to his prospect.

"You heard it from the boss, Princess."

I narrow my eyes at him, whatever his name is. "You wanna keep that patch, I suggest you keep me happy," I joke, but the way his face pales makes me wonder just how much power I might have.

Maybe being the club princess isn't all that bad.

The second he delivers my drink, I throw it back in one and excuse myself to the ladies'.

On my way back, I turn the music up that was playing quietly from the speakers on the bar, much to the annoyance of the crowd of older members who are watching sports on the flat screen on the other side of the clubhouse.

"Dance with me," I say, holding my hand out to Xander when I get to our table.

Hoots and hollers come from the rest of the guys.

"Get in there X, my man," Gunner jokes.

"Fuck you, Gun. I value my cock too much to put it anywhere near our princess."

"Oh, you did not just say that," I seethe, my hands on my hips as I glare at him.

Xander holds his hands up in defeat.

"It's true. Cruz and Prez would cut it off with the bluntest knife they could find if I step out of line."

I look over my shoulder and Cruz nods at Xander, proving that his previous words are more than true.

"Men," I sigh. "Come on. I want to dance. Just don't let your cock touch me," I joke.

I drag him into an open space and after a few minutes, a few other couples join us. We all happily dance together while the rest of the club watches our antics.

The alcohol hits me harder with every second that passes and my legs become less and less stable with every song that comes on.

"Whoa, you need to sit down," Xander says, his large hands clamping down on my hips to stop me face planting the dirty concrete floor.

"I'm fine, I'm—" My words are cut off when my eyes connect with his.

They might be blue, but that doesn't stop my mind from morphing them into a different green pair as he stares down at me.

"Emmie?" he whispers, clearly feeling whatever is crackling between us.

My arms land on his shoulders as I attempt to drag him closer to me. My surroundings vanished long ago. I don't hear the music or the guys who are probably warning Xander not to do anything for fear of Cruz putting a bullet through his brain.

All I can think about is that connection. What it was like when Theo kissed me the other night. How my entire body relaxed, yet tensed up incredibly tight at the same time. How I wanted to drag him closer but push him away. How he made me burn with lust and unfiltered hate at the same time.

I hate him. I do. I hate him. I just—

Everything happens so fast, I don't get to process the movement around me, the fact Xander's hands are no longer holding me up until my arse hits the unforgiving floor and the buzzing in my ears begins to fade.

Chaos ensues around me, but it takes my brain a little longer than necessary to actually see what's happening.

"Theo, no," I scream—or at least I think I do as I force my limbs into action and scramble to my feet. "Theo!"

Racing toward where he's got Xander pinned against the wall by his cut, I wrap my hand around his forearm in the hope of stopping him.

But I quickly discover that I'm too late.

Xander's already got a split lip, blood dripping from his chin and onto his white shirt.

"Fucking hell, Theo. Get the fuck off him."

I tug on Theo's arm, but he doesn't lessen his

grip on Xander at all. Instead, he steps closer, their noses almost colliding.

"If you touch her again, I'll fucking kill you. You got that, X?"

Xander doesn't cower at all despite the enraged fucking psychopath who's right in his face.

He's a fighter, and there's a good chance he could probably take Theo to the floor right now, but somehow, he manages to keep a cool head and just stare back at the blazing green eyes that are glaring pure fucking death at him.

"I stopped her falling on her arse, you dick. Something which you clearly didn't care too much about seeing as she hit the deck the second you touched me." Xander's eyes narrow at Theo, his voice unnervingly cool as he defends himself.

The clubhouse is in silence as every single person in the large space watches to see what Theo is going to do next.

I have no idea how much they know about him, but the anticipation that ripples through the room tells me that they're more than aware of just how dangerous he is.

Finally, Theo looks away from Xander and turns his burning eyes on me.

"You okay?"

Shaking my head, I blow out a frustrated breath.

"Fuck you, Cirillo. Fuck. You."

Turning my back on him, I grab my jacket and

bag from the chair I left them on and storm out of the clubhouse, concerned eyes following my every movement.

"Em, you okay?" Cruz asks softly, catching my upper arm to stop me.

"Yes," I hiss, shrugging him off. "I'm fucking fine. Thank you."

Dragging my arm out of his grip, I march toward the doors.

"Do not get on your fucking bike, kid."

Flipping him off over my shoulder, I swing the door so hard it crashes back against the wall.

I suck in a deep lungful of ice-cold air, suddenly feeling annoyingly sober.

There are bikes everywhere, which only makes Theo's Ferrari stand out that much more where it's been abandoned in the middle of the compound.

Ripping my bag open, I search for my Christmas present from Stella and unsheathe the blade.

Excitement oozes through my veins at the thought of his reaction.

Fuck him.

Fuck him to fucking hell and back with a cactus up the arse.

I surge forward with my fingers gripped tightly around the handle, ready to cause some damage.

I've got the point almost touching the perfect black paint of the door when his deep, booming voice echoes around the compound.

"Don't even think about it, Ramsey."

A smile twitches at my lips as the blade connects.

I glance over my shoulder, my eyes connecting with his wide, horrified ones as I drag the sharp tip of my knife along the side of his precious baby.

I don't stop until I hit the edge of the door. Then I pull the knife away, put its cover on and drop it back into my bag.

I could do more, but I'm pretty sure I just made my point. Loud and clear.

Turning to face him, I find him standing with his fists curled at his sides, his chest heaving and his eyes burning holes into mine.

I don't need to get closer to know that his usually green eyes are currently black and fucking deadly. I feel it in the tension that crackles between us.

Behind him stand Cruz, Xander, Gunner and a handful of other guys as they wait to see what's going to happen next.

All of a sudden, Cruz moves out of the way and my pops comes stalking through the crowd.

He glances at Xander, who's still got blood running down his chin before coming to stand in front of Theo, although his eyes are trained on me.

"What the fuck is going on?" he growls.

"Nothing, Pops. I've got it covered."

He looks me up and down, I assume checking for injuries.

"I can handle Theodore."

Theo's face hardens at my use of his full name, and Pops doesn't miss it.

Turning his back on me, he focuses on Theo, although Theo's eyes remain locked on me over Pops's shoulder.

I don't hear what Pops says to him, but Theo doesn't react at all—although his response, which I can lip-read, sends fire shooting through my veins.

"She's mine. I know how to get her in line."

"Oh no," I screech, stepping forward, but Theo is faster.

He sidesteps Pops and storms toward me, catching my jaw in a bruising grip and slamming me back against his precious car.

"Prez, you can't let him—" Cruz starts, but he's swiftly cut off by Pops.

"You will leave them to handle their business. Emmie is a big girl. She doesn't need a white knight."

My entire body trembles with anger as Theo's fingers cut into my cheeks, stopping my mouth from closing as he looms over me.

"What the fuck do you think you're doing?"

If he's expecting an answer then he's going to be bitterly disappointed.

Narrowing my eyes at him, I do the only thing my alcohol-fuelled brain can think of and I jerk my knee up fast.

Much more alert than me, he moves out of the way just in time.

"Did you want tonight to be your last one breathing, Hellcat?"

A growl rips up my throat as his face gets closer.

His nose brushes mine, and for the briefest moment, my eyes flicker at the sensation of him touching me so gently, so intimately. But then his fingers tighten on my hip, digging into my skin, and I remember that there's nothing fucking gentle or intimate about this.

"Get in the fucking car, or your grandfather, uncle and the dick who wants to fuck you are going to get a front row seat to me doing just that."

"They'd kill you," I hiss when he releases his hold on my face.

His laugh is wicked and full of spite. "Would they?" he asks, almost in amusement.

"Yes. I'm theirs, I'm—"

"Mine," he spits, his lips only a breath from mine. "You're fucking mine, and they know their place."

My brows pinch as my brain tries to compute his vicious words, but I don't get a chance to figure anything out because my feet leave the floor and I'm physically thrown into Theo's car.

"Don't make this harder than it has to be, Hellcat," he warns, batting my fighting hands away as he pulls the belt around me and clicks it into place.

"Any harder? I don't want to be in your fucking car, Cirillo," I scream in his face.

"No? Want me to prove you wrong?"

My eyes narrow, daring him to do just that, intrigued as to how he's going to make his point.

"Fine," he sighs, almost as if he's bored out of his mind.

Forcefully, he pushes my thighs apart, and before I can argue, he's cupping my pussy over my knickers.

"Fighting me makes you horny, Hellcat. Admit it. There's nowhere else you want to be right now."

"Like hell there isn't."

He chuckles, his eyes holding mine. It's malicious, and fuck if it doesn't make my cunt flood with need.

"I know you, Ramsey," he groans, slipping a finger beneath the lace that's covering me.

The second he discovers just how wet I am for him, a loud growl rips from his throat, his already dark eyes only getting darker.

Panicked, I turn to the entrance of the club, expecting to see everyone standing there watching, but to my relief, there's no one there.

"Shit," I hiss when Theo pushes his finger inside me, bending it in a way that makes me want to submit to him and whatever twisted plan he's concocting right now.

"See," he says, a smug fucking smirk pulling at his lips, "you don't want to be anywhere but at my mercy."

"Fuck you."

"You want that, don't you, Hellcat?"

He rips his finger from me, my body clenching in a pathetic and embarrassing attempt to keep him inside me.

My muscles ripple around nothing, desperate for what he could have given me so easily.

Lifting his hand, he traces my lips with the finger he just had inside me.

"You want me pushing into your cunt, don't you, Em? You want to be so full of me that you don't know where you end and I begin."

I shake my head, denying his words despite the fact that we both know they're true.

"I bet you're so tight. It'll feel like I'm ripping you in two. You want that?"

Again, I refuse.

"You want me to fuck you so hard, the only thing you can think about is how good it'll be when I finally let you fall. *If* I let you fall."

"I hate you." The words come out weak, my voice dripping with need from the picture he's just painted so clearly for me, instead of the biting tone I was hoping for.

"No, you don't. You just want to."

"Whatever. Let me out of your car. I want to go home."

He chuckles once more, and I feel the deep rumbling all the way to my toes.

"Yeah, that's not happening. You've got a date tonight, remember?"

"In case you hadn't noticed, Cirillo, I don't follow orders."

"No," he says, leaning in and sweeping his tongue over my bottom lip, tasting me. "You don't."

One minute he's there, almost kissing me and rendering me useless, and the next, he's slamming the car door on me and clicking the locks.

"What the fuck?" I scream, slamming my palms on the window as he casually walks around the front of the car.

He gestures something to someone inside the clubhouse, but I'm too furious and slightly mortified about what happened in full view of my grandfather that I don't even bother looking.

"Ready?" he asks the second his arse hits the seat and he turns the engine over.

"No, but something tells me that won't stop you," I sulk, crossing my arms over my chest and turning away from him slightly.

"Cute," he mutters, his eyes burning into my skin.

"Fuck you."

"Oh, I have plans. And as hot as it is to have an audience, I'm not sure those guys are the best choice."

Before I get a chance to respond, although I'm

not sure what I could really say other than to agree with him, he floors the accelerator and we fly from the compound, leaving anyone who might protect me from this deranged psycho behind.

"You need to relax, Ramsey," he says coolly when we're almost at his building.

"How'd you find me?"

He shakes his head, his grip on the wheel tightening as he takes a turn.

"Theo," I snap when he doesn't respond. "How did you find me?"

"Tracked you," he says as if it's totally fucking nothing.

It's exactly what I expected, and the reason I left my phone behind and turned it off.

"How? My phone is—"

He laughs, and the belittling tone laced through it fires me up.

"Don't laugh at me like I'm a fucking idiot, Theo. I fucking knew you'd do something insane like track me. That's why I left my phone at home. So how did you track me to the clubhouse?"

I glare death into the side of his face as he pulls into the underground car park of his building.

It's the first time I've been down here, but I'm too angry at him to bother looking around.

"How did you..." Realisation hits me. "You tracked my fucking bike. Unbelievable. Un-fucking-believable."

He just shrugs and pulls into a parking space.

"I'm not staying here with you tonight. I don't give a shit how many orgasms you intend to give me or how big your cock is. I'm fucking done with you. You're fucking insane, Theo. You're—"

His hand wraps around my throat, pinning me back against the chair and cutting off my air supply.

"Watch your fucking mouth, Ramsey. I have more than one way to stop it from spitting bullshit."

My lips purse and my teeth grind.

Leaning over the console, he gets right in my face once more.

His scent hits me, stronger than before now we're enclosed, and damn it, my mouth fucking waters.

"Better," he muses. "Think you can be a good girl until we're upstairs?"

My lip curls into a scowl, giving him a silent answer.

"No, I didn't think so."

25

EMMIE

The second he opens my door, I make a run for it.

I know it's pointless. I know he's faster, stronger, generally better at everything than me, but still, for my own sanity, I have to try. I need to know that I tried to escape this. Even if I don't really want to.

I might be fighting it, but I can't deny that a night with his rough touches, dirty words and skilled fingers, and hopefully cock, is exactly what I need.

"Get the hell off me," I scream, thrashing about in the hope of loosening his hold on me. It's futile and we both know it.

With one arm clamped around my waist, his other hand twists in my hair and drags my head to the side, exposing my neck.

"Keep fighting, Hellcat. It'll make your submission so much fucking sweeter in the end."

"You won't win, Theo. You won't break me," I cry as he sucks so hard on my neck I have no doubt I'll be attempting to cover the bruise for weeks.

"Watch me," he warns, spinning me around so I can see across the almost deserted car park.

My eyes land on a Kawasaki that's parked alongside some more fancy arse cars that I've never seen before.

"Whose is that? Yours?"

"Not yours, so stay the fuck away from it."

A wicked smile pulls up my lips.

"It is, isn't it? That's yours. You can ride a bike?"

"I can do a fucking lot of things, Em. Did you want to test me?"

"No," I say, allowing the anger to drain from my voice and my body to go lax in his arms. "There's only one thing I want from you."

My back bumps against his car.

"Oh yeah? Willing to admit you want me now, are you?"

His eyes hold mine and I can see suspicion swimming in them.

"I don't want you, Theodore. I just want your mouth."

Lifting my hand, I mimic his move from earlier and run my fingertip along his bottom lip.

He snatches it, sinking his teeth into my skin

until it burns with pain before his tongue laps at the ache, soothing it better.

"You want that, don't you, Theo?" I ask, tilting my head to the side. "You want to eat my pussy?"

He knows I'm playing him. He's not that stupid, unfortunately. But that doesn't stop his eyes from dilating with need.

"You want to spread my thighs wide and taste me until I'm crying out your name?"

"Hellcat," he groans, but I don't tone it down.

Two can play at this game, motherfucker.

Reaching out, I cup his hard dick through his trousers.

"Gonna try and deny just how bad you want it, Cirillo?"

"No," he states. "I fucking own what I want."

I shriek as he lifts me off my feet and drops me on the roof of his fucking car.

"Theo, what the hell are you—"

"Lie back," he demands, his voice low and dangerous as he grabs my knees and forces them apart.

My knickers are dragged to the side, the cool air of the garage flooding my burning hot skin.

"Oh God," I whimper. He's about to eat me on the top of his— "Oh, shit," I scream when his mouth connects with my cunt and he sucks hard on my clit.

My fingers twist in his hair in an attempt to

drag him closer—not that I really think that's possible.

He laps at me like a starved man as I writhe about on the roof of his fancy Ferrari, moaning like a fucking whore.

"Yes," I cry when he pushes two thick fingers inside me. "Yes, yes."

My release races forward, but he knows it and he pulls back just enough to stop me from falling.

"You're a cunt," I spit.

He laughs against me, sending shivers of pleasure shooting through my body.

"I'm so close," I whimper.

"I know. Trust me?"

I scoff. "Not a fucking chance, Cirillo."

"That's fair," he mutters before licking up the length of me once more.

My head spins with the vodka and the number of times he brings me right to the edge of release before pulling back.

I should have expected it and been ready for it, really. It seems to be his main brand of torture.

He starts up again, tonguing my entrance, when there's a loud bang somewhere behind me.

Arching my back, I hang my head over the edge of the car and look in horror as Daemon emerges from a door on the other side of the garage.

His eyes find mine in an instant and a wicked smile pulls at his lips.

"Theo," I snap, trying to drag his face from between my thighs.

"Evening," Daemon mutters, his eyes never leaving us as he gets closer. "Glad to see someone else is having fun tonight."

As he rounds the boot of the car, Theo finally looks up, but only enough to make the briefest eye contact with his friend.

He nods once before diving back for me and bringing me right to the edge once more, which only comes faster, knowing we're being watched.

Daemon pauses in another doorway and looks back over his shoulder.

My release just begins to crest when—

"Nooooo," I cry when Theo rips his fingers from inside me and lifts his mouth from my clit. "You're a fucking cunt tease, Cirillo."

Lifting his hand, he wipes across his mouth as he stares at my slick pussy as it clenches around nothing, desperate to rediscover my lost orgasm.

"You think Daemon's hard, wondering how you taste?"

I quirk a brow.

"Call him back. Let's find out."

He laughs darkly.

"I don't share my toys, Hellcat. Let's go."

The next thing I know, I'm flying, my arse is in the air, and I'm staring directly at his.

"Put me down," I demand.

"So you can try running again? No chance. In

case you didn't get the message earlier, you're mine, Emmie Ramsey."

"Pfft. Think again, knobhead. I'm not a thing. I don't belong to anyone."

The dark laugh that falls from his lips sends a shiver racing down my spine.

"You keep telling yourself that, Hellcat."

I'm still trying to cover my thong-clad arse as we make our way to the lift.

"Will you stop that?" he mutters, batting my hands away. "You're ruining my view."

"I swear to fucking God, I'm going to..." My words trail off when I look to the side and catch our reflection in the mirrored wall of the car. "Holy shit."

I watch him as he stares at my arse in the mirror, his finger trailing up my thigh until it dips between my legs.

His eyes are locked on where it disappears, and I writhe on his shoulder as he pushes it inside me.

"So desperate for my cock, aren't you, Hellcat?"

"Theo," I whimper, unable to deny the truth this time.

I'm so lost, watching the hard set of his face as he stares at himself fingering me that the ding of the lift startles me.

With his fingers still inside me, he carries me out of the enclosed space and toward his flat. I can't help but look toward the other end of the hall, half expecting Daemon to be watching us.

"Fuck, Theo. I need—"

"I don't care," he hisses. His voice is cold, and it probably should terrify me, but in contrast to that, my body practically vibrates with excitement. "You keyed my fucking car, Em. Why should I give you anything you need?"

"B-because you want to," I stutter when he curls his fingers just so.

His chest rumbles with something, but it's not a response I can make out. Instead, when he speaks, it's not at all what I'm expecting him to say.

"Give me your hand."

"W-what?"

"Hand," he barks. "Mine are busy." He palms my arse with his other, proving his point.

Spinning, he stops when the biometric pad to let us inside his flat is right beside me.

"I can get us in?" It's a dumb question, I'd already figured as much, but the words fall from my lips regardless.

"You were meant to be here waiting for me. How did you think you were going to get in?"

The fact that he's clearly stolen my handprint at some point barely registers over the shock that he's actually allowed me access.

No one has access to Theo's space. Since moving here, he's locked it down like Fort Knox.

My surprise renders me useless—well, that along with the way he's working my body and the fact that all my blood has raced to my upside-down head and is mixing with the vodka still flowing through my system, so I just reach out and press my hand to the pad.

It takes a second, but then it beeps, the little light turns green, and the sound of locks being disengaged hits my ears.

Holy shit. Theo really did give me access to his place.

That realisation hits me harder than I'm sure it should, and as he carries me inside, swinging the door closed behind us, I forget all about fighting as we move through his dark space.

He brings us to a stop on the other side of his living room. My feet have barely hit the floor, my body missing his fingers, before my back crashes against the floor-to-ceiling windows.

"Theo, what—"

His eyes are wild as they stare into mine and a shudder of desire laced with fear rips through my body.

Reaching into his back pocket, he pulls a knife out.

My mouth goes dry as I stare at it.

"What? You think you're the only one who gets to play with knives, Hellcat?"

I swallow nervously as he takes a step toward me. For the first time since I took a blade to his car, I'm seriously regretting it. What the hell was I thinking?"

"P-pleas—"

"Aw, look at you, begging for it," he drawls, cutting off what was going to be my demand for him not to hurt me.

Tucking the knife under the hem of my shirt, he drags it up, the fabric parting with ease until he gets to the slashed neckline that hangs down over my shoulder.

He drags both my jacket and my ruined shirt down my arms and roughly tugs them from my hands.

The cold glass behind me makes me shiver and my nipples harden beneath my bra. He can't see them for the padding, but it doesn't stop his eyes dropping as if he knows, as if he can see past my underwear and to exactly what he does to me. What his roughness, his darkness, his anger does to me.

My chest heaves as we stare at each other. If he's waiting for me to tell him to stop as he stands there with his knife poised to cause some damage, then he's going to be bitterly disappointed.

It might have been a thoughtless act, vandalising his car, but deep down, I knew exactly what I was doing, exactly what beast I was poking.

And it fucking worked, because he's right in front of me.

"What?" I taunt. "You gonna stop there?"

He surges forward, slipping a finger beneath the small bit of fabric holding the cups of my bra together and slices it clean through with his knife—only this time, he catches my skin, too.

I hiss as the burn hits me, my eyes dropping as blood pools at the small cut.

Theo stares at it, sucking his lip into his mouth, his teeth sinking deep into the flesh.

Just as I start to wonder if he's actually going to move, he lifts his hand and runs a finger down the cut. It stings, but I don't stop him as he drags his digit lower and writes a T with the blood on my stomach.

"You see that?" he asks, his voice so low it's barely more than a growl.

I nod, staring at his handiwork as another droplet of blood threatens to run down my body.

"You're mine, Emmie. Mine," he repeats, in case I didn't understand the first time. "The next time anyone touches you, a fucking Reaper, anyone... I. Will. Kill. Them."

I can't help but roll my eyes at him.

"Dramatic much. Jesus, Theo. It's not like you caught me fuc—"

"Don't," he warns, grasping me around the throat and pinning me back against the glass. "Don't even think about fucking any other fucking guy."

"Because you're so keen to do the job yourself," I snap, my body aching for the release he ripped from me.

"You want my cock, Hellcat?" he asks, his

crazed eyes holding mine as his grip on my throat tightens until I wonder if he's actually planning on me passing the fuck out.

"You know I do."

His eyes hold mine, some bizarre internal debate warring behind the dark and dangerous depths which confuses the fuck out of me, because ultimately, I'm just a girl standing here, asking for him to put his very obviously hard dick in me.

I'm not sure I really see the issue.

I have no idea what changes, or what decision he comes to, but one second he's lost in his own head and the next my skirt is around my waist and his knife is slicing into both my knickers and the skin above my hip.

"Argh," I cry out at the sting, but he doesn't stop, thank fuck.

The knife clatters to the floor as he rips his trousers open and violently shoves them over his arse, wrapping his hand around his huge cock and stroking hard as his eyes run over the length of my mostly exposed body.

"You did this. Just remember that," he warns before his hands wrap around my thighs and I'm lifted from my feet and pinned against the window with his hips.

His length teases my soaked entrance, and he groans, feeling just how ready I am for him.

"You been taking your pill?" he asks, and

without thinking about how he knows what kind of birth control I'm on, I nod.

Thank fuck I didn't plan on saying anything, because the second he thrusts his hips, the second his giant cock pushes inside me, all thoughts, words, sense, everything falls from my head as my body tries to adjust to what's happening below my waist.

"Oh fuck," falls from my lips as he pushes deeper, forcing my body to let him in.

"Relax, Hellcat," he groans in my ear as if he's in physical pain. "You were fucking made for me. You can take it."

Doing as I'm told, I blow out a long breath, and the second he feels me go limp, he thrusts forward, filling himself to the hilt.

I have no fucking idea where I end and he begins, and it's fucking everything.

Releasing one of my thighs, his fingers twist into my hair and he drags me so my nose touches the tip of his. His eyes hold mine. They're still dark, but I swear there's also some twisted excitement within them.

"You have no idea what you've just done."

Our breaths mingle as our chests heave.

I sense he's trying to tell me something important with that warning, but fuck, his cock is twitching inside me and the only thing I can think about is how it's going to feel when he moves.

Narrowing my eyes at him, I say six words that

are sure to get me what I want. "Fuck me like you own me."

His fingertips dig into the soft flesh of my thighs, and his nostrils flare a beat before he pulls out. Then on a roar, he slams back inside me.

"Theo," I scream as he hits me so deeply I can't decide if it hurts or not. "Fuck. Fuck. More," I cry as he starts pounding into me like a man possessed.

Dipping his face into the crook of my neck, he drags my head to the side and sinks his teeth into my skin.

I don't realise he's drawn blood until he moves me once more, slamming his lips down on mine, and I taste the copper on him.

It's dirty, and wild, and fucking everything I've been craving from him, everything I knew he was capable of long before I was even ready to admit that I wanted him.

"Yes," I cry, ripping his shirt open, sending buttons pinging off in all directions so I can sink my nails into his shoulders, spurring him on further.

26

THEO

Reality slips further and further away with every thrust of my hips, every clench of her muscles around my length, every one of her cries and pleas for more.

Releasing her hair, I push my hand between our bodies to find her clit.

She's so close, and as much as I might get off on denying her, right now, I need it. I need to feel that moment she falls over the edge and tries dragging me even deeper into her body.

Her slick skin slides against the smooth glass at her back. If anyone cares to look up, then fuck, they're getting one hell of a view right now.

My cock jerks inside her at the thought of being watched.

Fuck. If I didn't need her mouth on mine so badly, I'd take her from behind, force her to see the world that's just on the other side of the window.

Force her to see all those people down there who could be watching me make her mine.

Mine.

That one single word makes my chest swell.

I was trying—although weakly—to do the right thing.

Then she took that fucking knife to my car. I knew there and then that any good intentions I had for her had just flown out the window.

She's going to fucking pay for that.

All the positions I want to make her pay in, flicker through my mind.

Fuck, yeah. This entire penthouse is about to get christened in a whole new way.

Finding her clit, I pinch hard, making her cry out into our kiss.

"Come for me. Hellcat. I wanna feel you flooding my fucking cock."

Ripping her lips from mine, her head falls back as she races toward her release.

"Eyes, Emmie. I want you to look into my eyes and see who owns you while you fall."

Her pussy clenches, and only a second after her lids lift, her dark eyes finding mine, does she fall.

Her entire body locks up impossibly tight, almost sending me into my orgasm right alongside her, but I clench my teeth and force myself to ride it out.

I'm nowhere fucking near ready for this to be over yet.

"Fuuuck" I groan, watching as her pleasure takes over and her face falls slack, her eyes heavy, her full lips red and abused. "You're so beautiful when you come for me, Hellcat."

Her body is slick. Blood covers her from the bite mark I left on her neck and the cuts on her chest and hips.

Fuck. She's never looked better.

"Theo," she pants, coming down from her high, her body limp in my arms. "Fuck, that was—"

"Just the beginning," I finish for her.

With my cock still buried in her cunt, I pull her from the window, laying her back on the chaise end of the sofa, letting her arse hang off the edge as I drop to my knees.

"Holy shit," she gasps at the angle.

"Good, babe?" I ask, although it's completely unnecessary as her nails claw down my forearms when I roll my hips, grazing that spot inside her that makes her eyes blaze with need.

"Again," she cries.

"You don't deserve it," I tell her. Although the words might be true, it doesn't stop me from following her orders.

She laughs darkly. "After all the shit you've pulled, I more than deserve this, arsehole."

Skimming my hand down her back until I find where we're joined, I drag some of her juices over her arse and press one finger against her tight hole.

"Oh, Hellcat. That can certainly be arranged."

Her eyes widen in shock, her lips forming a little O as I push harder against her tight muscle.

"Anyone taken your arse before?"

She shakes her head slightly as my finger goes a little deeper.

Her pussy contracts around me and I start moving faster.

"Good. It's going to be mine, too."

My other hand finds her breasts, palming them roughly and pinching her nipples as I fuck both her holes.

She writhes against the sofa cushion.

"You gonna come for me again, Em?"

She nods in a rush. "Yes, yes," she cries.

"Want more?"

But before she can answer this time, my hand slides up until I've got her throat in a tight grip, cutting off her airway enough to make her head spin as my hips pick up speed and my finger slides deeper into her ass.

"Fuck. Theo," she cries, her back arched as she gasps for breath. "Yes. Fuck. Yes. Keep going."

My cock swells as she clamps down, her release imminent, and I know that I'm not going to be able to hold off this time, no matter how much I might want to keep this going all fucking night.

The second her release slams into her and she tenses, I fall right along with her, my cock jerking violently, filling her with hot ropes of cum.

"Emmie," I groan as I drown in what must be the most powerful release I've ever experienced.

My entire body trembles by the time I come down, my softening cock slipping from her cunt.

"Holy shit," Emmie gasps, sucking in huge lungfuls of air when I release her throat and sit back on my haunches.

The sight of my cum slipping from her body spurs me into action and I push two fingers back inside her.

"What the hell... shit," she cries.

"Sensitive?"

"Jesus. Fuck." She falls lax on the sofa, her arm hanging off the side as I slowly finger fuck her while pushing my cum back inside.

"T-Theo, I c-c-can't—"

"Wanna fucking bet?"

Pushing her further onto the sofa, I spread her legs wide and lick up the length of her cunt, tasting our mixed pleasure.

"Oh God," she moans, propping herself up on her elbows to watch me. "That's hot. Can you taste yourself?"

"Mmm," I agree with a moan that makes her shudder. "I can taste us. Fucking delicious."

Dipping my fingers back inside her, I lift them for her.

Her lips part without instruction, desperate to know what we taste like combined, but I don't let her have it. Instead, I paint our joined releases along her lips.

"Lick," I demand, watching her tongue lap at the wetness before I thrust both fingers deep inside her mouth.

Her long tongue swirls around my digits as I dive for her cunt once more, too addicted to her taste not to get her off again.

"Your tongue shouldn't feel this good," she cries, her hips writhing against me.

"You shouldn't taste this good."

I don't stop until her body is thrashing about and her juices are dripping down my chin and onto the sofa.

Only when she's done and coming back to Earth do I turn my head to the side and sink my teeth into her, giving her a matching brand to the one I've already put on her neck.

"Mine," I growl, licking at the wound, tasting the copper of her blood.

Her eyes meet mine. I see the argument within them. But it's too late.

She's already handed herself over willingly.

If only she knew exactly what that meant.

Her eyes drop from mine and take in my body.

"Jesus," she mutters. "I knew you were fucking psychotic, but I didn't realise you were a vampire."

She pushes to sit up, squirming as I'm sure the evidence of our session slips out of her.

I have to fight the need to push her back down to keep my cum inside her.

As if she can read my thoughts, she reaches out and cups my rough jaw.

"Don't worry, I'll be feeling it for a while."

My lips collide with hers. It's the only way I can express what her words make me feel, because even attempting to express it freaks me the fuck out.

She's a job, a little voice screams in my head.

All you've got to do is get her secrets.

And I will. I'll get all the information Dad needs to prove that she's not a part of this.

It's just what happens next that's up in the air, because the second she discovers the truth, and there's no doubt that she will, where will that leave us?

"You're insatiable," she mutters into my kiss.

"Any idea how long I've been waiting?"

"Yeah, actually, I do."

Lifting her exhausted body into my arms, I carry her through my flat, kicking open the door to my bedroom then stalking through to the adjoining bathroom.

"You gonna freak out on me this time?" Emmie asks before I put her back on the ground.

"That all depends."

"On?" she asks, her huge, dark eyes staring up into mine.

Her makeup is fucked and smeared all over her face, her lipstick probably all over mine too.

"On if you can keep your stupid comments to yourself."

She falls silent as she thinks, and I place her feet on the floor and turn the shower on.

"The shampoo," she whispers.

Reaching for her, I drag her under the water, watching as the blood that's smeared all over her skin begins to wash away.

Grasping her chin, I hold her eyes firm.

"Listen to me very closely, Emmie."

She nods, at least as much as she's able to with my firm grip.

"Aside from Stella, you're the only girl who's been here. And," I add, in case that wasn't enough, "you're the only girl who's ever going to be in here."

"B-but—"

"It's yours, Em. I bought it all for you."

Her lips part, and whatever it was she wanted to say dies on her tongue.

"The shampoo is good for brunettes." Lifting my hand, I twirl a lock of her dark hair around my finger. "There's even makeup remover above the basin," I confess. Kissing along her cheek, I brush my lips against the shell of her ear. "And tampons by the toilet."

"W-why?" she breathes, her entire face screwed up in confusion. "You hate me. Why would you do all that?"

I shrug, taking her hand and guiding it to my already hard cock.

"Does it feel like I hate you?"

She lets out a heavy sigh.

"I don't know what I think anymore," she admits.

A smirk tugs at my lips. "Orgasms that good, huh?"

She fights it, but it's no use. Her lips curl and she smacks me gently on the chest.

"Shut up, you idiot."

"That's better. I don't know how to take you when you're not hurling insults at me."

"Same. All this buying me shit is weird."

"Weirder than sneaking into your room and jerking off while you sleep?"

Her eyes flash with shock, although I'm not sure why, she damn well knew what I was doing. I guess it's just the fact that I admitted it.

"Y-yeah, actually. For you, it is."

I study her for a few seconds, taking in every inch of her face.

"What are you thinking?"

"Tell me something. Something no one else knows."

She looks away from me, her eyes focusing on something over my shoulder.

"I already have," she whispers. "I told you how I really feel about my mum."

My chest aches, remembering all the things she

said to me about how much she misses her, even though she knows she shouldn't.

"Something else," I demand.

She chews on her bottom lip for a few seconds, thinking.

"I think... I think that..." Her eyes come back to mine as if she needs my strength to say what she's thinking. "I think that maybe I don't hate you after all."

An unexpected laugh rips up my throat.

Wrapping my hand around the back of her neck, I pull her into my body.

"I'm pretty sure our friends would claim to already know that secret, Hellcat."

"Then I'd deny it profusely because this... us... right now... it's none of their business."

"Fuck yeah," I grunt before claiming her lips and setting about giving her another secret to keep from her friends as I make her scream my name against the marble wall.

27

EMMIE

I wake to a buzzing sound. I'm so relaxed that I almost put it out of my mind and pass back out, but then the body that's wrapped around me like a freaking spider monkey comes to, and he moves faster than I thought possible.

His heat leaves me, and I'm left cold and alone as he grabs his phone. The light of the screen makes me wince as he lifts it to his ear and I watch as he stands from the bed, bare as the day he was born, and walks toward the door.

"What's wrong?" he asks in a cold, angry voice that immediately makes my hackles rise.

Rolling onto my back, I pull the covers tighter around me, trying to retain some of his warmth.

I try not to think about how much I miss him already when he's only in the hallway. I refuse to be that girl, even if I know deep down that I already am.

"Fuck. I'll be right there," he says before walking back into the room and immediately pulling out a clean pair of boxers to drag on.

Damn shame, if you ask me.

I watch as he starts covering himself up before walking to the bed and leaning over me.

"I'm sorry, Hellcat. Business calls. I won't be long."

He drops the sweetest kiss to the tip of my nose that makes my heart flutter wildly in my chest.

"Okay."

"Go back to sleep. I'll be back before you know it."

"You'd better," I warn, sinking into his kiss when his lips find mine.

I'm on the verge of reaching for him and refusing to let him go, but I know I can't. A call in the middle of the night is never a good thing, so I reluctantly let him go and listen as he makes his way out of the flat.

I let out a sigh and curl back into the sheets, but I already know it's pointless.

I might sleep like the dead, but once I'm awake, that's it.

Forcing myself to stay put, I will my body to succumb to my exhaustion, but it's pointless. And less than ten minutes later, I give up, throw the covers off and swing my legs over the edge of the bed.

The coolness of the flat surrounds me, making goosebumps prick my skin, and I shudder, but it's not enough to dampen down the aches throughout my body.

Hell, he worked me over pretty thoroughly last night.

A smile twitches at my lips, because damn if it wasn't the best night of my life.

Reaching for one of Theo's hoodies that are neatly folded in his wardrobe, I pull it on and head for the bathroom.

As I step inside, images of the time we spent in here together last night fill my mind and it makes my temperature pick up.

The things he confessed, the way he kissed me, the softness to his touch after the brutality in both the garage and living room...

The memories of it now make my head spin almost as much as when it was happening.

While I'm sitting on the toilet, I look to the side, noticing a hidden panel. Pressing my hand to it, it opens just like the one by the shower, and sure as shit, inside sits a box of tampons. And not just any box, the exact same ones I usually use.

"Creepy fuck," I mutter to myself, but I can't help the smile playing on my lips.

Did he know I was going to end up here with him in the end? Was he just playing the long game?

I think back to some of the less than enjoyable

times we've spent together as we hurled insults at each other and generally hated that the other dared even breathe near us, and I can't help but wonder if this is all some twisted game.

Surely not.

Shaking my head, I force my stupid insecurities down, close the cupboard and finish up what I'm doing.

I don't know why, but I kinda thought that Theo would have slipped out of bed when I finally crashed only a few hours ago to come and clean up the mess in the living room, but as I flick the lights on, I discover that it still looks like something out of a crime scene.

Bloody handprints are smeared on the window, there are stains, which I can only assume are also blood, on the leather sofa, and when I step closer, I see droplets on the wooden floor.

Christ, no wonder my body aches like a little bitch. It literally looks like he mauled me out here.

Needing something to keep me busy while he's gone, I rummage through the kitchen until I find some cleaning products. All of them are full, and it leaves me wondering who actually cleans this place. I can't imagine Theo pulling on his Marigolds and donning a feather duster, although the thought makes me giggle as I gather up my findings and head back to the living room.

I remove the evidence of what happened the night before from the window before setting to work on the sofa with some anti-bac spray. I clean the floor the best I can in the absence of a mop, and I'm just about to take everything back to the kitchen when one of Theo's shirt buttons catches my eye.

Looking around, I spot more of them where they finally stopped after I ripped them clean from the fabric.

Getting on my hands and knees, I begin crawling around and gathering them all up.

I shouldn't care. I should leave them to make his left eye twitch in annoyance when he gets home. But some weird part of me doesn't actually want to piss him off for once.

As I reach for the one I can see poking out from under the coffee table on the rug, my hand hits something.

Grabbing it, I pull out a folder.

Thinking nothing of it, I place it right side up on the coffee table and grab the button—only when I stand, something about it catches my eye and it makes my heart jump into my throat.

On the front of the grey folder, in perfect penmanship, is my name.

Emmie Cora Ramsey.

"What the hell?" I mutter to myself. Placing the buttons in my palm on the coffee table, I perch my arse on the edge of the sofa, and with a trembling hand, I flip the folder open.

For the longest time, I just stare at the words

before me, confused, refusing to understand what they mean.

But when reality does finally slam into me, my stomach turns over and I have to run toward the bathroom to save puking on the floor I just cleaned.

I heave long after my stomach is empty. It's almost as if I can remove the memory of reading those words from my body if I vomit enough.

My entire body trembles with exhaustion from dry heaving, and my skin is covered in a sheen of sweat.

I barely feel the impact as I fall onto my arse and pull my legs up in front of me, hugging them to my chest.

I brought the folder with me in my panic, and I stare down at it like its mere presence offends me.

It does.

Or at least, what it hides inside does.

"It can't be true," I tell myself. It's a joke. It has to be. A stupid prank that one of the guys pulled for Christmas to wind Theo up.

But as I open the folder once more, I'm reminded by just how official the document before me looks.

And when I find a familiar signature at the bottom, I realise that this is very much real, and that my stupid concerns about this all being too good to be true earlier weren't stupid at all.

"Fuck," I hiss, mortified that I believed for even

a second that this could have been something real. That he really wanted me.

All this time, he was just playing me.

Making me trust him, getting all my secrets out of me, listening to me cry about losing Mum and how conflicted I am over it all.

Anger like I've never felt before surges through me and I jump to my feet. With the folder clutched to my chest, I pace through the flat, trying to figure out what my next move is going to be.

I have no idea where he's gone, but fuck waiting around here for him to get back and discover that I know everything he's been hiding from me.

"You're mine." His words from last night hit me like a freight train. *"You have no idea what you've just done, do you?"*

Another wave of nausea hits me.

That's why he didn't want to fuck me.

If he didn't, then he'd have an out. But now we've... now we've... I heave again, unable to process this overload of information.

All I know is that I need to get out of here now.

I need to get away from him.

My husband.

I pull on a pair of his boxers and sweats, tugging the strings almost as tight as they'll go around my waist to keep them up.

My boots are where I placed them as I tidied up, and I shove my feet into them angrily.

My entire body trembles with undiluted fury, the image of that signed wedding certificate as clear in my mind as if I'm still sitting in the bathroom, staring at it.

My breathing is ragged as I rip through the drawers of the cupboard by the front door in the hope of finding his key collection.

The one for his Ferrari is sitting on the top, and I quickly locate the Maserati one. But they're not what I want.

"Yes," I hiss when I wrap my fingers around the Kawasaki key and run from the flat, not even bothering to close the door behind me.

Fuck him. He deserves to have his fancy penthouse burgled after all this.

The lies. The deceit.

"Devious fucking cunt," I hiss to myself as I wait for the lift to start descending.

All the late-night visits, the tracking, listening to me openly bleed out over my mum the other night. All of it was a fucking game.

When was he going to tell me?

Was he ever going to tell me?

And more importantly... How? Why?

Why the fuck are we married? What's the point? What is he getting out of this?

Thoughts are still flying around my head at a million miles an hour as I emerge in the underground car park.

Only when I step through the doors, I realise that I'm not alone.

The beep of a car locking cuts through the silence before a middle-aged man wearing—I squint, not believing my eyes—his pyjamas, and carrying what I guess is a medical bag with his phone to his ear, rushes to the other side of the garage. To the door that Daemon emerged from last night.

I know I should get on Theo's bike and get the hell away, but suddenly, my need for some answers gets the better of me and I find myself following.

I hide in the shadows, watching as he makes his way through to another set of doors.

He clearly doesn't have permission to enter, because he has to wait for the locks to be disengaged. I can only assume that the person on the other end of the phone is allowing him access.

I know from listening to the guys' conversations that there's a basement gym in this building, but something tells me this man isn't here for his daily workout. Whatever this is, I'd put money on it being linked to Theo's mysterious middle-of-the-night call.

I rush to slip through the door behind him. I might have had access to Theo's flat, but I have no reason to believe he'd give me access to everything.

Lights flicker on as he makes his way down another set of stairs, heading deeper underground. Unease washes through me.

No one keeps anything good this deep underground.

Especially not the freaking mafia.

Telling myself that I've watched too much TV, I continue forward.

The buzzing in my ears is the only thing I can hear, and I can only hope that I'm being incognito, because the man hasn't once tried to look back.

When he hits the end of the stairs, he turns left, and it's not two seconds later that I hear a voice that sends a fresh bolt of anger through my body.

"In here," Theo says, his tone hard and cold. Nothing like the way he murmured in my ear only a few hours ago as he thrust inside me.

Silence falls around the sterile and cold space.

The floors and walls are all concrete. I can't help thinking it looks like some kind of underground prison.

Edging forward, I pass multiple closed doors with little sliding windows, which only solidifies my previous thought.

My heart is in my throat when I spot the open door, but now I've made it this far, there's no way I'm stopping now.

Holding the folder that's still in my hand tighter to my chest, I forge on.

I squint at the bright light when I turn into the doorway.

Everything I thought about this space rings true as I step inside what can only be described as a cell.

It's grey, cold, hard. Inhumane.

The man is in here, crouched on the ground, but it's not him I focus on. That would be the lying fuck I started to trust.

"Do you have something you need to tell me?" I ask, my voice piercing the heavy silence.

Theo startles, and after a beat, he turns to me with wide eyes.

"Emmie, you shouldn't be down here," he says calmly and void of any kind of emotion.

"And you should have told me about this," I bark, waving the folder in front of his face.

His lips part as if he's about to spin me another line when a deep, unfamiliar voice fills the room.

"I'm losing her."

Ripping my eyes from Theo's, I look down at the scene he moved away from when he realised I'd joined them.

For a couple of seconds, I'm unable to register what I'm looking at.

There's blood. So much fucking blood.

My stomach turns over at the sight of it.

But that's nothing compared to what happens when I get a look at the face of the person the blood belongs to.

"Mum," I cry, my eyes burning with tears as I stare at her lifeless form on the cold floor.

"I'm losing her." The doctor's words come back to me.

"NO," I scream, unwilling to let her go out like

this, whatever this is. I rush forward, falling down, abandoning the folder.

My knees collide with the unforgiving concrete, but I don't feel it. I feel nothing but undiluted panic.

"No, please. You have to save her, please," I beg as tears cascade down my cheeks.

Reaching out, I place a hand on Mum's free arm. Her skin is cold. As if she's already gone.

"No," I sob. "I need you, Mum. I fucking need you." I hate that those words are true. She's been nothing but a shit mother my whole life, but still, even now, I hold onto that stupid hope that something might change. "Please."

"You need to get out of Doc's way," Theo's flat voice says a beat before warm hands wrap around my upper arms, lifting me from the ground.

"Get the hell off me," I cry, thrashing around. "You need to fix this. You need to fix this now, you lying fucking cunt."

I kick out behind me, hoping to cause just some of the damage I'm imagining, but before I can connect with any part of him, pain shoots up my arm and everything goes black.

The last thing I see is Theo's lost and pained expression.

Emmie and Theo's story continues in DEVIANT PRINCESS.

Read D and Piper's story in my Rebel Ink series now. Start with HATE YOU

HATE YOU PROLOGUE

Tabitha

I stare down at my gran's pale skin. Her cheeks are sunken and her eyes tired. She's been fighting this for too long now, and as much as I hate to even think it, it's time she found some peace.

I take her cool hand in mine and lift her knuckles to my lips.

"It's Tabitha," I whisper. I've no idea if she's awake, but I don't want to startle her.

Her eyes flicker open. After a second they must adjust to the light and she looks right at me. My chest tightens as if someone's wrapping an elastic band around it. I hate seeing my once so full of life gran like this. She was always so happy and full of cheer. She didn't deserve this end. But cancer doesn't care what kind of person you are, it hits whoever it fancies and ruins lives.

Pulling a chair closer, I drop onto it, not taking my eyes from her.

"How are you doing today?" I hate asking the question, because there really is only one answer. She's waiting, waiting for her time to come to put her out of her misery.

"I'm good. Christopher upped my morphine. I'm on top of the world."

She might be living her last days, but it doesn't stop her eyes sparkling a little as she mentions her male nurse. If I've heard the words 'if I were forty years younger' once while she's been here, then I've heard them a million times. She's joking, of course. My gran spent her life with my incredible grandpa until he had a stroke a few years ago. Thankfully, I guess, his end was much quicker and less painful than Gran's. It was awful at the time to have him healthy one moment and then gone in a matter of hours, but this right now is pure torture, and I'm not the one lying on the hospital bed with meds constantly being pumped into my body.

"Turn the frown upside down, Tabby Cat. I'm fine. I want to remember you smiling, not like your world's about to come crashing down."

"I know, I'm sorry. I just—" a sob breaks from my throat. "I don't know how I'm going to live without you." Dramatic? Yeah. But Gran has been my go-to person my whole life. When my parents get on my last nerve, which is often, she's the one who talks me down, makes me see things differently. She's also the only one who's encouraged me to live the life I want, not the one I'm constantly being pushed into.

That's the reason I'm the only one visiting her right now.

When my parents discovered that she was the one encouraging my 'reckless behaviour', as they called it, they cut contact. I can see the pain in her eyes about that every time she looks at me, but she's too stubborn to do anything about it, even now.

"You're going to be fine. You're stronger than you give yourself credit for. How many times have I told you, you just need to follow your heart. Follow your heart and just breathe. Spread your wings and fly, Tabby Cat."

Those were the last words she said to me.

HATE YOU CHAPTER ONE

Tabitha

The heavy bass rattles my bones. The incredible music does help to lift my spirits, but I find it increasingly hard to see the positives in my life while I'm hanging out with my friends these days. They've all got something exciting going on—incredible job prospects, marriage, exotic holidays on the horizon —and here I am, drowning in my one-person pity party. It's been two months since Gran left me, and I'm still wondering what the hell I'm meant to be doing with my life.

"Oh my god, they are so fucking awesome," Danni squeals in my ear as one song comes to an end. I didn't really have her down as a rock fan, but she was almost as excited as James when he announced that this was what we were doing for his birthday this year. Although I do wonder if it's the music or the frontman who's really captured her attention. She'd never admit it, but she's got a thing for bad boys.

I glance over at him with his arm wrapped around Shannon's shoulders and a smile twitches my lips. They're so cute. They've got the kind of relationship everyone craves. It seems so easy yet full of love and affection. Ripping my eyes from the couple, I focus back on the stage and try to block out that I'm about as far away from having that kind of connection with anyone as physically possible.

I sing along with the songs I've heard on the radio a million times and jump around with my friends, but I just can't quite totally get on board with tonight. Maybe I just need more alcohol.

"Where to next?" Shannon asks once we've left the arena and the ringing in our ears has begun to fade.

"Your choice," James says, looking down at her with utter devotion shining in his eyes. It wasn't a great surprise when Shannon sent a photo of her giant engagement ring to our group chat a couple of months ago. We all knew it was coming—Danni especially, seeing as it turned out that she helped choose the ring.

Shannon directs us all to a cocktail bar a few

streets over and I make quick work of manoeuvring my way through the crowd to get to the bar, my need for a drink beginning to get the better of me. The others disappear off somewhere in the hope of finding a table

"Can we have two jugs of..." I quickly glance at the menu. "Margaritas please."

"Coming right up, sweetheart." The barman winks at me before his eyes drop to my chest. Hooking up on a night out isn't really my thing, but hell if it doesn't make me feel a little better about myself. He's cute too, and just the kind of guy who would give both my parents a heart attack if I were to bring him home. Both his forearms are covered in tattoos, he's got gauges in both his ears, and a lip ring. A smile tugs at the corner of my mouth as I imagine the looks on their faces.

My gran's words suddenly hit me.

Just breathe.

My hand lifts and my fingers run over the healing skin just below my bra. My smile widens.

I watch the barman prepare our cocktails, my eyes focused on the ink on his arms. I've always been obsessed by art, any kind of art, and that most definitely includes on skin.

I'm lost in my own head, so when he places the jugs in front of me, I startle, feeling ridiculous.

"T-Thank you," I mutter, but when I lift my eyes, I find him staring intently at me.

"You're welcome. I'm Christian, by the way."

"Oh, hi." A sly smile creeps onto my lips. "I'm Biff."

"Biff?" His brows draw together in a way I'm all too used to when I say my name.

"It's short for Tabitha."

"That's pretty. So… uh… how do you feel about—"

"Christian, a little help?" one of the other barmen shouts, pulling Christian's attention from me.

"Sorry, I'll hopefully see you again later?"

I nod at him, not wanting to give him any false hope. Like I said, he's cute, but after my last string of bad dates and even worse short-term boyfriends, I'm happy flying solo right now. I've got a top of the range vibrating friend in my bedside table; I don't need a man.

Picking up the tray in front of me, I turn and go in search of my friends. It takes forever, but eventually I find them tucked around a tiny table in the back corner of the bar.

"What the hell took so long? We thought you'd pulled and abandoned us."

"Yes and no," I say, ensuring every head turns my way.

"Tell us more," Danni, my best friend, demands.

"It was nothing. The barman was about to ask me out, but it got busy."

"Why the hell did you come back? Get over

there. We all know you could do with a little... loosening up," James says with a wink.

"I'm good. He wasn't my type."

"Oh, of course. You only date posh boys."

"That is not true."

"Is it not?" Danni asks, chipping in once she's filled all the glasses.

"No..." I think back over the previous few guys they met. "Wayne wasn't posh," I argue when I realise they're kind of right.

"No, he was just a wanker."

Blowing out a long breath, I try to come up with an argument, but quite honestly, it's true. My shoulders slump as I realise that I've been subconsciously dating guys my parents would approve of. It's like my need to follow their orders is so well ingrained by now that I don't even realise I'm doing it. Shame that their ideas about my life, what I should do, and whom I should date don't exactly line up with mine.

Glancing over my shoulder at the bar, I catch a glimpse of Christian's head. Maybe I should take him up on his almost offer. What's the worst that could happen?

Deciding some liquid courage is in order, I grab my margherita and swallow half down in one go.

I'm so fed up of attempting to live my parents' idea of a perfect life. I promised Gran I'd do things my way. I need to start living up to my promise.

By the time I'm tipsy enough to walk back to the bar and chat up Christian, he's nowhere to be seen. I'm kind of disappointed seeing as the others had convinced me to throw caution to the wind (something that I'm really bad at doing), but I think I'm mostly relieved to be able go home and lock myself inside my flat alone and not have to worry about anyone else.

With my arm linked through Danni's, we make our way out to the street, ready to make our journeys home, and Shannon jumps into an idling Uber while Danni waits for another to go in the opposite direction.

"You sure you don't want to be dropped off? I don't mind."

"No, I'm sure. I could do with the fresh air." It's not a lie—the alcohol from one too many cocktails is making my head a little fuzzy. I hate going to sleep with the room spinning. I'd much rather that feeling fade before lying down.

"Okay. Promise me you'll text me when you're home."

"I promise." I wrap my arms around my best friend and then wave her off in her own Uber.

Turning on my heels, I start the short walk home.

I've been a London girl all my life, and while some might be afraid to walk home after dark, I love it. I love seeing a different side to this city, the quiet side when most people are hiding in their flats, not flooding the streets on their daily commutes.

My mind is flicking back and forth between my promise to Gran and my missed opportunity tonight when a shop front that I walk past on almost a daily basis makes me stop.

It's a tattoo studio I've been inside of once in my life. I never really pay it much attention, but the new sign in the window catches my eye and I stop to look.

Admin help wanted. Enquire within.

Something stirs in my belly, and it's not just my need to do something to piss my parents off— although getting a job in a place like this is sure to do that. I'm pretty sure it's excitement.

Tattoos fascinate me, or more so, the artists.

I'm surprised to see the open sign still illuminated, so before I can change my mind, I push the door open. A little bell rings above it, and after a few seconds of standing in reception alone, a head pops out from around the door.

"Evening. What can I do you for?" The guy's smile is soft and kind despite his otherwise slightly harsh features and ink.

"Oh um..." I hesitate under his intense dark stare. I glance over my shoulder, the back of the piece of paper catching my eye and reminding me why I walked in here. "I just saw the job ad in the window. Is the position still open?"

His eyes drop from mine and take in what I'm wearing. Seeing as tonight's outing involved a rock concert, I'm dressed much like him in all black and looking a little edgy with my skinny black jeans, ripped AC/DC t-shirt and heavy black makeup. I must admit it's not a look I usually go for, but it was fitting for tonight.

He nods, apparently happy with what he sees.

"Experience?" he asks, making my stomach drop.

"Not really, but I'm studying for a Masters so I'm not an idiot. I know my way around a computer, Excel, and I'm super organised."

"Right..." he trails off, like he's thinking about the best way to get rid of me.

"I'm a really quick learner. I'm punctual, methodical and really easy to get along with."

"It's okay, you had me sold at organised. I'm Dawson, although everyone around here calls me D."

"Nice to meet you." I stick my hand out for him to shake, and an amused smile plays at his lips. Stretching out an inked arm, he takes my hand and gives it a very firm shake that my dad would be impressed by—if he could look past the tattoos, that is. "I'm Tabitha, but everyone calls me Biff."

"Biff, I like it. When can you start?"

"Don't you want to interview me?"

"You sound like you could be perfect. When can you start?"

"Err... tomorrow?" I ask, totally taken aback. He doesn't know me from Adam.

"Yes!" He practically snaps my hand off. "Can you be here for two o'clock? I can show you around before clients start turning up. I'll apologise now for dropping you in the deep end, we've not had anyone for a few weeks and things are starting to get a little crazy."

"I can cope with crazy."

"Good to know. This place can be nuts." I smile at him, more grateful than he could know to have a distraction and a focus.

My Masters should be enough to keep my mind busy, but since Gran went, I can't seem to lose myself in it like I could previously. Hopefully, sorting this place's admin out might be exactly what I need.

"Two o'clock tomorrow then," I say, turning to leave. "I'll bring ID. Do you need a reference? I've done some voluntary work recently, I'm sure they'll write something for me."

"Just turn up on time and do your job and you're golden."

I walk out with more of a spring in my step than I have in a long time. I'm determined to find something that's going to make me happy, not just my parents. I've lived in their shadow for long enough.

I look myself over before leaving my flat for my first shift at the tattoo studio. I'm dressed a little more like myself today in a pair of dark skinny jeans, a white blouse and a black blazer. It's simple and smart. I'm not sure if there's a dress code—D never specified what I should wear. With my hair straightened and hanging down my back and my makeup light, I feel like I can take on whatever crazy he throws at me.

With a final spritz of perfume, I grab my bag from the unit in the hall and pull open my door. My home is a top floor flat in an old London warehouse. They were converted a few years ago by my father's company, and I managed to get myself first dibs. They might drive me insane on the best of days, but at least I get this place rent-free. It almost makes up for their controlling and stuck-up ways... almost.

Ignoring the lift like I always do, I head for the stairs. My heels click against the polished concrete until I'm at the bottom and out to the busy city. I love London. I love that no matter what the time, there's always something going on or someone who's awake.

The spring afternoon is still a little fresh,

making me regret not grabbing my coat, or even a scarf, before I left. I pull my blazer tighter around myself and make the short journey to the shop.

The door's locked when I get there, and the bright neon sign that clearly showed it was open last night is currently saying closed.

Unsure of what to do, I lift my hand to knock. Only a second later, the shop front is illuminated, and the sound of movement inside filters down to me, but when the door opens it's not the guy from last night.

"Oh... uh... hi. Is... uh... D here?"

The guy folds his arms over his chest and looks me up and down. He chuckles, although I've no idea what he finds so amusing.

"D," he shouts over his shoulder, "there's some posh bird here to see you."

My teeth grind that he's stereotyped me quite so quickly, but I refuse to allow him to see that his assumptions about me affect me in any way.

"Ah, good. I was worried you might change your mind."

"Not at all," I say, stepping past the judgemental arsehole and into the studio reception-cum-waiting room.

"That's Spike. Feel free to ignore him. He's not got laid in about a million years, it makes him a little cranky." I fight to contain a laugh, especially when I turn toward Spike to find his lips pursed and his eyes narrowed in frustration. All it does is confirm that D's words are correct.

"Is that fucking necessary? Posh doesn't need to know how inactive my cock is, especially not when she's only just walked through the fucking door. Unless..." He stalks towards me and I automatically back up. I can't deny that he's a good looking guy, but there's no way I'm going there.

"I don't think so."

"You sure? You look like you could do with a bit of rough." He winks, and I want the ground to swallow me up.

"Down, Spike. This is Tabitha, or Biff. She's our new admin, so I suggest you be nice to her if you want to stop organising your own appointments and shit. I don't need a sexual harassment case on my hands before she's even fucking started."

I can't help but laugh at the look on Spike's face. "Don't worry. I'm sure you'll find some desperate old spinster soon."

He looks me up and down again, something in his eyes changed. "Appearances aside, I think you're going to get on well here."

I smile at him. "Mine's a coffee. Milk, no sugar. I'm already sweet enough." His chin drops.

"I thought you were our new assistant. Why am I still making the coffee?"

"Know your place, Spike. Now do as the lady says. You know my order."

"Yeah, it comes with a side of fuck off!" He flips D off before disappearing through a door that I can only assume goes to a kitchen.

"I probably should have warned you that you've agreed to work around a bunch of arseholes."

"I know how to handle myself around horny men, don't worry."

After finishing my A levels, before I grew any kind of backbone where my parents were concerned, I agreed to work for my dad. I was his little office bitch and spent an horrendous year of my life being bossed around by men who thought that just because they had a cock hanging between their legs it made them better than me. I might have fucking hated that year, but it taught me a few things, not just about business but also how to deal with men who think they're something fucking special just because they're a tiny bit successful and make more money than me. I've no doubt that my time at Anderson Development Group gave me all the skills I'm going to need to handle these artists.

"So I see. So, this is your desk. When you're on shift you'll be the first person people see when they're inside, so it's important that you look good. But from what I've seen, I don't think we'll have an issue. I've sorted you out logins for the computer and the software we use. Most of it is pretty self-explanatory. I'm pretty IT illiterate and I've figured most of it out, put it that way."

D's showing me how they book clients in when someone else joins us. This time it's someone I recognise from my previous visit, although it's immediately obvious that he doesn't remember me like I do him. But then I guess he was the one delivering the pain, not receiving it.

"Biff, this is Titch. Titch, this is Biff, our new admin. Be nice."

"Nice? I'm always nice. Nice to meet you, Biff. You have any issues with this one, you come and see me. He might look tough, but I know all his secrets." Titch winks, a smile curling at his lips that shows he's a little more interested than he's making out, and quickly disappears towards his room.

It's not long until the first clients of the afternoon arrive, and I'm left alone to try to get to grips with everything.

Between clients, D pops his head out of his room to check I'm okay, and every hour I make a round of coffee for everyone. That sure seems to get me in their good books.

"I think I could get used to having you around," Spike says when I deliver probably his fourth coffee of the day. "Only thing that would make it better is if it were whisky."

"Not sure the person at the end of your needle would agree." He chuckles and turns back to the design he was working on when I interrupted.

My first day flies by. D tells me to head home not long after nine o'clock. They've all got hours of tattooing to go yet, seeing as Saturday night is their busiest night of the week, but he insists I get a decent night's sleep.

Continue reading Tabitha and Zach's story
HATE YOU!

ABOUT THE AUTHOR

Tracy Lorraine is a *USA Today* and *Wall Street Journal* bestselling new adult and contemporary romance author. Tracy has recently turned thirty and lives in a cute Cotswold village in England with her husband, baby girl and lovable but slightly crazy dog. Having always been a bookaholic with her head stuck in her Kindle, Tracy decided to try her hand at a story idea she dreamt up and hasn't looked back since.

Be the first to find out about new releases and offers. Sign up to my newsletter here.

If you want to know what I'm up to and see teasers and snippets of what I'm working on, then you need to be in my Facebook group. Join Tracy's Angels here.

Keep up to date with Tracy's books at
www.tracylorraine.com

ALSO BY TRACY LORRAINE

Falling Series

Falling for Ryan: Part One #1

Falling for Ryan: Part Two #2

Falling for Jax #3

Falling for Daniel (A Falling Series Novella)

Falling for Ruben #4

Falling for Fin #5

Falling for Lucas #6

Falling for Caleb #7

Falling for Declan #8

Falling For Liam #9

Forbidden Series

Falling for the Forbidden #1

Losing the Forbidden #2

Fighting for the Forbidden #3

Craving Redemption #4

Demanding Redemption #5

Avoiding Temptation #6

Chasing Temptation #7

Rebel Ink Series

Hate You #1

Trick You #2

Defy You #3

Play You #4

Inked (A Rebel Ink/Driven Crossover)

Rosewood High Series

Thorn #1

Paine #2

Savage #3

Fierce #4

Hunter #5

Faze (#6 Prequel)

Fury #6

Legend #7

Maddison Kings University Series

TMYM: Prequel

TRYS #1

TDYW #2

TBYS #3

TVYC #4

TDYD #5

TDYR #6

Knight's Ridge Empire Series

Wicked Summer Knight: Prequel (Stella & Seb)

Wicked Knight #1 (Stella & Seb)

Wicked Princess #2 (Stella & Seb)

Wicked Empire #3 (Stella & Seb)

Deviant Knight #4 (Emmie & Theo)

Deviant Princess #5 (Emmie & Theo

Deviant Reign #6 (Emmie & Theo)

Ruined Series

Ruined Plans #1

Ruined by Lies #2

Ruined Promises #3

Never Forget Series

Never Forget Him #1

Never Forget Us #2

Everywhere & Nowhere #3

Chasing Series

Chasing Logan

The Cocktail Girls

His Manhattan

Her Kensington

75174224R00227

Your Invisible Inheritance

Nikki Mackay

REBEL
MAGIC

REBEL
MAGIC

Nikki Mackay has written an absorbing and helpful book on the use of Family Constellations in resolving personal and relationship issues. She helps the reader to uncover unknown influences from the past to resolve current issues. These may be linked to traumas unresolved by ancestral family members, including those we have never met. As a psychotherapist, I am familiar with exploring past family relationships to discover answers to present problems, but the use of Family Constellations as Nikki has developed this process, adds a deep level of knowing what has been unknown that may go back generations in your family. Nikki gives clear case examples and useful instructions for the reader to experiment with questions of their own.

Judi Ledward Hobbes, Psychotherapist.
BA (Hons) Psychology and Philosophy,
PG Dip Integrative Psychotherapy,
Member UKCP and BACP (before retirement)

Wouldn't it be wonderful if your life was simply about you, in the here and now, just this one life, to master your strengths and weaknesses? If only it was as simple as that! In this beautifully written book, Nicola Mackay describes with a rare and deep insight, how the inheritance from your descendants can weave layers of entanglements in your cellular memory and structure that unconsciously undermine you. Amazingly, using her inspired therapeutic techniques, you can heal all of the past and move on.

Your Invisible Inheritance provides the guidance for finding the missing pieces of your heart and soul as you acknowledge, honour, and express gratitude to those who have gone before you. Embrace them, as you thank them for their sacrifices, triumphs, and failures—they are your invisible inheritance. As you do all of this, your continued ascension is assured.

Patricia Iris Kerins DHP
Visionary Healer and Author
www.patriciairiskerins.com

Your Invisible Inheritance, Nicola Mackay's most recent contribution to the field of trauma, is a wise, enthralling, and far-reaching book that offers readers an in-depth approach to healing the legacy of suffering. After working for decades with individuals and communities, the author brings her unique and compassionate perspective to constellation work and ushers it into the 21st century. Mackay's book powerfully addresses the invisible roots of our fears—historical and ancestral—and the personal and communal damage they provoke. All humans desire safety and a sense of belonging. Around the globe we are witnessing how fear of *Other* dominates political landscapes. *Your Invisible Inheritance* provides a rich and useful model for healing our private and public wounds, one that promises to have an amazing impact on our lives.

Dale M. Kushner, M.F.A.
Author of *The Conditions of Love*
Blogger for *Psychology Today*

Your Invisible Inheritance is a wonderful journey of self-discovery. This book will take you through a rich exploration in the field of family constellations, explaining gently and carefully each concept along the way and making you long for more. At every step you will discover new dimensions of your family history and how your system of origin can influence and impact your current life and wellbeing. Take a dive, plunge into it, do the exercises, stop, breathe, and reflect. Allow the healing sentences to touch your soul. By the end of the book you will have discovered a treasure of new things about yourself and your past: your true, unique and unrepeatable invisible inheritance that shapes you and your journey into life. This book is your guide to honour your roots and your past. Enjoy the journey!

Cristina Muntean
Systemic facilitator in organizations
Founder of *Media Education CEE* Prague

You know that feeling when you haven't read anything really life-changing for ages? *Your Invisible Inheritance* is the answer to your transformational reading hunger. This is a gold mine of opportunity—for change, for happiness, for removing the weight of generations of pain. Here you will find the reasons and explanations for so many of your family and relationship conflicts, and then you'll be given a path to heal them. This is where your next metamorphosis begins. Shed that protective chrysalis—your time has come.

Sue Fitzmaurice
BA (Hons) Pol Sci, MBA
Author of *Purpose: The Elements of Purpose,*
Purpose 2: Making Sure Your Purpose Finds You,
and *The Smart Seeker's Guide to Spiritual Bullshit*

In honour of the untold stories of the forgotten dead and the forgotten living.

To the silent, unseen, missing, and excluded souls—you are remembered.

Note to the reader:

All names and some details within the shared examples have been changed to protect client confidentiality.

Also by Nikki Mackay

Non-fiction

*Between the Lines: Healing the Individual & Ancestral Soul
with Family Constellation*

The Science of Family: Working with Ancestral Patterns

Tarot for Understanding Love & Relationship Patterns Made Easy

Fiction

Dead Men Talking: The Beginning of the Black Light

Contents

You are surrounded by fields of influences, made up of not only your family and ancestors, but also the relationships and connections you have created throughout your life.

Questions for curious souls

Who are you?

What are your dreams? What are your hopes? What are your fears?

Have you ever wondered why you choose the things you choose? Why you are drawn to the people that you love?

In the moments of stillness when you are alone with your breath, your heartbeat, and the land underneath your feet, who are you?

Do you know the stories of who you are and where you come from?

Who you are in this moment is the result of a complex field of layers of energetic influence from people you have known and loved, choices you have made, and the family and ancestors that you come from. Their memories—the imprint of them—flow through your veins. Their fight to survive beats within your heart.

Your ancestors aren't some dim and distant spot in the depths of your family stories. Their absence is present with you right now. You are here because they were here.

'I want to ask you who you are. I want to know your story. I want to know your joy. I want to know your sorrow. I want to know what it took to be you, to stand where you are standing. And if it feels safe to look back at where you have come from. The journey from there to here. Please tell me. I want to know.'

This is the conversation I invite you to have with your ancestors.

Understanding, connecting, and engaging with the stories of those who have lived before us and shaped our world is a meaningful and empowering process in fully claiming our place in our own life.

Our ancestors and their choices flow through us. Their stories are woven into our souls in such a way that we can be unconsciously drawn to follow their footsteps, seeking to fulfil their hopes and dreams and holding them tightly as if they were our own.

Family and ancestral constellation allows us to explore and uncover these stories and our own inheritances.

It is these influences that impact your belonging and sense of self. It is the heaviness within your heart when your day is hard. It is the niggling feeling that something isn't quite right. It is the fear that grips you when things change unexpectedly and outside of your control. It is the unconscious belief that you are not enough.

This is your invisible inheritance.

What if the story you are living doesn't actually belong to you?

Introduction

Who we are in the present is knowingly and unknowingly influenced by the energetic field of influence that we belong to and that we come from. Our history lies coiled within us. The untold stories of our ancestors are present in our blood.

Family and ancestral constellation is a therapeutic tool that allows the invisible influences from the present and past to be made visible, acknowledged, and made whole. It allows us as individuals to uncover the hidden historical narrative that we are unconsciously holding. It creates a space for us to bear witness and give place to the trauma before fully and freely moving forward with our own life. It is the key to unlocking the missing puzzle pieces of who we are.

Everyone within the family and ancestral field of influence has a place and an equal right to belong. Everyone. Regardless of who they are, what they have done, or when they did it.

But who actually belongs within our own field and what are the entry requirements? This is more complicated than you may think. Take a moment to consider your own life. Think firstly of the obvious family connections: your parents, your grandparents, and siblings. Then allow your thoughts to drift back to your childhood friends and perhaps your first loves. Then keep going; think about your former partners, past and present friends, colleagues, and even close neighbours. Think about all the people you have had connections with through accidents or circumstances outside your control, car accidents or surgeries where perhaps you have been a victim of or responsible for someone else's trauma. All of those people have a place within your field of influence to a greater or lesser degree. Every one of them. And that's a lot of people.

From this perspective of beginning to see the vastness of your own energetic field of connections, take the next step and think about all of those same connections but from your parents' perspective, and your grandparents. And then your great grandparents. Including any wars or conflicts they were involved in.

Can you feel the breadth and depth of the field of influence flowing down to and through your personal place? All of those different points of connection and disconnection? Can you feel the potential of the chaos contained inside?

This is the starting point of understanding belonging. This is the field of influence that has invisibly shaped your choices and sense of place. This is part of who you are and where you come from, and when you are displaced or disconnected in some way within this field, this is the root of the disruption to the forward flow of your life.

Beyond the family we grew up with and the ancestors we heard stories about, we can be entangled and connected with many unseen influences.

This includes hidden loves of our ancestors, children who have been given away, traumatic deaths connected to war or violence, loyalties to other family lines and countries of origin the family has migrated from, as well as different and potentially oppositional religious belief systems that run throughout the untold historical narrative of your family field.

Invisible inheritance is not a small thing.

Creating a constellation is a process that aims to shed light on this. By working with your own historical narrative—the untold or silenced stories that you are unconsciously holding—you have the opportunity to disentangle your historical emotional trauma. This disentangling then flows from you to your family, to the community around you, to your belonging in the land in which you live, and finally to the collective that you are a part of. This is uniquely personal to you whilst simultaneously being much bigger than you, as it ripples out in waves through your field of influence.

Throughout this book we will create a map of these entanglements and find our way back to your place. One entanglement at a time. One constellation at a time. Your future self will thank you. Your descendants will thank you.

To see or not to see?

I love this work. It is the stories within our individual and collective historical narratives which fascinate me; being able to reanimate the little details of an experience as we bear witness to the story within our life or the lives of those we knowingly or unknowingly connect to—all of the joys and strengths as well as the pain and the sorrow. There is a liberation in the moment of witnessing, to step freely into our own place unencumbered by the past but still being able to see and acknowledge what has happened and our individual place within it.

And this is key: being able to see, witness and acknowledge the choices that were made in the past that have contributed to the present. This can be a hard thing to do for an individual, it is even harder within our collective experiences.

The emotions and trauma from the past are reanimated and re-experienced in the present as if we have been transported back to that moment in time. Not seeing, denying, detaching, perpetrating, and re-perpetrating, can seem to be an easier choice than to witness. However, not seeing also has its cost and that cost ripples down from the collective to the individual and vice versa. It is the heavy weight that hangs over you in the dead of night when sleep escapes you. Seeing, bearing witness, and acknowledging, require both courage and compassion. Can you truly look at who you are and where you come from? This book is an invitation to do that.

By looking at your own individual choices and the untold story narrative within your family field that you are in resonance with, you have the potential to not only liberate yourself from the trauma of the past but to contribute to a different way forward for each of us collectively. What do you choose? Where does your curiosity take you?

This book will allow you to uncover the invisible inheritance that is stopping you from finding your own place and moving forward with your life. It will help you find the missing puzzle pieces—those empty, aching spaces in the silent moments. It will change things; it will change who you think you are.

My unfolding field

I accidentally discovered family constellation as a therapeutic tool when I attended a class on the use of sound and voice in ritual. I found the experience of standing within a group constellation deeply moving and personally transformative. I was working as a clinical physicist within the NHS. I specialised in physiological measurement within neurophysiology and was working on my master's thesis into the possible effects of energy healing on the autonomic nervous system. I was fascinated that we as individuals could create a map of emotional entanglements within a 'field of influence' that could not only reveal the hidden influences of the past within our present, but that could also be disentangled in such a viscerally tangible way. I was immediately hooked. It was one of those moments that changes the course of your life and you didn't know it was missing from your life until it dropped right into place in your soul. Within weeks of that experience my life had turned upside down. My relationship ended, I moved home, and my work changed. Everything changed. But importantly, I felt free. That is the power of constellation. I have been learning about and working with constellation ever since.

In the two decades I've been managing a large therapy practice, I have repeatedly observed the impact of trauma from previous generations on individuals in the present. My clients come from all corners of the world, from different backgrounds, different ages, genders, and ethnicities. They are as diverse a group of people as I could imagine, but they all have one thing in common. The untold stories of their historical narrative weave through them all, from forgotten loves and broken promises to the inheritance of war and conflict trauma. Their stories are different, but the inherited presence is common. From these hundreds of stories and experiences, I've developed new approaches and theories that I'm delighted to share with you here.

1.

The beginning—who do you think you are?

The past is connected to the future through our place in the present moment, and forms our being. Where aspects of the past are unseen or unacknowledged, then the trauma from that past connects to our future via our place in the present and we become entangled in it.

Moving through a created constellation and your field of influence is, in essence, walking through ancestral and family souls, and should be done gently. The constellations reveal themselves slowly and should not be rushed. Presumptions and assumptions are completely ineffective. There are orders and structures within the constellation itself, but the way in which they are connected and interwoven is unique to each individual within each family field. As the constellation unfolds, patterns begin to appear, revealing the unseen, the unacknowledged, and the hidden loyalties.

One of the fundamental building blocks when exploring belonging, in terms of our family dynamic, is looking at the interaction between us as an individual and our family of origin. Our family of origin includes our parents, as well as our siblings, born and unborn, known and unknown. I will be using phrases such as *known and unknown*, and *seen and unseen* a lot in this book when discussing constellation.

> **Historical narrative:** This is the history of your family and ancestors. It is made up of the stories that you know that may not always be totally accurate, and the untold stories, the hidden pain, and silent trauma.

> **Unknown:** An event or person that has been kept secret from the rest of the family such as a child born outside of marriage and given away, of from an affair, abuse, or a rape that was never reported. So many things can stay hidden and silenced within a family.

Unseen: With this there is a more conscious choice at the root of the trauma to *not see.* This isn't necessarily from a malicious perspective. The death of a son or lover in war time, or perhaps the early death of a child, can be so painful that the only way to survive the pain in the moment is to *not see* the person that has died. This is not a healing choice. The *unseen* can also have more of a perpetrating edge particularly within relationship dynamics.

Influent Field: This is the dominant field of influence from the invisible entanglements that are impacting you in your life right now. It is made up of fields of influence from your family and ancestors, as well as connections you have made yourself through former and current partners and friendships.

The 'unknown' and 'unseen' are people or events within the untold stories in the historical narrative of your family and ancestral lineage that have been silenced, ignored, or excluded from their place within the family field. Prepare to change what is true about your sense of self and place. We are going to explore beyond the version of self and place that you have perhaps passively accepted, and look at what is actually there rather than what we accepted, hoped, or believed was there.

Beginning and belonging within the family of origin

Your mother and father are the gatekeepers to your ancestors and the field of influence that flows from them to you. The dynamic that exists between you and your parents is complex. So much information can be gleaned by setting up a simple created constellation with you and either or both of your parents. Your ability to see and be seen by your mother and father is key. If there is an interruption to this, it can be devastating and debilitating. There are many permutations of effect within this seemingly simple and basic dynamic. Perhaps an individual cannot see one or other of their parents and is pulled to 'look' at someone else within the family instead, or is excluding themselves from their place and belonging. Perhaps one or both of the parents is unable to see and acknowledge their child, holding a belief that it isn't safe for them to be a parent. The impact of even one of these entanglements can ripple into relationship patterns, work experiences, issues of being seen or heard, the ability to materially provide and sustain oneself, as well as impacting physical health and even fertility.

Once you have a sense of the root of the entanglements that you are drawn into, then the work to explore the details and themes within the entanglement begins. There are endless variations and combinations flowing through the family field, and through my private practice I have observed some recurring themes. The impact of relationships, broken promises, and lost loves, are ever present, as is the presence of war and conflict related trauma. The historical narrative of the untold stories of love and trauma is entangled through each of our family fields. Within every single relationship there is a conscious and unconscious relationship promise.

Even when a relationship ends, the relationship promise can remain entangled and have an influence on our present and future moments.

The relationship promise can survive long after the relationship itself dies; all of those exes are potentially still floating around your field of influence. And all of your ancestors' exes. Quite a thought isn't it?

Pause for a moment to think about that: every relationship promise and every story of love, betrayal, loss, or violence, will impact on future relationships of all kinds unless they are fully healed and released.

Unless the historical narrative of the trauma and relationship promises is acknowledged, and the stories told and released, then you will not be free to take your own place and belong, nor will you be free to love and be loved.

What is all this inherited stuff and where is it coming from?

In essence, constellation allows for the creation of an energetic map of all the connections and loyalties, known and unknown, within the field of influence upon us, where we can interact with and explore the entangled connections. Family constellation work, established by the late Bert Hellinger, is based on the principle of the interconnectedness of all things so that each person within a family, going back generation upon generation, has an equal place of belonging within that family. When someone in the family is excluded, or there is an event or entanglement that is not seen or acknowledged by the rest, then this has an effect on the family as a whole. Patterns, events, and trauma from the past are carried down and are repeated through generations, leaving an emotional, physical, and spiritual imprint on us, as we are compelled to follow the fates of those who have gone before us.

The entanglements and patterns that we observe and experience during a constellation all arise from displacement, exclusion, or self-exclusion. They are the missing and unseen memories within the field of the historical narrative that runs through each of us from our ancestors.

Feeling alone and lost is still a connection to the field of your belonging— it is just an entangled one.

In your isolation you are connecting with the presence of an absence, an inherited missing piece. True belonging exists outside of that. You exist outside of that.

This book is an exploration of my own observations, theories and practices that have grown from the original Hellinger system approach. For me, the field of influence and who belongs within that field of influence is much bigger than the traditional concept of family. In my experience, the field around us not only consists of the direct connections we have made in our own life, it is also made up of all of the souls who have been touched by the lives and choices of our ancestors. This connection flows through our blood and we have each inherited the cost of our ancestors' choices and actions: their acts of love and acts of hate, the promises kept and held tightly, as well as the promises that were broken. Constellation not only gives us a map of where we are in the midst of all the inherited entanglements, it also shows us the way forward. It gives us a way to actively disentangle the past from our present, and the keys to unlock our dreams and our hearts.

The Hellinger approach is often referred to as having its origins in established therapeutic modalities such as Gestalt therapy, family therapy, and Hellinger's background as a psychotherapist in Germany [1]. That is only part of the origin. Hellinger also spent sixteen years working as a missionary priest with the Zulus in South Africa in the 1950s and spent considerable time observing their ancestral healing and spiritual practice. There is an African concept called *Ubuntu*, referring to a universal life and healing force, which is found in all things. [2] It is based on the concept that an individual cannot be viewed as separate from the family and community they are part of. It is a way of thinking about what it means to be human, and how we as humans should behave towards one another. It is the ability to see the other with compassion—as human—thus making you human as well. [3] Archbishop Desmond Tutu describes ubuntu as meaning that 'my humanity is caught up, is inextricably bound up, in what is yours.' [4] This ethos is a fundamental part of the structure of family and ancestral constellation theory and lifts it out of a purely therapeutic context, connecting us with what is sacred.

What does it actually mean to belong? What does *belonging* mean to you? Is it acceptance of who you are? Is it being loved, and your love being accepted and cherished? Is it being seen and heard, both within your family and outside it?

Belonging is a very personal and intimate experience, and yet we do not exist in isolation. Our ancestors and their choices flow through our blood. Their stories are imprinted on our souls in such a way that we unconsciously follow in their footsteps, seeking to fulfil their hopes and dreams, and holding them tightly as if they were our own hopes and dreams.

Do you have autonomy over your life, dreams, desires, and choices? Or is it something you have to work hard for?

Have you ever felt stuck in some areas of your life? That something wasn't quite right? That the life you are living isn't fully yours?

Have you ever felt 'numbed out' in your relationships, as if part of you needs to escape or switch off in order to get through the day?

Has it felt as though it is only possible for one area of your life to go right at any one time? And that if things are going too well then there will be a price to pay for that?

What if all of those thoughts—those responses, those experiences—don't belong to you?

We accept that some stuff is passed down from our ancestors. Some health conditions are hereditary, along with eye colour and hair colour. We know that we can be genetically predisposed to certain things. We accept that materially we can legally inherit land, belongings, and bequests after the death of family and loved ones. What we are exploring and uncovering with family and ancestral constellation is the transgenerational inheritance of trauma and memories of trauma.[1] We are uncovering the invisible inheritance from the field of influence of our ancestors and those souls that they have entangled with. This is the invisible inheritance of the unacknowledged trauma, the untold stories, the broken promises, and the promises still being held, those that left one country for another and those that were left behind. These influences, more than anything, have silently shaped not only your perception of who you are but also the perception that others have about you. It has influenced where you see your boundaries, what your responsibilities are, and where your future dreams reside.

Can you see and feel who you truly are? What if you never really had your proper place? What if you are lost in the field of someone else's belonging? What if you are free-falling through someone else's life? Are the dreams you are aiming for actually yours? Who are you?

Belonging

Belonging is a basic human emotional and physical need.

There is a constant struggle within us to belong. When we have a sense of belonging, we are at peace. There is a need to belong in all aspects of our lives: within our families, our relationships, our work, our friendships, and the ancestral land we come from (particularly when that is different from the one we live on). When we don't feel that sense of belonging, we begin to feel excluded and on the outside. A separateness can be felt in our relationships and experiences. If our sense of belonging to our family is not strong and secure, then belonging will be sought in other ways. For example, through carrying the unacknowledged pain in a partner's family in an effort to earn a place there, often regardless of the cost emotionally, physically, mentally, or materially. A common example of this is when your partner's mother has lost children through miscarriage, abortion, or early death, you can be unconsciously representing the missing son or daughter for the mother and carrying the weight of her grief. This will

---

[1]Recent research [23] [24] has shown evidence of epigenetic transgenerational transmission of trauma, looking, for example, at the inheritance of holocaust trauma, and Native American genocide and trauma within current descendants of the American Civil War.

have an impact on you and on the level of intimacy between you and your partner.

So great is the pain of exclusion and not belonging that we entangle ourselves within our own deeper familial fates or the fates of others in order to feel we have earned our place.

I belong

The start and end point of constellation is belonging. It is the ability to say inwardly and outwardly "I belong" and for that statement to feel true. Understanding belonging is the cornerstone of understanding the placement, order, and structure of family constellation and constellation field theory. It is the cornerstone of understanding ourselves.

Ask yourself:

Do I belong? When do I feel whole?

What feels like home? When do I feel at peace?

Where is my safety? When do I feel free?

Is it internal or external to my place?

Do I have a place?

Is it just for me?

What is belonging?

In the most basic sense, it is the acknowledgement and acceptance of your place, both within your family of origin and the land you live on. However, there are many dynamics that we are unknowingly entangled with that can influence and disrupt these aspects of belonging.

One of the trickiest elements of the constellation process to get your head around is the tangible and often visceral experience of the unfolding of the influent field within a created constellation. This is where, by stepping into the map of relationships within the created constellation or by creating a constellation map of the relationships in our mind's eye, we experience and can articulate the emotional intricacies of an entanglement that is not our own and that comes from outside of us.

We step into the created constellation field and experience the energetic influences from a perspective outside of ourselves. This effect of the constellation results in the invisible influences—the invisible inheritance—being made visible.

There have been various attempts to explain and explore this phenomenological effect, the most popular being an explanation based on Rupert Sheldrake's [5] concept of morphogenic fields and morphic resonance. Sheldrake suggests that in morphic fields we find the presence of the past. We each, individually, have our own morphic field that is a part of the bigger morphic field of our family and ancestors, and in turn our family and ancestral morphic field is a part of the morphic field of the country that we live in. The country morphic field is in turn a part of the bigger collective field for each soul collectively. Within these fields is the inherited 'knowing' of our ancestors, both individually within our family, and collectively. Sheldrake uses morphogenic fields and resonance to explain the instinctive response to a 'knowing' field of influence that underpins each of our inherent responses. It is the same theory from within the animal kingdom and the natural world that explains how butterflies know when to migrate or how young birds know where their ancestral winter home is without being guided there.

Have you ever walked into a room and had an instant knowing about another individual? A recognition of their character and behaviours before they've even opened their mouth? Think of meetings at work or stepping into a crammed train carriage on the underground—have you ever had the instinct of who to avoid, of who feels dangerous, and who feels safe? Or the immediate and deep connection with someone after a few minutes of chatting—a recognition at a soul level that this person is one of 'yours'? That is the morphic fields at play. It is the unconscious recognition and reading of the resonance there. It is the knowing of who we are and where we come from.

Hellinger also refers to the active field of influence within constellation as the knowing or informing field. He argues in his concept of an extended mind that most of our being is based in fields of connectedness between us and other people outside of us, and not within us in isolation. [6] He states: 'Fields evolve in nature and are influenced by what has happened earlier. They develop habits in and of themselves and are transmitted from past members of the species through a nonlocal phenomenon called morphic resonance.' Through morphic resonance, the patterns of activity in self-organising systems are influenced by similar patterns in the past, giving each species and each kind of self-organising system a collective memory in the present. [7]

But what if the 'knowing field' that we are influenced by isn't actually ours? When we are rooted in an ancestral field of influence *that isn't ours* (perhaps an ex-partner's), or if we are rooted in a field of influence of one of our ancestors (maybe a great-great-grandmother), the reality of that ancestor's life becomes present within our own. We can unconsciously be living our lives according to their reality, their dreams, their fears, and their beliefs, and not our own. We can be reacting and responding not only to people in a train carriage or meeting room with a 'knowing' of who is safe and who spells trouble, but also reacting within the relationships we forge, and the dreams we cherish and follow. We may think they are our reactions and responses when they are anything but.

The constellation gives us a place and a way in which to explore the hidden patterns and loyalties from the past that are impacting on us in a present situation, that may be rooted unconsciously or unknowingly in the past. It gives us a tool to pop ourselves out of someone else's morphic field and back into our own.

How does constellation do that?

The objective of uncovering the unseen and unacknowledged trauma is to acknowledge it and give place to it, to shift the influent field—the morphic field—out of one of entanglement and discord and into our own individual field of belonging.

The acknowledgement of the unseen is not carried out from a place of judgement or belief, right or wrong, or in an attempt to impose our personal beliefs on the field as a whole. The goal is to acknowledge and disentangle existing entanglements not to create new ones.

The historical narrative can create an almost habitual re-enactment of traumatic memories that arise from these past entanglements.

Removing the emotional entanglements releases us from the burden of the traumatic entanglement, allowing our own individual experiences to shift.

In the setting up of a constellation, we enter a version of 'trauma time,' where time or events that we connect with are both non-linear and non-local. This means that within the created constellation, past and present are not separate and we experience them as we are influenced by them. For example, you may wish to explore your relationship with a current partner and find yourself in the field of influence of your great-great-grandmother who is carrying the broken promise of a lost love from a different country. The constellation provides a mapped-out representation of the emotional relationships that encompass the historical as well as the current narrative. It's a map of the jumbled, mixed-up loyalties around us.

Think again about morphic fields and influence fields. The fields are made up of internal parts relating to you, and external parts relating to the people in your ancestral field of influence. The lineage of belonging for you as an individual can be understood by quantum resonance theory. The simplest and perhaps most commonly known example of this is the forced resonance tuning fork experiment where a vibrating tuning fork forces a stationary tuning fork into resonant vibration when placed beside it. [8] The field of energy of one tuning fork influences another by its very presence.

This analogy helps us understand how entangled memories can be activated within us by the external influencing field of our ancestors when the external inherited trauma is in resonance with the internal entangled memory. As an example, if we experience a horrible break up and we are knocked out of place by it, we can unconsciously find ourselves connecting with our great-grandfather's pain at the tragic death of his fiancé, thus becoming embroiled with his field of influence. The result can be that we begin to live our life through his pain and lost dreams. We are then walking through our life feeling both the internal stuff (our own trauma at the end of our relationship) and external field (our great-grandfather's trauma) at the same time.

Within constellation theory, ancestral animators are the deeply held roots of an original entanglement that can pass, sometimes silently, from generation to generation. It is common for an ancestral animator to lie dormant within the relevant field and only become active through specific external triggers. Think of the ancestral animators like the vibrating tuning fork. An example of an ancestral animator may be an individual who has an unconscious belief associated with the cost of love. Perhaps a great-grandmother lost her husband in a war after he promised he would come back safe and she waited for him to keep that promise. The trigger might come for the individual in the present when their partner travelled for work, manifesting as a deep sense of fear and a lack of safety in love. It would surface from deep within their soul, adding a heaviness, or a burden, to the relationship.

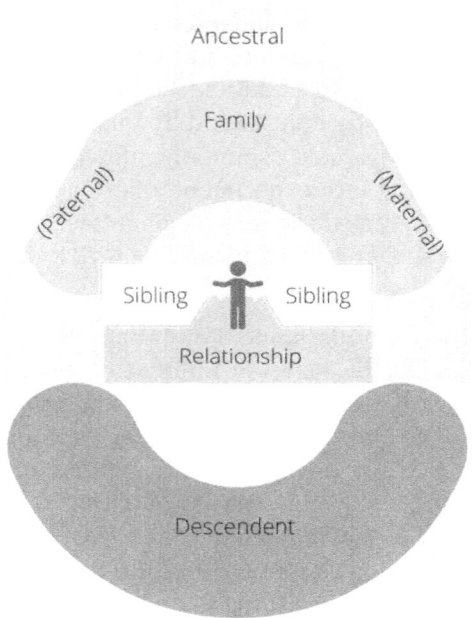

Image 1—Fields of influence

Main types of field of influence within the created constellation field

Family field—This is the connection with our mother and father and the close immediate generations around us, both in our childhood and in our present.

Relationship field—This is made up of intimate relationship partners. This field will include our previous partners, as well as the family influences of our previous partners. Your ex as well as your former mother-in-law and father-in-law all still have a place with you long after the relationship is over. Also taking a place here are any previous partners of your current partner, and in some cases the family influences of their previous partner. And reciprocally of course, you have a place in theirs.

Sibling field—This field is informed by our born and unborn siblings. However, it is significantly more than that. The sibling field is the filter through which we interact with our external world relationships. It can also be our springboard into belonging within another individual's family field, cutting off ties to our own if there is a lack of safety in belonging within our immediate family realm.

The sibling field itself is the animator for intimate, personal, and working relationships.

Individuals who form another family outside their family of origin, will unknowingly recreate the dynamics of their family of origin within the close friendship or 'in-law' bonds they create. For example, in the sibling field (the field of external relationship connections), you may be unknowingly representing your best friend's mother for them and your best friend may unconsciously be representing your grandfather. And this is the tricky part. If you are representing the absence of someone then you are not fully you, and they, as they represent an absence for you, will not be fully them. The friendship becomes entangled and weighted with the absence of the past.

Ancestral field—This can be current, close, or distant ancestral influences, and it is not limited to our own direct family. Included within this field are victims and perpetrators of murder, abuse, slavery, displacement and migration, and war. It includes financial influences and belief influences. This is a long list and we will work through all of it.

Descendent field—This is the forward-facing part of the field of influence and includes children, born and unborn, as well as the place for dreams, creativity, and work. It is what flows from you to the future, the active continuation of your line.

Influent field—This is the field that is directly influencing you in the present moment which may or may not be comprised of the previously mentioned fields. For example, in the case of an entangled individual, the influent field may be the ancestral field of a former partner rather than your own ancestral field.

Created constellation field—This is the field that coalesces during constellations and is the combination of the above fields for each person relating to the specific intention of the question being asked in the constellation.

What is happening within the created constellation field itself?

The depth and breadth of constellation theory can be challenging to grasp. How can the past have such an impact on the present? And why does constellation, as a therapeutic modality, work so effectively to map the points of influential trauma within a group or family system? There's no doubt the past has a bearing on the present, but we can't cherry-pick which parts of the past we are going to acknowledge and give place to. It all has a place. If we try to ignore or exclude something we become further entangled.

There are five elements we need to be aware of to be able to work with our invisible inheritance:

Entanglements—Constellations are not just concerned with the relationships between individuals within a single family or family field, but also the larger relationship dynamics between multiple blended families or family fields of different individuals or family groups. The concept of entanglement shifts the emphasis away from the idea that we as individuals are separate and existing in isolation towards a theory of the individual as part of a web of connections that spans across time and space. This concept includes the idea that emotions do not belong to us as an individual but can come from outside of us and be non-local to us and entangled with other people outside of us, in both the present and the past, knowingly and unknowingly. It is also the notion that our very being is defined by the connectedness between us.

Non-locality—Quantum entanglement is based on the idea that there can be non-local connections across time and space. This non-local connection includes our own family and ancestral field but is not limited to our biological family and ancestors. The groups and field influences of individuals that we, our partners, or ancestors have formed connection with, are also influential upon us even if we do not have any known and direct relationship to them. Non-local essentially means that we can be unconsciously connected to and entangled with the historical narrative and emotional trauma of someone outside of us.

Non-linear time—Within constellations we are exploring the influence of traumatic entanglements from past generations which contribute to the reproduction of trauma and emotional conflict in the present moment. The past trauma is experienced within the present as if it were happening within this moment in time. External factors such as the land you live on, the choices you make, as well as the individuals within your social circle, can contribute to the creation of entanglements that react non-locally and with a non-linear time context within your informing field of influence.

The combination of non-local and non-linear can be thought of as time travel in action. One moment you believe you are you, sitting having a coffee on a Saturday morning in London, but in reality, your choices are being shaped by your great-great-grandmother's first love from 1913 in a troubled and pre-war Vienna.

Bearing Witness—The act of bearing witness and giving place to the unacknowledged trauma within the historical narrative is both simple and complex. On an individual basis, it requires courage, compassion, and a willingness to see what was, as well as what is. The function of bearing witness is to honour the hidden or unseen parts within the created constellation space thus shifting the field of influence from the past to the present. This is achieved through the creation of the constellation as well as through the language of the constellation narration (as directed by the constellator), which are the phrases I will be guiding you to say throughout the book.

Directed Narrative—This is the power of language to disentangle within a created constellation. During the course of a constellation, whether in a group or an individual session, a language narrative will be introduced by the constellator within the created constellation space. The directed narrative has a very specific focus and is in alignment with the overall intentional question. What the language narrative does is move and release you from the influence of the informing field. In terms of quantum physics theory, the language narrative within the created constellation space provokes the response of a wave function collapse[2] within the influent field acting upon an individual, allowing them to step into their own place unencumbered by the weight of the entanglement from the previously influent field. Say for example you are unconsciously entangled with your great grandmother whose son was killed in WWI in France. We would work with the phrases *I can feel the weight of your grief. I didn't know I was holding this but I can feel it now. I have been trying to be him for you. But I can't be him. I am not him.* This gently moves you out of the field of influence from your great grandmother who is overwhelmed by her grief. Then we would work with phrases to her son: *You still have a place. I have been holding you within my place but you belong outside of me. You still have your own place. You haven't been forgotten. I remember you. I am not the only one who remembers.* These words and phrases shift the field of influence around you.

Through them you are able to consciously recognise the invisible influences that have been lifting you out of your place and into someone else's morphic field. They are powerful. As you say them, you will feel the movement back into your place.

The creation of a constellation needs to begin with the asking of a specific question. This question sets the *intention* that establishes the influent field upon the created constellation and the lens through which the constellation is experienced. Then there is the initial placement of the represented loyalties and emotional entanglements relevant to the question, which create an energetic map. This initial map can either be set up in your mind's eye or physically created using mats, or with people in a group-represented constellation. In this book we will work with creating constellations in your mind's eye, but if you choose to you can also set them up physically. The map you create within the constellation reflects your inner perception of the situation that you wish to explore.

---

[2] This concept of human beings behaving as 'walking wave function' and the use of language within wave function collapse is discussed by Alexander Wendt in his book 'Quantum Mind and Social Science' [10].

When an aspect of your historical narrative within your influent field is unseen, meaning that a significant emotional entanglement or event is hidden or non-visible within the field of influence, successive generations will unconsciously follow the fate of the unseen.

Events that took place during previous generations can have far-reaching implications for our individual present-day choices. War and violence, the loss of children, loss of partners, betrayal and divorce—even if the events happened centuries ago—can and will leave a subconscious imprint. The trauma of loss, anger, bitterness, and grief, when unacknowledged, can resurface at any point in the field of influence, often triggered at key points of change. The most destructive patterns are those rooted in anger, loss, and bitterness. Unseen influences can polarise a field into those who are willing to see the victims, often becoming aligned to them in a sacrificial way, and those who are unwilling to see them and react with perpetration and persecution in order to deny their existence. The trigger for the unseen is, most commonly, a loss or denial of place for us in the present. This can be an experience of not being seen or overlooked within the workplace, the end of our relationship, or even something seemingly joyful like a move of home. The trigger in the present around 'loss of place' can be something that appears quite simple, but the root of the trauma that influences the response can be heavy and destructive.

Within constellations, the most destructive entanglements commonly are the result of an event where an individual or group is responsible for taking the life of others. When those responsible will not look to the victims, the effects can ripple through the historical lineage, affecting many generations to come. War and violence and deaths resulting from them can also be devastating for many generations, for both victims and perpetrators, particularly if the perpetration is unacknowledged. We, the subsequent generations, are often drawn to an entangled association with the victims and will display behaviours or patterns that indicate that we are sacrificing ourselves in some way, giving up our place so that a victim or victims can be seen again. We carry the grief and guilt that was previously experienced. We can also be unseen by those around us, and thus feel that we don't have a place, which suggests that we are tied to unseen and displaced victims. Those of us who are tied to perpetrators, often experience great anger and can become entangled with destructive and violent relationships.

Giving place to a previously unseen aspect within a constellation not only shifts the field of influence but it also removes the burden from the family system. This symbolic acknowledgement is transformational: you are no longer carrying the burden of the entanglement and it now exists outside of you.

The entanglement, and the unseen aspects within it, are bigger than you, but you still have to take responsibility for your own choices that are *in resonance with it*. The influences from our ancestors flow down to us from generation to generation. The influences from our siblings and relationships flow around us. However, the connection with our own place, our own choices, our work, our dreams, and our children, flows forward from us. It is forward facing. It is the continuation of the family line and field. It represents more than the physical birth of children. It is also the starting point of belonging for our hopes and dreams. In the context of a constellation, the space for our dreams and our children, born and unborn, is very similar. It is what we offer to the world, what we create, and what we strive for. In that offering there is a need to accept that we are letting go a part of ourselves. What was once part of us, what comes from us, whether that is a dream or a child, now has its own place in front of us and is free to be seen and heard independently from us. We as individuals become entangled when our parents and ancestors are unable to do that.

Our own ability to fully accept and take our own place within our family field has an influence on the ability of our children, as well as our hopes and dreams, to have a place of their own, a place that is accepted freely by both them and us. This is the point at which we need to take responsibility for our own choices and actions, where we need to fully see, know, and accept where we come from, and our place in relation to (but also separate from) our origins. This is the tipping point where the flow from past to present switches to the flow from us to the future. The generations following on from us can be encompassed by children or other aspects of our creative self. Only when we accept who we are and where we come from and take our own place, can that which flows from us be free to be fully seen, heard, and acknowledged too.

Where are you standing now? Can you face your own future? Who are you in this moment and who do you choose to be moving forward?

When we are born into our family, we are entirely dependent on them for our safety and well-being as well as our belonging. There is an automatic acceptance of the truth of the family of origin that we are born into. In the vulnerability of infancy there is no safety outside of the perceived safety that comes through the acceptance of the family truth and the reality of the day to day existence within that family field. As we grow into our childhood and adulthood, the development of our own sense of truth occurs. Our own truth may not be in resonance with the family truth. In many cases this disparity will have a profound impact on our sense of safety and belonging. There can be an unconscious belief that as an individual we will lose our safety and belonging if we reject the family truth in favour of what is true within our own hearts and beliefs. In order to survive, it can appear easier to sacrifice aspects of our own truth and in turn aspects of ourselves in order to stay in alignment with the family truth. The consequences of this self-sacrifice can be severe, and if left unresolved and unhealed, will impact future generations.

And so...

In the moments of stillness and silence, when you are alone with your breath and the beat of your heart... who are you? And who is it that you yearn to be?

I invite you to walk with me, one constellation at a time, through your field of influence of the untold stories of your ancestors.

It is safe to stop and feel and heal and live. It is safe to thrive.

What do you choose?

How to use this book

The creation of a constellation begins with the asking of a specific question. This question sets the intention that establishes the influent field upon the created constellation and it is the lens through which you will experience the constellation.

When a constellation is created it reveals a map of all of the entanglements and interconnections that are knowingly or unknowingly affecting us in the present moment. It allows us to begin to see and feel all of the silent and invisible influences around us. It shows us what is standing between where we are and where we would like to be.

This map can either be set up in your mind's eye or physically created using mats or people in a group-represented constellation. In this book we will work with creating constellations in your mind's eye, but if you choose to you can also set them up physically with sheets of paper laid out on the floor. The map reflects your inner perception of the situation that you wish to explore.

When you are expanding a constellation in your mind's eye, you are creating an image or an energetic sense of something to represent whatever or whoever you are bringing in. For example, it could be a red heart to represent a space for love, or a broken heart to represent a broken promise, or a closed cardboard box to represent secrets. Go with whatever image, person, object, colour, or even absence of space that comes in for you. I have had clients use everything from a tree to sunlight, a spatula, or simply a sense of an energetic space, for visual representatives. Note what it is for you, without judgement, and gently carry on.

If it is difficult to see or physically experience the connection to your representative space, or perhaps the image is blurry or not fully formed, then that is an indication that that person or aspect is caught up in an entanglement or family dynamic that pulls them away from not only you but the family system as a whole. Again, note this response and gently carry on with the constellation.

After you have established the entanglements within the created constellation, I will gently guide you through the process of *disentangling,* through introducing the missing and unseen parts of your field, bearing witness to those parts, and then working with the powerful healing phrases.

Your responses to individuals that you are connecting with can be surprising. You are feeling what is going on from a different perspective, often for the first time. We are going to walk through the entanglements within your ancestral field together, one constellation at a time.

How present are you in your body?

Before you attempt any of the exercises in the book for yourself, please ensure that you take time to be grounded and as fully present within your body as possible. Our sense of groundedness and being present with ourselves is directly linked to our belonging. If we are displaced for whatever reason, it's harder to be present within ourselves. Observe without judgement how grounded and present you are before beginning, and then again at the end of any constellation work. This is particularly important with work undertaken in the mind's eye. It is essential to being able to discern the effect of the created constellation itself. Learning how it feels when the energy in your body is just yours, and how it feels when you are fully in your own place, is incredibly helpful and transformative. When you are not grounded and in your place, you are more vulnerable to the morphic field of your ancestors and their entanglements. Being grounded and present within your body and place is your strongest point for being seen, being heard, claiming your dreams, and moving forward with your relationships and your life.

This is what we are aiming to do together as we work our way through the different fields of influence in this book. The intention with any constellation work is to uncover any entanglements or dynamics that are impinging upon our ability to fully and freely take our place. So, entanglement by entanglement, we will slowly work through the field of influence of your invisible inheritance until you are truly home in your place as a free soul.

If there is no sense of place to begin with, then the exploratory exercises can be somewhat futile. Being grounded and present is tricky so don't beat yourself up if you find yourself drifting. Instead, notice the drifting and any internal resistance to the exploration of the field. That is helpful too. Knowing when it feels safe to be present and when it feels safer to drift up and out will deepen your understanding of what happens when you feel displaced in your everyday life and if that displacement is an internal movement or if there is indeed an external trigger.

What does being grounded feel like?

Close your eyes.

Take some deep breaths into your body and allow the energy and any tension in your body to settle.

Let your body begin to relax into the support of the chair or the floor where you are sitting.

Allow your focus to move up to the crown of your head and then slowly move your attention downwards from the top of your head to the tips of your toes.

Take another deep breath.

Take note of how comfortable or uncomfortable the sensations in your body feel.

Take note of any areas of your body that are drawing your attention.

How comfortable does your breath feel. Is it shallow or deep?

Focus on how present and in your body you feel, how grounded in the moment you are.

How grounded do you feel in your body?

How grounded do you feel in the present moment?

Pay attention to how this feels, as you will need to compare these sensations with those you feel during constellation sessions.

> You must meet yourself at whatever place you are in and be with yourself there.

It is important to manage your expectations of the experiences of this work. Some individuals find the process subtle and gentle and will strive to get it right. Others become lost in the field of emotions and can have strong physical or emotional responses to created constellations. You must meet yourself at whatever place you are in and be with yourself there, in how you are experiencing each moment rather than how you would like it to be or feel.

I recommend you keep a diary or a notebook beside you as we work through your own field of influence together via the exercises in this book. I will guide you gently through them as I would with a client. Take it at your own pace and give the process the respect it deserves. When you step into a created constellation field you are stepping into the memories, loves, joys, and traumas of your ancestors and their relationships. These are movements of the soul and there is a sacredness to this work.

2.

Discovering how to belong

We are all hard wired for belonging. It is essential to explore your individual sense of belonging and what that means for you. We can do this by firstly looking at the interactions between you and your family of origin. Many entangled patterns are created unconsciously with our family of origin. There can be a temptation to jump further ahead into more complicated and busy constellations with many different family members, partners, or animators, but this can be a distraction if the initial connection from you to either your mother or father is not comfortably established in some form. It doesn't have to be a soft, fuzzy, warm connection—that may not be possible, and if not don't worry, that isn't our aim here.

The paternal line and field

Your paternal line is the direct biological connection that flows from you to your birth father, to his father and to his father, and so on through the previous generations of the lineage. The paternal field includes the collective field influences from this direct line, individuals connected with that line, step-fathers, and any other significant non-biological father figures.

The connection with a parent is complex and will shift and change over time as the family field of influence also shifts and changes. We are going to begin by exploring your own individual connection to your birth father. Our starting point in beginning to understand your belonging is to look at your connection with him and the field of influence that flows from him to you. This is the paternal line and field—it influences the very foundations of your physical belonging and whether or not you can actually accept your place.

Having an understanding of the qualities of this connection—from you as an individual to your father, and in turn your shared lineage—can be an early indicator of other possible entanglement issues influencing your present situation.

> If a connection to your parents is not established, the fundamental entanglements will never shift.

If the basic connection from you to your father or mother has not been established at all, then it doesn't matter how many constellations we explore, the fundamental entanglements that are blocking and hindering you—impacting your love life or your relationship with your own children—will never shift. There will merely be an exchange of one set of entanglements for another. This results in feelings of being trapped, not being seen or heard, and generally not feeling enough. It is not a good place to be.

The role of the father and the male line

When we begin to explore our family dynamics through the lens of constellation, the role of the mother can appear to have a greater influence on the entanglements upon us. It can be easy to become entrenched in constellations involving the mother and the maternal line. This is in part because of the direct physical connection and bond between a mother and child during pregnancy, birth, and the early years of a child's life. The connection with our mother is influential over our emotional life—our ability to receive and give love is deeply influenced by her. The mother does carry more weight in terms of the family entanglements relating to emotional connection and emotional belonging, but the father and the paternal line are influential on our physical belonging, our sense of place in the world. Any entanglements within the relationship with our father can be devastating because they fragment our physical belonging and sense of self.

An interruption to the connection with our father, and to the paternal line and field, is an interruption to belonging both within our family of origin as well as to our outer world connections. Whenever belonging is interrupted, it changes how we are seen and heard by others in our everyday life and how we feel when we interact with others. The interruption can be anything from the end of your parents' relationship in your early childhood, resulting in a loss of connection with your father, to his inability to see you because of the weight of his own trauma. It can influence how safe we feel in a relationship or friendship. It's a big deal, but it is often overlooked because of the vibrancy of the emotional entanglements that come in through our maternal lineage.

The structure of a constellation—the point to aim for

When we begin to delve into the world of constellation and entanglements, we are not doing so blindly. There is a particular order and structure that flows down from our ancestors to us. This structure becomes disordered and entangled when points of trauma and events are unseen or unacknowledged in the generations before us, and the field of influence we are living through and being seen through, is not our own.

There is an optimal flow that we look to achieve within the constellation setting that is informed by the orders and structures of the field of influence upon us.

The main principles within any constellation are:

Belonging—This is where you as an individual source your belonging within your family field of influence, commonly from your birth parents but not always and nor does it have to be.

Balance—The family field itself tries to always be in a point of balance—this is why the roots of entanglements are created. If there is unacknowledged trauma within the field, it will impact the field as a whole and the generations that follow will knowingly or unknowingly pick up the entanglements in an effort to balance the field. There is an unconscious familiarity with the weight of an entanglement that can be associated with safety.

Structure—This is the order and flow within the family, the hierarchy of belonging that runs from the ancestors to the descendants.

The flow of belonging and order can be thought of as:

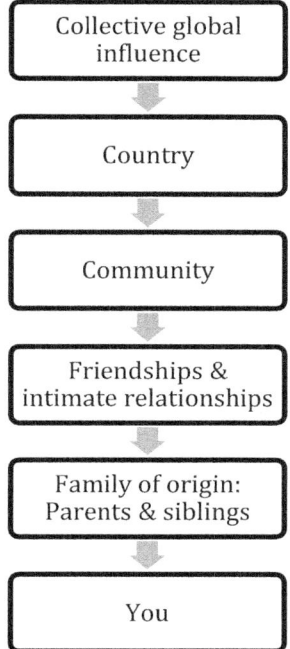

Image 2—The flow of belonging

The belonging for us as individuals flows to us from the structure of our family, our relationships, the community around us, and the collective global influences. The belonging is based upon the balance within each part and is most often seen through a lens of shared beliefs.

Think about the beliefs we often unquestioningly accept within the family we grew up with, and then, if perhaps those beliefs aren't in resonance with the beliefs that we and our partners or close friends share as we grow up, how these differences can create tensions or even conflict.

Everything from beliefs around relationship etiquette, parenting, political beliefs, to who is defined as belonging and who is defined as 'other,' are filters that are often put in place before we are born and that we may take years, decades, or a lifetime, to recognise as not being universal truths, but beliefs and perceptions that we choose or that have been chosen for us.

Our inherited beliefs can be cultural, religious, spiritual, political, personal, and even unconscious in nature. When our beliefs—the passport to our belonging and the structural order within the field—are not accepted and balanced internally within ourselves, then the field of influence will become disrupted. For example, if you have been brought up Catholic and then choose to become Buddhist. Or if your family does not believe in divorce and you choose, reluctantly or otherwise, to become divorced.

When our own beliefs are in opposition to our family or community, we can become displaced as we unconsciously try to balance that within ourselves.

In addition to our inherited and personal beliefs there is another very important factor that we need to be aware of.

If there has been migration or displacement—eg. moving to another country—within our family field of influence, then the belonging and the order within the structure of our family system is also disrupted. Can you think of points in your present or past family history, or your partner's family history, where there has been migration? This very common theme of displacement is one of the main reasons why it is important to consider our connection with our paternal line and field when beginning to work with our ancestral constellation, as any potential fracture through movement can severely impact on the individual sense of belonging of future generations.

These disruptions create the entangled memories that are passed trans-generationally and are invisibly inherited by us as individuals. It also affects how we see others and how we may perceive others as potentially dangerous for our belonging. Considering this cause-and-effect pattern on a global scale for a moment, the current geo-political situation may be more understandable.

Sacred holding and sacred sacrifice

When a constellation is created it reveals a map of all the entanglements and interconnections that are knowingly or unknowingly affecting us in the present moment. It allows us to begin to see and feel all the silent and invisible influences around us. It shows us what is standing between where we are and where we would like to be. When the map of entanglements and patterns is revealed, it can at first glance seem like a chaotic mess, however there is always an optimal flow within the family field that we can bring into balance through the constellation process. This is the structure of belonging.

Optimal flow is where the children look to and see the mother and the father. The mother whilst seeing her children, sees and follows the father, leading the children with her. The father creates a place for the family within his belonging and ancestors, thus supporting his partner and children.

This sounds a little archaic. I certainly thought that at first. However, it is important to remember here that we are looking at the flow between *parents* and *children* that has come down to us from our ancestors. Belonging within relationships outside of parenthood is different. The energetic contribution of a place of belonging in the paternal field by the father to the mother, is to *balance* the sacrifice and cost of becoming a mother and to create a place of safety for each soul.

There is a sacred transformation in becoming parents, for both mothers and fathers. The transformation from woman to mother is interwoven with sacrifice and pain. There is undoubtedly joy and love too, but at the core there is a deep vulnerability as your body becomes not just your own—part of your heart and soul now belongs with your child. In order to connect with the deeply sacred nature of the transformation into motherhood, not least within the birth process, but also within those early stages of a baby's life when they too are vulnerable and are utterly reliant on you, there needs to be safety. Deep, secure, and strong safety. This comes from the father. This sacred holding and offering of safety, and of a place to be held within the vulnerability, is the father's sacrifice and transformation from man to father. He holds her and he holds them, so she can lose and then find herself again within motherhood.

This is the balance. It isn't about her following him into a patriarchal system of belonging and losing her autonomy.

The structure of family is more complex now than it was for our ancestors. There may be step-parents, same gender parents, donor eggs, donor sperm, or surrogate mothers. But *how* people are made remains the same. There will always be the birth mother and the birth father. And how the birth father holds the birth mother so that she has a place to lose herself and come back to, influences the flow and structure of the field of belonging for the child. We may need to add in additional partners to the structure of the parents' relationship but *how the parents support and honour one another's place is key* and will determine whether or not the child's place is entangled. If the father is excluded or the mother doesn't feel safe, then that *will be* inherited by the children.

Within this concept of the optimal flow there is also a need to preserve the fact that the mother and father's relationship is separate to the relationship with the children and takes precedence over the relationship with the children. It exists outside of the relationship with the children and is an entirely different entity.

It doesn't matter how complex the relationship dynamics are outside of the birth mother and birth father's connection, or how many individuals are involved within their relationships, or the gender identity within those relationships, it all still exists outside of the relationship with the children.

In terms of the hierarchy and belonging within the family system, the relationship between the parents comes before the relationship with the children.

This means that the love that exists between the parents has a place and is also sacred. The love for the children comes after that.

Laid out in these terms, this makes sense, but for many people this seemingly simple piece is very often out of alignment, with the children being pulled into the relationship promise between the parents. And when it is out of alignment in one generation, it has the potential to disrupt the belonging of all of the generations that come after. Entanglements between family members form and will flow down the line creating a pattern or repeating an inherited pattern.

The father and the father's line are particularly important. They are influential on our physical and material belonging, on our sense of safety, on our ability to have and accept a place of belonging upon the land, and to be seen and heard within that context. This is no small thing. The culture and heritage of our ancestral land, encompassing religious, political and cultural beliefs, are ingrained in the unconsciously inherited memories of each of us as individuals. Each of us unknowingly carries the beliefs of those who have gone before us in our fields of influence. Oftentimes those beliefs can be in stark contrast to our personal beliefs, causing us to hit potholes on our forward paths as we actively attempt to be true to ourselves. The attempt can be anything from choosing a love outside the belief system of our ancestors, getting divorced, choosing to work in a field dominated by the opposite gender, or maybe choosing to follow a spiritual rather than religious belief.

Think about times in your own life when you have chosen yourself, or attempted to choose yourself, and follow your dreams. How smooth was your path forward? Do any bumps or potholes in the road come to mind? Can you choose to follow your own dreams without invoking old patterns of sacrifice and debt?

When I first started working with constellation, my experience was largely formed by Bert Hellinger, and his approach and my training with him. Constellation, as a therapeutic modality, was at its beginnings in Britain at that point, although it was firmly established in mainland Europe. My early experiences of constellation were dominated by the most commonly occurring patterns within groups and individual sessions, namely those affecting love and relationships, and the individual-mother relationship.

An individual's relationship with their mother is significant and deservedly holds an important place within the constellation field as well as constellation theory. However, I began to notice the absence of men and fathers from the focus of the constellations I was participating in or facilitating.

Where are all the men?

The men were part of the constellations but they were very much defined by their place within the dominant relationship patterns presented, such as an absent husband, or through an individual wishing to explore a relationship with an absent father. The only male-focused constellations that commonly occurred were those connected with the impact of war and conflict trauma. Aside from that, where were all the men? It wasn't an easy question to answer but it was one that I was determined to understand.

The basic principle of constellation is that each soul within the field of influence has a place of equality and *belonging, regardless of gender, choices made, actions undertaken, or beliefs held.*

As discussed, the theory of optimal flow within constellation is that the father's place is equal to the place of the mother and balances the sacrifice of motherhood with an offering of place, belonging, and safety. So why were the men absent within general family constellations?

This same absence of men and of the place of the father's lineage appeared throughout my learning, even when observing constellations facilitated by men. This seemed strange to me and out of kilter.

My understanding of the influence of the paternal line and field has deepened considerably over the last two decades and I've noticed a pervasive feature of this line and field is the presence of silence. And this silence is often accompanied by guilt and overwhelmingly traumatic entanglements to previous generations. The types of traumas range from the suffering of war, violence, or displacement and migration, as well as the perceived weight of broken promises within the field, whether those promises were emotional, intimate, or financial. These hidden entanglements appear time and again in the silence of this part of the constellation field. I believe the absence of the men within the constellation process is because it is very hard to look at and sit with such pain. The weight of the broken promises, particularly those relating to love and intimacy, open the door to a flood of messy, emotionally-rooted entanglements that draw the focus away from the deeper roots of fractured and displaced belonging. But there is a great cost to consciously or unconsciously choosing not to see the fractures within the field of the paternal and it affects us all individually and collectively.

The experience for us in the present time is of a significant number of silent, missing, and absent men in our lives. And this symptom of the deep-rooted entanglements within the paternal line and field also serves to exacerbate the entanglements experienced within the maternal line and field, which has a weighty influence on our emotional lives.

What this essentially means is that we have a silently fractured relationship with our father and that line, and we can find ourselves drawn into emotional relationships that are similarly fractured.

We can feel ourselves displaced or excluded within our relationships and friendships, and not being or feeling seen by our partner. That horrible feeling of not being enough, not being seen, and not being heard or valued, has its roots here within these entanglements. And this is a hard place to be, spinning our wheels in the quicksand of unhealthy relationships and trying to fix the emotional root when the real root issue is in an entirely different place.

But what has caused the silence and the displacement in the first instance? What is the collective entanglement that is so clearly filtering down to the individual family field experiences?

The lands in your blood

In my work, I have observed an influence on all parts of the constellation field from the psychohistory of different lands, and the greatest impact is on the father's and the paternal line and field.

Memories are held within the land and they can hold particular sway over the paternal line and the connection with the men in our life. These memories are held within our blood, passed silently from one generation to the next, and they become stirred at points of transitions, choices, and change, that are in resonance with our ancestors and their fields of influence. For example, if we choose to relocate, move in with a partner, buy a property, or change job, it can trigger the inherited belief that there has to be a sacrificing cost involved or that it isn't safe.

The aspects which consistently appear within constellations involving land and belonging of any kind are around displacement, the excluded, perpetration, the forbidden, and silence. These are highly emotive and heavy hitting aspects that are found scattered at various points in each of our family's histories. The silence that characterises the experience of the paternal within general constellation exploration appears as a collectively-rooted entanglement within the psychohistory of the land—an un-screamed scream.

Migration of some kind within a family historical narrative, whether through choice or otherwise, is not uncommon. If there is an unresolved trauma around the choice to move, the entanglement will be rooted to that time and with those ancestors, and their historical narrative will flow down the line to the present generation. It also flows from the collective belonging of a particular land or country to the people that knowingly or unknowingly belong to that land or country. This belonging can be in the present or the past.

Several generations may pass with the family, or a particular branch of the family, being established in the new land, however the first loyalty, known or unknown, will always be to the land of origin and to those left behind. (Similar orders of loyalty exist when constellating an individual who has been adopted. Their first loyalty will always be to the birth family, in particular the birth mother. They wait consciously or unconsciously to be seen.) And so it is with land, too. The land of origin within the ancestral line has greater influence upon the individual in question, particularly if there is an entanglement around the land, be it displacement, slavery, perpetration, betrayal, exclusion, or particular beliefs associated with the land of origin. It isn't necessarily the land itself; it is the unseen souls held within the land.

In exploring these influences within the constellation field there is a pattern that repeatedly appears. It is a triangle of:

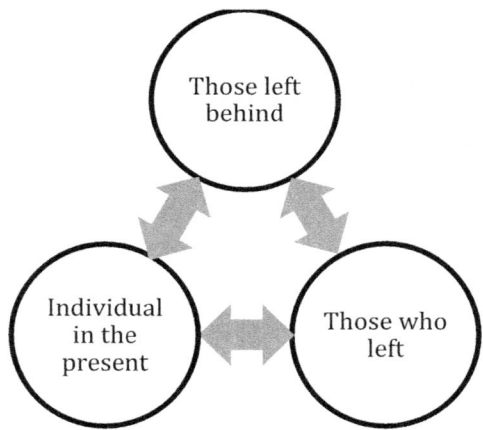

Image 3—Migration triangulation

In each and every constellation I have seen, the most animated and influential space was 'those left behind'. A historical narrative of migration within the individual and family context cannot be ignored in either the individual or the collective dynamics.

It is this triangulation that is the root cause of entanglements around a lack of compassionate response, or a sacrificing response on a personal level in intimate and family relationships, or to the current geo-political changes.

The past lives inside us. Think about who you are and where you come from. Do you know where your grandparents are from? Your great-grandparents? And the generations before them? Has there been movement within your family from one place to another? Were your ancestors ever forced to move? Did they lose their land or their livelihood? Can you imagine how difficult the move or moves were? It is impossible to uproot an entire family lineage and drop them into a new land without someone or something being left behind. Even if that is simply regret. And most commonly what is left behind is more than regret: it is the elder generations who cannot make the move; it is the early blossoming love that is left behind; it is the separation of parents and children. And it is these things that create the fractures within the field of belonging. It is the cost of this wound that rips the fabric of the family field and is carried forward.

Beginning to connect with your father

Take a deep breath.

Close your eyes and think of your father. In your mind's eye see him standing before you and take the time to really look and see him.

Feel your connection to him; feel it in your heart.

How does your connection to your father feel for you?

Is it comfortable?

Can you see or feel the connection to him?

Do you know who he is?

Do you stay in your body?

The paternal line is experienced quite differently to the maternal line, and as we've discussed, it is also often overlooked. Have a think about what it might feel like to change from boy to man to father. What sacrifices may be involved? What does the boy have to leave behind to become a man? What price does one have to pay to become a father?

The vast majority of participants on my group constellation sessions are women. The issues they are drawn to are many and far reaching, but an underlying element of the focus of the work for many of them is the dynamic between the masculine and the feminine within intimate relationships. I have observed a great reluctance within some women to actually look to and see the paternal line and field, and the great surprise at what they experience when they do choose to connect. This reluctance to look to the men is extended to the dynamic between men and women in current personal relationships. There is often a desire to focus on 'fixing' that relationship piece and not wanting to consider where the deeper root entanglements are really coming from.

This can appear as an undermining of the place of the men, as well as the role of the paternal field and line both within the constellation context and our everyday interactions. It can be an attempt to push the paternal line and field influence away—to make it disappear—so that we can perhaps feel safer within ourselves. What actually happens though, is that in choosing not to see or feel this part of our lineage we effectively reanimate the inherent patterns of perpetration within the informing field, thus exacerbating and attracting the very things we are trying to escape. We can't make something better by ignoring it. When this is an active entanglement, the perpetration shows up in all areas of our lives, not just in our personal relationships but we tend to feel it there most. It impacts drastically on belonging as well as our individual ability to trust love.

Doesn't that sound like something worth spending a little time working to change?

The role of the father is equally important to the role of the mother. When either is excluded, it impacts on the children and the subsequent generations. Your parents are the gateway to your ancestors and the dominant fields of influence upon you. When a member of the family field is excluded, other members of the family—that generation or future ones—will unconsciously attempt to redress the balance, creating our invisible inheritance.

When a mother cannot look to the father of her children with acknowledgement of his place, disordering the optimal flow, then the children will unknowingly carry the weight of that within themselves and they will be faced with an unconscious choice: they can either join their mother in bitterness and anger towards their father thus creating a pattern where they cannot accept their own place within the field, or they will reject the connection with their mother in order to be accepted by their father. There are many reasons why a mother cannot or will not acknowledge the place of her children's father: it may feel unsafe to do so, he may have betrayed her, he may way have walked away from her and the children, or she may have walked away from him and cannot look at her own choices.

We will work through all of those possibilities and other very common situations as we walk through your family field of influence and belonging, but I want to reiterate here: what we are looking for is the acknowledgement of the father by the mother, and of the mother by the father, to be between them. The responsibility for that is theirs. It is not about either parent being the fairy tale love of the other. It is about the acknowledgment of the indisputable, genetic, and biological truth for you as an individual that one is your father and one is your mother, and that you are not responsible for the dynamics of their relationship. What happened or is happening within their relationship belongs to them and is between them. Your place is outside that. You have plenty of your own choices that you are responsible for, and we will work through those too, however your parents' choices and relationship experiences belong solely with them.

Even the simple act of reading these sentences and understanding the essence of them will begin to move the field within you. That is a good thing.

When the acknowledgment of place from one parent to the other does not happen, the children and subsequent generations get displaced and embroiled in their parents and ancestors' pain. It is that simple and that complex.

Core connection with your father in your mind's eye

In creating this constellation, we are seeking to observe and feel into your own initial response to the acknowledgment of your place and your father's place. It sounds simple but just because a constellation is simple doesn't mean it isn't powerful.

Noticing that you can be consciously present with yourself before going into a connection exercise, but become ungrounded and distracted when attempting to connect with your father, is an obvious indication that you are unconsciously grounding yourself outside of your paternal line and field. This is significant information and a helpful puzzle piece to have because it will have undoubted consequences and entanglements associated with displacement and belonging, not necessarily in all areas of your life but certainly some. This important piece of the puzzle could easily be overlooked if time isn't taken to simply observe your own natural energetic state.

From our discussion of the how, what, and why of constellation we know that we need to have an intentional question before we step into the created field together.

The intentional question for this constellation is:

Is it possible to stay grounded and connected within my own place whilst connecting with my father?

The answer to this is revealing. If it is not possible, then it is an indication that there is an entanglement between you and your father, or within the paternal line itself.

Take some slow deep breaths into your body and notice how comfortable your breath is. When you feel ready, bring your father into your mind's eye, or imagine him standing in the room with you, and try to feel the connection to him in that way. Breathe into the connection and gently notice how the energy or any tension in your body is feeling again before checking in with the following:

> *Can you see him; are you feeling the connection to him?*

> *Where does he move in relation to you? In front of you? Behind you? Beside you?*

> *What happens in your body when you connect with him?*

> *Do you stay grounded?*

> *At what age are you seeing him?*

> *Do you stay the same age and in the present moment or are you shifting to an earlier point in your life?*

Try saying the following phrases out loud or internally in your mind's eye:

You are my father and I am your son/daughter/child.

I accept you as my father and I accept I am your son/daughter/child.

Parts of me are like you.

I accept the parts of me that are like you, but my choices are different.

My place is different.

How easy were the phrases to say?

Did they feel true for you in the moment that you said them?

Ideally, we are looking for you to remain comfortably present within your body and within the present moment, to be able to connect with your father, acknowledge his place, and simultaneously maintain your own sense of belonging and autonomy. Don't panic if this seems like a tall order. At this stage we are merely observing your responses and gathering information.

This is a useful tool you have just discovered that can act as a barometer for your belonging at any given point and can help you get back into your place and strengthen your belonging if you find yourself struggling. Take a moment to scribble down your thoughts and how it felt in this first constellation interaction. If it wasn't comfortable then we will seek to uncover the entanglement(s) impinging upon the connection as we work our way through the rest of the book, one step at a time, one entanglement at a time. We want to work towards it feeling comfortable and strengthening to say:

You are my father and I am your son/daughter/child.

You have a place and I have a place.

We are separate.

We each belong.

If this feels comfortable, then we are in a good place. If it feels uncomfortable, don't worry. We are going to look further at the connection between you and both of your parents, checking in to see if your place is indeed outside of the relationship between your parents, regardless of whether that relationship is still an active one or not.

Where does your unconscious loyalty lie?

With this next constellation exercise, we are seeking to strengthen our natural place of belonging as it comes to us from each of our parents, as well as the connection to the paternal field and the maternal field. This is another very powerful piece of work within a simple constellation.

The intentional question for this constellation is:

Is it possible to stay grounded and connected within my own place whilst connecting with both my mother and father?

You would think the answer to that intentional question would be yes, but it is not always as easy as it sounds. Your connection to each of them, and the lineage that flows through them, is not static. It shifts and changes as you move through your life; and your loyalty, if entangled, can also shift as you seek to move forward into your own choices.

Take some slow deep breaths into your body and repeat the grounding process, noticing in particular how comfortable and relaxed your breathing is. When you feel ready, bring your father and mother into your mind's eye.

Are you seeing or feeling the connection to them?

Are they standing side by side?

Can you see them both clearly or is one clearer than the other?

Where are you most drawn?

What happens in your body when you connect with them? Do you stay in the present moment or are you experiencing the constellation from an earlier point in your life?

Do you stay grounded?

Try saying the following phrases out loud or quietly in your mind's eye:

To your mother: *This is my father. I accept he is my father.*

To your father: *This is my mother. I accept she is my mother.*

My life comes from you both. I accept my life from you both.

How easy were the phrases to say?

Did they feel true in this moment?

In this constellation we are looking for an indication of the dominant loyalty potentially impacting you. If one of your parents is clearer than the other, then that would suggest the connection there is more comfortable and established. We would instead focus our next steps on the parent who is less clear, absent or displaced within the created constellation space as this indicates a heavier entangled loyalty. In the created constellation the easiest and clearest connection can, surprisingly, be with a parent that we don't necessarily have a positive emotional connection with in our lived moments. We are looking at the entanglements through the constellation—this isn't a reflection of the quality of the emotional relationship itself. If you find yourself propelled back to a point in your childhood, take the time to notice that without judging yourself. Gently close down the connection to the constellation and focus on your breath again. Take some time to write your experience down.

Making sure responsibility for your parents' relationship stays with them

With this created constellation we are exploring who is responsible for the relationship promise between your parents. Of course, the responsibility is between your parents and we would hope to observe this within your created constellation, but the reality is often different. Most of us would, on a conscious level, be horrified to be included in our parent's relationship, particularly as it means they are reciprocally embedded within our own intimate relationships. More on that later.

It can be tricky to let go of holding the weight of their relationship promise. This is because part of us may have unconsciously believed that continuing to hold responsibility for that promise is tied into not only our own safety and belonging but also to one or both of our parents' safety and belonging. That is a lot to carry energetically and it takes up a significant amount of space within ourselves, and that space is taken from the place where we hold our own relationship promises. Thinking of it that way might help to let the weight of the promise go.

In this next constellation we are observing the order within your family and seeking to bring the optimal flow in to place if it is absent. The intentional question for this constellation is:

Is my place outside my parents' relationship promise, and who is holding responsibility for that relationship promise?

When you are expanding the constellation in your mind's eye, create an image or idea of something to represent whatever space you are bringing in. For example, it could be a heart to represent a space for love, or a ring to represent a promise, or a white light to represent the unseen. Go with whatever image, person, object, colour, or even absence of space, that comes in for you.

Take some slow deep breaths into your body and notice how comfortable your breath is, working to ground within your body as much as you can. When you feel ready, bring your father and mother into your mind's eye or imagine them in the room with you and feel into the connection. When you have established a connection with them, bring in a space or representation of their relationship promise.

Where does the marriage/relationship promise go?

Is it a sense of them or do you have a visual image?

How do you feel when the promise comes in? Is it inside or outside of you?

Are your parents looking at the promise?

Do their positions change?

Do you stay grounded?

Of the three spaces where are you most drawn?

Are you in the present or have you gone back to an earlier time?

Try saying the following phrases out loud or quietly in your mind.

To your parents about the promise:

This is between you both.

I cannot carry this for you.

My place exists outside of this.

I am not the safety in your marriage/relationship.

This part is important. Take your time with it. Really breathe deep into your body and feel what happens when you work your way through the phrases. You are not the safety in your parents' relationship. It isn't possible for you to be that and also be free to live your own life. The internal resistance to this seemingly simple movement can catch us off guard, so if you find yourself feeling a little stuck or displaced just breathe into the discomfort, note your resistance, and gently move onto the next step.

To your father: *I cannot be my mother/her for you.*

To your mother: *I cannot be my father/him for you.*

With these phrases, within the created constellation field, we are opening up our energetic awareness to what is potentially influencing your parents' relationship promise from *outside* their relationship promise. The *her* and the *him* are purposely open to enable the movement to flow to your parents' former partners or indeed to their parents. Take some time to linger here in the relief of not having to be *her* or *him*.

If your parents are no longer together, if they are divorced, or if perhaps your mother didn't have a relationship with your father beyond the pregnancy that created you, then there is a little more work to do at this point. Regardless of the length of time of the relationship between your parents, there is a place for their relationship promise, even if that is just relating to the intimacy between them, consensual or otherwise. When that relationship promise is broken, or death has taken it, then the *broken promise* can very easily be inherited.

If your parents are no longer together then bring a space in for the broken promise and feel into the response within your body and your energy. Notice where it goes in relation to you and what happens to your grounding and connection to your parents.

Try saying the following phrases, preferably out loud—a bit of strength and determination in your voice will be helpful here.

The marriage/relationship promise between you is broken.

I leave the weight of that with you.

My place exists outside of your broken promise.

You are still my father. You are still my mother. I am still your son/daughter/ child.

No one has lost their place.

I exist outside of your marriage.

I exist outside of your betrayal.

I don't accept a place in your marriage.

I don't accept a place in your betrayal.

I am free.

Betrayal is a strong word. It is also a strong pattern with an often hidden root. If you have found yourself involved in betrayal within relationships, be they intimate or work related, then please try working through the above phrases a few times. Even if the dynamics of your parents' relationship are unknown to you or you cannot imagine either of them choosing betrayal.

Are you the same person today that you were a decade ago? Have you ever chosen something or done something in your past that would seem extraordinary to those who know you today? Our parents exist outside of being our parents. They live their lives outside of the lens through which we see them, and an inherited pattern of entangled betrayal can flow silently from one generation to the next. Moving the responsibility for the relationship promise is the first step in liberating yourself. It will also allow for a positive shift within them.

This simple series of short constellations reveals the placement of us as an individual in terms of our family of origin and whether or not the optimal flow and hierarchy within the field of influence has been observed. It allows us to discern the potential dominant entanglements unknowingly influencing our place and reveals our next steps in our journey through the family and ancestral fields.

If the optimal flow and placement of the relationship promise of your parents is entangled, then you are too.

These simple connection constellations can also be used to great effect to strengthen belonging and place once the order is restored. The field of influence is not made of hardened concrete, it is fluid. And as such, entanglements that have been previously dormant can reanimate quite easily. Knowing the simple steps to take to support your belonging can bring great comfort and strength in times of crisis. These are great tools for self-care, empowering you when faced with challenges in your everyday life.

Inherited displacement—promises and broken promises

Now we continue our exploration of the theory of the paternal line and field. What exactly are we doing in these constellations and why is it so important?

What exactly does it mean if the promise is not held by one or both of your parents and how does it impact you?

When you as a child are placed within the relationship promise of your parents, it creates a triangulation between three people—you, your mother and your father.

The theory around triangulations and inherited promises might at first seem complicated. What it essentially means is that instead of a relationship promise being held and honoured between two people, a third person gets pulled in, creating a triangle.

One example of when this can happen is when someone has an affair, which itself is a destructive entanglement. However, a triangulation with the relationship promise of the parents is more destructive because the *child* gets pulled out of their place as a child and into the broken promise between their parents.[3] This is an inherited promise and can trap the child within the parameters of the parents' relationship.

You will discover several different types of triangulation as we journey through the constellation field together, involving invisibly inherited promises.

I cannot emphasise enough how significant this particular triangulation relating to your parents' relationship promise is for your sense of self and belonging.

This inherited parental relationship promise is quite literally the gift that keeps on giving, because once it is established as an entanglement it flows forward down the line from generation to generation. It spreads like a

---

[3] I call this particular type of inherited relationship promise the *Paternal Line Triangulation* within the constellation theory that I have developed and teach.

virus, displacing generation after generation, and impacting not only belonging but also the freedom to love.

We are going to explore your paternal line connection to look for this particular inherited entanglement. It is easier, in the first instance, to begin one generation back, and look at where your father's belonging and place is in relation to his parents and their promise.

In this regard we are considering your father as a child looking at where his parents' relationship promise is held. In this way we can explore the dominant entanglements that are likely to come from him, how they affected your mother, and in turn their direct impact on you. We are looking beyond you to the potential entanglements within the field of your belonging that flows from your father to you.

What was the relationship like between your mother and father before you were born?

Was it just between the two of them?

What were you born into?

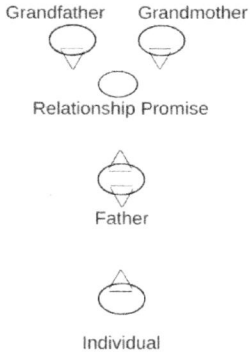

Image 4—Father and inherited relationship promises.

If there is discord between your father's parents—your grandparents—then your father can be pulled into holding *their* relationship promise with either *his* mother or father. There are different side effects within each scenario and we are firstly going to look for what happens when he gets pulled into holding the parental relationship promise with his mother—your grandmother.

The holding of this promise has an impact on your father's own availability within his own relationship promises. He will also energetically stay with his mother and her line and move away from his father and his father's line.

This might not seem like such a big issue outside of the obvious relationship limiting aspects, but it really is a big issue. It means that your father can't belong with his own paternal line, which influences belonging, and if he can't belong then you can't belong either. He will feel a pull to find belonging elsewhere, creating further entanglements. These entanglements will have a massive impact on you.

The easiest way for him to find belonging externally is through intimate relationships and to attract a partner who carries a similar pattern within their line. It can very quickly become painful, and this also has a massive impact on you.

If this is the case for you, it is essential to look at the women and men connected to your paternal line and to work with honouring and releasing the inherited promises—broken or otherwise—to honour the individuals and the land that haven't yet been seen, acknowledged, or honoured. This is what we are doing here.

The unseen individuals that are invisibly impacting you may not directly be involved with your father's line but may instead be represented within the unseen, and in particular unseen women.

The unseen women are those who were left behind holding the broken relationship promises, the women who have loved, lost, and haven't let go of the dreams that have died.

This triangulation with unseen and unacknowledged women will be particularly prevalent within your relationship field and we will look deeper into this in Chapter Five.

The inheritance of a parental relationship promise is undoubtedly the most common and toxic entanglement within the field of influence but it is not the only unhelpful dynamic to be found there.

The reversal of the father child relationship

In this dynamic, instead of the natural flow from parent to child, we observe a reversal of that, with the flow instead moving from child to father and so on. If this is the case for you then part of you will energetically stay with your father, limiting the choices you can make in your own life as you unconsciously strive to create and provide safety for your parent. You are in effect being a parent to your father as your father waits in his childhood.

An example of this would be where perhaps your grandparents' relationship ended when your father was a young boy, and his father walked out, cutting off contact with the whole family. Part of your father would be waiting in his childhood for his own father to come back to relieve him of the weight of the broken promise that he was carrying in his place. You would experience this, unconsciously, as your father not seeing you, and can unconsciously be drawn in to either replace your father's missing parent for him, or to carry the weight of the broken promise for him in his stead.

There can be a particularly poignant and difficult dynamic that comes in at the later stages of the parent's life when there is a natural shift in the roles of the family of origin as the son or daughter holds on to the parent, and the collective entanglements, in the face of death. But this dynamic isn't limited to that transitional stage of life and that is not what I am looking at here. This is where it is important to circle back to some of the simple constellations we stepped into at the beginning of this chapter, exploring your connection to your father and your ability to maintain your own sense of place and groundedness as you connect. Remember the phrases:

You are my father and I am your son/daughter/child.

You have a place and I have a place.

We are separate.

We each belong.

This potential entanglement is *why* they are so important to say from a place of grounded but separate connection as you stay in the present moment. If you find that either you or your father is time-travelling to either of your childhoods during this simple constellation then the alarm bells should be ringing. Take a deep breath and work to separate your energy out before moving forward.

The silenced men

So far in our exploration within this field we have looked at entanglements around the close generations of our paternal family of origin. The next commonly occurring entangled pattern takes us further back and deeper into the ancestral silence.

The reversal of the male line

The natural order within a family lineage that we would hope to see is a line of forward-facing ancestors, looking at their descendants all the way down to you in the present. But that isn't always the case.

A reversed line can occur when your father cannot see or be seen by his own father. When he cannot be seen, he waits, seeking out whatever unacknowledged trauma is pulling his own father away, and he tries to step into that for his father in an effort to be seen. This pattern of waiting and holding unseen trauma continues down the line, with the line all looking to the trauma in the past instead of towards the future and their own choices.

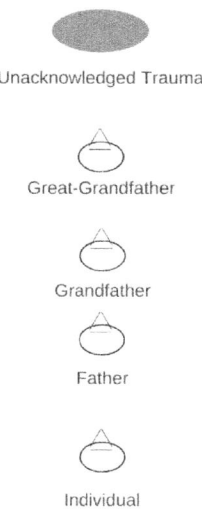

Unacknowledged Trauma

Great-Grandfather

Grandfather

Father

Individual

Image 5—Reversed paternal line

Commonly our fathers are pulled to other significant and missing men within the field of influence, often characterised by conflict or war related trauma.

Take a moment to think about that: the line of silent boys and men, each isolated within the trauma of violence and unable to reach out through the silence, each isolated within the weight of the unspoken pain. It is impossible to find a family untouched by war and conflict in recent generations. This silent lineage will be present in your family too.

The result is a fragmented and distorted line entrenched in deep pain. This creates the missing and excluded paternal line entanglements, where the line is reversed and the father cannot see his children, his partner, his work, his joy, or his dreams. Instead the father looks to the trauma and the missing souls, which results in a pull to the unseen and the dead. Therefore, the belonging—the sense of place and safety—is also fragmented and distorted within this reversed and fractured lineage.

Even when you are just beginning to talk about and feel into this pattern of reversal, the silent weight of the pain becomes almost tangible to us. It is a deep and sorrowful pain and we are going to gently walk through it, slowly honouring and remembering those who have gone before us.

In the following constellation exercises the focus is on observing whether or not an inherited parental relationship promise is a feature of the immediate field of influence upon you, and if so, gently working to restructure the field. Take your time with this. Some of these entanglements might have been silently held for generations and there is great healing power in taking the time to bear witness and truly feel into the connection, or absence of connection.

We are not doing this from a place of judgement, but simply to observe and witness. You don't have to agree with the choices and beliefs of your parents and ancestors. You simply have to see and accept that *they* made those choices.

The significance of a reversed paternal line

I regularly work with groups facilitating constellation. It never gets old for me. I love stepping into the field, uncovering the entanglements, and witnessing the healing. There is always resistance to working with the paternal line, but that doesn't stop me, because it is so important.

Bill participated in one of my general group family constellation classes held in France. He was an American married to a French woman and had settled in France with her. Throughout the course of the day he had been pulled into several different constellations as a representative. In each of his representative roles a theme emerged of him being excluded. He represented unseen men, a forgotten love, an abandoned child, and also silence, as the day's constellations unfolded. Even within the context of the group, I observed him holding himself back and he would actively give up his place for others. He arrived into the class a little late after one of the breaks and placed himself outside the circle of chairs where the rest of the group were seated. He was surprised when one of the other participants noticed him and invited him to take one of the unoccupied chairs. This interaction struck me as interesting in light of the roles he had held for others and I invited him to explore his own family field dynamics within the group.

When I asked him if he had a particular focus or area of exploration for the constellation he asked if he could explore why he felt he didn't belong in his family. The lack of sense of place was having an impact on his current marriage and his relationship with his children. He also felt it had been a contributing factor to the end of his first marriage.

With such a strong sense of displacement, the root entanglement is unlikely to be within the current field of influence around Bill in his present marriage, or even within his former marriage. The former marriage was with an American woman and Bill had lived with her in the United States for the duration of their marriage. There were undoubtedly entanglements within the current and former relationship that were exacerbating the root entanglement of displacement, however until the deeper root entanglements were uncovered and acknowledged the core dynamics would not release. Given his move from the United States to France for love, and his previous representative roles, I decided to explore the land influences within his family and ancestral field.

Both of Bill's parents were born in the United States, but looking further back down the family lines his maternal family originated from Scandinavia and his paternal family from France and Germany. In discussion about any possible links with war or military service, Bill shared that his maternal line had been involved in the American civil war and that his paternal line had been involved in WWI. From this information, we immediately get a sense of the possible root entanglement of the displacement that Bill was experiencing. The paternal aspects of both the paternal field and the maternal field were complex. I decided to include both of Bill's paternal line aspects as well as representatives of each of the countries connected to his family.

In the initial set up of the constellation, Bill placed himself, his mother, and his father, along with their marriage promise, in a tight triangle. Both parents immediately stepped back away from Bill though his mother still looked at him. The marriage promise stayed with Bill. Both parents were drawn to the oppositional aspects of the paternal line, i.e. the mother looked to the father's paternal line and the father looked to the mother's paternal line. In contrast, the paternal line representatives were drawn to the representatives of the different countries.

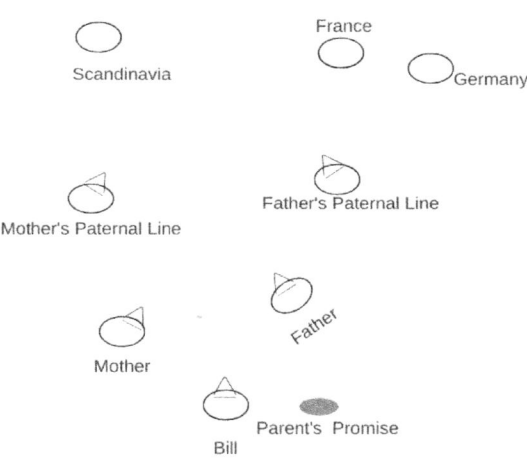

Image 6—Bill's initial constellation placement

This suggests, at the very least, an inherited parental relationship promise, with Bill holding the weight of his parents' marriage promise and representing his father for his mother. However, there was more complexity because of the pull that the oppositional paternal lines had for each parent. This suggests that looking at the trauma in the family field for each other was an unconscious part of their marriage promise, and Bill was holding responsibility for that too. This hints that there could also be a narrative of broken or unfulfilled promises in either or both paternal lines. The paternal lines are drawn to the countries of origin within the constellation.

In this context, the represented space is not just land or a country. It is a representation of the individual or individuals connected to that land or country that remain unseen or unacknowledged. It is very likely those left behind.

When representing an animating space such as land, it is a representation of the family members that are entangled within the represented space. Examples include 'those left behind,' 'those that didn't survive,' 'those that did survive,' and 'the cost of survival,' as well as those waiting in the land of origin for people to come home.

Entanglements around perpetration for place and belonging can be triggered within different generations and we observed this in the interplay between the two paternal line spaces. For Bill, this had a strong influence on his sense of safety and belonging and he struggled to carry more of the perpetration and the cost of the perpetration within himself in order to be safe and to belong.

When there is a shift from one country to another, this can create a series of effects within the family field, and some individuals will be drawn to see and acknowledge them at the cost of their own belonging. This is what Bill was doing. Others choose to not see and to perpetrate others in an effort to be safe and to avoid becoming an unseen victim.

Within this constellation the association that came through most strongly was the cost of a broken promise, particularly the promise from those who left to come back home and liberate those waiting behind.

When the dominant energy is of those left behind, then the cost of survival of those that survived, as well as the guilt carried for those left behind, can influence your ability to take your own place and be free to choose for yourself. This is essentially what we observed within Bill's constellation.

The entire focus of the constellation changed when the representatives for civil war and WWI were included. The civil war space was far more dominant. Bill and his parents, as well as the paternal line and broken promise spaces, were responding to it as if it were alive and in the present moment. When we observe such a response it is an indication that the unacknowledged trauma and the associated dead have yet to be seen. They have been carried forward silently from one generation to the next and experienced as if the war, and the threat of war and death, were still alive. This is the non-linear and non-local effect of the influent field in action. When spaces were brought in to represent the dead, the countries could not see them, and gentle work was undertaken to allow the dead to come home and to acknowledge the cost of the broken promise from both sides. This allowed for more balance in the field.

A further sense of peace and balance was achieved when Bill could connect with the different countries that were holding the space for those left behind, and say:

Parts of me come from you.

Parts of me are like you.

I accept those parts.

We're separate; you belong and I belong.

There is enough now.

I can't be them for you.

But I do remember.

You are remembered.

I remember you.

I am not the only one who remembers.

From this work, we can see some of the threads that weave in silently from the deeper paternal ancestral field. Often the historical narrative will be unknown but is still part of who you are and holds influence over you.

Where you come from, and the cost of the choices made by your ancestors around survival and love, stay silently present within you.

The cost of the choices made in the past, along with the unacknowledged pain of the paternal field in the present moment, can re-animate when we make a similar choice.

How did you feel reading through Bill's constellation? Can you connect with those left behind in the countries and places significant for your family? Does it feel safe to remember them?

Connecting with your father as he stands with his parents

Setting up a simple constellation to connect with your father and grandparents is a movement within the field of influence in and of itself. This is because, as you bring your father into your mind's eye, or imagine him there in the room with you, the field can be influenced by your perception of his existence as your father and no more, and your place as his child and no more. As we bring his parents—your grandparents—into the field, the influences that flow from them to him become clearer and we begin to see him as he is, rather than how we believe or want him to be.

This is also the portal to the paternal field. Every entanglement that exists within this field, known and unknown, flows around those three people. Take a moment to think about that, about the weight of the unknown entanglements that exist in this simple constellation.

We have collectively forgotten more than we will ever know about where we come from; yet we can begin to remember it here as we step into the created field with our father, grandfather, and grandmother. If they are displaced by the forgotten entanglements in any way, then so are we.

The intentional question for this constellation exercise is:

Is my father in his own place in relation to his parents and me, his child?

Take the time to work through the grounding exercise and centre yourself as much as possible. Take some slow deep breaths into your body and notice how comfortable your breath is. When you feel ready, bring your father into your mind's eye and when you have established the connection with him, bring each of his parents into the created constellation as well.

Can you still see him?

Can you see your grandmother?

Can you see your grandfather?

What happens in your body when you connect with your father?

Do you stay grounded?

At what age do you see him?

Do you stay in the present moment?

Where are your grandparents in relation to you and your father?

Try saying the following phrases out loud or in your mind:

To your father:

It is safe for you to be my father; it is safe for me to be your son/ daughter/ child.

The line has survived.

The line has continued.

To your grandparents:

I accept my place in the line. I honour your name. I accept my name.

Little phrases with big effect

With this exercise, if the phrases are comfortable to say and feel true, then you can be assured that there is a sense of place and belonging within you and that is very much what we are aiming for here. It is important to explore whether you can stay grounded and within your own place as you connect, and if you are able to do so as an adult or if you are having to shift back to the place of a child in order to do so. If that is the case, then there is an indication of contracts or the inheritance of promises associated with belonging. If the phrases with your father feel uncomfortable or untrue then this is an indication of a reversed or fractured paternal line.

Note any areas of discomfort. You can circle back to the simple connection and belonging constellations when you have completed this chapter exploring the deeper entanglements in this part of your field of influence.

Remember the great value of seeing an entanglement. The very act of seeing and feeling the entanglement begins to disentangle you from it. [9] That is why this work is so powerful—it allows these invisible pieces to be made visible.

Displaced love—when your father cannot connect with his mother

To further explore the potential of an inherited parental relationship promise in your field of influence, we must explore the dynamic between your father and his mother.

Take some slow deep breaths into your body and notice how comfortable your breath is. When you feel ready, bring your father into your mind's eye and when you have established the connection with him bring in your paternal grandmother. This is a really important connection for them and for you.

Where is your father in relation to you and your grandmother?

Can you see your grandmother?

What happens in your body when you connect with your father?

Do you stay grounded?

What happens if you bring in something to represent your grandparents' relationship promise?

Where does it go in relation to your father and what happens to your connection with him?

Do you stay in the present moment?

Phrases to your father about your grandmother:

I can't be her for you.

I can see her, but I cannot look at her for you.

You are not a child in this.

I see you waiting for her; you don't need to wait anymore.

This is where we dig a little deeper into the 'her' we made reference to when we were exploring who was holding the relationship promise between your parents. If you cast your mind back to that early constellation, we were ensuring that your parents' relationship promise was between your parents and outside of you. Most commonly though, it is being held by the child—in this case, you. And if it is being held by you, the likelihood is that one or both of your parents have inherited promises or broken promises from their own parents. That is what we are looking at clearing here. Because if part of your father is waiting in his childhood—if he is waiting to be seen by his mother—then it's highly likely that you, his child, are mothering that part of him. In this entanglement you are not your father's child—you are instead his mother. And that is not an arrangement that works well for anyone.

The phrases we have used here are to explore a potential dynamic whereby your father may be waiting in his childhood in order to belong or to be accepted. An acknowledgement of the weight of that entanglement can be enough to begin to move it for you, for him, and for your descendants. And stop you being his mother.

I see how strong you are; I see and feel your strength in me.

Your place is not forbidden.

Your place is not a betrayal.

My place is not forbidden.

My place is not a betrayal.

You belong.

I belong.

These phrases allow for the gentle separation and restructuring of your field of belonging. This is a soft introduction to the truth that your father's place is just for him, that it is safe for the line to continue, and for him to step out of his childhood. In turn, you can stop being his safety and step into your own place. A positive shift for everyone.

What happens when you say the phrases? Can you feel the movement within the words?

This is so important, as not only are you talking to that part of your father, you are talking to the part of you that connects in with that part of him. The part of you that associates 'waiting to be seen' and 'waiting to be enough' with safety and belonging. Because if it is here in one of your core relationships that defines your belonging, it will show up in other important relationships too. For example, in the partners we are drawn to, an acceptance that waiting to be enough for someone to love us or see us can be normalised, when in actual fact it is utterly destructive. This little big entanglement in our belonging can lead us into relationships where we believe that if we just keep giving, then maybe our partner will change, maybe they will begin to love us.

Do you recognise that pattern? This is where it begins. Work this constellation as many times as you need to. This is for you.

Make sure that you feel in your heart the truth of:

My place is not forbidden.

My place is not a betrayal.

I belong.

Take a break here before you step into the next part of the paternal field. Walk around outside or stomp about your home. Feel your belonging within your physical body, not just in your mind.

What happens if there is a blocked connection between your father and his father?

In this next constellation exercise, we are seeking to gently disentangle the roots of a possible reversal within your paternal line. We can do this by acknowledging the place of your grandfather and the connection from your father to him. If both can be seen and acknowledged by you whilst being able to maintain your own sense of place, then a movement towards healing the line can begin.

This is a deeply healing and restorative movement that can be used to strengthen your sense of place and belonging.

If it is not possible to connect directly with your father and grandfather, because the relationship doesn't feel safe or because of how you feel about them and the choices they have made, then starting at a softer point of connection several generations back can be very helpful. This is about you and strengthening your sense of place and belonging within the paternal line. It does not matter how far back you have to go to find that soft point of connection. Work with what feels most supportive for you in this moment. It doesn't matter if you don't know the stories of the line that far back—allow your body responses to guide you. Where does it feel safe for you to connect?

Begin as always with some gentle grounding and breathing. When you feel comfortable, bring your father and grandfather, or ancestors if the connection is safer, into your mind's eye. Allow yourself to simply observe and feel your response to the line appearing in front of you. Keep your focus on your own energy and sense of place, trying as much as possible to stay present with yourself. If you need to stop, then just stop.

Try saying the following phrases out loud or in your mind.

To the grandfather or ancestor within the line:

I honour you.

I honour your place.

I honour your land.

I honour your beliefs.

I honour you.

You do not need to stay a child. You belong. You have a place on the land that is just for you. I have a place in the land that is just for me.

Work your way gently back, one generation at a time, through the ancestors, from the point at which you started.

You might find that you can establish a soft point of connection with one ancestor and then the connection and flow will just drop away, and you will experience the absence of a connection instead. This is what a fractured paternal line feels like. It is literally broken, and you will experience the broken connections as you work through it. It can feel quite unsettling to go from a place of love and supported connection to an absence, so take your time to go through it gently from a place of compassion for both you and them. Establishing this safe connection with the paternal will support you in uncovering the deeper entanglements within the field. Take a note of the point or person in the line that feels the most comfortable for you. Remember it. Feel it in your body. This is a point we will come back to as part of your safety and belonging as we move forward.

If an attempt is made to explore deeper, more painful entanglements without your safety and belonging being first established, then it will be much harder for you to process and you are more likely to detach or disengage from the rest of the work. What we are doing in this chapter is bringing in as much safety and belonging as possible so that we can effectively explore and clear the entanglements that are impacting your present and future.

It is worth every moment of the hard work.

Being enough

When you carry the burdens of those that go before you, not only do you sacrifice yourself and your own place, but you can prevent the dead from moving on and finding peace. I think it is safe to say that your intention wouldn't be to hold onto the dead. The pattern is not released it is perpetuated.

Our sense of belonging, desires, drive, and ambition, have strong connections with our father and our paternal line. The roots of addictive behaviour and self-destructive patterns—such as alcoholism, drug addiction, depression, and suicide—can also be found here, as this is linked to our father's ancestral lineage.

When our father or other significant individuals from our paternal line are missing, detached, or rejected, then this line is weakened. We are weakened. We experience this through an unsettled connection with the absence of their presence. It is hard to reconcile that within ourselves without consciously choosing to work with it.

Any issues and burdens about ourselves and others are potentially linked to our emotional entanglements within the paternal line. The beginning of a solution is to look to the paternal line with an open heart, to see the sacrifices therein and accept them, and then accept our own place in the line. This is often more complicated than it sounds because the things that have happened to fracture the line in the first place are not easy things to reconcile. But we are not doing this from a place of judgement or indeed forgiveness. We are doing this from a place of witnessing and acceptance that the painful stuff happened.

The paternal line

Connecting with the broader paternal line and expanding on the work from the previous constellations is an incredibly helpful process to engage with. If we can connect with the existence of the line itself, rather than the individuals that make up the line and their choices—which may be the antithesis of our own choices and beliefs—it will create a space for acknowledgement and connection of the paternal line that is free from the weight of the entanglements within it. It is difficult to undertake this if there is already any judgement or resistance within you towards your paternal field. For this reason, it is again helpful to pick a soft and safe point of connection to the line. You don't have to go directly through your father if it doesn't feel safe. In this acceptance, I am not suggesting that you take responsibility for the actions, beliefs, or choices that were made, rather an acceptance of their actions, beliefs, or choices, and a separation of theirs and yours. You are only responsible for your own.

Begin with grounding yourself in the present moment. Have an awareness of the land under your feet and the breath that flows through your body. When you feel ready, bring your father, your father's father, father's grandfather, etc, into your mind's eye, or a more muted sense of your paternal ancestral line. Continue to breathe consciously into your body and feel the land underneath your feet.

When you can feel the connection to the line opening up in front of you begin to say the following phrases out loud:

I honour you.

I honour your land.

I honour your name.

I honour your sacrifices.

I honour your place.

I honour my own place.

I accept my own place.

Take a moment. And then a deep breath, and say the last three phrases again. Allow yourself to really feel them.

I honour your place.

I honour my own place.

I accept my own place.

Then breathe into your body and notice your connection to the land underneath your feet. Use this constellation to help support yourself when you are feeling lost or displaced. It is powerful. If honour feels too charged a word to use in this context, then try working with *I acknowledge you* or *I accept you.*

This is a powerful act of bearing witness and a deeply healing movement. It is worth getting out of your own way and seeking the softer point of connection within the line. You are claiming your belonging back. This is for you.

Resistance runs deep

It can be very difficult to overcome the pain and anger involved in the fracturing of the family field, particularly in relation to the paternal field. A constellation won't always come to a point of peace and balance whereby all aspects and all representatives within the created constellation can witness and accept the unacknowledged trauma, and that isn't necessarily the aim or intention behind the work. Constellation as a therapeutic tool allows the invisible parts to become visible and shifts our awareness away from how we perceive the dynamics of a situation, to the reality and truth of how things actually are or were. Seeing an entanglement begins the process of disentangling it.

This isn't always a comfortable process, but there are times when sitting in the discomfort of a truth can highlight where our own responsibilities begin and end. We are not at the mercy of the ancestors. We have our own choices and responsibility for those choices. Yes, those choices are influenced and sometimes limited by the historical narrative but that does not alter our own personal responsibility.

Sometimes the hardest work comes not with the identification of the entanglements in the field, but in the ability to let them go and accept what happened in the past as we embrace our present moment.

Acceptance of the actual historical narrative in our family field as it is, not how we would like it to be, is important and key to forward movement for each of us. We don't have to agree with the choices that were made in the generations before us, but we do have a responsibility to *accept that these were the choices which were made*, to witness and acknowledge what happened, and also witness the choices or actions from within our own family field connections that contributed to an event or trauma. In the act of acceptance and witnessing, there is a release, but part of that release involves letting go of the entanglement, and the responsibility of the entanglement, that you have been knowingly or unknowingly carrying.

There can be a comforting familiarity to the weight of an entanglement. There can also be a sense of power and dominance that comes with holding the responsibility for the entanglements within the historical narrative, particularly when the narrative is associated with conflict or traumatic violence. The power that comes with holding the perpetration in the field can be seductive and an individual may choose to continue carrying the weight of the narrative rather than allow a movement towards peace and healing. I have observed this within both group and individual constellations.

Being unable to let go

One such example was with a group participant, Andrew, who wanted to explore the anger he was experiencing in his personal relationships. He had challenging relationships with both his wife and son. When the constellation was set up it became clear that Andrew wasn't able to see either his wife or son. Despite initially placing his wife and son close to him within the created constellation, he found himself unable to stay beside them. He physically stepped back and withdrew and began to look from outside the constellation. Both representatives for his wife and son were able to see him but felt unable to reach out and connect with him. They also didn't feel safe in his presence which was upsetting for Andrew to witness as he felt this was a true reflection of their shared reality. The mother and son drew towards one another for support which further displaced Andrew and he felt anger when he looked at them.

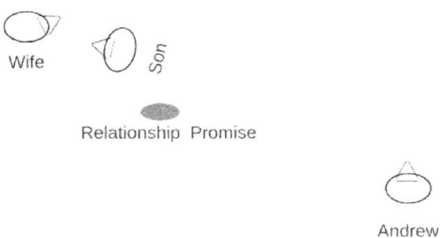

Image 7—Andrew self-excluding within the constellation

Bringing in the wife's parents and former partner allowed more appropriate distance between the mother and son. The son could stop being his mother's safety; he could see she had safety outside of him and it disrupted any dynamics that would contribute to an inherited parental relationship promise; however Andrew showed no response to the movements in his wife's family field.

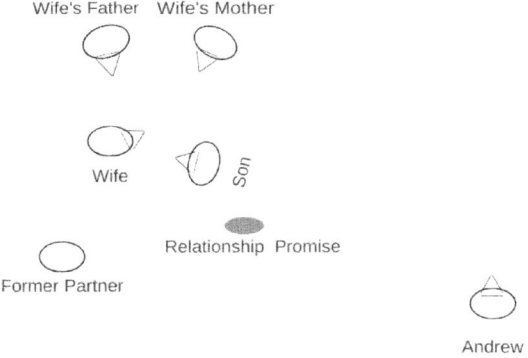

Image 8—Andrew's son moving out of being his mother's safety

In our initial conversation before setting up the constellation, Andrew revealed that he had a particularly difficult relationship with his father. As he spoke about his father, the raw emotion in his voice and demeanour was palpable. Andrew was angry with his father who he experienced as distant and absent. Further questions revealed that the paternal line was connected with Poland in WWII. At this point in the constellation, after ensuring that there was safety for Andrew's son in terms of his belonging with his mother and her field, I brought in representatives for Andrew's father, grandfather, and the land in Poland.

There was an immediate response to the inclusion from Andrew, his wife and son. Both the wife and son moved to stand with the representative for Poland and Andrew's grandfather stood between Andrew and his wife and son, blocking his connection to them. Andrew's father also moved to stand beside the representative for Poland.

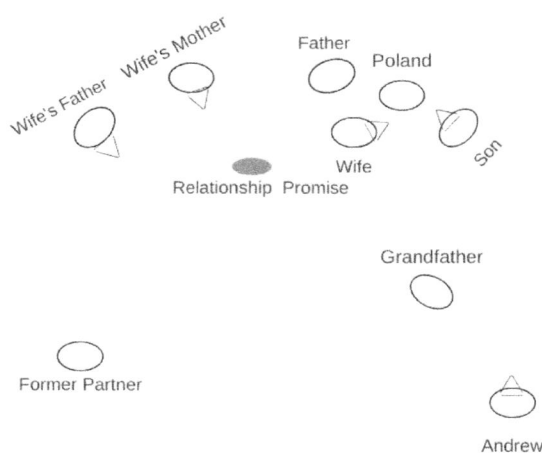

Image 9—Andrew refusing to engage with his line's past

It was clear, given the responses with the field, that there had been a betrayal and loss of life. Representatives for broken promises, persecution, and the dead were included, which brought peace to everyone else in the constellation, but not Andrew. He continued to display anger towards the other representatives and chose to hold onto that anger even when there was a softening in the connection between the dead, Andrew's grandfather, and the land in Poland.

Andrew communicated that the grandfather and his brother had collaborated with the Nazis against their own community in order to keep their own family safe. He was angry and deeply shamed by this. There was complexity within this constellation around the victim and perpetrator dynamics as well as the appearance of the triangulation with those left behind. However, the movement within the constellation was physically stopped by Andrew. Even after revealing the hidden influences within the field that were at play, and working to disentangle the triangulation between the community in Poland (those left behind/victims), those who left (Andrew's Grandfather/perpetrator), and the surviving generation (Andrew's father), Andrew was still unable to look at his father and grandfather, or his wife and son, without judgement and anger. He was physically holding on to the power of the entanglement. I asked him to try to acknowledge the life that flowed from his grandfather, to his father, to him, and then to his son, by saying:

I honour your place.

He refused. I asked him instead to say:

I see your place.

Again, he refused. I then asked if he would consider bowing his head in acknowledgement of the line that he comes from, including the land in Poland. Again, he refused.

I stopped the constellation shortly after having worked a little more with Andrew's son, who could see and acknowledge his lineage and the cost of the choices made, to ensure that the son wasn't looking at the paternal line on behalf of his father.

So much moved within Andrew's constellation, and the feedback from Andrew's wife was very positive around the relief it brought for both her and her son. However, Andrew was still experiencing anger and its isolating effects. This is where being able to see and accept the choices that were made by the ancestors is so important.

We cannot change what happened—this is a fact—but we can witness it and let go of carrying the cost of it.

The letting go part is an individual choice and sometimes we need to get out of our own way.

Exploring belonging

Once we have established a connection to the paternal line or paternal field, then we can begin to explore the concept of belonging itself in a little more detail.

A simple meditation with your breath and the phrase *I belong* can be helpful for revealing any potentially unacknowledged entanglements. It is a small phrase and it seems like it should be easy to say, but saying it and believing it, feeling the truth of it, can be hard. Is it easy for you to say that phrase? What happens when you do?

What feels like home?

Where is your safety?

Is it internal or external to your place?

Do you have a place?

Is it just for you?

Answering those questions when you are just considering the energy and emotions in your own body and sense of place upon the land is one step. Opening the field up a little wider to bring in your father and paternal line is another step. What happens when you do that?

Can you still say *I belong?*

Does it feel the same?

What feels like home now?

Where is your safety now?

Is it internal or external to your place?

Do you still have a place?

Is it just for you?

What happens if you try to say *I accept my place upon the land. I accept my place in the (your surname) line?*

Does it feel true?

Does it feel comfortable?

There is no place for judgement here. If it doesn't feel comfortable then just note that and gently work with the words and your breath.

Where and who are you when you look at your parents?

Here we take a deeper look at the weighty and unpleasant inherited parental relationship promise and what it means for your sense of place and belonging. The resultant influences on your relationships are explored fully in Chapter Five.

Attraction between individuals is complex. The desire to belong, to have a place within a family dynamic, even if that family dynamic is not in resonance with our own family of origin, can be a significant unconscious motivation within our relationships. If we feel excluded by or from our own family then we will knowingly or unknowingly seek a place to belong in someone else's family.

In relationship dynamics we tend to be attracted to people where there is a similarity of fate or entanglement in their field of influence, where their stuff feels similar to our stuff. It is very often the case that the heavy entanglement that is in part excluding us from our own family is replicated and echoed within our partner's family field.

If our relationship with our father is toxic and it doesn't feel safe to be a part of the family, then we can be drawn to a partner that has strong victim-perpetrator dynamics and a lack of safety somewhere within their field of influence too.

Say for example that their great-grandfather was abusive and violent to his wife and it was held as a silent secret where it wasn't safe to see or acknowledge the trauma. It is common that the price of belonging within a partner's field is to carry this heavy burden or fate and to hold responsibility for it. In this case it would be you unconsciously representing the abused and silent great-grandmother. A heavy price to pay for belonging.

I have undertaken countless sessions where this mirroring of fates appears, including similar points of betrayal within parents' or grandparents' relationships, ancestors being killed in the same conflict in the same place, loss of farmland, as well as traumatic deaths of significant family members. I want to be clear here, unconsciously representing the unacknowledged trauma in someone else's family doesn't heal anything. It just creates another layer of entanglements for you and the next generations to work through.

The inheritance of promises and broken promises

By the very nature of the paternal field, patterns and broken promises can be passed silently from generation to generation, with the children seeking to belong in an entangled line by carrying these heavy fates into either their maternal line or into a partner's line.

Any entanglement within the paternal line will automatically disrupt the sense of place and belonging within the line. I cannot emphasise that enough. However, once these entanglements are acknowledged and disentangled the paternal field becomes a great source of strength and support. It stops being your Achilles heel and starts being your superpower.

The influent field from your ancestors is not just made up of trauma. It is full of amazing, strong, creative, and wonderful people with stories of joy, happiness, and dreams.

It is just that the entanglements tend to drown that out. That doesn't mean that it doesn't exist. And that place for joy exists for you *and* your ancestors. You are here because they were here. The line is more than the pain and the trauma. Choosing to see it can transform it.

This is why the constellation exercise to connect with the essence of the line itself is so important. It is that transformative. Think of all of the belonging stuff that you can nip in the bud by taking the time to look at where you come from and the simple acts of connecting and remembering.

Positive paternal parts—hope and joy within belonging

I have worked with the positive support of the paternal lineage as a tool for support in many client sessions, particularly with women who do not have a strong inherent sense of their belonging and place within their own paternal field. In such cases the entangled connection that they have with the paternal line is replicated throughout their other significant relationships such as the relationship with a partner or child.

One client in particular, Audrey, had experienced a difficult relationship with her father, having been passed repeatedly from the care of her mother, to her father, and then to other family members during her childhood.

She initially chose to work with constellation to try to improve her relationship with her husband and sons and to gain more confidence in her chosen career. There was complexity in all areas of Audrey's family field. The trauma of her childhood was the tip of the iceberg in terms of the historical narrative within the family. There was a history of alcoholism, drug abuse, and violent trauma, within the maternal and the paternal lineage. Audrey had managed to find solidity and belonging for herself through her marriage however she was also unconsciously carrying the unseen trauma within her husband's family field as a way of earning that belonging.

Before beginning to disentangle some of the historical narrative from Audrey's family of origin it was important to establish her own separate place and belonging both within the context of her marriage promise but also outside of it. She felt safe within the marriage as a married 'Henderson woman' (Henderson being her husband's surname). In order to support that, I guided her through some simple constellations to acknowledge the marriage promise between her and her husband and each of their own separate places. I then asked her to work with her husband, her father-in-law, and her grandfather-in-law. Saying to each of them in turn:

I see and accept your father within you.

I see and accept your father's name within you.

I see and accept your father's land within you.

I see and accept your father's work within you.

I see and accept your father's blood within you.

I see and accept your father's sacrifices within you.

I see and accept your father's place.

I see and accept your place.

I see and accept my own place.

You are a free Henderson man and I am a free Henderson woman.

This brought much relief for Audrey as we gently worked back from the connection with her husband, to her father-in-law and beyond. At each step we were effectively weaving together the lineage of the paternal, their individual places, and Audrey's own place. This allowed her to witness and see the line without carrying the burdens of the line. Her confidence, and sense of self, improved dramatically with this work and we were able to explore some of the more traumatic narratives within her family history and personal relationships from an established point of safety and belonging. This also meant that any aspects of her own family field that changed from her perspective, did not go on to alter the sense of belonging within the marriage for either her or her spouse.

What happens if you try that with your own partner? Can you feel the shift within the field?

Have you thought about your belonging in terms of your partner's field of influence? Names hold power. Trying saying the phrases to your partner in your mind and notice any shifts or changes in your body and breath.

Missing men and unknown fathers

It can be hard to connect to the male line when there is a separation between the parents, or if we don't know anything about our father or even who he is. In such cases the person in question can feel incomplete or feel a sense of loss in areas of their life.

> An advantage of constellation therapy is working with certain parts of the field even when there is no knowledge of the individual family members.

We can work with the fabric of the field and work to acknowledge the unseen and missing—which is healing—taking back those missing puzzle pieces.

The existence of fractures within the paternal line and field is common yet rarely acknowledged, even in situations when some of the details of the narrative within the field are known. The existence of the fractures can often be carried forward knowingly and the weight of them straddled between the seen and the unseen parts of a family or individual. For example, if the grandfather died in a war and no one speaks of it. Or if the great-grandfather walked out on his family and never returned. The impact of such fractures can be limiting, and it is often the desire to push forward—to become free and unburdened as an individual—within a specific context such as a work promotion or relationship crisis, that brings the wounding fractures to light.

Paul had been a client over a period of years and would come for individual sessions periodically when he was experiencing a crisis situation to utilise the support of constellation for himself and his family members.

He would be very careful about the context and the focus of the work to ensure that we stayed within the boundaries of the present generations of the family. He wouldn't allow himself any space to focus on the constellation field from his own perspective. He was deeply in service to his wife and four children and was only ever interested in clearing just enough, to allow for forward movement for all of them, despite my encouragement to try to look at his own place and the weight of what he was carrying.

At a point during our work he experienced drastic changes in his work environment which threatened the financial security of his family. It was this change that forced him to look more deeply at his own place in the family he had created, and at his paternal line and field.

The known narrative of Paul's family of origin involved a fracturing of the paternal line and field. His great-great-grandfather had disowned and disinherited his son, Paul's great-grandfather, because he fathered a child out of wedlock with a young girl who was in the great-great-grandfather's employ as a maid. The disowned great-grandfather did not acknowledge the pregnancy at the time nor the son that was born to the young girl (who was also dismissed from her post in a state of disgrace). Paul's grandfather was the son. He went on to serve in the British Army and did not have a relationship with his father. He married and had children and also had several affairs.

Paul's father was conceived as a result of one of those affairs. Paul's father was never acknowledged by his own father. He wasn't even given his name. Instead he was brought up with his mother's surname and was only consciously connected with his maternal influenced paternal line. He too refused a relationship with his own son and left Paul's mother. The heavy entanglements of shame, loss of place, exclusion, denial of place, and servitude, that silently dominated the paternal field were not secret. They were known but they were heavy burdens for Paul to bear. He accepted the mantle of unseen man willingly as if he had no choice. The impact of the shame and the choices from the historical narrative of the family held him in a place of servitude and enslavement. It was only at the point that the family he'd managed to create for himself became threatened that he felt able to explore the threads in the fractured paternal line.

Paul was unknowingly representing the disinherited and excluded great-grandfather, as well as the cost of the broken promises of his grandfather. He carried a surname that was not fully true for him. His grandmother's maiden name was Lovatt and he was living his life as a Lovatt man. Part of him was indeed a Lovatt man but he was also more than that. The connection with the fractured and forbidden paternal was imperative to establish and to allow Paul to let go of the narrative of exclusion, punishment, and servitude, that he was unconsciously carrying.

Through a series of constellations, we worked with the reconnection to his paternal line and field. The initial set up of the constellation was clearly fractured. None of the men in the line could look at their own sons, however there was a clear and direct link between the great-great-grandfather and Paul. It was not necessarily a positive one.

I am not him.

I will not be him for you.

His choices are not my choices.

I cannot look at him for you and I cannot look at you for him.

Parts of me come from you.

Parts of me are like you.

My blood is your blood.

I feel you denying my place.

I survived.

My survival is not a betrayal.

My life in this is innocent.

The choices you made caused pain.

I accept you made those choices but I do not agree with your choices/beliefs.

I cannot carry the cost of your choices for you.

I leave them with you.

My choices are different.

We repeated this work with each of the men in the line. At this point we also had to bring in representatives for the women who were not acknowledged by the men as well as the broken promises there. This was very emotional for Paul and had a deep and positive influence on his relationship with his own wife. After this work the line was able to acknowledge more compassionately the existence of the different generations, however Paul was still holding the responsibility for the safety within the line. We worked from the great-great-grandfather through to the connection with Paul's own father to help to strengthen the place of the line.

I honour your father within you and I honour him within me.

I honour your father's name within you and I honour him within me.

I honour your father's land within you and I honour him within me.

I honour your father's work within you and I honour him within me.

I honour your father's blood within you and I honour him within me.

I honour your father's sacrifices within you and I honour him within me.

I honour your father's place.

I honour your place.

I honour my own place.

You are a Baldwin man and I am a Baldwin man.

I am a free Baldwin man.

I am claiming my place.

I am coming home.

Can you feel the ripple run through you as you read those words? Try saying the phrases using all the names you know of within your family field and see how it feels for you.

This was not an easy piece of work for Paul to do. He had to navigate his way around the silence, secrets, shame, and broken promises, when his ingrained habit was to accept and be invisible. However, the changes that resulted from his dedication and hard work were incredible. He was able to stabilise his working life and transform his relationships. His sense of who he was and where he came from was deeply altered. His confidence grew and his choices and dreams became his own. This is the power of the paternal line.

He did not have to accept the choices of the previous generations as being right and true, or accept their beliefs as his own, and neither do you. He had to accept that choices had been made, and beliefs held, that were outside of his place and yet he still had a place. It changed his life. Try stepping into the paternal field yourself. You won't regret it.

The missing men and the forgotten dead

It would be impossible to encounter a family living in the world today that does not have a connection to war. It flows through each of us.

In families where there has been violent perpetration associated with war and conflict, whether this is suffering perpetration or the active perpetration of others, the generations that follow will be drawn to the fates of the unseen within the untold stories of the historical narrative. Their silent stories will be flowing through you and this invisible inheritance shows itself in certain ways.

There can be an unconscious desire to display behaviours or patterns that show that we are sacrificing ourselves or in some way giving up our place so that the victims or the unacknowledged may be seen again. We may also carry the grief and the guilt that has previously been unexpressed within the family. Does that sound familiar?

Within the constellation setting I often see someone who is unseen by those around them, someone who feels that they don't have a place. They are tied to the unseen and displaced victims.

There are also those that are tied to the perpetrators, who can experience great anger and draw this towards themselves and become entangled with destructive and violent relationships, or be the perpetrator in a violent relationship. Once you become aware of the patterns at play it becomes easy to spot them either within ourselves or in our friends and family. And when we know they are there, then we can actually do something about them. The influence of the missing and forgotten dead within our family, connected to war and violence, is immense. There are more forgotten dead than there are living.

Those of us who are tied to the perpetrator or who have that fate within our family can, as an attempt to address and balance this, become involved in the field of healing. This can be through the medical profession, social care, or alternative and complementary therapies. We can experience chronic burnout as we attempt to heal others as a way of bringing peace to our own family lines. Unfortunately, we are at no point addressing our own family entanglement; we instead are faced with an endless queue of individuals who require energy and support and we quickly find ourselves becoming weaker and weaker. This too is a form of self-sacrifice to appease the familial entanglements. It really isn't helpful, and it perpetuates the patterns of sacrifice in an unbearable way.

Remembering the dead is so important. When they are not seen and they are not at peace then they have an effect on the living as if they were still alive.

When the circumstances of their death are such that they have sacrificed their life so that others may live, there is also a pull from us to them in the present. If they have sacrificed their life for their beliefs or their country, or indeed if someone has taken a life in such circumstances, it adds an extra dimension to the entanglement and the pattern that inevitably flows down our family lines. Life is precious but if another's life is not valued and we are tied to that fate, then we may find ourselves unable to value our own life or to accept the sacrifice of others. We are unable to submit to and accept the fate of the unacknowledged and forgotten dead.

Honouring the forgotten dead and choosing to remember

Peace comes when the victim and perpetrator can be seen and acknowledged within their respective family fields—when they have a place. In turn, family members are able to look to both the victim and the perpetrator and accept that this is part of who they are, and so with this act the system becomes whole again with a movement towards peace.

This is deep work. Take your time here.

Step into this constellation when you are feeling as fully present in yourself and your body as you possibly can. Remember we are stepping into old wounds and immeasurable grief here.

Take a little time to ground your body and settle your breath. Noticing how comfortable and present you feel in this moment. When you are ready, bring your father, grandfather, and greater paternal field, into your mind's eye.

Once the connection with the father and grandfather have been established bring in a representation for land.

Gently scan down the energy in your body and notice:

Can you still see your father?

Can you see your grandfather?

What happens in your body when you connect with them?

Bring in a space for war:

What happens when you bring in a space for war?

Do you stay grounded?

Where does it go in relation to you?

Where does it go in relation to your father?

Where does it go in relation to your grandfather and the paternal line?

Now bring in a space for victims:

Do you stay grounded?

Where do the victims go in relation to you?

To your father?

To your grandfather and the paternal line?

Now bring in a space for perpetrators:

Do you stay grounded?

Where do the perpetrators go in relation to you?

To your father?

To your grandfather and the paternal line?

When you are ready, feel into saying the following phrases either out loud or to yourself:

I bear witness to your pain.

I bear witness to your sacrifice.

I bear witness to your suffering.

I don't need to sacrifice in order to be safe.

I don't need to perpetrate in order to be safe.

I don't need to choose between victims or perpetrators.

For me there is another way.

To the victims:

I see you.

I am not holding judgement of you.

For me your lives are of value.

This was not done in my name.

I bear witness to your fate.

I accept your fate.

You haven't lost your place.

You still belong.

Parts of me are like you; I accept those parts.

My fate is different.

I take my place in honour of you.

To the perpetrators:

I see you.

I am not holding judgement of you.

For me your lives are of value.

This was not done in my name.

I bear witness to your fate.

I accept your fate.

You haven't lost your place.

You still belong.

Parts of me are like you; I accept those parts.

My fate is different.

I take my place in honour of you.

Notice the response and release with each of the phrases and if any parts still feel sticky or uncertain. If they do feel sticky, then go back over it. Notice too that I am using identical phrases for both the victims and the perpetrator spaces. This is because they are so intertwined, and we are consciously stepping into a healing movement, not judgement. This is a more complex constellation and you may need to work through it a number of times.

With each new constellation a different layer of the field will move, and you will become more aware of your own place on the land.

The unconscious belief that we have to choose between becoming a victim or becoming a perpetrator is a tricky one to shift but this work is the beginning of the healing process.

I mentioned earlier that there are more forgotten dead than there are people within our field. Shifting our focus there and allowing ourselves to step into the grief and sacrifice is an important step, but we can also tend to the forgotten dead in other ways. Whether we light a candle in their honour, visit a gravesite or battlefield, speak the names of the dead, or simply set the intention:

I remember you.

You are not forgotten.

I remember you.

I am not the only one.

I remember your place as I take my place.

The words and language that we use in constellation are powerful. Well done. You have worked your way through your paternal line and field.

Once you have established the basic foundations of the root of the entanglements that you are drawn into within the paternal field then gentle work can be undertaken to disentangle and strengthen the field as well as your place within it.

The theories around the paternal line hold a fascination for me. They are often overlooked in today's climate in favour of the emotional dominance of the maternal line and yet we cannot truly be free and accept our own place until we have acknowledged, explored, and accepted where we come from in our paternal line and field.

Once this hard work (and it is hard work) is completed in our core belonging, we will be able to bring a depth of confidence of belonging into each and every interaction we have. We are well on our way to belonging within our own place, and from that place being free to love and be loved. It is not easy work, but I believe this goal is worth the time and effort invested to achieve it.

3.

How we learn to love

Emotional belonging

The seat of our emotional belonging and the root of so much of our invisibly inherited relationship stuff resides in the emotionally weighted connection with our maternal line and field.

Our mother gives birth to us. Life comes from her. A rejection of our mother and an inability to accept the connection that comes from her to us, can have serious consequences in all areas of our life. It can essentially lead to a rejection of life itself as we become thoroughly entangled and stay focused on the dynamic with her instead of participating in our own life.

Take a moment to let that sink in.

If you are unable to get past the fact that your mother is the woman that birthed you and that part of you comes from her, regardless of the quality or dynamics of the relationship between you, then you will forever be embroiled in an unconscious energetic battle with her, and that has the potential to limit *all* areas of your life. I kid you not.

This perpetual entanglement of struggle manifests itself in the commonly held belief that we are not enough and not worthy of love. The belief that our mother didn't give us enough love or do enough for us, with a simmering undercurrent of frustration and anger around not being seen—is any part of that sounding familiar? It certainly isn't comfortable.

If this is the case, then there is often an unconscious waiting to be seen by our mother that goes along with such beliefs. A waiting to be judged to be enough. To be worthy of love, worthy of being heard or even seen.

This disruption of the mother-child relationship leads to some common but highly destructive patterns that I have regularly observed in my practice. The natural order and flow in childhood is for children to take from their parents and for parents to give. The connection with our mother and the maternal line is linked firmly with our ability to emotionally belong and to be free to choose to love.

It is also influential upon creativity, emotional communication, and sacrifice. If it is disrupted or entangled in any way then we suffer greatly with our self-worth and confidence. We can lurch from one relationship to the next or suffer in an emotionally vulnerable relationship in the hope that we will eventually be loved.

It can be an easy kneejerk response to say that you want different parents, that your parents weren't good enough, and that you didn't receive enough from them. But this is the equivalent of stating that you want a different life, that your life isn't good enough, or that it is not enough.

Parts of you can wait in your childhood at the points where you were wounded by your mother and father.

You can unconsciously hold yourself at those points or are held there by the entangled field. This is another example of the non-linear, non-local, shapeshifting, time travelling quality of the influent fields acting upon us.

Unconsciously staying in an entanglement displaces you both emotionally and physically and that is not a good thing. It certainly won't help with your emotional belonging in your friendships and relationships if part of you is stuck waiting in your childhood, because the people you are drawn to and who are reciprocally drawn to you, will also be stuck in their childhoods.

Blame is very often placed with the parents. Sometimes understandably and justifiably, this can appear to be the most natural response in circumstances of abuse, addictions, anger, and other traumatic experiences and patterns. I am not belittling those experiences whatsoever. I am not asking you to forgive an abusive parent.

Instead I am asking you to consider the acceptance that at a basic biological level they are your parent. That is all—an acceptance of that fact, leaving the weight of the rest of it with them, and not waiting for them to be different, or unconsciously waiting with the past in the hope it will change—a powerful acceptance of who they are and an even more powerful acceptance of *who you are*—an acceptance of your own place and that you exist outside of them.

You cannot change your parents. They are who they are. Just as you cannot change who the mother or father of your own children are. It is simply not possible. Resisting the fact that your life comes from them will only achieve a perpetuation of exclusion, grief, pain, numbness, and dissatisfaction within you, and that will flow from generation to generation. It helps no one and the inheritance of trauma continues unabated. Why not change the pattern?

If the connection to your mother can instead be acknowledged gently, with an acceptance of lineage and the indisputable biological link—with of course the caveat of the difference in choice, belief, and fate for you as an individual—then you will become free, with nothing to hold you back in life.

It sounds too good to be true but it isn't—it actually works. The only fly in the ointment is that it isn't always easy to look at who you are and where you come from. It takes courage and vulnerability. Sometimes the familiarity of an entangled connection can feel safer because it is more familiar than the absence of it. But if we do not step bravely into the field of influence of our ancestors and bear witness to who we are and where we come from, then the same cycle of trauma will keep on keeping on.

If we cannot acknowledge or accept it all as it is, then we will continue to perpetuate the same patterns within our life and we will pass them on to our own children. Our children will be unconsciously drawn into the cycle of entanglement as the line continues.

This is the piece that tends to shift it within even the most reluctant and entangled of folks—if they won't do it on behalf of themselves, they will certainly undertake this work with the courage of a warrior on behalf of the children.

It is essential to explore your maternal and paternal connections before stepping into explore relationship constellations. We will do that in Chapter Five, but please resist the temptation to jump ahead. I haven't structured our walk through your field of influence in this particular order without good reason.

If we cannot see our own parents, then there is a real limitation placed on how much of our partner we can see and connect with.

In some cases, the limitations can be so severe that there isn't space for a partner in our life at all. We will be drawn into seeing our partner's maternal and paternal entanglements instead of our own, which further adds to the potential for exclusion and displacement. Taking the time to work through these pieces with your own father and mother will make the world of difference.

Examples of constellations involving an individual and their mother are ubiquitous. It is an entanglement that is repeatedly experienced and can become reanimated depending on your personal choices in love, family, and work. This can make it appear as though everything from your perspective is your mother's fault, though this is not the case at all and not what I am saying here.

What I am saying is: when there is an entanglement in the relationship with your mother, then you as an individual are more susceptible to further and more complex entanglements in love, creativity, and emotional belonging.

The exploration of the connection between you and your mother is a simple movement to step into, yet deeply emotional and highly significant. The dynamics that exist in the relationship from mother to child are so complex and ever changing, from both perspectives. The field of influence is not static; it is fluid and changes as we change and as our family field changes.

It is worthwhile regularly checking in with your sense of place and belonging with regard to your own maternal line and field through a simple connection constellation with your mother. Your emotional belonging depends on it.

Simple mother connection constellation

This is one of the most common starting points for many more complex constellations, yet the simplicity of the movement between you and your mother is deeply healing in and of itself.

Given how significant the relationship is in terms of the flow of the constellation and the influent field, there can be internal resistance to exploring the connection. Take your time with this constellation and feel what happens within you and around you when you step into the constellation. Notice, without judgement, any resistance within yourself.

The intentional question for this constellation is:

Is it possible to stay present within my own place and connect with my mother in the present moment?

Begin by taking time to ground within your physical body as much as possible and notice how deep or shallow your breath is. When you are ready, bring your mother into your mind's eye and breathe into the connection with her:

> *Where does she go in relation to you?*
>
> *Can you see her or are you feeling the connection to her?*
>
> *Do you stay grounded and present in your body?*
>
> *What age are you seeing her?*
>
> *Do you stay in the present or do you time travel to an earlier point?*
>
> *What emotions come up for you?*
>
> *Does it feel safe to connect with her in this way?*

When you are ready try saying the following phrases either out loud or into yourself:

You are my mother and I am your son/daughter/child.

I accept you as my mother.

I accept I am your son/daughter/child.

I accept my life as it comes from you.

You are my mother and I am your child.

Does it feel comfortable and true to acknowledge the place for each of you and the truth of the flow of your relationship? With this exercise, one of the key aspects to observe is whether there is difficulty with the phrase *You are my mother and I am your child,* and if the opposite of that appears to be true energetically. It might seem like a strange thing to check in with, but if you are entangled then you can hold the place of a mother as your mother stays a child. This is more common than you might think and is an indication of the reversal of the maternal line and is a very common entanglement with quite troublesome ripples.

If it feels difficult in this initial connection, try introducing the phrases:

You are my mother and I am your son/daughter/child.

And I am more than your son/daughter/child.

I exist outside of you and you exist outside of me.

That should give you a little more room to breathe in the connection and allow you to move forward to the next step.

Reversal of the maternal line

When there is an interruption to the natural order and flow from mother to child in the maternal line, this results in the reversal of the line itself.

Instead of the connection flowing from mother to child down the line, it flows back from child to mother through the generations to the original root cause of the reversal and entanglement. The root cause might be something like the death of a child in the previous generations, or perhaps the forced adoption of a child out of the family when the mother became pregnant outside marriage. This is a very common occurrence in the historical narrative of our family fields.

There are a number of possible scenarios within the family field that will create a reversed line entanglement, but the features of the reversal remain the same.

The child waits to be seen by the mother, but the mother cannot see the child as she is pulled to look to her own mother who in turn cannot see her and is looking beyond her towards the previous generations within the maternal line and field. It is similar to the reversed paternal line that we discussed in Chapter Two, but the resulting entanglements are quite different.

A common symptom of the line reversal is the switching of the roles of mother and son/daughter/child. This is where the child takes on the role of parent and holds safety and emotional safety for the mother, effectively sacrificing their own safety and emotional belonging.

There are two classic responses to a reversed maternal line:

Anger and perpetration—this is characterised by a need to exclude our self from our mother and the line in order to find a safe place to belong. In this scenario we can attempt to join and belong to a different maternal line and field, perhaps through a relationship or close personal friendship. There we will become embroiled with their family entanglements in exchange for being seen and accepted.

Sacrifice and servitude—this is characterised by waiting to be seen by our mother. There will be attempts to carry the heavy fates within the close family field that our reversed line of mothers is pulled to. This is often typified by either endeavouring to replace or carry the unseen and missing children, or replacing the lost loves and unconsciously holding the broken promises and dreams. We will internally carry the pain within the line and try to replace all that has been lost, driving ourselves to breaking point.

With the **anger and perpetration** response we exclude ourselves and become displaced looking for an earned belonging through carrying someone else's trauma stuff in a relationship or friendship. With the **sacrifice and servitude** response we stay with our mother and her lineage, often stuck as a child or at a certain point in our childhood, and carry the weight of the trauma in the field. Neither response is helpful from an emotional belonging perspective. It is deeply wounding.

Aspects of the reversal—a grandmother's love

So often in sessions with clients, when there is a difficulty in the relationship with the mother, the client will describe their relationship with their grandmother as the true point of comfort and safety in their childhood. Their relationship with their grandmother is more positive and supportive than the relationship with their mother.

This sets a little bell off in my head because this is a classic indication of a reversed maternal line. Do you recognise that in your own family field too?

This reversed loyalty can occur for a number of reasons but most commonly it happens with known early or traumatic deaths of children, as well as with unborn or missing children in the untold stories of the historical narrative of the line. (Missing children can refer to miscarriages, abortions, or adoptions, both known and unknown.)

In this case the mother will energetically or emotionally give her children to her own mother to replace the missing children within the line and field. This giving away of the children excludes her as a mother to her own children, and it repeats from generation to generation, forming an historical narrative within the maternal line and field. There is so much grief and pain here and it is hard to sit with the heaviness of it.

There are so many missing children in each of our family fields and so many grieving mothers, separated, isolated, and displaced from one another.

The weight of the grief has a detrimental impact on belonging. The experience of feeling unseen and given away, literally or emotionally by our mother, is not an easy thing to move forward from with all parts of ourselves intact.

In order to heal this and emotionally belong,
the root entanglement must be honoured,
witnessed, and acknowledged.

The unseen, missing, or lost children must also be given their place and be seen.

If this does not happen then you are likely to experience a sense of exclusion and displacement within your own emotional relationships and working life. You may feel yourself unworthy of love or success. And that is a very hard way to move through life. It can destroy confidence and one of the above two responses of **anger and perpetration** or **sacrifice and servitude** will kick in.

If you find yourself feeling angry and resentful towards your mother, take the time to gently work through the constellation exercises, because you are most likely carrying the unexpressed grief and pain from the unseen within your lineage. This is bigger than your mother—it will not have begun with her.

The anger can hint at a connection with a heavier root entanglement and will easily permeate other areas within your life and choices. Most destructively, it can deeply hamper your ability to love and be loved. The kneejerk response is to look away and not engage with it, but if you take a deep breath and try stepping into the connection, even if it is an absence of connection to begin with, you will find the keys to release yourself and your heart.

Dream a little dream for me

Dreams are important. They are special. They are part of what makes us who we are, what we hope for, move towards, and attempt to manifest in our lives. Every one of us has dreams ranging from places to travel to, careers to forge, books to write, finding the perfect home or the perfect love, to dreaming of a houseful of children.

But what happens if the dreams we are holding tightly aren't really ours? Do you ever feel like you have to finish off one last thing before you are free to follow your dreams? And the goal posts on that one last thing keep changing? Or do you feel as if you are trapped in a career that doesn't feel right to you, but you have worked your whole life to get there?

The inheritance of dreams is an entanglement that occurs within both parental field aspects, although it is most commonly observed within our maternal lineage.

It shows up as the sacrifice of our own precious dreams entangled with an unspoken promise or contract, that has passed down the line, to fulfil the broken or unfulfilled dreams of the previous generations. It is a painful entanglement, tinged with the loss of hope and bitterness of the ancestors intertwined with our own.

There is a cost associated with motherhood.

There is the obvious physical and emotional cost and strain on a woman as she transforms from woman to mother, but the cost goes beyond that. In previous generations becoming a mother would herald the end of whatever work or career the woman had established for herself. Her time would have to move away from herself and her own dreams and flow to her children. For some women this was a very conscious and happy sacrifice and indeed part of their dreams overall. However, for other women, a stronger sense of sacrifice and unfulfilled dreams takes a place alongside the children. The loss of autonomy over our dreams can be a bitter pill to swallow. The place of the unfulfilled dreams can be quite tangible for children in the line, especially if they are not fully within their own place. The children, particularly within a reversed line, can become drawn to carry and follow the mother's dreams in place of their own dreams as they wait for her to see or love them, especially if, for example, they carry an inherited parental relationship promise or are unconsciously giving their place to a missing child.

It can appear to us as children, that holding the sacrificed dream is a debt that needs to be paid in order to belong or to be worthy of love. The awareness of this debt can even begin in utero within fractured and reversed parental lines and so it can feel very familiar and safe as time goes on.

Is your maternal line reversed?

We are going to gently work our way through the connections in your maternal line now. I am sure there are little alarm bells ringing in resonance with some of the effects of a reversed line. Now is the time to bear witness to what is actually there within your line and give place to the unseen and the unacknowledged.

Begin by taking time to ground within your physical body as much as possible and notice the pattern of your breath.

The intentional question for this constellation is: *Is my maternal line reversed and are my mother or I entangled with her parents?*

When you are ready, bring your mother, your grandmother, and your grandfather into your mind's eye and breathe into the connection with them, noting your response to each:

Where are each of them in relation to you?

Where do you feel pulled?

At what age are you seeing each of them?

Can you stay present in your body?

What emotions, if any, are coming up for you?

The first aspect I want you to explore is what is happening in the connection between your mother and her father. If your mother has moved towards your grandfather instead of staying in her own place, then this is a sign that she is holding a relationship promise or secret with him. And that is not helpful for any of you. Gently work with the following phrases to her and your grandfather:

I don't accept your choices as mine.

I don't accept a place in this relationship promise.

This will help to establish a separation and a boundary around belonging. We can further support that boundary by the following movement from you to your grandfather:

I see you hiding.

I cannot keep your secrets for you.

I don't need to earn my place by holding your secrets, I already belong.

I understand that some of these phrases that I am guiding you to work with may seem a little strange. Remember that there is a function behind them: *to release the field of influence around the entanglement.* The phrases and the language within constellation literally move and shift the field of influence upon you and help you drop back into your own place, disentangled. Your parents and grandparents exist outside of being your parents and grandparents. Think of all of the choices that you have made and the secrets that you are perhaps holding—your parents and grandparents are no different. Now try to gently work through those phrases again.

We're not working with the phrases from a place of judgement or anger; stay present with your heart as you work through the constellation, and try to say them from your heart.

Now we need to move on to explore a possible reversal within your maternal line. You may already have formed an opinion on whether or not your line is reversed, however I suggest you try working with the following phrases to your mother regardless of whether or not you feel your line is reversed. Try it and notice how it feels. Notice any resistance from inside you or outside you. Remember what we are doing here is looking for the unseen within your line. Your sense of safety can falsely be associated with the entanglements themselves and it can sometimes feel dangerous to step into the field and truly witness. Take a deep breath and bravely say the phrases to your mother. Then breathe again. And again. Take time to notice whether or not the statements feel true and if you have any accompanying physical responses to them:

I see/feel you giving me to her (grandmother).

To your grandmother:

I cannot be them for you.

I cannot replace what you have lost.

I am your grandchild.

I am not your child.

Take a moment for yourself here.
This is deep work and you are bravely going where none of your ancestors have gone before.

Take time to honour yourself and your place within all of this. This is a significant movement.

When missing and unseen children are present within the close generations, or the historical narrative, it leaves its mark on those who come after. *I cannot be them for you* is a big little phrase. The 'them' is the missing children, and the grief can be huge. If you find yourself having a strong emotional response but a limited release from the entanglement with this exercise, don't worry, that is quite normal. This is just one step on our path forwards. It will move.

Seeing the unseen children

We've talked about the presence of unseen children within your line as a potential cause of a root entanglement that contributes to the creation of a reversed maternal line. We haven't talked about the unseen children themselves and why they are so important.

Unseen children, for the most part, are real souls. Some of them have lived and breathed and played, some of them only for a short period of time. Others were miscarriages, abortions, and children that were perhaps a dream in the heart of their mother or father. The collective energy of the unseen children in your field of influence when you yourself are unseen or displaced can be somewhat overwhelming. *They represent and carry the weight of the unacknowledged grief and pain of generation upon generation of mothers and children.* They often wait in the silence to be seen, loved, accepted, and given place. If the waiting that typifies them is in resonance with your own personal entanglements, then the connection with the unseen children within your field is even more important. We must walk gently through this part of the field; the unacknowledged trauma runs deep.

In the presence of grief

Begin by taking time to ground within your physical body as much as possible. Notice your breath and any tension present within your body.

Remember to go with whatever image, person, object, colour, or even absence of space, that comes in for you as you are setting up the constellation in your mind's eye.

When you feel ready, bring your mother, your grandmother, and a representative space for the unseen children, into your mind's eye and breathe into the connection with them, noting your response to each:

> *Is it possible to stay grounded and present when you bring the unseen children into the created constellation space?*
>
> *Can you feel them within your space or outside of your space?*
>
> *If you have a visual or emotional connection, is one aspect clearer than the other?*
>
> *What emotions are coming up for you as you connect with your created constellation?*
>
> *What happens if you bring in a space to represent secrets beside your grandmother and mother?*

When you feel ready try saying aloud the following phrases to your mother:

I know there would have been others.

It is okay.

I can see them, but I can't see them for you.

I see part of you following them; I can't stay with the others for you.

I cannot hold your responsibility as a mother.

I am your daughter/son/child; I am not their mother.

I am not your mother.

If your dominant experience of this constellation is the connection to the unseen children themselves, and you feel them within you, then work directly with them saying:

I see you.

I feel you.

You have a place and I have a place.

We each belong.

These phrases allow us to tap into the essence of any entanglement present between you and your mother that is influenced by unseen children. It allows us to open up to the possibility of unseen siblings as well as the existence of unseen children within the historical narrative of our ancestors. It will feel charged. It may feel overwhelming. It may feel numb. All of that is okay.

We are beginning to witness with this exercise, and there is no right way and no wrong way to experience it. The important thing is to notice how it feels for you—how present you can stay with it, and whether you get pulled back to your own childhood or perhaps displaced altogether.

You might find your connection to your own unborn children coming in here, and you can softly acknowledge them with the above phrases too. We will be exploring your connection to your born and unborn children in chapter six.

Acknowledging the unseen and missing children is another act, similar to the forgotten dead within the paternal line and field, where the tending of the forgotten and missing can move into our everyday lives in small but poignant ways. For example, we might light a candle to honour the children, place pebbles in our home or land to mark their place, or plant something in the earth to honour their lives.

Entangled mothers and daughters

Clara, a 52-year-old English woman, had a very entangled relationship with her mother. She had a closer relationship with her father and this allowed her to maintain her sense of place within the family. The connection with her father also gave her some relief from her tricky relationship with her brothers and to some extent her mother. However, after her father's death when she was 39, the relationship with her mother deteriorated to the point of estrangement.

From Clara's perspective, she had been excluded from her place in the family because of her non-relationship with her mother. She decided to embark on a series of individual skype sessions in order to explore this and to ensure that the relationship with her own son and daughter would not be impacted. Her daughter in particular had a positive relationship with Clara's mother, her grandmother, and Clara did not want her to feel trapped in the middle between them.

From the description of Clara's experience thus far we can determine a number of key things. The fact that there was a softer relationship with her father that somewhat shielded Clara from the relationship with her mother, suggests that Clara was part of an inherited parental relationship promise with her parents and their marriage promise. This means that Clara was holding aspects of her parents' relationship promise with her father and potentially unknowingly representing his mother and former love for him. This created a block in the relationship between her and her mother, who would have unconsciously felt threatened by the women that Clara was unknowingly representing. You can feel the complexities that are already present just by the simple entangling act of carrying part of the relationship promise. This is how easy it is to become lost in the family field and the narrative of our ancestors.

This is not the only potential entanglement present. From Clara's description of the positive relationship between her daughter and mother we can also deduce that there is a likelihood of a reversed maternal line. Which means that Clara, within her place as a daughter, was not only entangled with inherited relationship promises that were exacerbated by the death of her father, but she was also displaced by the reversal of her maternal line. Her daughter was, in part, unconsciously taking Clara's place with her mother and receiving the love that Clara did not. Complicated? Yes. Immovable? Thankfully no.

There was an immediate sense of relief for Clara after our initial skype appointment when we identified and cleared the entanglements around the inherited parental relationship promise. However, the biggest sense of emotional change for Clara came with the work around her reversed maternal line. In the initial session, when I asked Clara to bring the connection to her mother and father into her mind's eye, it was very uncomfortable for her. Her mother presented as large and dominant whilst her father was smaller and almost childlike. Clara felt threatened by her mother's presence. When I asked Clara to bring in a space or representation of her parents' marriage promise, the dynamic shifted. The connection with her father became more solid and Clara felt bigger and stronger. She was holding the promise. This was felt by her as positive and familiar, but it was not a helpful entanglement for Clara and was hugely limiting.

The entanglements became clearer with the introduction of her paternal grandmother and her father's first love, and we worked to clear the entangled and inherited broken promises there. It was only after this had cleared that Clara was finally able to look at and attempt to connect with her mother. The connection however was not reciprocated either in the constellation context or in Clara's day to day life. It became clear that there was indeed a reversed maternal line.

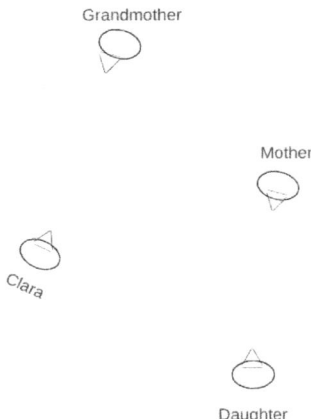

Image 10—Clara and her reversed maternal line

When Clara's 20-year-old daughter was brought into, and placed within the constellation, she was pulled between her mother and grandmother. The grandmother could see her granddaughter, but she was still refusing to acknowledge her daughter. I asked Clara to bring in a representative for her maternal grandmother and the aggressive energy from Clara's mother faded. The focus shifted to Clara's grandmother. The grandmother could only see Clara and not her own daughter. A mirroring of Clara and her daughter's situation.

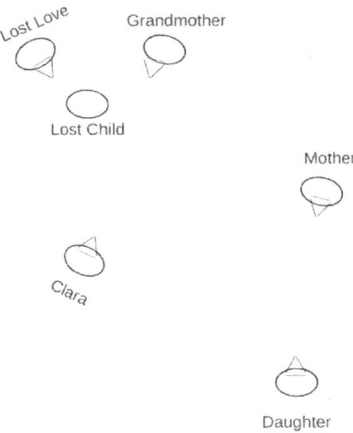

Image 11 - Clara and the influence of the unseen

We worked to acknowledge the place of the grandmother:

You are my grandmother and I am your granddaughter.

I am not your daughter; my mother is your daughter.

There was resistance and grief from the grandmother to these statements of truth. It was clear from the resistance that there was unacknowledged trauma of some kind for the grandmother before the birth of her daughter. Given the dynamics present in the previous paternal line triangulation, I brought in a space for a lost love and an unseen or unacknowledged pregnancy relating to the grandmother before her marriage to Clara's grandfather. The deeply held grief released dramatically for the grandmother and passed through Clara.

We gently worked to firstly acknowledge the unseen child from Clara's perspective:

I recognise you.

I have been holding you in my heart.

You have your own place.

You are not a secret anymore.

I am not you and you are not me.

We are separate and we each belong.

This eased some of the grief that Clara was experiencing. I then asked her to shift her focus to her grandmother. The grief once again intensified. We worked with the following:

I have been holding your grief tight.

I have been holding your regrets tight.

I have been holding your pain tight.

I have been holding your anger tight.

I have been holding your guilt tight.

I have been holding your losses tight.

I have been holding your death tight.

I bear witness to your grief.

I bear witness to your regrets.

I bear witness to your pain.

I bear witness to your anger.

I bear witness to your guilt.

I bear witness to your losses.

I bear witness to your death.

I honour your grief and I let this go.

I honour your regrets and I let this go.

I honour your pain and I let this go.

I honour your anger and I let this go.

I honour your guilt and I let this go.

I honour your losses and I let this go.

I honour your death and I let this go.

The powerful words allowed Clara to step back and separate from her grandmother's grief and to have a stronger sense of her own place.

They are not words to be skimmed over. Stop here and say the words out loud, and feel the rhythm of them within your own field.

Within Clara's constellation, we then revisited her connection with her mother.

I can see this now too.

This wasn't your fault.

I feel you waiting for your mother to see you.

Not all of her survived this.

I feel you giving me to her.

I feel you trying to replace what she lost so that she could see you.

I can't be the missing child for her or you.

You are worthy of love and I am worthy of love.

It is safe for you to be my mother.

It isn't a betrayal.

It is safe for me to be your daughter.

It isn't a betrayal.

I am choosing to let this go.

You can choose that too.

I leave that choice with you.

You can probably feel the deep exhalation that came with the phrase *I leave that choice with you.*

After this work, Clara and her mother have reconnected positively and are taking tentative steps forward in their relationship. The scope of the sessions is greater than the snapshot I have shared here. The important aspects to note are the complexity of the root cause of the maternal line reversal, and the need to clear the holding of her parents' relationship promise before the maternal line could be addressed. This is where our father line and field work come in from Chapter Two, along with the importance of belonging.

> If there isn't a clear sense of physical belonging in the field, then it is difficult to identify and heal any entanglements around emotional belonging. You cannot have one without the other.

This work also helped to transform Clara's place in her own marriage as well as her relationship with her children. It was incredibly powerful. The unacknowledged trauma relating to unseen and missing children within the present and historical narrative is huge and affects every one of us. Clara's experience is not unusual.

How did you feel reading through the unfolding of Clara's constellation? In particular, how did you feel reading the phrases to her grandmother? Could you feel the connection to your own grandmother begin to come in for you? Take a moment and read through the phrases again, out loud, and feel the energetic response within your heart.

With the acknowledgement of potentially deep grief, I find that lighting a candle in honour of the grief itself, as well as the unseen, can be another, sacred way to support the unfolding and healing.

Emotional belonging within love and relationships

We need to talk a little more here about relationship promises. They don't just come into play for couples who are married and have children.

Every emotional relationship is characterised by a relationship promise between the people involved, whether it is an intimate relationship, a friendship, or a working relationship.

There is a need to explore whether the promise that is in place between a couple actually belongs to them. This is important. Think back to Clara and the weight of the entanglements that came in through simply holding responsibility for aspects of her parents' relationship promise.

Promises held by a parent, grandparent, or previous generations, where there is an unresolved entanglement, can and will flow down the line and be held in place of your own wishes and desires about love.

That is a huge unconscious sacrifice to be making. In such cases, the promise held is most definitely not a couple's own and it is essential to bring in the root of the broken or unfulfilled promise in order to clear the entanglement. We discuss the deep complexities of relationship patterns fully in Chapter Five.

Our maternal field influence on relationships, love, and parenthood, is generally characterised by us unconsciously:

Staying within our parent's marriage promise.

Giving our children away, figuratively or literally, to replace those who have been lost within the previous generations or the historical narrative.

Holding a belief that we need to be alone in order to be responsible for the historical narrative, either waiting for a love to return or perhaps waiting with the family land.

Experiencing a non-acknowledgement of our place by our previous or current partner.

Experiencing a non-acknowledgement of our mother by subsequent partners/wives of our father.

The stepmother dynamic, whereby our stepmother, if not secure in her place with our father, will knowingly or unknowingly seek to displace our mother as well as us and our siblings. This creates a heavy entanglement for everyone.

A lack of safety in having children or claiming creativity.

Do you recognise any of those unconscious choices within yourself or other members of your family? If you do, then take note of where you can see those choices, both internally, and externally around you.

The maternal line influence on love

If we are struggling in our love life, we wouldn't automatically look for an invisibly inherited entanglement between our self and our mother. It isn't the obvious place where we would choose to begin to explore, or the relationship we would want to firstly focus on when considering our love lives. It may even be the last place you want to look, but it can hold the missing keys to unlocking patterns within love and relationships.

Sharon was a client who had initially participated in a group session focusing on her career and dreams. Her circumstances were complex. Her family, going back several generations, were from Guernsey, one of the Channel Islands located between Britain and France. When we first started working together, she was living in London and having issues in her working life as well as in her relationship with her fiancé. Her relationship with her mother, who lived in the family home in Guernsey, was very close. Her mother's health was beginning to deteriorate, and Sharon made the decision to move back to the family home to care for her. She took the decision to resign from the job that she was unhappy in, and she felt positive about her choice. Her relationship with her fiancé deteriorated alongside her mother's health. At the point at which her mother had to be admitted to a hospice her fiancé chose to end the relationship. Shortly thereafter, Sharon's mother passed away. Sharon became withdrawn and isolated in the months that followed. She found it difficult to leave the confines of her family home, which she had inherited, and could not contemplate leaving the island. At that point, she contacted me to arrange a series of individual sessions. The obvious place to begin is the exploration of Sharon's grief around her mother's death.

Although this created a little breathing space for Sharon it became clear that there was more than grief influencing her present situation. When Sharon worked on the connection with her mother in the constellation, she lost a sense of her own place and identity. This shifted only slightly with the acknowledgment of their separate places:

You are my mother and I am your daughter.

That will never change.

You still have your place and I still have mine.

We are separate.

We each belong.

Bringing in her grandmother and great-grandmother gave some relief to Sharon, particularly her great-grandmother, however they too were held tightly within Sharon's place. She had no awareness of herself in her constellation, only them and the land in Guernsey. I asked Sharon to bring in a representative for a promise between her great-grandmother and the land and this opened up the constellation. There was finally a movement outside of Sharon and she began to have a stronger sense of her own body and place. She was however very drawn to the promise and I asked her to say *I recognise you. I have been holding you* to explore whether the statements felt true. They did, and her connection with the land strengthened to the point of her feeling a magnetic pull downwards and it became difficult to stand. This pull downwards is characteristic of a pull to the historical narrative of the dead, a loyalty to them and their unfinished stories. This is not a good land connection to have despite it being a strong one. It pulls us into unconsciously sacrificing parts of ourselves, our dreams, and our choices. In the place of our sacrificed dreams we hold the unfulfilled dreams and hopes of the dead. We become energetically stuck in someone else's life.

I asked Sharon if there had been any lost loves connected with her great-grandmother. I asked her this because of the combination of experiences she was having, most notably the holding of a promise that originated outside of her, the pull to the land, the narrative of the dead within the land, and the loss of identity as a woman in her line. She shared that her great-grandmother had been engaged before the marriage to Sharon's great-grandfather but her fiancé, a young fisherman, had died at sea. We brought him in and he looked to Sharon and the promise rather than the great-grandmother. Part of Sharon's great-grandmother had been holding on to the promise to wait on the land for him to return and this promise to be the one who waits had passed from one generation to the next. When we brought in Sharon's ex-fiancé he immediately went to stand with the promise and Sharon's great-grandmother's first love.

We worked gently with the great-grandmother:

I can see this now.

I can feel how much you both lost.

This promise was between you both.

I have been holding it for you.

I have been holding it so you could be free.

But it doesn't belong with me.

Death has taken the promise.

And then the young fisherman:

She couldn't wait for you anymore.

You didn't survive.

Death took you and the promise.

I can't be her for you.

I can't be the one who waits.

This is between you both.

I am letting it go.

You can let it go too.

We then worked with the women in the line:

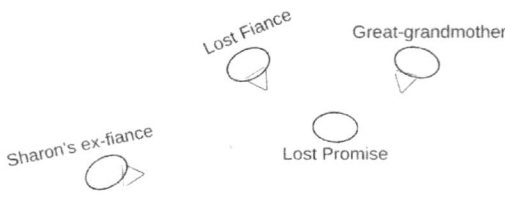

Image 12—Sharon and the inherited lost love

I am a De Voille woman.

I am a free De Voille woman.

I can be the first free De Voille woman.

It is safe for me to love and be loved.

It is safe for me to walk upon this land as a free woman.

It is safe for me to leave this land.

It is safe for me to return to this land.

This land isn't death for me.

Love isn't death for me.

These phrases within the constellation setting are very powerful. Try them yourself with your own name. *As loudly as you can.* Claim that place as a free woman, a free man, or a free soul.

Sharon was able to move forward freely with her life. She chose to stay on the island in the family home as her base but regularly travelled to London for work and has begun to date again.

Connecting with our parents

The responsibility for invisibly inherited promises doesn't always come from deep ancestral places.

The pull towards broken promises in the field around us can be exacerbated when we as individuals are placed, or take a place, inside our parents' relationship promise rather than outside it. Surprisingly this connection with the relationship promise of our parents, and our place in relation to it, is fluid. It shifts and changes with the field of influence around us and the choices we make for ourselves as we move through our life.

Claiming more solidity in our sense of place *outside* our parents' promise sounds simple but it requires the acknowledgement of place for each of our parents as well as our own place, and that isn't always easy.

Try to step into the connection just now for yourself. Gently ground into your breath and body before you begin, and when you are ready, bring your mother and father in front of you or into your mind's eye. To begin with, notice the response within your breath and body. When you feel ready try working with the following phrases:

I accept my life as it comes from you.

Your relationship is between you both.

My place exists outside of it.

I leave your relationship with you.

My place exists outside of it.

I am not the safety in your relationship.

I am not responsible for your relationship.

My place exists outside of it.

It is essential that these phrases feel clear and true. If they do not, or if you feel yourself drawn to either or both parents, then it's imperative to revisit the simple mother and father connection exercises and gently work to acknowledge and separate.

Doing this work now will make it significantly easier to step further into the field of influence around you. If you don't, then some of your hard work will be flowing to support your entanglements rather than release them.

When your mother is holding a broken promise for her father

Sharon's experience of unknowingly holding a promise from the unfinished stories within the historical narrative of the field of influence is a common one. It is transformative to explore the threads around broken promises. From our walk through the paternal field we know the significance of an inherited parental relationship promise. Viewing the inherited promise through the lens of the maternal line allows us to explore the broken promises from the perspective of the unseen women in the field, and there tends to be quite a lot of them. This is important work to do, because if there is a dominance of broken promises and unacknowledged women within your field of influence, then the dominant maternal line for you can come from the *unseen women* rather than your biological maternal line. Take a moment and think about that.

> If your field of influence is littered with broken promises that you have a propensity to be drawn into, then your instinctive loyalty will be to the unseen women in the field rather than to your mother and her line. This is a big deal.

This essentially means that your unconscious loyalty and belonging can be with the women who have been displaced in your historical field of influence and their unfinished stories will be woven into your belonging and your heart.

To explore if this is happening within you, we need to look at the connection between your mother and her father, your maternal grandfather.

Begin again, by taking time to ground within your physical body as much as possible and notice the pattern of your breathing and any tension present within your body.

Our intentional question is:

Where are the unseen women when I connect with my mother?

When you are ready, bring your mother and your maternal grandfather into your mind's eye and breathe into the connection with them, noting how you respond to each:

Is it possible to stay grounded and present when you bring them both in?

Can you feel them within your space or outside your space?

If you have a visual or emotional connection, is one aspect clearer than the other?

Is your mother closer to you or to your grandfather?

Then when you are ready, bring in a space for broken promises associated with your maternal grandfather, taking some time to note any changes in your energy or breath.

What happens in your body?

Where does your focus go?

Can you feel the broken promises within your body or outside your body?

Gently try saying the following phrase to the broken promise space:

I didn't know you were there, but I can feel you now.

Does that statement feel true?

The space for the broken promise will hold the former partner(s) connected to the promise. We are talking to the unseen women here. The broken promise space is a gateway to them.

When you are ready, try saying the following phrases to your mother:

You are not responsible for this broken promise.

I see you taking a place within it.

I see you holding it in your marriage promise.

I am not responsible for this broken promise.

I don't accept it; I exist outside of it.

There is safety for me outside of it.

There is safety in letting it go.

I am choosing to let it go.

Take a little time here to sit with your breath and your heartbeat. How do you feel? What memories or emotions are coming up for you? What parts of your life are popping into your thoughts right now? Do you need to work through the constellation again?

Exploring your direct maternal line and the lineage of the unseen women

There can be a lot of resistance to releasing an entangled broken promise, both internally and externally. The weight of the anger and grief of the unseen women can seem intractable. Where we have an unconscious loyalty to the unseen women instead of to our known maternal line, then there is a need for us to tread carefully through the created constellation space.

Following on from our created constellation with you, your mother, and your grandfather, alongside the place for a broken promise, the details of the promise itself need further exploration. Giving place to and witnessing all aspects of the broken promise allows for much needed movement within the field of influence.

The broken promise is literally a vessel of unfulfilled dreams, hopes that were lost or betrayed, and often deep anger and the grief of voices that have been silenced or unheard. The sense of loss and grief is intensely held.

In previous generations, the cost of being an unseen woman, to find oneself on the receiving end of a broken promise, or to be a hidden or secret love, would most often result in a loss of place and safety. Being cast out of the family or community was likely. From this exclusion, a silent continuation of hidden displacement can exist and flow through the influencing historical narrative. Any exploration of the details of entanglements around broken promises and the presence of unseen women can become emotive.

It is helpful to begin a created constellation with land as an animating space for your belonging, as well as bringing in land to support the known maternal lineage and the unseen women. It all comes down to belonging. And everyone belongs. Everyone.

Begin as always with some gentle grounding and breathwork and then, when you are ready, bring in a representation of land for yourself. Take time at this point to breathe into your body and feel the land under your feet, noticing what land it is and how easy it is for you to take your place upon it.

Then when you feel comfortable bring into your mind's eye a representation for your mother and her line, and a space for the unseen women, ensuring that there is a representation of land for each aspect. This may feel uncomfortable to set up within your mind's eye and if you feel it is too difficult to navigate internally then set up a physical constellation with mats, sheets of paper, or markers.

Gently work with the following phrases *out loud* to your mother, the maternal line, and the unseen women, in turn:

I see you.

I see your place.

Parts of me are like you.

Some of my choices are like your choices.

Then to all simultaneously:

My choices are my own.

My loyalties are my own.

I don't need to choose between you.

You each have a place and I have a place.

My place exists outside of this/you.

You don't belong with the forbidden women.

You don't belong with the excluded women.

You don't belong with the silent women.

You don't belong with the unseen women.

I don't belong with the forbidden women.

I don't belong with the excluded women.

I don't belong with the silent women.

I don't belong with the unseen women.

My place is just for me.

This is an important movement. Take time to ensure that you can work through the above phrases and still stay present within your body and place upon the land. Say it out loud with your eyes closed and then again with your eyes open. Notice how you are saying it—is it from your heart? Or are you pushing the connection away with the phrases? Try to gently connect with your heart and repeat the phrases, allowing yourself to fully feel them.

When it feels stable—and you may need to repeat the process more than once—then it is time to look at what flows forward from you.

> This is about your own future, your dreams,
> and your children, born and unborn.

This forward-facing part of the field of influence is yours, and yet with entanglements to the unseen women and the inherited broken promises, sacrifice of the forward-facing aspects of ourselves is common. When you feel ready, and it may take a few attempts rather than immediately, bring in spaces for your children born and unborn, or your dreams. Dreams and children, born and unborn, all occupy the same space that flows forward from us.

Gently work with the following phrases out loud to each represented aspect of mother and unseen women in turn:

I am a mother/parent/dreamer now too.

These are my children/dreams.

The line has survived.

Their place is not forbidden.

To your children or dreams:

This is part of who you are.

This is part of where you come from.

Your place(s) exists outside of it.

You don't belong with the forbidden.

You don't belong with the excluded.

You don't belong with the silent.

You don't belong with the unseen.

It's okay if we are different.

Within this movement your focus should be on maintaining your sense of place and grounded belonging when facing forward, and for the phrases to feel clear and true.

If this is not the case, then it indicates a deeper entanglement and the need to explore a little further. Take a little time to note the phrases or places where things feel sticky for you before moving on. There is no place for judgement here; you are bravely choosing to see the trauma that has been unseen. That in itself begins healing.

Witnessing yourself within your emotional belonging

It is important to manage your expectations of the experiences of this work. Some individuals find the process subtle and gentle and will strive to 'get it right'. Others become lost in the field of emotions and can have strong physical or emotional responses to created constellations.

> You must meet yourself at the place you are,
> and be with yourself there.

You must meet yourself at whatever place you are in, and be with yourself there—with how you are experiencing each moment, rather than how you would like it to be or feel. Don't underestimate the deep power of witnessing yourself and your truth. It can change your emotional belonging.

Witnessing yourself in connection with your mother

Let's check back in with the connection to your mother now that you have worked your way through part of the maternal line and field.

Take some deep breaths into your body. Notice how your breathing feels, if it feels deep or shallow. Scan down your energy slowly, from the top of your head down to your toes, how does the energy in your body feel? Are you feeling grounded or detached?

Close your eyes and think of your mother. In your mind's eye, bring her in and see her standing before you.

Feel your connection to her. Breathe in that moment. How does it feel for you?

Is there a difference to your breath? To the energy or tension within your body? Are you feeling or seeing the connection to her? If you are seeing the connection, is it blurry or is it clear?

Are you seeing her at the age she is now or are you seeing her at another time?

What comes into your mind as you look at your mother?

What emotions, if any, are you feeling?

Bring in to your mind's eye something to represent the fates or entanglements that she carries. If you are struggling to visualise something, then simply see or feel a space beside her for those fates.

How do you feel when you bring that space in and shift your focus there? Does your breathing pattern stay the same? Does your energy stay with you in your body or do you feel heavy? Or detached?

Is it easier to focus on your mother or the space for the fates that she carries? Which is clearer or easier to feel?

What happens when you bring in her mother behind her?

The point to aim for is to be able to comfortably say:

You are my mother and I am your son/daughter/child.

I accept you as my mother.

I accept I am your son/daughter/child.

I accept the parts of my life that come from you.

These simple phrases can be incredibly difficult and challenging.

Depending on your response, you may wish to bring in other family members or animators from the exercises in this chapter, such as the unseen, or promises or secrets. It is important to work through the process slowly and gently whilst observing and witnessing your physical and non-physical responses. The subtlety of the field and your response to it are all part of the constellation process. You are gathering information and knowledge about yourself and your connection to your belonging. And in that lies power.

Sharing the witnessing

It can be easier to explore this in a paired constellation. A particularly helpful exercise is to set up a constellation where you represent your mother and another person represents you as a child. You can try this with a friend; someone you trust and feel comfortable with.

Try standing about a metre apart, facing one another in the first instance, and simply look in to each other's eyes or at the very least facing one another. What unravels from that point on depends very much on the entanglements of you and your family.

Changes of interest to note down:

Inability to maintain eye contact—This shows us that it isn't safe to be seen within the connection. The line is reversed, or the loyalty is with the unseen.

Inability to look in direction of child/mother—Again, this shows us that it isn't safe to be seen within the connection. The line is reversed, or the loyalty is with the unseen.

Inability of either party to remain standing—This shows us that the loyalty is with the dead and the deep historical narrative.

One or other of you looking fixedly at the floor or distant point beyond the other—Again, this shows us that the loyalty is with the dead and the deep historical narrative.

Emotional releases—This shows there is a shift in the field of influence, a response to being seen and witnessed.

After a few minutes the child representative says *yes* to the mother representative.

The reason we work from the child's perspective when you are representing your own mother is to allow you to feel her response, rather than to simply rely on observation or a preconceived notion that you maybe already hold.

There can be anger from children towards their mother when they feel that they are not being seen or are being given away by the mother to her mother or ancestors.

In this paired exercise where you represent your own mother, the experience is invaluable in allowing you to feel the entanglement from a different perspective *outside of yourself*.

The reversal of a line can be seen in the physical constellation when the mother cannot see the child and either looks to the floor or turns away from the child. It can be very painful for the child to observe this within the constellation setting and using the above exercise to experience it from your mother's perspective can gently shift the awareness from a sense of loss into a sense of understanding. When there is an understanding of the entanglements at play, and how strong a hold they can have, then change can follow. When we experience first-hand the weight of the dead, or the grief, or the pain, it begins to release from within our hearts. A little piece of ourselves can be claimed back. Always we are looking for the invisible parts of the influences—what isn't being seen, acknowledged, or heard.

Is it safe to be a mother?

Eva participated in a group constellation workshop in Scotland. Her primary intention for attending the general family constellation class was a difficult relationship with her own mother. She found it challenging to even acknowledge the place of her mother when describing her situation to the group. The relationship with her mother had been physically and emotionally abusive. As she attempted to speak her story, I observed the sense of detachment that overcame her when she tried to talk about her family of origin. I asked her to describe her relationship situation. As she described her relationship with her husband, she became more relaxed and clearly was able to ground her energy in her body as well as steady her breathing. This shifted again when I asked her if they had any children. It emerged that Eva had been pregnant but unfortunately the pregnancy had been ectopic and the pregnancy had to be terminated. In the course of the surgery, a fallopian tube also had to be removed. Her husband still wanted to try for another baby however Eva believed that this was no longer possible. As she spoke, I felt that the three aspects of the relationship with her mother, the relationship with her husband, and the loss of their child, had become entangled.

I set up the initial constellation with Eva, her husband, their marriage promise, the child from the ectopic pregnancy, and her mother.

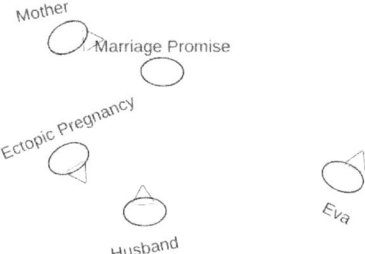

Image 13—Eva excluded from her place as a wife and mother

The marriage promise representative immediately moved to stand beside Eva's mother, Eva withdrew from her husband and the child, and her husband was focused on the child and Eva's mother. This is not ideal, as it shows us that Eva's mother has a place within the marriage promise, and that the connection between Eva and her husband was hampered by this. It was clear there were inherited promise entanglements at play.

I then brought in representatives for *guilt* and *abuse* as animating spaces to discern their effect within the constellation field.

This shifted the constellation considerably and Eva stepped back into the field moving towards abuse and guilt. The representatives for abuse and guilt moved towards the child and the child was drawn to them. This is a reversed maternal line with the child waiting to be seen by her mother.

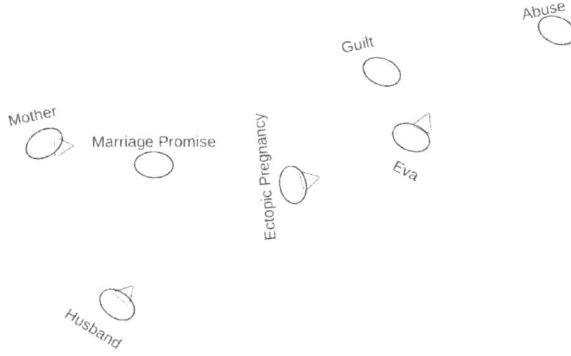

Image 14—Eva acknowledging the weight of the guilt

This was very distressing for Eva. The mother however was buoyed by the inclusions and began to behave erratically, moving around the constellation area. I included an additional representative for *secrets* alongside the mother which calmed the energy down. I started to work with the relationship between Eva and her mother:

You are my mother and I am your daughter.

Part of my life comes from you.

I accept that part of my life comes from you.

But your choices are not my choices.

Your beliefs are not my beliefs.

Your secrets are not my secrets.

I am not you.

This was very difficult for Eva to say and she was very resistant to the phrases. However, the impact on her child and her husband was liberating. They were able to move away from the representatives for abuse and guilt that had been encircling them and were standing closely looking at Eva. Eva was not yet able to turn to look at them.

I asked Eva to try saying:

I am a mother now too.

And at this point Eva's grief spilled from her. She hadn't allowed herself to acknowledge the pregnancy or to accept her place as a mother. She dropped to her knees within the constellation after saying the words. This dropping down into a kneeling position is an indication of returning to an unacknowledged trauma from childhood. *Abuse* and *guilt* moved closer to her as she held memories from her childhood. I asked her to say:

I have been looking at myself through you.

I have been looking at myself through your abuse.

I have been looking at myself through secrets.

I blamed myself for you.

I am a mother now too.

I haven't become you in motherhood.

I haven't abused my child.

I feel you taking my place in my marriage.

I feel you taking my place in my motherhood.

I don't agree.

I am taking back the parts of me you have.

I am giving back the parts of you I have been carrying.

I then asked Eva to repeat the previous phrases:

You are my mother and I am your daughter.

Part of my life comes from you.

I accept that part of my life comes from you.

But your choices are not my choices.

Your beliefs are not my beliefs.

Your secrets are not my secrets.

I am not you.

This piece of work opened up the constellation for Eva and the marriage promise began to move back towards her and her husband.

I then asked Eva to look at abuse and guilt and say:

I see you.

I see your place.

I won't look at my place through you anymore.

I am more than you.

I let you go.

At this point Eva was able to turn around and look at her husband but she was still finding it difficult to look at her child. I gently walked her towards the representative for her child and asked her to say:

Even though it is hard I can see you.

I am your mother and you are my child.

I accept you.

Part of me went with you.

Not all of me survived.

I have been looking at you through abuse.

I have been looking at you through guilt.

But you are more than that.

I accept you as my child and you can have me as your mother.

It is safe for me to be your mother.

This took a long time to work through. There was a lot of fear in this for Eva particularly around her acknowledgment of herself as a mother, but with each word she became stronger and was able to move closer to her child, finally embracing the child. I included a safe representative from Eva's ancestral maternal line which also helped support the movement.

I then included a representative for future children for Eva and her husband. She could see the place for future children when she and her husband stood together with their marriage promise, with the support from the ancestral maternal line, and with their lost child beside them.

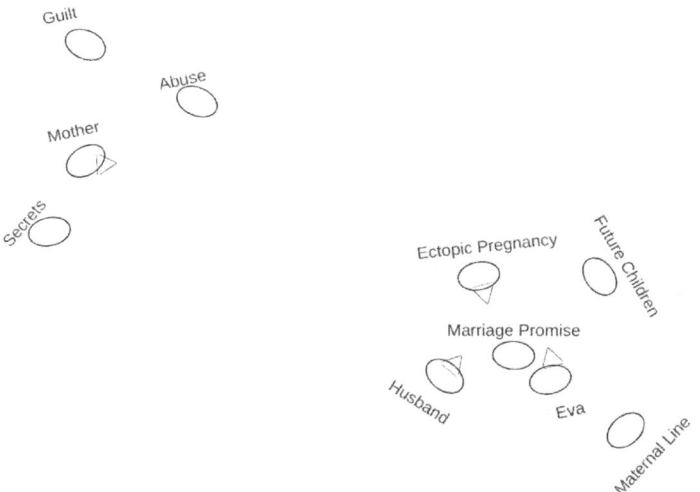

Image 15—Eva supported and seen in her place

I asked Eva to firstly say to her child:

You will always have a place in my heart and in our hearts.

You haven't been forgotten.

It is safe for me to be a mother.

It is safe for me to have other children.

Your death wasn't a punishment of me or you.

It is safe for there to be other children.

You will always be my first child.

I then asked her to turn to her ancestor and say:

I accept my place as a free mother.

I accept the parts of me that come from you.

I have been looking at myself through my mother.

But her mothering is not my mothering.

There is no place for abuse in my mothering.

I am making a different choice.

At this point the constellation shifted, and Eva, her husband, their child, and yet to be born children, were able to embrace. I stopped the constellation at this point and spoke with Eva. I suggested that she continue to work with some of the phrases to support the forward movement of accepting that there can be safety for her in being a mother. A year later I was delighted to meet their baby boy. This was a highly complex constellation and yet a deeply healing one. It was only possible to unravel by being present with the subtle movements of the field both within and external to Eva. *The details and slow movements are not only significant, they are essential to this work.* The entangled inheritance from Eva's mother had bled into the relationship with her husband, and into her beliefs around the safety of motherhood. This is the depth of the invisible inheritance and the potential for what we are able to transform through the power of our created constellations.

Take some time to read back through Eva's example and the healing movements. Particularly if you have experienced a miscarriage, ectopic pregnancy, or abortion, yourself. Claim your place as a mother or father, perhaps lighting a candle for the missing children and the grieving parents within your own field.

There is deep bravery in doing so and healing the vulnerability within. Allow the phrases to speak to your soul, say them aloud from your heart and feel the field around you respond.

Acceptance

Our connection with our mother and the mother's line can be the starting point for the judgements, opinions, and beliefs that we have about the world and ourselves. It is also the storage place for our will and willpower.

An acceptance of life as it flows down to us essentially equates to an acceptance of our place. If there is a rejection of this then the sense of place is weakened and can lead to patterns of exclusion. When patterns of exclusion exist then we are limited, with aspects of ourselves being unseen or unheard. When we are unseen or not heard—for example if our voice feels silenced—then those who are able to see or hear us often carry a similar fate or entanglement within their own dynamics. Or where someone else has perpetrated a fate that is in resonance with our invisible entanglements and is seeking to unconsciously repeat that same pattern, then they too will be drawn to those unseen elements within us. This does not bode well.

When we connect with our mother, the comfortable point that we aim to reach is to be able to *see her as she really is,* to see and acknowledge what she carries in terms of *her* place within the family, and her connection to our father, and to be able to accept our life from both her and him.

If it is difficult to see or physically experience the connection to your mother, or perhaps the image is blurry or not fully formed, then that is an indication that your mother is caught up in an entanglement or family dynamic that pulls her away from not only you but the family system as a whole.

The importance of the simple exercise to connect with your mother cannot be underestimated. It is not a one-time only exercise. It is a useful gauge for observing the connection to and relationship with the whole maternal line and field. Gently working with this over a period of time can transform your sense of emotional belonging in both your inner and outer worlds.

Well done. You have walked through the constellations within your maternal line and field and have released much of your invisible inheritance. Your physical and emotional belonging will have changed.

You are your parent's child, and you are more than their child. You are also not that child anymore. Your place and life exist outside of your parents.

We have established a good and solid base to move forward from and explore your place, and the relationships around it. Take a little time here to read through your notes and think about how you felt when you were in your constellations. Do you notice a pattern in the types of entanglements that came up for you? Or have memories of your relationships with people outside your immediate family been coming up? You are claiming your own place and your own future. This will stir up emotions in your everyday relationships in the family that you have created, as well as in your friendships and working relationships. This is what we will explore next.

4.

Being seen and unseen—finding the missing pieces

We are now going to step into another interesting part of the constellation field and look at your place in relation to your siblings, both born and unborn, as well as known and unknown. It might seem strange to think of the relationship that you have with your siblings, or your feelings about being an only child, being significant for how you communicate with your friends, colleagues, partner, and partner's family in the present, but there is a very direct influence.

You can't choose your family, can you?

The fields of influence swirling around us come firstly from our paternal and maternal lines, which pull us into our close family dynamics and all of the entanglements there. This is our inner world of belonging within our family system.

The sibling field is different. It is the filter through which we interact with our outer world, and that outer world is made up of our friendships and personal and work relationships. It is the part of the field influenced by the relationships that we *choose* to form, and it has some interesting differences and quirks.

If there is a lack of safety in being able to belong in our own inner family field through our parents, then the sibling field can be our gateway to belonging outside of that.

When we are *displaced* within the line and order of our siblings, then we are also closer to the weight of the untold stories of our ancestors, particularly the victim and perpetrator entanglements that can be a strong feature of those stories. The entanglements from those stories then begin to inform our experience of our relationships and whether we are seen, heard, and loved.

When there is a desire to escape from our family of origin or to belong outside of our family, then we can recreate our sense of family belonging in our close personal friendships, intimate relationships, and working relationships. This makes sense, right? We are hard wired for connection and belonging, and when we don't have or feel love in our family, we need to feel and share that love somewhere else. Our friends become more important, and our work can help give us a purpose and strengthen our sense of self. That pride in being seen for a job well done or the warmth of sharing an evening with your best friend—those warm fuzzy feelings all come from sibling field influences. We build and recreate a family to belong to. We find our place outside our family.

It doesn't sound like a bad thing to do, to have friends and a work that you throw yourself into, and on the face of it is isn't, but recreation is exactly what we are doing *if we are entangled*, because when we have a recreated family outside the family of origin, we will also recreate the dynamics of the family of origin that we're escaping from.

This is because we are drawn to and repelled by the field of influence of the individuals around us. Remember the morphic fields and tuning fork examples from chapter one? This is it in action.

We are unconsciously drawn to the familiarity of weighty entanglements within others, because on an unconscious level they represent safety and belonging.

Our recreated family act as representatives for us, and us for them. For example, you may be unknowingly representing your best friend's mother for them and they may be unconsciously representing your grandfather. And this is the tricky part.

If you are representing the absence of someone then you are not fully you, and they, as they represent an absence for you, will not be fully them.

The friendship becomes entangled and weighted with the absence of the past. And this takes us into the dynamics of the seen and unseen, the perceived cost of belonging and the inheritance of work, dreams, place, and promises. That's a lot of stuff to have in your friendship and it will bring you close to one another.

This closeness sounds like a positive thing, and parts of it are; I'm not trying to pour cold water on your precious friendships. What we need to address is the fact that if you are knowingly or unknowingly representing and recreating family and belonging in your close friendships, because of your sibling field, then there is a hidden cost to that. It is transactional—we unconsciously buy our belonging by holding the pain or trauma for the other person or representing whatever is missing for our friend. This transactional aspect of our friendships is related to the concept of the relationship promise that exists in each and every single relationship we have.

This can all work really well for both you and your friend as long as you both stay entangled with the same stuff in the same way. However, if one of you shifts some of your stuff then it starts to get messy.

If, for example, part of the stuff you were unconsciously asking your friend to hold was connected to not being or feeling seen by your mother, and you worked on that stuff and no longer needed your friend to hold it for you, then it shifts the dynamics of the promise between you. It is no longer balanced. This will seriously upset your friend because your friend will experience that as a betrayal; they will be seeing you through the lens of whatever person or stuff you are unknowingly representing for them. All of the pain or anger that they feel about that person or part of their family will be rained down upon you.

Have you ever had an intense friendship like that? Where you meet and feel so connected—a kinship—as if you've known each other for ever? It's easy to hang out with them; everything can be going great for months or even years, but then something changes for one or other of you, and then wham!—it all changes.

The hurt for both of you is amplified because you are unconsciously creating belonging for one another and the shift in the balance of the friendship will feel, on some level, like a loss of belonging or place. Do you recognise this is in any of your friendships or in the behaviour of a friend? Have you watched them cycle through a new best friend every few months? The root of this is a lack of belonging in the family field.

Our close friendships can act as representatives within the family of origin for the known and unknown entanglements, as can our work colleagues. Work colleagues and associates will also represent the missing or unseen aspects; however they tend to be a little messier because they generally represent our sibling relationships directly.

The direct representation can be of either our known and born siblings, or the missing and unknown siblings. If you have a tricky relationship with one or more of your siblings, take a moment to think about your work colleagues just now. Think about the colleagues that you have difficulties with or the ones that get right under your skin. Now compare their behaviour and your response to them to your sibling interactions. Do you see any patterns? Brenda from accounts may just be representing your sister. Or the person who is constantly claiming credit for all your hard work may be representing a missing sibling.

This direct representation of our siblings within our working relationships can trigger aggressive relationships and victim perpetrator dynamics within our workplace and it can be horribly unpleasant.

When you are rooted in the sibling realm rather than the parental, then the minutiae of everyday living and interaction can be amplified.

Hey, that's my place!

One of the most helpful and gentler explorations of place and belonging can come in with the sibling line. *Your place within the order of your siblings can and does influence various aspects of your life.* In terms of the theory of the constellation field, your sibling line is ordered from the eldest, the first conceived, to the youngest, the last conceived.

The **older siblings** can bear the brunt of the outer lying entanglements and dynamics that flow to us through your parents, such as a pull to your parents' previous partners as well as broken promises from your ancestors. The **younger siblings** are influenced more by the immediate parental structure, made up of parents' dreams and work dynamics and the threads that come in around the need to belong and have enough. This can and often does pull in patterns in the ancestral field linked with war losses, conflict, and servitude dynamics.

When you do not hold your appropriate place within your family of origin and within your sibling line, then you are displaced within the line. This means that you are more likely to be pulled to the deeper and heavier entanglements within the field of influence upon you. It makes you more vulnerable to the inherited trauma in the field of influence around you.

This is because there is a need to earn your place. There is an unconscious knowing that things aren't quite right and an inner desire to change that, for it to feel safer and more secure.

An unconscious belief is created that our safety and belonging can be earned through the service of missing siblings around us, to our close family members, or in a greater service to the older ancestral influences. That service can include displacing ourselves in order to give the missing a place, which exacerbates everything, as we are then in the scenario of recreating our entangled family through our friendships. It is exhausting and also why our lack of relationship with our brother, or the inner sibling yearning of an only child, is much more than it might first seem on the surface.

When there are losses of children, whether it is miscarriage, abortion or the death of a child, then the system as a whole is impacted.

The impact of the presence of the soul of a child conceived and lost within weeks is still influential on the other siblings or family members, to a greater or lesser degree, depending on the other entanglements within the family field of influence.

In some families the effect will be minimal if the other siblings are very present and grounded in their own place and the parents see and acknowledge their children—all of their children. If, however, there are complexities present within the relationship dynamics between the parents, then the influence of even such a short life can be significant.

The place where we enter our family of origin sets the tone for our experiences in our formative years.

If our parents have struggled to conceive and we are born after a miscarriage or a number of miscarriages, then the pain and grief connected with the earlier loss doesn't just go away, it will imprint itself on us. If our parents do not acknowledge their pain and grief then we step in to hold that for them, and the pull to the unseen becomes established and normalised for us.

I have been talking about the sibling field around you. Now I want to talk about your actual siblings, known and unknown, the line of siblings that exists from eldest to youngest, and your place in that line.

Your place within your family is interwoven around your connection with and to your siblings. Your place within your family in relation to your sibling line in many ways defines your place in life.

Imagine the effect of holding a place in your sibling line that does not belong to you. Imagine standing in the place of the eldest child, with all the expectation that goes along with it, when you are in fact the second or third child.

Missing siblings can have an impact on the surviving siblings in terms of our emotional communication with our other born siblings, as well as with our parents, and also in our ability to communicate effectively, and succeed in the world outside of the family.

I didn't know you were there

When we think of our siblings, we tend to think only of those that are born and who we share our mother and father with. The idea that other people can belong in our sibling line can be jarring. Time and again I have had clients push back against including known step-siblings and this is a warning bell for me.

When you resist the inclusion of a known sibling, whether that is a step sibling or not, then there is an underlying reason—commonly that it doesn't feel safe, or there is a sense that there isn't enough for everyone.

But only including the born and unborn children will give a limited or skewed perspective. Pregnancies, births and losses, both known and unknown, from previous relationships of your mother and father *do belong* in your sibling line order.

When you have difficulty in relationship patterns, in belonging within relationships, or even with fertility, then the previous partners and any possible pregnancies relating to your father become key.

If you have difficulties in work, creativity, freedom of choice, or in connection with your own children, then your mother's previous partners and any pregnancies become more relevant.

The pregnancies and siblings that connect to your mother will tend to be more readily present within your field because of the fact that all of you will have originated from the same womb, creating a more physically direct connection to the field.

Who are the missing?

Generally speaking, with the term *missing sibling* I am referring to a child that is missing through miscarriage, abortion, still birth, or untimely death. The missing children belong to our family, even if the miscarriage was in the very early stages of pregnancy and the mother herself was unaware. The energetic imprint of the child or children will still be there, and their absence felt by us.

There can also be the influence, under certain circumstances, where the dream or desire to have a child has gone unfulfilled by someone, and the resulting grief, pain, and anger, holds the space of a child within our sibling line. This tends to be linked to an unresolved relationship with our father, where the potential mother hasn't let go of what could have been and sees us, the children who come after, as if we should have been their child.

Types of missing siblings to be aware of and their possible impact on you:

Miscarriage—Influences loss of voice and your place.

Abortion—Influences loss of belonging, victim-perpetrator dynamics, anger and abuse.

Missing twin—This influences your ability to sustain an intimate relationship, as well as your work and career fulfilment.

Missing triplet—This is characterised by aggressive relationship patterns and delineation of victim-perpetrator dynamics between the surviving twins.

Unacknowledged primary/secondary families—Where one or other of your parents has children with another partner that are held as secrets. This is characterised by a pull from you to hold secrets or stand with the unseen. It can also be linked with either the perpetration or creation of secrets.

Early deaths—There will be an association with strong grief and depression, and often a pull to addictive behaviours in relationships or lifestyle choices.

Adoption—This is polarised into either taking the place of someone else, usually in a working dynamic, or self-exclusion of your place.

IVF—Complex patterns combining all of the above entanglements are seen with IVF. The degree of influence is dependent on your parents' ability to acknowledge their own grief and pain.

Death of a dream of a baby—This has an impact on daughters in particular within fertility and relationship patterns. With sons it can create a desire for a string of short term, intense relationships ending with betrayal.

Where is your place?

It is my experience that both born and unborn missing siblings are influential upon the sibling line. The degree to which they are influential can vary greatly, however they still have a place of belonging in the line and have an impact on us, the born siblings.

This is where the exploration of something as seemingly simple as the sibling line becomes a trigger for transformational change and healing for each of us as individuals. The weight of secrecy in any unacknowledged pregnancy is unknowingly carried by us and our other siblings that have an acknowledged place within the line.

Consider the effect it might have if you are born into a place in your family where you are believed and are perceived to be the first born, when in fact your mother has had children or abortions before you, that are perhaps unknown to your father. It is a secret. You are born and take your place holding that secret.

When a pattern of acceptance of secrets and secrecy, and to some extent betrayal, is established at birth then it can become natural to seek out or attract the energy of betrayal in other relationships.

And it continues through you, into your relationships with your partner and your children.

I didn't know

When a parent has had an affair and a child is conceived, the resentment of the betrayal of the relationship promise, as well as the sense of rejection from the conceived child, can be carried by us within the context of our sibling line. This sense of either accepting or denying the place of an illegitimate sibling is an entanglement that can flow into our working and intimate relationships, the ownership and acknowledgement of our work, success, financial reward and security. All of this can be limited and negatively influenced by the unseen entanglements of our sibling line.

The depth of complexity and the potential transformation from within sibling line constellations is often overlooked and misunderstood. It is so much more than filling in the blank spaces in our childhood and within our sibling line. It is the microcosm of belonging within the field of influence.

If we allow it to, it will display the effect of the unseen men, women and children within the field, the cost of broken promises, the reversal of the parental lineages, as well as the inherited relationship promises.

A really common entanglement that I have worked with repeatedly, is the uncovering of an unknown and unseen sibling connected to the former partner, known or unknown, of one of the parents of an individual.

Deborah had asked to work with her family field in a group constellation in the United States. Her primary focus was her relationship with her sister who was emotionally volatile and suffered periods of mental instability. When we talked a little more about her family of origin, she also shared that her older brother had committed suicide and that she had a younger sister who was struggling with addiction issues and was estranged from the family.

The first step in any sibling line constellation is to establish the relationship to, and order of, the known siblings from the shared parents of the individual's mother and father, but also to be mindful of and include any siblings from previous or subsequent relationships.

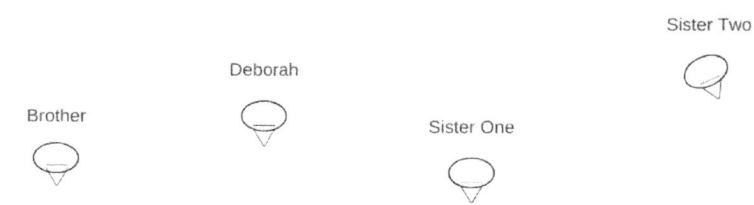

Image 16—Deborah's known sibling line

The initial sibling line was created. In the first instance Deborah set the line up with each of the four siblings, including herself, tightly packed together. This is a sign of a lack of safety and a need to defend against external attack. However, after a few moments the representatives began to drift apart. This movement was very distressing for Deborah. The spaces and gaps that appeared within the sibling line and the associated behaviour and response of each sibling representor was revealing.

Her brother and known younger sister both behaved similarly. They each attempted to step outside the confines of the sibling line and their gaze was cast downwards. When I asked them to describe how they were feeling in the place that they were each representing within Deborah's family field, they were both monosyllabic and weighed down by the emotional trauma in the field.

Deborah became further agitated as she witnessed her siblings succumbing to the weight of the trauma. Her youngest sibling is unseen, not only by Deborah but also by the other two siblings. She could have been in a different room and remained as visible to them. When I asked the representative to describe her experience, she was overwhelmingly angry. She was angry with her siblings for not seeing her, or being aware of her suffering, and she was also unwilling to acknowledge that they were suffering too.

Each individual sibling within the line was trapped in their own experience of pain and suffering; they could each only see themselves, creating a hierarchy of victimhood within the line. Nothing could be seen outside of that internal perspective, aside from Deborah, who was attempting to pull the disparate threads of her sibling line together and push everything else away.

It was clear that there was a historical trauma influencing and affecting the siblings within the constellation. My initial observation was of the weight of the unseen within the field, and the impact in particular on the eldest sibling, Deborah's brother. He was literally unable to stand in his place. At this point I included a representative for a missing sibling who could have been born before him. This meant that he would not have the weight and the cost of being the first in the line when it clearly wasn't his place. His response was immediate. He was able to step forward into the line, however the pull downwards and the emotional weight were still very obviously present within him.

The representative for the missing and unacknowledged sibling was agitated and simultaneously drawn towards and repelled away from the presence of the brother. This response is an indication that the siblings within Deborah's line are influenced by the emotional entanglements belonging to their parents.

Including a representative for the mother of the unseen sibling polarised the response of the line. Deborah's own personal response was very strong.

She became antagonistic towards the unseen mother and very territorial about her place within the line. It was clear that the mother of the unseen sibling was not Deborah's biological mother. Deborah only wanted to acknowledge the place of her known born siblings. I brought in representatives for her mother and father, the relationship promise between the parents, and the broken promises between her father and his former love.

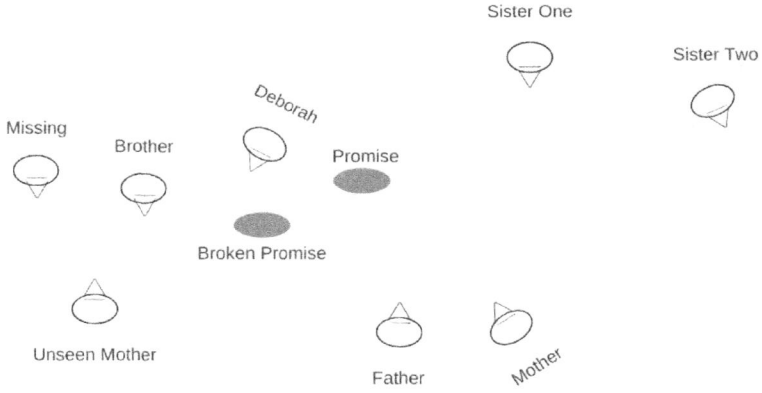

Image 17—Deborah connecting with the unseen former love and missing sibling

With each new represented space, the intensity and aggressiveness within the line dissipated. The weight and the cost of the promises and broken promises were being held by the siblings. Adding places for the previously unseen aspects, such as the former love, the relationship promises, and the broken promises, began the process of liberating siblings from the field of influence of the unseen, excluded, and broken promises. It moved the weight of the previously unacknowledged trauma from within the line to outside the line, and the siblings who were holding it became free.

Within this constellation there were entanglements around the weight, cost, and debt of the broken relationship promises, however there was a further, more sinister influence. For Deborah's sister and brother, along with the missing siblings, there was an overwhelming and all-consuming pull to the dead. This was compounded with Deborah's own aggressive behaviours, and the polarisation of anger and numbness within the line hints at deeply rooted and unacknowledged entanglements, with violent trauma and perpetration of place within the field of influence of Deborah's ancestors. Uncovering and healing the inherited relationship promises would have a strong and positive impact on Deborah's emotional belonging and relationships, however the root of her anger and aggressive behaviour lies outside of that. It is rooted within the ancestral inheritance of trauma.

The responses of the women both within the sibling line and the generation before were very telling. There was a tremendous amount of pain in the interaction between the father's former partner and her child, and then subsequently between her and Deborah. A snapshot of the significant movements is illustrated.

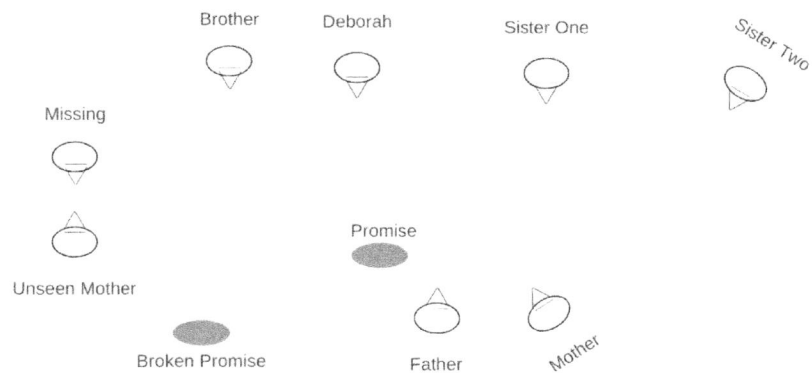

Image 18—Deborah and the inheritance of promises

You can see from the illustration that both the broken relationship promise and the marriage relationship promise moved towards Deborah.

This was not an easy movement and the representatives for each of the animating promise spaces were dominating and aggressive.

In this complex constellation, the most effective place to begin working with the language of the entanglements is the dynamic between the known seen and born siblings—in particular Deborah—and the unseen former love of her father. This is because the weight of the broken promise between the former love and Deborah's father is animating the betrayals within the victim-perpetrator aspects of the paternal line and field, as well as creating an inherited relationship promise. This blocks the relationship between Deborah, her siblings, and her mother.

It was very difficult for Deborah to acknowledge the unseen woman, and also for the unseen woman to look directly at her. The connection softened when I asked her to look at and connect with the unborn sibling conceived by the woman and her father. This is the strength of the sibling line and field work.

> Even in the most polarised of lines and fields, there is an unconscious awareness of the truth of acknowledging the place of another, and that doing so does not detract from our own place.

Creating a space for Deborah to look and experience the truth of her previously unknown sibling's existence allowed her to let go of some of the unconscious entanglements she had been carrying that were about the need to perpetrate through anger in order to have a place and be safe. Within this movement there was a connection between the formerly unseen lover and Deborah.

I didn't know you were there, but I see you now.

I am beginning to see your pain.

I am beginning to feel your pain.

At this point the connection between the two softened and they truly saw one another. The father, who had been silent up until this point, slowly began to move towards his daughter and his former love.

Papa, I have been carrying this for you.

I have been carrying the guilt for you.

I have been carrying her pain for you.

I can't do it anymore.

It is killing me.

At this point the father and former love embrace silently for a long time. The woman broke the embrace spontaneously saying *I let you go* and stepped back from the father whilst still maintaining contact with her unborn child. The focus of the entire sibling line shifted.

The entire line relaxed and each was able to step more fully into their own place of belonging without the need to perpetrate or sacrifice.

For Deborah, in the post constellation space, the biggest and most significant shift for her was letting go of the weight of the responsibility for her siblings and their safety. She no longer felt the need to fight in order to keep them and herself safe. She began to look beyond the survival mode she had been living in, and her external field relationships blossomed as a result.

How did you feel reading through Deborah's constellation? Was it comfortable to witness the unseen and missing siblings along with the unacknowledged partners? Can you imagine what might be there, waiting, within your own sibling line?

Choosing to see

We will now explore your belonging and place by stepping into your own sibling line. Before you step into this particular constellation, take time to explore how you see yourself in relation to your siblings.

How is the communication and connection between you and your different siblings experienced? Is there any animosity or breaks in contact or communication between you and your siblings?

The sibling line can become more complex with children from previous or subsequent relationships for either or both of your parents. It can be tempting to disregard any influence from step-siblings, however in my opinion this is a big mistake. The reluctance to acknowledge the place of siblings who we share one parent with taps into a deeper resentment that very easily flows into our intimate relationship choices in a limiting and destructive way.

If you are particularly resistant to including known step-siblings into your sibling line, then try to set up the constellation without your step-siblings and allow yourself to feel the difference before and after their inclusion. What you will find is that the acknowledgement of another person's place does not cost you your own place. It does not cost anything. Each and every single person has an equal right to belong, to be seen and to be heard. The simple movement from the heart of seeing and acknowledging someone else's place is sacred, and it is utterly free.

In your mind's eye, place yourself within your sibling line of known living siblings, starting with the eldest on your right-hand side, through to the youngest on your left-hand side, or ending with yourself if you are the known youngest.

Work with your breath as you do this, remembering to take slow deep breaths as you work your way through the line and feel your connection to each sibling in turn. For example, if you are the third of four children you will have your two older siblings next to you on your right-hand side and the youngest next to you on your left. As you sense your place amongst them, work through the following questions:

Do you feel balanced on both sides of your body?

Do you feel lighter or heavier on one side compared to the other?

Can you feel your feet; do you feel grounded and within your body?

Do you feel comfortable in this, your natural state?

If you know of any missing siblings through your family history or previous therapeutic work, then add them in to the sibling line at this stage. So, if you know that your mother had a miscarriage before you, or if she shared any stories of miscarriages or abortions from previous relationships, you can place them at the point in time they occurred within your sibling line.

If you feel lighter or heavier on one side, or unbalanced, then it is often a sign of missing and unacknowledged siblings within the line. I have noticed that it is often the case that if there is a particularly difficult relationship with a sibling or siblings then there is a hidden dynamic of a missing sibling at play.

Connect with your sibling line through your mind's eye or through sensing and feeling your way along it by noticing your physical and emotional response. Begin to add in a missing sibling into the line in the places that feel blank, numb, or uncomfortable for you. As you do so say to them:

I didn't know you were there.

I can see you now.

We each belong here.

You have a place within my heart.

You have a place and I have a place.

Check in again with how you feel physically and emotionally. Keep working your way down the sibling line adding in any missing siblings until you feel that it has come to a point of balance. Take your time— you are doing powerful soul work.

When you feel you have reached that point of balance and you feel at peace within it, then it is time to acknowledge and honour each of your siblings in turn and to also affirm your own place in the line.

You can do this in your mind's eye or through lighting candles to honour each sibling. (You will need a small candle or tea-light for each sibling.)

Start with the first child saying:

You are the first and I am the (your place) and light the candle for them.

Then:

You are the second and I am the (your place) lighting a candle for them too and so on down the line. When you are lighting the candle for yourself say aloud *I am the (your place) and I take my place.*

You can repeat this acknowledgement exercise whenever you feel the need to. It is very supportive during times of transition because not only does it soothe our own sense of place, it soothes the field of influence around us.

For only children, or individuals who have been adopted

When you are unsure if there are any missing siblings, or if you have been adopted, or if there is uncertainty over whether or not any other siblings exist, then the focus when working your way through the potential sibling line is very much on how you feel and react throughout the process.

As you work through the initial steps to calibrate your internal reactions and responses, take time to notice how you feel on each side of your body, add in a sibling where you feel there is a gap or a space. Gently pay attention to how you respond emotionally and physically until you feel grounded, at peace, and fully balanced within your place.

Reconnecting with who you are

Once you have found and accepted your place within your sibling line it is interesting to notice how you feel reconnecting with your mother and father and the maternal and paternal lines beyond them.

Connecting with the parents and the ancestral lines is often easier and more comfortable when you are secure and grounded within your own place in the sibling line.

I do my work in your honour.

I take my place in honour of you.

I accept love in my life in honour of you.

I bear witness to your dreams as I follow my own.

Abortion

To say that the impact of abortion on the constellation field is significant would be an understatement. There is so much to consider aside from the obvious physical and emotional trauma on those knowingly and unknowingly involved.

From the effects I have observed within constellation it appears that when a child is aborted the relationship between the father and mother of the child will often end or irrevocably change. The siblings before and after the abortion are also affected, and *if the mother in particular does not see the aborted child, the other siblings attempt to do this for her* in an effort to bring peace to the family field and safety to their own place.

Part of the mother also goes with the aborted child—ie. part of her dies too—and connection with any subsequent children is hampered by this fracturing of her soul. It affects her ability to see the rest of her family and will often also have a terminating effect on aspects of her creativity.

In order to restore the balance to the family system, the aborted child must be seen by both the mother and father and given their own place. This is difficult to do.

It is very common for the born siblings to see the child instead of the mother and father. Seeing the aborted child can be a healing movement but only from the place of one sibling acknowledging and honouring another.

> If you are seeing and acknowledging your aborted sibling then that is a significant and deeply healing thing to do, but if you are seeing them on behalf of your mother or father then that is not good for anyone—it is an entanglement.

The loss of children through miscarriage at any stage also draws part of the parent (the mother in particular) towards death and the unacknowledged dead within the untold ancestral stories in the field. In turn, the surviving children—you—make some attempt to redress this for her.

There are distinctive characteristic markers of the presence of abortion within the sibling line. The most obvious is the experience of the lack of safety for the born siblings who are conceived directly after the aborted sibling. The womb itself doesn't feel safe and the trauma of the former pregnancy can be inherited.

Louise participated in a group constellation in Britain. Her intention for attending the workshop was to explore the crippling anxiety and fear that she experienced in her working life and personal relationships. She felt most safe in the background when, in her words, she was able to 'wear her cloak of anonymity.' However, this desire to remain safely anonymous was at direct odds with her need to be seen in her personal relationships and friendships and to be recognised for her hard work and success in her career. She described the experience as being pulled in multiple directions at the same time with a strong need to be seen, heard, and valued, which was simultaneously underlined with a root fear of being seen and heard. She talked about repeating patterns of betrayal and emotional abuse in both her working and personal life. I asked her to describe her version of her relationship with the family that she grew up with and she described difficulty in the emotional connection with her mother in particular. She had grown up with two siblings, an older brother and a younger sister. She found it difficult to connect with her older brother and felt unseen by him and threatened by his displays of anger towards her and her younger sister. She felt very protective of her younger sister although did not experience a reciprocal sense of care and love in return. She described a positive connection with her father though again the connection with him felt weighted and burdened. From her description, they connected when the two of them were alone and there were no other family members present, but the connection seemed to disappear and she became unseen when any of her siblings, mother, or external family members, were present.

I decided to explore the presence of missing siblings within her sibling line. I made this decision because of her description of the repeating patterns in her work and personal relationships, in combination with the dynamic between her and her family of origin.

If a pattern of experience is replicated time and time again within the external field influence of work, friendship or relationships, then the original root entanglement is most likely to be found within the field of influence of the family of origin, rather than within an unacknowledged or still active broken relationship promise.

Her experience of her place and voice as unseen and unheard also points us towards exploring the sibling line which is clearly replicating within her sibling field relationships. I asked Louise if she knew of any miscarriages or abortions within her sibling line but she could not remember and became quite emotionally overwhelmed at this point. I asked her to choose representatives from the group for her older brother and younger sister and we began to gently work with the sibling line constellation.

Image 19—Louise's known sibling line with the influence of the missing

Louise placed her brother and sister directly next to her, standing shoulder to shoulder with her, however it was impossible for the three of them to remain in close proximity. Each of them was drawn downwards and it became physically difficult for them to remain standing upright. Their gazes were fixed on the floor and their shoulders were hunched forward. The longer they stood within the created constellation space the more pronounced the pull downwards became.

As I have previously mentioned, this physical response within the created constellation space of a pull downwards is an indication of an unconscious loyalty to the unacknowledged dead.

The elder brother moved away from his two sisters and there was a visible relaxation within his body and an exhalation of his breath as he did so. This is an indication of him excluding himself and his sisters from the belonging within the sibling line. In contrast, the weight of the entanglement upon Louise and her younger sister became heavier. The younger sister slowly moved to hide behind Louise and again there was a physical relaxation within her as she withdrew from her place of belonging, not to the same extent as the brother but there was more strength in her stance. In contrast Louise's legs began to buckle and the pull downwards became even more pronounced. This is a visual illustration of the cost of Louise's belonging within the sibling line as she holds the weight of the unacknowledged entanglements within herself, her body, and her place.

From these initial movements within the constellation it was immediately obvious that there were missing siblings within the line that were carrying, or entangled with, unacknowledged trauma. I placed a representative into the line in between the brother and Louise within the space that had been created with her brother's movement away and Louise's physical submission to the heaviness within the field. The representative took a moment to centre themselves within the sibling line and almost immediately began to physically shake and tremble. Neither the brother nor the younger sister could or would look towards or acknowledge the missing sibling; Louise unconsciously mimicked the shaking and trembling of her sibling, however she could not turn to look. When I asked her to acknowledge the representative for the missing sibling by saying *I didn't know you were there. I can see you. I can see your place,* she began to weep.

Both Louise and the missing sibling representative were physically shaking but Louise would not look at the sibling; instead she focused on me. I asked Louise again to say the phrases *I didn't know you were there. I can see you. I can see your place* and to try to look at the sibling. At this point she spontaneously said *I did know. I did know you were there. It wasn't safe to look. It isn't safe to look.*

It was very clear from the dynamics present and the fear response for both the missing sibling and Louise that the missing sibling had been aborted and there was a significant amount of unacknowledged trauma around the conception and abortion, as well as entangled persecution elements within the greater field of influence historically. In order to move this from the children within the line I asked Louise to say *I didn't kill you.* The speaking of this phrase transformed the energy within the created constellation space. Louise broke down, not with the weight of the entanglement but rather from the release of the unconscious trauma that she had been holding. Her missing sibling dropped beside her and her elder brother and younger sister began to turn to look although they did not move back into their place within the line. Louise could now say *I can see you. I can see your place,* which softened the energy within the line a little more however there was still a rigidity to the positioning of the born siblings, and Louise and the missing sibling remained on the floor. The constellation unfolded further with the inclusion of the mother and father of the born siblings.

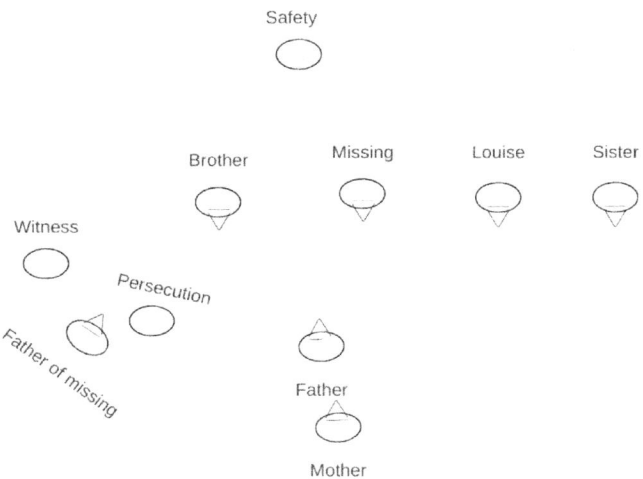

Image 20—Louise and the cost of the missing sibling

However, the father was fixated on Louise and could not see any of the other siblings. It was clear from his stance that he could not or would not acknowledge the missing sibling. He was holding tightly on to the mother's hand in an effort to stop her turning away from the children within the line. The mother's gaze was fixed to the floor and she was not fully present within the created constellation space. She continued to try to turn around and would then attempt to hesitantly step forward towards Louise and then be repelled back. It was clear that she was drawn to heavy traumatic entanglements both within her own generation and the previous generations of her line and was carrying a weight of guilt around that. When I asked the father if he could see the missing child he became very agitated. I decided to place a representative for a different father of the missing child and also placed an animating representative for *persecution* within the field.

The father of the missing child and the persecution space immediately recognised one another and gravitated towards one another. There was a strong response to this within the constellation. The father stepped in front of the mother to protect her and the children within the line stepped further outside their places. I added further animating spaces for *safety* and *witness*. In order to move the entanglements that Louise and the siblings were unconsciously carrying, I asked Louise to say to her missing and clearly aborted sibling:

Your life is innocent.

My life is innocent.

This wasn't your fault.

This wasn't my fault.

Louise's mother was then able to face and address the persecution space supported by *witness* and *safety*:

You can't have my children.

You can't have any more from me.

This is over.

The victims aren't forever bound to be victims.

The perpetrators aren't forever bound to be perpetrators.

At this point the father of the aborted sibling broke down and dropped to his knees. Persecution and witness went to stand with him. There are several key and complex entanglements that we can discern from the unfolding of this constellation.

Firstly, it is likely that the missing sibling that was connected to the dominant loyalty entanglement from Louise's perspective was not conceived from Louise's biological father. Secondly, it is also likely that the conception occurred as a result of rape or sexual violence. Thirdly, the violence of the rape remained unseen and a secret and became entangled from the mother's perspective (and therefore also from the children's perspective) with persecution dynamics in the historical narrative of the family field, very possibly connected with war or violent trauma.

We can discern this from the father's inability to acknowledge the place of the unseen child, his desire to protect his wife, and the movements of persecution and the missing sibling's father within the constellation. However, we must also remember the focus of the constellation and the intention with which Louise set up the created constellation field—to explore the connection with any missing siblings in her line and their impact on her safety and in turn her ability to be seen and heard.

From what we observed in the constellation it was clear that the missing sibling was aborted and that the weight of persecution around the conception—from both the conception itself and the persecution in the field—was unacknowledged within the mother. In such situations, the safety in the womb for the subsequent conception and pregnancy is overlaid with the loss of place and safety of the former unborn sibling. This informed Louise's relationship not only with her mother but also her elder and younger sibling. It is also important to note how Louise and the missing sibling resonated within the created constellation field. Louise was tied to the sibling's fate and was holding the cost of the trauma with the sibling. She was in essence waiting for the persecution to come back and find her (from both the abortion and the historical trauma) as well as carrying the guilt and shame.

The constellation was complex, and time was spent disentangling aspects of the relationship with the mother and father as well as the guilt within the field. However, for the focus of our exploration here the key point is the impact of unacknowledged abortion within the sibling line and the loss of safety that dominates the subsequent born children.

Post constellation, Louise shared with me that her mother was raped by a family friend. The rape resulted in a pregnancy and the pregnancy was terminated. Louise's mother grew up in London, however her family were originally from Romania and moved to London to escape the second world war. Many of her family members left behind didn't survive. After the constellation, Louise received a phone call out of the blue from her brother and they tentatively began to connect once more. She spent further time disentangling herself from the weight of the broken promises between her parents, along with the acknowledgment of the missing siblings, and her anxiety has dramatically improved.

The sibling field and its outer world connections

The sibling influences animate our personality traits, foibles and everyday interactions with colleagues, friends and lovers. They are the cornerstone for the way in which communication is experienced and projected.

The siblings within our family have individually cast their loyalties to the entanglements present both inside and outside the family system.

Opposing entanglements and different perspectives, such as the victim and perpetrator dynamic, can and do lead to painful interaction in the present generations of siblings and their relationships. Not only that, but the difficulties or absences in the realm of the siblings is rippled out and replicated within the communications in our working relationships, friendships, and to some extent our intimate relationships.

I am not them; you are not them

Lisa had attended a group constellation in London. She had come along with a friend having never heard of constellation before and had found the experience of representing fascinating. She contacted me to arrange a session to explore some difficult experiences she was having in her workplace. She worked in finance and was part of a team of four people that reported to the same manager. She was having problems with one colleague in particular who she felt was continually undermining her place within the team. In team meetings she would talk over Lisa and interrupt her, she would exclude her from emails, withhold critical information, and had gone as far as presenting Lisa's work to their manager as her own. Whenever Lisa tried to talk to her about it privately the colleague would aggressively deny it, but in front of the other colleagues she would appear calm and pleasant pretending that the issue was just in Lisa's imagination. She was at the end of her tether.

I asked Lisa if she had any siblings, and at first she said no, however when we went on to discuss her relationship with her father, she shared that he had been married before and had a daughter, Hannah, with his first wife. Her father had left his first wife when Hannah was two years old. He had been having an affair with Lisa's mother and she had fallen pregnant with Lisa. The relationship didn't last, and he left Lisa's mother when Lisa was also two years old for a different woman. Lisa was very reluctant to think of Hannah as a sibling and even thinking of her as a stepsister was tricky for her. I explained, even though it might seem to be something of a tangent, that I wanted to explore the connection between her and Hannah. I felt it was significant for her current work situation.

When Lisa brought Hannah into her mind's eye she immediately tensed up. She experienced Hannah as being large, dominating, and very angry. Lisa felt herself become small and she physically curled into herself. She couldn't look at Hannah and had to look away. I asked Lisa to say to Hannah:

It is hard to look at you.

But I can see you.

You were before me.

This softened the connection a little and Lisa was able to look at Hannah. I asked her to bring in a space or a visual to represent the broken promise between her father and Hannah's mother. She saw a broken, bleeding heart and Hannah was clutching it in her hands and holding it out to Lisa. Lisa became quite distressed by this and shrunk further into herself. I asked her to say:

I didn't take him from you.

I am not him and I am not my mother.

I am Lisa.

I was just a child in this too.

You are not responsible for their broken promise.

I am not responsible for his broken promises.

You have a place and I have a place.

We each belong.

Our places exist outside of the broken promises.

Our places exist outside of the betrayal.

This eased the tension between them a little more and Lisa's breathing began to relax, however she still felt anger coming towards her from Hannah. I asked her to say:

I can feel part of you has been waiting in your childhood.

Part of me has been waiting there too.

He isn't coming back.

I didn't take him from you.

I didn't get more of him.

He couldn't see me either.

He left us too.

The cost of the broken promises belongs with him.

We have both been holding that.

I am making a different choice.

I am choosing to let it go; you can let it go too.

I accept you as my sister and you can have me as your sister.

There was huge relief in this movement for Lisa. The connection with Hannah was significantly softer and Lisa was able to stand tall instead of shrinking and trying to hide. At this point I asked Lisa to bring the difficult colleague into the constellation. The colleague stood beside Hannah, and Lisa's body and breathing tensed up again. I asked her to say to the colleague:

You have been looking at me through Hannah.

You have been looking at me through her anger.

I have been looking at you through my father's guilt.

Lisa relaxed with this. It was clear that the colleague had been representing Hannah within Lisa's external field and this had been the root of the aggressive behaviour. With external field entanglements when a friend or colleague represents a family entanglement for us, we will always reciprocally be representing an aspect of their family field. I worked the following narrative with Lisa to the colleague:

I feel your family's guilt in this.

I have been holding their guilt within my guilt.

I won't be guilty for them or you.

I am not guilty in this.

There is no debt between us.

The debt belongs with you.

Lisa audibly exhaled as the entanglement eased. The colleague's influence dissipated from the created constellation leaving just Lisa, Hannah, and their newly cleared connection. The acknowledgement of the place of her elder step-sibling, in the absence of the weight of the guilt from her father's choices, meant that the connection with Hannah became a source of strength. Lisa no longer had to unconsciously defend or justify her place. The hook that her colleague had been drawn to in the morphic field was no longer there and Lisa was able to flourish within the team.

Something as simple as an exploration of a tricky sibling relationship can transform the external field connections. What comes up for you if you think about your relationships with your siblings now? And if you think about the possibility of siblings unborn or unknown? How does it feel to acknowledge the possibility of their place?

Understanding the missing parts

To understand the impact and influence of the sibling field it is essential to have an understanding of the basics of constellation theory and the interaction and interconnectedness of the informing field: that each individual within a family has an equal place and an equal right to belong, to be seen, and to be heard.

When an individual, event, or trauma is not acknowledged, then there will be those in the family field that are pulled to that individual, event, or trauma. There are those of us that see and carry, and there are those of us that are repelled, who refuse to acknowledge or allow others either consciously or unconsciously to carry the fate in their stead.

From this original point, entanglements are created that are passed from one generation to the next with either the pull to carry or the pull to exclude. The entanglements create patterns of behaviour around pain and exclusion with great influence upon the familial relationship bonds. The individuals, events, or trauma connected to the original entanglement are represented knowingly or unknowingly by us, our family field members, and the generations that follow.

We can become a conduit for the missing, the seen, the unseen, the victim, the perpetrator, the enslaver, the enslaved, the promise, the mother, the father...

A common entanglement within the sibling realm is that associated with a missing twin. Having a missing twin is common—one in three pregnancies begin as a twin pregnancy. This phenomenon is known as Vanishing Twin Syndrome, [10] and the vanished twin spontaneously aborts early within the pregnancy. Depending on the historical narrative of the family field, the effect of a missing or vanished twin can be debilitating, particularly within personal relationships.

When we lose our twin, part of us holds a place for them, waiting for them to come back and to feel that level of closeness again. We look for it in our intimate relationships and can often have a series of intense monogamous relationships that never feel quite right for us. That is because we are unconsciously looking for our twin and our partner can never be that person for us, no matter how hard either of us try.

Robert participated in a group constellation session in Scotland. His intention was to focus on his relationship with his wife. They had been together for ten years, but the relationship had deteriorated and they had jointly decided that a divorce was the best way forward. It was a hard decision for them to make; they still loved one another but the closeness wasn't there anymore.

Robert described their relationship as being more like brother and sister, rather than husband and wife. He wanted to work with a constellation to ensure that the divorce was as amicable and gentle as possible for both of them. I was curious about the dynamics of the relationship as it was clear in the way that Robert spoke of his wife that he still loved her.

I set up the constellation with Robert, his wife, and their marriage promise. Robert set it up initially with them facing each other, with the marriage promise beside them. Neither of them could look at the other, they were both looking off to the side, but they were holding hands. There was a strong sense of grief for both of them.

I brought in a representative for divorce. There was an immediate response within the created constellation space. Robert and his wife stepped closer together yet still could not look at one another, and the marriage promise representative began to weep. The divorce representative slowly moved towards the marriage promise.

The bond between Robert and his wife was clearly very strong. I asked them to say to one another:

I am choosing divorce.

They both found it very difficult to say and the weight of grief within the field became stronger. I then asked them to say to one another:

I can't be them for you.

This phrase transformed the energy immediately. They were both able to look at one another for the first time. I decided to place two further representatives within the created constellation space. One to represent Robert's missing twin and one to represent his wife's missing twin. The effect was incredible. They each turned and embraced their missing twin, holding them tightly and crying. I asked both Robert and his wife to say to their twin:

Part of me has been waiting for you.

It was hard when you left.

I have been looking for you.

It is hard to live without you.

I blamed myself.

My survival felt like a betrayal of you.

Choosing to love felt like a betrayal of you.

I have been holding your absence in my heart.

This moved the weight of the grief and both Robert and his wife were able to stand with their twin and say to each other:

I have been looking at you through them.

I have been looking at you through their absence.

I don't need you to be them for me anymore.

I can't be them for you.

You are worthy of love and I am worthy of love.

It isn't a betrayal of them to love and be loved.

Then they each said to their twin:

I honour your place as I take my place.

I honour your place as I love and accept love.

With this healing movement the divorce representative slowly moved away from the grouping of Robert, his wife, their missing twins, and the marriage promise. Robert and his wife slowly stepped towards each other and held hands again, looking one another in the eyes, and were able to say:

I see you.

I see who you are.

I accept you as you are.

You are enough and I am enough.

I stopped the constellation at that point as it was clear that the movement of the disentanglement connected to the missing twins needed time to settle before any consideration could be given to divorce. Robert and his wife decided to stay together and their relationship is still going strong; they are much closer and no longer feel like one another's sibling.

How did you feel when you read the phrases from Robert's constellation? If you felt moved with the inclusion of the missing twins, then try repeating the twin phrases again but this time to a space for your twin in your mind's eye:

Part of me has been waiting for you.

It was hard when you left.

I have been looking for you.

It is hard to live without you.

I blamed myself.

My survival felt like a betrayal of you.

Choosing to love felt like a betrayal of you.

I have been holding your absence in my heart.

This is a common and deeply limiting entanglement. Take the time to gently work through the phrases from your heart.

Safety in being you

In some cases, it can be too painful for us to accept and acknowledge our place within our family field or to accept our life as it flows to us from our mother and father. This can occur when there is recent or ingrained trauma within our family that is under the surface and unacknowledged, or if it isn't safe to belong within our family.

In such cases it can be easier to exclude our self from the family field and to attempt to earn a place in someone else's family field. The easiest way to do this is through a relationship and this is a significant influence on relationship patterns.

However, our relationship field can be similarly complex. There is a cost to belonging to such a field of influence. The closeness of the friendships forged is often intense in nature, as is our dedication to our chosen profession. There is a need to earn a place in this created family structure through the mutual carrying of fates. What is actually happening is the members of this created field represent for one another the missing, the seen, the unseen, the victim, the perpetrator, the enslaved, the promise, the mother, and/or the father, within each of their family fields of origin.

It is a safe place to root oneself only if the representing of fates is mutual and continuing. If there are changes, such as the forming of an intimate relationship, or the healing of a trauma within the field of origin, then the safety that we have fabricated within the created field of belonging can be threatened or even destroyed, often at great emotional cost.

What I want you to take away from the explorations of the sibling field is how transformational it is to acknowledge the place of the missing and how very simple it is to do.

The resistance we feel to acknowledging the missing, doesn't belong with us. It too is inherited. The acknowledgement of another person's place does not cost you your own place. It does not cost anything. Every person has an equal right to belong, to be seen, and to be heard. Not only does it not cost you anything, you can benefit from this seemingly small act. It moves you out of belonging in a place that has to be bought and instead roots you within a belonging that is free.

Choosing to see is a radical act of kindness.

5.

The inherited cost of love—are you free to love and be loved?

Love, and our very human need to love and be loved, is the driver for so many people seeking clarity from constellation. Even when we know it is possibly not quite right for us in our heads, our heart follows the trail of the entangled broken promises and it can be very hard to resist the promise of love even if that promise isn't real. The relationship field and the patterns associated, hold some of the most complex entanglements.

This is because of the very nature of a relationship. It literally joins two different family fields together whilst simultaneously animating the previously held seen and unseen promises and contracts within those family fields.

Cast your mind back over some of the weddings you have been a guest at. There is the ceremony, but I want you to think about and remember what happens afterwards, at the celebration breakfast, lunch or dinner, where the family and friends of the happy couple are drawn together in one space focusing on the couple's relationship. All of the parents, siblings, aunts and uncles, grandparents, various cousins, school friends, college friends, maybe an ex-partner or two just for good measure. All of those people gathered together in one room. Sometimes with the inhibition loosening addition of alcohol.

Sometimes it gets a little fractious, occasionally it gets a little rowdy, a little angry, and sometimes it is just plain wild. Great care is generally taken by the couple over the seating plan. Hours can be spent poring over it and deciding who should be sat next to who, who needs to be kept as far apart as humanly possible lest war break out. We have all experienced a wedding party that has become a little heated, or at least heard tales of such happenings. There is always some relief at being able to say goodbye at the end of the evening.

This hotbed of heated emotions and simmering undercurrents is a pretty accurate representation of the family and ancestral field influences that are bearing down on your love life, and your choices in love, every single moment of every single day from you and your partner's (and former partners') families.

It can be the family wedding from hell that you can't just say goodbye to and walk away at the end of the night. This particular party doesn't end. It doesn't stop entangling you unless you choose to stop, look, feel, and disentangle yourself.

Love at its best is simple, a pure movement with acceptance from the heart. The dynamics of love however, are thoroughly complicated.

When we are born, our bonds of loyalty are to our family, to our mother, our father, our siblings, and our ancestors. As we grow older the ties and bonds that we create become more complex and intricate and spin out from us like a spider's web.

There are two different types of relationship pattern to be aware of.

The first involves entanglements that we have participated in creating through our own relationships with our current and former partners, where promises and broken promises from former relationships get carried into our next relationship.

The second involves entanglements that come from beyond us. It is the inheritance of the promises and broken promises of our ancestral field.

The common denominator in both types of pattern is the inheritance of the relationship promise. It comes to us either through our own relationship lineage or through our ancestral lineage. And quite often from both types of lineage all at once.

The promise

There is a conscious and unconscious relationship promise at the core of every single relationship. Every single one. This promise exists regardless of whether it is an intimate relationship, a friendship, or a working relationship.

In general, the promise will represent the known and unknown, seen and unseen, aspects of our relationship and commitment to one another. It is created at the start of our relationship and becomes more clearly defined with each stage of commitment. When the relationship is based purely on the connection between us and a partner, the promise should be relatively clear and easy for each of us to see and acknowledge. But that isn't always the case. There are influences from both of our previous relationship lines, as well as possible ancestral influences and inherited promises from both of our ancestral fields. Quite the gathering of stuff.

If the dynamics of our relationship have changed, then the promise too will change, or rather the connection we have to the promise will change. Instead of feeling like a symbol and gesture of love and devotion, it can become a weight—a constraint—and something that we desire to break free from.

It can become a source of anger, pain, or guilt. It is important for both you and your partner to be able to see and accept the different aspects of the promise as well as see, and feel seen, by one another in order for love to survive and thrive.

If your relationship is having a rocky patch it is very important to check in with and gently tend to the relationship promise space between you and your partner. You may each be looking at different versions of it.

It is only when the importance and value of the love at the start of your relationship is acknowledged, when the relationship and the relationship promise itself has a place, that a movement towards healing can occur.

Being able to be present with this, to acknowledge what was in the past, will allow both of you to be present in the now, rather than being pulled into unfulfilled dreams and hopes and the loss of what might have been.

Similarly, if you are single and would like to be in a relationship with a new partner, ensuring that there is actually a place for a new promise is very important. That space can be filled with old broken promises from your relationship lineage and your ancestors, which blocks you from stepping into a new relationship.

Please form an orderly queue

Our relationship line is the series of connections that is held by us to each and every previous partner, from the first love through to our current or last partner. The strength of connection and influence of former partners in the line will vary. The strongest influence will often be with our first love, and then following on from that any marriages and engagements.

Intimate relationships will also have more impact than non-intimate, however the weight of the dreams of how things *could* have been is also significant. Due to the nature of relationship pattern entanglements, some previous partners of your current partner (or previous partner) can also influence or indeed hold a place themselves in the relationship line. Your ex, or your partner's ex, could well be having an influence on your relationship right now.

Say for example your current partner was in a serious relationship with someone else before he met you. It ended because she cheated on him with someone else. Your partner hasn't quite got over it yet and is holding the pain of that betrayal and broken promise, unable to let it go. That broken promise will be the lens that your partner sees *you* through. Not only that, but that broken promise will be held within *your* relationship promise. And their ex will also have a place in your relationship. In all parts of your relationship. Including your sex life. Similarly, parts of your exes will be in there too.

This feature of inheritance within our relationship lineage can be quite a shock. Unless you are impeccable with your energy, your exes stay in your life and you stay in theirs. It is that simple and that disturbing.

The inherited promises from our ancestors pull us out of our own relationship lineage and shapeshift and time-travel us to theirs. As we have discussed previously, the most toxic entanglement within the whole constellation field is the inherited parental relationship promise. It acts as a portal to all of the broken and unbroken relationship promises within the historical narrative of our ancestral field of influence and we become thoroughly entangled with the broken promises. Finding our way forward can feel like we are wading through thick mud.

Family and ancestral influences upon relationships

Each of us has a mother and a father. This is a biological fact, but it can be one that is difficult to accept emotionally. The ability to accept our place as it comes to us from our parents, shapes the foundation of our life and our future potential and choices. Knowingly or unknowingly we each hold a sense of our family that influences our actions, decisions, and responses, within our own lifetime as well as for the generations to come.

As we interact with another person, whether in a working relationship, a friendship, an intimate relationship with the opposite sex, or an intimate same sex relationship, we are influenced by our own origin within our own individual family system, and our place in relation to our maternal and paternal family lines, as well as the field of those we interact with. We bring the entanglements within those lines with us, like a backpack filled with other people's stuff.

The longer our relationship lasts, the more likely we are to become influenced by the pattern of previous long-term relationships within our family and ancestral fields and the promises that have been made and broken by our ancestors. Our own promise gets gradually eroded by the weight of theirs.

Some common relationship entanglements occurring as a result of inherited ancestral promises are:

First Love ties—the intensity of our first love. It's often our first outer field connection, and a strong bond with someone who sees the you that your family cannot or will not see.

Secrets—When it is not safe to be seen by your family or perhaps by your partner's family. In this case part of us can be cut off or sacrificed in order to hold a place in the relationship.

Betrayal—This can be the cost of breaking a promise in a relationship. It can create an imbalance within our place so that we need to balance that by holding a place for betrayal in any subsequent relationship. This can take many forms. Some of the most common I see include aspects of the following in the historical untold stories of our ancestors or in our present:

The need to wait for someone to come back.

Having place/love stolen or unacknowledged.

Not being enough.

Ties to the person involved in breaking the promise.

For example, if we feel guilt over ending a relationship with someone with whom we had fallen out of love, but they were still in love with us, this can feel like a betrayal. If we are not comfortable in choosing ourselves or if we cannot look at the choice we have made, then we can displace ourselves through the effort not to look. We can get tangled up in the untold stories of betrayal in our ancestral field of influence and can hold a place for that in our next relationship.

Loss of place—This can happen through betrayal, but also through exclusion, when we are faced with having to choose between love and family, friendships, work, beliefs. The ancestral inheritance is at play here with an unconscious belief that there is a debt to be paid if we choose ourselves.

Sacrifice of belonging—This can be an introductory thread into abusive relationship and enslavement or victim-perpetrator patterns following on from loss of place. It is the carrying of death or a particularly heavy fate for another in order to earn a place.

Tied to previous partner/parent of partner—resulting in only attracting relationships with unavailable people, or lack of intimacy with those who are also similarly entangled.

Forbidden—belief system differences. Beliefs of not being enough, tied to secrets within the workplace, friendships, or with family members. It can show up if, for example, you have been brought up as Catholic and you fall in love with a Jewish partner.

Price to be paid—This is linked with loss of place but also when there is part of you or your partner that needs to be sacrificed in order to have love. Perhaps there is a need to relocate, the sacrifice of dreams, fertility issues, loss of voice, an unconscious allegiance with secrets, and the presence of silent and unseen men and women.

Guilt—of breaking a promise. You consciously or subconsciously may believe you played with someone's feelings in a previous relationship and then you accept punishment for this in subsequent relationships.

Shame—This can be from within us if we cannot reconcile a choice we have made, or an acceptance of shame placed upon us. It is highlighted in the need to carry a broken promise forward in our own relationship lineage or through our invisible inheritance.

Ownership and servitude—In return for safety, a place, an escape, or a recreation of the family field, there can be a pull into this dynamic. In deeply rooted entanglements, it can present as a pull to death within the historical trauma and untold stories in the field of influence.

Ancestral Promises—The promises and broken promises, loyalties and secrets, associated with the family dynamics of us and our partner, and our previous partners, that come to us through our own relationship lineage and the inheritance.

Mary came for some individual sessions because she was unhappy with the level of intimacy and emotional communication in the relationship with her husband. Mary and her husband Thomas were both in their late fifties and they had both been married previously. They had only been married for one year although they had been together for six years. Prior to the marriage, the relationship between them had been very close. They had enjoyed spending as much time as possible together and she described them as feeling like teenagers in love. It was hard for her to comprehend the change between them after the marriage ceremony. She explained that it seemed to change from the day of the wedding. On their honeymoon to China, a dream holiday for both of them that they had spent months happily planning, she felt as though she were on holiday with a stranger. At first, she put it down to the stress of organising a wedding, however several months passed by and they seemed to drift further apart. She described it as trying to communicate with one another through a wall of water.

Unexpected and unwelcome changes within a relationship after its formalisation, whether through marriage or moving in together, are not uncommon. It generally indicates that there is at least one other promise still active for one or other of the partners.

I initially set up the constellation with just Mary, Thomas, and their marriage promise, to observe the loyalties between them and to explore whether or not there was actually a place for each of them with the other within their relationship.

Relationship Promise

Image 21—Mary's initial relationship constellation unable to see or connect with her partner

Mary initially set up the constellation with her and Thomas standing side by side with the marriage promise in front of them. However, she placed Thomas on her left-hand side, meaning that she was on the right. Generally, in relationship constellations between men and women, the male stands to the right of the female. This comes from the concept of the optimal flow within constellation theory and the structure and hierarchy of belonging within the field. However, in Mary's constellation this was reversed. It was also very uncomfortable for them to stand closely beside one another, although she had placed them as standing shoulder to shoulder. Neither of them was able to look at the marriage promise. Instead they were each being pulled to look outside of their relationship and Mary became quite distressed as she witnessed this.

I decided to bring in a space for Thomas's first wife. The relationship had ended badly ten years previously when Thomas discovered that she had been having an affair with one of his friends. In the aftermath of the separation his sense of betrayal was further compounded when his father allowed his ex-wife to move in with him along with her new partner.

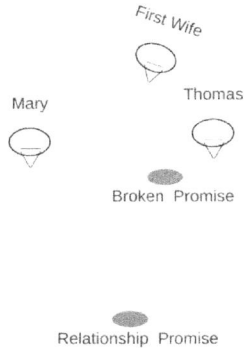

Relationship Promise

Image 22—The former promises influencing Mary's relationship constellation

Within the constellation there was still a very strong connection between Thomas and his ex-wife although it seemed to be driven by her and not him. The ex-wife was also fixated on Mary rather than Thomas. I placed their broken marriage promise within the created constellation field and it too drew a lot of energy and focus from both Thomas and Mary. It has clearly been unconsciously held by Thomas and Mary within their marriage promise.

Mary addressed Thomas's ex and worked with the narrative of:

You are no longer his wife and he is no longer your husband.

The promise between you is broken.

You made a different choice.

We won't hold your broken promise in our marriage.

You can't have my place as a Smith woman (Smith being Thomas's surname).

I won't be you in this.

Mary then spoke with Thomas:

I can feel the betrayal here.

I recognise betrayal.

I am not her.

I won't be her in this marriage.

Her place is outside of this.

There is no shame in your divorce.

You haven't lost your place as a Smith man.

You are a free man and I am a free woman.

This cleared the entanglement with Thomas's ex-wife, however the statement about Mary being a free woman didn't quite ring true. I moved Mary to stand on Thomas's left now that he had let go of his former marriage promise. Although Thomas could now comfortably see and connect with Mary, Mary was still unable to look at Thomas, and to her distress was still pulling away to look outside the relationship. I brought in a space for Mary's former husband and their marriage promise.

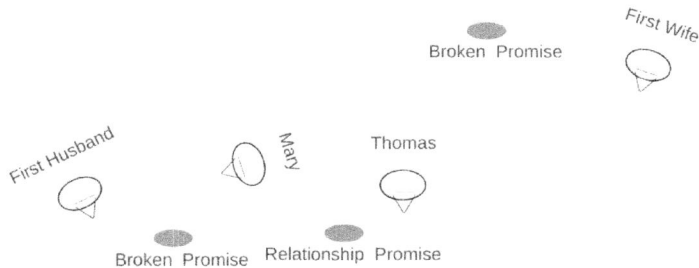

Image 23—Mary acknowledging her own previous choices

This brought a little more ease to the relationship and Mary was able to stand a little closer to Thomas. We then worked with the narrative from Mary to her ex-husband:

You were my husband and I was your wife.

The promise between us is broken now.

I chose divorce.

You haven't lost your place and I haven't lost mine.

Again, there was some relief, particularly with Mary's ex-husband, but Mary herself seemed more agitated and couldn't make eye contact with either her former or current husband and was instead pulled to look away. There was a strong sense of guilt and secrecy around Mary and I remembered the charge of energy within her when she worked with the narrative:

I recognise betrayal.

I asked Mary if there had been someone else for her during her marriage to her former husband. She broke down at this point and began to cry. I placed a space for her lover within the constellation and the relief for Mary was immediate.

We worked with him with the narrative of:

I don't need you to be my escape anymore.

I don't need you to be my guilt anymore.

There is a place for love with me.

That love doesn't need to be a secret.

There is no shame in the love I have.

I am ready to let you go.

I am ready to take myself back.

Mary's relationship with her ex-husband had been a hard and emotionally abusive one. She met her lover, Dan, at work and they struck up a friendship which quickly grew into something more significant for both of them. For Mary, he reminded her of what it felt like to be truly seen by someone else. She had felt so unseen in her marriage for years. She gradually remembered who she was through the relationship with Dan and her confidence slowly came back. She found the courage to end the relationship with her husband and also decided to end the relationship with Dan. She wanted to be alone in order to heal. However, she had then carried the weight of the guilt and the secrecy into her marriage with Thomas. All of the broken promises, betrayals, and secrets had taken a place in their marriage promise. However now the two of them could stand side by side looking at their marriage promise:

There is a place for you with me.

There is a place for me with you.

I am your wife and you are my husband.

Our love has a place.

Our friendship has a place.

Our intimacy has a place.

This is just for us.

There was a little more follow up work to do with the ancestral narrative of broken promises however the most significant pieces had moved, and Mary and Thomas were able to recapture the happiness and freedom within their love that existed before the marriage vows were taken.

Where are your loyalties in love?

Entanglements within your relationship line can be observed quite simply in a created constellation. It is simple, but it isn't necessarily comfortable. What we need to do is make a list of each and every person that you have been involved with. Every single one, even if you don't want to remember them, or if you can't remember their name, or if it doesn't seem that significant to you as you cast your mind back. Write it down anyway. It is important.

It is important to note here that the process of remembering or acknowledging the significance of previous loves or partners begins a movement in and of itself. Some of us will only have had one or a couple of significant relationships, in which case the process of remembering and acknowledging is simpler though not necessarily easy. Some of us may have had many more, and it can be painful to sit in acknowledgement of that and the choices that went along with each, however it is a necessary and important part of our process. There is no place for judgement. Be gentle with yourself.

Exploring your relationship line

Before stepping into the created constellation and observing the flow between you and your previous and current partners, first notice any changes within your breath or the tension in your body as you bring each of the partner representatives into your mind's eye. Scan down the energy in your body again and take note of any changes. If it feels too much to visualise or feel the connection, you can place sheets of paper on the floor to represent each partner space. This will give you a little more distance as you connect. It can be surprising how intense the connection with an old and forgotten love can feel.

If you have a long line of people to work through then take your time with this. Don't rush your way through it in one day. Start at the beginning and gently, step by step, one promise at a time, work your way down the line.

Some connections will be easy and soft, some less so. You might be surprised at the depth of feeling in some of the connections that didn't really seem that important at the time. This is because your former partner might be holding on to you as the one that got away. So many of the influences upon you are from outside of you. It is worth the time and effort to clear your relationship line in this way.

When you are ready, take a deep brave breath and step in front of the line of your former partners.

Are you able to see each of them? Is your gaze pulled downwards? Has your posture shifted? How do you feel simply standing in front of your relationship line? What emotions come up for you? Does it feel comfortable?

Now I want you to shift your focus to your first love and take some slow deep breaths into your body. Then try to say:

You were important for me.

What happens when you say that? What happens to your posture, your breath? How does it feel? Can you look at them? Do you feel seen? Is there rejection or anger present or is there a sense of peace?

You have a place in my heart.

Again, notice your response and if that statement feels true.

What we shared has gone now. What was between us has changed.

The promise between us is broken.

These phrases can be difficult and challenging. And the difficulty can come as something of a surprise, especially if it is a partner from many years ago. Allowing time and space for a depth of connection to occur, in spite of the discomfort or awkwardness it may bring up, will allow the block to move by giving place to what was, it's importance, and the reality of your present situation. Remember here that we cannot bring someone into the constellation that isn't already there. You are not opening a can of worms; this was all already within and around you, you just weren't consciously aware of it.

What we are doing is allowing you to feel and witness how much you may have been unconsciously holding from your past, and creating a space to let that go. And that is a very good thing.

If there is difficulty in acknowledging that the relationship promise has been broken then that is an indication of a deeper-rooted entanglement, either because you are not ready on some level for the relationship to end, or because of an entanglement held within the family or ancestral field rather than your relationship line.

I am letting you go.

Please let me go too.

These statements can reveal whether or not you are actually ready to let go of your previous love. The ties that bind can be very strong and it is often surprising where you can get stuck. The power and grip of dreams created together, but that remain unfulfilled, can be limiting to your future relationships, and a pattern of service to an older dream can become established.

It is also important to note your partner or former partner's representative response, whether or not they are willing to let go of you. Do you feel trapped or stuck when you connect with them? If there is a reluctance from them to let you go, then further work on acknowledging the importance of 'what was' is needed, as well as an acknowledgement of the shared dreams that no longer have a place in your present.

I am taking back the parts of me you have.

I'm giving you back the parts of you that I have been carrying.

It is important for you to be fully present in order for this movement to be effective. Taking time to work with your breath and stay grounded throughout will make this much easier.

You cannot hold the place for love with me.

Please leave space for another.

In order for full intimacy to be experienced within your current relationship, the space for love within your energetic field must either be free (but have a place), or be occupied by your current partner. Similarly, for your partner with whom you are intimately involved, there needs to be a mutual place and space for intimacy shared with you or else intimacy and sex will be diminished, stilted, or possibly even forbidden.

In the process of exploring your relationship line, other entanglements impinging on relationships may become apparent.

When dipping in to look at your previous relationships and the relationship line, notice how open or filled or available the space for a partner is. Where the space is held can be revealing. Is there a space for love? What price, if any, has to be paid for that love? Is it forbidden? Does the space for love truly belong to you or is it being held for another family member?

Try saying, strongly and clearly:

I am choosing love.

It is safe for me to love and be loved.

Because it is absolutely true.

Inherited promises and their hidden cost

Anne had been working with one to one individual constellation sessions with me every few months, over several years. We had worked together exploring various aspects of her family field, and her place within it, however her original intention for beginning to work with family constellation was to explore difficulties in her relationship with her daughter. Anne explained that her daughter was the eldest of four children for her and her husband. They had a tricky relationship, but it had worsened considerably after her daughter's marriage two years before. Anne and her daughter had become estranged and her daughter cut off all contact with Anne and her husband, although still maintained some limited contact with her siblings.

The timing of the estrangement occurring after the daughter's marriage is significant. It is an indication that somewhere in the mix there are inherited relationship promises.

When I asked Anne about her relationship with her husband, she became quite emotional. It was a difficult relationship for her. They were very young when they began their relationship—she was seventeen and he was twenty. They had been dating for a few months when he abruptly ended the relationship and began to date someone else. It was at this point that Anne discovered she was pregnant. Her whole world changed. Her own parents disowned her and threw her out of the family home. They were devout Christians and the conception of a child outside of the sanctity of marriage was unacceptable for them. Her now husband's family also reacted very angrily and insisted that their son marry Anne and that the two of them live within their family home until they could afford a home of their own. They did not welcome Anne into the family, but instead she was treated as a woman of ill-repute who had trapped their innocent son and she was made to feel an outcast for the two years that she lived there.

The birth of her daughter did nothing to soften either set of parents' attitudes towards her, although all four grandparents acknowledged and behaved softly towards their granddaughter. Her husband reluctantly ended his new relationship and married Anne. Both sets of parents and her husband focused their anger onto Anne, blaming her for the pregnancy and the disruption to their lives. As Anne spoke about this the shame placed upon her some thirty years previous was still palpable. There was no anger within her at the way she had been treated, and she physically withdrew into herself when she spoke about it. It hadn't appeared to cross her mind that what happened to her then was still impacting her in the present.

There are several significant potential entanglements to note here that are identified from conversation with Anne.

> The already difficult relationship with her daughter deteriorated after her daughter's wedding suggesting a relationship entanglement root as opposed to a direct maternal line entanglement.

> The forced marriage as a result of pregnancy after the relationship had already ended.

> The loss of place within her own family which would have drawn her to unconsciously seek a place in her husband's family.

> Denial of place based on belief.

> The further denial of place from her husband's family. She only existed as an unseen mother.

> The forced end of her husband's relationship with another woman.

> The placement of blame upon her by all involved.

All of this points to root entanglements within the relationship field that were not only impacting Anne's relationship with her daughter but also potentially her own sense of place and worth.

In our discussion on constellation theory relating to relationship patterns, an important first step is to establish that the relationship promise or marriage promise exists only between the two people within the relationship. In this case the marriage promise between Anne and her husband is highly likely to be holding various entanglements relating to her own family, her husband's family, and her daughter's place. It is also important to consider whether or not her daughter is holding the marriage promise within her own marriage. So, from the perspective of the intentional question of:

What needs to be cleared to heal the relationship between Anne and her daughter?

I decided to first set up a simple constellation to explore the dynamics between Anne, her husband, her daughter, and the marriage promise.

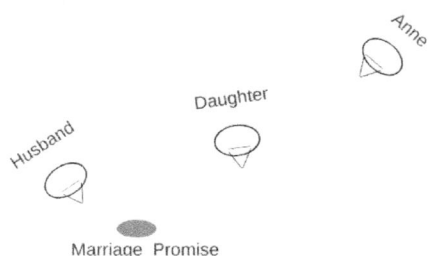

Image 24—Anne displacement by her husband and daughter

It was immediately clear that all was not well. There was a strongly established loyalty between her husband and daughter. The two of them stood together side by side along with the marriage promise. The daughter was effectively in Anne's place and Anne was on the outside of the relationship looking in from a point of exclusion. She found it difficult to stand straight within the created constellation space and could not make eye contact with anyone. Again, the sense of shame and guilt was palpable within the constellation field. Anne's daughter looked to her with judgement and anger. Her husband could not look at her or acknowledge her. The representation of the marriage promise was very heavy and clearly held more than the now obvious paternal line triangulation that was displayed between the father and daughter. The daughter's place was inside the marriage promise, not outside it. Therefore, her sense of belonging was also rooted within the marriage promise, and whatever entanglements were held within it, and also held by her unconsciously, were impacting all her relationships, not just the relationship with her mother. In order to uncover and move the entanglements it was essential to first take the daughter out of the marriage promise.

I am your mother and you are my daughter.

This is your father; you are his daughter.

The marriage promise is between us.

Your place is outside of it.

Your place has always been outside of it.

I don't need you to be the safety in our marriage.

I don't need you to be my safety.

The connection between Anne and her daughter began to soften with the biggest response coming with the phrases around safety. There was still a reluctance from both the daughter and the father to move away from one another.

Your life in this is innocent.

There is safety for you outside the marriage promise.

You are not the wife in this—you are the daughter.

This narrative brought further relief for both the daughter and Anne however the father was still displaying anger and would not let go of his daughter. At this point I brought in a space for the woman Anne's husband had been in a relationship with directly before their marriage. The daughter immediately relaxed and was able to step away from the father saying:

I can't be her for you.

I am not her; I am your daughter.

I feel your anger.

I cannot hold it anymore.

I cannot hold your promises or broken promises.

They belong with you.

I am leaving all of this with you.

This allowed the daughter to be disentangled from the marriage promises between her parents and also from representing her father's lost love. At this point the daughter could fully face and make eye contact with Anne and acknowledge her as a mother.

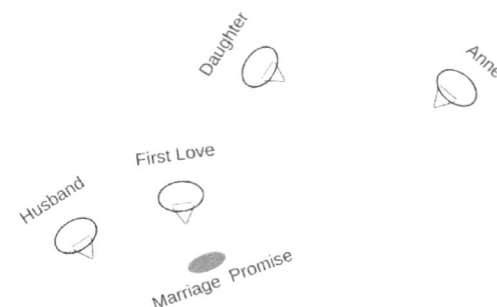

Image 25—The inclusion of the former love in Anne's constellation

From the image, you can see that although there is now a connection between the mother and daughter, they are still unable to move freely towards one another because of the entanglements within the field. The father's ex-love is now standing beside him and both are looking at the marriage promise. The high level of comfort in the belonging alongside one another and the proprietary nature of the holding of the marriage promise suggests that the relationship between Anne's husband and the ex-love was more established than initially described and also potentially continued after the marriage between Anne and her husband. I decided to explore this further and asked Anne to work with the narrative:

I see the betrayal here now.

It isn't a secret anymore.

And then to the ex-love:

You cannot have my place.

My place is just for me.

I have a place in this marriage as his wife.

I have a place outside of this marriage as a free woman.

I feel what you lost; he made a different choice.

This was hard for me too.

This allowed the ex-love to step further back and although there was relief in the movement for Anne and the woman, Anne's daughter remained tense. The woman had shifted her focus from Anne's husband and the marriage promise to Anne's daughter.

This is my daughter.

I won't give her up for you.

I won't give up my place as a mother.

I am her mother and she is my daughter.

It is safe for me to be her mother; it is safe for her to be my daughter.

At this point the ex-love could completely step back and Anne and her daughter could move towards one another. The connection between them was much improved and they were able to embrace one another, however the phrases *It is safe for me to be her mother; it is safe for her to be my daughter* had been very difficult for Anne to say and did not feel fully true. There was still distance between Anne and her husband although the daughter was no longing filling the space between them, however she continued to look back at her father as though unsure of the safety for each of them if she truly stepped outside the marriage promise.

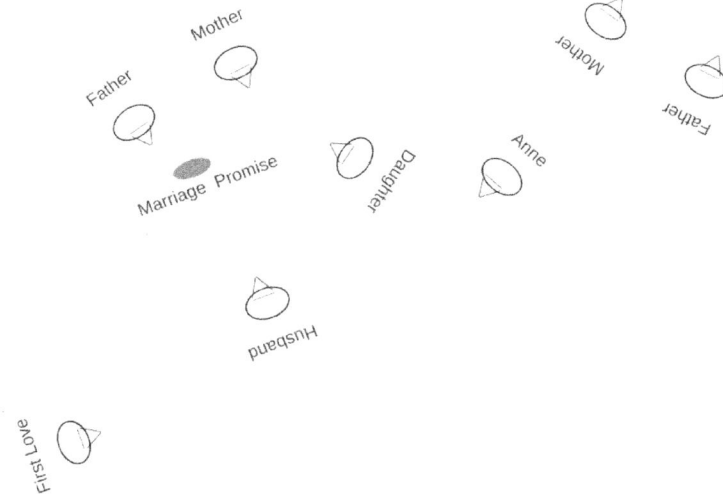

Image 26 - Anne's belonging as an unseen woman

When the entanglements around children and previous partners being held within a marriage promise are cleared, yet there are still obvious blocks to connection within an established, albeit strained, relationship, it points to a deeper historical influence of entanglement within the family and ancestral field. This potential for family and ancestral influences was highlighted in the initial conversation with Anne as she described both parents' response to the unplanned pregnancy, the forced marriage, and the disownment. I included both sets of parents into the created constellation.

Anne's parents turned around and would not acknowledge Anne, her daughter, or indeed any other aspect of the created constellation. This is clearly the root of a very heavy entanglement that is influent upon Anne, however her daughter was not drawn to her maternal grandparents and was instead drawn towards her paternal grandparents and their grouping with her father around the marriage promise. Bearing in mind the focus of the intentional question, to explore the root of the block in the relationship between Anne and her daughter, it was important to focus on the paternal line and not the maternal.

Anne repeated the narrative used with the ex-love:

This is my daughter.

I won't give her up for you.

I won't give up my place as a mother.

I am her mother and she is my daughter.

It is safe for me to be her mother; it is safe for her to be my daughter.

But this time to her mother and father-in-law and with the addition of:

I will not carry guilt for you.

I will not carry shame for you.

I will not be your unseen woman.

I will not be your silent woman.

I am a free woman.

This is not your marriage promise.

It is between my husband and I.

Your places are outside of it.

My daughter's place is outside of it.

This created enough movement and space for Anne to take a place beside her husband and to be seen by both her husband and daughter. It was clear that there was more within the field that needed to move however enough had been cleared within this first session to allow a space for Anne's relationship with her daughter, as well as an affirmation of her own place as a wife, mother, and free woman.

After this initial session Anne experienced a dramatic and very welcome change in the relationship with her husband. She described it as being truly seen by him for the first time in over thirty years. There was tentative communication with her daughter and the beginnings of healing in their relationship. Anne decided to continue to work within the constellation field and more work was carried out over a number of sessions to further uncover and heal the entanglements that came from both family ancestral lines. Part of that included a deeply moving constellation around the uncovering of unseen women and mothers within her own maternal line. There was a history of forced adoption within her mother's family and their strong Catholic belief system. It was after this session that Anne reported back to me that her and her daughter were fully reunited. The puzzle piece that needed to move was to disentangle her daughter from the place she was holding in the marriage promise. The rest flowed easily from there.

Intimacy, please?

The level of intimacy we experience in our relationship is influenced and subjected to the same orders of entanglements as relationships themselves.

When you are not in your place within the family system, then this has an impact on how you physically experience your world on an everyday basis. Quite simply, if you are not in your place then you are not in your physical body and you are not fully present. If you are not fully present and grounded in your body, then the level of intimacy that you experience with your partner will be severely limited and diminished. This is because parts of you can be left with either a previous partner or with a previous partner's family entanglements.

This means that your ex, and ex-in-laws, can be influencing your sex life in this present moment! Do you really want to be giving your ex-mother-in-law a place in your bedroom?

Unfulfilled hopes and dreams are the killers of intimacy. Where a previous partner holds on to anger around the end of a relationship, the way in which the promise was broken or the betrayal of the intimacy of what was shared becomes very significant. As the spurned partner, we can hold onto a piece of that relationship and a piece of our partner.

This inability to let go means that a little of the space for love is lost within us. The space is filled with the past, with anger, fear, and betrayal. We will see that before we see anything else and we will also see that before we see any new partner.

The energetic imprint of our previous partner will be placed upon any new love and we will also see the traits of the previous betrayal superimposed. Our new partner will begin to represent the traits of our previous partner and can actually take on the baggage of any unfulfilled dreams or work carried by that former partner.

Does that ring any bells? Have you ever felt like you've met the perfect guy and then a few months in the same old patterns start to show up? Have you ever wondered why you always end up with the same sort of partner? This is the inheritance of the broken promises in our relationship line.

Our new partner fills the space that our previous partner held, and if this is not identified and acknowledged then they continue to do so, even after our relationship ends, unconsciously acceding to another's fate. This again highlights the importance and need to clear our relationship line, discerning not only the seen promises but also the unseen. Who wants a Groundhog Day relationship with all of their exes?

I see you breaking your promise.

I see your betrayal.

I bear witness to it.

I leave it with you.

I see you breaking (have broken) your promises.

I leave your broken promises with you.

I am not in service to you.

You do not have my loyalty.

I will not pay the price of your betrayal.

We are separate.

I have my own place and it is just for me.

What is the origin of the promise?

The attraction between two people is complex and goes way beyond the physical realm. The desire to belong, to have a place within a family dynamic, even if that family dynamic is not in resonance with our own family of origin, can be hugely seductive.

In relationship dynamics we tend to be attracted to individuals where there is a similarity of fate or entanglement in the system. It can be the case that the heavy entanglement that is in part excluding us from our own family is replicated and echoed within our partner's family field. It is common for the price of belonging to be carrying this burden or fate, and to hold responsibility for it, and generally it will be a heavy weight to bear.

One example that I commonly observe is where the maternal line is reversed. This is the pattern we talked about in chapter three where an entanglement can be created where we give our children to our mother in an effort to appease her loss and pain.

What this creates is a pattern where we sacrifice ourselves and our desires, effectively giving up our place to the unacknowledged trauma our mother is entangled with. A new partner can earn or buy a place within the new family by taking a place in the reversed line. We can take the place of the mother to the child, and so instead of holding the place of partner they become mother, and the true mother feels free. In some cases, the true mother steps into our place of partner further complicating the dynamic. This has a devastating impact on the level of intimacy achieved and possible within our relationships.

It also severely limits the communication in our relationships. What is often very difficult to comprehend is when we find ourselves cast in the role of mother instead of lover. This aspect of the promise will often only be revealed to us after a significant commitment has been made either by way of marriage or co-habiting.

We will often make excuses for what we are experiencing because we do not wish to acknowledge or see the truth of the relationship as it now stands for fear of losing that precious place of belonging, as well as the perceived risk associated with the breaking of a promise.

It can be very challenging to explore blocks in intimacy and affection within our relationships and constellation is a highly effective and gentle way to do that.

Healing intimacy after betrayal

There is a need to explore whether the promise between you and your partner actually belongs to the two of you. If you found parts of your relationship lineage tricky or uncomfortable to work with, or if you know of betrayal within your or your partner's relationship line, then it is worthwhile doing a little extra work here.

> Within a created constellation, simply observing whether it is comfortable for you to stand beside your partner can reveal a lot.

The physical spaces within a constellation are a representation of the emotional connections and entanglements. If it isn't easy to imagine them standing alongside you, and you feel the need for a little space, then often the distance that you need to move away will be the distance required to leave space for another person or another promise.

We have discussed the emotional impact of such spaces being held within the relationship, however there is also a very strong physical impact on your relationship intimacy.

When the bond and promise within your relationship is not grounded in the present, then it is very difficult for the two of you to be grounded in one another physically. One or both of you are being pulled to other places or people.

This means that it may feel forbidden, not possible, or simply too difficult, to be fully present physically with one another. And in any act of physical intimacy the natural response becomes to not be present and to emotionally detach, drift, and effectively leave your body. This does not make for great sex.

There is general perception that grounding your energy in your body and being present is an easy thing to do. However, many people, if not most, find it challenging and something that must be learned rather than a natural state of being. There are many interruptions that can come in between your energetic awareness and an awareness of your body. The spacy, not quite present, time slipping by throughout the day, feeling can be a common one. It can happen from a very young age, particularly if there has been childhood illness or trauma associated with death within the family. In such cases it becomes natural and can feel safer to not be present, to always be ready to escape elsewhere even if that is just into your thoughts.

Physical intimacy can feel like a threat to safety. Allowing someone to be physically close to you can feel dangerous depending on the entanglements and fates that you carry.

In situations where you are tied to your first love, your physical focus will always be with that person. You will have to effectively leave your body in order to be physically intimate with another person. It is possible that this will also feel like a betrayal, and so you may actively seek out relationships where your partner is physically absent or already in another relationship.

In situations of serial relationship patterns, where there isn't clarity around the ending of the relationship, a part of you can be left with each of those former partners. Part of you may be left with each and every one of your ex partners, connecting you to them in the present whilst simultaneously pulling you away from where you want to be and who you want to be with.

This unconscious fracturing of self can be connected to a desire to hide— to not be seen—where love feels forbidden or something that can't be comfortable or enjoyable. In such cases you can leave a part of your intimacy with each respective partner but will in turn take something from them. What you take from them will be a burden or heavy fate— some of their stuff—effectively releasing your partner from their inherited entanglement. If this is the case for you, then you have probably experienced your previous partners going on to form committed relationships with their next partner, as they have managed to unburden themselves with you and are free.

Sex, intimacy, and affection can feel, or can be perceived to feel, forbidden with any one of the entanglements we have discussed. It can feel threatening to begin to explore this aspect of your relationships. Working to strengthen your connection to your own place and physical body is the simplest and least threatening place to begin to help clear any blockages or entanglements around physical intimacy.

Gently notice your response as you work through this next exercise.

This is my body; I claim it

Sit straight in a hard-backed supportive chair with your feet on the floor comfortably placed a hip width apart and facing forwards.

Rest your hands on your knees.

Focus on the natural rhythm of your breath.

Shift your awareness to the point at which the breath enters your body.

Let your focus sit in that place with your breath for a moment.

Next allow your focus to drift over your body from the top of your head to the tips of your toes.

Continue to allow your breath to come and go naturally.

Move your focus to your hands resting upon your knees.

Gently increase the pressure of your hands against your knees and on an outbreath push your knees apart.

On your next in breath push your knees back together.

Repeat this movement, naturally following your own breath's rhythm as you do so.

This exercise is particularly useful and effective for training yourself in a very simple way to ground the energy in your body and to also be fully present in your body. By working with the breath in combination with movement of the lower half of the body there is no choice but to be fully present in the moment. It is then possible to feel into how long the process takes, how comfortable you are during the process, whether any emotions or physical responses are triggered and also for how long after the exercise is finished you remain fully present and engaged.

The more often you practice this movement, the easier it will be for you to stay present with your body and emotions. By knowing and understanding what it feels like to be comfortably in the moment with your breath and your body, you will be able to discern any shifts or changes from that state.

Creating a place for love

There is something special about working within the constellation field to support a couple within their relationship and to remove any blocks that are standing in their way of committing to one another. Relationship dynamics can be very complex, and a couple can be entangled from so many different places—former partners, inherited promises, unacknowledged former loves, etc. Sometimes things can slot into place easily though and it is always a pleasure to facilitate such a constellation.

Rachael came to see me to work on her relationship with her partner Bill. They had been together for six years and had bought a home together a few months previously. Rachael was frustrated as although they had committed to one another financially, Bill actively avoided any conversation about marriage. Rachael was convinced that he was scared of marriage and although she described them as being very much in love, she felt there was an invisible barrier within their relationship when it came to the next steps (for her) of marriage and children. She wanted to remove the invisible barrier.

She described her former relationships as having a similar pattern of men not wanting to commit, and when the relationships ended, they would then go on to marry the next girlfriend. She was really concerned about this happening again, although did agree that the relationship with Bill was different as it had lasted much longer, and they had a form of commitment through their shared home.

In any relationship constellation, the first step is to explore the relationship promise between the couple and how comfortable it is for the couple to stand together side by side, looking at whether the promise is actually between the couple in question or if there are other aspects being held within it. The initial placement of the mats used in the individual sessions is revelatory. I always ask the client to place the mats as they feel they are connected to one another in the present moment.

Image 27—Rachael's initial relationship constellation with both partners pulled outside of the relationship promise

Within the initial constellation it can be seen that the placement is adversarial to, rather than supportive of, one another. Rachael placed them at opposites side of the relationship promise and when I stepped into the field neither one was looking at the other. They each were pulled to look behind them. It did not feel uncomfortable to be across from one other, quite the opposite, but the most dominant loyalty was clearly not to one another. This pull backwards, for each of them, is suggestive of an unseen aspect in the former generations rather than an unacknowledged partner. I decided at this point to bring in spaces for each set of parents.

Image 28—The mirroring of the family entanglements in Rachael's constellation

Each set of parents, who were both still married to one another, mirrored the other set. There was a similar shared entanglement. This is not unusual; we are drawn to partners and friendships where there are similar entanglements and dynamics within the historical narrative of the family field. This similarity of entanglement where they are both entangled with one parent is why the relationship had managed to flourish in the way that it had thus far. The relationship promise was balanced between them and their unconscious promises. Though the invisible barrier to more traditional commitment was still there.

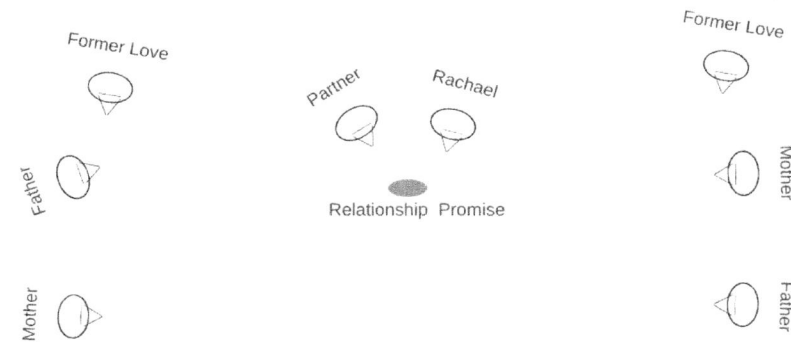

Image 29—Rachael and her partner coming home to one another

With Rachael's parents, her mother was unable to stand beside her father and her father was reaching out for someone else. Rachael was drawn towards her father and pulled away from Bill. Reciprocally, Bill's mother was looking for someone else and would not look at either her husband or her son. Bill was focused on his mother and could not engage with his father. There are three significant aspects to note within this.

1. Rachael is unconsciously holding the place of her father's former love and isn't fully free to hold a place within her relationship with Bill because of that.
2. Bill is within an inherited parental relationship promise where he is waiting for his mother to see him.
3. As Bill waits to be seen by his mother, he is unconsciously representing her lost love.

I began with Rachael's family and included a place for the former love of her father along with a place for that broken promise. Rachael became very emotional when the former love was present. We worked with the narrative:

I didn't know you were there.

I can feel your place now.

I can feel what you lost.

There was a significant emotional release at this point.

This promise was between you both.

It is broken now.

You are more than the broken promise.

I am more than the broken promise.

I didn't take him from you.

He made a different choice.

And then to her father:

Part of me has been holding this for you.

I can't hold it any more.

You have a responsibility here.

There was a movement between Rachael's father and his former love. At this point Rachael was able to say:

It is safe for me to have love in my life.

I haven't agreed to be alone for either of you.

I don't have to choose between love and my family.

I don't have to choose between love and safety.

I am choosing love.

I will remember you as I choose love.

Rachael was then able to turn around and face Bill. At this point she became aware for the first time how far away from her Bill was in the constellation, and she became distressed. This awareness comes as the balance within the relationship promise between the two of them changed. She was no longer entangled within her own line, and the aspects within the unconscious promise between the two of them no longer held that entanglement, and as a result the promise was now unbalanced. When working within a relationship constellation of a couple who are together and want to stay together, it is essential to work with both family fields in order to maintain the balance and integrity of the promise. If I had ended the constellation at this point Rachael would have been freed from the weight of her father's broken promises however the promise between her and Bill would become untenable and the relationship would have suffered as a result.

In the context of the intentional question that we are working with here, Bill's field is a little more obviously entangled. I brought in his mother's lost love and the grief from the mother was tangible. We worked with a similar narrative to acknowledge her grief as it was an echo of the unseen woman's grief connected to Rachael's father:

I can feel the weight of your grief.

I can feel what you lost.

I can see this but I cannot look for you.

Bill has been looking at this for you.

Bill has been trying to replace the lost love for you.

He can't do that anymore.

He can't be him for you.

He isn't him.

He is your son.

The mother was able to turn around at that point although she still remained closer to her lost love. Bill was able to take a step back and look at Rachael. Rachael then worked with the narrative to Bill:

This wasn't your fault.

You are not responsible for your mother's grief.

I feel you waiting for her to see you.

I feel you waiting in your childhood for your mother to see you.

You don't need to wait there anymore.

You can be seen.

You are not a boy in this; you are a man.

Our love is not a betrayal.

There is a place for our love.

It is safe for you to have love in your life.

You don't have to choose between love and your mother.

You don't have to choose between love and safety.

I am not your mother; I am your partner.

There is a place for you with me.

There is a place for me with you.

This is part of who I am.

This is part of who you are.

Their place exists outside of our love.

Their place exists outside of our promise.

It is safe for us to choose love.

It is safe for us to have children of our own.

It isn't a betrayal.

At this point Rachael and Bill were able to stand next to one another comfortably and both see the relationship promise that was just for them. All of this took place in one session. Rachael emailed shortly after the session to share that she had discovered that her father had been engaged before he married her mother and broke off the engagement when he met her mother. They both felt guilty about it as they had begun their relationship for a period of time before he ended the engagement. She also shared that Bill's mother had fallen very deeply in love with a young man whilst she was at university, but he was killed in a motorbike accident. The weight of the grief was still present with Bill's mother as she spontaneously shared the story with Rachael shortly after the constellation session. Such occurrences of sharing family secrets and making the invisible connections visible, is not uncommon after a constellation session and it is always interesting to hear about the ripples afterwards. Three months later Bill and Rachael were engaged. They are now married and have a young daughter. The invisible barrier has gone. Rachael's constellation was a fairly simple and not too deeply entangled one. That is not always the case.

Choosing to love freely

It can feel daunting to step into a created constellation to explore the connection between you and your partner or a space for a future partner.

What if it doesn't feel safe? What if you find out something you don't want to know?

If you feel nervous, take same slow breaths into your body and then gently and bravely step in. As you do so, remember that when we step into a constellation we are seeing and feeling what is already there. We might not be able to see it or consciously acknowledge it in our everyday, but we are living it regardless of whether know it or not. Be brave. It'll be worth it.

I want you to bring your partner into your mind's eye or imagine them in the room with you. Take a little while to breathe into the connection and notice where they are in relation to you and whether you can see them or if you are feeling the connection to them instead.

How easy does it feel? Are you struggling? Is there any resistance?

When you are ready try saying:

You are my husband and I am your wife.

or

You are my partner and I am your partner.

or

You have a place with me and I have a place with you.

or

You have a place in my heart and I accept a place in yours.

Notice how you feel when you say the phrases that are right for you, if it provokes a change in the connection, or if it changes where you are placed in relation to one another, whether you can see one another, and if you are both present and grounded within your bodies.

Do the phrases feel true when you say them? Were any of them tricky?

Scan down your body and energy and notice how you feel. Do you still feel like yourself?

What we ideally want to achieve is for you to be able to look at your partner (or the place for a potential partner), seeing the place of their parents, grandparents, and ancestors, as well as the place of any previous spouses or partners and children, and say:

I see this is part of who you are.

I see this is part of where you come from.

I accept this is part of who you are.

I accept this is part of where you come from.

I can't look at this for you, but I do accept it.

Then to be able to bring your own parents, grandparents, etc, and the place of any of your previous partners and children, and say to your current or future partner:

This is part of who I am.

This is part of where I come from.

I don't need you to look at this for me.

I can see this.

Let's try that. Start by bringing in your partner, or future partner space, and a space for your promise. And then your family and exes and children, and their family and exes and children. Saying loudly and clearly:

I see this is part of who you are.

I see this is part of where you come from.

I accept this is part of who you are.

I accept this is part of where you come from.

I can't look at this for you but I do accept it.

This is part of who I am.

This is part of where I come from.

I don't need you to look at this for me.

I can see this.

And we are not done yet. We want to take another step forward and tell our partner about all of the family and ancestral stuff, as well as their past choices and ours:

All of this has a place.

But it has no place in our relationship (or marriage) promise.

Our promise is just for us.

Our relationship (or marriage) is just for us.

There is a place for you with me.

There is a place for me with you.

And then breathe. Feel into what happens in your body. Feel what happens in your heart. How does it feel when the space is created for just you and your partner or future partner? Does it feel safe? If not, don't worry, you've just moved quite a lot of people out of your space. It will take a little while for it all to settle. To support that settling movement try saying:

It is safe for me to love and be loved.

It is safe for you to love and be loved.

We are not finished yet. I want you to feel into that space for the relationship promise next.

Where is it and how does it feel?

This is a really important part of your relationship. It basically acts like the contract between you and your love. It holds your promises of what you will do and what you absolutely will not do. It is unique to you and your partner. You *both* get to decide the bits that go in there.

The promise will also evolve, grow, and change as you and your partner grow and change. That is also a good thing but the promise itself needs to be tended with care.

Who you both are in the first flush of your relationship will not be the same as who you are two, ten, or twenty years down the line. And holding your old promise when it doesn't fit you any more is leaving the door of your relationship open to the inheritance of other old promises in the field of influence around you.

Take some time now to tend to that promise space, regardless of whether you are single and looking for love, newly loved, or thirty years in. Choose to love freely with the terms that fit you and your love. You don't want your future self to find out that you have inadvertently agreed to a promise that isn't right for you.

Remembering that the relationship promise itself acts as a contract, some phrases you might want to try out are:

I see and accept your way is different to my way.

I see and accept your voice is different to my voice.

I see and accept your work is different to my work.

I see and accept your safety is different to my safety.

I see and accept your place is different to my place.

You have a place in my heart and I have a place in yours, but we are still separate.

We each belong.

What happens when you read through the words to create the ideal relationship promise?

If you have been together for a while, then have a place for the original promise and one for the promise of where you are now.

Which version of the promise are each of you looking at? If there is a different promise focus for each of you, then this will impact the intimacy within the relationship as well as the communication.

When healing an existing relationship, the promise as it existed at the start of the relationship, as well as the promise as it exists now, must be given a place.

It is important for both of you to be able to see the different aspects of the promise, as well as see and feel seen by each other.

Try gently saying:

For me this promise has changed.

For us this promised has changed.

There is (or can be) a place for a new promise.

If you find it hard to do this then we need to do a little more work to explore the blocks that sit in the way of this movement. It is only when the importance and value of the love at the start of your relationship is acknowledged, when the relationship and the relationship promise itself has a place, that a movement towards healing can take place.

Being able to be present with this and to acknowledge what was in the past, will allow both of you to be present in the now rather than being pulled into unfulfilled dreams and hopes and the loss of what might have been. This loss of dreams can be rooted in your own life or part of your ancestral inheritance.

This piece of work is special and I believe it is sacred. Honouring the place for your promise in this way is a gift to you and your partner. Quite a few of my clients have shared this work with their partners and have gone on to incorporate the words into their wedding vows. That is truly choosing to love freely.

When love hurts

Of course, we don't always get a 'happy ever after' and not all relationships last. What do we do when our relationship ends, or we want to end our relationship? How do we safely break a promise? What happens to all of the love, hope, dreams, and pain?

The end of relationship is more than a relationship not working and more than you or your partner making a different choice. It is the breaking of a promise or contract between two people and their family fields.

If the promise or contract between you and your partner hasn't been acknowledged clearly, and the breaking and ending of it isn't acknowledged and seen, or if there is a silence around the relationship itself, or if parts of the broken promise are unseen, then the promise can still have an impact on one or both of you as if it were still in place, effectively tying both of you and your future fates together.

If your relationship hasn't ended well or if one of you is still holding onto the other (and that can be them holding on to you—something you may be oblivious to), then part of you stays connected and committed to that person. Saying that this is not a good thing is an understatement. This is where the entanglements in your relationship lineage come from and it can get horribly messy.

The effect of this in your everyday life is that you are not fully available, that not all of you is free to love and be loved. Any relationships that follow will inevitably be with people who are also not completely available. This can be either in the sense of a similar unknown but still very active commitment to a previous partner, or by knowingly becoming involved with a partner who is already married or otherwise committed to someone else. Messy.

The promise that is made within a relationship, particularly a relationship that has been formalised in some way, either by a marriage, living together, or through having children together, can hold a place itself within the constellation field. And when it is over and done with, and that dream has died, that is not something you want to be dragging around with you.

Constellation to support divorce

In western society, over half of all marriages end in divorce and divorce is now generally thought of as commonplace. But it is a very recent phenomenon. It is only in the last few decades that it has been possible for women to petition for divorce. In certain faiths it was forbidden and would having been a devastating and shameful event for both families involved. This historical narrative of divorce trauma is why, even in cases of an amicable divorce, there is such a strong response from the surrounding family fields to divorce.

The reasons for a strong field response to divorce are complex. Perhaps in some cases it is the first divorce in the family that has been petitioned by a woman. In previous generations this would have been impossible. Divorce would have been perceived as being dangerous, particularly for the woman, and the loss of name, land, place, and belonging, can appear in the constellation with a pull to unseen, silent, excluded, and forbidden women, with a resulting separation and exclusion from the family's belief system. There may also be a narrative of punishment and shame flowing silently through the field of influence.

The usefulness and immediacy of effect of constellation in supporting individuals through the painful process of divorce always strikes me. I have worked with countless clients at various points of the separation and divorce journey and seen constellation transform something that has been crushing, excluding, and oftentimes intractable, into something more peaceful, with a space for resolution and belonging.

The impact and cost of divorce within the constellation setting, in terms of emotional belonging and freedom, is far greater on women than on men.

I do not mean to say that divorce is easier on men than on women or that there isn't an emotional cost to men. What I am saying is that within the three fundamental building blocks of constellation—namely: belonging, balance, and structure (the set-up of the accepted structure within the constellation field and field of influence that collectively flow down to affect us as individuals)—involves a sacrifice by the woman and her place within her family of origin, in order to accept a place within her partner's family field of origin.

Belonging—for however long the marriage or relationship lasts—is consciously and unconsciously derived from her partner's family field. What happens then when the relationship ends? Even if the split is amicable and her choice, there is a great cost and impact upon her belonging.

There is a conscious and unconscious loss of place which if left unchecked can mean being relegated to the realms of the unseen, silent, excluded, and forbidden women that exist within the historical narrative of the untold stories of her family field. And that is why the cost of divorce, within the constellation setting, is considerably higher for women.

Sarah came to see me when she was in the midst of a particularly painful divorce. She and her soon to be ex-husband Jonathan had been married for twenty-four years. They had an eighteen-year-old son who was still living in the family home before he headed off to college. Sarah was American and Jonathan was Scottish.

They met when Jonathan went to the United States to travel after he finished his university degree. They fell in love and Sarah moved her life to Scotland to be with him. Jonathan's family had roots in the United Kingdom that went back several generations. Sarah's ancestral lineage was a little more complex.

This is often the case with countries like the United States which have a strong migrant history as part of their collective narrative.

Her paternal line went back to Poland and Russia. Some of her ancestors had left Europe and moved to the States after the first world war. She had never been to see the descendants of the family who were left behind in Eastern Europe and they were very rarely spoken of when Sarah was growing up. Migration within the historical narrative of the family is very common. As we have discussed in chapter two, there is a particular triangulation that occurs that can have an extremely destructive impact on belonging. This is the migration triangulation of:

Those who left, those left behind, and descendants in the present

This triangulation is a ubiquitous one. It is not always active but can become animated or re-animated when belonging or safety is threatened.

For women going through the process of divorce and finding themselves emotionally, physically and spiritually displaced, it can be a destructive and unexpected root of trauma that becomes entangled with the present trauma of the divorce.

Add to that the historical associations and cost of divorce within the family narrative, particularly around belief and belonging, and you have a heady emotional and traumatic mix.

When Sarah came to see me the divorce process was well underway. Jonathan had been having an affair with a family friend for a number of years. Unfortunately, their son had discovered the affair and it was he who had told Sarah what had been happening.

To Sarah's surprise, Jonathan's mother and father, with whom she had previously had a positive relationship, closed ranks and were cutting her out of the family and refusing to communicate with either her or her son.

Jonathan's family were Catholic although he considered himself agnostic. Sarah had been brought up without a religious family belief. She described both her parents, who were now deceased, as atheist. However, going back to the family roots in Eastern Europe the family also had ties to the Catholic church. This background is significant.

The Catholic church in particular is very dominant within the context of relationship constellations. Divorce is not easily recognised within the field of influence of the ancestral narrative that is overlaid by the belief system of the Catholic church. This, combined with the presence of the migration triangulation, was weighing very heavily on Sarah and she described herself as feeling unseen and silenced in all areas of her life since the shocking discovery of her husband's ongoing infidelity. She also felt that it was impacting on her relationship with her son, who had become more withdrawn and uncommunicative as the separation and divorce unfolded.

We worked through a series of constellations together. As a rule of thumb, within a divorce constellation, you are essentially reversing the process of the creation of the optimal relationship promise, so that the relationship promise is just between the couple in question, the couple can see one another, and the relationship promise acknowledges the family and ancestors of each other as having a place and that that place exists outside the relationship promise. The place of any children is also seen by both of them and also exists outside of the relationship promise. The place of any former partners from each of their respective relationship lines has to also be seen and exist outside the relationship promise. However, when a relationship is ending, it tends not to be a relationship that has the optimal relationship structure and balance within the constellation context. It certainly wasn't present within Sarah's relationship constellation.

I wanted to get a sense of the loyalties and entanglements that were most dominant for Sarah in her present moment. In the initial constellation, I decided to try to keep it as simple as possible and to only include Sarah, Jonathan, the marriage, the promise, divorce, and betrayal.

In keeping the initial constellation relatively simple it is possible to discern through the animating spaces of marriage promise, divorce, and betrayal, where the dominant influences were coming from in the field, and what needed to be seen in order for Sarah to be seen and liberated from the entanglements she found herself weighed down by.

I brought in betrayal as an animator because of how she described the extra-marital affair, her in-laws' treatment of her, and her fear that this was the emotion her son was experiencing. Betrayal within the family field is as rife as migration and can have serious undertones of silence, guilt, punishment, and shame. The initial constellation was revelatory. Both Sarah and Jonathan were also behaving as animators, in that they were holding or representing other individuals, known and unknown, within the family field. Jonathan was very dominant and aggressive whereas Sarah became small and withdrew into herself. The betrayal was connected to Sarah rather than Jonathan, which Sarah found surprising and wanted to deny, however when I asked her to say to the betrayal space:

I recognise you.

You are familiar.

There was a relaxation in her body and a recognition of the truth of that. There was however no change in her demeanour, placement, or energy, within the created constellation space. She still remained small and vulnerable.

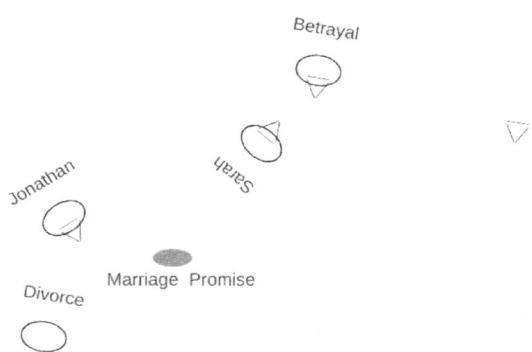

Image 30—Sarah and the cost of betrayal in the influent field

The divorce and marriage promise remained with Jonathan. Bringing in his parents and a representative of the Catholic church reduced his aggressiveness and dominance somewhat. From this we can deduce that there are two dominant entanglements at play, one from each of their respective fields. Despite Jonathan's energy dropping, the aggressiveness in the field had not moved and Sarah felt persecuted and vulnerable.

I brought in her own parents and an animating space for the ancestral land associated with her. This gave her a little more strength, but she still remained small. In order to move the persecution energy, I had Sarah work with the following narrative towards her mother-in-law:

This is my divorce.

You cannot have it.

Sarah was surprised at the strength in her words and the immediate shift within her. The mother-in-law moved away from the divorce. We continued:

I can feel the anger in your marriage.

I can feel the grief within you.

I feel you looking at this divorce.

It isn't your escape.

I won't be the safety in your marriage anymore.

And I won't be your escape.

This is my divorce.

You cannot have a place within it.

I will not give up my place for you.

Your beliefs are not my beliefs.

This changed the field significantly for Sarah. There had clearly been a holding of her in-laws' marriage promise within her own marriage. She had also been unconsciously earning a place within her relationship, as well as the land in Britain, by holding onto the anger and the pain. Divorce was coveted by her mother-in-law but denied a place because of her beliefs.

It was quite apparent that her father-in-law had also strayed from his marriage vows. Sarah, having been made aware of her husband's infidelity and then choosing divorce, was a threat to the women in the field who also desired that but felt or were unable to choose it. This opened up a raft of secrets and betrayals within Jonathan's lineage, however the focus of the constellation was to support Sarah within the divorce so in order to disentangle further we worked with the following narrative to Jonathan:

I see this now too.

I feel how much I have held in our marriage promise.

I won't hold this anymore.

I am choosing divorce.

You are no longer my husband and I am no longer your wife.

I am leaving this with you.

This movement freed Sarah further and there was significant relief. She was however still energetically small and vulnerable within the created constellation.

This is another common occurrence. As the woman releases herself from the place she has held within her partner's family field, she unconsciously begins to seek out a place of belonging back within her own paternal lineage. However, the place that she finds is often the place of her father's child rather than the place of an adult woman.

When she turned to face her parents, she began to weep. We worked with the following narrative:

I am still your daughter and you are still my father.

I am not a child in this; I am a woman.

There is no shame in this divorce.

It isn't dangerous for you.

It isn't dangerous for me.

I haven't returned as a child; I am coming home to my place as a free woman.

I am a free Nowak woman (Nowak being her maiden name).

These are powerful words. If you have experienced divorce yourself, how do you feel when you read them? Try saying them aloud using your own name.

This narrative shifted the energy for Sarah in terms of the smallness and vulnerability. However, it was very difficult for her to say *I am a free Nowak woman,* and when she tried there was a clear pull towards the ancestral land animator. This ancestral land animator is significant because of the migration triangulation and it was representing those left behind in Eastern Europe. The constellation opened further when I brought in spaces for those left behind and those who left. The betrayal animator was also drawn over to the animating land space, along with the Catholic church animator that had previously been associated with Jonathan's family.

This is an indication of an entanglement of betrayal and guilt in the family's land of origin. It was rooted with those left behind who had not survived the trauma of the conflict at that time. We gently worked to uncover the invisible parts of the entanglement, the most dominant of which were the unseen women connected with those left behind.

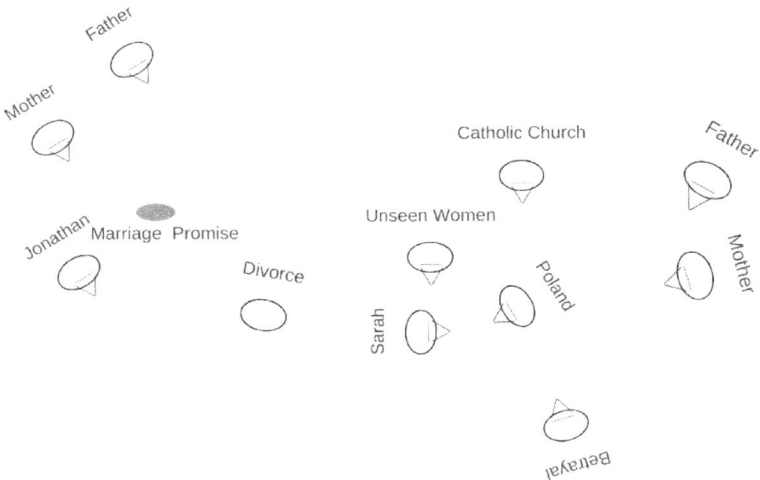

Image 31—Sarah's constellation showing the cost of love and belonging

I didn't know you were there, but I feel you now.

Parts of me come from you.

Your blood is my blood.

I feel the silent women within you.

This divorce isn't dangerous for me.

I am not being hunted.

This isn't death for me.

I don't need to be hidden in order to be safe.

And then to the land itself, Sarah's father and those who left:

The hidden women have been walking with me.

The silent women have been walking with me.

The unseen women have been walking with me.

The excluded women have been walking with me.

The forbidden women have been walking with me.

The wild women have been walking with me.

I feel their support.

I accept their support.

Their support runs through me.

I can't be them for you.

I have my own place on the land.

I am a free Novak woman.

They are now free Novak women.

I claim my own place.

I remember them as I claim my own place.

The movement here for Sarah was dramatic. She was able to stand fully within her place on the land, with the support of the ancestors, and for the first time fully see and face her soon to be ex-husband and their impending divorce. There was more hard work ahead, but this was the turning point for her and it was a key moment. She was no longer an unseen woman. She was a free woman. I will always remember the look of peace and belonging within her as she took her place. The divorce was no longer her nemesis. It was her freedom.

I urge you, if you are divorced or going through a divorce, to work through Sarah's phrases and make them your own.

Claim your freedom. This is your life. You are owned by no one.

Navigating divorce gently

When you are exploring divorce for yourself it is important to set up the initial created constellation space mindfully. The constellation space must include both you and your partner, with a space for the relationship promise as well as the divorce. We also need to bring in the parental influences for each of you.

It can be quite daunting to step into this constellation and I would suggest mapping it out with sheets of paper or coloured squares if it feels too much to connect with in your mind's eye.

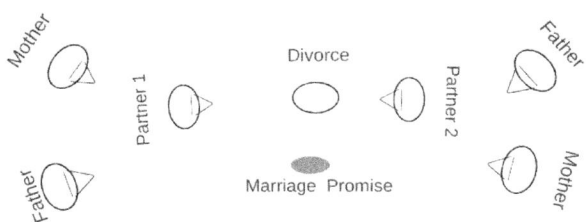

Image 32—Sample divorce constellation

When you are ready, and everyone is in place, take a deep breath and try saying:

I am no longer your husband/wife.

You will still be a free (insert surname(s)) man/woman.

I will still be a free (insert surname(s) woman/man.

You will still have a place and I will still have a place.

Take time to breathe into and notice the shifts as you speak the words. If you feel tense or find yourself rushing through, then stop. Take a deep breath and work through the words again. We want them to feel true and for you to be able to stay grounded and present in your body as you say them.

Then, if you are a woman who is getting divorced, I want you to say, very clearly, to your paternal line and field:

I am coming home.

I am coming home as a free woman.

I am not coming home as a child.

I include these phrases as women can become trapped at this point, as we saw in Sarah's example, and it is easy for us to lose a sense of our belonging. We may unconsciously believe, or there may be a historical narrative to support the belief, that we may only retain a place in our paternal line of origin as either a child or an excluded woman.

Shifting this unconscious historical narrative is crucial. Not only is it limiting to be unconsciously holding the place of a child, but if our childhood was unsafe or traumatic then we become trapped in yet another layer of trauma. This simple movement lifts us out of that potential pitfall.

Then to both of your parents and ancestors:

I chose this divorce.

This divorce is not dangerous for me.

I haven't lost my place.

I haven't lost my name.

I haven't lost my safety.

I still belong.

You can't have a place in my divorce.

Well done. Take some time here to note how you feel. This is hard work. Take some slow deep breaths and say:

I am (your name).

I belong.

I am free to love and be loved.

There is a place for love with me.

If you feel at all wobbly then pause, take a deep breath, and say those phrases again. Say them as many times as you need to. They are true.

Ancestral animators of the field

When someone in your field of influence is unseen and their story isn't told, or if their voice is unheard, then the generations that follow unconsciously recreate the fate of the unseen. This forms an unconscious historical narrative that can attract or repel members of the field. The events of previous generations have far-reaching implications on present day choices. The trauma of loss, anger, bitterness, and grief, when unacknowledged, can resurface at any point in the field of influence. Often this is triggered at key points of change such as births, deaths, and unions.

The unfulfilled promises and dreams act as ancestral animators and are not limited to our family of origin. These ancestral animators can trigger an unconscious alignment with the historical narrative and untold stories, and the shape shifting, time-travelling nature of the field is activated. The most destructive patterns are those rooted in anger, loss, and bitterness.

These can be found in:

Ancestral in-laws

Former partners

Spurned partners

Secret loves

Excluded loves

Hidden betrayal

It can feel as though you are being thoroughly thwarted when you are unknowingly entangled with an ancestral animator. 'Love is cursed' or 'my family is cursed' are common descriptors for those of us who are particularly entangled with them. There is a need to go back before we can move forward.

Within the constellation setting the most common theme that appears is where we are tied to the fate of someone who has gone before us who is not at peace within the realm of the dead. The prevalence of the dynamic of victim and perpetrator within the constellation setting is extraordinary.

The entanglement that is created from an event where someone is responsible for taking the life of another yet will not look to the victim, is a very strong phenomenon, and the ripples that flow down the family lines can affect many generations that come after.

The events that create such an entanglement do not have to be some great family secret. Everyday situations of war and violence and the deaths that occur due to them are devastating for many generations of a family, not only in terms of the victim's family but also the family of those responsible.

In families where there has been perpetration of others, we, the generations that follow, are drawn either to the fates of the victims or the perpetrators.

If we are drawn to the victims then we will display behaviours or patterns that indicate that we are sacrificing ourselves in some way, giving up our place so that the victim or victims may be seen again, along with carrying the grief and the guilt that has previously been unexpressed within the family. Or we perhaps become unseen by those around us and feel that we don't have a place. We are tied to the unseen and displaced victims.

Not all of us are tied to the victims. Some of us are tied to the perpetrators, and when that is the case we will often experience great anger and draw this towards ourselves, becoming entangled with destructive and violent relationships, either as the victim or the perpetrator. These patterns form the untold stories within the historical narrative of our family field and can be triggered at any point.

The trigger is not necessarily restricted to similar events, it can be emotional in nature. When we feel ourselves at risk or are perhaps experiencing a victim-perpetrator pattern in our relationship or work, then our unconscious response can be to align with the historical narrative, and we react as if we are in a life or death situation in the present moment even if we are not.

In other words, when we are entangled with unacknowledged trauma connected to victim-perpetrator patterns and feel threatened, emotionally or otherwise, then our system reacts to the threat by shape shifting and time travelling us back to re-live the death or trauma of our ancestors. Their life or death story becomes ours.

Looking for love and not finding it

Imagine having to leave your home and country behind you as a rebellious teenage girl—all that you have ever known and loved. Not all of your family are able to come with you. Your grandparents are too old to make the harsh journey, and your uncle doesn't agree with your father's fears and decides to hold onto the familiar safety of the farm that has been in the family for generations. He does not want to deprive his infant sons of their heritage. The young man that you love and hoped to marry cannot come with you. His family do not hold the same political beliefs as your father and they do not believe that the war will reach the village. They do not believe the stories that are being told of pogroms and violence and death. He cannot leave them behind to work the land without him. Imagine the horrible and impossible choices that were made to leave or to stay. Imagine being that young woman. Being sixteen and in love and having to leave the young man you dreamed of marrying, and all that felt safe and familiar. All of the dreams and hopes of the future left behind, finding yourself in a new town, in a new country, where everything, including the language and the culture, are different. Imagine finding out that your father was right. That the war did come. And that the young man who held the part of your heart that you left behind had not survived. Your grandparents, your uncle, his young sons and the farm all gone. Could your heart survive that? Could you make your way in a new land, grieving for all that was lost? Imagine that the best way forward for your family now was to forge loyalties with other families finding themselves in the same situation in this new world, in this new land. What stronger loyalty is there than the bonds of family? A marriage is arranged for you with the son of a more affluent migrant family. This family is lucky, their medical skills are sought after, and they have managed to ingratiate themselves within this new world. The son however is not a happy soul. He too has left behind his heart. And whilst you mourn and grieve for what you have lost, he chooses instead to nurse his anger and bitterness. He keeps it hidden from his family and from yours. Only the two of you share the intimacy of his rage within your marriage, this marriage that keeps your family safe but sacrifices all that is left of you. You cannot bring yourself to look upon the children born from him with love. For you, when you see them, you are reminded of pain and loss. You distance yourself to survive and hope that they can do the same. Love for you becomes something that is cursed; it was left with the dead.

This story is real. It happened countless times to countless souls. The characters and losses are different but the dynamics of those left behind and those who left remain the same. The point that completes the triangle is the individuals in the present, the descendants. Sometimes the entanglement is with those left behind, sometimes with those that left, sometimes both. The impact of the entanglements can be devastating.

Anna came to a group workshop in the United States. Her intention was to work on her love life. No matter what she did or how hard she tried, her relationships always seemed to follow the same pattern. They would start out well and the men would seem kind and interested in her. But as the relationship progressed, the connection between them would deteriorate and they would become controlling, and in some instances abusive. At this point she would end the relationship and take a little time on her own to heal. As she described her experiences to the group, she said she felt as though she was cursed. She had the ability to turn a kind and happy man into an angry and abusive one within the space of a few months. She was trying to joke and laugh as she talked about it however the pain and confusion within her were clear. When Anna spoke about the women within her maternal line and field it was not with softness and affection. She spoke of a difficult and cold relationship with her mother and a softer yet still distant relationship with her grandmother. She also spoke of her grandmother's experiences of her emotionally abusive mother, Anna's great-grandmother.

The great-grandmother's marriage had been a long and unhappy one, but it was the last known marriage within the maternal lineage of her family that had actually stood the test of time. Each and every other marriage or significant relationship had been cut short, either through early deaths or in more recent generations through divorce. Anna smiled again and tried to make a joke about the family curse on love.

The sixteen-year-old girl in the story you have just stepped into was Anna's great-grandmother's story, and Anna was holding it tightly within her heart. Although she was not that young woman in the story, she was unconsciously representing her, her lost hopes and dreams, and the painful reality of her abusive marriage that was the price to be paid for the family's survival in America.

Anna's version of her great-grandmother was of an abusive and cruel woman who made her daughter's life miserable and drove away all who tried to love her. That version changed considerably when Anna stepped into the created constellation field.

Until that point no one within Anna's family knew of the suffering and abuse within the great-grandmother's marriage nor how much of her heart was left behind in Russia. The guilt and cost of her survival, whilst those that were left behind suffered a violent death, was silently held and unconsciously passed from generation to generation, along with the unconscious belief that love is not safe.

That love and sacrifice are one and the same. That it is only possible to be safe and have a place for your dreams when you are alone.

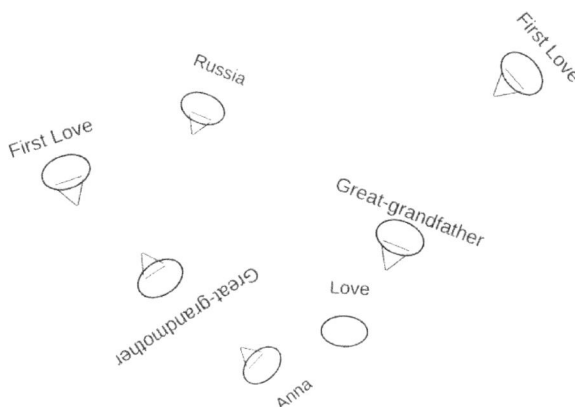

Image 33—Anna's inheritance

In the created constellation you can see the strong entanglement between Anna, her place for love, and her great-grandmother. Her great-grandmother looks for her lost love left behind in Russia. Her great-grandfather will not look to his lost love, but instead he looks to Anna and the place for love within her life. Anna struggles under the weight of her great-grandmother's pain, waiting for her to see her and how much she has carried for her. It is an intractable entanglement. There is some relief within Anna as the structure of the field she has been unconsciously living in is revealed, however she has no awareness of her own place for love. All she can see is her great-grandmother and her lost love. And as she looks to them, love is claimed from her by her great-grandfather.

The language narrative used within the constellation begins to move and loosen the entanglements.

I can see this now.

I can feel this now.

I have been holding your pain tight.

It is safe for me to have love in my life.

It doesn't always cost this much.

Death has taken your marriage promise.

You are free in death.

You can go home now.

You can be together now.

You can choose love now.

And then to the great-grandfather:

I feel what you lost.

I can feel your anger.

She (the great-grandmother) didn't take it from you.

I didn't take it from you.

I can't be her for you.

I can't carry forward the sacrifice.

It is safe for me to have love in my life.

It doesn't always cost this much.

The realisation within Anna of the cost of the continuation of the line hits her hard. She can see her great-grandmother from a completely fresh perspective.

I see your sacrifice.

I witness it.

It is remembered.

I don't need to be hidden in order to be safe.

I am a free woman.

I am a free Russian woman.

I am a free American woman.

I am free to choose love.

This constellation was pivotal for Anna. It didn't change the hardships that her mother and grandmother experienced in their childhood nor the cost of love within the line. However, giving place to and witnessing the sacrifice of the previous generations shifted the weight of the unacknowledged trauma within the family line.

Looking beyond the accepted truth to the actual story freed not only Anna but it also freed the generations of unseen men and women within her family field. She felt a lightness of being that she hadn't experienced before. She was free to choose herself and to choose love. From her perspective, the curse was broken.

There are many similarly entangled descendants of trauma in the present who find love is blocked, or who are fated to follow the patterns of those gone before.

When you scratch the surface of stories within the family field, you uncover lost loves, forgotten loves, the forbidden, abandoned and excluded.

We often only see our family and ancestors through the role that they hold within the family: mother, grandfather, great aunt, great-grandmother. But each life lived was full of dreams and hope, sometimes fulfilled and sometimes painfully lost. Each story from their past, when unacknowledged or unseen, becomes our story in the present.

Work through Anna's constellation as if it were your own. This *will be* a part of your own invisible inheritance. This will be flowing through you in some way. Notice who and what stands out for you from Anna's story. Working with this can free your future love and your future dreams.

Remembering the dead is important. When they are not seen and they are not at peace, they have an effect on the living as if they were still alive. When the circumstances of their death are such that they have sacrificed their life so that others may live—if they have sacrificed their life for their beliefs, or their country, or if someone has taken life in such circumstances—it adds an extra dimension to the entanglement and the pattern that inevitably flows down the family lines.

When the victims are not seen, we within the generations that follow, can be drawn to them. We make unconscious efforts to bring them to light by sacrificing aspects of ourselves, whether that be success in our material life, denying ourselves love, or through our physical health. When the perpetrator does not take or accept responsibility, when they cannot see or face their victims or the victim's family, then they become very big and influential energetically. They overshadow other members of their family, making them feel small. We in the generations that follow that are tied to the fate of a perpetrator, can carry a great anger that will flare up within us. We can energetically tower over our family members and friends. There can be a compulsion to become involved in destructive, violent or manipulative relationships, either as the victim or as the perpetrator. And so the patterns are carried forward until the unseen are seen, and the stories that haven't been told are witnessed. Instead of being free to live and exist in the present we are instead unconsciously living and experiencing life through the historical narrative.

Honouring your ancestors

The ancestral animators are the deeply held roots of an original entanglement that can pass, sometimes silently, from generation to generation, and trigger the historical narrative. They aren't necessarily rooted within our own field of origin. When we are aligned to the unseen men, women, or children, in either our own maternal and paternal fields or a partner or previous partner's maternal and paternal fields, then the pull to the ancestral animators becomes established. It is also common for an ancestral animator to lie dormant within our field and become animated by us when we choose love or another dream for ourselves.

The unseen held within our field of influence are often deeply wounded and lost souls, and their wounding can be interwoven with our own.

I invite you to connect with the unseen in your ancestral field, remembering that the connection to the unseen very probably exists outside of your known family.

Light a candle in honour of them and try saying very clearly and consciously from your heart:

I see you.

I feel you.

I have been holding your wounds within mine.

I am (your name).

I am a free soul.

Each of you are free souls.

It is safe for me to love and be loved.

I can choose love without living your story.

Sit quietly. Listen to the silence. Listen to the beat of your heart. Feel your presence in the absence of theirs, in this stillness you have created.

You have created a space to love freely. This is yours. And it is sacred.

6.

The forward flow—healing the ghosts of the past to be present to the future

The continuation of your line and field

The influences from our ancestors flow down to us from generation to generation through the gateway of our parents. The influences from our siblings and relationships flow around us. However, the connection with our children and dreams, flows from us to them. It is future facing. It is our legacy.

It is more than the physical continuation of our family line through our children—it is the starting point of belonging for our hopes and dreams, our inheritance to our descendants. It is what we offer to the world, and in that offering there is a need to accept that we are letting go of a part of ourselves. What was once part of us, what we create, and what comes from us, now have their own place in front of us, outside of us, and are free to be seen and heard independently of us.

That can be really difficult to get our head around. It is this struggle to let go and separate that fuels the invisible inheritance. We have been working with entanglements where our ancestors have struggled with this forward flow and separation. Now it is our turn. One day, in the not too distant future, we will be the ancestors looked at by our descendants. What would you like your inheritance for them to be?

Our own ability to fully accept and take our own place within our family field has an influence on the ability of our children, as well as our hopes and dreams, to have a place of their own, a place which is accepted freely by both them and us.

This is the point at which we each need to take responsibility for our own choices and actions—where we need to fully see, know, and accept where we come from, and our place in relation to but also separate from our origins. We are more than the child of our parents. We are more than the product of our invisible inheritance.

This is a tipping point for us, where the flow from past to present switches to the flow from us to the future generations.

Only when we accept who we are and where we come from, and take our own place, can that which flows from us be fully seen, heard, and acknowledged.

Whose truth are you holding?

When we are born into our family, we are entirely dependent on them for our safety and well-being as well as our belonging. There is an automatic acceptance of the truth of the family of origin that we are born into. In the vulnerability of infancy there is no safety outside of the perceived safety that comes through the acceptance of the family truth and the reality of the day to day existence within that family field. The truth can include:

It isn't safe to be seen.

It isn't safe to be a mother.

I have to carry my father's regrets in order to be safe.

I am responsible for holding the pain of others.

It isn't safe to trust love.

There can be entanglements present within our immediate family of origin and family field that we can be born into, or perhaps experience in utero, that will predispose us to perpetually carry the pain or trauma of others in order to navigate safety for ourselves, and these form part of the family truth. Some common yet destructive occurrences are:

Lack of safety in the womb after abortion or miscarriage.

Separation from our mother at an early stage.

Separation from our father at an early stage.

The end of our parent's relationship.

Either or both of our parents establishing new relationships.

Violent or sudden death within our immediate family field occurring either when we are in utero or in early childhood.

When there is a belief or lived reality of 'not enough,' linked to money, safety or love. And this can be either in utero or in early childhood.

Conception through rape or abuse.

As we grow into our childhood and adulthood, we develop our own sense of truth. Our own truth may not be in resonance with the family truth and this disparity may have a profound impact on our sense of safety and belonging.

There can be an unconscious belief held within us that we will lose our safety and belonging if we reject our family truth in favour of what is true within our own hearts and beliefs.

In order to survive, it can appear easier to sacrifice aspects of our own truth and beliefs, and in turn aspects of ourselves, in order to stay in alignment with the family truth. The consequences of this self-sacrifice can be severe.

Karen began working with me at a point of transition in her life. Her children, a son and a daughter in their twenties, were fully grown and had left home. They were living their own lives outside Britain where they had been brought up. Karen's relationship with her husband Charles, from her perspective, had grown stale and distant over the last ten years, and she was questioning what she wanted to do with the rest of her life. She was struggling to see a happy future for herself in her current situation. She felt as though she had lost all sense of who she was and didn't know what her dreams were anymore. There was a childlike quality to Karen's energy and communication. She experienced a sense of extreme vulnerability as she tried to look forward within any created constellation and did not have a sense of her own autonomy.

We began exploring Karen's relationship with her husband in the initial constellation. I wanted to observe where the loyalty was for each of them and also if it was possible for Karen to have a place for, or any sense of her dreams when her husband was within the created constellation space.

We began with bringing in spaces for Karen, her husband, and their marriage promise. Although Karen placed the marriage promise in front of her and Charles, neither of them could look at it or acknowledge it, and there was a significant physical distance separating Karen and Charles.

Image 34 - Karen with no place for her dreams

It was quite clear from observing this initial constellation, before even introducing the animator for Karen's dreams, that there were outside influences on their marriage and marriage promise. Because of Karen's description of the marriage and her original intention for the session—to explore her sense of loss of self and autonomy within her dreams—it is likely that the influences upon Karen and Charles originate from the family ancestral influences, as opposed to the lineage of former partners.

I brought in representative spaces for each set of parents and their associated marriage promises. Neither Charles' parents nor the promise made any impact on the dynamic between Karen and Charles within the context of Karen's intentional question. However, the addition of Karen's parents and their promise caused a strong response within the constellation field.

Karen shifted so that she was more able to connect with and be close to her father, effectively turning her back on Charles and their own marriage promise. Karen's mother and her parent's marriage promise moved possessively towards Karen's and Charles' promise.

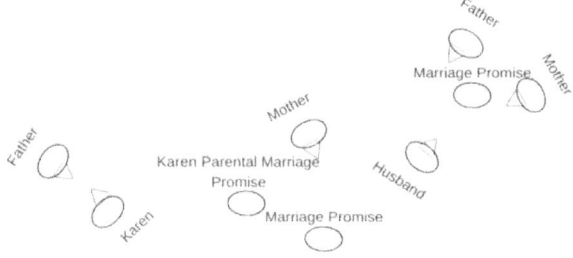

Image 35—Karen and the burden of belonging

Karen's parents' marriage had been a turbulent one. They had both been involved in significant relationships before they were married. Karen was aware of this because her mother would often refer to her father's great love and infer that Karen and her mother played second fiddle to that. When Karen spoke about her experiences of her childhood, she recited them as statements of fact; there was no inner questioning of the validity of the statements. Physically and energetically she shrunk back into herself. Connecting with the memories of her childhood pulled her into those entanglements and she became small as a result. There was a clear pull for Karen into the unseen, secrets, and acceptance of a truth, that was not in alignment with her own personal truth, nor was it supportive or nurturing for her.

The significant aspects in this constellation to note are Karen's shift of loyalty to her father from her husband, which simultaneously pulled her to become smaller and without voice, as well as the abandonment of her husband and marriage promise to her mother and her parents' marriage promise.

This is a deeper dynamic that is more than an unconscious holding of an inherited relationship promise. We can identify that by the way in which Karen responds to the inclusion of her parents and the lack of a mirroring response within her husband's family field.

We must remind ourselves at this point that the relationship promise will always seek to be balanced and that there is often mirroring of entanglements within the historical narrative of the fields of respective partners.

We do not observe that here, suggesting that the entanglements for Karen are rooted before her conscious awareness of intimate relationships, and are directly linked to safety and love, or more specifically the perceived cost of safety and love.

I interrupted the constellation at this point to refocus the created constellation field to explore what we had uncovered. In order for Karen to have a sense of her own self and purpose in her present, she needed to be able to claim back the parts of herself that were entangled in her childhood and with her parents.

In this next constellation, I included spaces for Karen in the present moment as well as her childhood, her mother, her father, the family truth, and Karen's own truth.

The undercurrents that were felt in the former constellation were more overt in this constellation. Karen, both in the present and in childhood, had no connection to or awareness of her own truth. The family truth was in front of Karen's childhood and in effect blocking the connection to her parents. Both aspects of Karen were again fixated upon her father though her father could not see her. He was looking outside the created constellation. Karen's mother was displaying anger towards both Karen in her childhood, and Karen's father. Standing within this highly intense created constellation space, before beginning to disentangle the threads, was helpful for Karen. There was a familiarity to the weight of the chaos presented and a relief that the chaos was finally being seen.

We worked firstly with the connection between Karen in the present and her childhood self. There was a weight of guilt within the connection and it was clear that a part of Karen had remained in that childhood place, waiting for her father to see her. The following phrases introduced some separation for Karen's childhood self:

Your life in this is innocent.

This is not your fault.

You haven't created this pain.

You haven't created this death.

In this you are a child.

You are more than their unseen truth.

You are more than the unacknowledged pain.

You are more than the grief.

You are worthy of love.

You are worthy of belonging.

You are worthy of safety.

At this point Karen was able to integrate her younger self into her present self.

We were then able to acknowledge the pain within Karen's childhood as she felt her father draw away from both her and her mother, and his pull towards death. I brought an animating space in for death in the place that Karen's father was fixated upon. Karen became very distressed at this point as her father continued to turn away from her and attempt to move towards death. We worked with a narrative of:

I accepted your truth as mine.

It isn't true.

It wasn't true.

You were wrong.

Your truth is not my truth.

I don't believe you.

I am not that child anymore.

I am a free woman.

I thought I had to accept your truth.

I felt you dancing with death.

I thought you would stay if I accepted your truth.

Your truth wasn't safe for me.

I am choosing my own truth now.

Both Karen and her father were finally able to look at and accept one another. There was significant relief in this for Karen although the undercurrent of guilt remained. I gently shifted her focus towards her mother who at this point had become further enraged at the softening in the connection and acceptance between Karen and her father.

The quality of the connection between Karen and her mother was different in this constellation in comparison to the initial constellation. She was not fully in her place yet as an adult in the connection with her mother, but she had certainly moved on from the paralysis of childhood. She was able to discern her mother's anger as well as her distress.

It wasn't true.

I didn't exclude you.

You weren't displaced by me.

You weren't excluded by me.

That wasn't true.

I lost him too.

My father couldn't see me either.

You are looking at me through your version of this but it isn't true.

It wasn't true then.

It isn't true now.

I believed you.

I believed that he stopped loving me, but it wasn't true.

He was my father and I was his daughter.

The love between you died but he never stopped loving me.

There is a place for your truth and a place for my truth.

Our truths are different.

I am choosing my own truth

There is a place for my own truth.

I am worthy of belonging and that has a place in my truth.

I am worthy of safety and that has a place in my truth.

I am worthy of being chosen and that has a place in my truth.

I am worthy of being seen and that has a place in my truth.

I am worthy of being heard and that has a place in my truth.

I am worthy of being loved and that has a place in my truth.

I am worthy of being valued and that has a place in my truth.

I am enough and that has a place in my truth.

This was a pivotal moment for Karen as she was able to let go of both her unconscious belief that she was responsible for her father's safety and the belief that part of her had to wait for him in her childhood to hold back his unconscious draw towards death. This then created the space for her to explore the truth that she had unconsciously accepted from her mother—that her father had stopped loving her and that she was not worthy of love or safety and all that goes along with that.

This is very deep work and this shifting of unconsciously held truths and beliefs can allow the integration of our childhood self into our adult self. Karen's father died in the days after her marriage to Charles and she had silently held onto the belief that his death was the cost of her choosing love and her own dreams.

This was contributing to the fear and loss of self in the present as she attempted to look forward to her own future. She became entangled and was propelled back to her lost inner child. It is important for such a transition to be fully integrated before any next steps, and I encouraged Karen to take a little time for herself and to work with the narrative around the unconsciously held beliefs before we went on to tackle her relationship with Charles and her future choices.

How did you feel reading through Karen's constellation? Did the weight and the chaos from her childhood feel familiar? Some of the truths we accept unquestioningly in childhood can stay silently hidden in our hearts. We are going to gently explore what truths are there for you, both in your childhood and your present.

Family truths and secrets

It is important to remember here, that we as children accept the reality of the world that we are born into, and the family that we are born into, as the only reality and the only truth, and there is great vulnerability in that.

Often what is perceived to be a truth in a family is only one version of a particular family story—the safest version that the parents are able to share, or the version that they inherited from their parents.

As adults we can still unconsciously hold some of the family truth within us even if we consciously know it to be not true or safe for us. If some of the choices we make as adults are not in alignment with the family truth then we can be triggered by root entanglements within our own field and our relationship field. This is because some of what we may choose for ourselves, that is right and true for us, would be perceived as a betrayal within the greater field of influence of our family and ancestors.

There are different types of truths that can be held within a family. Some examples are:

The truth of one political, spiritual, or religious belief.

The truth within relationship promises and gender beliefs within relationships.

That safety only comes with non-acknowledgement of trauma, pain, or grief.

That place and belonging has to be earned through sacrifice.

That place and belonging has to be earned through perpetration.

That the maternal or paternal line isn't safe or should be excluded.

That the child has taken the mother or father's dreams from them.

That the child is responsible for the safety of the family.

That happiness and love is a betrayal.

The power of your truth is not my truth

Think for a moment about your version of your parents. As you look back at them from the age you are now and see them as you saw them as a child, how does it feel? Does the truth that you believed and accepted as a child still feel true?

Take some slow, deep breaths into your body. Notice how present and grounded you feel in this moment. When you are ready, bring your parents into your mind's eye. Breathe into the connection and pay attention to where they go in relation to you and how it feels.

I want you to bring spaces in to represent their truth in your childhood and their truth now.

Next bring spaces in to represent your truth in your childhood and your truth now.

Take the time to notice what comes in for each part. Don't worry too much about what visual or sense of space comes in, focus instead on how it feels for you as you breathe into the connection. Do you stay present in your body or are you drifting back to your childhood?

Now gently work with saying:

It isn't true.

It wasn't true.

You were wrong or *For me, you were wrong.*

Your truth is not my truth.

I don't believe you.

I am not that child anymore.

There can be a cost to seeking a different truth or holding a different truth to that of our parents and family of origin. Most commonly that cost is exclusion and loss of place or the *belief* that there will be exclusion and loss of place.

When we work with *you were wrong* or *they were wrong* in the above constellation process, to a parent or ancestor, it isn't from the perspective of judgement or blame. It is simply creating a place and a space for your own truth, which is important for clearing the root entanglements and moving into acceptance of who you are.

Releasing your younger self

If you found yourself getting stuck in the different versions of truth or you felt yourself drifting back to childhood, then a little work to connect with yourself as a child can be really helpful.

Take a moment to settle your energy and bring a representative for yourself as a child into your mind's eye. Notice at what age you are initially connecting with yourself as well as the impact on your body and breath.

Gently work with saying:

Your life in this is innocent.

This is not your fault.

You haven't created this pain.

You haven't created this death.

In this you are a child.

You are more than their unseen truth.

You are more than the unacknowledged pain.

You are more than the grief.

You are worthy of love.

You are worthy of belonging.

You are worthy of safety.

Your truth can be your own.

Your truth is your own.

Some of the phrases may be more challenging to work with than others, and that is okay. Take your time and notice any resistance within you as it occurs and gently continue to work with this part of yourself.

It can be helpful to bring in a separate space for safety within your created constellation field. There is no place for judgement in this—take your time and work through the constellation as many times as you need to.

It is safe for life to move forward

The acceptance that there can be a place of safety in living, dreaming, and creating can be far more challenging than it sounds, and the need for safety and to feel safe is paramount. This is the point at which we can find ourselves potentially entangled with the patterns of our paternal and maternal line and fields that we have discussed so far. We'll view them now from this new perspective.

The big three

There are three transformational events which create ripples throughout our entire field of influence and they are **deaths**, **marriages** (or formalisation of a relationship), and **births**. Dormant entanglements become reanimated with any of these three, and it can become challenging to remain free from the entanglements that are stirred back to life. Some examples of big three examples are:

Becoming pregnant and miscarrying knowingly or unknowingly.

Becoming pregnant and terminating the pregnancy either through an agreed choice, without the other parent's knowledge, or being forced to choose an abortion.

Becoming pregnant, giving birth, and keeping the baby.

Becoming pregnant, giving birth, and adopting the baby through choice or forced choice.

Becoming pregnant, giving birth, and the baby not surviving or dying very young.

Following a dream to study or work in a particular area.

Following a dream to create a business.

Bringing safety into your transition from child to adult to parent is so important, and this is why, from the perspective of you to your parents, we have worked with such phrases as:

It is safe for you to be a mother/father.

It is safe for me to be your son/daughter/child.

The point that we are now exploring the field from has shifted. You no longer have a place as a child in this. You are an adult and hold your place as an adult. This is where the importance of the belonging aspects of the paternal line come to bear.

I belong.

I accept my place.

My place is just for me.

We also want to move into being able to say:

It is safe for me to live.

It is safe for me to be a mother/father/parent.

It is safe for me to dream.

It is safe for me to create.

The transformation from woman to mother to grandmother

The point of transition from woman to mother is a vulnerable one. Our everyday lives in the present are very different to the everyday lives of our ancestors. We are pulled in so many directions. There are so many things on the to-do list and the expectation that we can do it all, have it all, be it all, and look good doing it. It's impossible.

The sacredness of the transition into motherhood is often overlooked or simply squeezed out through lack of time. The lack of time and sacrifice of time that is a natural part of motherhood, can be rejected consciously and unconsciously as we try to keep all the plates spinning. And sometimes it is the older generations that carry the burden of that.

What happens when it is the daughter trying to give her mother the responsibility of the children so that she can have more time for herself? What happens when it is the daughter who tries to reverse the forward flow of the maternal line when motherhood costs too much?

For grandmothers, when their daughter or daughter-in-law consciously or unconsciously expects them to continue the sacrifice of time associated with motherhood instead of accepting that natural sacrifice themselves, they can be catapulted into entanglements of servitude and enslavement within the family field.

The mother in question can be attempting to remain a child themselves instead of becoming a mother, another thread leading us back to the importance of safety and belonging.

The transformation from man to father to grandfather

The transition from boy to man to father is also vulnerable, particularly in the case of a fractured paternal line.

There is a weight of responsibility in becoming a father, not only to the mother and child, but also to the line itself. If the paternal line is reversed or fractured, it does not provide the inherent safety and belonging needed to support the man in his place as he transitions into fatherhood and as he also attempts to support and give place to the mother.

In the transition from father to grandfather, an entanglement can be re-animated around there not being enough, with a need for someone to have to die or give up their place in the line in order to make room for the new generations.

This is an entanglement often associated with the reality of there not actually being enough food, safety, or security, in a childhood experience of war, migration, or trauma, or an existence of that entanglement in the historical narrative of the untold stories.

The weight of unconsciously co-parenting as a grandparent

Tina had been a client for a number of years and would use both individual sessions and group work to support her as and when she needed to. She had worked hard on her relationship with her mother, which had been a difficult and challenging process. Part of her determination had been a deep desire to prevent any entanglements flowing from her to her own children and future generations. *This stops with me!* was her personal mantra. She was disconcerted to feel the weight of those entanglements resurface when her own daughter became pregnant. With growing concern, she observed her daughter morph into someone she didn't recognise anymore.

From Tina's perspective, her daughter Dana was refusing to take responsibility for being pregnant, or prepare a space for the arrival of her child, and was attempting to pass the weight of that onto Tina. This worsened after the birth of Tina's granddaughter and Tina became torn between wanting to love and protect her granddaughter Nina, and the weight of the expectations that Dana was placing on her.

We explored the dynamic during an individual session. Tina's experience is not an uncommon one.

Time was spent acknowledging Tina's relationship with her mother and the grief there, but the deepest movement came with acknowledging the belonging, balance, and flow, within her maternal lineage. We worked with Tina's connection to her daughter Dana with the narrative:

I had to make sacrifices in order to be your mother.

I had to make sacrifices in order to keep you safe as a child.

I chose to do that.

In spite of the cost, I chose to do that.

I do not regret that choice.

You are not a child anymore.

I will not stay in sacrifice for you.

I have given enough.

I have already sacrificed my time.

I have already sacrificed my choices.

I have already sacrificed my dreams.

For me, it was part of being a mother.

You are a mother now too.

This is yours now.

I cannot be a mother for your child.

I am her grandmother and there is great joy in that for me.

I will not bring sacrifice into the joy.

Motherhood changes a part of who you are.

I cannot protect you from that change.

You can't have a place with me as a child.

You have left and I have let you go.

I create (some) safety for your child but I will not be safety for you.

I was responsible for your safety when you were a child.

But you are not a child anymore and my time is my own again now.

I have earned this time; it is mine.

I am doing something special with it.

I will not follow you back into sacrifice.

Your time is not more important than my time.

My time is important too.

My life is important too.

I am still your mother, but I am also more than your mother.

Others see me as more than your mother.

I will not give that up for you.

It is precious for me.

This narrative was transformative for Tina. It allowed her to step back from her daughter's fear of motherhood and the associated cost of that. She was able to take her place as a grandmother and embrace the joy of it.

This movement is highly significant not just for Tina but for the transition from parent to grandparent in general. The structure of belonging within family and community has changed and deteriorated in parts of our culture and as a result, the honouring, as well as the acknowledgement of the place of mothers and fathers, has diminished.

The cost and natural sacrifice is also not acknowledged however the impact of this does not always stay with the new generation of parents. It ripples and spreads throughout the field and the grandparents find themselves encumbered and trapped within the role of perpetual service of parenthood.

This takes nothing away from the joy of grandparenthood at all. Some of the phrases in Tina's constellation may seem a little harsh, but their purpose is to disentangle the relationships to allow for a clearer place for love, connection, and joy, between all of the generations. If you are in Tina's position, work through those phrases for yourself.

You will not lose your children or grandchildren if you do, but you may lose parts of yourself if you don't.

Responsibility

In constellation work there can be a temptation to keep the focus on the choices that our family and ancestors have made and look at the resulting entanglements with a sense of judgement and perhaps anger at the generational impact. *Why am I the one that has to heal the family? Why is my family so crazy? Why is it always me?* are questions that can be frequently uttered, rhetorically and indignantly, by some clients. Unfortunately, those clients are missing some subtle but very important points of constellation theory and practice.

The purpose of the constellation is not to look at the choices and the events of the past through the advantage of our present knowing, casting judgement and anger at what has happened. It is to look and see with compassion, to give place to the missing and the silent, the perpetrated and perpetrators, remembering that each and every soul belongs, and has an equal place of belonging, regardless of the choices that have been made.

> Patterns don't flow down from generation to generation because your ancestors decided you are the one that needs to pay for the pain of the past. They pass down because an unconscious choice is made by the next generation to carry that which is too heavy or too painful to see within the previous generations.

You are a participant in this. Responsibility is important.

You may be carrying responsibility for pain or trauma that has nothing to do with you but often it will be entangled with some of your own choices that perhaps have similar echoes or resonance from either the victim or the perpetrator perspective.

What are you responsible for? Can you see the consequences of your own choices and accept responsibility? Or are your descendants looking at that for you?

What do you need to take responsibility for?

Take a moment to think about your own life here: all of the friendships and relationships you have been involved in, your working life, places you have worked and left, your family, and promises you have made and broken. There will be a lot there. You can't move through life without connecting with others in some way, shape, or form. You also can't make choices in your life that will please everyone, and nor should you, but being able to see the cost of the choices made and promises broken is key.

What happens when you work with the following phrases?

I am responsible for my own choices.

I see the cost of the choices I have made.

I see the cost of my parents' choices.

I see the cost of my ancestors' choices.

I accept the choices they have made.

I don't agree with all of them, but I do accept what they have chosen as their choice.

I leave the cost of their choices with them.

I accept the cost of my own choices.

I feel guilt.

I feel anger.

I feel shame.

I was wrong.

It was an impossible choice.

I broke a promise.

I broke a trust.

I caused pain.

It doesn't have to be a betrayal.

These phrases are used within the constellation narrative to provoke and observe a response rather than from a judgemental perspective. *They are not sticks to beat yourself with.* Rather they are keys to release you from the guilty prison of not seeing.

As the line and field continues, you transition from child to adult, with the next generations looking back at you for confirmation of their place as it flows from you to them, regardless of their personal beliefs around the choices you have made. *You* become the gateway to the ancestral field. That forward flow is interrupted if you are unable to fully take responsibility for who you are in the present moment. Can you bravely do what some of your ancestors weren't able to do? Can you be the first in the family field to look at who you are and where you come from? What do you choose for your legacy?

A field of broken dreams

There is a space that exists between the realms of the ancestors and the realms of the descendants. It is the space that we have to transition through as we turn *from looking at our parents and ancestors from the place of a child, and face forward to our future and our descendants as an adult.*

This transitional space, in between the realms of our ancestors and descendants, is the gateway to the root entanglements that have overtaken the parts of ourselves that we have lost. And we can lose those parts of us in lots of ways.

When we break a promise in a relationship and we feel guilty about it, and then we unconsciously choose not to see that broken promise, we leave a little bit of ourselves with our ex in the effort not to see. When we betray a trust and it doesn't sit comfortably, we leave a little piece of ourselves with that person. If we are betrayed in a relationship, or if we lose our job that we have worked so hard for, and we feel ashamed, then we can cut off that part of ourselves in an attempt to forget, to not see.

With each piece of ourselves that we lose or are cut off from, we detach a little more from our place, we lose a little more of our sense of self. And as that happens, we are drawn into this transitional field space. We are drawn to the broken dreams, broken promises, and betrayals that look and feel like the parts of ourselves that we don't want to see anymore. We become entangled with the pain of the ancestors that feels like our pain.

It is like walking through thick, heavy mud. And very quickly we become stuck there, looking back at the ancestors whose pain feels like ours. We hold their pain instead of our own and we stop facing forwards. We stop seeing our dreams. We are entangled. And we are entangled because we cannot face the cost of our own choices.

This is where we must remember that the patterns we experience are not perpetrated down the line from one generation to the next. There is no thought to the cost of not seeing your own pain, there is just the simple response of survival or submission.

There are choices outside of survival or submission. However, *we must see our own pain* in order to see the choices that exist outside of survival and submission. If we can't do that, then anger and perpetration will fester within us, and each of our personal interactions will be viewed through the victim-perpetrator lens.

As victims of this, we can become the perpetrator whilst still believing ourselves to be the victim. This is not our best self. And it isn't easy to sit with.

This transitional field can be composed of:

> Unfulfilled dreams

> Displacement and fractured belonging linked to war, migration and violent deaths

> Broken and betrayed promises

> Unseen and missing children

When a parent can't wish their child well

Traversing the transitional field can be tricky. That movement from holding the place of a child and looking at our parents and ancestors from the perspective of childlike innocence, to becoming an adult and realising that our parents and ancestors are more than our version of them, or even our expectations of them, can be hard.

The movement from child to adult, from adult to parent, then parent to grandparent, is a complex one. We can grow fond of the lack of responsibility that the place of the child affords us, and the desire to hold on to the place of the child within the field can overtake everything, even the place and happiness of our own children.

This was the case for Beth. I had been working with Beth on and off for a few years. We started our therapeutic relationship when Beth started having skype sessions to explore her anger.

She was in her early fifties at that time and married. She had an adult daughter, Sophie, from her first marriage. Her first husband, Raymond, had died in a car accident when their daughter was five years old. Beth did not cope well with her husband's death. It had not been an easy marriage and the decision to have a child was one her husband had pushed for. Beth had not wanted to become a mother and she held anger towards him for dying and leaving her to raise their daughter alone. So much so, that she broke down after his death and left her daughter with her parents for a couple of years.

In that time Beth travelled across the United States and met and married her second husband, Peter. Beth's daughter did not get on well with her stepfather. In fact, none of Beth's or Raymond's family approved of Beth's second marriage to Peter. Sophie's childhood was characterised by the fallings out between Beth and the rest of the family. Sophie spent time living with both her maternal and paternal grandparents as she grew up and only visited with Beth and Peter during the school holiday periods.

The skype sessions with Beth were tricky. She was entrenched in her position as the victim and was intent on holding onto that perspective as tightly as she could. The focus of most of Beth's anger was her mother. She carried a quiet rage that she couldn't seem to let go of.

As we worked together it became apparent that Beth's maternal line was reversed, meaning that Beth's mother wasn't claiming the place of mother but instead was giving Beth to her own mother, Beth's grandmother, instead. In addition to that there was also an inherited parental relationship promise at play.

Beth was unconsciously holding a place within her parents' marriage promise, and was energetically replacing her mother for her father, whilst also simultaneously and unconsciously representing the unseen women in his life before he married Beth's mother.

It sounds complicated and it was complicated. However, such entanglements are not unusual. What was unusual was the attachment that Beth had developed to the entanglements, and the inner power that came to her from holding and replicating the entanglements, particularly with the unseen women on both her paternal and maternal lineages. This was the root of her anger.

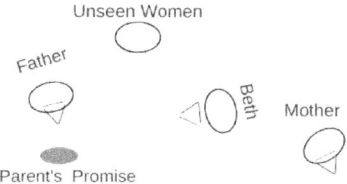

Image 36—Beth and the loyalty to the unseen women

The illustration details the entanglements with Beth's immediate family of origin. We worked to release Beth from her parent's marriage promise and to acknowledge her place outside of it by working with the narrative:

This is between you both.

I have been holding this for you.

I can't be the safety in your marriage.

I can't be the anger in your marriage.

I can't be the regrets in your marriage.

In the session there was relief and release in the moment for Beth, however when she noticed that it felt lighter, she braced against the movement. We then looked briefly to the relationship between Beth's mother and grandmother, but Beth became quite resistant and opted to delay and revisit it in the next session instead.

In the subsequent session Beth reported that there had been a significant shift in the connection with her mother, from her mother's perspective. Her mother had attempted to engage more directly with Beth. She was reaching out and trying to connect with her. This appeared to only fuel Beth's anger *How dare my mother think she can try to talk to me about my life after all this time!* was the thrust of the initial discussion in our session.

In exploring the created constellation, it appeared that Beth was aligning herself with her father and the unseen women, although outside of the marriage promise, and behaving aggressively towards her mother and grandmother.

From the language that Beth was using, the way in which she was holding herself energetically, and the way she was interacting in the session, it was apparent that she was not an adult woman in the created constellation—she was a child.

She was also energetically quite big, and her energy was aggressive and perpetrating, indicating that it wasn't just her energy that was flowing through her within the created constellation field—she was also representing others.

Because of the anger and dynamics we were dealing with, as well as the knowledge from our discussion in session one about her lack of connection with her own daughter, it was likely that Beth was representing unacknowledged and unseen children within the historical narrative of her ancestral family field.

At this point though, there was zero interest from Beth in exploring the relationship with her daughter nor her first or current husband.

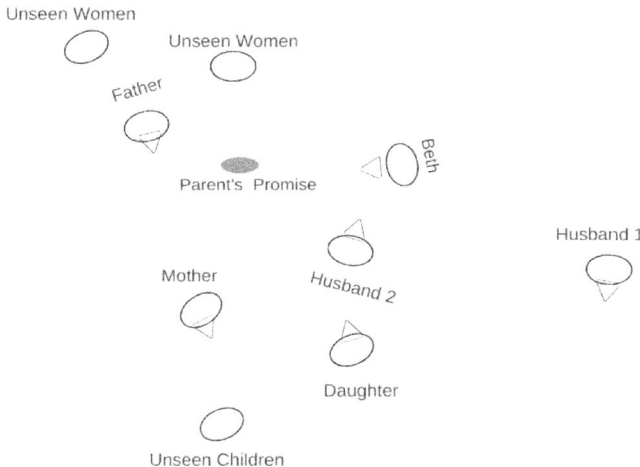

Image 37—Beth choosing not to let go

In the illustration, it is possible to see the daughter waiting to be seen, and the displaced second husband stepping into her daughter's place as another unseen or unacknowledged child.

It was impossible for Beth to work with the narrative:

You are my mother and I am your daughter.

I suggested trying:

Part of my life comes from you.

This phrase would have allowed Beth to work with the simple biological truth of that, but there was too much anger and resistance for her to be able to touch that truth.

Bringing in the unseen children associated with Beth's maternal line, as well as the unseen women connected with Beth's father, was transformative.

There was a strong lineage of forbidden children and forced adoption within her mother's strongly Irish Catholic lineage. There were also places for unacknowledged children relating to her father's previous loves and extramarital affairs. There was a deep softening within Beth as we worked with the children.

I didn't know you were there, but I can see you now.

I have been holding you tightly within me.

I have been holding their beliefs (the church) within me.

I have been holding their fear and anger within me.

There was a releasing of the broken promises connected with the unseen women and their belonging, along with their secrets, and for the first time Beth dropped into her place in the absence of what she had been carrying. And then she noticed the shift within herself. And the resistance came in once more. The familiarity of the anger and rage felt safer for her than the absence of the entanglements.

I suggested some exercises for her to work with in between sessions, in order to support the shift into an association for safety outside of the anger and rage.

However, when Beth came back for the next session she had chosen not to work with the exercises; instead she had embraced the anger. I decided to work directly with her sense of place in the present moment with the narrative of:

I am not a girl in this.

I am a woman.

I can be a free woman.

I can be a free wife.

I can be a free mother.

And to also directly explore the dynamic that came in when she connected with her daughter Sophie. It was very difficult for Beth to work with saying:

I am your mother and you are my daughter.

She spontaneously said:

I didn't want to have you. You have taken too much. You should be giving to me, not taking any more of me.

It felt more natural for Beth to say *You should be my mother. You should be my safety. You took my place from me.* Beth did notice how ungrounded and angry she became when she stepped into her spontaneous phrases and how much more ease there was when she could instead work with:

Even though it was hard, I am your mother and you are my daughter.

You have a place and I have a place.

Neither of us are children anymore.

There is enough now.

But for Beth there wasn't enough.

Even though we uncovered the root entanglements of the 'not enough' dynamic with the forbidden and displaced unseen children she was not ready to let go of the familiarity and the power that came with the rage and the sense of debt.

She was also unable to acknowledge her daughter's place as being outside of her, separate and free. She was stuck within the transitional field and on some level was choosing to stay a child, looking at her mother and waiting for her mother to acknowledge her suffering, despite the fact that the root of the suffering she was holding came from the narrative of trauma within the line rather than from her own direct experience of trauma.

When someone makes such a choice, to hold on to the rage or whatever the entanglement is, there is little to be achieved in constantly going over the same constellation again and again. In Beth's case she wanted to continue to work with her mother and her daughter and where she felt wronged by them. It was an unconscious attempt to re-perpetrate or to reanimate perpetration within the field and it would have been inappropriate for me to continue to work with Beth in that vein.

I suggested the exercises to continue working with, where Beth had felt and experienced the release within the field, but ultimately her choices are her own and she has to choose to let go of what she has been carrying. Unfortunately, she wasn't ready to do that.

When the entanglement can be reversed

It is however very possible to clear such a dynamic. Louisa came to see me for a one to one session in Scotland. I hadn't worked with her before and she hadn't had any previous experience of constellation. I was in the area to facilitate a group workshop and had agreed to work individually with a couple of people.

Her intention for the session was to work on the relationship with her daughter, Lola. They had been estranged for a couple of years and Louisa did not know where or how she was. She was full of regret for the difficulties in their relationship and desperate to make amends.

They had fallen out over her daughter's choice of partner. When we set up the initial constellation, Louisa's family of origin entanglements were very similar to Beth's. Her maternal line was reversed as was her paternal line. There was an inherited parental relationship promise between Louisa, her father, and her paternal grandmother, and it was clear that there had been inheritance of ancestral relationship promises that had impacted Louisa and her daughter's relationship.

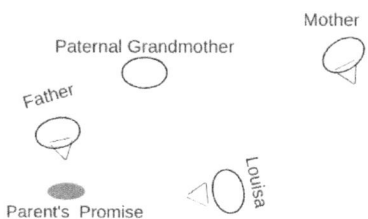

Image 38—Louisa and the influence of the unseen

The illustration shows the similarities between Louisa's situation and Beth's.

Working gently to clear Louisa from carrying the responsibility for her parent's marriage began to soften the connection between her and her daughter. The trickiest part came with the inherited ancestral promises and the reversed paternal line.

Both Louisa and Lola were pulled to the entanglements and the entrenched sacrifice was very strongly present. Louisa at first did not want to clear the anger between her and her paternal grandmother, who had been abusive to her when she was a child.

The grandmother resented Louisa's place and Louisa was not ready to release her own anger yet. Part of her was standing in her childhood and waiting for her father to see her. There was a strong need within Louisa for him to see how abusive the grandmother had been, and to see how much she had carried for him. However, when she realised that her daughter Lola was also entangled and that the anger and sacrifice were in fact being held between them, she immediately let go of her place as a child and stepped into her place as a woman and as a mother.

I have been looking at you through my childhood.

I have been looking at you through my own anger.

I have been looking at you through my pain.

Part of me was asking you to hold that with me.

Part of me was asking you to hold that for me.

I couldn't see that then, but I can see it now.

I don't need you to hold that anymore.

I don't need you to hold my childhood.

I am not a child in this.

I am a woman.

I am a free woman.

I am a mother.

I am a free mother.

You are my daughter.

I don't need you to stay in your childhood and I don't need to stay in mine.

There is safety outside of that.

There is enough safety for each of us.

We then worked to ensure that none of the broken promises from the previous generations or Louisa's relationship line were being held within her daughter Lola's marriage.

There is a place for love with you.

You are worthy of love.

I accept that you are free to choose love.

You don't need to choose between being a daughter or being a wife.

You are a free woman.

Louisa was massively relieved at the end of the session and quite tearful. She had worked very hard in our short time together and I gave her some suggestions of exercises to support the shifts within her field of influence. She left hopeful that her daughter was now free, and was also exhausted after her first experience of constellation. It can be very hard work.

Six months later I received an email out of the blue from Louisa. Her daughter had spontaneously contacted her after the session, and they had exchanged a couple of very emotional phone calls. Louisa was delighted to learn that she was to become a grandmother and wanted to let me know that she was continuing to work hard on her own sense of place as well as the line that flowed onwards from her. She remained hopeful that the phone calls would eventually lead to a meeting in person and she would be able to be a part of Lola and her husband's life and the new life of her soon to be grandchild.

The sparks of hope amidst the pain and trauma of the entanglements are why I love working with constellation as much as I do.

When there is a true and clear intention to let go, then magic can happen. Hope is very important.

Stepping into your transitional field space

Now it is time to step into your own transitional field space and to see and feel what is there for you. This is a big step and feeling some resistance within yourself is quite normal. Gently breathe through it.

If you take a moment now to focus on your breath and your body then take some slow deep breaths and allow your attention to drift from the top of your head down to your toes. Notice how present you feel within your physical body, and if you can stay present within your body or if your energy drifts upwards and out.

Can you bring in a sense of the ancestors behind you and the space for descendants before you?

What happens in your body when you do this?

Do you remain grounded and in the present?

Do you shift back to ground in your childhood?

Do you move forward to stand with the descendants?

Can you bring in a place for your own dreams?

Feel how comfortable it is to say:

I don't need to earn my place through sacrifice.

There is no place for sacrifice within my dreams.

Bringing in support from the different parts of the informing field is essential to be able to fully step into your own place and allow the future to flow forward from you.

First bring in a space for yourself and take some slow deep breaths into your body.

Then behind you on the right hand side, feel/see the connection with your paternal line and work with saying:

I honour you.

I honour your land/my land.

I honour your name/my name.

I honour your sacrifices/my sacrifices.

I honour your place/my place.

Now behind you on the left hand side, feel/see the connection with your maternal line and work with the following phrases:

I can see you.

I can feel you.

I feel the parts of me that are like you.

I accept the parts of me that are like you.

I honour your dreams as I follow my own.

Now bring a space in for your dreams in front of you and breathe deeply into your body and your land connection.

Then to the paternal and maternal lines behind you as you look forward:

I accept my place from you.

I am worthy of support.

There is a place for support with me.

I accept support.

And I support others.

I am choosing myself/to live.

I am free.

My dreams are free.

Can you see your dreams? Do you stay in your body? Do the phrases feel true?

If any part of it feels tricky, or you feel stuck, then gently work with saying:

I don't need to earn my place through sacrifice.

There is no place for sacrifice within my dreams.

I honour you.

I honour your land.

I honour your name.

I honour your sacrifices.

I honour your place.

I can see you.

I can feel you.

I feel the parts of me that are like you.

I accept the parts of me that are like you.

I honour your dreams as I follow my own.

I accept my place.

I am worthy of support.

There is a place for support with me.

I accept support.

And I support others.

I am free.

My dreams are free.

Then to your dreams:

I accept you.

What is happening when you can't see your children or the place for your unborn children and dreams?

When the place for children—born and unborn—or dreams, cannot be seen, then this is an indication of an entanglement where we are wholly or in part staying as a child. It can be hard to accept our place, and that the freedom to choose our own dreams exists in addition to that place. It can also be hard to acknowledge the place for dreams that our own children, or the children within the field, generally have.

Instead the children can seem threatening simply because they are evidence of the continuation of the line, and that doesn't always feel safe. They can be associated with our own death and we can hold the belief that there isn't enough when we see them. It is not easy to sit with this part of ourselves. Beth couldn't. There was safety for her in the anger. Don't give yourself a hard time for feelings that come up in this transitional field space. The very fact that you are reading this means that you are ready for this to change. Don't judge yourself for the trauma that you are entangled with.

Exploring blocks to forward facing

Gently scan down the energy in your body and notice how you are feeling as you prepare to step into this constellation. Take some slow deep breaths. When you are ready, gradually work to bring in a place for:

Children born and unborn

Land for you

Land for the children born and unborn

Notice what happens in your physical body and how it feels emotionally. Breathe as deeply as you can into your connection with land. When you feel ready, work with saying the following to the children born and unborn:

You are not death for me.

I am not death for you.

Your freedom is not stolen from mine.

My freedom is not stolen from the ancestors.

Your dreams are not stolen from mine.

My dreams are not stolen from the ancestors.

I do not need to stay a child.

I do not need to hide from death.

I do not need to hide from my dreams.

I accept the place of my dreams.

I accept you as my descendants.

I accept my place with the land.

I do not need to be the unseen for you.

I do not need you to be the unseen for me.

It is enough that I live.

It is enough that you live (or exist).

It is enough that I have a place.

It is enough that you have a place.

It is enough that I dream for me.

It is enough that you dream for you.

Take a deep breath and draw focus and energy back to yourself and your body. Feel your body and the land underneath. Be present with yourself in this moment. Feel the weight of the entanglements drop from you—the expectations of the dreams of others and their hopes, all going back to them. The place for your dreams and hopes are with you, and the place for the descendants and all that flows from them. This is what you have been working so hard for. This is yours. This is for you. You are worthy of this.

When you are fully present with yourself again and you can feel the field settle around you, then it is time to check in with the connection between you and your dreams, between you and the forward flow. It doesn't have to be today. Take your time. When you are ready, place sheets of paper in front of you to represent:

Dreams

Hope

Love

And any other forward-facing aspect you would like to bring in for yourself. You could add children, a partner, or creativity—whatever you would like to move towards for you.

My dreams are my own.

My choices are my own.

My soul is free.

I am choosing myself.

It isn't a betrayal.

I hold/ have held a belief that I am not enough.

I hold/ have held a belief that I am not worthy of love.

I hold/ have held a belief that I am not worthy of being healthy.

I hold/ have held a belief that I am not worthy of being seen.

I hold/ have held a belief that I am not worthy of being heard.

I hold/ have held a belief that I am not worthy of belonging.

I hold/ have held a belief that I am not worthy of my dreams.

And then:

I feel the place where I held those beliefs within me.

I feel how tightly I held them.

They do not belong with me.

They belong outside of me.

I won't hold those beliefs anymore.

I am letting them go.

Pause here and take some slow deep breaths into your body. Look at the sheets of paper you have placed in front of you. Take another deep breath and say out loud:

I am enough.

I am worthy of love.

I am worthy of being healthy.

I am worthy of being seen.

I am worthy of being heard.

I am worthy of belonging.

I am worthy of my dreams.

I am a free woman/man/soul.

I am (your name); I have my own place.

There is a place for safety with me.

There is a place for support with me.

There is a place for security with me.

There is a place for love with me.

There is a place for hope with me.

There is a place for dreams with me.

There is a place for healing with me.

Take some time to sit with your notebook and write down how it felt and how it feels now, in the post-constellation space. Look through the notes you have made.

> Who you are now is not the same as
> who you were at the start of this book.
> Your soul is lighter, and the souls of your family
> and ancestors are lighter.
> And the souls of your descendants will be lighter.

You have bravely stepped into the field of influence around you and chosen to see and witness the unseen stories of your ancestors. You will no longer be living their story within your life. You have done that. Curiosity, bravery, and courage have led you here. And this is just the beginning. This is the start of your life as a free soul.

What does your story look like?

Who are you now?

Who do you choose to be?

Where do the dreams in your heart take you?

Final Thoughts

You are here because they were here

The unacknowledged and invisible trauma within our ancestral field forms the structure of who we are and how we live. Constellation is an amazing tool for shifting that structure and the system of our belonging to give place to the missing and absent memories and trauma that we hold entangled within us.

Once we have found these entanglements, and they are acknowledged and disentangled, then our ancestors become a great source of strength and support.

Their stories stop being your Achilles heel and start being your superpower. Cast your mind back over what you have learned and uncovered within your own invisible inheritance. Look through your notebook. Take the time to witness your own hard work. And it was hard work. It took bravery and courage to step into the field of your ancestors and choose to see what was there. That can be the easy bit though. What can be harder is to let the weight of the entanglements go, to step into who you are in the absence of the entangled trauma and invisible inheritance. A little voice in your head can whisper:

Who am I if I let this go?

Is it safe to let this go?

Is it a betrayal to my ancestors for me to be this free?

Am I strong enough to let this go?

Yes, you are strong enough to let this go. If you are strong enough to hold the weight of the entanglements for the number of years that you have, then you are strong enough to let them go.

It takes huge strength to continue to strive forward with your life, continually choosing to show up, to love, to participate, to try, to heal, whilst holding the weight of the invisible inheritance. You wouldn't be reading this book if you didn't want to shift the weight of the entanglements.

Think of the space within you that has been filled with the invisible inheritance? Think of the strength it took to hold that and still strive to be you. Now imagine what you can do when all of that strength and capacity that encompasses you can be used, not to hold trauma, but to hold your dreams? Who are you if you let the entanglements go? Wouldn't you like to find out?

When we work with constellation, we clear a pathway forward for ourselves and our descendants. We create a new picture of who we are and where we are in our present moment, and we have a clear map of where we come from and where we want to move forward to.

The influent field from your ancestors is not just made up of trauma. It is full of amazing, strong, creative and wonderful people with stories of joy, happiness and dreams. It is just that the entanglements tend to drown that out. That doesn't mean that it doesn't exist. And that place for joy exists for you *and* your ancestors. You are here because they were here. The lineage of your ancestors is more than their pain and the trauma, and choosing to see it can transform it.

The potential for transformation and change from the individual through to the collective is massive. Our focus on this journey has been the unacknowledged trauma but that does not mean that there is only trauma there.

Now you can look back to your known and unknown ancestral lineage and say:

Part of me comes from you.

Parts of me are like you.

I accept those parts.

I feel your strength supporting my strength.

I feel your hopes supporting my hopes.

I feel your love supporting my love.

There is a place for each of your dreams and there is a place for my dreams.

I accept your support as I follow my dreams.

I remember you as I follow my dreams.

You are not alone in this. It doesn't matter how far back you have to go down your known family lines, or if indeed the soft, sweet point of connection comes from the unseen or unknown folks instead. Within that field of influence there are people cheering you on, and that is your superpower. In the same way, you look to your dreams and your descendants with hope, love and good wishes. You are their cheerleader; you are part of their superpower, and in doing so you also become your own superhero.

Who do you choose to be?

What is your joy?

What are your dreams?

Will you choose to live your life as a free soul?

My aim with *Your Invisible Inheritance* is to open up the magical web of constellation to you so that you can begin to incorporate it into your own everyday life. In every moment you can consciously choose to be you living your own story.

What do you choose?

A bigger picture

Think about the power of all the things that we celebrate within our families and our communities. Think about the power of remembering and honouring what was and what has been. Everything from celebrating a wedding anniversary to honouring years served in the military, to remembering a loved one after they have passed. Think too about the cultural and collective remembrance and celebrations. Perhaps Independence Day on the 4th of July, or Remembrance Sunday within Europe on the 11th of November to commemorate the end of the first world war, or Martin Luther King Day on the 3rd of January, or Holocaust Memorial Day on the 27th of January. All of these memories and moments are significant on an individual and collective basis. They have an emotional charge, and knowingly or unknowingly help to define the structure of who we are.

As we connect with those memories, both individually and collectively, we are in effect animating their field of influence upon and within us. Our sense of belonging is enhanced by the individual and collective honouring and remembrance.

Think now of the weight of all of the absences of those things that are not remembered—the trauma that has not been witnessed, where history has been rewritten or ignored, the emotional trauma of someone who is excluded and displaced, through to the weight of collective unacknowledged trauma. We know how big the ripples are from the pain of something like a broken relationship promise or the unacknowledged death of a child within our individual family and ancestral fields— imagine the weight of that in the collective: the cost of war, broken political promises, and deep cultural betrayals; everything from enslavement, land grabs, mass migration and terror events. Can you begin to feel it? It seeps into each of us as individuals from our collective experience of non-acknowledgement.

This unacknowledged and invisible collective trauma also forms the structure of who we are and how we live in destructive ways. The belonging of each of us individually and collectively can be negatively impacted by the invisibility of the collective unacknowledged trauma. But as we chip away at our own individual invisible inheritance, we begin to uncover our connection to the collective stories. Because these stories— this history—comes from our ancestors.

The collective influence of the untold stories of the past is within us, influencing our relationships and personal choices as we experience our sense of belonging through the unconscious lens of unacknowledged collective trauma.

For me, constellation and the disentangling of the root traumas brings sparks of hope to situations that feel desperate and overwhelming. By looking at who we are and where we come from as individuals we are contributing, in no small way, to a greater collective shift.

We are shifting the lens through which we see and experience others and how others see and experience us. And if we focus on the collective dynamics and choose to participate within that arena then we are also simultaneously contributing to our own individual healing. It's a win-win. Constellation allows us to advocate for the forgotten dead and in doing so we can transform the lives of the forgotten living. For me that shines a light of hope into the darkest of places. My sincere intention is that it sparks hope within you too.

Appendix

Therapeutic applications

Constellations are a method for transforming negative, conflictual relations and blocks to the invisible entanglements that we are each influenced by, as well as a tool for understanding the hidden and invisible influences upon an individual or group.

As a therapeutic modality, constellation can contribute to a clearer understanding of the emotional experience of an individual or group and highlight a potential new path forward with a choice for a new future. If there is unacknowledged trauma, debt, or violence, within the field, it will impact on the field as a whole, an impact that has potentially rippled across generations. The representatives placed within the constellation form a map of interconnections and loyalties. By looking at the order and structure of what is being presented, and the verbal or non-verbal responses of the represented spaces or physical representatives, it is possible to gain a deeper understanding of the core root influences on an individual or situation.

Constellations are based on a theory that every person or group has a place and an equal right to belong—the interconnectedness of all things. The entanglements and patterns that are observed during a constellation arise from displacement, exclusion, and self-exclusion.

They are the missing and unseen memories within the field of the historical narrative of the untold stories. The constellation makes it possible to explore the hidden patterns and loyalties that impact on a present situation that may be rooted unconsciously or unknowingly in the past.

The objective of uncovering the unseen and unacknowledged trauma is to acknowledge it and give place to it; and to shift the influent field out of one of entanglement and discord and into the field of belonging for the individual in question.

The acknowledgement of something or someone that is unseen is not carried out from a place of judgement or belief, or right or wrong, or in an attempt to impose a personal belief on the field as a whole. It is only possible to acknowledge and disentangle existing entanglements, not to create new ones.

Constellation process outline

There are several steps taken when creating a constellation for an individual or group:

1. Formulating an intentional question—this is derived from the individual client, the group, or a collective focus.

2. Determining the significant aspects of the intentional question that should be included in the initial constellation.

3. Creation of the initial constellation—placement of the representors, symbols, or mats, within the created constellation space.

4. Facilitation of the constellation by the constellator alongside the client or group, introducing the missing aspects of the field relating to the intentional question as the constellation unfolds, and incorporating the use of spontaneous and directed language narrative to shift the influent fields.

5. Analysis within the constellation as it unfolds by the constellatory; a reading and understanding of the patterns and entanglements presented and gentle movements within the field to disentangle and release.

6. Post-constellation analysis with the client or group if appropriate. This can include suggested further individual work that the client can undertake to support themselves or more in-depth analysis of a collective constellation.

Facilitation in active constellations

Constellation facilitation is a complex process. It involves the observation and in-constellation analysis of the visible and non-visible parts. The placement of particular represented spaces may seem to indicate that the constellator has the ability to manipulate the constellation space and influence the outcome. However, the purpose of the constellation, and indeed the very nature of the relationship between the constellation and the informing field, is to reveal what is actually there rather than what we believe or want to be there. If an aspect is included or inserted into the constellation field that is inappropriate, inconsequential, or simply wrong in terms of the focus of the intentional question, there will be no recognition of the inserted aspect by the rest of the field. It literally will have no place. The process of constellation facilitation requires a deep understanding of the structure and order within the constellation field of influence.

Types of constellation

An individual or group constellation should begin by establishing the reason or intention for the session. This is the setting of the intentional question that is the lens through which we will then view the created constellation field. This can be trickier than it would initially seem. Individuals come to constellation for a variety of reasons. Some individuals are in crisis in a particular relationship and wish to explore the hidden dynamics. Others are experiencing physical or emotional pain and discomfort and wish to uncover the root.

Some may feel blocked or stuck in a relationship or place of work and others are simply curious about their place within the family and wish to explore and strengthen their roots of belonging.

A constellation will not always come to a point of resolution and balance within a session and that cannot be the focus or the goal. It will not always come to a point of peace. The purpose of the constellation may be for a secret to be revealed, or for a connection or entanglement to be seen as it actually is. The individual may need to spend time in acceptance of this in their everyday life and reality before the field can move towards peace. A constellation may need to be interrupted at a certain point to allow space for integration. The inner knowing of the flow of constellation comes with a respect of the pace of the flow, the details as well as a respect for the family or individuals in question. There can be great value in the 'not knowing' within the constellation field, as well as allowing a space for the discomfort and previous cost of the trauma of the entanglements themselves.

There are different ways in which to work with constellation both individually and within a group setting.

Individual constellations—in person

Constellating on an individual basis can be done using a number of different representative tools. My personal preference is to work with mats to represent the different aspects of the constellation to be explored.

Other options range from small figures to plain markers, similar to checkerboard markers.

My practice is to ask the person I am working with to choose a mat for themselves and a mat for each of the persons, themes or influences we are initially bringing in to the constellation. I then ask the individual to place their own mat first—somewhere in the room that they feel drawn to—and decide in which direction they wish to face. I then ask them to place the other mats in the room according to where they feel they are in relation to them. Thus a spatial representation of their emotional connections. This creates a living, energetic map or web of the interconnections and loyalties involved, both known and unknown, and allows for the invisible to be made visible. I then stand on each mat in turn to discern the pulls and loyalties within each place before asking the client to take their place and gently moving the constellation forward.

Individual constellations—telephone or video call

This is similar process to the individual in person constellation with the mat representatives, but it unfolds in the mind's eye. Time is spent at the beginning of the session establishing the area to be explored and I ask some general questions about their family of origin, current relationship, and work situations. Then after helping the individual to ground as much as possible within their body I begin to bring in the different people, themes and influences into their mind's eye.

This is done one step at a time as opposed to setting up an initial constellation in person with the different aspects all being present at the beginning. What I find interesting is the ability of the individual client to stay present throughout the process.

With the in person individual sessions, the advantage is that a perspective can be given on the different pulls and loyalties present within the field, however this can also be distracting for the client and there can be resistance to feeling or seeing what is there if it is different to their own expectations. There can be surprise at their response to individuals or to certain situations. When there is an entanglement, a common response is to detach or leave the body, to escape. This presents an opportunity for the individual to feel what is going on from a different perspective, often for the first time.

With the distant telephone or video sessions, all movements are made from the individual's perspective. As each representative is brought into their mind's eye, then they experience their response directly and have to be present within their body in order to do so. I believe that in some ways the movements can be deeper from the individual's perspective. The only disadvantage comes if there is an inability or reluctance within the individual to open themselves to the fates of entanglements that may be influencing the other representatives, though this response is rare and may be handled with skill and practice.

Group constellations—active group representatives, spoken

Within a group constellation my general practice is to ask the individual to choose representatives from the group themselves and to also represent themselves within the constellation.

In some cases, depending on the particular issue being explored or the vulnerability of the client I will ask them to choose a representative for themselves too. I will also place additional individual representatives as the constellation unfolds. Careful observation of the responses of the group witnessing the constellation can reveal members of the group who have similar entanglements within their own field of influence. Those who have similar entanglements will either be emotionally drawn into the constellation and be visibly moved, or will detach, attempting to remove themselves from the energetic unfolding.

This in my opinion is one of the truly fascinating aspects of constellation. When a constellation has been set up to explore a dynamic in an individual's family, the representatives who have been placed within that constellation will often find themselves in a role that has resonance for their own family and ancestral dynamics. As they react and respond within this separate constellation, they are also subtly shifting the dynamics of their own. To clarify, this is not and should not be their primary focus or intention, but nevertheless it is the effect that begins to ripple through as the constellation moves. So too for the individuals witnessing the constellation. They in turn can be unconsciously bearing witness to events and happenings within their own field and this can provoke the emotional trauma or clearing of those particular events as the influence of the entangled fields shift and change.

Some constellators do not value the therapeutic role of representing within constellation as much as 'having your own constellation done.' However, on this I have to disagree. Yes, exploring your own constellation is highly effective and invaluable, but can sometimes also be a jarring, confusing, and discombobulating experience. It is often in the hours and days following a constellation that the clarity comes in and the confusion lifts. With representing, the energetic shifts can be subtler, and the clarity of connection at the time and in the moment can be clearer and present. It can be a gentler process and just as valid. Representing allows the layers of the unseen and silent within the influent field to be gently cleared. It also affords the opportunity for them to safely observe the patterns at play before stepping into the constellation itself.

The constellation unfolds as the representatives engage with the influent field within the created constellation field and take on the characteristic loyalties, both known and unknown of the position they hold. It is a movement of the soul and must be worked with gently and slowly.

Group constellations—active group representatives, unspoken

The power of the movements can clearly be seen with unspoken representation in both larger groups and paired work exercises. Silently feeling, engaging, and moving within the constellation field can be excruciating, depending on the intentional question, but the capacity for bearing witness is immense. It is something that many individuals will resist and this in itself is worth noting and drawing their attention to after the exercise. What is unacceptable to them about silence? Does it hold a fear or is it related to their voice and a need to be heard? If you suggest that their use of voice in this particular therapeutic space is a perpetration upon the others, what is their response?

Pre-created constellation

This is a useful tool for allowing an individual experience whilst in the space of the group energy. Mats can be used to set up a constellation that the participants can then step into and move through, exploring the different elements as they go. Taking note of their inner and outer reactions. Very useful for sensitive issues or where a group of people hold similar threads of entanglement within their lineage. I often employ this technique at the end of group work to bring participants back into their body and to their own individual place and field of influence within the created constellation field.

Unfolding at the right pace

Within each type of constellation, a decision must be made as to how closely to explore the details of the entanglement within the constellation. This is influenced by how present the individual is in their everyday life and in their body, how vulnerable they feel, and how ready they themselves are to see the details. You may have an understanding of what the possible roots and influences of the entanglement are upon someone else however if they are not ready to face that then you could create further distraction, chaos, or pain for that person. What may seem like an insignificant and small step for you may seem huge for them. Meet them wherever they are and work with them from that place.

Recommended Reading

R. Sheldrake, The Presence of the Past: Morphic Resonance and the Habbits of Nature., Icon Books., 2011.

F. M. Boring, Connecting to the Past., North Atlantic Books, 2012.

B. Hellinger, Acknowledging What Is: Conversations with Bert Hellinger, Zeig, Tucker & Theisen Inc., 1999.

B. Hellinger, Love's Hidden Symmetry: What Makes Love Work in Relationships, Zeig, Tucker & Theisen Inc., 1998.

B. Hellinger, Peace Begins in the Soul: Family Constellations in the Service of Reconciliation, Carl-Auer, 2003.

U. Franke, In My Mind's Eye: Family Constellations in Individual Therapy and Counselling, Carl-Auer, 2003.

D. van Kampenhout, Images of the Soul: The Workings of the Soul in Shamanic Rituals and Family Constellations: The Workings in Shamanic Rituals and Family, Carl-Auer, 2001.

B. Brown, Braving the Wilderness: The quest for true belonging and the courage to stand alone, Vermilion, 2017.

M. Wolynn, It Didn't Start with You: How Inherited Family Trauma Shapes Who We Are and How to End the Cycle, Penguin, 2017.

B. van der Kolk, The Body Keeps the Score: Mind, Brain and Body in the Transformation of Trauma, Penguin, 2015.

References

[1] I. ,. H. P. a. Z. A. W. Stiefel, "Family Constellation — A Therapy Beyond Words.," *Australian and New Zealand Journal of Family Therapy,* vol. 23, pp. 38-44, 2002.

[2] Christian B.N. Gade, "What is Ubuntu? Different Interpretations among South Africans of African Descent.",*" South African Journal Of Philosophy ,* vol. 31, no. 3, p. 487, 2012.

[3] S. Edwards, "A Psychology of Indigenous Healing in Southern Africa.," *Journal of Psychology in Africa.,* vol. 21, p. 335–348., 2011.

[4] D. Tutu, No Future Without Forgiveness, Rider & Co, 1999.

[5] R. Sheldrake, The Presence of the Past: Morphic Resonance and the Habbits of Nature., Icon Books., 2011.

[6] F. P. Mayr, Consciousising Relatedness. Systemic Conflict Transformation in Political Constellations., European PhD Dissertation International Studies in Peace, Conflict and Development, 2010.

[7] Sheldrake, The Rebirth of Nature: The Greening of Science and God, 1990.

[8] O. Hiroaki, "Resonance frequency-retuned quartz tuning fork as a force sensor for noncontact atomic force microscopy.," *Applied Physics Letters,* 2014.

[9] K. Fierke and N. Mackay, "To 'See' is to Break an Entanglement: Quantum Measurement, Trauma and Security," *Security Dialogue,* Forthcoming.

[10] A. Devi, "Vanishing Twin Syndrome.," *Research& Reviews: A Journal of Health Professions.,* vol. 4, pp. 27-29, 2014.

[11] N. Mackay, The Science of Family: Working with Ancestral Patterns, O-Books, 2009.

[12] N. Mackay, The Science of Family: Working with Ancestral Patterns, 2009.

[13] N. Mackay, Between the Lines: Healing the Individual & Ancestral Soul with Family Constellation, 2012.

[14] F. Ruppert, Trauma, Bindung and Familienstellen: Seelische Verletzungen verstehen and heilen. Munich., 2005.

[15] F. M. Boring, Connecting to the Past., North Atlantic Books, 2012.

[16] A. Wendt, Quantum Consciousness and the Social Sciences, CUP, 2015.

[17] N. Mackay, Autonomic nervous system changes during Reiki treatment: a preliminary study., The Journal of Alternative and Complementary Medicine, 2004.

[18] S. Schwartz, "Nonlocality, Intention, and Observer Effects in Healing Studies: Laying a Foundation for the Future," *The Journal of Science and Healing,* 2010.

[19] S. Schwartz, The Manipulation of Perceived Reality Through Nonlocal Intention, 2017.

[20] M. Fisher, " (2015) 'Quantum Cognition,'," *Annals of Physics,* Vols. 362,, pp. 593-602, 2015.

[21] K. Fierke, "Consciousness at the interface : Wendt, Eastern wisdom and the ethics of intra-action.," *Critical Review,* vol. Vol. 29, pp. 141-169, 2017.

[22] K. M. Fierke and F. Antonio-Alfonso, "Language, entanglement and the new Silk Roads," *Asian Journal of Comparative Politics,* vol. 3, no. 3, pp. 194-206, 2018.

[23] N. Kellermann, "Epigenetic transmission of Holocaust Trauma: Can nightmares be inherited?," *Israel Journal of Psychiatry Related Sciences,* no. 50, 2013.

[24] P. MA, "Intergenerational Trauma: Understanding Natives' Inherited Pain," Indian Country Today Media Network, 2016.

Acknowledgements

Thank you to all the people who have worked with me both individually and in groups over the last couple of decades. It takes courage and vulnerability to look at who you are in the midst of the inherited entanglements, and it has been a privilege to step into that with you. Thank you to my own parents, family and ancestors; your stories have been present with me in the process of writing this book in ways I never envisioned at the beginning.

To everyone who read, re-read, and then read again, the different versions as it slowly emerged—Oona, Chris, Tara, Suzanne, Mike—I am deeply grateful for your patience, good humour and sarcasm. Also very thankful for Sue Fitzmaurice at Rebel Magic Books and her enthusiastic approach to editing.

The conversations with K.M. Fierke in attempting to bridge the interdisciplinary language gap between systemic therapy, quantum physics, and social science, have been invaluable in shifting my own thinking about the 'how?' of constellation.

A special thank you to my partner Mike for his support, and the long, mental health preserving conversations in the pub, and to my son Jasper for his encouragement, confidence, and computer design skills.

Nikki Mackay BSc MSc is a Family and Ancestral Constellation therapist and teacher. She previously worked as a Clinical Physicist within the NHS, specialising in neurophysiological measurement and exploring the efficacy of energy healing on the autonomic nervous system. She has a busy therapy practice and teaching school based in Western Europe and the United States and offers training, workshops and individual family constellation therapy. Since 2016 she has been exploring the possibilities and boundaries of constellation at a macro level working with the International Relations Department of a university in Scotland looking at using constellations as a tool for peace and reconciliation in global conflict, as well as researching the normalisation of hate and the roots of racism with groups in the United States.

nikki@nikkimackay.co.uk
www.nikkimackay.co.uk

REBEL
MAGIC

www.rebelmagicbooks.com

Printed in Great Britain
by Amazon

59322868R00165

PUBLIC PRIVATE PARTNERSHIPS IN IRELAND

Manchester University Press

IRISH SOCIETY

The Irish Society series provides a critical, interdisciplinary and in-depth analysis of Ireland that reveals the processes and forces shaping social, economic, cultural and political life, and their outcomes for communities and social groups. The books seek to understand the evolution of social, economic and spatial relations from a broad range of perspectives, and explore the challenges facing Irish society in the future given present conditions and policy instruments.

SERIES EDITOR
Rob Kitchin

PUBLIC PRIVATE PARTNERSHIPS IN IRELAND

Failed experiment or the way forward for the state?

Rory Hearne

MANCHESTER UNIVERSITY PRESS
Manchester and New York

*distributed in the United States exclusively
by Palgrave Macmillan*

The right of Rory Hearne to be identified as the author of this work has been asserted by him in accordance with the Copyright, Designs and Patents Act 1988.

Published by Manchester University Press
Oxford Road, Manchester M13 9NR, UK
and Room 400, 175 Fifth Avenue, New York, NY 10010, USA
www.manchesteruniversitypress.co.uk

Distributed in the United States exclusively by
Palgrave Macmillan, 175 Fifth Avenue, New York,
NY 10010, USA

Distributed in Canada exclusively by
UBC Press, University of British Columbia, 2029 West Mall,
Vancouver, BC, Canada V6T 1Z2

British Library Cataloguing-in-Publication Data
A catalogue record for this book is available from the British Library

Library of Congress Cataloging-in-Publication Data applied for

ISBN 978 07190 8487 4 hardback

First published 2011

The publisher has no responsibility for the persistence or accuracy of URLs for any external or third-party internet websites referred to in this book, and does not guarantee that any content on such websites is, or will remain, accurate or appropriate.

Typeset in Minion
by Action Publishing Technology Ltd, Gloucester
Printed and bound by
CPI Group (UK) Ltd., Croydon, CR0 4YY

Series editor's foreword

Over the past twenty years Ireland has undergone enormous social, cultural and economic change. From a poor, peripheral country on the edge of Europe with a conservative culture dominated by tradition and Church, Ireland transformed into a global, cosmopolitan country with a dynamic economy. At the heart of the processes of change was a new kind of political economic model of development that ushered in the so-called Celtic Tiger years, accompanied by renewed optimism in the wake of the ceasefires in Northern Ireland and the peace dividend of the Good Friday Agreement. As Ireland emerged from decades of economic stagnation and The Troubles came to a peaceful end, the island became the focus of attention for countries seeking to emulate its economic and political miracles. Every other country, it seemed, wanted to be the next Tiger, modelled on Ireland's successes. And then came the financial collapse of 2008, the bursting of the property bubble, bank bailouts, austerity plans, rising unemployment and a return to emigration. From being the paradigm case of successful economic transformation, Ireland has become an internationally important case study of what happens when an economic model goes disastrously wrong.

The Irish Society series provides a critical, interdisciplinary and in-depth analysis of Ireland that reveals the processes and forces shaping social, economic, cultural and political life, and their outcomes for communities and social groups. The books seek to understand the evolution of social, economic and spatial relations from a broad range of perspectives, and explore the challenges facing Irish society in the future given present conditions and policy instruments. The series examines all aspects of Irish society including, but not limited to: social exclusion, identity, health, welfare, life cycle, family life and structures, labour and work cultures, spatial and sectoral economy, local and regional development, politics and the political system, government and governance, environment, migration and spatial planning. The series is supported by the Irish Social Sciences Platform (ISSP), an all-island platform of integrated social science research and graduate education focusing on the social, cultural and economic transformations shaping Ireland in the twenty-first century. Funded by the Programme for Research in Third Level Institutions, the ISSP brings together leading social science academics from all of Ireland's universities and other third-level institutions.

Given the marked changes in Ireland's fortunes over the past two decades it is important that rigorous scholarship is applied to understand the forces at work, how they have affected different people and places in uneven and unequal ways, and what needs to happen to create a fairer and prosperous society. The Irish Society series provides such scholarship.

Rob Kitchin

Contents

Tables and figures

Abbreviations

AIB	Allied Irish Banks
CABE	Commission for Architecture and the Built Environment
C & AG	Comptroller and Auditor General
CAW	Celtic Anglian Water
CIE	Coras Iompar na hEireann
CIF	Construction Industry Federation
CUPE	Canadian Union for Public Employees
DART	Dublin Area Rapid Transit
DBFOM	Design, Build, Finance, Operate, Maintain
DBFM	Design, Build, Finance, Maintain
DBF	Design Build and Finance
DBO	Design Build and Operate
DCC	Dublin City Council
DHCDA	Dolphin House Community Development Association
DIT	Dublin Institute of Technology
DOEHLG	Department of the Environment, Heritage, and Local Government
GDP	Gross Domestic Product
GGB	General Government Balance
GNP	Gross National Product
HSE	Health Services Executive
IAG	Informal Advisory Group
IBEC	Irish Business Employers Confederation
ICTU	Irish Congress of Trades Unions
IIB	Irish Investment Bank
IT	information technology
LEA	Local Education Authority
NDFA	National Development Finance Agency
NESC	National Economic and Social Council

NRA   National Roads Authority
NSW   New South Wales
NTR   National Toll Roads
OECD   Organisation for Economic Co-operation and Development
OPW   Office of Public Works
PFI   Private Finance Initiative
PMDS   Performance Management Development System
PPP   Public Private Partnership
PSB   Public Sector Benchmark
RFQ   Request for Qualifications
RFP   Request for Proposals
RPA   Rail Procurement Agency
SIPTU   Services Industrial Professional and Technical Union
SMIF   Secondary Market Infrastructural Funds
SPC   Special Purpose Company
SPV   Special Purpose Vehicle
TD   Teachta Dala
TUPE   Transfer of Undertakings Protection of Employment
VEC   Voluntary Education Committee

Introduction

The new, eleven storey, Criminal Courts of Justice Complex stands majestically and imposing on Parkgate Street at the entrance to Dublin's Phoenix Park. Its extremely impressive circular shape has a bronze and layered glass veiled frontage. Opened in November 2009, it contains twenty-two courtrooms. It was designed, built and financed by, and will be managed through, a Public Private Partnership (PPP) between the Irish state (through the Courts Services) and a private consortium led by Australian multinational Babcock and Brown (who also bought the privatised Irish Telecommunications Company Eircom in 2006). At a completion cost of €140 million, it was €30 million over budget. However, rather than paying for the project on commencement of the process, the Irish state instead will pay for it through annual payments (of approximately €21 million) to Babcock and Brown over the twenty-five-year duration of the contract.

The Irish President, Mary Mcaleese, spoke at the official opening of the Courts Complex in January 2010 and described the 'splendour and character' of the new building, asserting that, 'by investing in such a building, by insisting that it must be the very best, not simply to look at but to work in and to be in for all users, whether judges or judged, that tells us a lot about our character and our values'.

Despite a low level of public awareness about PPPs, they have become an important part of Ireland's social, political and economic landscape. The practical experiences of this new form of public services and infrastructure delivery, however, have neither been detailed publicly to any considerable extent, nor has the real cost and long-term implications been investigated in sufficient depth. In particular, there has been little research undertaken into the impacts of PPPs on the sections of Ireland's society that are affected by low incomes, poverty, low standards of education and health and other social issues as a result of the country's intense social and economic inequalities. Government capital expenditure in the areas of social protection, such as social housing regeneration, education and healthcare facilities, affect these populations most acutely. Look at, for example, O'Devaney Gardens. It is a flats complex in Dublin's inner city. It is one of many local authority estates in Ireland where residents have suffered intense socio-economic inequalities, particularly social exclusion and poverty.

O'Devaney Gardens and other similar inner-city flat complexes built in the 1950s and 1960s initially enjoyed a decade or two of stability. This ended during the 1970s and 1980s as deindustrialisation led to high rates of unemployment and poverty in these areas. The communities became further disadvantaged and destabilised by the heroin crisis in the 1980s. The estates deteriorated due to inadequate estate management by the local authority landlord, Dublin City Council (DCC). This situation was compounded by ill-conceived housing policies such as the 'surrender grant' that provided a financial incentive to tenants to buy a house elsewhere if they relinquished their council flat. Further adding to this problem were DCC's allocation practices, which meant it was required to house the most 'at-risk' people on the housing waiting list. They tended to be individuals and families affected by the most serious social issues and inequalities. Moving them into these already disadvantaged estates simply deepened the challenges. Such policies led many tenants, often working families and community leaders, to move off the estates. This then led to a reduction in the social mix, which was previously more balanced. Thus, the estates became concentrations of, in many cases, the most vulnerable in society. This had a detrimental impact on the communities and demoralised the remaining residents. It led to the social housing sector becoming increasingly residualised and availed of a narrower social mix, restricted to the lower income groups and the more vulnerable in society (Drudy and Punch, 2005; Fahey ed., 1999; Redmond, 2001, 2002). Attempts were made in the late 1980s and early 1990s to refurbish some of the estates through the Exchequer-funded Remedial Works Scheme.

By 1995, over 12,000 units had been refurbished nationally, notably Ballymun and Fatima Mansions. However, the schemes failed to have a significant effect on the overall regeneration of the estates as the policies were restricted to external physical renewal, thus neglecting problems within the housing units and, in particular, the deep social and economic inequalities that affected the residents. In the late 1990s, therefore, local authorities began to explore the possibility of the complete demolition of the estates and the rebuilding of new housing with community facilities and additional support services as part of large-scale 'regeneration' plans.

Compared to the rest of Irish society, there was very little 'trickle down' of wealth to people in these areas during the years of high economic growth from 1995 to 2007, known as the period of the 'Celtic Tiger'. The Celtic Tiger refers to the period of rapid economic growth in Ireland that began in 1995, slowed down in 2001, and picked up pace again between 2003 and 2007. During this time, Ireland experienced an unprecedented economic boom, with gross national product (GNP) growth rates ranging between 6 per cent and 11 per cent from 1995 to 2000 and then averaging around 5 per cent from 2000 to 2006.

The concentrations of people, suffering from many social disadvantages for example in education, employment and health, in places such as Dublin's inner-city flats complexes, manifest the intense socio-economic inequality that persisted and indeed worsened in Ireland during the Celtic Tiger era. In 2006, Ireland ranked first of the fifteen countries in the European Union in terms of earnings inequality, with the top 1 per cent of the Irish population owning 20 per cent of the nation's wealth, 17 per cent of the population was classified as being at risk of poverty, while the percentage of children living in consistent poverty actually increased in 2006.

The areas had high concentrations of populations affected by unemployment, early school leaving, low levels of attendance at third-level education and of those classified as at highest risk of poverty, including, particularly, lone parents. As the drugs crisis[1] and poverty continued, areas such as Fatima Mansions, St Michaels Estate, St Theresa's Gardens and Dolphin House unfortunately only came to public attention when the media carried the generally negative stories on gang and crime-related activities. Conditions reached such a crisis point on one estate that, in May 2010, the residents of Dolphin House – the flats complex in Dublin's south-west inner-city area of Dolphins Barn – campaigned publicly using a human-rights-based approach in order to highlight their issues. Many residents had been severely affected by inadequate housing conditions. For example, some flats had serious sewerage problems with a constant foul odour that was so strong it made residents nauseous. The sewerage spurted up over the grids on the drains in the front of their flats where their children played. It invaded their sinks and baths. Sometimes when they or their children were having a bath, the sewerage burst up through the plug-hole and spread into the bath water. There were also serious problems of damp and mould in many of the flats, which appeared to contribute towards the poor health of the tenants, such as re-occurring chest infections, pleurisy and asthma. At the most basic level, their kitchens were too small to seat a family for dinner and, therefore, they had never had a Christmas dinner at the one table together in their own home. The residents summed up their circumstances succinctly when they described how 'the Celtic Tiger never knocked on our door'.

There were still, despite the conditions, very strong vibrant communities within these areas. This was evident in the significant number of residents who wished to remain living there. They highlighted their strong historical family ties to the areas, commitment to their communities and local solidarity and support. Their parents and grandparents originated from the city centres and local areas, living in tenement flats and working in local industry. Such strong community and family ties have proven to be vital supports in their daily struggle against social isolation and poverty. Many residents described how identity, history and culture were much valued and worth fighting for.

On the 2 August 2001 the Department of the Environment, Heritage and Local government issued a circular (HS 13/01) to all local authorities in relation to regeneration plans for these areas which stated:

> Local authorities should consider the extent to which additional housing supply can be brought on stream through Public Private Partnerships between local authorities and private developers utilising suitable local authority lands. These lands would primarily be lands in areas where there is already a significant concentration of social housing.

The PPP was to involve local authorities entering into a contract with a private developer where the public land was transferred over to the developer in order to build private residential and commercial units that it could sell. In return, the developer was responsible for the provision, generally on site, of a negotiated amount of social housing and/or community facilities. These would be funded by the future sale by the developer of the private units at either market or 'affordable' rates. These new PPPs would thus provide for the redevelopment of the estates at 'zero financial cost' to the Exchequer. They would also provide, in line with government policy, a greater mix of housing types in these areas. This has been identified by government and policy advisors as a key method of reducing social exclusion. Some of the development gain from the projects was to be used to fund significant social regeneration plans that traditional, state-funded, regeneration had not provided. The projects would bring about 'a bright new future' for the residents of the areas, at a much quicker pace than direct state investment:

> In order to make a reality of better social housing, the government will ensure that new housing is designed and planned on quality principles, includes an appropriate housing mix and provides necessary social infrastructure ... PPP's have the potential to deliver housing in a faster period without compromising on quality and we will continue to encourage this approach where appropriate. (Former Taoiseach, Bertie Ahern, speaking at the launch of the Dominick Street flats complex regeneration PPP, 2006)

By 2008, this 'new future' through regeneration had been promised for at least twelve local authority flats complexes in Dublin's inner city. Other regeneration projects using a similar PPP model were also being planned across the country in places such as Limerick, Sligo and Kildare. In Dublin's inner city, construction had commenced on the Fatima Mansions PPP project and the contract had been signed with the preferred bidder (Bernard McNamara & Co.) in the O'Devaney Gardens project. In the St Michael's Estate and Dominick Street projects the contract had also been awarded to Bernard McNamara & Co., while other estates, including Croke Villas, St Theresa's Gardens, Charlemont Street and Dolphin House were preparing for commencement of the PPP process.

However, the property market crash in 2008 resulted in the projected profits for developers from the sale of the private residential and commercial units being significantly reduced. The reality facing the residents living on these local authority estates, amongst whom were some of those worst affected by the socio-economic inequalities in Irish society, was that they were no longer living on high-value sites that had motivated this PPP model. The regeneration of their estates was no longer economically viable, from a commercial perspective, through the PPP model. The projects had become too 'risky' for the developers to undertake. On 19 May 2008, DCC announced that negotiations with the developer, McNamara and Co., in relation to the PPP regeneration projects of St Michael's Estate, O'Devaney Gardens and Dominick Street, had collapsed. On 1 December of that same year, DCC announced that the three regeneration projects 'are no longer viable under the Public Private Partnership process that had been envisaged' because of the economic downturn. DCC stated that it would take over the projects and try to deliver them another way. As a result, there have been considerable delays in the projects and, as of June 2010, construction has not yet commenced on any of the collapsed projects.

The communities that were long-promised regeneration could not withstand more disappointment and delays. In O'Devaney Gardens the residents had entered the regeneration process with enthusiasm, optimism and in good faith in 2004. Six years later, there was still no sign of their project commencing. The estate deteriorated rapidly as tenants lost hope in regeneration and transferred off the estate. DCC did not re-allocate the vacated units and instead boarded them up. This made the estate look even more run-down and the vacant areas became an attractive space for anti-social behaviour to take place. The remaining residents in O'Devaney Gardens suffered from a downward cycle of vandalism and despair and, as of June 2010, there were only 100 occupied flats out of an original community of individuals and families that were housed in 278 flats.

O'Devaney Gardens is located just a five minute walk from the Criminal Courts Complex. Understandably, then that the residents were seething with anger at the apparent injustice of their estate being allowed to fall into disrepair while this great court building, that they walked past every day, grew taller and taller, and was even completed ahead of schedule. So, while a ceremony of fanfare and pomp took place at the opening of the Courts Complex, some of the local residents from O'Devaney Gardens held a protest outside. They raised a salient point that challenged policy makers, government and DCC in relation to the prioritisation of public spending in the Celtic Tiger Period. The residents explained that it was quite possible that some of the youth of O'Devaney Gardens, hardened by the despair at their decrepit housing conditions and lack of opportunities, could get involved in crime. If they did this, then, in all likelihood, they would be apprehended and receive their sentence in their neighbouring building – the wonderful and impressive new Courts Complex. In many ways, the different trajectories of development of these two PPP projects indicate much about the character, values and priorities in Ireland in the first decade of the twenty-first century. As one of the residents stated: 'What does it say about the government that it can ensure that hundreds of millions of euro were available to successfully build new courts that can send our children to prison, but it couldn't provide the funding for the regeneration of the estates where our children have no playgrounds or hope?'

Such contrasts and inequitable outcomes were not restricted to this example. This is apparent from the varied experiences of the PPP process since its inception in Ireland in 1998. Such developments and impacts associated with PPPs in the delivery of public schools,[2] social housing estate regeneration, waste-water/water treatment plants, road and rail infrastructure and incinerators in Ireland are the key subject matter detailed in this book. The book will investigate the PPP process from its inception in Ireland in order to provide overall analyses of the Irish state's rationale for the introduction of PPPs, of their outcomes generally and of their impacts on the state and public services and infrastructure delivery in Ireland.

The research for the book involved an investigation into a number of case-study PPP projects, which were selected as a representative sample from the various state sectors that had developed PPPs by 2005. The primary information sources were gathered from a very substantial number (155) of individual interviews with key stakeholders, and extensive participative research, undertaken between 2005 and 2010. The stakeholders were at a state policy level (central and local government institutions) and at individual PPP-project level. They included central government department officials, local authority officials, elected representatives, private-sector PPP companies, consultants and advisors, trade unions representing public- and private-sector workers employed in PPPs, employees working on the PPP projects, local authority tenants and community workers. A significant amount of the data was gathered as part of the author's Ph.D. research[3] and from participant observation in the development and decision-making process of community organisations and structures involved in the PPP projects.[4]

Before commencing the detailed analysis of PPP projects in Ireland it is necessary to provide a short introduction to the role public infrastructure and services play in the economy and society, the subject matter for Chapter 1.

Notes

1 The high rates of heroin addiction that emerged in the 1980s in Dublin's inner-city areas of high deprivation continued to rise in the 1990s (Bissett, 2009).
2 In Ireland, schools are divided into private fee-paying schools and public state-funded schools. The majority of the state-funded schools are, as detailed later in Chapter 4, managed by religious orders. A much smaller number of state-funded schools are run by the state-supported educational committees and non-religious boards of management.
3 The Ph.D., 'Neoliberalism and the Irish welfare state: Public Private Partnerships in schools and social housing' was conferred by Trinity College in June 2009.
4 The author has been employed as a regeneration community co-ordinator in Dolphin House since July 2007. This allowed the author to gain access to the various perspectives and experiences of key local activists, community workers and DCC officials.

1

Public Private Partnerships

This chapter begins with a brief description of the roles of public infrastructure and services in a society and an economy and then provides a detailed introduction to the development of PPPs, in Ireland and internationally, along with a contextualisation of their emergence within the phase of neoliberalism from the 1970s to the 1990s.

Public infrastructure and services

Infrastructure facilitates the production of goods and the supply of services. The proper provision and maintenance of public infrastructure and supply of public services are essential if a society is to develop and grow in a manner conducive to providing high standards of living. Vital public economic and social infrastructure spans a wide range of utilities from transport systems (roads and public transport), drinking water and waste-water services and health facilities to modern energy and communications networks. Public infrastructure supports economic productivity, competitiveness, improves health and well-being and contributes to sustainable development and the generation of sustainable communities. It also protects our environment, can address the pressures of climate change and the limits on the supply of oil, and provides opportunities and venues for social engagement and enjoyment.

For example, the quality of the transport infrastructure, such as rail and road connections, determines the ease with which people can interact within and between towns, villages, cities and rural areas. It impacts on travel-to-work times, which can have a major effect on people's quality of life. Furthermore, public amenities, such as parks and cultural facilities, are necessary to provide a high quality of life in local urban areas.

Additionally, social infrastructure has a key role to play in addressing economic and social inequalities by promoting social inclusion and improving the quality of life of those affected by such inequalities. For example, the provision of social and affordable housing can address the needs of those who cannot afford to cover the costs of purchasing their own home, and also the problem of homelessness. It can also address the provision of specific accommodation needs, such as those of travellers, as well as improvements in the housing conditions of the most vulnerable (including older people, people with a disability, those in existing social housing estates).

High-quality health services are another vital aspect of social infrastructure. In particular, access to high-quality health services and its infrastructure is vital to a range of vulnerable groups. It is an essential ingredient to improve their quality of life, to prevent deterioration in their circumstances and to the maintenance of good health, all of which are a prerequisite to the full participation of citizens in the social and economic life of society. Vulnerable groups include children in need of care and protection; persons with disabilities, including those with mental illness; people, including young people, who are homeless; drug users; and the elderly. There is a well-observed relationship in Ireland and internationally between health status and income levels, especially for lower-income populations and groups affected by social issues and disadvantages. The potential improvement in health status arising from investment in social infrastructure and services can also contribute to a greater participation by disadvantaged groups in education and in the labour force, thus helping to break the cycle of disadvantage and poor health over the longer term (Government of Ireland, 2007).

Many international studies have shown that investment in infrastructure and services also stimulate economic activity through the creation of employment and through the mechanism of the multiplier effect. Such investment has been a central part of Keynesian approaches implemented by various European governments in the post-War period from the 1940s to the 1970s and has been continued by governments to a varying extent since then. This has generally entailed stimulating demand (through investment in public works, state enterprises and the welfare state).

The Irish government's *National Development Plan, 2007–2013* (Government of Ireland, 2007, 5) states that productive infrastructure is, 'a key element in the promotion of competitiveness and the generation of sustainable economic growth and employment, contributes to regional development and assists environmental sustainability'. It is, therefore, of fundamental importance for national industries and businesses if they are to operate efficiently, innovatively and flexibly. This has become very important, particularly since the 1980s when the international policy framework was altered to reduce controls on capital mobility in order that it could find optimum investment opportunities.

Ireland's historical underinvestment in such physical and social infrastructure combined with rapid economic and population growth resulted in a considerable infrastructural deficit that was reaching crisis point by the late 1990s. The *National Development Plan, 2000–2006* (Government of Ireland, 2000a), which explained that Ireland's significant infrastructural deficit threatened to inhibit economic and employment growth, was the government's investment programme for the period and covered most major planned investment by the state in physical capital, education and training and research and development. It outlined €57 billion of state, private and European Union investment on education, roads, public transport, health services, social housing, rural development, industry, water and waste services, childcare and local development.

This was the first of such Plans in Ireland to include, as a significant component, PPPs, which were expected to play an important role in the delivery of the Plan, comprising 5 per cent (€2.85 billion) of total spending. In November 2001, Charlie McCreevey, the Minister for Finance at the time, explained that the government's aim was to 'help embed PPPs as an important pillar of public capital procurement and the provision of quality public services'.

PPPs develop in Ireland

Since being elected in 1997, the Fianna Fail-led government began to pursue, in a more vigorous fashion than previous governments, the policies of neoliberalism and privatisation (O'Toole, 2003; Sweeney, 1999). Neoliberalism, which is analysed in much greater depth in later chapters, is a market-driven approach to economic and social policies and includes the privatisation of state assets, the liberalisation of markets and fiscal austerity (often through reducing taxes and public spending). Providing strong ideological support for this approach was Fianna Fail's minority coalition partner, the neoliberal political party of the Progressive Democrats. In its second year of office, following representations by the Irish Business Employers Confederation (IBEC) and the Construction Industry Federation (CIF), the government undertook an investigation into the potential of addressing the public services and infrastructure deficit through private provision mechanisms such as PPPs rather than through the traditional direct state-provision model (Central PPP Unit, 2006c). To do this, it commissioned private consultants and PPP advisors Farrell Grant Sparks to produce a report into the benefits of PPPs, their potential application to Ireland and the necessary steps required by the government to start implementing them.

PPP projects, the government stated, were being introduced to provide public services and infrastructure at a more rapid pace and with greater efficiency and value for money than traditional, direct, state-provision methods. From a budgetary accounting perspective, PPPs were attractive as the investment could be recorded 'off-balance sheet' and thus would not affect the government's official debt ratio. This meant Ireland could more easily maintain its fiscal position in line with the conditions set down by the European Union's Stability and Growth Pact. This applied to countries in the Eurozone that had agreed targets designed to promote fiscal discipline. The targets involved maintaining an annual deficit of no more than 3 per cent of gross domestic product (GDP)[1] and a debt-to-GDP ratio of no more than 60 per cent.

The Farrell Grant Sparks report, 'A report submitted to the Inter-departmental Group[2] in Relation to Public Private Partnerships' (FGS, 1998) was the first major work on PPPs in Ireland. It concentrated on the positive benefits and experiences of PPPs and the private sector internationally, and provided an analysis of the theoretical benefits. The Farrell Grant Sparks report recommended that the benefits of private-sector involvement, as identified by international private- and public-sector proponents, could be established in practice in Ireland through testing specific pilot projects in a number of areas of public services and infrastructure. These included:

- toll roads (Drogheda, Western Dundalk bypass, Southern Cross, Southeastern motorway, Northern Port);
- light rail infrastructure (section of the LUAS project);
- a sewerage or water treatment scheme;
- a solid waste facility;
- schools, tertiary colleges (a new build in one – or a number – of appropriate schools and third-level colleges).

In June 1999, in line with recommendations from the Farrell Grant Sparks report, the government approved the development of pilot PPP projects in the transport, environmental services and education sectors. The Pilot Programme[3] (Table 1.1) included projects identical to those proposed in the Farrell Grant Sparks report.

The trade union representatives who were part of the PPP Informal Advisory Group (IAG) consented to the introduction of PPPs, unlike their counterparts in some other countries. The IAG was set up under the Social Partnership Agreements[4] in order to facilitate the exchange of views and information by the various social partners in relation to the development of PPP projects. The membership of the IAG includes IBEC, the Irish Congress of Trade Unions (ICTU), CIF and Forfás as well as the main government departments and agencies engaged in the PPP programme. The IAG has played a key role in developing the PPP programme.

Table 1.1 Irish Pilot PPP programme, June 1999

PPP project	Projected procurement start date
Post Primary Schools Bundle	2000
Cork School of Music	2000
M50 Second West-Link Bridge	2000
N4 Kilcock to Kinnegad	2000
Dublin Light Rail	2000
N25 Waterford Bypass	2001
N7 Limerick S.Ring 11	2000
Dublin Thermal Treatment Plant	2001
Ballymore Eustace Water Works	2001

Source: Central PPP Unit (2006a).

Following their introduction, the government promoted the PPP approach intensely through the provision of considerable institutional support at central and local state levels to enhance the public sector's capacity in this area. These included setting up a Central PPP Unit in the Department of Finance to lead, drive and coordinate the PPP process. The key functions of the Central PPP Unit are to develop the legislative framework, to give technical and policy guidance to support the development of PPP projects and to disseminate best practice. This was done in accordance with the recommendation made by Farrell Grant Sparks (1998) that a discrete government unit should be set up to oversee and advise on the PPP process, which would then 'roll out' expertise to comparable units in other departments. The institutional support also included the creation of such PPP Units in a number of other key government departments in 1999. Government support was publicly demonstrated through the high-profile backing from key government Ministers.[5] For example, in November 2001, Charlie McCreevey TD, the Minister for Finance at the time, at the launch of the Framework for Public Private Partnerships stated that:

> this has been a good year for the Public Private Partnership process ... how much we have achieved in developing PPPs in Ireland in a relatively short time ... we are actively exploring the scope for initiating PPP pilot projects in other areas, including health ... this Framework will serve as a key building block for the successful development of PPPs in Ireland in the future.

Furthermore, in October of that same year, Martin Cullen TD, the then Minister for the Office of Public Works, at the Second Annual Public Private Partnership Global Summit in Dublin, explained that it was not a matter of waiting for completion of the Pilot PPP projects before proceeding with other PPPs, rather it was 'intended that the pilot projects will set the basis for subsequent projects'. Outside of the Global Summit on PPPs a hundred or so trade unionists, anti-toll motorway campaigners and global justice campaigners protested against the introductions of PPPs. They feared that problems associated with PPPs across the world, particularly in the UK, such as cost overruns, privatisation and reduction in employee conditions, would also be experienced in Ireland. Their concerns did not make any impact on the government's intentions to rapidly develop and implement this new policy. Indeed, Budget 2004 stated that the government aimed to increase PPPs proportion of total capital investment from the 3 per cent level it was at in 2004 to 15 per cent by 2008. The government set further ambitious targets in the *National Development Plan, 2007–2013*, which provided for some €13.35 billion in PPP-funded capital investment of which €11.2 billion was in respect of projects funded by annual payments to the private consortia. In addition, over €1.9 billion of PPP funding in the Plan was planned to be in respect of toll-based investment in the roads area. PPPs, therefore, have been implemented and expanded at a remarkable pace in key sectors of the Irish state, at central and local government levels, displacing direct public-sector service and infrastructure provision.

Explanation of the Irish state

References to the Irish state in this book include the entire institutional infrastructure of the public and civil services and elected government at both central and local levels. The broad public sector in Ireland consists of the public and civil services. The civil service comprises the permanent staff of the fifteen government departments (for example the Department of Health and the Department of Education and Science) and certain agencies or offices. The agencies include, amongst others: the Office of the Revenue Commissioners, the Central Statistics Office, the Office of the Comptroller and Auditor General (C & AG), the Courts Service of Ireland, the Office of Public Works and the Office of the Ombudsman. The wider public service generally consists of specialised staff, such as teachers, doctors, police, army or those staff within agencies who, while not formally part of a department, provide services on behalf of the government.

A state authority under Irish law refers to a Minister of the government, a local authority, the Commissioners of Public Works in Ireland, the National Roads Authority (NRA), the Health Service Executive, universities, institutes of technologies, Voluntary Education Committees, the Courts Service, harbour authorities, Bus Atha Cliath – Dublin Bus, Bus Éireann – Irish Bus, Coras Iompair Éireann (CIE), the Rail Procurement Agency and the Digital Hub Development Agency.

Local authorities operate under the aegis of the Department of the Environment, Heritage, and Local Government (DOEHLG). Each local authority is responsible for the delivery of certain services, such as environmental protection, waste management, housing, water supply, sewerage and certain aspects of road transportation, while all local authorities are governed by a council made up of elected councillors. A large percentage of local authority expenditure, both capital and current, is provided by central government, which has resulted in considerable central government control over, and influence on, local government (OECD,[6] 2008).

In 'traditional' or 'direct' public provision and delivery of services and infrastructure, a state agency finances a capital service or infrastructure project using either existing tax income or by borrowing, either designs it 'in-house' or contracts a private company to design it and then, in most instances, contracts a private construction firm to build it. It then hires public employees to maintain and operate the physical structure once completed. However, in PPPs, a private company (usually a consortium formed specifically for the purpose of bidding on a project) provides, or takes over the design, building and/or financing and maintenance of a completely new public service or infrastructure project, such as a hospital, road or school that would otherwise have been provided through the traditional public-sector model. PPPs therefore can take many forms, but generally entail a 'sponsoring' state agency (government department, local authority, state or semi-state body) contracting or procuring a private company to design, build and/or finance and/or manage/maintain a public service or infrastructure for up to thirty years. Therefore, rather than the project being financed at the start by the Exchequer through capital investment and the running costs being funded from annual budgets, the private sector provides the finance for the project. This facilitates the state to pay for the project over an extended period of time through a series of annual payments to the private partner.

Expansion of PPP projects

The actual quantity and value of PPP projects that were developed in various sectors over this short period of time is very considerable. For example, the total outstanding commitments of central government departments and agencies in respect of large contracted PPP projects were estimated at just over €4.27 billion at the end of 2008. Roads comprised 54 per cent of that figure; the area of arts, sport and tourism, 17 per cent; courts, 14 per cent; education, 13 per cent; and local authority projects, 2 per cent (although this figure does not include any amounts that local authorities committed from their own budgets). One can see the extent of PPP development clearly in Tables 1.2 and 1.3, which summarise the various sectors in which projects, of a value exceeding €20 million, were developed by 2010. While PPP projects of less than that value exist across the public sector, the government only classifies projects over the value of €20 million as PPPs. Therefore, for the purposes of this book, the PPPs referred to are almost all in excess of that figure.

Government figures showed that, in 2010, there were at least ninety identified PPP projects, twenty-seven of which were in operation, twenty in construction and forty-three at procurement stage. The projects were valued at between €8 billion and €16.3 billion (including €4 billion on rail transport, €2.5 billion to €5.5 billion on roads, €450 million to €2.25 billion on education and €630million to €2.2 billion on water/waste-water services).

Table 1.2 Number of PPPs in operation, construction or planned in Ireland as of 2010

Project		Operation	Construction	Procurement/ planning	Total
Roads	DBFOM	7	5	3	15
Wastewater/ water treatment	DBO	9	6	10	25
Education	DBFM	7 (5 schools)	4 (schools)	17 (14 schools)	28
Light Rail	DBFOM	2	2	5	9
Courts/Prisons	DBFM	1		2	3
Accom	DBFM 1	4	5		
Redevelopment/ regeneration	DBF	1	1	1	3
Waste to Energy	DBFOM	1		1	2
		27	20	43	90

Notes: 1 DBFOM: design, build, finance, operate, maintain.
2 DBFM: design, build, finance, maintain.
3 DBF: design, build, finance.

Source: Adapted from Central PPP Unit (2005, 2007, 2008, 2010); C & AG (2009); NDFA (2009).

The projects include nine operational PPPs in the transport sector (seven operational road projects and the Dublin Light Rail System – LUAS, which has carried more than fifty-million passengers since it commenced operation). It also includes nine operational water/waste-water treatment plants. A significant amount of outsourcing of local government services has also taken place, particularly the outsourcing of local authority refuse collection services, such as the provision of a waste recycling service to the four Dublin local authorities, although these tend to be valued at under €20 million.

Government policy, as Table 1.2 demonstrates, promoted the PPP model particularly in the area of Irish education. In that sector, five new post-primary schools, referred to as the 'Grouped Schools Pilot PPP Project', were completed in 2003 as a twenty-five-year design, build, finance and maintain (DBFM) PPP contract between the Department of Education and Science and Jarvis Plc (through the consortium Schools Public Private Partnership (Ireland) Ltd.). Two other projects were operational by 2010. These include, first, the National Maritime College of Ireland (a twenty-five year contract to provide and maintain a third-level college for education and training in merchant marine and naval service studies, which has a capacity to cater for 750 students and was completed in October 2004) and, second, the Cork School of Music (a twenty-five year contract involving the construction of a new building to house the Cork School of Music, which can accommodate approximately 400 full-time third-level students and 2,500 part-time students and was completed in mid-2007). The total outstanding commitment under these contracts, as of 31 December 2008, was €554.4 million (C & AG, 2009). The five schools[7] represented the largest grouped PPP project completed to date in the education sector. In July 2006, due to Jarvis's financial difficulties, Hochtief PPP Solutions (Ireland) Ltd bought out Jarvis's interest in the schools project.

In 2005, the Minister for Education and Science announced a plan to provide a further twenty-seven new schools (twenty-three post-primary and four primary schools in twenty-two locations) through PPPs. The first 'Bundle' of schools went to the market in 2006 and was expected to be completed by September 2010. In 2006, the Department announced a second 'Bundle' of six schools on five sites in counties Cork, Limerick, Kildare, Wicklow and Meath. Then in June 2010 a third bundle of eight schools, to be delivered by PPP, was announced, providing accommodation for approximately 5,560 students.

Table 1.3 Details of PPPs in operation/construction/planned in Ireland as of March 2010

Department/ responsible body	Project name and private consortium awarded contract	Indicative value (€ million)	Project phase
	Road Concession (contract for 30 years)		
DCC and Dublin Port	East-Link		In operation since 1984
National Roads Authority (NRA)	M 50 upgrade West-Link		In operation
	N1/M1 Dundalk Bypass (Celtic Roads Group)	340	In operation since 2005

	N4 Kilcock/Kinnegad (Eurolink SIAC and Cintra)	550	Operation since 2005
	N25 Waterford Bypass (Celtic Roads Group – National Toll Roads (NTR), Dragados, Ascon/BAM)		Operation since 2009
	N8 Rathcormac/Fermoy Bypass (Direct Route)	320	Operation since 2006
	N6 Galway/East Ballinasloe (ICON)		Operation since 2009
	N7 Limerick Southern Ring/ Tunnel (Direct Route)		In construction 2010
	M3 Clonee/Kells (Eurolink)		Construction 2010
	M7/M8 Portlaois/Castletown (Celtic Roads Group)		Construction 2010
	M50 upgrade II (ICON)		Construction 2010
	M1/M4 motorway service areas –Tranche 1 (Tedcastle/Pierse/ Applegreen)		Construction
	N11 Arklow/Rathnew		Procurement
	M11 Gorey/Enniscorthy		Procurement
	N17/18 Gort/Tuam		Procurement
	Light Rail, operate and manage and DBFOM		
Rail Procurement Authority	LUAS (Veolia Transport)		In operation since 2003
	LUAS Docklands extension		Operation since 2009
	LUAS Cherrywood extension		Construction
	LUAS Citywest extension		Construction
	LUAS Bray/Fassaroe		Design
	Lucan LUAS	1 billion +	Planning preparation
	Metro North, 18km, DBFM	1 billion +	Preferred bidder stage
	Metro West, 34km, DBFM	1 billion +	Planning preparation
	Dart Underground Interconnector DBFMO	1 billion +	Market soundings

Department/ responsible body	Project name and private consortium awarded contract	Indicative value (€ million)	Project phase
	Education DFBM (25–year contract)		
Department of Education and Science	5 new post-primary schools (Hochtief)	274	In operation since 2002
	National Maritime College of Ireland	51.3	In operation since October 2004
	Cork School of Music	205	In operation
	Schools Bundle 1: 4 new post primary schools (Macquarie)		In construction
	Schools Bundle 2: 5 new post primary schools and 1 new primary school (Macquarie)		Contract signed
	Schools Bundle 3: 7 new post primary schools and 1 new primary schools		Procurement
	Third-level Bundle 1: 6 new buildings in 4 third-level institutions		Procurement
	Third-Level Bundle 2: 6 new buildings in 2 third-level institutions		Procurement
	Third-level Bundle 3: 4 new buildings in 3 third-level institutions		Procurement
	Redevelopment/regeneration DBF		
DOEHLG & DCC	Fatima Mansions redevelopment (Elliot Maplewood)	100–250	In construction
	Redevelopment of Greystones Harbour DBF (Sispar)		Construction
	Decentralisation		Deferred
Grangegorman Development Agency	Relocation of Health Services Executive and Dublin Institute of Technology (DIT) on to Grangegorman DBF		Procurement

	Water/waste-water treatment plants DBO (20/25–year contract)		
DOEHLG and relevant local authority	Dublin Bay Drainage Scheme (Anglian)	300	In operation since July 2003
	Wexford Main Drainage (Brent)	20–50	In operation
	Cork Main Drainage Treatment (Degremont)	50–100	In operation since 2004
	Dungarvan Sewage Treatment (ABV)		In operation since 2007
	South Tipperary Bundled Water Drainage (Earth Tech)		In operation since 2006
	Donegal Sewerage (Veolia Water)		In operation since 2008
	Balbriggan/Skerries Sewerage (Earth Tech)		In operation since 2007
	Portlaois Sewage Treatment (Earth Tech)		Operation since 2009
	Sligo Main Drainage (Anglian Water)		Operation
	Balbriggan/Skerries Treatment plant	20–50	In construction
	Waterford Treatment Plant (Anglian Water)		Construction
	Clareville (Limerick) Potable Water Treatment Scheme (Veolia Water/AScon)		Construction
	Meath Grouped Villages Waste-water (EPS)		Construction
	Donegal B		Appraisal
	Mullingar Sewerage (Veolia Water)		Construction
	Arklow Potable Water Treatment		Procurement
	Shanagh Sewerage (Dragados/ Sisk)		Construction
	Thurles Potable Water Treatment Plant		Procurement
	Wicklow Sewerage (Veolia Water)		Construction
	Waterford Grouped Towns Treatment		Tender
	Letterkenny Sewage Treatment		Tender
	Gwedore Sewage Treatment		Tender
	Navan/Mid Meath Water Treatment		Tender

Department/ responsible body	Project name and private consortium awarded contract	Indicative value (€ million)	Project phase
	Barrow Water Extraction and Treatment		Tender
	Portrane/Donabate Sewerage		Tender
Waste to Energy DBFOM			
DOEHLG	South East Region Waste Infrastructure		Appraisal
Dublin City Council	Dublin Waste to Energy (Dublin Waste to Energy/ Covanta ltd)		Construction
Courts/Prisons DBFOM			
Courts Service	Criminal Courts of Justice Complex (Babcock & Brown)		Operation since 2009
	Courts bundle		Procurement
	Munster Prison Complex		Assessment stage
	Thornton Hall relocation of Mountjoy Prison		Procurement
National Network for Radiation Oncology DBFOM			
Health Services Executive	(Four large centres in Dublin, Cork, Galway and satellite centres in Waterford and Limerick		Procurement
Accommodation projects DBFOM			
	National Conference Centre (Spencer Dock)		In construction
	Abbey Theatre		Project team
	National Concert Hall		Project heam
Outsourcing			
DOEH&LG & four Dublin local authorities	Waste management and environmental services (Greyhound)		Operational since 1997

Note: DBO: design, build, operate.
Source: Adapted from Central PPP Unit (2005, 2007, 2008, 2010); C & AG (2009); NDFA (2009).

Public investment in infrastructure

It is important to highlight that in a number of areas, including the schools sector, there has been demonstrable improvements in public economic and social infrastructure in Ireland over the last ten years as a result of substantial Exchequer investment. For example, the government invested €9 billion of public finance in schools, hospitals and, buildings and equipment related to public administration between 2000 and 2008 (€3.5 billion of which was spent on the education sector alone). Similarly, in the area of transport €14.5 billion was invested in roads in the same period, resulting in substantially upgraded major inter-urban routes. There was also a major enhancement of public transport, including both national rail services and commuter services, such as the LUAS, the doubling of peak capacity on Dublin's city rail line (the DART) and major investment in the Intercity Rail Network.

Over the period of the *National Development Plan, 2000–2006*, €10.4 billion was invested in the housing area. This provided an additional 31,000 local authority housing units and 9,000 voluntary and 12,400 affordable housing units. The sum of €3.1 billion was invested in environmental infrastructure projects, including the completion of hundreds of water service projects comprising waste-water and water supply and infrastructure management and rehabilitation. The health sector also received Exchequer investment of over €3.3 billion during the period of the Plan, including the provision of over 1,300 inpatient and day treatment places in hospitals across the country, and of primary and community care, particularly for older people.

Under the *National Development Plan, 2007–2013*, the government planned to invest €184 billion to fund numerous projects and initiatives throughout the country to address deficits in infrastructure and social services. This was the largest and most ambitious investment programme ever proposed in Ireland and included €54.6 billion for public economic infrastructure, covering, for example, the upgrading of the road network, the public transport system in line with Transport 21, especially in the Greater Dublin Area, water and waste-water infrastructure, waste infrastructure, the availability of broadband services, energy supply and the delivery of the decentralisation programme. The decentralisation scheme planned to provide regional development through relocating central government offices and services to towns and villages across Ireland.

The Greater Dublin Area comprises the four Dublin councils and the counties of Kildare, Meath and Wicklow, all of which experienced dramatic changes in terms of population and economic output through the 1990s and 2000s. These changes have brought challenges in infrastructure capacity, particularly in terms of a high reliance on car transport and long-distance commuting, traffic congestion, major increases in the cost of housing and inadequate environmental services.

The Plan also included a plan to invest €49.6 billion for social inclusion measures, €33.6 billion for social infrastructure (housing; hospital infrastructure; primary and community care facilities, particularly for the elderly; prisons; courts; sport, culture and community infrastructure) and €25.8 billion for human capital (schools, training, higher education). This resulted in the total annual level of public investment in infrastructure in 2008 in Ireland being more than 5 per cent of GDP, which was about twice the rate in the OECD and was the highest rate in the EU 15.

Problems emerge in projects

A surprising aspect of the rapid expansion of PPPs in Ireland has been the absence of major research, investigations or analysis of their initial outcomes, in particular any verification of whether or not their stated benefits were materialising in the initial pilot projects. Furthermore, a substantial proportion of the information available relating to their development has been written by private- and public-sector entities that have strong interests in promoting and developing these projects, such as national PPP agencies, private consultancy companies, legal firms and financial equity investors. It was quite difficult to find objective information that undertook a critical assessment of the selection process, development and outcomes of PPPs in Ireland. The few studies that have been carried out to date have found that the experience of PPPs in Ireland to date has been mixed (Bissett, 2008; Bradley and Allen, 2001; C & AG, 2004, 2008; Dillon, 2004; Hearne, 2006, 2007; Kay, 2002; Reeves, 2001, 2005).

The C & AG developed a detailed 'value for money' appraisal of the schools project, *The Grouped Schools Pilot Partnership Project* (C & AG, 2004) and of the Criminal Courts of Justice Complex PPP Project (C & AG, 2008). The report on the schools project revealed that, while the Department of Education and Science initially calculated an expected saving of 6 per cent for the PPP schools, the actual projected cost of the deal, according to the C & AG's calculation, was 8–13 per cent higher than through a conventional state-funded approach.

The examination of the Courts of Justice Complex looked at how the Courts Service evaluated the project in the course of its development and at the negotiation of the deal. It also identified lessons that could be applied to future projects where procurement by PPP is proposed. The examination stated that the National Development Finance Agency (NDFA) indicated that the projected cost of the final courts PPP deal would be around 6 per cent less than the cost of conventional procurement. It is noteworthy that the report also queried aspects of the financial modelling undertaken to assess the value for money of the project.

Kay (2002) and Reeves (2005) highlighted the lack of accountability in PPPs and argued that the private sector was more likely to adopt projects involving public services and infrastructure that boosted their shareholders' returns than engaging in projects that met the long-term needs of society. Sweeney (2004) questioned the assumption made by PPP proponents that the private sector can undertake public projects more efficiently and more cost effectively than the public sector in light of the problems that have been experienced to date in recent PPP infrastructural projects.

Privatisation (the sale of public assets) and commercial, market-oriented practices and policies have been introduced into the public sector across the world, in part because of the desire of neoliberal governments to reduce the conditions, power and influence of workers and their trade union representatives (Harvey, 2005). This has been accomplished to a certain extent through the introduction of private operators into the public services, which has significantly lower levels of trade unionism and quality of employee conditions (Allen, 2007; Whitfield, 2006). There has, however, been no research undertaken to date into the extent to which such neoliberal policy objectives, including the reduction in the quality of conditions of employment and trade union influence in the public sector, were motivating factors in the Irish government's decision to introduce PPPs. Nor has there been research to determine how the employment conditions of public- and private-sector employees were affected by PPP arrangements. The ICTU (ICTU, 2005, 3) stated that 'PPPs pose a serious threat to the delivery of future public services by public service staff' and were concerned that in order to increase investor returns, private-sector operators would achieve 'value for money' through savings and cost cuttings in the form of placing a downward pressure on the wages and conditions of staff. Therefore, ICTU believed, as a condition of involvement in PPP projects, private-sector companies 'must apply industry or national norms for pay, pension and conditions of employment, including equality and health and safety obligations and should be required to grant recognition and bargaining rights to the appropriate trade unions for the relevant sectors' (ICTU, 2005, 3).

They also expressed concern in relation to consultation with employees in the development of PPP projects and during their operational phase. It is surprising that ICTU's analysis did not contain a broader critique of PPPs contextualised within the wider development of neoliberalism and privatisation policies in Ireland. This, perhaps, is a manifestation of the consensus that had been reached with the trade unions in relation to the introduction of PPPs as part of the Social Partnership Agreements.

The international experience

The experiences in the United Kingdom, Canada and other countries that implemented PPPs and privatisation much earlier and more intensely than Ireland highlight that many benefits attributed to PPPs have not been satis-factorily achieved in practice. In a similar fashion to the Irish experience, the outcomes of PPPs internationally were very worrying, particularly from a social equity and public service perspective. PPPs, or Private Finance Initiatives (PFI) as they are called in the UK, were first introduced by the Conservative government in 1992 and their use has been expanded across the world since then. Their implementation has led to an intense debate interna-tionally about their appropriateness for use in the development and provision of public services and infrastructure. Problems identified in some of the projects (particularly PFI schools and hospitals) included poor 'value for money' and service delivery, reductions in public-sector capacity and demo-cratic accountability, the creation of a two-tier workforce, increased costs and increases in user charges.

Furthermore, rather than improving service standards, public-sector morale has been lowered, there has been reduced 'diversity' in service provision, the private sector profiteered by 'cherry-picking' the delivery of the most financially advantageous services and effectively neglected the most socially disadvantaged. Reflecting the extent of the problems PFIs faced in the UK, the finance spokesperson of the Conservative Party, George Osborne MP, who subsequently became Chancellor of the Exchequer after the 2010 British general elections, questioned their continued use. Prior to the 2010 election, he stated that a Conservative government would abolish the PFI model and replace it with an alternative one for funding major infrastructure projects. He criticised PFIs for lacking transparency, failing to genuinely shift risk on to the private sector and leaving the UK taxpayer committed to a repayment stream totalling £206 billion, with the peak bills due in 2017:

> The government's use of PFI has become totally discredited, so we need new ways to leverage private sector investment ... Labour's PFI model is flawed and must be replaced. We need a new system that doesn't pretend that risks have been transferred to the private sector when they can't be, and which genuinely transfers risks when they can be. (George Osborne MP, quoted in *The Observer*, November 2009)

In Australia, the New South Wales (NSW) government cancelled the PPP tender for the construction and operation of an A$3.5 billion, seven-kilometre, metro rail line in Sydney on which the government had already spent close to A$300 million. It was the fourth major PPP contract to be terminated in a ten-year period in Australia. A road tunnel project was cancelled in 2006 and the project was sold the following year for A$680 million – well below its original cost of almost A$1 billion. These results are in line with the outcomes of similar privatisation-type policies, such as the privatisation of the national telecommunications company of Ireland (Eircom), the rail network in the UK, electricity systems in the United States and Europe and water companies in the UK (which have neglected even to take adequate precaution against drought).

In the Latin American countries of Bolivia and Argentina, the water systems of some major cities were privatised in the 1990s. The private water companies that took over the systems significantly increased water charges and cut services to the poor, leading to popular protest and a subsequent cancelling of the private contracts by the governments. In 2004, the Swedish coalition government banned the privatisation of hospitals, amid fears that the expansion of private health would damage the public health system. Such negative outcomes have led to the mobilisation of considerable opposition across the world, particularly amongst trade unionists and local communities, against further privatisation attempts. This has also included direct opposition to mechanisms identified as forms of privatisation and neoliberalism, such as the introduction and expansion of PPP or PFI projects.

Privatisation and neoliberalism

PPPs, however, have been found to have a deeper, broader and more specific impact than privatisation. Indeed, it was in the face of the growing opposition to the negative societal impacts of overt privatisation policies that PPPs were identified by governments and private-sector proponents as an important mechanism to continue the neoliberal privatisation of public service delivery, and the welfare state more generally. PPP and PFI introduce aspects of neoliberalism such as commercialisation and marketisation directly into the welfare state and public sector, which could contribute to deterioration in the quality of and accessibility to services and exacerbation of inequality and poverty.

It is argued, therefore, that while PPPs might not appear as outright privatisation, when all public services and entire infrastructure are handed over to the private sector, this is leading to a process of *privatisation by stealth* of the remaining public services and infrastructure (Monbiot, 2000; Whitfield, 2001). For example, the private consortiums that finance and operate PPP and PFI projects are large global multinational companies. Therefore, PPP projects are facilitating the transfer to such commercial entities of control over, and responsibility for, the operation and provision of key aspects of public services and infrastructure. One aspect of this is that public services become commodities traded on international asset markets, bought and sold for profit, between various private equity investors and commercial businesses. Take the Criminal Courts of Justice in Ireland, which is no longer contracted with the original private consortium, Australian investment firm Babcock & Brown. The company was placed into liquidation in August 2009 and the management rights of its PPP fund (including the Irish Courts Project) were then sold to a management company, Amber Fund Management Limited. That fund now administers the PPPs through a company listed on the London Stock Exchange called International Public Partnerships, which has over £2 billion of PFI and PPP assets across the world. The company's website describes the projects in a way that is clearly aimed at attracting investors and achieving a strong return for their share-holders. It describes their 'portfolio' as comprising fifty-one 'high-quality PPP/PFI projects' with more than 99 per cent of the revenues 'government-backed, providing strong contractual certainty of future cash flows and 100 per cent of the portfolio is underpinned by concessions let by government bodies in top-tier OECD nations'. Included in the portfolio are PPP projects in the UK, Australia, Canada, Germany, France, Belgium, Italy and Ireland. This is the company that now holds the Criminal Courts Complex contract.

The fascinating, and indeed most worrying, aspect of this is that the public partner in this project, the Irish state, had no input into, influence or control over this procedure of contract sale and transfer. This process of buying and selling public assets as internationally traded commodities could have significant implications not just for the provision of the public services and infrastructure, but also for the democratic control by national govern-ments over the services for which they have the responsiblity to provide to their public.

Another example of the extension of global multinational control over Irish public services and infrastructure is the case of Dublin's newly constructed LUAS light rail system. The LUAS is a PPP operated by Veolia Transport Ireland. Veolia Transport Ireland, however, is a subsidiary of Veolia Environnement, a global multinational service provider, with over 336,000 employees and a recorded revenue of €34.6 billion in 2009.

Global trade rules governed by the World Trade Organisation, obliging national governments to irreversibly liberalise markets for services on a global scale, support this trend. PPPs are playing a strategic role in this process of capturing public services and assets for private investment and capital accu-mulation.

To date in Ireland there has been no wider critique of such privatisation and the neoliberal impacts of PPPs. There has been no detailed research into their role in the neoliberal transformation of the Irish welfare state at central and local levels, such as their impact on the fundamental role that the Irish state and public sector plays in the development of society and the economy. This reflects the political and social consensus around the introduction of

PPPs, represented most clearly by their inclusion as part of the Social Partnership Agreements. It is also a manifestation of the general trend toward neoliberalism in Irish politics and state institutions.

The little opposition that has been raised to PPPs has emanated from local communities and individual sections of trade unions. This book, therefore, fills this gap in information and provides an important critical analysis of PPP policy and outcomes. It is of importance given the historical juncture that the development of PPPs reached in 2010 in Ireland. The pilot projects were almost complete and a new phase of expansion of PPP projects was underway.

The book also presents an investigation into the underlying reasons and factors that influenced the Irish government's decision to introduce PPPs, in essence, why and how the Irish state chose PPPs as a model of procurement. It provides an analysis of the motivations, values and principals that lay behind the decision to introduce these PPPs, and addresses the fundamental question of why and for whom were PPPs really introduced. Were they about addressing the need for accessible public services or more about providing private companies with new avenues for profit making and capital accumulation?

To what extent has the introduction of PPPs been influenced by and facilitated the Irish neoliberal policy trajectory and the neoliberal restructuring of state institutions in Ireland, as has been the case with PPPs internationally? In other words, how much of their origins and development were about undertaking a fundamental market-oriented transformation of how Irish public services and infrastructure are provided? The outcomes of PPPs have raised the essential concern of whom do Irish public services now serve: the people or large international private commercial companies?

The book also investigates whether trends associated with such policy trajectories in other countries are present in Ireland, such as negative impacts on access to high-quality public services, workers' employment conditions, democratic accountability, community participation and consultation.

It then analyses the role PPPs are playing in the evolution and development of the Irish state and provides an important account for those outside Ireland who are looking at the 'Celtic Tiger' model and what remains of its broken economy to see what can be learned from the Irish PPP experience. The evidence is analysed in order to answer the fundamental question, namely whether PPPs are an effective and appropriate option for the delivery of quality, affordable, public services and infrastructure that meet social needs.

The following chapter (Chapter 2) provides an overview of the historical development of socio-economic policy in relation to the welfare state, Keynesianism, neoliberalism and the emergence of PPPs internationally.

Chapter 3 then provides a comprehensive account of the underlying reasons for the development of PPPs in Ireland. Chapters 4, 5 and 6 then provide a detailed analysis of what the outcomes have been to date in relation to the Grouped Schools Pilot PPP Project (Chapter 4), the regeneration of social housing estates (Chapter 5) and a summary analysis of PPPs developed to date in Ireland (Chapter 6). It looks at PPPs in terms of whether or not the Irish government-stated benefits of PPPs – including an accelerated delivery of service and infrastructure provision, increased 'value for money' in the development of infrastructure and services and improved quality of service and enhanced public management – materialised in practice.

This is of considerable importance for public policy in relation to the delivery of public services and infrastructure generally, given the dearth of existing empirical evidence to ascribe the much-lauded benefits of PPPs in this area. The history and experience of their development to date in Ireland provides important lessons for socio-economic planning and policy. This book provides, for the first time on Ireland, an insight into the Irish PPP experience, and also looks at some important lessons that have been learned from their short history in this country, thus contributing to the debate about the future of the public sector, required reform and privatisation. This is discussed in detail in Chapter 7.

Notes

1 GDP is the value of all final goods and services produced in a country in one year.
2 The Inter Departmental Group comprises representatives of all public service bodies (government departments and state agencies such as the National Roads Authority) engaged in PPPs. Its primary role is to bring together key decision makers to ensure that there is coherence and consistency across the public services in advancing Ireland's PPP programme (Central PPP Unit, 2006b).
3 It should be noted that Ireland's first PPP project, the East-Link Toll Bridge between NTR, Dublin Port and DCC was established in 1984 and in 1990 the West-Link was established.
4 These were various agreements between the social partners that included the main employer's group, the government and trades unions that took place from the 1980s until the 2000s.
5 A government Minister is a politician (TD) elected to the Irish Parliament (Dáil) who has been appointed by the Irish Prime Minister (Taoiseach) to be in charge of a signif-icant public office at a national level, such as the Department of Education and Science or Department of Health. Most government Ministers are members of the govern-ment's decision-making committee, the cabinet.
6 The Organisation for Economic Co-operation and Development (OECD) brings together the governments of countries committed to democracy and the free-market economy. Its membership includes 30 countries, 27 of whom are described as high-income countries by the World Bank, and include, amongst others, Ireland, Austria, Belgium, United Kingdom and the United States of America (OECD, 2008).

7   The schools and their relevant school enrolments are as follows: Ballincollig (County Cork) 1,000 pupils, Clones (County Monaghan) 500, Dunmanway (County Cork) 700, Shannon (County Clare) 600, Tubercurry (County Sligo) 675.

2

The welfare state, neoliberalism and Public Private Partnerships: the international experience

> The (Cholera) epidemics of 1832 and 1848 killed 140,000 people. Cleansing action by no one individual could ever be certain to be enough. The role for government was clear. This required collective action. It meant property rights needed to be disregarded and land compulsorily purchased, both big issues for a laissez-faire time. The Victorians took up the challenge by legislation, then accompanied by the great feats of Victorian engineering. In 1858 Parliament responded to the 'Great Stink' emanating from the River Thames by sanctioning Bazalgette to build 83 miles of sewers to prevent the deposit of raw sewage. The Manchester waterworks had begun in 1847 and by 1875 most of Liverpool's housing had water closets connected to sewers. (Blair, 2006, 1)

Thus explained former British Prime Minister Tony Blair how, it was only action undertaken by the state that could adequately address such profound public health issues that arose in the nineteenth century. Similar public health issues and concerns existed in Ireland, at the time a colony of the UK, and indeed across Europe. In the early decades of the twentieth century, the existing *laissez-faire* free-market system that relied on an uncoordinated mixture of local municipal providers, private operators and family systems was failing to provide a solution to the emerging social needs, including considerable health and housing problems, of an increasingly urbanised population. Those in power promoted the primacy of the free market and argued that such social problems were the responsibility of the individual and that the state should not intervene. Their approach was based on the classical economics' theory that society and the economy should be organised according to the decisions of the 'hidden hand' (as identified by classical economist Adam Smith) of the market. The free market, once it was left alone, unregulated and un-interfered, by governments, would bring about the optimum level of demand and supply of goods and services in an economy.

However, as conditions worsened for the mass of the population, demands for social reform began to be organised around social movements such as trade unions and social-democratic, socialist and communist political parties (Bourdieu, 1998; Harvey, 1989).

As a result of these crises, the development and growth in nation states and the pressures for reform, national states across Western Europe gradually began to assume greater responsibility for addressing economic and social problems that had once been considered individual or voluntary affairs. They began to develop and co-ordinate national and local public services and infrastructure (Kirby *et al.*, 1984; Pacione, 1990).

In a similar manner, the economic and social crises resulting from the 'Great Depression' in the 1930s, in the main caused by unregulated capitalism and free-market policies, led to further demands for government intervention (Harvey, 1989). In 1936, John Maynard Keynes' ground-breaking book *The General Theory of Employment, Interest and Money* was published (Skidelsky, 2009). In it, he argued for a model of central demand management where governments would invest in the economy to develop industry, maintain full employment and use redistributive taxation to fund high levels of welfare spending and thus minimise the impacts on the economy of the inherent 'boom' and 'bust' cycles of market capitalism.

Other more radical theorists (social democrats, Marxists, socialists and other state-planning theorists) also criticised the free-market model because it identified a demand for goods and services only when it was expressed through a financial demand. The free market, therefore, would only provide for publicly needed services such as transport, health and education when they had a financial aspect, that is when they were profitable for private capital and business to provide them (Kirk, 1980).

Thus in the 1940s, following World War II in particular, governments across Western Europe and in the USA took core responsibility for the provision of essential public services, infrastructure and welfare away from the private sector and free market. This was done on the basis that the private market could not be relied on to provide such essential components of the economy and society. They, therefore, constructed a variety of welfare systems involving an expansion of public expenditures and direct state provision in education, housing, transport, healthcare (including public hospitals and the provision of water and waste-water infrastructure for public health), defence services (such as law and order), macro-economic management institutions, roads, parks and public spaces. This was also undertaken in order to appease popular revolt and trade union strikes, to try and stave off the influence of Russian communism and to save capitalism from its inherent market crises. It was, in ways, a class compromise between workers, the state and owners of capital.

Governments thus developed 'Keynesian' and 'welfare state' models of economic and social development designed around a negotiated balance of state, market and democratic institutions to guarantee peace, inclusion, well-being and stability. It centred on redistributive politics, including some degree of political integration of working-class representatives in the form of socialist Labour parties and trade unions. The role of government and the state under this period of Keynesianism in Western Europe was expanded on an unprecedented scale and the state, both central and local, began to play an active role in addressing social need through its provision of such public services and infrastructure (Castells, 2000; Esping-Andersen, 1999; Harvey, 2005; Kirk, 1980; Pierre and Peters, 2000).

Varying types of welfare state developed in this period depending on their specific blend of Keynesian and market policies. Three broad types can be generally classified, including the liberal (adopted by Anglo-Saxon countries), social-democratic (Scandinavian countries) and conservative (Continental Europe) welfare state models. Scandinavian countries developed the most extensive Keynesian and welfare state models, followed then by France, Germany and the UK. This included the nationalisation of private companies, state-led planning and state ownership of key sectors (for example coal, steel, and automobiles), the development of universalism in the provision of public services and addressing inequality and social risks.

In the UK, for example, Clement Atlee's post-war government (1945–51) sought to address the chronic inequalities in public service availability and quality by proposing a comprehensive system based on the principle of universal access to services. It aimed at ensuring that all citizens, without distinction of status or class, were offered the best standards available in relation to a certain agreed range of social services. Underpinning this was the principal that the central state would be the guarantor of universal access to social services of the highest quality based on need and not the ability to pay and that the services would be mostly funded by general taxation and delivered primarily by the state itself.

Over the following decades, the West experienced a period of high economic growth and state expansion. Public-sector providers became increasingly characterised as providing a wide availability of public services, good working conditions and strong public trust (Esping-Andersen, 1999; National Economic and Social Council, 2005). Furthermore, the public sector became obliged under national and international laws to provide financial transparency, tackle inequality and social exclusion and improve access, participation and planning in delivery of services. It was also required to improve employment conditions, including staff involvement and union recognition and involvement in industrial relations frameworks.

However, the oil crises of 1973 and 1979, along with the serious economic crises and rising unemployment in the late 1960s and 1970s combined with the exponential growth in public spending that had been taking place since World War II led to Western governments facing huge fiscal crises. The UK government, for example, had to be bailed out by the International Monetary Fund in 1975. Inflation surged, ushering in a global phase of 'stagflation' lasting throughout much of the late 1970s. Keynesian policies were criticised and blamed for the crisis by followers of free-market orthodoxies, such as Margaret Thatcher in the UK and Ronald Reagan in the USA. This new wave of policy makers, government leaders, academics and 'Think Tanks' were advocates of free-market policies that came to be referred to as 'neoliberalism'. They were heavily influenced by the right-wing theorist Friedrich Hayek and other proponents of free-market approaches emanating from the Chicago School of Economics (Brenner and Theodore, 2002; Callinicos, 2003; Harvey, 2005).

Neoliberal theory and policies were founded on the theories of classical free-market economics. The advocates of neoliberalism argued that the unprecedented expansion of the state in the form of 'big government' was the main cause of the economic crises in the 1970s as it had required government borrowing to increase beyond sustainable levels, while simultaneously restricting the private sector from certain sectors of the economy. This, they claimed, was choking the potential for economic growth. The solution was radically to transform the role and form of the state by reducing state intervention and prioritising the primacy of the market. The neoliberals believed that the increase in the role of the state through the Keynesian period, particularly the increase in the number of socialist-oriented governments, threatened the very system of capitalism and, therefore, there was an urgent requirement to re-organise the economy and society according to free-market principles (Gill, 1995; Hall and Pfeiffer, 2000; Leys, 2001; Stiglitz, 2002).

Theory of neoliberalism

Neoliberal theorists advocate that all political and economic practice should be based on the classical economics' theory that the 'hidden hand' of the market is the best way to organise society. According to neoliberalism therefore, human well-being is best advanced by liberating individual entrepreneurial freedoms and skills within an institutional framework characterised by strong private property rights, free markets and free trade. The role of the state and governments in this model is principally to create and preserve the private property and free-trade framework through guaranteeing the proper functioning of free markets. The military, police and judiciary guarantee this system, by force if necessary. Furthermore, it seeks to bring all human action into the domain of private markets. Therefore, if markets do not exist in areas such as land, water supply, education, health-care, social security or waste, then they are to be created, by state action if necessary (Kirk, 1980; MacLaran and McGuirk, 2003).

In this neoliberal model of the economy, the ideal state only plays a distant, supervisory role, regulating what businesses want regulated and intervening exclusively in cases of market failure. It should have little or no part in the production of goods and services, and competition is to be intro-duced into all areas of the economy, into the heart of the state itself, and subsidies to private and public companies or services should not be allowed. Once markets are created, state intervention in them should be kept to a bare minimum because, according to the theory, state intervention will distort the accurate functioning of the market as the state cannot possibly possess enough information to second-guess market signals (prices) and because powerful interest groups will inevitably distort and bias state interventions for their own benefit, particularly in democracies. Markets are held to be efficient, whereas governments are not. If markets are unregulated, they will ensure the optimum economic, and therefore social, outcomes (Brenner and Theodore, 2002; Callinicos, 2003; Harvey, 2005; Kirk, 1980).

The fundamental role of the state under neoliberalism, therefore, is to ensure the correct conditions exist for private-sector economic growth. In these conditions, private capital (investment) can make sufficient profit to provide a significant return for its shareholders and to re-invest in further businesses, thus continuing economic growth. This process of private capital accumulation is the underlying motor of the free-market capitalist system (Allen, 2007; Whitfield, 2006).

Neoliberalism advocates that equality and poverty are best solved by market solutions through extending the reach and frequency of market trans-actions into all sectors of the society and economy. It asserts that continuous increases in productivity, resulting from the application of the free market delivers higher levels of living to everyone. Under the assumption that 'a rising tide' of economic growth 'lifts all boats' or results in a 'trickle down' of wealth from the creators of wealth (private enterprise) to the rest of the economy, neoliberal theory asserts that the elimination of poverty, both domestically and worldwide, can best be secured through economic growth provided through free markets and free trade. Therefore, while personal and individual freedom is guaranteed, each individual is held responsible and accountable for his or her own actions and well-being, extending to the realms of welfare, education, healthcare, pensions etc. Neoliberalism asserts that individual success or failure is conceived to result from personal attrib-utes or failings and not to derive from any failure of the system, such as class inequalities generally attributed to capitalism (Castells, 1993; Esping-Andersen, 1999; Harvey, 2005; Kirk, 1980).

Therefore, a central objective of the neoliberal political ideology is the dismantling of the existing state institutional arrangements and political compromises that focus on wealth redistribution, such as the welfare state and its public services, improved labour standards and increased trade union influence, associated with Keynesian approaches and the welfare state (Bourdieu, 1998; Brenner and Theodore, 2002; George, 2004; Harvey, 2005).

Marketisation
The dismantling of the welfare state was to be undertaken through privatisation and the imposition of market mechanisms, the private sector and market ethos and disciplines through a process of *marketisation* of the public services. Marketisation would be done through, amongst other methods, deregulation (introduction of a diversity of providers through competition between them at every level of delivery), the contracting out of services to the private sector and the transfer of assets and services to private ownership and/or control and the introduction of user charges.[1] The neoliberal government would only regulate and monitor the private sector, which would deliver and operate public infrastructure and services. Private-sector delivery, it was claimed, would improve service delivery, effectiveness and increase cost efficiency once the public sector ensured that the right conditions were in place, such as ensuring there were no barriers to market entry, that there was transparency over the results of the competition and that there was a regulatory framework that ensured these conditions were respected (Allen, 2007; Callinicos, 2003; Harvey, 2005; Whitfield, 2006).

Services such as health, education and social services, which had been predominantly provided in a non-market environment, should be opened up to private providers. The underlying rationale is that the lack of a price (or market) mechanism in these public sectors meant that it was difficult for the providers of these services to effectively gauge and, therefore, adequately meet demand. This was reinforced by the absence of competition between providers and a reliance on public funding:

> As a result of this environment, producers may have difficulties in responding adequately to evolving users' needs, such as the growing demand for long-term healthcare. Suitable policy measures, which could be explored in several public services, include the opening up of markets, the introduction of user choice, linking public funding more closely to performance as well as user payments such policy changes may contribute to better and more targeted services in several areas, and may help enhance efficiency while also achieving key public policy objectives. (OECD, 2005, 13)

A key aspect of neoliberalism, therefore, is convincing the public to accept that they have to pay for public services through user fees, even if they were previously free at the point of delivery (Allen, 2007). Overall, then, neoliberal theory postulates that in relation to the delivery of public services and infrastructure:

- Competition in the delivery of services reduces the overall cost of providing public services.
- The private sector is more efficient than the public sector in providing and managing public services and infrastructure.
- The labour market requires de-regulation and trade union power to be limited in order to ensure labour market flexibility.
- Individual choice in public services improves the quality of services.
- Choice reduces inequality because market forces are a more equalising mechanism than the state and government, which can be influenced by political voices.
- Local authorities and public bodies should be restricted to planning and regulating services in order to create the space for the private sector to develop more innovative ways of delivering services.

Such restructuring of the Keynesian welfare state reduces the proportion of profit that is allocated to the social wage (state revenue expended through public services and labour costs) and, thus, increases that proportion retained by private enterprise for return to its shareholders and also provides new opportunities for private capital investment and accumulation (Brenner and Theodore, 2002; Harvey, 2005; Whitfield, 2006).

Implementing neoliberalism

Through the 1980s, a dramatic transformation of welfare state policy agendas, supported by international institutions, such as the OECD, World Bank and International Monetary Fund, occurred in the USA, Latin America (most notably Chile under the Pinochet Dictatorship), the UK and, to a lesser degree, in Germany and other European countries. Margaret Thatcher's Conservative government, elected in 1979, implemented neoliberalism to a greater degree than any other Western European government at the time and indeed since. State involvement in the UK economy was reduced, state assets, particularly social housing and public utilities, were privatised, the free-market ideology was promoted, labour markets were deregulated and trade union power reduced. Fiscal deficits were reduced through spending cuts rather than tax increases and the tax system was re-designed away from progressivity (Harvey, 2005).

The collapse of Communist states in Eastern Europe, the fall of the Berlin Wall and other international geo-political events gave George Bush, in 1990, the context to state that a 'new world order' was emerging. Neoliberalism became the dominant political and ideological form of capitalist globalisation. This was recognised in 1990 when the term 'Washington Consensus' was coined to describe ten policy areas where neoliberalism had been universally accepted by global decision makers (Srinivasen, 2000; Williamson, 2000; World Bank, 2000).

Marketisation policies were introduced as part of the 'reform' of the welfare state, including compulsory competitive tendering of certain public services. This was a market-testing programme that required state agencies to tender out services to the market to facilitate competition from private-sector providers. It would also provide a cost comparison between providing services 'in-house' and purchasing them from a private provider. This and other forms of public service management, such as 'new public management' principles, were introduced in order to bring about tighter controls on public spending, implement private-sector management principles and mechanisms, which were viewed as the optimum, into the organisation and activities of the public sector in order to make it in line with the private sector and provide more effective and accountable services.

At local government level, across Western Europe and North America, the pressure to adopt neoliberal policies and the resultant reduction in central government funding combined with deindustrialisation and suburbanisation meant that the provision of public services became secondary to the prioritisation of the needs of capital and business. Attempts were made to restart economic growth as a solution to the social and economic crises, which had become particularly acutely manifested in inner cities, through the provision of local tax incentives to private developers, land grants for development, direct and indirect state subsidies to large developers and corporations, cost cutting to services, the privatisation of infrastructural facilities and services and focusing on 'marketing' or 'selling' the city to business and tourists (Brenner and Theodore, 2002; McGuirk and MacLaran, 2001).

Reform agenda
Indeed much of the new policy direction under neoliberalism was implemented as part of the aforementioned framework of 'reform' of the Keynesian, social-democratic, welfare state, focused, in particular, at the cost and effectiveness of public services. This 'reform' agenda garnered considerable public support for the neoliberal project because of the unprecedented problems that the welfare state faced. Through the 1970s and 1980s, it suffered increasing criticism from the public for cost over-runs and poor 'value for money', insufficient accountability and transparency, being inflexible regarding individual circumstances and demands for consumer 'choice', being overly bureaucratic with administrative labyrinths and hierarchies and

not catering for, or respecting, minority groups (OECD, 2008). Public services appeared to be designed in the interests of the providers rather than the public end users, and were unable to deal with emerging crises. Other criticisms included issues with the traditional bureaucratic culture in the public sector, emphasising compliance with rules rather than improving efficiency and effectiveness of performance, poor employee motivation and a lack of flexibility to innovate. Centralised state power structures also hindered local modes of delivery and accountability that further stifled incentives to innovate, to take responsibility for services and to push for better outcomes (Esping-Andersen, 1999; National Economic and Social Council, 2005; Pierre and Peters, 2000).

Furthermore, despite economic progress in the period, low incomes, unemployment and low levels of educational attainment persisted for working-class and poorer populations. The welfare state was unable to address the emerging problems of mass unemployment in this period and was seen, not just by neoliberals, but from broadly 'left' political-economy approaches, as requiring considerable reform in order to address the urgently needed economic adjustment and job growth.

In addition, while the welfare state was notably successful in minimising many of the risks of poverty, new inequalities emerged through the 1980s and 1990s, in part because of labour-market and demographic transformation. The post-war welfare state had been premised upon assumptions about the family structure and labour market that had become largely invalid. There was a growing disjuncture between existing institutional arrangements and emerging risk profiles. The welfare state was not responding to new economic realities as people faced new, and more intense, social risks. New marginal strata or 'under classes' emerged, such as lone parents, migrants and marginalised youth, as the nature of the family was transformed. The welfare state was, in many ways, unable to respond to new demands for labour-market flexibility, youth programmes, education and employment training skills, racial issues, childcare support and addressing the resource inequality between household types (Esping-Anderson, 1999; Giddens, 1993).

Negative outcomes of neoliberalism
The implications of the dismantling of institutional structures associated with the welfare state under neoliberalism was profound on those who most relied on, and needed, state services, mainly the poor, working classes and users of public services, such as council tenants and many public-sector employees. Forms of social solidarity that put restraints on profitable private capital accumulation and investment, such as the welfare state and its associated public services, independent trade unions and other social movements that acquired influence, were undermined and reduced. There was also an increas-

ing imposition of user fees, for example waste and water charges and a reduction in the quality and accessibility of public services, which all added considerably to the financial burdens of the poor (Bourdieu, 1998; Brenner and Theodore, 2002; George, 2004; Gill, 1995; Whitfield, 2006).

Furthermore, state regulation that had aimed at improving worker conditions was reduced in order to facilitate labour flexibility. As a result, across Europe workers' rights and conditions were reduced and there was a weakening of trade union organisation and a loss of trade union membership. The most extreme examples of this were provided in the USA and the UK, where Ronald Reagan and Margaret Thatcher respectively reduced the power and influence of trade unions from certain key public sectors and, as a result, negatively impacted workers' rights and conditions. This was most apparent in the confrontation with previously powerful groups of workers, such as the American Air Traffic controllers in 1981 and the British Miners in 1984.

It has been in the context of diminished personal resources derived from the labour market that the neoliberal determination to transfer all responsibility for well-being back to the individual has had doubly negative effects. As the state withdrew from welfare provision and diminished its role in arenas such as public healthcare, education and housing, which were once fundamental to social-democratic states, it has left large segments of the population exposed to impoverishment. The social safety net has been reduced in favour of a system that emphasises personal responsibility. The overall result is that under privatisation and neoliberalism, social inequality has increased to unprecedented levels, with the share of national wealth going to the wealthy rising substantially, while that going to labour and the poor has declined. Since the 1980s, most countries have registered increases in inequality (Harvey, 2005). This has had a negative impact on key quality-of-life indicators, not just for the poor, but for all classes in society (Wilkinson and Pickett, 2009).

The neoliberal restructuring of central and local government levels in terms of institutional forms and socio-political consequences has been highly uneven, varying significantly, both socially and geographically. The degree of implementation of neoliberalism can be seen to depend on each country's particular history, the extent to which the government embraced this new order, how neoliberalism fitted with an individual country's and region's frameworks of political-economic regulation and the extent of political struggles that resisted these policies (Brenner and Theodore, 2002; Brenner et al., 2005; Harvey, 2005). For example, in Germany, Sweden and France the trade unions remained strong, public services were not privatised to the same extent as in the UK and social protections remained in place. The development of neoliberalism in Ireland followed its own individual path and processes (discussed in detail in later chapters). Harvey (2005) compared, for example, the results of sustained neoliberalism in the UK versus a country such as Sweden where neoliberalism was not implemented to the same extent. Sweden ranked third in the world for life expectancy versus the UK, which was twenty-ninth; the poverty rate in Sweden was 6.3 per cent versus 15.7 per cent in the UK, while the income of richest 10 per cent of the population was 6.2 times that of the bottom 10 per cent in Sweden, compared to the UK where the figure was 13.6 per cent.

The emergence of Public Private Partnerships

Neoliberalism replaced Keynesianism and welfare state policies in the 1990s as the dominant orthodoxy amongst policy makers across the world, particularly in the deregulation of the financial sectors, capital markets, labour controls and the opening of key sectors of the economy to competition. However, significant opposition amongst workers and the general public to the negative outcomes associated with privatisation, particularly in the area of health, and the increasing poverty outlined above made complete privatisation of the welfare state difficult to achieve. This was most notable in education, healthcare, social services, universities and the state bureaucracy (Whitfield, 2001, 2006). As a result of this public opposition, privatisation was then redefined by neoliberal advocates who claimed it was restricted only to the sale of assets and that the process of marketisation in the public sector was different from privatisation and was little more than the application of the principles of a mixed economy (Blair, 2006; FGS, 1998). This process of 'marketisation', as explained earlier, centred on the greater involvement of private capital and market mechanisms within public services and infrastructure, which had traditionally been planned, delivered and financed by the state. It entailed an increase in private-sector involvement in public governance, such as government decision-making, legislation and policy formation to a much greater extent than previously existed. Increased competition between the public and private sectors, commercialisation of public services and the creation of markets within public services were part of this process. Market reform mechanisms, involving sanctions such as restructuring or the closure of 'inefficient' public providers, were imposed in the public sector in order to make it more 'efficient'. Public-sector managers were encouraged to copy private-sector organisational structures, such as performance management, and to focus on efficiency, productivity and savings targets. The values and ideals of social rights that informed public-sector values and priorities were undermined by a market ethos. Under this process, public service users became 'clients' and 'consumers'. These policies of 'neoliberalism by stealth' were promoted in governance, public services and infrastructure throughout the 1990s by conservative governments and then continued under the social-democratic governments of New Labour in the UK, Clinton in the United States, Schroder in Germany and by key international institutions, such as the IMF, OECD and the World Bank. In Europe, the EU created new competition rules in the area of public-sector tendering as part of the process of completing the internal market from 1992, while Eurozone member states had to follow new tighter budgetary rules under the European Stability and Growth Pact.

PPPs emerged during this period as a key mechanism to implement this process of market reform of the welfare state (Monbiot, 2000). New policy mechanisms such as PPPs were not referred to as privatisation, but instead branded as 'partnerships' (FGS, 1998). In this way, PPPs and other neoliberal initiatives could be continued in public services without raising the opposition that outright privatisation would have done.

As referred to earlier, private finance initiatives (PFIs), the term for PPPs in the UK, had first been introduced by the Conservative government in 1992. The New Labour government, elected in 1997, firmly embedded PFIs as a major source of funding for, and reform of, the provision of public infrastructure and services by expanding the concept to a broader range of infrastructure and services, including many of the core welfare state systems, for example services administration, education, housing, defence and criminal justice systems. Labour's first Act of Parliament in 1997 was to clarify the legal basis of PFIs and to initiate a review on how to accelerate their rate of implementation.

While the private sector had been involved throughout the twentieth century to varying degrees in state provision of public services (for example, having being contracted to build schools or roads and the delivery of energy and waste services and infrastructure), PFIs marked a radical departure from such traditional delivery in the extent to which the private sector was involved (Gill, 1995; Monbiot, 2000; Sweeney, 2004; Whitfield, 2001; World Bank, 2000).

Public Private Partnership definition

As defined in the opening chapter, a PPP project generally entails a 'sponsoring' state agency contracting a private company (generally a consortium bringing together a number of companies for a specific project) to design, build and/or finance and/or manage/maintain a public service or infrastructure for a defined period of time, often between twenty-five and thirty years. The elements within the scope of the project may include some or all of the following:

1 design of service/infrastructure;
2 build/construct/extend/renovate capital assets;

3 provide finance (for example provide/secure private equity and borrowing, collect user charges);
4 operate assets (for example facilitate management, employment of services staff);
5 maintain assets over contract life. (C & AG, 2008)

In terms of how PPPs are defined in legislation and policy, one can look to the Irish government's *Policy Framework for Public Private Partnerships: Working Together for Quality Public Services* (PPP Informal Advisory Group, 2001), where PPPs are classified as an arrangement or project where the following key characteristics are present:

- shared responsibility for the provision of the infrastructure and/or services with a significant level of risk being taken by the private sector, for example in infrastructure projects, linking design and construction with one or all of the finance, operate and maintain elements;
- long-term commitment by the public sector to the provision of quality public services to consumers through contractual arrangements with private-sector operators.

The Irish State Authorities (Public Private Partnerships) Act 2002 further clarified this and enshrined PPPs into Irish Law as a 'Public Private Partnership arrangement' between a state authority and a private 'partner' for the performance of functions of a state authority in relation to:

(i) the design and construction (building, refurbishment, maintenance, repair, improvement, demolition, extension and replacement) of an asset, together with the operation of services relating to it and the provision of finance, if required, for such design, construction and operation; or
(ii) the construction of an asset, together with the operation of services relating to it and the provision of finance, if required, for such construction and operation; or
(iii) the design and construction of an asset, together with the provision of finance for such design and construction; or
(iv) the provision of services relating to an asset for not less than five years and the provision of finance, if required, for such services.

The Act also specified that a PPP can involve the arrangement of the transfer of a state asset to a private partner. The PPP 'shall operate to confer on the private partner the functions of the State Authority', the Act noted. Under PPP procurement, therefore, parts of the public sector would no longer be responsible for direct infrastructure provision, service delivery and management of a public infrastructure and/or service. The public sector's role would be restricted to specification of the *outputs* required from the service and/or infrastructure and monitoring of its performance over the life of the PPP contract: 'The key contrast between PPPs and traditional procurement is that the private-sector service provider is responsible not just for asset delivery, but for overall project management and implementation and successful operation for several years thereafter' (PriceWaterHouseCoopers, 2005, 12).

PPPs are classified according to their various contractual forms but generally involve one of the following types: design, build and operate (DBO), design, build and finance (DBF), design, build, finance and maintain (DBFM) and concession-type PPPs (PPP Informal Advisory Group, 2001).

Design, build, operate (DBO)
In a DBO PPP, the private-sector partner designs and builds the public facility to meet public-sector performance requirements and is remunerated directly from the Exchequer for this aspect of the project, as would be the case with conventional procurement. The private sector is responsible for both operating and maintaining the facility for a predefined period, at the end of which responsibility for the asset is transferred back to the public sector. DBO contracts do not include a requirement that the private sector funds the project. Generally, contracts that have been classified as DBOs have also included a requirement that the asset be maintained. This is most often used in the provision of water and waste-water treatment facilities.

Design, build and finance (DBF)
This is generally used in asset transfer situations, where the public-sector contribution to the project includes provision of an asset (usually land) with the private partner developing the asset. Such projects are usually of shorter duration than other PPP projects and examples include social housing and urban regeneration.

Design, build, finance and maintain (DBFM)
This model is typically used for accommodation projects, such as schools and hospitals. The private-sector partner is responsible for maintaining the asset through the provision of ancillary support services, such as cleaners, while the state still provides the core services, such as teachers, nurses, doctors etc. In the majority of these projects, the state purchases or owns the site and issues the private partner with a long-term license for the duration of the contract, solely to enable them to deliver the required services as outlined in the output specification. In other cases, the private sector leases the asset back to the

public sector. The private consortium is responsible for designing, building, maintaining and financing the facility. It recovers its costs principally out of payments from the public sector, usually through annual payments from the Exchequer over the term of the contract, known as unitary payments, together with some potential for generating third-party income from user charges. Typically, part of this unitary (or all-in) payment amount is fixed over the life of contract, with the remainder varying in line with price fluctuations (usually the Consumer Price Index). The split between the fixed and variable elements varies from project to project. These payments are subject to satisfactory performance of the private partner in providing agreed facilities to the required standard. It is stated that at the end of the contract ownership of the facility transfers back to the state. These projects may also be referred to as DBFO PPPs.

Concession

A concession PPP project is one where a state authority enters into a DBFO or DBFM arrangement with a private-sector provider for the delivery of services whilst giving them the licence to levy a charge for the use of that service, that is the users of the service pay fees to the private-sector partner. The private-sector partner recovers its investment through user charges, sometimes referred to as 'third-party income' and sometimes through state subvention as part of the deal. The level of subvention requested generally represents the difference between estimates of the income that will be obtainable from the third-party user charges over the life of the contract while deducting the cost of delivering the asset/service in order to identify any funding gap. Concession projects allocate demand risk to the private partner. The state authority must consider how to address a scenario where the numbers of users may exceed expectations and the private partner may have the potential to earn 'super-normal' profits, for example in toll road arrangements. The state authority can address this by including a profit-sharing arrangement within the contract whereby a proportion of the user charges collected above certain specified limits will be remitted to the appropriate state authority and/or the Exchequer and where only a marginal benefit accrues to the private-sector partner for excess users above a certain ceiling (C & AG, 2008; FGS, 1998).

Long-term operate contract/outsourcing

This is used to contract out to the private sector the provision of a new service in a sector traditionally dominated by the public sector, for example in the provision of refuse collection and disposal and light rail services.

Increase in implementation of Public Private Partnerships
Through the 1990s and early 2000s, there was a significant increase in the use of PPPs across the world in a wide range of sectors, ranging from environmental services to healthcare provision and education in hospitals, schools, urban development and regeneration companies, outsourcing and other varieties of PPP models (Economist Intelligence Unit, 1999; Monbiot, 2000; Osborne, 2000; Payne, 1999; PriceWaterHouseCoopers, 2005; Whitfield, 2006). There was a growing acceptance amongst policy makers that PPP arrangements could be used as an additional and complementary instrument to meet infrastructure and public services needs (Audit Commission UK, 2003; European Commission, 2003). In 2004 and 2005, around 206 PPP deals worth approximately €42 billion were completed worldwide, of which 152 projects valued at €21 billion were based in Europe. By 2006, they had been expanded to a value of approximately €100 billion across Europe. Geographically, PPPs have remained concentrated, with the UK accounting for two-thirds of these deals and Spain and Portugal accounting for 9 and 10 per cent respectively. When PPP activity is considered as a percentage of GDP, the UK, Ireland and Portugal have, respectively, the greatest levels (PriceWaterHouseCoopers, 2005).

In the EU, PPPs have principally been developed in the transport (roads and light rail), water, environment (water/waste-water and waste), education (particularly school projects in the UK, Germany and Ireland) and health sectors. The UK has Europe's largest and most sophisticated PPP programme. Over 640 PFI projects with a total capital value in excess of £49 billion have reached completion. These PFI contracts have been signed in over twenty sectors and have translated into over 500 operational projects, including 230 new or refurbished schools, 185 new or refurbished health facilities and 43 transport projects. As of April 2007, over 340 projects, each with a capital value of over £15 million and a combined capital value of over £45 billion, were completed and operating. A sum of £206 billion of public money is committed over the next sixty years to PFI projects. PFIs were the main source of funding from the UK Department of Education for new schools and tertiary education institutions. One of the main organisations involved in the advancement of PFIs in the UK, Partnerships UK, is a PPP formed by the British government in 2000.

PPP proponents' rationale
The principal stated reason for the use of PPPs by their proponents, such as the European Commission, the World Bank, private consultancy firms and national governments, is that they can address the considerable public infrastructure and service deficits that have built up in recent decades. A key mechanism would be through providing access to finance (additional capital)

from the private sector, which permits a greater quantity of public services and infrastructure to be delivered than would otherwise have been possible through direct Exchequer funding alone. It also supports an increased delivery of infrastructure without immediately adding to the government debt. It is also argued that by allowing the private sector to generate additional third-party revenues from the commercial utilisation of public-sector assets, PPPs can reduce the amount of public-sector expenditure required for subventions in public-service provision. Additional revenue may also be generated through improved and effective asset utilisation, such as the disposal of surplus assets (European Commission, 2003; Institute for Public Policy Research, 2001; Osborne, 2000; World Bank, 2000).

Furthermore, because PPPs involved the private sector to a much greater degree than in traditional delivery models, they would provide public infrastructure and services at greater speed, efficiency and 'value for money'. This would be achieved through private-sector innovation, better management skills and harnessing private-sector expertise, which would lead to increased efficiency through the higher productivity of labour and capital resources, which, in turn, should result in better quality and lower costs of services. PPPs also enhance public management by transferring responsibility for providing the public services to the private sector, which enables officials within central and local government to act as regulators and focus upon public service planning and performance monitoring instead of carrying the 'burden' of the day-to-day management of delivery of public services (Economist Intelligence Unit, 1999; Osborne, 2000).

The Irish Government Departmental PPP Units outlined five of these benefits that would accrue in handing over greater responsibility to the private sector to provide and deliver public infrastructure and services, through such PPPs:

- better value for money and cost effectiveness through (a) optimal risk transfer and risk management, which would harness private-sector efficiencies and (b) the ability to exploit public-sector assets and services through user charges and asset transfer;
- greater levels of delivery of services and infrastructure through access to private finance;
- greater speed and efficiency of delivery of individual projects;
- innovation;
- improved quality of services. (Department of the Environment PPP Unit, interview, 2006, 2010)

These benefits would be achieved through:

- payments linked to performance over the lifetime of the project;
- long-term contracts whereby bidders focus on the whole life-cycle cost of projects and not just on the upfront capital costs;
- construction times post contract being faster as the private sector is incentivised to complete the project in order to begin to receive the ongoing regular payments;
- private-sector innovation and commercial and management expertise;
- a contractual framework to allocate risk to the party that can manage it best;
- allowing for a number of appropriate projects to be developed simultaneously as the capital costs can be spread over the longer term;
- efficiencies from integrating design and construction of public infrastructure with financing, operation and maintenance/upgrading;
- competition and greater construction capacity (including the participation of overseas firms);
- accountability for the provision and delivery of quality public services through an incentivised performance management/regulatory regime. (Department of the Environment PPP Unit, interview, 2006, 2010)

Another stated benefit of PPPs is that public-sector participation in a project may offer important safeguards for private investors, in particular the stability of long-term cash flows from public finances. The EU Commission (2009) stated that PPPs could offer capacity to leverage private funds and pool them with public resources to deliver shared policy objectives, such as combating climate change, promoting alternative energy sources as well as energy and resource efficiency, supporting sustainable transport, ensuring high level, affordable healthcare and delivering major research projects. It was also claimed that the global expansion of PPPs would be very beneficial for European public works and utility companies in gaining important government procurement contracts outside the EU (European Commission, 2009).

PPPs were also expected to increase the speed in which capital projects were brought to development by transferring the design and construction responsibility to the private sector, which in combination with payments linked to the availability of a service would provide significant incentives for the private sector to deliver capital projects within shorter construction time frames than the traditional model (European Commission, 2003; Payne, 1999; PPP Informal Advisory Group, 2001; PriceWaterHouseCoopers, 2001a; World Bank, 2000).

Value for money and risk transfer

According to their proponents, a mechanism by which PPPs provide greater value for money and better quality of service over that achieved under traditional procurement is through the introduction of competition between providers, service innovation and performance incentivisation. The competitive bidding process within the procurement and tender processes provides, in theory, greater value for money as competition amongst bidders lowers the cost as each bidder aims to provide the most economically favourable bid.

It is argued that the experience of privatisation shows that many activities, even those traditionally undertaken by the public sector, could be undertaken more cost effectively with the application of private-sector management disciplines and competencies. By exposing the provision of public services to competitive tendering, PPPs would enable the quality and cost of such services to be benchmarked against market standards, thereby ensuring the most cost-effective methods were employed. In addition, value for money would be achieved through optimal *risk transfer* from the public to private sector. This, according to PPP proponents, is the principal mechanism by which PPPs achieve value for money. The PPP theory of risk allocation is underlain by the key tenet of new public management and neoliberal theory that the private sector is characterised by greater innovation and commercial and management expertise than the public sector and, therefore, is better able than the public sector to manage certain risks (Economist Intelligence Unit, 1999; FGS, 1998).

Risks are aspects of the delivery and provision of public services and infrastructure, including the design, planning process, construction cost overruns, maintenance of the infrastructure or service, service demand (volume and usage) and project financing. Other risks include technology and obsolescence risk, regulation and legislative risk and residual asset-value risk.

The problem with traditional delivery, according to PPP theory, is that the public sector delivers too much of the process directly and, therefore, optimum efficiency will only be achieved when the public sector allocates the maximum risk (that is responsibility) within public infrastructure and service delivery to the private partner. This would then achieve optimal risk transfer and, therefore, optimal efficiency in terms of value for money and quality of service delivered. Optimum risk allocation takes place where the government only assumes those risks which it is best able to manage and allocates the remaining risks to the private sector (FGS, 1998; PriceWaterHouseCoopers, 2005). The assumption of the risk of projects running over budget is one such risk:

> What happens if the project runs over schedule? Who does it cost money to? In traditional models the public pays –in PPP it's the private sector. That's the

price of the risk that's built into a PPP. In traditional procurement, when the project goes belly-up the taxpayer pays for it. In PPP, you still pay for it but you pay down the road rather than upfront. It's like car insurance: in PPP, you pay for the risk but hope you never have to use it. It's there as a fall back. (Central PPP Unit, interview, 2006)

The government must pay (referred to as 'risk premium') the private sector for each aspect of risk it takes on, so there is a point at which risk transfer becomes too costly and ceases to represent value for money. The greater the uncertainty around the risk, the greater risk premium the private sector will charge to compensate for the uncertainty. The government, according to PPP proponents, gets value for money by paying this extra amount to the private sector because in the instance where such risks are realised the private sector will be contractually bound to take responsibility for paying for the associated extra costs (Murray, 2006): 'Risk transfer is the justification of the use of private finance: if the private partner puts crap (sic) paint on the walls that makes it hard to clean, then they suffer for it (Central PPP Unit, interview, 2006).

Value for money is also achieved in PPPs through the inclusion of commercial incentivisation or performance management target systems, such as penalty clauses within PPP contracts. These are aimed at guaranteeing the delivery of the aspects of services and infrastructure that are transferred to the private partner. This is more difficult to achieve in traditional direct delivery models as public-sector officials and unions resist such performance models as excessively market oriented.

PPP theory states that these incentivised payments should be dependent on the private sector's meeting specified performance criteria. Under PPP projects, payment to the private-sector contractor should only occur if the required service standards are being met on a continuing basis. If the service or asset does not meet the required standard set by the state, the incentive and/or penalty performance mechanism will result in reduced payments to the private operator. The theory is that the public sector only pays when high-quality services are delivered, and thus value for money and efficiency is ensured by giving the risk to the private sector. In theory, then, in return for providing 'on time' efficient and faultless services, the private-sector supplier would receive regular payments throughout the operational phase of the PPP to repay the debt incurred in designing and building the facility, cover its working capital and maintenance costs, repay its equity investors and provide a reasonable profit for its investors (Audit Commission UK, 2003; FGS, 1998; PriceWaterHouseCoopers, 2005).

The typically long-term nature of a PPP that includes operational and maintenance provision is aimed to ensure the private-sector partner develops an integrated, long-term solution to providing the project. Because the private sector is the one responsible for maintenance over the life of the project, it is therefore incentivised to generate design and management models that would provide high-quality infrastructure that minimise mainte- nance requirements and costs over the whole life of a project. This 'life cycle approach', theoretically, should lead to a reduction in the overall cost of the project to the state procurement agency.

The financial test to assess whether the PPP model offers value for money compared to traditional procurement is a specialised analysis that compares the predicted costs of a PPP project with traditional public procurement. This analysis is called the *public-sector comparator* or *public-sector benchmark* (PSB). The PSB should be a comprehensive estimate of the cost (including risk valuations) of procuring those elements of the project for which the private sector is to be invited to tender in the PPP contract. In this way, the PSB serves as a direct, like-with-like comparator for the private-sector bids and, at evaluation stage, forms the basis for the value for money assessment of the highest-ranking bid. In Ireland, this value for money test is required before any PPP project is given permission to go ahead, to show that the PPP mechanism provides greater value for money than traditional procurement (Central PPP Unit, 2006a).

Access to finance

The various ways in which PPPs provide additional finance to the public sector was described as an important mechanism that could facilitate state authorities to continue to provide services and infrastructure that otherwise may not be possible in a period of reduction in Exchequer capital spending. The additional finance could be raised from the private sector using private equity investors, through the ability to raise third-party income, through the unitary payment mechanism, which defers full payment, and through the ability to record the cost of the PPP project as 'off-balance sheet'.

These were important for European governments, which did not want investment in capital expenditure to impact on debt levels, in particular due to the principles of economic convergence and fiscal restraint enshrined in the Maastricht Treaty and as part of Eurozone membership. PPPs, through their access to private funding, therefore, were introduced to facilitate an increase in expenditure on public services and infrastructure that would not require an increase in Exchequer funding, initially at least due to the annual payments and off-balance sheet recording mechanisms.

Through the mechanism of unitary payments, PPPs allow the public sector to translate upfront capital expenditure into a flow of ongoing service payments over the life time of a project as the borrowings required to fund the project are in the hands of the private sector, which 'enables the public sector to proceed with projects at times when the availability of public capital may be constrained, thus bringing forward much needed investment' (Department of the Environment PPP Unit, interview, 2006).

In the Irish case, it was explained that it was easier for individual government departments to commit to such a mortgage-type PPP payment to pay for a public project rather than wait for the full capital subvention from central government. This was despite this process being a more expensive source of funding over the long term, as explained by a private-sector PPP advisor (interview, 2006): 'This is the driving factor for PPP. There is only a limited pot: it's easier to manage a stream of payments than pay full capital costs up-front.' Similarly, the Department of the Environment (interview, 2010) stated that, 'one of the disadvantages of traditional infrastructure delivery is funding. The advantage that the PPP form of procurement has over traditional procurement is the opportunity for an accelerated delivery through the use of private funding.'

In February 2004, Eurostat published new guidelines regarding the statistical accounting of PPP projects for the purposes of calculating the General Government Balance (GGB). The Irish government interpreted the Eurostat Guidelines (Central PPP Unit, 2006a) as re-affirming the position stated in the Farrell Grant Sparks report (1998) that the assets of privately financed PPP projects are not required to be recorded on the government's balance sheet and, therefore, are effectively 'off-balance sheet' in the National Accounts (Central PPP Unit, 2006b). This means that when a government purchases services from a private-sector operator who built and financed the investment, or in PPP projects that are fully funded by user charges, only the annual unitary payments of the government to the operator has an impact on the GGB, thus allowing an 'off-balance sheet' recording of the overall cost of the project. Debts raised to fund capital expenditure, which would normally be included as part of the national debt could, therefore, be transferred to special purpose vehicles[2] (Central PPP Unit, 2006b).

Eurostat stated, though, that this will only be the case provided the private-sector partner carries the majority of the financial and construction risk and carries either the demand or the availability risk. Therefore, a PPP that passes greater risks (i.e. greater privatisation of public-sector responsibilities and roles) over to the private sector has a reduced impact on the GGB and, clearly, will be favoured by governments. Overall then, this 'off-balance sheet' effect allows PPPs to be treated as current expenditures taken over a significant time period rather than up-front capital expenditures.

International outcomes: a critical appraisal

A number of critical trends have been discovered in PPP projects in operation which demonstrate that many of the aforementioned benefits have not been achieved in practice and, in fact, the outcomes to date are very worrying from a public-service perspective (Grubnic and Hodges, 2003; IPPR, 2001; Leys, 2001; Murray, 2006; Shaoul et al., 2002). There are disconcerting examples from the UK, the country with the most extensive PPP experience, where their introduction and outsourcing have not improved service standards, but instead lowered public-sector morale, reduced 'diversity' in service provision – as the private sector profiteered by 'cherry-picking' the delivery of the most financially advantageous services and effectively neglected the most socially disadvantaged – and there was insufficient democratic accountability of privately operated services (Monbiot, 2000; NESC, 2005; Whitfield, 2001). Other problems identified include reductions in public-sector capacity, the creation of a two-tier workforce, increased costs and increases in user charges (Grubnic and Hodges, 2003; Murray, 2006; Shaoul et al., 2002).

Furthermore, in cases of privatisation across Europe, it is not clearly proven whether private-sector management techniques have in fact been superior to those employed in the public sector or that services provided by the private sector were more efficient. As explained in the introductory chapter, there have been systemic failures of privatisation. Studies suggest that there is no conclusive evidence to show that private-sector operated services automatically lead to better services (Florio, 2004; Parker, 1997).

A number of government-commissioned reports have been carried out into the outcomes of PFIs in England, Scotland and Northern Ireland (Audit Commission UK, 2003, 2009; Audit Commission Scotland, 2002; Partnerships UK, 2004; C & AG, 2004). As noted earlier, the Audit Commission UK, the UK government's spending auditor, undertook research in 2003 into seventeen PFI schools and compared them to twelve traditionally funded schools and found that while PFI offered potential benefits, 'this study ... shows that the (PFI) process did not as a matter of course guarantee better quality buildings and services or lower unit costs' (Audit Commission UK, 2003, 42).

The Report also found that while the UK government cited better value for money coupled with design innovation, better risk management and long-term commitment of funding for maintenance as major advantages of PPP schemes, not all of these benefits were evident and some would not be achieved in the projects without significant changes. Unit costs between the studied projects varied widely, with no clear-cut difference between PFI and traditional schools in either construction or running costs.

Furthermore, the Audit Commission UK (2003) and Partnerships UK (2004) studies of PFIs in UK schools found little evidence that more investment had been made upfront to reduce longer-term maintenance costs in the majority of the schools.

The Audit Commission UK (2009) follow-up study investigated PFI school and hospital projects in England and found that key elements of the tendering process had not improved and in some respects had worsened. It explained that the success of some PFI projects has been matched by some notable failures; most notably, major Information technology (IT) projects. It also highlighted that the failure in 2007 of the Metronet PPP project, London Underground's infrastructure company, raised many questions about the viability of the PPP model (Audit Commission UK, 2009).

Whitfield's extensive and pioneering research into PFIs in the UK also found that the rationale for such PPP projects in terms of a lack of alternative finance being available, value for money, efficiency, risk transfer and private-sector vision and innovation had not yet been proven (Whitfield, 2001, 2006).

Such poor outcomes of PPPs and PFIs have led to considerable opposition across the world, particularly amongst trade unionists and local communities, to their introduction and expansion. Unison, the UK's largest trade union, ran a 'Positively Public' campaign against PFIs and in favour of quality in public services and recognition of the role of public service employees. In Canada, negative experiences of PPPs led the Canadian Union for Public Employees (CUPE), the country's largest public-sector union, to set up a 'P3 Alert' in 2002: a monthly newsletter containing information on negative experiences of PPPs and campaigns for public-sector alternatives (www.cupe.ca). In 2007, the Federation of Canadian Municipalities stated that there was not sufficient evidence to prove PPPs were better than traditional procurement. In that same year, the world-renowned architect Moshe Safdie withdrew from the Montreal PPP hospital project because of his deep reservations about the quality of design in such projects.

A study by Murray (2006), which focused on DBFM PFI and PPPs in the UK and Canada, found that they were in fact less cost effective, timely and transparent than traditional government procurement processes. It also found that PPPs were being implemented and promoted by governments, despite the absence of objective evidence that they were a superior option to direct provision.

Value for money

Murray (2006) found the value for money assessments, the public-sector benchmarks, used in PPP projects had limited use as they were too subjective, susceptible to manipulation by vested interests, too complicated and so consistently withheld from appropriate public scrutiny and that they could only be of any legitimate use if they were to be done by the relevant country's public auditor general. The Audit Commission Scotland (2002) found that the PSB comparison, on its own, could not provide decisive evidence of which method achieved the best value for money.

Significant controversy, therefore, surrounds the objectiveness and inaccuracies associated with compiling a PSB, particularly in relation to the methodology used in PSB analysis, such as the use of discount rates and the value of risk transfer, which have both been found to have been manipulated to favour PPPs.

PSB analyses use a 'discount rate' to calculate the current value of future payments to be made by a state body to a PPP consortium. This is reasonable because factors such as interest rates and inflation change the value of money over time. However, the way discount rates have been used in PSB analysis has been found to be incorrect and inappropriately biased in favour of the PPP option as they have greatly understated the current cost of future PPP contract payments. Small variations in discount rates resulted in large differences in the total estimated costs of projects (Murray, 2006; Pollock and Price, 2004).

Farrell Grant Sparks (1998) similarly noted that while the unitary payments mechanism in PPPs may appear cheaper in the short term, signing up to such projects on a significant scale will build up future payment commitments for a government. In addition, the assumption that a government would pay for a project upfront in the case of traditional procurement, instead of financing it over time at the government's borrowing rate, greatly overstates the relative cost of traditional procurement.

In relation to risk evaluation, the Audit Commission Scotland (2002) found that the cost advantage between the studied PPP projects and the PSB was narrow, and in most cases the risk adjustment figure resulted in the PPP option being cheaper. The Audit Commission looked at six of the current twelve partnership schools projects in operation in Scotland. The six projects were for sixty-five schools. In five of the six projects studied, the PPP construction costs were higher than the public-sector comparator and in all six cases the operating costs of the PPP option were higher than the public-sector comparator.

However, in every case that the Audit Commission Scotland investigated, PPP had been judged to offer a saving over the public-sector alternative. This revealed that the public authorities constructing the PSBs weighted the risk transfer so that the analysis found in favour of the PPP option. The Commission noted that this was probably the case because if the PPP scheme's costs had not been lower than the public-sector comparator estimate, the project was unlikely to receive permission to proceed and the opportunity to obtain new buildings or refurbishment would have been lost. In all but two of the schemes in the sample, the cost advantage of the PPP option relied on the estimate of the cost of risks transferred.

The report by the Comptroller and Auditor General Northern Ireland (C & AG Northern Ireland, 2004), *Building for the Future*, studied the delivery of the first PPP school building projects in Northern Ireland. The six 'Pathfinder' projects, were DBFM PPPs with a twenty-five-year contract. The

C & AG Northern Ireland found that three of the initial bids for the PPP projects were cheaper than the public-sector comparator. At contract close, there were only two that were cheaper, one was the same and three were more expensive. The overall saving was only 2.6 per cent below the public-sector comparator.

A study of fifty-five planned PPP schools in the Canadian province of Nova Scotia found that the completed PPP schools were more expensive than traditional schools and, contrary to PPP theory, the state retained the majority of the risk. Only thirty-nine schools were completed with the remainder taken back into the public system due to cost over-runs, poor building standards and inadequate accountability (CUPE, 2007). The variations between the government's estimate that savings would be made using a PPP, and the reality that PPP added costs, led the Canadian government's auditor to suggest the government had overestimated some costs in the traditional model to make the PPP seem more attractive than it actually was, as was found to be the case with Scottish authorities.

Similarly, the study of PFIs in Britain by Pollock et al. (2004) found that the value of risk transfer in PFI deals varied in absolute terms but was fairly consistent in the degree to which it marginally favoured PFIs in the value for money analysis. It found that, in all cases studied, the risk transfer almost equalled the amount required to bridge the gap between the public-sector and the PFI project. This suggested that the function of risk transfer was to disguise the true costs of the PFI and to close the difference between private finance and the much lower costs of conventional public procurement.

Murray (2006) also questioned whether there is, in fact, a meaningful transfer of risk in PPP projects. A PPP consortium typically exists for only one project; therefore, if the project experiences major difficulties, the consortium can go into bankruptcy. In order to complete the PPP project, or continue its operation, the government has to intervene to cover remaining costs – this obligation being established by the legal concept *force majeure*. The Audit Commission UK (2003) noted the insufficient risk transfer in the case of school PPPs as, if there is a major problem with a school building, the LEA (Local Education Authority) must intervene if the PPP provider fails to respond appropriately because it is the LEA's responsibility to provide the education service. Furthermore, the private sector is skilled at evaluating risks and will charge the government expensive rates for any of the risks it takes on (Deloitte, 2007). The healthy profit margins in PPPs demonstrated that firms were not taking on risks at a loss and, if anything, the private sector was charging a significant premium for risk transfer (Murray, 2006).

The Northern Ireland Association of Teachers and Lecturers argued that PPP contracts, which lock schools into long-term private procurement and facilities contracts, did not make logical sense and did not provide value for money. For example, the C & AG Northern Ireland (2004) report found a significant disparity between planned and actual enrolments in two PPP schools. In one school, Balmoral, the enrolment was approximately 58 per cent of that originally envisaged when the PPP contract was signed, and, as a result, the taxpayer was paying for some 500 school dinners in a school of fewer than 200 pupils. This issue of planned and actual enrolment can, therefore, become a major issue because, if enrolment drops, the state is tied into paying for an unused asset. This demonstrated the inflexibility and potential lack of value for money in PPPs:

> At a time when redundancies of teachers, classroom assistants and front line education staff are rife, it is astonishing that money is being wasted, hand over fist, for services that aren't needed. When PPP contracts run for 25 or 30 years, there is no way of knowing today what the needs will be in 5 years, let alone 30 ... The folly of private sector are being funded extravagantly from the public purse ... whilst front line teachers are losing their jobs, and having their conditions squeezed, there is no risk to the private sector in PPP. As happy as pigs at a trough wouldn't even begin to describe it. (Northern Ireland Association of Secondary Teachers and Lecturers, 2006, 1)

Infrastructure and service delivery

The complex procurement process involved in PPPs has led to significant delays in the implementation of projects, particularly at the outset of PPP development in a sector. For example, the C & AG Northern Ireland (2004) found that the initial procurement phase for PPP projects took longer than traditional provision, although the construction time was shorter. The Audit Commission UK (2003) also found that the initial PPP school projects had not been delivered more quickly than non-PPP schools.

Although buildings and facilities are not core services, like teaching or nursing, they are vitally important within the education and health systems. For example, studies have shown that children's learning is strongly affected by their physical environment. A study carried out into schools in Canada in 1993 concluded that the condition of physical facilities has a direct impact on learning (CUPE, 2006). Students are likely to judge the importance or relevance of their educational experience by how well facilities are maintained. In schools, the quality of teaching environments and the amount of daylight in classrooms improves pupils' achievement.

According to the UK Department of Education and Skills (2007), PPPs in schools can directly raise educational standards by improving school buildings and classroom facilities. This improves the environment in which learning takes place and ensures schools are properly equipped to deliver a modern curriculum. It is very significant, therefore, that there was mounting evidence for poor-quality buildings and associated services in PPP schools.

The UK Commission for Architecture and the Built Environment (CABE,[3] 2005) found that although PPP procurement can, in theory, deliver good design, it had often not achieved this in practice. The Report *found* that, 'the vast majority of PFI buildings commissioned to date have not been designed and built to a high enough standard and public service delivery suffers as a result' (CABE, 2005, 1). Furthermore, the Audit Commission UK found that a sample of PPP schools 'was, statistically speaking significantly worse than that of the traditionally funded sample on four of the five quality matrices (architectural design, building services design, User productivity, ownership costs, detail design' (Audit Commission UK, 2003, 13).

A report undertaken by CUPE (2007) on PPP schools in Nova Scotia, Canada, cited several problems with facilities run by the private sector, such as the problem of uncertainty about responsibilities between the school, local government board and the private operator, which left problems unresolved for long periods of time. These included questions concerning who would provide rubbish bins, look after lights and heat, the fixing of soccer fields, water quality (including arsenic in the drinking water), fixing problems with flooding and the payment of insurance premiums (CUPE, 2007).

Commoditisation

PPPs have also facilitated the creation of new markets for financial capital (for example, various equity investment funds) through the creation of secondary financial markets where PPP projects can be refinanced or the PPP consortia can sell or trade equity stakes in their various PPP projects. Once an infrastructure project is built and operational, many of the project risks (such as delays in construction) are no longer relevant. Completion of the riskiest phase, the construction phase, of the project successfully means that the post-construction PPP is an extremely low-risk investment.

Reducing that risk further is the fact that the multi-decade operating agreements in a PPP provide the private contractor with a guaranteed client (annual payments from the state procurement agency). This creates opportunities for the private consortium to negotiate with the funder of the project (for example, financial institutions such as a bank or investment bank) to reduce the annual financing costs, as funders are prepared to offer better terms for projects with lower risks, that is they are prepared to refinance projects at a much lower interest rate on the project's debt from investors. Refinancing then facilitates lower annual financing costs, which increases the returns (profit) that can be paid to the private sector's shareholders. Changes to the terms of the loan can increase the contractor's profit by as much as eighty per cent. The investment market also considers that, in the operational phase, the project will have significantly increased in value, which makes PPP contracts attractive investment opportunities, thus further enabling the private sector to expropriate this increase in value. The secondary market in PPP refinancing and investment is a stark example of the exploitation of public resources where gains in the value of public assets are expropriated by the private sector. In the UK, there has been a growing trend for investors to sell their share of the consortium after construction ends, thus achieving windfall profits (Deloitte, 2006; Murray, 2006; Audit Commission UK, 2003; Whitfield, 2006).

Conclusion

This chapter has shown that the roll out of PPPs internationally has been strongly influenced by neoliberal ideology and its proponents' approach to the state and public services. It has also unpacked the fundamentals of the free-market, neoliberal, philosophy and some underlying associated weaknesses in relation to addressing social and public necessities.

In countries that have pioneered PPPs, this new method of delivery has been promoted for its potential to provide greater Value for money, efficiency and access to finance than traditional public-sector delivery models. However, the evidence from the practical outcomes of these public private projects in the UK, Canada and elsewhere points to considerable problems. The following chapters investigate to what extent these trends are evident in the development and outcomes of PPPs in Ireland.

Notes

1 User charges may be generally defined as direct charges paid to the private-sector partner by third parties who are not the government, for example hard tolls paid by motorists (Central PPP Unit, 2006b).

2 A number of different private-sector parties can be involved in the delivery of a PPP project over its lifetime. The normal practice is for these parties to form a consortium. On award of a PPP tender, best practice would require that this consortium would form a financially robust Special Purpose Company or Special Purpose Vehicle (Central PPP Unit, 2006b).

3 CABE advises central, regional and local government in the UK on architecture and urban design and helps to formulate planning policy, and best practice design.

3

Trends in the historical development of the Irish state, public services and infrastructure

It shall be the first duty of the government of the Republic to make provision for the physical, mental and spiritual well-being of the children, to secure that no child shall suffer hunger or cold from lack of food, clothing, or shelter, but that all shall be provided with the means and facilities requisite for their proper education and training as Citizens of a Free and Gaelic Ireland ...

The Irish Republic fully realises the necessity of abolishing the present odious, degrading and foreign Poor Law System, substituting therefore a sympathetic native scheme for the care of the Nation's aged and infirm, who shall not be regarded as a burden, but rather entitled to the Nation's gratitude and consideration. Likewise it shall be the duty of the Republic to take such measures as will safeguard the health of the people and ensure the physical as well as the moral well-being of the Nation. (Democratic Programme adopted by the First Dáil (Irish Parliament), 21 January 1919)

The Democratic Programme of the First Dail outlined the economic and social principles that were intended to underpin the first Irish government. Its aim was the improvement of the people's health, education and welfare, for the first time by a government of the Irish people after hundreds years of foreign rule and oppression. The Programme was strongly socialist in character, reflecting the input of Thomas Johnson, the leader of the Labour Party at the time.

In return for its input into the Programme, the Labour Party did not contest the 1918 elections, deciding instead to allow the election to be a ballot on independence from British colonial rule. The Programme was passed by the Dáil on the same day as the declaration of the Irish Republic and the outbreak of the Irish War of Independence. That struggle for independence resulted in the offer of a Treaty to the people of Ireland by the

British government. The Treaty proposed not full independence for the whole of Ireland but instead an independent state of twenty-six counties, with the remaining six counties in the north of Ireland staying within the British Empire. The Treaty divided Ireland. Irish society, and the various political parties representing it, took conflicting positions either for or against it, leading to a bloody Civil War from 1922 to 1923. As a result, the country came to be dominated by the positions, views and actions taken in relation to the Treaty, the Civil War and the issues surrounding the struggle for national independence.

Fianna Fail and Fine Gael (in their various formations), the two main parties representing opposing sides in the Civil War, became the two largest political parties in the early decades of the newly formed Irish state. The Labour Party did not feature, as it refrained also from contesting the 1921 elections. Thus, the social and economic ideals raised in the Democratic Programme, that the Labour Party most strongly espoused, came a distant second to the politics of nationalism represented by the two largest parties. As both Fianna Fail and Fine Gael, in contrast to the aspirations of the Programme and the Labour Party at the time, were broadly conservative or 'centre right' in their economic, political and social outlooks.

Every government since the foundation of the Irish state in 1922 has been led by either one of the two conservative parties. Therefore, in contrast to other European countries, Ireland did not have a social-democratic or socialist government in power that developed Keynesian policies and a welfare state. Although, in reflecting on their populist approach to politics, Fianna Fail's and Fianna Gael's brands of conservatism were complex, and both developed policies that spanned a wide range of ideological perspectives. This included, in the case of Fianna Fail in its early years, radical agrarian land and banking reforms.

Despite these few radical policies, the dominant political, social, economic and cultural perspectives in the Irish state in the first half of the twentieth century were conservative, predominantly free-market oriented, nationalist, deeply influenced by the conservative Roman Catholic Church and reflected the rural, agrarian focused, population (Allen, 2007; Bartley and Kitchin, 2007; Coakley and Gallagher, 1999; Kirby, 2002).

In the decades after independence, the Irish state enacted the politics and policies of nationalist 'self-reliance' and thus played an important role in developing the public sector, particularly state enterprises. For example, in 1933, the Fianna Fail government established the Irish Sugar Company by nationalising a private company, set up a state bank and, in 1937, established a national airline, Aer Lingus. Irish shipping, Irish steel, Coras Iompar na h Éireann (CIE), Ireland's state-operated bus and rail company and other state-run companies were set up in the 1940s (Allen, 2007). The Taoiseach at the time, Sean Lemass explained that these actions were not part of an ideological agenda of expanding the role of state. Rather these companies were set up only where considerations of national policy were involved, or where the projects were beyond the scope of, or unlikely to be undertaken by, private enterprise (Sweeney, 1999). The population also suffered intense poverty in this period as the state pursued conservative fiscal policies and engaged in an economic war, up to 1938, with Britain, its main trading partner.

In February 1948, after sixteen years of Fianna Fail being in power, a new government was elected on a platform of major change. It was formed as a coalition between a number of political parties including Fine Gael, the Labour Party, Clann na Poblachta, Clann na Talmhan and the National Labour Party. In 1949, a proposal was put forward within the government to progress a welfare state and universal health system along the lines of that being developed at the time in Britain and other parts of Europe. However, this attempt to develop state-run public services was halted immediately due to the strong influence of the Catholic Church hierarchy and a number of elite professions. Noel Browne, the Minister for Health at the time, attempted to develop comprehensive postnatal care in the social welfare system in the form of the Mother and Child Scheme, which proposed the introduction of free maternity care for all mothers and free healthcare for children up to the age of sixteen. However, an alliance of the Catholic Bishops and the medical elite opposed the Mother and Child Bill being prepared by the government (Allen, 2007). They insisted that the government could not provide free care for all mothers and it would have to include a 'means test'. They also stoked fears of socialism being introduced through this form of 'socialised' medicine. The depth of involvement of the Catholic Church hierarchy in the early decades of the Irish state was manifest starkly in this instance.

On 12 April 1951, the then Taoiseach, John A. Costello, informed the Dáil that owing to objections to the Mother and Child Scheme outlined in a letter he received from the Catholic hierarchy he had ordered Minister Browne not to describe the Scheme as government policy 'unless and until you have satisfied the hierarchy'.

The weight of opposition from the Church and medical profession was too strong, and support for the plans was withdrawn by other members of the government. As a result, Browne resigned in April 1951. In his resignation statement, he told the Dáil that:

> I had been led to believe that my insistence on the exclusion of a means test had the full support of my colleagues in the government. I now know that it had not. Furthermore, the Hierarchy has informed the government that they must regard the mother and child scheme proposed by me as opposed to Catholic social teaching.

The government collapsed the following month and Browne's proposals were never implemented as originally envisaged.

Ireland continued its course of social exceptionalism, where public social spending remained very low while its European neighbours increased such spending and developed extensive public services, including schools, hospitals, transport and welfare provisions (NESC, 2005). The Catholic hierarchy also opposed the free public secondary schools service introduced in 1968. These events unmistakably demonstrated that the Catholic Church's position and concept of the 'family' as being the single most important pillar of Ireland's national system of social protection was also the *de facto* policy of the Irish state (Allen, 2007; NESC, 2005). The Church, therefore, was facilitated to continue the role it had undertaken in Ireland since the 1800s of providing, managing and staffing many public services, including hospitals, secondary and primary schools, psychiatric hospitals and so on, with the state paying the wages of the lay employees (Kirby, 2002).

As a result, along with Flanders (northern Belgium), Ireland was also an outlier among EU countries in the extent to which private religious and voluntary bodies were involved in the delivery and management of public services and infrastructure. For example, in 2001 Ireland had 63 per cent of its secondary students enrolled in predominantly publicly funded but privately managed institutions, only 10 per cent of which were institutions receiving more than 50 per cent of their funding from private sources (NESC, 2005).

The state did, however, play an important role in housing provision with local authorities becoming increasingly important providers of housing in Dublin and in other urban centres during the first half of the twentieth century, when public housing represented between 50 and 70 per cent of the total new housing being built (Drudy and Punch, 2005).

During the 1970s, Ireland experienced improved economic growth and the population grew in size and became increasingly urbanised (the proportion of the population classed as living in urban areas grew from 46 per cent in 1961 to 55 per cent in 1981) (Bartley and Kitchen eds., 2007). Public expenditure and the Irish welfare state were significantly expanded in this period. This was pursued with the assistance of finance obtained by borrowing undertaken by the Fianna Fail government of 1977 and continued by the Fine Gael–Labour coalition government that came to power in 1982 (Finlay, 1998). Public spending increased from 10.7 per cent of GDP in 1980 to 13 per cent in 1985. However, international and domestic economic crises through the 1980s resulted in unprecedented levels of national debt, unemployment, inflation and emigration (O'Riain and O'Connell, 2000; O'Toole, 2003; Sweeney, 1999). Unemployment increased from 7.3 per cent in 1980 to 17.3 per cent in 1985 and remained at 16.6 per cent in 1993. In 1986, a staggering

75,000 people emigrated from Ireland. The Exchequer debt doubled between 1981 and 1985 to 134 per cent of GNP (NESC, 2005).

The proportion of people in poverty also consistently increased in that period. In 1973, between 15 per cent and 18 per cent of the population lived on half the average income and by 1980 this had increased to 23 per cent (Kirby, 2002). In 1985, Ireland had the third worst level of poverty in the EU with 22.9 per cent of the population in poverty and by 1987 Irish GDP was only 63 per cent of the EU average (Bartley and Kitchin eds., 2007; NESC, 2005). Such intense socio-economic problems led to political instability, tension and conflict between the state, employers and unions. This resulted in the Fine Gael–Labour Party coalition government, which had been in power for five years, falling apart in January 1987. The Labour Party withdrew from the government as it refused to be part of severe budgetary cuts in spending that Fine Gael claimed were required in order to reduce the public debt.

Fiscal retrenchment and neoliberalism

Fianna Fail won a majority of Dáil seats in the resultant general election of 1987 and formed a government that responded to the economic and social crisis by orientating public policy in a neoliberal direction through policies of severe fiscal retrenchment (Allen, 2007; O'Toole, 2003). In the 'Tallaght Strategy', the government was given permission by the principal political parties in opposition to do whatever it deemed necessary to solve the economic crisis. A corporatist model of social policy was developed based upon co-operation between government, market and civil society in order to facilitate the transition to, and the implementation of, this new radical policy direction (Kirby and O'Broin eds., 2009). From 1987 onwards, this took the form of national Social Partnership Agreements between the social partners (the main employer's group Irish Business Employers Confederation (IBEC) and the Construction Industry Federation (CIF), the government and trades unions represented by ICTU). The agreements centred on the trade unions consenting to wage restraint, lower taxes on businesses and minimal state spending in return for the expectation of economic growth in the future when unions would be able to bargain for gains for their members. The unions also supported this process as a mechanism to curtail the introduction into Ireland of the policies of privatisation and reduction in trade union rights and influence that had been occurring at the time under the Thatcher government in Britain (Allen, 2007; Kirby, 2002; O'Riain and O'Connell, 2000; Whelan and Masterson, 1998). In addition to wage issues, other issues such as income tax and social welfare were important constituents of the agreements (Kirby, 2002).

NESC's (2005) seminal work on the classification and development of the

Irish welfare state revealed the extent to which the public social protection infrastructure programme bore the brunt of fiscal retrenchment during this period as the new Minister for Finance, Ray MacSharry, implemented severe cuts in public expenditure. The levels of public capital investment in housing, education and health fell precipitously from 1985 until the early 1990s. Spending in education almost halved in real terms between 1986 and 1991, despite student numbers increasing at secondary and third levels up to the early 1990s (NESC, 2005). In health, investment levels were more than halved and the government undertook a rationalisation and closure of hospitals with the effect that 4,000 in-patient beds were removed from the system between 1984 and 1988 and a further 2,000 beds were removed between 1991 and 1993. In the decade between 1980 and 1990, the overall acute bed capacity in public hospitals was reduced by almost one-third (OECD, 2008; Tussing and Wren, 2006). By 1988, health spending had declined to 58 per cent of the EU average and throughout most of the 1990s remained below three quarters of that average. For example, the proportion of GDP spent on health fell from 7.72 per cent of GDP in 1980, to 5.72 per cent of GDP in 1990 and over the twenty-seven years from 1970 to 1996 Ireland invested on average each year 63 per cent of the EU norm on health services (NESC, 2005).

In 1989, the impetus for such neoliberal policies was strengthened by the entry into the Fianna Fail government of the Progressive Democrat Party, which resolutely espoused free-market policies. Fiscal conservatism in budgets and economic adjustments were continued through the early 1990s. This was also undertaken in order to satisfy the Maastricht convergence criteria for Economic and Monetary Union and in preparation for adopting the euro as the new currency. These required, as explained in Chapter 1, the ratio of the annual government deficit to GDP to not exceed 3 per cent and the ratio of gross government debt to GDP to not exceed 60 per cent. Ireland was also required, after 1997, to follow the conditions laid down under the EU Stability and Growth Pact, which became the overriding framework for Irish budgetary policy, and required the public finances, as measured by the General government balance, to be kept close to balance or in surplus.

The policies of fiscal conservatism and the agenda of radical reform of the public sector through privatisation were intensified after 1997 by the newly elected Fianna Fail–Progressive Democrat coalition government. It reduced the rates support grant that supported local government finances and gave greater powers to the local authorities to charge for services (O'Toole, 2003). In practice, this was an invitation to local authorities that required funding to impose local service charges and to move away from providing free public services, such as waste collection and water provision. At the central state level, between 1997 and 2007, many state-controlled sectors were deregulated and opened to competition from the private sector, and state-owned companies in Ireland were commercialised. This was also as a result of the greater liberalisation of markets enforced under EU legislation.

Notably, the national airline, Aerlingus, was privatised in 2006, and the sectors in which the state rail and bus companies (CIE, Bus Éireann and Dublin Bus), the state owned Electricity Supply Board and the national postal service, An Post, operated were all opened to market competition. Significant commercial providers of health services, medical insurance, childcare, elderly care, secondary- and third-level education and other forms of social protection entered the market in Ireland over this period (NESC, 2005; O'Toole, 2003, 2009; Sweeney, 2004; Tussing and Wren, 2006). There was also an increase in the contracting out to non-commercial, non-governmental organisations of non-core functions to private companies, for example waste collection and recycling, the mandatory safety assessment of private vehicles and the management of on-street parking and clamping in Dublin City, and the provision of some social services was contracted out to non-commercial, non-governmental organisations.

Public-sector reform
From the 1980s onwards, there was also growing demand from the Irish public for public service reform similar to that experienced internationally. A process of reform then began in 1984 with the government introducing the Strategic Management Initiative, which aimed to improve the quality and accessibility of public services, staff mobility and the use of technology.

A subsequent Strategic Management Initiative was introduced in 1994 to continue this process. It included the social partners and introduced many necessary reforms, such as the creation of Customer Service Charters, the Performance Management Development System (PMDS) and Output Statements to help improve the focus on performance and the use of performance information for decision making and value-for-money evaluations (through the 1993 Comptroller and Auditor General Act). This process was developed further in the report by the Department of the Taoiseach *Delivering Better Government* in 1996 (Department of the Taoiseach, 1996) and then formalised in the 1997 Public Service Management Act. These policies and initiatives were aimed at making government departments and state agencies more efficient and transparent in policy formation, decision-making and service provision; more responsive to the public (customers); and increasingly performance-oriented through the effective management of resources and strategic planning (OECD, 2008). Greater accountability was provided through the Freedom of Information Act 1997, which gave, for the first time, access to the public to detailed information about the work being carried out by the civil and public services. It challenged the tradition of secrecy and the closed nature of the Irish civil service that was inherited from the culture of the British colonial state institutions and continued by state institutions after Independence.

There were also attempts to introduce these reforms at local government level through, amongst other strategies, setting up local partnership arrangements. These were implemented in order to address the inability of local authorities to respond creatively to new challenges and due to perceived inefficiency, reports of corruption and the authorities' bureaucratic distance from citizens and the associated failures to engage with, or satisfy the needs of, local communities. Under the local government reforms of 1996, local authorities were to replace their traditional emphasis on regulating and controlling activities to a more proactive, results-oriented and collaborative approach to delivery and development of services. The reforms drew heavily on the neoliberal new public management approaches, particularly adopting models from the US and New Zealand. They aimed to replace what were generally viewed as inert bureaucratic structures by more pro-active globally responsive and user-oriented forms of governance. They sought to instigate management practices in public service provision that were more business like, competitive, responsive and open to civic involvement. The reform models also proposed to achieve this by implementing performance evaluation through 'managerialism'. This would involve new public management, administrative and financial mechanisms linking funding allocations to the evaluation of performance. These were facilitated by setting targets and indicators, introducing service-level agreements, regulation, decentralisation and neoliberal approaches, including privatisation and PPPs (Kirby and O'Broin eds., 2009).

However, reform attempts did not meet public requirements, and demands gathered pace as the severe deficits impacted on the Irish population in a more acute manner through the 1990s.

Case study of neoliberalism in practice: the housing sector
The transformation towards neoliberalism of Irish state institutions at both central and local government levels can be viewed with particular clarity through the lens of the local authority housing sector. There is an extensive body of literature that details how the traditional public policy philosophy of 'public' – or as it is more commonly referred to 'social' – housing provision, which emphasised local governments' redistributive role as a public housing authority and regulatory role as a planning authority, was transformed in a neoliberal trajectory over the period from the 1980s to the 2000s (Drudy and Punch, 2005; Kelly and MacLaran, 2004; Punch *et al.*, 2004; Redmond and Russell, 2008).

Historically, local authorities were given the responsibility to carry out most of the development, provision, regeneration and maintenance of social housing in Ireland. This involved local authorities directly building or purchasing housing stock. The units were then rented at subsidised rates to tenants. New tenants were allocated units from the local authority's social housing waiting lists.

The neoliberal approach introduced since the 1980s, however, sought to minimise the direct provision of housing by local authorities and rather asserted that the state's role was to facilitate and encourage such provision by the private sector, in particular private developers, through a variety of policies. These included reducing the amount of direct building of social housing by local authorities, providing tax incentives for development, fast tracking planning permissions and undertaking re-zonings on a large scale (Drudy and Punch, 2005).

The number of dwellings rented from local authorities in Ireland, which had steadily increased to reach 125,000 in 1961, dropped consistently thereafter to 88,000 units in 2002. This resulted from the provision of strong incentives to leave local authority housing for owner-occupancy, for example mortgage interest relief and the 'surrender grant' introduced in the mid 1980s which offered £5,000 to tenants who relocated to private housing and thus gave up their existing local authority tenancy. The public housing stock was also significantly reduced by a policy of sales to tenants at discount. In total, over 230,000 public housing units (out of a total stock of 330,000) were transferred into the private market in this way. This was, in effect, the biggest privatisation of state assets since the foundation of the state with the 'sell-off' of more than half of all the public housing stock and it represented a major transfer of wealth from public bodies to private individuals (Sweeny, 2004). This is manifest in the fact that while local authority housing comprised 15.5 per cent of all residences in 1971, this figure had plummeted to 9.7 per cent by 1991 and a mere 6.9 per cent by 2002 (Drudy and Punch, 2005).

Insufficient central government funding for the building of new social housing meant that public capital investment by local authorities through the 1980s and 1990s focused on the refurbishment of their existing housing stock (Blackwell, 1988; Norris and Redmond eds., 2005). Central government also introduced urban renewal legislation in the mid 1980s that implemented various planning incentives such as tax designations and facilitated the setting up of PPPs in the form of local urban development agencies. These were separate entities to local authorities and were used as mechanisms to drive the development and regeneration of urban areas, for example the Custom House Docks Development Authority, which was responsible for regenerating a central Dublin site.

Planning was encouraged to become more pragmatic, flexible and results oriented, focusing on creating the right conditions for investment in areas that were identified to have the highest potential for success in encouraging inward investment and speculative property development. The experience of

Irish local authorities in cities such as Dublin was similar to that of US and British cities where the shift towards such entrepreneurial, market-led approaches to city planning and development was strongly influenced, and to a certain degree imposed, by the severe underfunding and neoliberal policy direction from central government (McGuirk and MacLaran, 2001).

EU subsidies and the Celtic Tiger

Successive *National Development Plans* developed by Irish governments, which covered six-year period (1994–1999) and seven-year period 2000–2006), adapted to EU policies in order to leverage financial support through, amongst other schemes, the Structural and Cohesion Funds. This fund targeted support at the poorer parts of the EU that required structural adjustment support to prepare for, and adapt to, the 'Single Market'. This influence of EU policy led to a more systematic, strategic and long-term approach to national public infrastructure investment (Bartley and Kitchin eds., 2007). Indeed, the extent of the fiscal austerity of the 1980s and 1990s and the potential negative impacts on public services were mitigated by this expansion of EU Structural and Cohesion Funds in the late 1980s. Through the 1990s, Ireland was a net beneficiary of EU funding and received, on average, €2 billion per annum during this period, receiving 6.3 per cent of the country's GDP from the EU in 1991. Net receipts peaked in absolute terms at €2.5 billion in 1997 when about 8 per cent of the Irish government spending budget was provided by EU sources. The *National Development Plans* up to 2006 were allocated €14.33 billion in EU structural/cohesion funding (Bartley and Kitchin eds., 2007).

The funding helped to address the deficit in investment in public infra-structure projects, welfare and training. Without the support of the structural funds, congestion in public infrastructure and constraints in third-level education would have severely limited the recovery and subsequent develop-ment of unprecedented growth in the economy after 1995 (FGS, 1998).

The EU funding, economic growth and the prioritisation afforded to capital spending through the *National Development Plans* contributed to a significant recovery in public spending in the late 1990s (Government of Ireland, 2000a). In education, for example, the level of real capital spending had attained its 1985 level by 1997. In housing, it was only by 2002 that public capital investment was beginning to approach the level it had been before the decline of 1987. However, despite the increase in social spending during the 1990s, it nevertheless accounted for declining shares of GNP and GDP until about the year 2000. Social spending as a ratio of GDP and GNP is frequently used as an indicator of a country's 'welfare effort'.

The total social expenditure declined from 19 per cent of GDP in 1990 to 17.5 per cent in 1997, the lowest in the EU. In 1992, Ireland was spending 23 per cent of its GNP per capita on social protection, but this fell to 19 per cent by 2001. Nevertheless, this allowed an increase of 46 per cent in real terms in per capita social spending over the same period. The evidence is that Ireland made a greater 'welfare effort' in the period of severe fiscal austerity in the late 1980s than in the opening years of the twenty-first century (NESC, 2005). Social spending per capita in Ireland in 2001 was the lowest in the EU, along with Greece, Spain and Portugal, at 60.5 per cent of the EU 15[1] average. The important aspect to be deduced from these figures is that the rate of increase in public social spending did not keep pace with the rate of economic growth during this 'Celtic Tiger' period.

Furthermore, population increases (growing by 16.8 per cent between 1996 and 2006 to 4.23 million inhabitants) combined with unprecedented private housing development and rising levels of inequality (manifest in areas of severe deprivation being marginalised from the benefits of economic growth) meant that significant public expenditure increases did not address the considerable public infrastructure and services deficits that had emerged. The deficits existed in environmental services (to meet new standards set by EU Directives in relation to water/waste-water treatment and integrated waste management), roads and public transport. It was also acute in capital investment in various types of social infrastructure such as public services providing social protection, including schools, social and affordable housing, day-care centres for people with intellectual or physical disabilities, crèches, medical centres and so on. Table 3.1 identifies the principal items of public capital expenditure that were delivering social protection in 2002 (NESC, 2005).

Expanding or creating such infrastructure requires long-term planning and, as a result, is a slower process than increasing 'front line' services and, therefore, requires sustaining a high level of capital spending on carefully selected projects over an extended period of time. Investment in these sectors was required to facilitate the provision of a higher level and improved standard of social protection services (NESC, 2005). The infrastructure deficit was, therefore, constraining the capacity to deliver much-needed public services aimed at social protection.

The deficits were exacerbated by the historic underinvestment in infrastructure, particularly the fiscal retrenchment in the late 1980s. This meant that the existing public infrastructure and services were unable to respond to the increased demands of the period (NESC, 2005; OECD, 2008). For example, with regard to the stock of Ireland's public capital, that is economic and social infrastructure, Ireland ranked quite low in the closing years of the twentieth century compared to the OECD and European averages (NESC, 2005). International Monetary Fund data show that Ireland's stock in public capital had actually fallen over the period from 1987 to 2000 by 10 per cent (Department of Finance, 2007).

In the housing sector, the market focus of housing policy and government reduction in spending on direct social housing provision created a situation whereby private housing supply in the late 1990s and early 2000s reached historically high levels nationally, for example over 60,000 units were completed in 2003, while the national social housing waiting list reached 48,000 households by 2005 (Drudy and Punch, 2005).

Table 3.1 Public capital expenditure on social protection in Ireland, 2002

Type of social protection	Department	Public expenditure €M
Local authority housing, voluntary housing and shared ownership	Environment	1,364
Pre-funding of future pension liabilities	Finance	1,035
Schools and other educational institutions	Education and science	564
Prison buildings and equipment, courthouses, probation centres	Justice, equality and law reform	61.5
Childcare	Justice etc.	23

Source: NESC (2005).

The rationale for the introduction of Public Private Partnerships

The concept of PPPs as a means to deliver public services and infrastructure emerged in the late 1990s as an important mechanism to respond to the infrastructure deficit and demands for public-sector reform while also facilitating the government's preferred policy trajectory of neoliberalism.

The primary reasons that underlay the Irish government's decision to introduce PPPs, according to the Central Government PPP Units (Department of Finance, Department of Education and Science, Department of the Environment), were that they would address the public infrastructure and service deficit more rapidly than would have been achieved by traditional procurement alone. They would also provide the necessary reform of traditional methods of public service and infrastructure delivery in the key areas of greater 'value for money', speed, efficiency and improved quality of service provision. It was asserted that PPPs would achieve this by accessing additional finance and introducing private-sector management expertise and skills to deliver and operate public projects more efficiently – skills in which the public sector was judged to be deficient. It is clear from the evidence detailed in this chapter that neoliberal justifications and theoretical benefits, similar to those outlined by international private- and public-sector PPP proponents detailed in Chapter 2, underlay the Irish state's decision to introduce and develop PPPs. These factors and processes are unpacked and outlined in this chapter.

Infrastructure deficit

The state believed that there was a need for Ireland to do what other Western European countries had accomplished in the 1960s in terms of investing significantly in public infrastructure. In the mid to late 1990s, investigations were being undertaken by various arms of the Irish state into new mechanisms of financing that would yield the substantial investment that was necessary to address rapidly the infrastructure deficit:

> There was broader political recognition that the infrastructure deficit was the key issue ... We had to fast track it, we had to build an awful lot of stuff, we had to try and find all the resources we could and not just financial resources but management resources. In a sense, we are doing what Germany did in the 1960s. We are catching up with forty years of underinvestment in capital infrastructure ... We were looking at different ways of getting money to add to existing funds. (Central PPP Unit, interview, 2006)

The Department officials explained that infrastructure development was essential if Ireland was going to continue to provide a positive environment for foreign investment and maintain its competitiveness in an increasingly globalised economy, and thus allow the high rates of economic growth to be sustained. This requirement was identified as a primary reason why the Irish government should implement PPPs in the influential Farrell Grant Sparks report (FGS, 1998) and by a private construction industry representative (interview, 2007) who sat on the PPP Informal Advisory Group: 'The growth in the economy is in shops, housing, hotels, leisure facilities etc. The productivity of our economy is curtailed by an inadequate infrastructure. Unless we address that bottleneck, we can't sustain growth.'

Furthermore, Ireland's traditional source of capital expenditure, the EU structural transfers, began tapering off after 1998 as Irish GDP transformed from 74 per cent of the EU average at the beginning of 1993 to exceeding the EU average in 1998. This made it ineligible for Objective One[2] status and substantial funding support.

A representative of Ireland's second largest political party, Fine Gael, advanced this rationale: 'as the scale of the infrastructure deficit facing the country became clear, and the huge strain on public finances that addressing the deficit would cause, it (PPP) was a mechanism to provide funding and allow for the rapid completion of major projects' (Fine Gael representative, interview, 2006).

For example, the Irish school infrastructure required considerable investment after decades of underinvestment (DOES, 2006a; Government of Ireland, 2007). There was considerable demand for investment in building new schools due to the growth in the school-going population in rapidly developing areas and in specialist accommodation provision to cater for pupils with special needs and to cater for diversity from both the growing Educate Together and Gaelscoileanna sectors. In particular, investment was required to facilitate amalgamations and rationalisations, especially at post-primary level due to the reduced role of the church in relation to trusteeship. The principals in the PPP schools explained that the infrastructure deficit, which had resulted in substantial numbers of school buildings needing refurbishment or replacing, was an influential factor in their decision to support the introduction of PPPs in the schools sector.

PPPs, according to the Irish government officials interviewed for this research,[3] would provide additional funding through private-sector finance and, therefore, further accelerate the expansion of infrastructure and services to meet the growing deficit beyond what was possible if the state relied on Exchequer funds alone:

> Importantly, in a national context, the injection of private finance (through PPPs) will accelerate the delivery of the public capital programme designed to remedy Ireland's infrastructural deficit ... Ireland has undergone a remarkable economic transformation since the publication of the *National Development Plan* in 1999. In the same period, much progress has been made in developing our physical infrastructure. However, the pace of economic growth has placed enormous pressure on that infrastructure. In the case of the Department of the Environment, rapid economic progress, combined with large-scale housing development, placed additional strains on the water and waste-water systems. (Department of the Environment PPP Unit, interview, 2006)

Similarly, the Department of Transport explained that PPPs were introduced in the roads sector because, it claimed, the government did not have the finance to build all the roads that were required.

It was also argued, in line with the neoliberal view on the deficient capability in the public sector and the state, that the twenty-first-century Irish state neither had the capacity for nor the willingness to fund the investment required to address the public infrastructure and service deficit. PPP Unit Officials asserted that it would 'not be appropriate' for the state to undertake the extent of investment required to provide, and manage, public infrastructure and services.

In line with their support for Social Partnership, the Irish Congress of Trades Unions (ICTU) representative on the PPP Informal Advisory Group explained that Irish trade unions accepted the argument that the level of infrastructural development required was too high for the state to undertake. Furthermore, the state did not have the employees in these sectors and, fundamentally, had expressed no interest in developing such new infrastructure and services itself. The state was moving away from 'doing' things and instead would 'monitor, plan and design' (ICTU IAG representative, interview, 2006). For example, the investment necessary for the planned Metro project in Dublin was considered to be 'too much' for the Irish government to undertake and, therefore, the only mechanism that would ensure its development would be a private-financed PPP project:

> There was always a sense that it [the Metro] was too big to commit to with capital expenditure. There was serious concern at the time of what impact it would have on the government balance sheet, whether Ireland would be breaching the Maastricht criteria or not. We were then asked to bring the Metro forward and do a business case for it; there was an underlying assumption that it would be a PPP. There was always a feeling in the Department of Finance that unless it's a PPP it is not really going to happen. (Rail Sector PPP Unit, interview, 2006)

The genesis of the Metro occurred, therefore, with no public debate and no possibility that it would be publicly funded or operated. Furthermore, the development of this major public infrastructure and service was being led by private capital investors:

> It was something the private sector would put money on the table and finance. This, along-side the guidelines and reported success of PPP in the UK, led in 2000 to the Metro becoming a project. It was almost a given it would be a PPP and there was never any real debate given the sheer scale with such a significant capital cost and its origins. (Rail Sector PPP Unit, interview, 2006)

If we examine this situation on a deeper level, it can be extrapolated that the failure of successive governments to provide public infrastructure and services, such as housing, schools, roads etc., to the required standards and at the required rate of provision, created a situation in which the private sector, through PPPs, was viewed as a more reliable route to guarantee the provision of public services and infrastructure by civil and public servants. As a result of the failure of governments to invest in public infrastructure, a new market was created for private investment and enterprise.

It is also important to highlight that, due to a rapid growth in GDP, the fiscal restraints that provided a strong impetus to introduce PPPs in other countries did not pertain when PPPs were initially introduced in Ireland. The Exchequer's position was such that it could have funded considerable infrastructural projects itself at the time (FGS, 1998). Some real pressure on public expenditure did re-emerge through 2001 to 2003 as a result of slower economic growth, but this dissipated again from late 2003 onwards. The government, at that stage, with relatively healthy fiscal conditions could still have undertaken borrowing to provide the necessary additional funding. However, government fiscal policy was focused on reducing the national public debt and restricting public borrowing in line with EU, Maastricht and Growth and Stability Pact guidelines. This, along with the government's desire to promote growth in the construction sector, was a principal motivating factor for the introduction of PPPs, according to former member of the Public Accounts Committee, Green Party Senator, Dan Boyle (interview, 2006):

> The main motivation to introduce PPPs has been to engage in 'off-balance-sheet' bookkeeping, as infrastructure produced in this way is not counted as part of the budget debt ratio that is part of the Maastricht criteria that determines membership of the euro currency. A second cynical reason is that it allows Fianna Fail to claim that it is delivering on behalf of one of its key support groups – the construction industry.

PPPs would thus allow the continuation of neoliberal, fiscally conservative policies of restricting government borrowing and spending on public service and infrastructure provision, and, therefore, facilitate the budget surpluses that existed to be redirected toward more short-term, electorally favourable, developer and construction industry supportive policies, such as reducing income, capital and corporate tax rates, and providing tax incentives for the development of private hotels, hospitals, property etc.

Deliver at greater speed

At the time of introduction of PPPs, the government, along with opposition political parties from across the political spectrum, was expressing 'frustration' with the slow delivery, inefficiencies and cost overruns of public-sector projects. The allocation of design and construction risk to the private sector, combined with payments linked to the availability of a service in PPPs were expected to address these issues and provide 'significant incentives for the private sector to deliver capital projects within short construction time-frames' (Department of the Environment PPP Unit, interview, 2006).

This 'frustration' with delays in public-sector delivery was also expressed by centre-left political parties. According to Jan O'Sullivan Labour Party TD, and a member of the Dáil Education Committee, PPP projects were introduced 'because of a failure to make the public system more efficient in terms of addressing the need for school accommodation within a reasonable time period, and because of the ideological make up of the government'.

Private-sector benefits

The justifications and reasons provided by Irish government officials for the introduction of PPPs were remarkably similar and, in many instances, exactly the same as those given by private-sector proponents outlined in Chapter 2 reflecting the influence of the private sector and subscription to neoliberal perspectives among the state officials. Again, the fact that PPPs were introduced at a time of budget surplus is an indication that their introduction was strongly influenced by the government's neoliberal belief in the superiority of private-sector delivery. The construction sector IAG representative explained this clearly in interview (2006):

> PPP came to Ireland when the Exchequer was in a healthy state. The necessary infrastructure could have been provided directly by the state. They thought the involvement of the private sector would provide innovative design solutions and better management of the infrastructure.

The adherence to the neoliberal ideology was also emphasised by Senator and businessman Fergal Quinn, speaking in the Seanaid Debate on the National Development Finance Agency Bill, in 2006:

> There must, therefore, be another justification for taking the more expensive [PPP] route. Whenever I raise this issue, I am overwhelmed by neither the quantity nor quality of the replies. I suspect for many people, the justification [for the introduction of PPPs] is ideological. It is rooted in a belief that the private sector always produces the best and the most cost-efficient result. As Members might expect, I am a great champion of the private sector, but even I find it difficult to accept that proposition without any firm evidence to support it in particular cases.

Strong political support was given to this ideological perspective on the role of the state from the Minister for Finance who introduced PPPs, Charlie McCreevey TD, and the government TDs from the Progressive Democrats. They advocated that the management of public services and infrastructure was beyond the capability of the public sector. The PPP Unit Officials from the various government departments also expressed this view. It would be through the direct involvement of the private sector in the entire process of planning, design, development and provision of public infrastructure and services in PPPs that would provide greater speed of delivery, efficiencies, optimum value for money and much higher standards than the state could undertake directly. This was evidenced most clearly in the candid and profoundly radical statement by the Department of the Environment PPP Unit (interview, 2006) that PPPs were introduced in order to facilitate the transformation of the role of the Irish state from one of direct provider of infrastructure and services to a mere regulator and monitor: 'By transferring responsibility for providing public services to the private sector, government officials will act as regulators and will focus upon service planning and performance monitoring instead of the management of the day-to-day delivery of public services.'

The state expected PPPs to achieve the objectives outlined above through the introduction of private-sector methods and ethos in the public sector such as the insertion of market-based principles of competition and 'incentivised performance' in the delivery process. PPP projects, therefore, were introduced to 'get things done' by changing the 'mindset' of the public sector away from being 'inflexible, slow and inefficient'. They were perceived as being effective and progressive because they could achieve many projects that would not otherwise be undertaken by the public sector. A key mechanism for this would be getting the input from the private sector into the public-sector delivery process, as, according to Central PPP Unit Officials, civil servants are over cautious and have a *'can't do'* attitude instead of a *'can do'* one. The Officials also expressed the view that local authority staff have very negative attitudes to the transformation of service delivery and, therefore, the PPP method was introduced in order to help the state bring about such necessary reforms.

For example, PPP facilitated the introduction of performance management systems and performance-based measures into the rail sector through the LUAS light rail contract. It had not been possible to include such incentive measures previously in the rail sector as it was operated by the state company, CIE. The absence of such commercial incentives in public-sector management, which meant that the public infrastructure and service providers 'stayed in business' regardless of what happened with the projects, was strongly criticised:

> The private sector skills and management expertise (that PPP brings in) are those which would be associated with managing business activities that survive or fall by reference to financial returns in the market place. Public servants do not typically work in such a commercial environment and would not therefore be practitioners of commercial business activity. Employing private enterprise to deliver some types of services at a particular cost, which cost is subject to a competitive process, has an incentive structure which is linked to the business entity's own private financial position; this incentive structure cannot be replicated for obvious reasons within the public sector. (Department of the Environment PPP Unit, interview, 2006)

PPPs would achieve value for money through exposing new and existing areas of state responsibility to market competition. The necessary aspect of this process, as noted by the Central PPP Unit official, is the provision of profit-generating opportunities for private investment:

> You give out risks to get more people to bid on projects – to get competition and therefore to reduce what we are charged. If we are too aggressive in our transfer of risk, then there's no competition – it's a judgment call based on market soundings and experience. Private companies do not come in unless they can make a profit. (Central PPP Unit official, interview, 2006)

Furthermore, the financial institutions rather than the state would be allocated the responsibility to guarantee adequate provision of the public service. It was explained that because the banks are often the principal financial providers for PPP consortia, they would ensure that the projects are operated to the required standard. This is because the banks, in order to guarantee the receipt of its interest repayments from the private consortium, would ensure the private operator provided the adequate quality and level of service required for receipt of the annual payments from the state. Thus, according to the state officials, private financial institutions would be better regulators of the projects than the public sector. It was also expressed that because the public sector did not have the requisite commercial imperatives or skills, in part as a result of the policy of cut-backs in the 1980s and on-going public-sector employment embargos (Allen, 2007; Sweeney, 2004), it would not be able to deliver the infrastructure or services the state required. Waiting to develop the experience and skills within the public sector from the ground level up to management was considered to involve too much of a delay given the urgent need for such infrastructure and services. PPPs would introduce the required private-sector experience and skills in the necessary time frame. Rather than building up skills, capacity and expertise within the public sector, the government, therefore, decided to get the private sector to provide these through PPP projects:

> There was the desire and realisation that in certain sectors the public authori-
> ties couldn't recruit and maintain the personnel required to run the
> infrastructure, for example in the local authority area where a very large invest-
> ment was needed in waste-water treatment infrastructure plants and the plants
> were increasingly sophisticated from a technical point of view ... We need to
> build skills up within the public sector. In the late 1980s cutbacks, the public
> sector lost a lot of skilled people and now mainly the capability is not there
> unless they set up project teams with proper resources. (SIPTU National
> Industrial Secretary, interview, 2006)

For example, the collection of dry recyclable refuse in Dublin City in the late 1990s required the establishment of a new collection and recycling service as none existed at the time. While DCC had been involved in the collection of waste for many decades it had never been involved in dry recycling. In order to provide such a recycling service, a significant amount of investment in infrastructure was required to provide collection and materials recovery (for example the bins, recycling facilities etc.), the segregation of material, the extraction of contamination and then marketing it to find an end-user to recycle it. Local authorities, traditionally, did not have experience in that area and it was for that reason that DCC contracted out the dry-recycling service, through a PPP. Similarly, the Ringsend incinerator was selected as a DBFM

PPP pilot project by the government to be operated by the private sector as the public sector had no experience of providing or operating such infrastructure.

The general opinion of the senior civil servants at central and local government levels interviewed for this research provide an important indication of the extent and intensity of their lack of confidence in the ability of the Irish public sector to deliver high-quality and efficient services.

Lack of choice in the implementation of PPPs

Another important aspect to the introduction of PPPs has been the extent to which there appeared to have been no real choice and democratic input around the development of projects. As a result of the government decision to pursue the PPP approach, designated sectors within local authorities and government departments were informed that proposed public infrastructure and service projects in their sector, with an initial capital expenditure exceeding €20 million, would have to undergo a PPP feasibility assessment before commencement. While this was, in theory, to assess whether or not a project was suitable for the adoption of such an approach, the practical experience for certain government departments and local authorities was that the proposed project would only receive funding if it was undertaken through the PPP route.

PPPs in social housing estate regeneration, the Grouped Schools Pilot PPP Project, the Wexford and Wicklow local authorities' waste-water treatment plant and the LUAS and Metro projects provide examples of the practical implementation of this policy. The development of these projects illustrate that PPPs were adopted as the method of delivery on the basis that there was no other option available to the state authority or agency to access central government funding. The message was that the PPP method would have to be used if a specific project was going to proceed.

For the Department of the Environment (PPP Unit, interview, 2010), and consequently the relevant local authorities, 'the main driver' for the introduction of PPPs, 'has been the government policy requiring PPP arrangements to be considered for all major infrastructure projects'. PPP project managers and community representatives involved in negotiations surrounding the regeneration of DCC social housing estates via PPPs explained that they were informed by the Department of the Environment that state finance was not available to fund their regeneration projects. Therefore, their projects would not be developed if they did not adopt the PPP method. For example, DCC was informed by the Department of the Environment in 2003 in relation to its request for funding for the regeneration of St Michael's estate that the financial climate in relation to public finances at the time had changed and the Department recommended that PPPs should be investigated as a method to produce regeneration faster and cheaper. Therefore, DCC introduced and developed the social housing regeneration projects through the PPP mechanism because of the unavailability of government funding to provide it by any other route. Their hands were effectively bound by central government imposed policy. This left it with no option but to pursue the PPP method despite the fact that that model would require the reorientation of the regeneration plans away from the wishes and needs of residents toward the requirements of the private developer and financial capital. The ensuing projects would involve the sale of valuable public land, the dislocation and destruction of inner-city communities housed on the estates and a reduction in the quantity of social housing units located within those communities (detailed later in Chapter 5).

The inadequacy of government funding for the provision of new infrastructure, such as schools, also influenced local actors, such as school principals, to adopt the PPP route of delivery. This was because this route was perceived as guaranteeing the provision of a new school as it obviated the delays of waiting for the Department of Education and Science to allocate funding through traditional mechanisms. The Minister for Education in 2002, with an education budget showing a 14 per cent reduction, outlined in the Dáil the reality that, if the PPP route was not adopted, fewer schools would be built or refurbished:

> Five schools are to be built by PPPs at a cost of €10 million per year for several years. We now have those schools; if we had to pay for that out of capital funding, it would have cost €70 million and many fewer schools would be built or refurbished under the capital programme. We must look at ways, other than the traditional ones, of building schools and the PPP is the way forward. PPPs provide a top quality school with no maintenance costs for twenty-five years as the company will provide that. Less is withdrawn from the capital budget because the initial outlay is less, therefore, more schools can be built. (Dempsey, 2002)

In the case of water and waste-water treatment plants, the Department of the Environment stated that PPPs were not necessarily the only option and every project was to be tested on its own merit. However, it was claimed that when one local authority submitted a proposal through a traditional mechanism, keeping it within the local authority, the Department refused to fund it. It was believed that the project was refused funding because the proposal was not done using a PPP approach. This reveals that, in some cases, actors at central government level, whether officials or government ministers, were imposing the PPP mechanism at local government level, irrespective of the preference of local authority management for the projects to be procured through traditional mechanisms. The dependency of local government on central government was, therefore, being used as an important mechanism by the Irish Central state to undertake the neoliberal restructuring of state institutions.

Commercialism, neoliberalism and the role of the private sector

Irish government officials also explained that, as detailed by private-sector proponents in Chapter 2, PPPs were introduced because they could provide greater value for money and funding than traditional delivery mechanisms by facilitating the conversion of public services, infrastructure and assets into income-generating commodities. This included the introduction of user fees, such as road tolls and rail fares and the privatisation of local authority land in regeneration projects. This income would further reduce the amount of Exchequer funding required to invest in new services and infrastructure:

> The private sector may be able to generate additional revenues from third parties, thereby reducing the cost of any public-sector subvention required. Additional revenue may be generated through the use of spare capacity or the disposal of surplus assets. (Department of the Environment PPP Unit, interview, 2006)

Through the application of these income-generating mechanisms, PPPs would facilitate the implementation of a central neoliberal policy objective of creating market opportunities for the private sector within public govern-ance, services and infrastructure (Bourdieu, 1998; Brenner and Theodore, 2002; Harvey, 2005; Whitfield, 2006). The Irish government's application of such mechanisms provides evidence to support the hypothesis of geo-political economy academics, such as David Harvey, that neoliberalism facilitates 'capital accumulation through dispossession' from public services, service users, employees and taxpayers (Harvey, 2005, 178). For example, PPPs in roads facilitated the introduction of user fees. PPPs in local authority housing estate regeneration was set to facilitate the commercial realisation of the market-value of public land by and for private developers, who would, in return, finance the provision of social and community aspects of regeneration of former local authority housing estates:

> PPPs can capitalise in a cost effective and socially progressive manner on the escalation in the value of urban lands in public ownership ... these projects are financially neutral for the Exchequer, as the private sector is providing public housing in return for development rights on the remainder of the sites. (Department of the Environment PPP Unit, interview, 2006)

A further example is provided in the rail sector, where the Rail Procurement Agency (RPA) entered into PPPs with developers to provide public rail infrastructure and services adjacent to their developments, thus capturing some of the development gain that went with providing high-quality public transport.

Public-sector employment conditions

Another aspect of this process of neoliberalisation was the aim to reform conditions of employment and reduce the influence of trade unions within the public sector. This rationale was found to be underlying the decision of the Irish state to introduce PPPs. For example, the contract to operate and provide the infrastructure for Dublin's light rail service, LUAS, was outsourced to the private sector through PPPs. It is posited that this was undertaken so that the trade unions, which were a powerful force within CIE, would not be as influential in the future: 'It was breaking the hold of the unions. It was to overcome the perception that Dublin's public transport is often interrupted by industrial action. With a PPP, a union member's job is on the line if they disrupt as the company is penalized for an interrupted service under the contract, and could even lose the contract' (Rail Sector PPP Unit, interview, 2006).

This policy decision resulted in unfavourable changes to the rights and conditions of the new private-sector employed rail drivers in comparison to the public-sector drivers. For example, on employment LUAS tram drivers were obliged to sign a 'no-strike' contract. No such contract existed previously within the public sector. According to the trade union representatives interviewed, this measure and other conditions contained in the LUAS drivers' contract were intended to send a signal to the militant public-transport workers that, if they took industrial action too often, then their service would also be privatised:

> SIPTU's deal to represent the LUAS workers had the price of the 'no-strike' clause. It wouldn't have been allowed by their members; it would have been a sell-out to privatisation. We all have to stand back from the ideological approach. It was to show the public transport workers if you cry wolf too often you'll get a LUAS. (ICTU representative, interview, 2006)

This reform of employment conditions for the worse would not have been possible to apply to directly employed public-sector workers due to the levels of trade unionism and established conditions and standards in the public sector. It appears that the introduction of PPPs may well have been influenced by the government's aim to reduce the influence of trade unions within the public sector and to develop more flexible, competitive, neoliberal-type work practices than those that exist in the traditional public sector.

Increasing role of the private sector

The private sector played an important role in influencing the development of PPPs in Ireland. For example, in 1998 the IBEC and the CIF made a joint submission advocating PPPs to the Department of Finance. The document was drawn up by a committee composed of representatives of National Toll Roads, Allied Irish Bank, engineers and several legal and finance organisations. Private-sector advocates involved in the promotion and development of PPPs internationally, including Farrell Grant Sparks, PriceWaterHouseCoopers, KPMG and Deloitte and Touche, also played a central role in promoting and effecting the introduction of PPPs through their reports and information sessions commissioned by the Irish government. These groups clearly stood to gain commercially if such projects were adopted on a large scale in Ireland. The government commissioned these private consultancy companies to undertake reports and develop guidelines to facilitate the development of PPPs in areas of the public sector previously restricted from commercial involvement. The PPP Unit in the Department of the Environment (interview, 2006) stated explicitly the important role played by such reports. According to the Unit, the government decided to use and encourage PPPs principally because of 'two important Reports published in the late 90s/early 2000, both of which concluded that there was scope for PPPs in Ireland, the Farrell Grant Sparks report (1998) and a PriceWaterHouseCoopers report (2001)'.

The private-sector consultants emphasised to the government the importance of introducing PPPs in order to rapidly address the infrastructure deficit. Criticism of, or cautionary lessons from, international experiences of PPPs were rarely mentioned in the reports. For example, the government-commissioned Farrell Grant Sparks report concluded that such PPPs were required because, even if a considerable proportion of the service and infrastructure deficit were to be met from the projected Exchequer surpluses in Ireland, 'it is hardly conceivable that the total requirement will be dealt with in this manner' (FGS, 1998, 21).

The Department of Finance appointed PriceWaterHouseCoopers (PWHC) in 2001 to undertake a review of the effectiveness of the PPP method in order to build on the 'significant progress' made in the first few years of adopting the approach. Their *Review of PPP Structures Report* (PWHC, 2001a) analyses Irish government PPP activity up to that date, provides theoretical justifications for further expanding the PPP programme and outlines the policy framework required to increase the rate of implementation of such PPPs in Ireland. PriceWaterHouseCoopers were also commissioned by the Department of the Environment in 2001 to produce a report on how that Department could develop a framework within which PPPs could be advanced in Ireland in the roads, water and waste sectors. The report entitled

'*A Policy Framework for Public Private Partnerships*' (PWHC, 2001b) provided general contextual information on PPPs and specific procedural guidance in relation to the delivery of infrastructure using such an approach. The report concluded that there was considerable potential for the use of PPP models in Ireland and that there was an even greater need for such PPPs given the macro-economic developments that had occurred in 2000 and 2001 since the launch of the Irish Pilot Programme. These included inflation in the construction sector, a slowing down in economic growth and consequent tightening of public finance and increased demand for infrastructure investment outside of what had been planned in the *National Development Plan, 2000–2006* (for example, the Dublin Metro). PriceWaterHouseCoopers (2001b, 11), therefore, recommended that 'it is possible that the increased use of private finance, enhanced competition and better value for money associated with PPPs will provide an effective means of dealing with these new challenges'.

They were also given the opportunity by the Irish state to highlight the positive experiences of PPPs from the UK and elsewhere in private sessions held with Irish local authority senior management and government departments. This exposed Irish government officials to biased presentations of the principles and benefits of PPPs. This might explain why Central PPP Unit officials pointed to the international experience of PPPs as being generally positive and made few references to the need for an Irish model to avoid the mistakes made internationally. In this way, despite considerable international evidence of negative outcomes from PPPs, the Irish government appeared satisfied to take the perspectives of international private-sector proponents without any critical analysis. The private sector also played a significant role in the genesis of individual PPP projects, such as the Metro, the LUAS and the Grouped Schools Pilot PPP Project.

In fact, private firms exerted pressure directly on the public sector to adopt PPPs. For example, the Grouped Schools Pilot PPP Project was not included in the original programme of Irish pilot projects. However, 'a large international bank' gave a presentation to the Department of Finance on how PPPs could be used very successfully in education projects. The Department of Finance then approached the Department of Education and Science about including schools in the Pilot Programme. The Department of Education and Science itself then became very active, initially at least, in promoting the possibility of developing PPP schools to the private sector: 'the Department of Education and the Department of Finance actively promoted PPPs and encouraged companies to set up in Ireland because of the amount of work that was to be tendered using the PPP model' (PPP private operator, interview, 2006).

Clearly then, the Irish state's awareness of and interaction with private-sector consultants and companies was a key influential factor in the adoption and development of PPPs. They were also promoted to the Irish government and state Officials at an international level by governments, particularly the UK government, and international institutions such as the European Union, United Nations and the OECD that advocated the potential for private companies. For example, the development of PPPs was supported by links and co-operation between Irish government PPP Units and their comparable units in Northern Ireland. It was also aided by the strong support from the EU Commission for PPPs and the United Nations' PPP organisation.

The intense promotion of PPPs by private companies and consultants to the Irish state, as outlined above, revealed the importance of this potential market to private business investment and capital. It demonstrates how the sizable public infrastructure and service deficit that resulted from decades of underinvestment combined with other factors, such as rapid economic growth had through the 1990s and 2000s been identified by neoliberals as a potential market opportunity to promote new avenues for private capital accumulation (Allen, 2007; Harvey, 2005; Klein, 2007). From a neoliberal standpoint then, PPPs were expected to play an important part in the *neoliberalisation* process of opening up the welfare state and its public service and infrastructure provision to global and domestic businesses:

> There has obviously been a deficit in investment in infrastructure in Ireland, both north and south of the border spanning health, education, justice, the courts and housing. That has created a huge opportunity for those of us involved in the sector, again both north and south of the border. (Investment Banker, speaking at 3rd Annual Irish PPP Policy Forum, 2007)

Irish state support for and promotion of PPPs

Along with the Farrell Grant Sparks report in 1998, a number of other high-profile reports also put forward cases for the implementation of PPPs in Ireland. Among these, the *Bacon Report* (Bacon & Associates, 1998) on house price developments advocated PPPs in areas of physical infrastructure, such as roads, sewerage, water facilities and social infrastructure. The various stakeholders involved in Social Partnerships also recommended and endorsed the use of PPPs in new infrastructure or service projects within the National Economic and Social Council during 1999, the Social Partnership Agreement 2000, *Programme for Prosperity and Fairness* (Government of Ireland, 2000b). That Agreement tasked the Informal Advisory Group with developing a framework to guide the PPP procurement process (ICTU, 2005). The resultant *Policy Framework for Public Private Partnerships: Working Together for Quality Public Services* (PPP Informal Advisory Group, 2001) outlines how the government aimed to embed PPPs as an important pillar of public capital procurement and the provision of public services.

In order to provide optimum support for the development of the PPP process, the government established, along with the Central and Departmental PPP Units, a website (www.ppp.gov.ie) and a new Centre of PPP Expertise in the National Development Finance Agency (NDFA). The Central PPP Unit was set up to facilitate the process by developing the general policy framework, including the legal framework, within which PPP projects operate. It provides central policy guidance to departments and other state authorities to ensure the process works effectively given that not every department would, necessarily, have acquired the level of expertise to develop and implement such projects. It also chairs both the Interdepartmental Group and the Informal Advisory Group on PPPs (Central PPP Unit, 2006b).

The *Review of PPP Structures Report* (PWHC, 2001a) classifies the phase of Ireland's development of PPPs up to 2001 as *'programme mobilisation'* with progress made in *'market development initiatives'* to create interest amongst national and international private-sector providers and the creation of *'deal flow'*. PPP 'deal flow' describes the rate and quantity at which new PPP projects are put out to tender in the market by public authorities and then reaching contract closure.

By 2001, at policy level, the report notes, the focus had already started to shift towards the use of PPPs to provide a range of other elements of social and community infrastructure, such as social housing, schools, colleges and healthcare facilities. The report also notes that there had been a highly visible political commitment to the approach with the clear backing of the Taoiseach, the Minister for Finance and senior Ministers. Therefore, it states, Ireland had moved effectively through the mobilisation phase 'harmonising the key requirements of visible political leadership and commitment to deliver progress on market development, deal flow and stakeholder engagement'. This, the report notes, 'has embedded PPP as a procurement method across government allowing the mechanism to play a full role in a changing environment for the delivery of public services (PWHC, 2001a, 17).

The government established a Cabinet Committee on Infrastructural Development Including Public Private Partnerships, which, following the General Election in May 2002, was reconstructed as the Cabinet Committee on Housing, Infrastructure and PPPs. It was chaired by the Taoiseach and met quarterly. The overall aim of these actions was to promote the benefits and opportunities of PPP projects nationally in order to increase the PPP deal flow. The Central PPP Policy Unit, in consultation with other PPP Units and the Social Partners, produced a PPP Communications Strategy in 2002. The strategy further demonstrated the commitment of the government to vigorously promote PPPs. The key stated objective of the strategy is to develop a profile, both nationally and internationally, to inform firms and stakeholders of the existence and possible applications of PPPs in Ireland. The

Communications Strategy aims to 'correct misunderstandings and misinformation on PPPs and maintain an information resource centre. It will also help to create and maintain a competitive market for PPPs by attracting top class national and international firms' (Central PPP Unit, 2002, 9).

The key messages the strategy sought to publicise include the fact that PPPs are not a means of 'privatisation by the back door', that Ireland is developing an extensive pilot programme, that value for money must be achieved in projects and that, because the programme is being undertaken on a pilot basis, it involves an ongoing learning, evaluation and revision process (Central PPP Unit, 2002). The government also introduced three important pieces of enabling legislation to ensure that state departments and agencies would have the power to enter into PPPs, be supported through the process and that opportunities for developing projects would be enhanced (Central PPP Unit, 2006b). The first piece of legislation introduced was the Transport (Railway Infrastructure) Act 2001, which facilitates private-sector participation in the development of the public rail sector in Ireland. The Act established the Rail Procurement Agency (RPA), which is an independent statutory public body with responsibility for procuring new metro and light rail infrastructure and services through concessions to the private sector, joint ventures and PPPs, rather than through the traditional approach. Secondly, the government enacted the National Development Finance Agency Act, 2002, to establish the National Development Finance Agency which, amongst other things, would assess optimal financing for public investment projects (including PPPs), such as those set out in the *National Development Plan* and other infrastructure priorities. Thirdly, the state authorities (Public Private Partnership Arrangements) Act 2002 facilitates the 'fullest possible participation' by Irish state authorities in the PPP process (Government of Ireland, 2002) by providing certainty to the powers of Irish state authorities to enter into PPP projects and also gives local authorities power to enter into joint ventures, such as PPP projects, with the private sector. According to the government, the Act contributes to the creation of an environment in which PPPs can flourish as a method of public procurement (Government of Ireland, 2002).

Conclusion

This chapter indicates that considerable effort was invested by the Irish state in providing the institutional arrangements and political support necessary to rapidly expand the development of PPPs in Ireland. Furthermore, the development of such projects were underlain by an expectation and belief, on the part of the government and state officials, that the private sector would provide greater amounts of finance to address the infrastructure deficit and would provide higher-quality and more efficient public services and infrastructure. This would be achieved by facilitating a greater involvement of the private sector in the policy making and governance of the Irish state and public service and infrastructure delivery than existed previously. The process underlying the introduction of PPPs can, therefore, be analysed, using a geopolitical economy approach, as contributing toward the trend of *neoliberalisation* of the Irish state at the level of public governance, service and infrastructure provision. It also reveals the important role that PPPs were expected to play in providing new avenues for profitable private investment (capital accumulation) by the private sector. This reflects trends associated with the process of neoliberalisation of the state internationally (Brenner and Theodore, 2002; Peck and Tickell, 2002).

Notes

1 Austria, Belgium, Denmark, Finland, France, Germany, Greece, Ireland, Italy, Luxembourg, Netherlands, Portugal, Spain, Sweden, United Kingdom.
2 To qualify for Objective One status the GDP per capita for a region or country within the EU must be below 75 per cent of the EU average. The recognition of Objective One status is usually accompanied by structural funds support from the European Community as part of its regional policy.
3 The methodology for the research provided in this book, including an outline of the various actors that were interviewed, is outlined in Chapter 1.

4

Outcomes of the Grouped Schools Pilot PPP Project

Introduction

> Failures of privatised companies, such as Railtrack, have proved that the private sector does not deliver effective services or value for money. Once services are run for private profit, the quality of care is reduced and the public service ethos is replaced by the profit motive. The first 14 PPP hospitals, for example, saw bed reductions averaging 30 per cent and cuts in clinical staff budgets of 20 per cent. (National Union of Teachers, 2003, 1)

> We are left with broken machines and structural problems like leaks that render the hall unusable. This year it's been ongoing for six weeks ... I rang the private operator help line but got nothing ... I am like a nut case as it impacts on us. If I'm ready to eat the phone, am I focused on the kids? For a school this size, the teacher on the ground has more to do. You are chasing everyone, but it's nobody's job. I wouldn't touch the PPP model with a barge pole. (PE Teacher in one of the Irish PPP Schools, interview, 2006)

The requirement for the provision of new school buildings and the modernising and upgrading of existing ones reached a crisis point in Ireland in 2007 when hundreds of children in areas of rapid population growth, such as the urban commuter areas around Dublin, could not attend school at the start of the new year because there were insufficient places in schools for the number of children that had reached school going age in those areas. From the early 2000s onwards, many schools, particularly in the larger towns and cities, had struggled to deal with the lack of adequate buildings, with some children spending their entire school years in prefabricated buildings, squashed into tiny classrooms, in playgrounds where they were not allowed to run because the space was so that tight they bumped off each other and with outdated and insufficient facilities, such as information technology (IT) equipment, physical education (PE) areas, science materials and laboratories.

The historical lack of investment in Irish schools, accentuated during the public expenditure cuts in the 1980s and 1990s, meant that, despite investment increasing by 600 per cent between 1992 and 2006, from €94.1 million to €644.6 million, these problems remained in the 2000s. The requirement for new schools and extra classroom space and equipment resulted from a rising population nationally, a changing social and cultural environment and the need for special education provision and to reduce class sizes.

The revised Primary Curriculum applied further pressure for the provision of appropriate facilities to teach all subjects, particularly in the areas of science and physical education. It is well documented internationally that the good condition of school buildings and provision of the appropriate facilities are essential to provide a high-quality education system, particularly to enable the implementation of a broad and balanced curriculum. At post-primary level, there was also demand for updated facilities with the introduction of revised subjects, such as technology and art that have specialist IT and equipment requirements, as well as improved facilities for the practical work required by the post-primary science syllabus and support for the completion and assessment of practical coursework for the Leaving Certificate examination.

PPPs were identified as an important mechanism to meet these infrastructure requirements in both a rapid and cost-effective manner. A PPP Unit was set up within the Department of Education and Science[1] to promote and support the development of PPP projects in the education sector. The Unit, as explained in Chapter 1, has overseen the development of a number of projects including the Grouped Schools Pilot PPP Project, which entails five schools that have been in operation since 2003. The school sector has proven to be one of the key areas for the development of PPPs in Ireland and as of 2010 a further twenty-seven schools were planned to be delivered through this mechanism.

As outlined in Chapter 3, the Department's stated rationale for developing schools through the DBFM PPP method was that it would:

- provide access to extra funding through private finance;
- provide greater value for money in delivering schools;
- improve the speed of delivery;
- provide higher standard buildings and better maintenance/operation of the schools than traditional provision;
- relieve school principals and staff of the responsibility for managing school buildings and allow them to concentrate on their core education functions;
- lead to new ideas and private-sector innovation on school design through an output-based competitive approach;

- achieve better 'third-party' use of state-funded school buildings outside of regular school hours. In summary, there would be greater involvement of the private sector in the provision, management and maintenance of school buildings.

Under the terms of the PPP contract, the private company is required to, within a specified timeframe of delivery, construct the schools and provide all fixed and loose furniture and fittings, including, inter alia, computers, PE equipment, musical instruments and woodwork and metalwork equipment etc. It is also responsible for maintaining the buildings and grounds over the twenty-five-year life of the contract, and to manage and pay for all of the schools' premises services, such as waste management, cleaning and security over that period. The PPP was expected to guarantee that the building will be provided 'on-time' and achieved using high-quality materials because the private company loses financially if it is delayed and will be responsible for addressing any maintenance issues that might arise from poor-quality materials being used in its construction. The academic management of the school remains with the school authorities and the state retains legal ownership of the property (DOES, 2006a).

In the Grouped Schools Pilot PPP Project, the private operation was taken over from Jarvis Ltd by Hochtief Ltd in 2006. The Department makes annual payments of €11 million per year to the private partner over the contract life, totalling an estimated €283 million (€150 million in net present-value terms). These payments were to be conditional on the private operator meeting agreed availability and service levels.

In 2004, the C & AG undertook a detailed analysis of the projected value for money of the project and found that the PPP route was more expensive per unit cost per square meter than direct provision (C &AG, 2004). The analysis, however, only examined the stages of development of the project up to the point where the contract was signed with the private company. It did not cover an assessment of the operation or quality of equipment and buildings provided and did not, therefore, assess whether or not the schools achieved the additional objectives outlined by the Department. This chapter provides an assessment of such outcomes. The evidence gathered from the research into the case-study PPP schools is presented in Table 4.1. The rest of the chapter details the quality of the school buildings and equipment provided and whether or not value for money was being achieved. It then looks at the speed of delivery, operation of the schools to the agreed service standards (quality of maintenance and management by the private operator of the school), the impact of the deal on the role of the school principals and the impact and extent of 'third-party' or 'non-school/community' use of the school buildings.

A number of important impacts, such as the commercialisation of the schools, community use and changes in employee conditions, are then outlined. Finally, the findings in relation to the fundamental question of PPPs' suitability for schools, evidence of neoliberalism and the implications of these findings for the Irish government's planned PPP programme in the schools sector are presented and analysed.

Quality of design, buildings and equipment

Building design and layout

From an aesthetic perspective, the PPP schools look fantastic. They are large spacious buildings with a modern design and excellent features. The classrooms are significantly larger than those provided in a traditional school. The increased size of the schools includes greater circulation space (corridors etc.), which contributes positively to the general school atmosphere. This has resulted in an improvement in the discipline of pupils according to one school principal who believes that the greater space means less incidents of 'trouble' in the corridors and classrooms as there are less children 'bumping off each other in the corridors'. The physical size and design of the school buildings are a benchmark for other schools and provide a model that affords pupils an environment that facilitates learning. As one school principal explained:

> The school is physically excellent – spacious and bright. The classroom space is much bigger and the practical rooms are big and wide. The corridor space is fantastic. The facilities are fantastic. The teachers have a nice environment. We worked in portacabins before. Now everything is within the one building; the IT structure is great, the facilities, labs and workshops are very positive.

The *Whole School Evaluation Report* (DOES, 2006b) for one of the five schools found similar advantages, including the additional facilities beyond what would be traditionally provided in a school funded by the Department. For example, it has six science laboratories, four dedicated computer rooms with 300 computers across the school and enough classrooms for teachers to have their own base rooms. There are also office facilities for a number of teachers with specialist roles. The school also has a performing arts area and music room, as well as a full-sized gymnasium and fitness suite. A large cafeteria provides food for the student population. Outdoor facilities include six tennis and basketball courts, a pre-existing astro-turf pitch and a sand-based playing pitch capable of accommodating full-scale football or hurling matches. The other four schools have a similar impressive range of facilities.

A comparable analysis with traditionally provided schools is made difficult by the fact that even though the PPP schools are, on first observation, highly satisfactory, a large part of their successful impact is the 15 per cent increase in space over traditional schools. This raised a question of how much the benefits highlighted in the five PPP schools are attributable to the PPP model *per se* and how much relates simply to the increased space over that of traditional schools. Thus, it could be maintained that the design innovation, so often lauded as a positive attribute in PPPs, in this case study was simply the expansion of the size of traditional schools.

Despite their aesthetic standards, Table 4.1 provides details of significant design and structural problems found in the schools. For example, there was visible subsidence at the side of one school with the footpaths around the school building sinking and cracked. The extensive subsidence of the school grounds has caused problems with the sewage system, rainwater drainage and to the sports field and basketball court. The C & AG's 2008 Audit of the five PPP schools also found this to be the case. Poor lighting design and acoustics was a problem identified in three of the schools. In these schools, some of the corridors and classrooms were quite dark to the extent that they required electric lighting even on sunny days.

Four of the five schools had problems with the design of the stage/hall area. This negatively impacted on their ability to provide for drama and, as it is the assembly area, for occasions that bring both the whole school and the wider community together. The design of some of the stage and canteen area were not suitable for school use. In one instance, the school had to buy an additional portable stage as the existing stage was too small for use by the children in a play. They also had to buy their own lights and sound system, which all came out of the school budget. The principals also highlighted evidence of poor heating design, which has contributed to school utility bills. There were significant issues with noise levels in the metalwork rooms to the point that teachers and pupils believed it was a serious health and safety issue. Furthermore, in some of the science rooms, the gas was located inside the classroom in gas cylinders with no air extraction system. School guidelines state that gases should be stored externally and piped in but there was no specification in the contracts for the private company relating to the storage of gases.

There was also evidence of poor design of the woodwork rooms with dust extractors also being inadequate. Electric sockets were located in the middle of the classroom floors which was completely impractical. One school had to convert an additional classroom to a music room because the music room provided was poorly designed. The schools, therefore, were experiencing considerable problems on a day-to-day basis as a result of design and construction issues.

Furthermore, while the schools visually appeared impressive on first examination, closer investigation of the inside floors, doors and ceilings revealed a different picture. There were problems with gaps between the doors and windows and their frames, the floors were lifting in places, the bricks were cracking on the walls and the doors were creaking. Incredibly, in four of the schools, there were leaks in the roofs of the PE halls.

Consultation with principal and teaching staff

These design problems in the schools resulted, in part, from the inadequate consultation with the teachers and principals from the schools. The PPP process is required to include the 'social partnership' principles of consultation, such as stakeholder participation in the original and ongoing decision-making process, and accountability. The guidelines for consultation with stakeholders[2] in the PPP process was outlined in Section 7 of the *Framework for Public Private Partnerships* produced by the PPP Informal Advisory Group (2001), which stated that there should be extensive consultation and open communication in respect of PPP projects. In particular, public service employees should be informed at the earliest possible stage of proposals for the introduction of PPPs and of any significant developments throughout the process. According to the guidelines they should also have the opportunity to contribute positively to the development of projects, and this partnership approach should be maintained throughout the project's lifetime.

However, principals and teachers from the schools were not satisfied with the extent of consultation they had in the PPP design, planning and development processes. This resulted, in part, because of the PPP requirement to treat the schools as a single 'bundle' with one design model being applied to all five schools. Schools were therefore being designed in a way that was not necessarily suitable for the requirements of each individual school. In addition, the 'output-based' approach in a PPP contract meant that the Department was less prescriptive in what was required for the school, with the expectation that such an approach would bring the benefit of attracting new ideas from the private sector in terms of innovative design. This was unlike a traditionally procured school, where the design brief from the Department would specify the exact details of the school building, such as the size and layout of the rooms. For example, one principal explained that they had requested additional practical rooms (for woodwork, art etc.) and specific changes to the planned practical rooms. Their suggestions were not acted upon and, as a result, after construction they had to convert an ordinary classroom into an extra art room. This school felt that this was a significant problem, as it is located in a disadvantaged area where the demand for practical subjects is traditionally very high.

Similar design problems due to the lack of consultation emerged in the

Table 4.1 Overall evidence from the Grouped Schools Pilot PPP Projects

School	Design	Building quality	Equipment quality	Maintenance	DOES monitor	Third-party school use	Workers' conditions	Impact on principal
1	Excellent, but: heating problems, poor acoustics in stage area. Lack of chemical extractors	Large, spacious, bright, but PE hall has 15 leaks. Problems with building subsidence	Poor, esp. metalwork. Machines unusable. Problems with woodwork dust extractor. IT problems	Very poor. Helpdesk delays	No evidence	Issue with vending machines. Poor community usage	Worsening of conditions for some staff	Increased workload
2	Excellent, but: poor art room design. Poor design of stage area. Designed according to teacher in class, not school	Large, spacious, bright, but PE hall leaking	Mixed. Some very poor, e.g. lathes. Art room paint substandard. Poor equipment for staff room	Not satisfactory. Helpdesk delays, gym equipment not fixed	No evidence	Issue with vending machines. Poor community usage	Worsening of conditions for some staff	Freed up time, but not to extent DOES claimed
3	Excellent, but lights have to be on all day in some classrooms. Poor design leading to heat loss. Poor acoustics in metalwork room	Large, spacious, bright	Mixed, but poor woodwork and metalwork equipment	Very satisfactory *But* Not satisfactory & delays (acc. to teachers)	Poor	Issue with vending machines. Poor community usage	Worsening of conditions for some staff	Reduced workload. Very happy with it

4	Excellent, but: dark corridor, lights have to be on all day in some classrooms, poor design of stage/assembly area. Heating problems. PE dressing rooms very small	Large, spacious, bright, but PE hall roof leak. PE hall floor lifting. Bricks cracking	Mixed. Poor metalwork and woodwork. Dust extractor problems. Poor PE equipment (English standard). IT problems.	Not satisfactory. Delays, Gym equipment not fixed	Poor	Issue with vending machines. Poor community usage	Worsening of conditions for some staff	Reduced workload, but 'its not my school to manage, it's the private operator's'
5	Excellent, but: poor design of stage area, poor location of prayer room, poor acoustics of machine rooms, not enough natural light in tech. drawing room	Large, spacious, bright, but PE hall roof leaks	Mixed. Metalwork equipment continuously breaking down. Problems with dust extractor. Motor burned out of sander after three weeks	Very Satisfactory (Acc. to principal) yet abandoned helpdesk system. Not satisfactory (acc. to teachers)	Poor	Issue with vending machines. Good community usage	Worsening of conditions for some staff	Reduced workload, but noted the contract needs to be tighter and enforced

other schools. For example, another school had a problem with the fact that the computers were provided in the classrooms on the presumption that the teachers were based in a particular classroom but, in that school, the students remained in class while the teachers moved between the classrooms. This meant that the computers and other equipment were left unattended for the period of time while the teachers transferred to other classes, resulting in the equipment being damaged.

The experience of the Grouped Schools Pilot PPP Project shows that no two schools have the exact same requirements and that the building of schools through mono-design bundles can therefore lead to considerable difficulties, as this approach is not flexible with regard to the needs of individual schools. Consultation with each individual school is necessary to discover its teaching, staff and pupils' requirements, how it operates and to investigate if the proposed building can be structured around that plan, as opposed to, as one principal put it, 'the schools are being told by the Department and PPP company, here is your building now structure your school accordingly'.

It was interesting to observe during the research that a notable divergence emerged between the views and experiences of the principals, who were much more positive toward the PPP outcomes, and the teachers who had a more negative experience. Teachers, in particular the practical-subject teachers, appeared more aware of the many day-to-day workings of the schools' facilities and fittings, while the principals appeared, understandably, slightly removed and more focused on higher-level management issues. For example, there was a much higher level of dissatisfaction in relation to the outcomes of the consultation process amongst teachers, with teachers in four of the five PPP schools feeling excluded from the design and development process. The teachers were led to believe at the initial discussion stages that they were going to have a significant input into the planning of the schools. However, after a private company had been selected as the preferred bidder they were given a copy of the plans and then told to submit changes and modifications. They suggested some small changes, but they were informed that these were not considered due to the financial implications as only cost-neutral design changes were possible. The evidence from the schools demonstrates that their input certainly did not appear to have been acted on.

They felt that the objectives of the private operator were prioritised over the teachers' educational requests. They were also excluded, they believed, because many of their proposed design changes would have affected the speed of completion of the projects and, therefore, jeopardised the provision of the schools exactly on time. This was a vital issue as the reputations of the Department's PPP Unit, the PPP company and others and, indeed, the future of this PPP model were dependent on the first bundle of PPP schools being delivered 'on-time' and 'on-budget'. Many of these design problems, the teachers believed, could have been avoided had the teachers, the ones with the practical expertise, been involved at an earlier stage of the design and procurement process. One of the PE teachers summed up their frustrations:

> Our opinion was ignored. We got no real input into the design. We were shown plans and made recommendations but, for example, we asked for a viewing area in the hall but you can see here now there's no viewing area. We spent time drawing up equipment lists but they were completely ignored. There is no value of the opinion of teachers on the ground. The [education body] were representing the Department for us in negotiations with the private consortium but they seemed more interested in bowing to the private operator than listening to us.

Another issue that arose time and again was that facilities provided for in the schools appeared not to be designed for educational uses. For example, a lot of the gym equipment provided was not practical for children, as the private operator had provided adult-based equipment that could be used after school hours as an income generator. This reflected a similar trend that emerged in PFI schools in the UK where some aspects of the design of the school were not appropriate for educational use and instead had been designed to meet the commercial needs of the private operator. Another reason for this is that the private companies that were involved in PFIs were found not to have much experience in designing educational facilities. It appeared those designing and constructing the schools were not aware of the important educational design features that schools require.

Equipment provision

According to the Department, principals and teachers, the overall quality of the equipment supplied to the five schools was generally of a high-quality standard. Staff in all five schools commented positively on the great number of computers in the staff room and around the school. However, in all five schools there were also instances where the quality of equipment supplied was poor, particularly in relation to the practical subject areas of metalwork, woodwork, art and PE. Some of the equipment led to health and safety issues for staff and students, such as parts of the woodwork lathes breaking off the machines. Further health and safety issues arose from the low level of protection provided on some of the machines in the metalwork area.

Furthermore, the pottery kilns in some of the art rooms were not appropriate and there was a lack of ventilation preventing their use (C & AG, 2008). The kilns supplied by the PPP company were internally ventilated and the manufacturer had stated that exhaust flues were not required. However, the general practice for traditional schools would have been that a canopy would be provided to allow for ventilation (C & AG, 2008).

Some of the equipment was so sub-standard that it affected the ability of teachers to provide lessons and had to be replaced. But they were replaced only after intense pressure was placed on the private company by the individual teachers and schools. The problem was caused by the fact that, in some instances, the private operator fitted out the schools with what teachers described as cheap equipment, which might have reduced its costs but was substandard as a result. The fact that the private company was responsible for sourcing the equipment also led to a situation where equipment was provided on the basis of lists given by the Department and not according to what individual schools and teachers required. The issue in this instance was that the Department's lists were completely out of date. Most affected by this were the practical subject areas as these have changed their syllabus significantly as a result of equipment, technology and industrial developments. As a result, the equipment required in 2010 is very different from what was specified to be provided in 1990. In traditional schools, the school or teachers would identify and source the required equipment according to what was needed in that year. It is a more flexible and suitable arrangement than the PPP where the operator provided the equipment without reference to individual class or teachers' requirements. This pointed to the problems that can arise from the PPP model where the private sector is given the responsibility to source the required equipment. The Department did accept there had been some initial problems concerning the delivery and quality of some equipment for specialist classrooms and that it was to blame in some instances, such as the issue of equipment lists.

It took a considerable amount of effort on the part of the principals and teachers to get the inappropriate, faulty and below-standard equipment that had been supplied replaced, as initially the private company refused to do so. It was a 'war of attrition', according to the teachers, who felt that it was very stressful for them on a personal level, particularly as they reported that they were intimidated from complaining. For example, one teacher provided evidence of a letter from the private operator threatening to sue the teacher if complaints continued about the standard of the equipment provided. The schools were made to feel, by both the private operator and the Department, that each school was the only one of the five schools with any problems.

The teachers felt let down by these experiences because they had been informed at the start of the PPP process that such maintenance or equipment problems would not be their responsibility and therefore no time would be wasted trying to deal with such issues. However, the reality was that any time they had a problem they found it very difficult to get the private company to resolve the problem. The teachers believe that the contract was not sufficiently specific, and, therefore, the private company had wriggle room to do what a private business does – make profits by lowering costs, apparently, in this case, through the provision of cheap, and, as a result, unsuitable and inferior equipment. One school even had to engage engineering inspectors to prove that the equipment was unusable. One teacher explained:

> There were bits falling off the lathes each week. Twelve months later we got three new lathes but the replacements were also of poor quality. We waited for a year for the drill and mill to be operational. Three years on, one lathe is still not commissioned. It's never been sorted. There is a higher risk of accidents. We are still missing the full complement of equipment. We can't use an important machine that's worth €10,000 as there are bits of it missing. I raised the problem with the private operator but initially I got no response. I'm tired of this. I'm not interested in writing to them any more. It doesn't have any effect.

In another school, they had no hand tools for three weeks, which affected the junior certificate and leaving certificate classes with the result that the teacher and students had to come in after school in order to catch up on lost time.

It appears that, in order to reduce costs, the private operator only put in the standard of equipment fulfilling only the basic criteria and therefore much of it was not of an educationally sufficient standard. This is clearly an example of the conflict that can arise in these projects between the educational requirements of a school and the private operators' necessity to keep costs low in order to maximise commercial return.

Value for money

As detailed in the introductory chapter, the C & AG report (2004) found that, in a comparison between the unit cost of one of the PPP procured schools (Ballincollig community school) and the unit cost of a conventionally procured school (Kilcoole), the conventional approach was cheaper than the PPP route by a margin of 8–13 per cent. These findings contradict the Department's calculations that the PPP model would be cheaper and better value for money. The main difference between these figures relates to the fact that both the Department and the C & AG used different residual value estimations for the schools in their public sector benchmark (PSB). The Department assumed that the schools provided by conventional means would have useful lives of thirty-five years. However, in contrast to this the life span of the school buildings proposed under the PPP deal were assured to be around fifty years. This biased the PSB in favour of the PPP option and, therefore, cast doubt on the accuracy of the assumption of different useful lives (C & AG, 2004).

The C & AG report also found the projected unit costs of construction in Ballincollig were about 26 per cent higher than the projected equivalent unit costs in Kilcoole. Most of the unit cost differences were attributable to costs associated with the PPP form of procurement, including charges associated with risk transfer, increased scope of work to accommodate facilities management and to provide for third-party income generation and increased professional/legal/financial fees. However, the PPP Unit in the Department makes the case that this increased cost is based upon the whole life-cycle investment model. This is centered on increased expenditure aimed at providing superior buildings that would require less maintenance over the life time of the building. A private company that was part of the consortium delivering one of the school bundles explained that this is also a key mechanism of how the state achieves value for money through a PPP as the contract includes maintenance of the schools for twenty-five years, thus resulting in the standard of materials used being a lot higher than traditional projects as items are chosen to last. On this basis, the private operator is contracted to transfer the schools back to the state in perfect condition after twenty-five years, saving the Department the cost of having to re-build or refurbish the school as is the case with many traditional schools that are not built to such high standards or maintained over their life to a high standard.

The C & AG also found that the Department assumed a unit cost of construction for the conventional procurement model of €2,115 per square metre, including VAT, in its PSB. This compares to the PPP bid proposal cost of €2,073, including VAT. But the Department's own cost norms for construction of schools by traditional procurement at the time was around €1,800 per square metre, including VAT (almost 15 per cent lower than the assumed unit cost) (C & AG, 2004). The Department also failed to include VAT in the estimated €71.6 million construction cost of the PPP proposal, while the estimated cost of construction by conventional means was VAT inclusive. As a result, the Department failed to compare projects on a similar cost basis. The comparison should have been based on a total construction cost estimate for the PPP proposal of around €80 million, rather than the €71.6 million figure that was used. The C & AG also criticised the Department's PSB cost comparison as the project cost estimations should have included whole life-cycle costs for both models – both capital costs and running costs over the project life. The results of the C & AG analysis suggest that schools could be provided with comparable useful lives to those offered in the PPP deal through conventional procurement at costs equivalent to conventional procurement (C & AG, 2004). Furthermore, the Public Accounts Committee 2006 Report on its Oireachtas Hearing into the Grouped Schools Pilot PPP Project states that the Department negated the possibility of undertaking a true financial comparison as the space provided in the PPP schools was 15 per cent greater than conventional schools. The Department had carried out the PSB on the basis of a 35,000 square metres school but it should have undertaken the comparison on the basis of a 30,000 square metres school (the traditional size of a school). The Public Accounts Committee and the C & AG noted that in order to test whether the PPP gave better value for money it would have been necessary to keep all other conditions as they were. However, the Department had introduced too many complex variables, such as size, to enable such an accurate comparison.

The Department also failed to take account of the fact that the cost of borrowing involved in the deal with the private operator was higher than the cost achievable through direct Exchequer borrowing. Also excluded were the costs of conducting the PPP procurement and bidding process itself (for example the private operator's bid cost for the Cork School of Music alone was £1 million). This process is very complex as it involves putting together a contract that ensures the guaranteed provision of all aspects of the construction and maintenance of the schools over the twenty-five years. As a result, public bodies spend considerable sums of money on consultants to advise them in this process. For example, the Department spent a staggering €236,000 on legal and financial advisory services related to the schools project and €395,000 related to the College of Music project (C & AG, 2004).

The additional facilities did not generate the expected income and indeed appeared to be a cost to the school. For example, the five PPP schools were to receive a proportion of the income generated by the private operator from catering, vending machine and third-party usage of the school facilities. The contract provides for a guaranteed minimum to each school, in respect of income from catering and vending, averaging €2,800 in year one and increasing to €3,500 (plus indexation) from year three onwards. Profits from third-party usage of the school facilities outside core education service requirements (after deduction of associated expenses such as increased staff, heating and insurance costs) was also supposed to be shared on an equal basis between the school and the private operator. However, principals in two of the PPP schools expressed concern that the private operator had not given the school its fair proportion of the income and it transpired from the C & AG Audit (2008) that, in fact, no school had received such payments.

The school principals believed that the private company was trying to generate costs that could be invoiced to the school equalling the amount the company was supposed to pay the schools from income from the canteen and vending machines. The C & AG Audit (2008, 94) supported this experience noting that: 'It was the practice of the original PPP company to deduct any amounts due for work commissioned by the school principal which was outside the scope of the contract from any income due to the school from vending machines placed in the school.'

Furthermore, there was considerable unease in all five schools that expenses relating to the private operator's use of the school for income-generating purposes were being paid for by the schools. The vending machines and gyms, for example, had a high demand on electricity, but it was the schools, rather than the private operator, that paid for the electricity relating to their use. In addition, the schools were originally fitted with cables that could carry large amounts of electricity, well above what normal schools would use (500 versus 127 kilo volt amps), to operate the various income-generating facilities (for example gym fitness suite, canteen, vending machines etc.). The standing charges relating to these cables were very expensive and were charged to the school. The principals were highly critical of the failure of the PPP company to take responsibility and pay such expenses, and they also criticised the Department for not ensuring that the private company paid for them. The C & AG Audit (2008) also noted that the principals were concerned about the failure of the original PPP company to provide energy management and efficiency reports to assist the schools to reduce costs. The current PPP company has engaged with the school principals in order to minimise energy usage.

The schools also paid for the disposal of refuse which was generated from the private operator's canteen and other income-generating facilities. This frustrated the school principals, particularly given that the contract stated that the private operator was to pay for all of the schools' premises' services, such as energy and waste management, cleaning, catering, security, parking and telecommunications.

School principals were given the impression at the start of the PPP project that all maintenance issues would be paid for by the private operator. However, the reality was that they had to pay for significant costs in this area. For example, traditionally, a school would have hired and paid a once-off maintenance contractor to carry out work, such as electrical or plumbing problems. In the PPP, the private company organised it but quoted prices over and above what would have been expected for simple maintenance, such as the fitting of a new electricity socket. Thus, any maintenance provided by the private company outside of what had been specified in the contract turned out in practice to be a more expensive method for the school than the traditional method of the school principal hiring the relevant repair person directly.

Many of these extra costs can be attributed to the involvement of a 'for-profit' private operator in the maintenance and operation of the schools. There was a requirement for considerable profit to be provided from the payments from the Department given that the expected rate of return to the investors involved in the Pilot Schools project was estimated at 13.7 per cent (C & AG, 2004). This profit had to be generated from the schools. The involvement of the commercial private sector, therefore, resulted in the logic of the maximisation of profit being applied to elements of the day-to-day maintenance of the schools. This profit is an additional cost to schools over and above what existed in the traditional model and money which otherwise could have been available for the school.

Risk transfer

According to the Department, an important benefit of the PPP method was expected to be the transfer of risk, in relation to time and cost overruns, to the private sector rather than leaving the Department liable for the potential additional costs of school projects. In the PPP contract, the state retained the demand risk, while the design, availability, construction and maintenance risks were transferred to the private partner. The Department estimated that if it procured the Grouped Schools by conventional means, design and construction and operational risks would result in adding an estimated €8.3 million in net present value terms to the cost of the procurement. This additional risk-related cost accounted for 6.9 per cent of the overall estimated cost of the procurement of the schools by conventional means. This, according to the C & AG, was a low percentage of the overall cost and indicated that, in fact, the level of risk transfer contained in the project was limited. This is one of the key principles of PPPs, namely that the optimum risk is transferred to (or retained by) the partner that can best manage the risk. The fact that the demand risk (the estimation of the enrolment capacity of the school), one of the most significant risks, was retained by the Department further limited risk transfer. This risk was retained because the Department would have had to pay the private sector a considerable amount if it transferred it to the PPP company as it would have charged an exorbitant amount to cover any potential losses if pupil numbers changed significantly.

The C & AG demonstrated in the case of the Ballincollig PPP school that part of the reason why the state ended up paying more than it would have under conventional procurement was because it transferred responsibility for managing the building to the private sector but retained this demand risk itself. Ballincollig was planned to cater for 1,000 pupils, but enrolment for the first year was only 580 pupils, for the third year 613 and was still only 600 in 2008. However, payments to the private operator by the Department were not reduced, despite the lower than planned pupil enrolment in the school. Similarly, the school in Dunmanway, Co. Cork, was constructed with the capacity for 700 pupils, based on an estimate of future enrolment demand, but the actual number that enrolled in the school in 2003 was 635 and fell then to 566 by 2006, while the planned enrolment for the school in Tubbercurry, Co. Sligo, was 675 but the actual enrolment in 2006 was only 512 pupils. In Shannon, Co. Clare, the school was planned for 600 pupils but enrolment reached 700 in 2006. It is unclear whether the PPP company negotiated an increase in the annual payment to deal with that increase.

The C and AG's finding that there was an 8–13 per cent cost differential between PPP and conventional schools is very significant and casts considerable doubt on the evidence base that underpinned the rationale for the use of PPPs in the provision and maintenance of schools. The high cost of the annual 'unitary' payment to the private company could affect the overall long-term affordability of the project. Furthermore, if that cost differential continues in future bundles of planned PPP schools, it could have a significant impact on the state's ability to provide further new schools or refurbish existing schools as the more schools are provided under PPPs, the fewer new schools can be provided overall, assuming a static budget.

It is also interesting to note that the external consultants that advised the Department in 2000 at the commencement of the PPP process on whether or not private-sector financing should have been used for both the Grouped Schools and the Cork School of Music projects advised that privately sourced finance might represent an additional cost relative to the public-sector cost of finance. However, the consultants still recommended that private financing should be included as part of the PPP project (C & AG, 2004). This inclusion of private financing, even at additional cost, reflects the Irish government's enthusiasm and strong ideological commitment to greater private involvement in public infrastructure delivery through PPPs.

Speed of delivery

One of the other key motivations for the Department to introduce PPPs was the assumption that it would provide the infrastructure 'on-time' and more quickly than traditional mechanisms. This was achieved in the delivery of the Grouped Schools Pilot PPP Project. The private company explained that the faster delivery time was achieved through the PPP's contract mechanism, which sets clear dates for completion and no matter what happens during the project this completion date must be adhered to, otherwise the private client will be penalised financially. This provides a guarantee that the project will be delivered on time. The Department claimed that the schools were built in half the time of traditional methods, however, the C & AG (2004) noted that the total time for the procurement was three and a half years versus the traditional time of four to five years. This demonstrated that the PPP route was really able to provide a school anything from six months faster to actually taking a similar time to the traditional route. This contradicts the Department's claim that the PPP schools were built 'in half the time' of a traditional school. It represents almost a zealous exaggeration of the benefits of PPP by the Department's PPP Unit, a trend that emerged in relation to the way the Unit positively described the PPP schools.

Despite this, the Department itself emphasised the speed and innovation of delivery it was achieving through traditional procurement in its 2006

Schools Building Programme (DOES, 2006a). Two schools designed by Department architects were built as part of a Pilot Project in 2003.[3] Following completion of the design phase, tenders were sought in the traditional manner for the construction of the new schools. Construction commenced in late 2002 and was completed in 2003. The Griffeen Valley Educate Together School, Lucan, was also delivered on time and within budget through a combination of traditional and modern system-build technologies executed on a fast track five-month building programme.

Maintenance and management

Traditional school management

In Ireland, there are over 3,200 primary level schools and 750 second-level schools. The operation and management of the schools is very different from most countries as the majority are privately owned and managed by local religious trusts through patron bodies. The principal of the school is responsible for the day-to-day operation of the school and he/she answers to the Patron who may manage the school personally or appoint a person or group, such as a Board of Management to act as a manager.

Funding for all schools is provided largely by the central government through the Department. For example in 2006, the Department spent €7.7 billion on education of which over 70 per cent was for salaries and 8.5 per cent for capital expenditures. The Department also sets the general regulations for recognition of schools, prescribes the national curricula and establishes regulations for the management, resourcing and staffing of schools. At the primary level, it is Boards of Management of the individual schools that are responsible for managing the schools and the overwhelming majority are run by either the Catholic Church or one of the other faith denominations, with bishops or other faith leaders being the patrons of schools. In multi-denominational schools, the patron is usually the Board of Trustees of a limited company, such as Educate Together. Secondary schools have three types of management and ownership arrangements. Voluntary secondary schools are privately owned and managed and include fee-paying and non-fee-paying schools. They are under the trusteeship of religious communities, boards of governors or individuals. Vocational schools and community colleges are owned by the local vocational education committees (VECs). Their boards of management include VEC representatives and parent, teacher and community representatives. They are largely funded by the Department. The third arrangement is community and comprehensive schools which were established in the 1960s. Many of these schools were established as the result of the amalgamation of voluntary secondary and vocational schools. They are managed by boards of management which are representative of local interests, and funding is provided entirely by the Department to cover teachers' salaries, educational costs and general building and support services (heating, lighting, cleaning, secretarial and administration costs, caretaking, security, etc).

The funding provided for these schools includes the services of a full-time secretary and caretaker. The majority of schools in excess of 500 pupils have funding for a second caretaker and part-time secretarial assistance. School budgets also provide an allocation in respect of cleaning services (C & AG, 2004). Three of the schools in the Grouped Schools Pilot PPP Project are community schools and two are community colleges.

Since the 1990s, there has been a significant move away from the dominance of the religious orders in the management of secondary schools due to the decline in the status of the church in Irish society and the steep fall in the number of vocations to the religious orders. In addition, falling church attendance has led to a reluctance on the part of main churches or religious orders to step up and become patrons for schools in newly developing areas where it is unclear what the likely religious persuasion of the majority will be. Given the growing ethnic diversity and demand for a non-Catholic Church dominated education system, parents (both Irish and new immigrants) are increasingly choosing to opt for non-denominational or multi-denominational schools, such as Educate Together schools.

Management and maintenance of PPP schools

In the PPP schools, the private operator obtains a significant involvement in the management of the school building. The operator becomes responsible for 'facilities management' (that is tasks that principals and staff were responsible for in traditional schools, such as maintenance and management of the school buildings and some equipment, caretaking and cleaning and after school use of buildings). This is a key departure from the traditional school model. The ancillary staff, such as caretakers and cleaners, are no longer employed by the school and under direct control of the principal but are now employed and directed by the private operator. The private company operates a 'helpdesk' system from its central offices for teachers and principals to report items requiring attention by faxing or emailing the private operator, which then allocates the necessary task to their local employee (caretaker or cleaner) or a contractor. In a traditional school, if a difficulty arose with some aspect of the building, the principal or teacher contacted the caretaker who would then address it. Along with the helpdesk, the private company's area facility manager is to visit the schools once a month to assess how maintenance and management is working.

The experience of principals and teachers under this system has been very mixed regarding the quality and level of maintenance and management being provided by the PPP company. The responses received from principals to the C & AG Audit (2008) 'raised some doubt as to the extent to which the required maintenance and management services are fully provided'.

The primary research undertaken for this book found that two school principals were very satisfied with the level of maintenance and stated that it was maintained to a higher level than in their old school. They explained that the PPP company had a very different maintenance strategy in place in comparison to traditional schools, with comprehensive maintenance plans for each week and each year with everything managed by the company. The principals explained that this means in practice that, if a teacher comes to the principal with a facilities problem, the principal just emails the helpdesk and, obviously, does not have to go looking to find a caretaker and organise what needs to be done. They felt that it was a very good model for addressing any facilities problems that arose and having them dealt with. The principals stated that the management structures in a traditional school would not have the expertise to provide this, and, furthermore, it was highly unlikely that the Department would generate such templates for the proper maintenance of traditionally run schools.

Despite these positive experiences, the principals in the other three schools were concerned with aspects of maintenance and management. Furthermore, the teachers in one of the two schools where the principal had been very satisfied with the maintenance had in fact problems with the system. Therefore, four out of the five schools were found to have experienced some level of poor maintenance by the private company. The helpdesk reporting system was identified as a major problem, in particular in relation to the poor response from the private company in dealing with on-going maintenance issues that were reported and which impacted on the day-to-day operation of the schools, such as the replacement of faulty equipment. These problems have also been identified in PPP schools in the UK and Canada. In these instances, it was highlighted that such problems emerged, in part, because of the private operators' focus on reducing costs in order to ensure a profitable return to their investors.

So, while the PPP contract stated that the buildings, equipment and fittings had to be fit for purpose, the original private company, in clear contravention of the contract, sometimes refused to take responsibility for rectifying the problems that emerged. The problem in some of these instances centred on disagreements between the schools and the private company over the standard of equipment provided. Problems also arose in relation to establishing which equipment/fixtures supplied by the company were provided for in the contract under a 'supply-and-maintain' arrangement and thus were to be maintained by the company and which were under a 'supply-only' arrangement and were thus to be maintained by the school.

In one school, the company claimed that any plug-in appliance was 'supply-only' and, as a result, the school had to spend €60,000 on a new dust extractor for the woodwork room. The principals also complained that the Department never supplied them with a list of what equipment was provided under 'supply-and-maintain' and that was 'supply-only', and this meant the schools were disempowered in the disagreements with the private company because they had to rely on the company to tell them what was 'supply' and what included 'maintenance'. The C & AG Audit (2008, 96) also found this to be the case and affirmed that 'as the schools did not receive a detailed listing of the items appropriate to each category, the company effectively decides the matter in each instance'. The schools felt that the Department should have been more responsive to them in relation to this difficulty. According to the C & AG, the Department is clarifying the matter, using its records and those of the current PPP company, and, when it is resolved, will provide a list to the school principals (C & AG, 2008).

The original private company also claimed that some of the maintenance problems were arising as a result of vandalism and that it was therefore the school's responsibility to pay for the repair. However, the schools claimed that the maintenance issues were resulting from normal levels of 'wear and tear' and therefore, under the terms of the contract, were the private company's responsibility. This led to a tension between both parties, as the schools believed the company was consistently promoting the vandalism explanation. These issues could develop into major difficulties in the future if they are not addressed, as more maintenance problems emerge in aging buildings. These concerns in relation to equipment and maintenance should be addressed as a matter of urgency according to the Whole School Evaluation Report undertaken into one of the PPP schools:

> Complexities due to the subcontracting of some supply and maintenance issues, as well as uncertainties for the school management around the overall agreement between the department and the private operator have all added to the challenge of successfully managing resources. It has also been the case that any alterations to original specifications, from storage space to matters relating to voltage or phone line changes, have been both complex and expensive considerations. (DOES, 2006b, 1.4)

Another example of the problems that arise from the lack of clarity over roles of responsibility for maintenance was evident in two of the schools which reported that the private company stated that it was not its responsibility to maintain the gym machines. The schools had no funding to get the machines serviced themselves, so, when some of the machines broke down, the PE teachers tried, unsuccessfully, to mend the equipment themselves. As a result, the equipment lay idle, as machines were out of order for prolonged periods of time. The PE teachers were also frustrated with their failed attempts to get poor standard and unsuitable equipment replaced. For example, when they asked the company to replace sports mats, which were not child appropriate, it did so only on condition that the company would not have the responsibility to maintain the new ones. This is clearly against the spirit of a PPP, where the costs of replacing or repairing fixtures and equipment that do not meet the specifications of the contract are supposed to be borne by the private operator.

The PE teachers were shocked when the roofs of the PE halls in these spectacular new buildings leaked when it rained. The floors were seriously damaged as a result. Again, there was evidence in this instance that the private company was slow in rectifying the problems, despite the teachers logging the requests on the helpdesk. A teacher explained that when the floor of the PE hall is not up to standard, as a result of the rain damage, niggling at the back of the teacher's mind will be question: 'what if something happens to the pupils as a result of a damaged floor – is it my fault?' The teachers stated that, as a result, when they could, they took the PE lessons outside and let the new hall lie idle. In addition, while the schools now have very impressive playing pitches, the maintenance of those pitches was very poor. For example, in the spring time one of the schools logged a request with the private company for the pitch to be fertilised, but this was not done until mid-July – when the school was closed for the summer! It appeared that the contract specifications for ongoing maintenance were very poorly thought out from the public-sector perspective. The impact of these problems was articulated clearly by a very frustrated PE teacher quoted at the start of this chapter:

> We have a state-of-the-art gym, yet three out of ten machines are broken. The step-machine has been broken all year. When things go wrong with the IT or serving these machines, it is drawing on the school's central funds, it cuts our budget as the money has to come from somewhere. My heart is broken with this PPP. The buck doesn't stop anywhere. It's crazy. They are not interested in what the teachers on the ground have to say. We are the ones who know how to manage kids. Yet we are left with broken machines and structural problems like leaks that render the hall unusable. This year it's been ongoing for six weeks. I had two leaving cert. classes and could only use half the hall: it was crazy. I rang the private operator help line but got nothing … I am like a nut case as it impacts on us. If I'm ready to eat the phone, am I focused on the kids? For a school this size, the teacher on the ground has more to do. You are chasing everyone, but it's nobody's job. I wouldn't touch the PPP model with a barge pole.

The resistance on the part of the private company to accept responsibility for facility provision and management issues was a recurring theme amongst the school principals and teachers interviewed. They had considerable difficulty in getting the company to accept that the problems existed and then getting them to carry out the necessary repairs. This demonstrated further the limited transfer of risk that took place in these PPP project and provides further evidence undermining PPP theory, which states that the private sector should pay the costs when a risk materialises.

Detailed analysis of the operation of the helpdesk

The PPP changes the nature of the relationship between the principal and their ancillary staff. The helpdesk system meant that there was no on-the-ground management system for the private operator and their representative only called on a school on average once a month. Schools, however, work on the basis of personal relationships between staff, pupils and the school community. The *Whole School Evaluation Report* (DOES 2006b) supported these findings and noted that the process in place to facilitate often simple matters of maintenance or repair involved excessive paperwork and sometimes delay which management had little control over. Teachers and principals interviewed reported the response time from the private operator to problems logged on the helpdesk as unsatisfactory.

A teacher in one school described how the printers were consistently broken. In one instance, they logged it fifteen times and there was still no response despite it being the busiest time of the year while pupils were preparing for exams.

There was a clear lack of information and understanding at a school level of what was included in the contract and which party was responsible for dealing with issues. As explained earlier, the private company claimed that certain problems were not its responsibility and the schools could not challenge this as they did not possess the information from the Department to certify whether this was true or whether it was a case of the company avoiding the expense of addressing the issue. For example, the system of emailing the helpdesk to ask for routine procedures to be carried out in the school, such as the opening and closing of certain rooms etc., was a 'logistical nightmare' according to one teacher. For example, there is a partition door/divider between two large rooms that serves for after school study in the school, but the private company had to be emailed to get the caretaker to open the divider. The company then stated that the divider was not designed to be opened daily. The school had done a lot of work getting a supervised after-school study session set up for the children and that was the only room big enough to do it in. Because of the refusal of the company to open the doors, the school had to move the study session to a smaller room which has impacted on the number of children that can partake in supervised study. Similarly, the doors could not be opened at the school play as the caretaker had not been emailed to open them. This demonstrates the difficulties that exist trying to get basic things done in a PPP school which would be done by the caretaker in traditional schools. Many of the teachers were disillusioned and stated, at times, that they would prefer a traditional Department school.

Furthermore, in one school where the principal had described the maintenance system as working effectively, he had actually changed the system of reporting problems back to the traditional method of going straight to the caretaker with an issue. Initially the principal had logged all the problems to the helpdesk but he described that system as 'bureaucracy gone mad'. So the school phased it out and they are now doing it the 'logical way', where the principal and teachers go straight to the caretakers if there is a problem and bypass the helpdesk system.

There was also a problem with the internal communication system in one school. The intercom could be heard well in classrooms and in the hall but could not be heard in the social dining area. As a result, if the principal wanted to call a student or announce a message, it would not be heard in the social dining area. The principal had been logging the problem for at least six months, but it still had not been fixed satisfactorily. The deputy principal noted that the system in a Department school was better where they had more of a free rein to get someone in to fix things in the school.

These instances demonstrate clearly how, in PPP schools, the basic school infrastructure is privately controlled. This results in considerable frustration on the part of school staff. A further example is provided in the case of problems with the lack of litter bins and lids in one school. In order to get extra litter bins, the school had to make a request to the private company and then wait for its decision as to whether it believed they were needed or not. Even getting notice-boards erected in a class room became a difficult procedure as schools could not do this, or any similar changes, without permission from the private operator. The experiences and feelings of the school staff emphasise clearly that the building was not publicly owned and locally controlled, but most definitely owned and controlled by a private company. According to the principals, even the students were very aware it was a privately operated school and not directly *their* school.

Information technology system

In comparison with traditional schools, the five PPP schools were fitted out with a very high-specification and state arrangement as part of the contract. However, the IT contract did not cover the testing of software or its installation. To have the software installed, the schools had to pay, what they believed were, expensive fees to the private company. For example, in 2006 it cost €100 per software test and the cost of installing software on the computers was €20 per computer. In one school, there were 300 machines and at €20 each that would have totalled €6,000, a significant additional cost to a school budget.

Students and teachers who had the capacity to install the software were not permitted to do so because the company stated that it would interfere with the machines, again making it clear that the private company had primary control in the everyday running of the school. The problems were exacerbated by the fact that the subcontracted IT company was based in Dublin and unable to respond rapidly to the schools' problems given their diversity of locations at large distances from Dublin. Moreover, the IT maintenance contract with the company was only specified to last three years. Once this terminated in 2006, it left the schools with a large computer network with no maintenance support from the company or the Department and, as a result, it was going to be very expensive for the schools to continue providing computer facilities to their pupils. This has limited the ability of pupils and staff to use the computers. Adding to the difficulties was the fact that the phone system in some of the schools was dependent on the IT system. Therefore, if there was any issue with the phone systems, the schools had to organise any maintenance and pay an additional fee to another private company.

The extent of the problems with the IT system was reflected in the Department's decision not to renew the IT contract with the company and to remove IT contracts from the new bundles of PPP schools. In future, the PPPs will get the same IT systems as traditional schools, where the school receives funding to provide IT according to their own schools' specific requirements.

This evidence from the school principals, teachers and ancillary staff clearly demonstrates that there were considerable problems and dissatisfaction with the equipment, maintenance and management by the private company. These experiences were refuted by the Department's PPP Unit. Part of the reason for this is that the PPP Unit only has a procurement function and, therefore, found it difficult to find the capacity to monitor whether day-to-day issues such as equipment specifications and maintenance issues existed to the extent the schools claimed. According to the Department, its active intervention along with a clear communications strategy has alleviated the initial 'teeting problems'. Similarly, the Public Accounts Committee 2006 report stated that the problems had been ironed out through dialogue between the Department, schools and the company. However, the *Whole School Evaluation Report* (DOES, 2006b) stated that significant problems remained to be addressed:

> On a practical level ... difficulties have arisen, and remain unresolved within the PPP agreement, in relation to matters like equipment supply and maintenance, the quality of some items which have been supplied and, in places, omissions from the originally anticipated fit-out of rooms ... These issues

collectively present an ongoing challenge for the management of resources. (DOES, 2006b, Section 1.4)

Furthermore, it noted that the health and safety matters relating to the school building 'should be rectified immediately' and that the 'complexities and difficulties in relation to the joint-management and upkeep of resources within the PPP process ... should be addressed as a matter of urgency' (DOES, 2006b, Section 1.4).

This evidence highlighted a fundamental problem with the PPP model, namely that it is very difficult to address problems that arise after the contract is signed, that is if problems emerge during the operation of the school and it is deemed by the public client that the contract is unsuitable, it is very difficult and costly to then change specifications. This highlights the importance of getting the contract exactly right at the start. The individual specificity and breadth of variety of each individual school's requirements demonstrated that the PPP concept of operating a bundle of schools from the same contract turned out to be an impossible task and, overall, should be deemed unsuitable for the school system.

Relieving principals of responsibility

By introducing PPPs into school provision, the Department expected to reduce the school principals' responsibility for, and time spent on, managing the school building. These projects would, therefore, facilitate principals to concentrate, to an even greater extent than previously, on their core educational duties. While four of the five school principals did state that they were 'generally satisfied' with the extent to which their responsibilities were reduced (mainly due to the fact that if something in relation to the facilities needed attention, it was not their problem), overall this was true to a much lesser extent than was hoped for.

The principals were happy with aspects of the system where, for example, the caretakers would follow a facilities issue up themselves and there was not an everyday necessity for the principals to contact plumbers or carpenters, as is the case in traditional schools. Furthermore, the private company is the employer of the caretaking and cafeteria staff, so matters like their terms of employment, contracts and wages are not issues for in-school management or the board of management. The presence of the company's representative during fire drills and of its facilities manager, once a month, is an important support in the management of the school's resources. The management of the old pre-PPP schools was, according to the principals, a huge undertaking requiring skills that they often lacked. A PPP, therefore, brings in much needed building management expertise.

However, all five principals stressed that they now had *additional* responsibilities, which do not exist in traditional schools, such as trying to manage
the school according to the specifications of a legal contract, which is very
large and complex. Furthermore, three of the principals explained that the
PPP did not relieve them of responsibilities to the extent that was initially
promised as they still have to run and maintain the building. From graffiti to
litter, to minding equipment and looking after lockers, they are all still the
responsibility of the principal. These are important areas that influence
student's discipline and attitudes to litter etc. that affect the general ethos and
atmosphere in the school. For one school principal, the PPP was 'an absolute
failure' in this regard as he felt that nothing had changed for him between the
old and new school, except there was now a constant challenge of trying to get
the company to carry out adequate maintenance and respond to problems
that arose in relation to the building.

Surprisingly, these three principals did not even have a copy of the
contract to help guide them in relation to managing the relationship with the
private company. They were informed by the Department that they could not
get access to it due to commercial confidentiality clauses in the contract. The
principal in another school explained that he did manage to get the contract,
but it was only after a year into the operation of the schools. However, the
contract was written, he explained, in a 'legal speak', and, as a result, was
difficult to read and understand. It therefore proved impossible to enact on a
practical basis; 'the reality is that a school can't be managed on a day-to-day
basis from a contract written up by a boardroom of lawyers'.

Department monitoring of PPP contract performance

In order to guarantee contract compliance in the event that the private
operator does not deliver on its service obligations, significant financial
penalties are included in the contract. Therefore, if the company failed to
provide, for example, equipment to adequate quality or maintenance to a
sufficient standard, a penalty was to be deducted from the annual payment
from the Department.

This follows PPP theory, which states that private-sector payment, and
consequently its profits, should be linked directly to service delivery
outcomes. In this way, the profit motive is inserted into the service delivery
process in order to ensure the service is provided, and at the required
standard. In theory, then, the private company does not generate returns
unless the service is available at the quality specified. This would therefore
ensure that maintenance and other issues for which the company is responsible would be undertaken adequately. Furthermore, the fact that the private
sector's overall profit also depends on returning to the state high-quality
schools at the end of the contract life should ensure that the schools are well

maintained from the start. The private contractor explained that this is what happens in practice. When they made their bid for the PPP contract, they included the projection of what would be required to guarantee the building for twenty-five years, and assessed what it would cost to maintain the building over its entire life cycle. From their perspective, the accuracy of that projection is the risk the private sector takes on. If they get it right, they get their profit at the end of twenty-five years, and the Department gets the schools well managed and maintained.

The evidence, however, for the period of operation of the five schools by the original private company, was that the Department did not monitor the fulfilment of contract specifications and did not issue any fines to the company in relation to failures to abide by contractual requirements. This was despite the overwhelming evidence in international PPP projects that such monitoring was an important issue in ensuring contract compliance.

The principals would ring the helpdesk and report a task. Each task would then have a different timescale within which the private company had to resolve it. But the Department appeared to have no structure in place for checking whether the tasks were done within the specified timeframe or done to a sufficient standard. In addition, the principals were told that if something was broken, the company had two days to fix it or else penalties would be paid. Yet in one school, the toilets were unusable for three weeks and no penalty was paid. This is clear from analysis of the annual payments made to the PPP company by the Department, in respect of the five schools for the years from 2003 to 2006, which shows no evidence of deductions, despite the clear evidence that breaches in the delivery of maintenance, equipment and other contract specifications as outlined in this chapter had taken place. As the C & AG Report notes: 'there were a number of quality failures which, when taken in aggregate, could have resulted in deductions' (C & AG, 2008, 95).

The original PPP company had not recorded any of these quality failures (C & AG, 2008) and, therefore, the payment stayed the same at around €10.1 million per annum. Within that figure, the fees paid for facilities management (including building management and maintenance, cleaning etc.) actually *increased* each year from €1.1 million in 2003 to €1.4 million in 2006 (C & AG, 2008). These payments are made on receipt of an invoice in respect of each school and a report from the company indicating that any problems that had arisen had been resolved or were being dealt with. Furthermore, a formal Liaison Committee comprising the five principals and representatives of the Department and the PPP company met on a regular basis during 2003 and 2004 during the difficult 'bedding-in' period.

However, the Department decided to discontinue that at the end of 2004 and handed matters over to the company in order to allow the schools and the company to meet locally and to use the helpdesk to address day-to-day problems (C &AG, 2008). The Department, therefore, was paying the company the annual unitary fee despite not checking whether it had carried out its contract duties. This logic of a private commercial service provider monitoring the delivery of their own service was very poor practice from a public-sector perspective. The C & AG Audit (2008) also found that there were issues relating to whether or not the verification procedures followed by the Department provided adequate assurance regarding the full delivery of contract services for which the annual payments were being made:

> There would appear to be insufficient communication between the Department and the project schools with regard to performance issues. While an abridged version of the PPP company's monthly report is sent to the schools, the Department does not seek a response or confirmation of performance from them. (C & AG, 2008, 95)

The principals explained that they, along with the teachers, pupils and ancillary staff are the ones that have to live with the daily reality of the problems in the schools and, in their experience, the absence of in-school monitoring by the Department of the private company's delivery of contract specifications was an important contributory factor towards the on-going issues of poor maintenance and management.

Monitoring is obviously vital in such a situation where a private company, whose primary objective is to maximise returns to its shareholders, could, if it so wished, try and increase its profits by cutting back on its obligations to provide certain services (Whitfield, 2001). The Department had failed to set up the proper structures to monitor the projects, which meant that it could not apply any fines because it did not have the mechanisms to prove that the private operator had not fulfilled its contractual obligations. The reality was the Department did not invest the necessary resources in monitoring the implementation of the contracts to ensure that they were the high-quality projects it asserted they were.

A teacher pointed out her frustration with the impacts at school level of the Department's inadequate monitoring:

> The people negotiating the deal are not on the ground here today; they weren't putting a bucket under the drops last week. The PPP doesn't facilitate us. Teachers are not in the picture; we are even less so than in a Department school because their (the Department) head turns another way when the (company) is involved.

The Department perspective

The Department is delighted with the outcomes of the Grouped Schools Pilot PPP Project, but accepts that, in the first two years, there were quite a lot of difficulties, and ensuring the enforcement of contract specifications was difficult. For example, the contract states that the grass should be cut at least twelve times a year in the schools. So the company cut it in one school twelve times a year, but did not cut it short enough. The children then could not run properly in the grass, which made it difficult for them to play sports. Fortunately, the Department had specified that the blades of grass could be no more than 150 millimetres in length after being cut. In order to ensure it was done properly, the Department officials had to travel to the school and go out on to the playing pitch with rulers to ascertain the length of the grass and prove it had not been cut to specification. The efficiency of the PPP mechanism must be questioned when it leads to waste of public-sector official's time on such farcical situations.

The problems arose also because the people who were responsible for the everyday management of the project (school principals) were not part of the procurement negotiations. The Department stated that, as a result of this, it would like to see the contract managers (principals) involved at the heart of the contract tendering process between the Department and private bidders. The Department also accepted that it had not included adequate specifications within the contract that tied the private company into being responsible for certain issues. This resulted in what might be considered 'small' problems, which the schools were left to deal with, but in reality the problems impinged significantly on the everyday running of the school. For example, the contract did not specify that the litter bins should have lids. As a result, no lids were provided and birds picked all the rubbish out of the bins and made a mess around some of the schools.

For new PPP schools, the Department has insisted that school staff are given adequate training and user-friendly guide that explains the contract by the PPP company for the purposes of the staff's understanding of what is supposed to happen and of the way in which services are to be delivered. It is hoped that the confusion involved in the Pilot Projects will be overcome by providing such a user-friendly guide for the school principals. However, the evidence to date shows that a contract can never cover every situation that might arise, which again highlights the difficulty of using a commercial contract to operate a school.

Given this experience, it is incredible that the Department has requested the private company and local school management to again use the 'self-monitoring' system in the new bundles of PPP schools. Rather than trying to monitor every aspect of the contract, the emphasis is to be on developing the relationship between the company and the school and 'as long as there isn't major issues' the DOES 'won't go racing to the contract' (DOES, 2007).

Given the evidence outlined above, there is a fundamental problem in the contracting out of such responsibilities to 'for-profit' commercial private companies. The company in the PPP schools appeared to have undertaken the tasks set out in the contract at a level that required the minimum cost, even if that meant the service was substandard. This finding has considerable implications for the continued application of PPPs in public infrastructure maintenance contracts as it highlights major difficulties that can arise.

'Third-Party' use of schools

Each of the five schools has an annual allocation of 350 hours of access to the school, outside of normal school hours, which can be utilised for either school usage or made available for community use with the schools keeping any income earned. Furthermore, the PPP company is contractually required to source other 'Third Party' use of the schools outside these hours. Aside from the 350–hour allocation and the normal school day, the school is therefore, effectively, a private building. This has impacted on the schools in a number of important ways. Considerable concern was expressed about this by principals in four of the schools. Their experience was that because the PPP allocates the responsibility for the majority of out-of-hours use of the school facilities (namely PE halls, gym, soccer pitches, classrooms etc.) to the private company, there was a reduction and restriction in the control and use of the schools for important school and community events, such as parent–teacher meetings and public meetings on topics of importance to the wider community.

For example, one school had an issue with obtaining an allocated time on a weekend from the company to allow it carry out Assessment Tests for the incoming first year students. The private company stated that the hours on a Saturday or Sunday were equivalent to double time out of the school's yearly hour allocation, which impacted on the ability of the school to carry out some after school activities.

This focus of the private company on making money from 'third-party' out-of-hours use of the schools meant, in some instances, that the parent–teacher meetings had to finish at the exact time scheduled by the company, as the hall had been rented out from that time onwards. Such meetings generally require flexibility around the length of time they take, because parents often run late or discussions need to take time. No such flexibility is permitted in this model. In one school, the private operator used the sports hall most nights from six to ten in the evening.

Principals expressed their disappointment that the schools were not being used by the community as much as was the case in the old schools. A significant factor in this was the high rent the company charged. The perception amongst the local community was that it was now a 'privately controlled' school rather than a community school. This was accentuated by the necessity for the community to formally contact the company, through the 'faceless' helpdesk, in order to get access to the school. This was unlike the situation in the old school where a community group could arrange it directly with the principal with whom they were familiar.

In one school, the basketball and athletics clubs had used the gymnasium in the old school facility, and they naturally encouraged local children to enroll in the school. The gym was adequate and had wide community usage on a grace and favour basis. The school's Board of Management decided that the principal could make decisions on what basis to give out the use of the gym. However, with the PPP, the private company increased charges and local volunteer-run clubs could not afford to use it, and the school started to lose children to other schools as a result.

The principals believed that the schools, which are some of the finest facilities in the areas, should be at the centre of the community. But despite some of the local areas being bereft of such facilities, the schools felt they could not encourage the use of their facilities because the schools effectively belonged to the private company. It is now no longer a community facility, but a commercial facility. As one principal explained:

> We wanted to start up a basketball club in the school but the hall is too expensive to hire. This is not a wealthy community. It's not commercially viable for the operator to open the school without an income, therefore a lot of the time we have an underutilised resource. It's purely commercial now. Traditionally, it was a vocational school. This has had an impact on the community. It is not serving the community in the way a community school should ... It should provide for the community, not just from 9 a.m. to 4 p.m. We do have to be careful with our given allotment of 350 hours. It's easy to eat into them. I'd love to give it to smaller organisations, such as playgroups, to use. I'd love to see it used more and I wouldn't charge as much.

The C & AG (2008) Audit supported this evidence noting 'the low level of usage of the schools by the community', while in a similar description the Whole School Evaluation Report stated that, 'the lack of full control over school resources has, in a number of practical ways, remained a challenge for the management of the school. With restricted access to the school in the evening time, it has become more difficult for the school to make its facilities available to the local community, something which has been a significant cause of concern' (DOES, 2006b, Section 1.4).

The Public Accounts Committee (2006) also expressed concern that the renting out of the schools had turned the schools into a commercial enterprise. It noted that there was unease generally about the commercial use of schools, particularly given the fact that schools were considered to be an integral part of a community. It criticised the PPP because it involved a disengagement from the relationship with the wider community, and recommended that clear guidelines be established on the use of schools by community groups outside of regular school hours.

Clearly then, even from a commercial perspective, the results of the third-party usage was poor. The expectations regarding the renting out of school buildings, sports facilities, gyms and so on had not been realised.

Overall, these incidences demonstrate that having a school privately operated and maintained was not ensuring that the community had maximum use from it. It also highlighted the impact of the conflict between a private operator's need to make a profit and a school's primary role in the provision of a public service to the local community.

Vending machines

Another income-generating facility for the private company is the vending machines that are installed in each of the schools and from which children can buy sweets, drinks and snacks. On completion of the schools, there was immediate concern on the part of principals, teachers and parents in relation to the use and quantity of vending machines installed by the private consortium in the schools. The unease arose from a general concern about healthy eating and particularly the consumption of sweets and sugary drinks by children, which has been linked with the trend toward obesity in children in Ireland and across the developed world.

In the PPP schools, the contract gave the private company full control over the vending machines, their location and their food and drink content. In one school, for example, there were two vending machines directly outside the door of the PE hall. The schools asked the private company about having healthy food the machines and some of the schools asked if it could get rid of the vending machines completely. They argued that the machines ran counter to what a school should be about, that is healthy eating and living, and that they indeed contradicted what the schools themselves were teaching in terms of encouraging children toward a healthy eating lifestyle.

The schools were also concerned about the impact of the commercial advertising of these unhealthy products in the schools, as the outsides of the vending machines were emblazoned with Coca Cola advertising. The situation was only changed when the schools agreed to pay the private company compensation to remove the vending machines – because it was a change in the terms of the contract agreed between the Department and the company. This also demonstrated that the reason the machines were not removed earlier by the company was because of their commercial value in providing an income. The Department did acknowledge the extent to which the vending machines ran contrary to the ethos of the schools and, as a result, in the second bundle of school PPPs, vending machines have been left out of the contracts completely and they will be the responsibility of the school's Boards of Management.

Private operator employee conditions

Trade unions have expressed concerns in relation to the conditions of employees, including both those being transferred from the public sector to the PPP companies or those newly employed by the company. The evidence from the interviews with the ancillary staff (caretakers, cleaners and canteen workers and some administrative staff) employed by the original private PPP company demonstrated that significant issues had arisen. For example, the company refused to give wage increases that the workers were due under National Wage Agreements, refused to transfer pension contributions and also gave significantly increased workloads to employees.

In 2005, the private company operating the schools at the time employed sixty-four staff of which twenty-three had transferred from being employed either by the Department of Education and Science or Voluntary Education Committees (VECs). In the transfer from their former employers to the private company, the terms and conditions of the employees were to remain the same under TUPE regulations.[4] However, the conditions for some staff worsened after transfer. In 2004, the company informed its employees who had transferred from public service that it would only pay benchmarking (annual increases due to employees under the National Wage Agreements that would automatically be paid in the public service) once the employees accepted the revised conditions. The revised conditions for the caretakers and cleaners included changed starting times, moving from fortnightly to monthly pay, revised payments for emergency call outs, changes to annual and sick leave accrual and a reduction in availability of overtime, which had been a vital source of income to the workers in the pre-PPP schools. The change to monthly pay meant considerable hardship, as family budgets and personal needs were geared towards receiving pay on a fortnightly basis. The cleaners also stated that they used to work for the entire year in the old school, but now they were laid-off for the period of school holidays, with a resultant reduction in pay, along with the stigma of having to go to the social welfare office to receive income supplement.

The cleaners joined the trade union, SIPTU, for support in their claim to retain the pay and conditions that had been promised to them prior to transfer. There were also issues with workers being told they were no longer entitled to the state (public-sector) pension and the transfer of the staffs' pensions from their former employers to the private company did not take place properly. This problem arose because there is no legislation relating to the transfer of public service pension schemes to a private operator under TUPE guidelines. One caretaker explained the impact of these changes generally:

> It's now all about profit. It's ok for managers and the business. They'll get top money, but people like us on the ground get nothing. We were better employed in the Department of Education. We were promised that, if anything, everything would improve when we transferred, and not get worse like it has.

In June 2004, SIPTU made a claim to the original private company for the payment of benchmarking wage increases on behalf of caretakers and cleaners in three of the PPP schools. The dispute was not resolved at a local level and became the subject of a conciliation conference under the auspices of the Labour Relations Commission. At a Labour Court hearing in August 2005, the private company accepted that it gave a commitment in 2002 to honour any agreements on terms and conditions, including pay that had been in place prior to it employing the staff, but only for those employees who transferred out of the public service (Labour Court, 2005).

The Labour Court then ruled in December 2005 that the cleaners be paid the benchmarking and be allowed, in the circumstances, to remain on fortnightly pay. This shows the importance of union representation for these vulnerable workers: 'if we didn't have the union to fight for benchmarking, we wouldn't have got it' (Cleaner, interview, 2006). The impact of union membership was demonstrated by the experiences of the cleaners who were non-unionised in one of the other PPP schools. They were forced to accept the monthly pay system as part of the benchmarking increases. Furthermore, a canteen worker in that school would only be interviewed out of 'ear shot' of her manager. She explained she was nervous of being interviewed for fear of being reprimanded. She explained that they were not unionised, that they had received a wage review annually but their wages had been frozen since the private company had been reportedly in financial difficulty. She explained that she had worked in the old school, but the conditions in the new school were worse and the wages lower:

> I don't get a proper break. I used to get paid for my break, but now I don't at all. I was out sick and then when I came back I was informed my hours were cut. I'm in for six and a half hours, but I only get paid for six hours ... All the staff should be on the same standards – but they're not. The new ones are worse off than those of us coming down from the VEC. If you're working for the government, you should be paid a government wage.

It was evident from the interviews that a two-tier workforce had developed as new staff were brought in on lower wages. For example, a cleaner in one school who had been newly employed by the private company, claimed that she was discriminated against in that she did not receive the benchmarking increase and was on €1 less per hour than the existing cleaners.

Furthermore, in the new PPP schools the conditions of work were more difficult as they did not have the same quality and quantity of cleaning materials. In one school, they were only allowed access to a limited amount of cleaning detergent. In another, the vacuum cleaners were broken and just patched up with tape. The cleaners had to wait for them to completely stop functioning before they were replaced by the company, and, as a result, they could not clean the carpets as well as they should have been. This was not hygienic for the children and staff.

The workers explained that they used to feel that their jobs were secure as they were in employment within the public sector, but after transferring to the private company they felt much greater insecurity about this. In particular, they were fearful of being replaced by staff that would accept lower wages. As a result, they advised other workers against transferring from the public sector.

It is clear that unless there is legislation for each item to cover the transfer of employees from public to private operators, such significant problems will arise repeatedly in these situations. A reasonable question posed by one of the workers was about how fair it was that employees are negatively impacted by a decision by the state, that they had no input into, to change its method of procurement.

This reflects a trend in privatisation, where the private operator saves money by increasing the workload of employees and reducing wages. It will be important to examine the treatment of employees in the second bundle of PPP schools to ascertain if this trend continues (Whitfield, 2001). This is particularly critical because the facilities management aspect of the contract will be undertaken by Sodexho, a French Multinational Corporation, about which concerns have been raised about the quality of service provision and treatment of employees (CUPE, 2007).

It is also very noteworthy that the employees of the private company felt that the company's main priority was commercial gain and not the smooth running of a public school. This has serious ramifications beyond the immediate conditions of the ancillary staff and, again, brings into question the suitability of a commercial company being centrally responsible for the management of a public school building and its associated facilities.

Privatisation and neoliberalism in the schools

A significant body of evidence has been presented to support the contention that the use of PPPs in the five schools entailed some of the negative aspects associated with the international experiences of privatisation and neoliberal policies in public services. This includes the introduction of commercial, 'for-profit' values into the Grouped Schools through, for example, the hiring out of schools and a resultant reduction in community use, for-profit canteens and the installation of vending machines, as well as the significant role that the private company has in the control, maintenance and management of the schools. Furthermore, the theory that the private sector is more efficient than the public sector, which underlay the introduction and use of PPPs, was demonstrated in some instances in the Grouped Schools Pilot PPP Project to not materialise in practice. The following sections present further analysis of how the PPP model facilitated the neoliberalisation of the provision of public schools in the Grouped Schools Pilot PPP Project.

Commercial ethos

The introduction of a private company into the school environment led to a conflict between two distinct sets of values, or motivations. The school's primary motivation is educational while the private company views their involvement in the schools as a business and, thus, is primarily driven by the desire to make a return for their shareholders and therefore has commercial or profit motivations and values. The schools felt that, in the initial stages, the private company did not understand how schools operate as it is a very different system from a commercial entity.

The problem centred around schools being generally non-profit oriented, and, as a result, the staff engage in many supportive activities on a voluntary basis, for example trying to fix problems that arise even if they occur out of school hours, supervising activities in their own time, such as sports and discos etc. In contrast, the school principals and other staff believed that the private company viewed all interactions from a profit-maximising perspective.

In summary, it could be argued that the private-sector logic of profit maximisation led the private company in the Grouped Schools Pilot PPP Project to adopt a strategy that reduced spending on facility management services, reduced staff salaries and benefits, charged higher than normal amounts for any extra maintenance and introduced user fees for 'third-party' use of the schools, so that it could then increase its rate of return. Employees experienced an intensification of these pressures when the original private company went into financial difficulties from 2004 onwards.

New market for capital

PPPs created new markets for private investor capital evidenced from the number of large, international, private companies involved in their provision and management. They included construction companies (for example Ascon), international banks (for example Barclays), accountants and advisors (Farrell Grant Sparks) and international operators (Jarvis Plc and Hochtief). The increasingly important role being given to the private sector in the delivery and planning of public education services and infrastructure was also demonstrated at the Second Annual Irish PPP Forum in 2006, where the panel presenting updates on PPPs in the Education Sector was chaired by Michael Flynn, the Director of private accountancy and financial advice company Deloitte. The panel also included the President of Cork Institute of Technology, the head of Infrastructure Origination in the Bank of Scotland and a Senior Partner in Farrell Grant Sparks.

The importance of the Irish schools PPP market as a business opportunity was further evidenced by the delegates at the Annual PPP Forums, which included companies involved with education PPPs in Ireland and Europe such as Equion (financial investment company), SMIF (Secondary Market Infrastructural Funds), Barclays bank, and Inisfree ltd (which owned, at the time, over 300 schools and hospitals in the UK and was the biggest owner of schools and hospitals outside the UK government).

A key aspect of neoliberalism, the conversion of public services and assets into commodities that can be traded between private companies on international markets, was evident in the re-financing and sale of equity by Jarvis Plc in the Irish PPP schools. This occurred through a complex process of contract sale and transfer. The Special Purpose Vehicle (SPV) in the Grouped Schools Pilot PPP Project, the Schools Public Private Partnership (Ireland) Ltd, involved Jarvis Plc and Barclays Private Equity. In 2006, Jarvis plc sold 50 per cent of its equity in the Grouped Schools Pilot PPP Project to SMIF (Secondary Market Infrastructural Funds) and 50 per cent to Barclays Bank. Such 'secondary market' investors in PPP projects have been criticised in the UK for 'sweating' public assets. This takes place where the private company that purchases the PPP contract receives a fixed income from the government. Efficiencies and, therefore, cost savings, are increased by making the employees or the service do more for less investment.

Early evidence of 'sweating' in the schools PPP project was visible in the reduction in employee conditions and reduced spending on maintenance. There clearly is potential for further 'sweating' when the project is re-financed. Jarvis sold the facilities management contract to Hochtief Ltd. Therefore, Hochtief is now a joint partner in the SPV with Barclays Private Equity in relation to the operation of the five schools. This, again, highlights the circumstance that arose in relation to the Criminal Courts of Justice project that PPP contracts can be agreed with one private consortium, while a completely different company may, in a relatively short time, end up being the private operator. There is also inadequate accountability of the service provider as, due to commercial confidentiality clauses and the lack of open reporting mechanisms by commercial entities, it is not clear which company is the private operator. The Department, however, was not concerned about these arrangements because, in its view, the equity provider (the bank) would ensure that, regardless of what private operator was in place, a high-quality service would be provided in order to guarantee the continued receipt of annual payments from the state.

Intensifying neoliberalism

The private sector was seeking further implementation of commercial aspects within PPP schools such as linking the performance management targets to, for example, the level of funding available for an individual school or introducing competition between schools for government funding.

The manner in which the Department developed the second bundle of PPP schools indicates that it was adopting such an intensified neoliberal model of school delivery where the commercial aspects will impact on core welfare state services such as teaching and school governance. For example, the second bundle is more closely modelled on the UK-based Building Schools for the Future Programme, which includes Local Education Partnership structures of school governance that bring the private sector directly into school delivery and management. The Local Education Partnership is a PPP that provides schools and is 80 per cent controlled by the private sector with a local authority and Partnership for Schools (a new Department for Education and Skills body) each with a 10 per cent stake. The Local Education Partnership not only delivers facilities management, but also provides other services such as educational support, school transport and introduces market-oriented performance measurements in teaching and education standards. For example, in some of the Local Education Partnership schools part of the private operator's fee is based on measurable improvements in exam results (UK Department for Education and Skills, 2007; Whitfield, 2006).

This model has been criticised by teacher unions for extending private-sector control and involvement in the management of schools and provision of teaching (Whitfield, 2006). The Irish DOES has suggested that this structure could be introduced in Ireland and it would facilitate the creation of larger PPP projects with a greater number of schools, which could further advance the development of the PPP school programme.

PPP inflexibility
PPPs are generally a very inflexible model of provision of public services due to the length of time of the initial contract and the considerable time needed to change any contract specifications, as well as the expense involved. While it is possible to build in opportunities to change service requirements within a contract, this is only cost effective to the public sector when the changes are reasonably predictable, as unpredictable changes are considered high risk and therefore charged at an expensive rate by private-sector partners. Changes to the contract requirements during the operation of the schools can therefore be very expensive as the PPP contractor is in a strong position in negotiations over contractual changes (Deloitte, 2006). The public sector then faces the option of paying a very high price for changing the contract specifications or else retaining a contract that fails to meet its needs.

This has serious implications for PPPs in the schools sector as school buildings and facilities cannot be divorced from the educational activity that takes place within them and there are constant changes required to improve education standards. For example, the Irish government's school building programme is continually adapting to meet new and emerging curricular needs and requirements under new legislation such as recent provisions for special education needs. It is likely during the duration of the twenty-five and thirty year PPP schools' contracts that there will be further legislation and other shifts in educational policies that may affect how the buildings are used and what is required of them. However, the Irish state could face considerable costs if it tries to apply these changes, if they are outside the contract stipulations. This was evident from a number of instances in the Grouped Schools Pilot PPP Project where the schools faced paying significant costs to the private company for changes in the electricity systems, replacing equipment and, as noted earlier, had to pay compensation to the company in order to get the vending machines removed from the schools.

The decision to transfer aspects of responsibility of the operation of schools to the private sector cannot, therefore, easily be reversed even if significant changes are required or major issues arise. Indeed, the Audit Commission of Scotland (2002) recommended that state education providers are best placed to deal with such changes as the state will continue to be responsible for the core education service and will retain control over key areas such as setting education policies and determining enrolment and catchment area policies. Therefore, they should retain control over these aspects as they are better placed than private companies to plan for, and mitigate, the impact of any significant fall in demand or changing requirement for school services.

Conclusion

According to the Department its objectives relating to the Grouped Schools Pilot PPP Project were achieved and five excellent schools were delivered 'on-time' and at the agreed contract price. PPPs, according to the Minister for Education and Science Mary Coughlan, are an innovative way of delivering quality facilities: 'The PPP model allows the schools' management and staff to concentrate on their core educational duties and it is a particularly attractive feature of the process' (Minister for Education, 2010).

However, the evidence outlined in this chapter from the case-study research contradicts this. It has revealed a previously un-reported level of concern on the part of principals and teachers in the five PPP schools relating to a number of aspects of the project. In the first instance, concerns were raised in relation to the value for money of the schools as significant extra costs emerged for the schools in the operational phase. This is very note-worthy, as it was the principal reason for the introduction and use of PPPs.

Furthermore, the most significant finding of the C & AG (2004) report was that the PPP model was more expensive than the conventional model because of extra costs that are central to the PPP form of procurement. Further adding to the cost of the PPP model were the costs of private finance which was more expensive than Exchequer-borrowed finance and the additional cost of private-sector profit. The requirement of the private company, as is normal for a private business with shareholders and equity investors, to maximise its returns led to attempts to implement opportunities for income generation and cost reduction in certain circumstances, even if they appeared to result in reduced service quality or a compromising of the public-sector education ethos. This also led to a commercialisation of the schools with a resultant loss of the school management's and, therefore, public-sector control over the schools and, very significantly, a reduction in community use of the schools. The original private company appeared to avoid the transfer of key risks on to itself and instead leaving them to be the responsibility of the schools. This was evident from the fact that, in the first instance, there was evidence that the company provided cheaper and consequently a poorer quality of materials in building and equipment, which could be very expensive for the school and the Department in the long term. Secondly, the company did not accept responsibility for instances where operational risk materialised such as serious maintenance issues and, in fact, passed the cost back to the schools. This proves that certain risks were not transferred successfully to the private company. Furthermore, the significant financial penalties that were included as part of the contract for the event that the private operator did not deliver on its service obligations were not used.

This demonstrated that while PPP theory states that risk is passed over to the private sector by ensuring it is incentivised to manage that risk efficiently, the application of the incentivisation scheme (through the penalty mechanism) did not take place in the PPP schools. The private operator could therefore maximise its annual return of approximately 13.7 per cent.

Optimum risk transfer also only takes place when the partner to which the risk is transferred, in this case the private company, has greater expertise in managing that risk. However, there was substantial evidence that the original private company did not have greater expertise in managing design, fit out and maintenance risks. The lack of knowledge and expertise in relation to educational needs on the part of the private company was evident from the poor school design which led to acoustics, lighting, stage and class room layout problems, and maintenance and management problems (Table 4.1). In addition, the reduction in workload and responsibility for school principals did not occur to the extent to which the Department had hoped it would as the private operator was not as efficient in managing and maintaining the schools as had been expected. The PPP did not prove conclusively to be providing a high quality service and in some instances it appeared to provide a poorer service than direct public provision.

This suggests that the cost of transferring the risk of maintenance and operation of schools to the private consortium should have been ascribed a higher cost than it was in negotiations with the bidders. This would have increased the cost of the PPP method within the PSB undertaken by the Department and would have added to the evidence that the conventional approach was more cost effective. It can therefore be asserted that, given the Department's long history in building and managing schools, it would clearly have been both cheaper and would have provided for better quality if the schools had been provided in the conventional manner, albeit with a considerable increase in capitation funding to ensure the highest possible quality service was achieved.

Following the takeover of the schools contract by the current PPP company (Hochtief) in July 2006 a number of changes have been made by the Department and the company in response to the problems outlined in this chapter. This includes a member of the Department's technical and professional staff visiting each school on a quarterly basis to gather feedback on the operation of the school building. The Department also agreed to recommence the Liaison Committee meetings to deal with other issues from September 2007 (C & AG, 2008).

Despite its statements to the contrary, the Department also acknowledged the substantial problems that arose in the Pilot project by providing a number of improvements to the contracts for the second bundle of PPP schools. These include ensuring a greater involvement of school principals from the outset of the PPP process, starting at preferred bidder stage. There is also an increased level of monitoring by the National Development Finance Agency (NDFA) of the construction and 'fit out' phase. As referred to earlier, a 'user-friendly' version of the contract will be provided by the PPP company to the schools and to the Department. Based on the experience gained from the Pilot Schools, all future projects of this kind will be standardised and the same area norms and IT provision will apply to all schools regardless of the method of procurement.

The drive to further develop PPPs in the education sector was evident in the rapid pace of procurement and development of the additional PPP bundles. For example, by February 2009 the third bundle, which includes eight schools, was at the pre-procurement stage and outline planning applications were submitted to the relevant local authority. It was expected that the schools would be delivered by 2013. In June 2010 it was announced by the Minister for Education and Science, Mary Coughlan TD, that the NDFA had signed the contract with Macquarie Partnerships for the second bundle which will provide six schools with places for 4,700 pupils. They are also DBFM PPP contracts for twenty-five years of duration. The schools include the first PPP primary school, Gaelscoil Bheanntraí, Co. Cork, which will provide 200 pupil places. The other five include Bantry Community College, Co. Cork, which will provide 700 pupil places, Kildare Town Community School, providing 1000 pupil places, Abbeyfeale Community College, Co. Limerick, providing 850 pupil places, Wicklow Town Community College providing 1,000 pupil places and Athboy Community School, Co. Meath, to provide 950 pupil places. The schools are to be constructed by Pierse Contracting and John Sisk & Son Ltd. The construction period will be approximately eighteen months, during which time it is expected that in excess of 1,000 construction workers will be employed across the project sites. The Minister promised the public:

> That staff and students in all six schools can look forward to using the most up-to-date designs and facilities ... In each location the new school will ensure the students in those centres will be able to access a broad subject range ... The principle of 'everything works' applies under the PPP process – classrooms, laboratories, specialist equipment, heating and lighting all have to be available every day ... The six new schools will be available by the end of 2011. (Minister for Education, press release, June 2010)

It will be important that research is undertaken to ascertain whether or not the cautionary lessons from the Pilot projects are applied successfully and if the Minister's promises become a reality.

These bundles form a considerable part of the €540 million that was included in the *National Development Plan, 2007–2013* for first and second-level school modernisation through PPPs which equated to 11 per cent of the total planned investment in this area. €595 million was also planned to be invested through PPPs at third-level institutions. This highlights the progression of PPPs in the schools sector and indicates the important role that PPPs will play in the future of Irish education. It also demonstrated that the Department is one of the leading Departments in the delivery of infrastructural projects under the government's PPP Programme.

From their origins, the Irish school PPP model was influenced heavily by the UK school PPP model. As detailed earlier in this chapter, it appears that the Irish government and the Department is aiming towards a situation where PPP occupies, just as in the UK, a very important role within public school provision and management. This would have very significant consequences for the Irish public education system if the experiences of the Pilot project were to be replicated in further PPPs developed.

In Ireland, as noted previously, school provision has historically been paid for by the state but delivered in many instances by not-for profit (private) religious and voluntary institutions. Rather than seeing the decline of the role of these institutions as an opportunity to develop a dedicated system for the public provision and management of schools, with the higher quality and more equitable outcome that this would entail, the Irish government is instead following a policy trajectory, evidenced through PPPs, in line with neoliberalism. The changes through PPP are clearly a form of privatisation, contrary to the claims of the government. These changes are not happening all at once, as the government is anxious to avoid the confrontations which have taken place between public-sector workers, parents and private companies in other countries (Monbiot, 2000). But nonetheless, the general process of the *neoliberalisation* of the school infrastructure in Ireland has been introduced through PPPs. The Grouped Schools Pilot PPP Project and the proceeding bundles of PPP schools involve a transfer of a very substantial level of responsibility for the maintenance, management and control of school buildings and ancillary staff from the state and not-for profit private sector to the for-profit private sector. This can be described as nothing other than a process of privatisation.

In light of the evidence outlined in this chapter, Irish government plans to expand PPP use for the delivery and maintenance of publicly funded schools should be questioned. Rather, the positive experiences gained from the Pilot Grouped Schools Pilot PPP Project, such as the 15 per cent increase in space and extra IT facilities, should be applied to all new traditionally funded schools.

Notes

1 Hereafter referred to as the 'Department' in this chapter.
2 Stakeholders in the project include employees and their trade unions, local community groups, public representatives, interest groups and the public at large.
3 One is in Tullamore and one in Raheen in County Laois.
4 The Transfer of Undertakings Protection of Employment Regulation (TUPE) is based on an EU Directive 2001/23 and involves protection for the rights of employees on the transfer of employer (ICTU, 2005).

5

Spinning the wheel: the regeneration of Dublin's inner-city estates through Public Private Partnerships

> Dublin City Council are not addressing either how we are living or the anti-social problems. When they are offering tenants a way out, the residents are running out. There is no upkeep or maintenance being put into the flats. Dublin City Council are basically running the flats down ... bit by bit they are breaking the community and the community spirit is broken ... The lights keep getting smashed on our landing and hall and the electrician doesn't come out for days, so you can't see in front of you walking in your hallway. I am intimidated and I have family as back up in the flats, but people in their eighties, how do they feel about what's going on when they have no family left? It's because the Council want people out. (Charlemont Street resident, interview, 2007)

Estate profiles and emergence of regeneration

DCC has approximately 25,000 social rented dwellings of which approximately 16,000 are in the form of flats in large complexes in the inner city (Norris, 2005). As explained in the introductory chapter, most of these flats complexes were built in the 1950s, 1960s and 1970s to provide new housing to those living in inner-city tenements. The residents moving in to them were thrilled with their new homes, which were considered luxurious, with a separate toilet and bathroom, and very spacious. After two or three decades of stability, the building of strong communities and relatively good conditions, the estates deteriorated rapidly in the 1980s and 1990s due to rising rates of unemployment, the resulting poverty and the heroin epidemic. The physical conditions also 'dis'-improved due to inadequate maintenance and upkeep of the estates, while housing allocation practices that transferred tenants most affected by social issues off the waiting lists into the estates added to the instability and high levels of social issues (Drudy and Punch, 2005; Redmond and Russell, 2008).

These factors, combined with offers of the 'surrender' grant, led many residents, often those with employment, to relocate off the estates, leaving concentrations of the more vulnerable and lower-income residents behind. Refurbishment schemes in the late 1980s and 1990s failed to have a significant impact on the considerable physical problems of the flats and the deep-rooted social and economic inequality, while the drugs crisis ravaged the estates.

This chapter investigates the experiences of ten flats complexes, with a total of 2,469 units that were designated for PPP regeneration by DCC (Table 5.1). There is a particular focus on the experience of the St Michael's, Fatima Mansions, Dolphin House and O'Devaney Gardens projects, as they provided the majority of evidence for the research that underpins the detailed analysis presented.

Fatima Mansions is located in Dublin's south-west inner city, at the back of St James' Hospital, and is the oldest of the estates, being built in 1949 with 394 flats. Across the road from Fatima Mansions, located on the banks of the Grand Canal, is the largest of the studied estates, the Dolphin House complex, which was built in 1956, and sits on 18.5 acres and comprises 436 units. Heading towards the city centre, off Cork Street, just a fifteen-minute walk from Dolphin House, is St Theresa's Gardens, which was also built in the 1950s, with 346 units. Just five minutes walk towards the city centre along Cork Street is the smaller, sixty-unit, Chamber Street complex. The Bridgefoot Street flats with 143 units is also nearby, located off Thomas Street, very close to the famous Guinness Brewery. Continuing along the Grand Canal in an eastward direction from Dolphin House, along the South Circular road, just off Harcourt Street in the city's salubrious office district and close to the famous city-centre park of St Stephen's Green is the smaller estate of Charlemont Street. It was built also in the 1950s, with 181 units.

Heading then westward along the Grand Canal out of the city leads to St Michael's Estate in Inchicore, one of the newest of the estates, built in the 1970s with 346 units. Across the River Liffey on the city's north side lies the O'Devaney Gardens complex with 278 units, also built in the 1950s, and located near Phoenix Park off the North Circular Road. Then, there is Dominick Street, built in the 1960s, on Parnell Street in the heart of Dublin's north inner-city shopping district with 198 units, and, finally, the smallest of the estates, Croke Villas, built also in the 1960s with eighty-seven units and sitting in the shadow of the famous stadium of Irish Gaelic Games, Croke Park.

There are basic design problems with the flats complexes that have meant they are not suitable for many aspects of modern living. For example, they are smaller than the local authority guideline size (introduced by the Department of the Environment in 2007), and many of the kitchens are tiny and the sitting rooms are not big enough for a dinner table. They have inadequate community facilities, insufficient parking spaces, accessibility problems (there being no elevators or fire escapes in any of the estates), no private open space, such as balconies or gardens and they tend to be isolated from

Table 5.1 Case study – local authority estates in Dublin's inner city

Estate	Year built	Location	No. of original units
South city			
Dolphin House	1956	South Circular Road, Royal Canal, Dublin 8	436
Fatima Mansions	1949	South-west Inner City, Dublin 8	394(1986) 270(2000)
St Michael's Estate	1970s	Inchicore, Dublin 8	346
St Theresa's Gardens	1952	Cork St, Dublin 8	346
Charlemont St	1959	Harcourt St, Dublin 2	181
Bridgefoot St	1964	Guiness Brewery, Dublin 8	143
Chamber St/ Weaver Court	NA	Cork St, Dublin 8	60
North city			
O'Devaney Gardens	Late 1950s	North Circular Road, Dublin 7	278
Dominick St	1961/70	Parnell St, Dublin 1	198
Croke Villas	1961	Croke Park, Dublin 3	87

surrounding neighbourhoods. In Dolphin House, the play and community facilities include a playground area with broken swings and a burnt out see-saw, a football pitch that is unplayable as it covered in broken glass and a community centre in a temporary portacabin structure. Most of the estates have only one drive-in entrance leading to an 'island' effect. The sewerage and drainage systems in some of the complexes also experience considerable problems, causing overflows and foul odours.

The open plan design of the estates is a significant contributory factor to an increase in persistent anti-social behaviour,[1] such as drug dealing (Sheridan Woods, 2008), which has also been exacerbated by the inadequate responses of the Gardai and DCC. A resident of the newly regenerated Fatima Mansions explained why significant change was necessary:

> The residents wanted new housing and better conditions; they were living in terrible conditions, with damp in their flats, poor maintenance and there was a lot of anti-social behaviour in one place within the complex. They wanted a better way of life.

These communities suffered for decades as a result of the high levels of inequality in Irish society. Even during the economic boom, they continued to suffer from high unemployment, dependency on social welfare, lone parent poverty, child and elderly poverty and high rates of school drop-out and very low rates of third-level education (Bissett, 2009; Sheridan Woods, 2009). The concentration of large numbers of vulnerable individuals and families with alcohol and drug addiction problems on some of the estates also made it difficult to address these problems. For example, in St Theresa's Gardens, it was estimated in 2006 that in excess of 80 per cent of the working-age population depended on social welfare as their primary source of income, 72 per cent of the overall population was at or below the age of 35 and less than 0.5 per cent of the population was in third-level education, compared to a third-level progression rate of over 80 per cent in wealthier areas of Dublin (Nurture, 2007). Similarly, Dolphin House had a very high economic dependency ratio of 48 per cent in 2007, with a very high proportion of residents in receipt of social welfare income and a similar lack of achievement of third-level education, with only one person between the ages of eighteen and twenty-two years in full-time education in 2006.

As a result of these factors, the demand for regeneration from communities has increased over the last decade. Surveys in Dolphin House (2008) and St Theresa's Gardens (2007) indicated that a majority of residents on the estates desired complete demolition and regeneration:

> We need regeneration badly. There are the dreadful repairs, dreadful maintenance and dreadful anti-social behaviour regarding drugs, and the sewage is crawling out of the flats – it's reaching the second and third floors. There is a lot of structural poverty around here. (Dolphin House resident, interview, 2008)

In a similar manner, the residents of the Charlemont Street estate explained their urgent need for a new start:

> We are one of the twenty-five most deprived areas in the country. We want it knocked down. We want our kids to be able to bring their friends from school here, to have somewhere decent to live. That's what's happening now with the regeneration ... so we are not coming up the stairwells and there is beer cans and shit and urination everywhere. (Charlemont Street resident, interview, 2008)

However, the Celtic Tiger did not leave these areas untouched. The value of the land where the estates were located escalated considerably from 1996 onwards, as a result of the general rising value of land in Dublin's inner city. These were high-value locations close to inner-city employment opportunities, on good transport systems, including the LUAS light rail (the line runs close to Fatima Mansions, Dolphin House, Charlemount Street and St Michael's Estate) and office and shopping districts (Charlemont Street and

Dominick Street). The development potential of the sites attracted the interest of those who were amassing wealth and power during this era: developers, banking financiers and the central government and its DCC colleagues.

PPPs were implemented as a way of realising this land value for private developers and the government through radical 'regeneration' plans involving complete demolition of the flats complexes and the building of new public, private and affordable housing along with community facilities. This chapter provides an analysis of the outcomes of these partnership regeneration projects, with a particular focus on the experiences of the residents living on the estates. Their accounts reveal the harsh underbelly of the free-market philosophy of the Celtic Tiger period. The government and developers turned up at their doors, not to offer support, but to take the land upon which their homes were situated, which had become some of the most valuable real estate in Europe.

Irish social housing and regeneration policy

The Department of the Environment is the central government department in Ireland that is responsible for setting policy and law in relation to social housing provision and the standards for housing conditions. Local government housing authorities, such as DCC, and voluntary housing associations, such as Respond, are then delegated, under the various housing acts, the day-to-day responsibility for the provision and maintenance of social housing. The *National Development Plan, 2007– 2013* explains that government housing policy is underpinned by the position that, 'good quality housing is fundamental to the social and economic development of the country and the economic well being of its people. As an important component of national infrastructure, housing is central to social development, competitiveness and ultimately economic growth' (Government of Ireland, 2007, 12).

Indeed the social housing sector is identified as one of the key 'social protection' areas of capital investment in the Plan. The provision of accessible and affordable housing is a key policy objective in addressing poverty and social exclusion (Combat Poverty Agency, 2002). The government's Housing Policy Framework (DOEHLG, 2005) aims to build sustainable communities that are 'places where people want to live and work, now and in the future. They meet the diverse needs of existing and future residents, are sensitive to their environment, and contribute to a high quality of life. They are safe and inclusive, well-planned, built and run, offer equality of opportunity and good services for all.' In relation to social housing, the framework noted that 'it is not acceptable that the social housing domain should be compared unfavourably with private housing development' and in order to make a reality of better social housing, the government promised, among other actions, to ensure that the management and maintenance of social housing estates are prioritised, rolling out a programme of regeneration for all run-down estates nationwide and a programme of other remedial works to improve local authority housing (DOEHLG, 2005).

However, alongside this stated support for the development, promotion and regeneration of social housing was the practice of moving away from direct state-led provision towards support for the private housing market.

An example of private market intervention was the increasing use of income support to assist tenants in the private rented sector through the supplementary welfare allowance (Drudy and Punch, 2005). Furthermore, in December 2002 the government amended Part V of the Planning and Development Act 2001, which had required, as a condition for planning permission, private developers to transfer up to 20 per cent of their sites to local authorities for the provision of both social and affordable housing. The Act was amended, due to lobbying by developers, to allow local authorities to opt out of enforcing the on-site 20 per cent rule and instead allow approval of Part V status if the developer gave the local authority land elsewhere or the financial equivalent of the value of the land transfer. Many local authorities have used the Amendment to opt out of enforcing the 20 per cent social housing rule and, therefore, Part V has had a minimal impact in providing social housing (Kelly and MacLaran, 2004).

In line with this policy trajectory, the government began to promote PPPs as the mechanism to achieve its policy of regenerating social housing estates. These involve private developers taking a central role in the delivery of the projects. In 2001, as detailed in Chapter 1, the Department of the Environment issued an instruction to DCC to pursue the proposals it had for regenerating a number of inner-city flats complexes through this model. As the property market boomed, the number of projects being planned expanded rapidly. By May 2008, for example, DCC was engaged in, or planning, the regeneration of at least twelve large local authority estates in the inner city (including the flats complexes outlined above) through this mechanism. Construction commenced in 2004 on Ireland's first PPP in the housing sector, the Fatima Mansions project. The private partner was a consortium between the building contractor P. Elliott & Company and developer Moritz Holdings Ltd. The other estates were at various stages of the PPP procurement process (Table 5.2). Before detailing their status, and providing analysis of the projects, it is worthwhile outlining DCC's explanation of what the various phases within the development of a PPP project were to be.

DCC explained that a PPP should include a feasibility study by the City Council Project Management Unit that provides a draft outline of heights and densities etc. and possible yields from the site in relation to various private, social and community uses, and the resulting proposals for redevelopment.

Table 5.2 Stage of PPP project as of May 2008

Estate	Project status
South city	
Dolphin House	PPP Feasibility Study
Fatima Mansions	Contract signed with Elliot/Morris. Construction started 2004
St Michael's Estate	Castlethorn/McNamara selected as preferred bidder
St Theresa's Gardens	RFQ advertised 2007
Charlemont St	RFQ advertised 2007
Bridgefoot St	PPP assessment stage
Chamber St/ Weaver Court	PPP assessment stage
North city	
O'Devaney Gardens	Contract signed with Castlethorn/McNamara 2007
Dominick St	McNamara selected as preferred bidder 2007
Croke Villas	Bennett Ltd selected as preferred bidder

The procurement process then commences with the advertising of the project in the *European Union Journal* and at least one national newspaper.

Archaeological, utilities and soil analysis studies are undertaken along with 'community consultation', which includes the completion and signing off of a community charter that details the agreement between DCC and the community of what should be in the project in relation to social housing units, community facilities and aspects of social regeneration. The detail of the project is then publicly advertised through a Request for Qualifications (RFQ) to potential developers. This is to be undertaken within the first year. A shortlist of interested developers is drawn up from the applicants that respond to the RFQ. These short-listed bidders are then notified, met with and then issued with a tender document, the Request for Proposals (RFP) that outlines in greater detail what the project will entail. They are requested to submit masterplans that detail how they would achieve the contents of the RFP.

An assessment panel is then set up to decide which of the plans submitted by the short-listed bidders best meets the criteria, that is to select the preferred bidder. The local authority's Project Management Unit then undertakes a process of negotiation with the preferred bidder to develop a PPP contract covering architectural, planning, financial and legal agreements. The contract is then signed as a legal agreement between the local authority and the private developer (or consortium). This was expected to take up to two years from the commencement of the procurement process. Once the contract is signed, a planning application is prepared and submitted to the relevant authority. Once planning approval is obtained, demolition is undertaken and construction expected to begin within a year.

By May 2008, then, in relation to these DCC PPP projects, the contract had been signed with the McNamara/Castlethorn development partnership for O'Devaney Gardens and the same consortium had been selected as the preferred bidder for the St Michael's estate. McNamara & Co., on its own, was also the preferred bidder for Dominick Street. McNamara & Co. is one of Ireland's largest building and development companies. The company is owned by a well-known Fianna Fail supporter Bernard McNamara.

The preferred bidder, Bennett construction, was selected for the redevelopment of Croke Villas. The St Theresa's Gardens and Charlemont Street projects were at the stage of the RFQ. Other estates including Bridgefoot Street (143 units) and Chamber Street/Weaver Court (sixty units) were at PPP assessment stage. Dolphin House, the largest local authority complex in Dublin City aside from Ballymun, was at the feasibility study stage. Nationally, other local authorities, such as Sligo and Kildare County Council, were investigating the potential of PPPs.

The government, the Department of the Environment and DCC viewed the PPP projects as 'flagships' and 'catalysts' for the future physical, social and economic regeneration of areas in Dublin and across Ireland (Fatima Regeneration Board, 2005; Government of Ireland, 2007; DCC, 2006). The *National Development Plan, 2007–2013* further dedicated €255 million of capital funding on PPPs for housing, and intended that the 'successful' model of PPP regeneration developed by DCC and other PPP arrangements such as the Affordable Housing Initiative, which involves the making available of state land to private developers to provide private affordable housing, would be expanded to develop other projects throughout the programme period (Government of Ireland, 2007, 12).

The need for research

In a similar fashion to the general literature on PPPs in Ireland, there was, until the latter part of the 2000s, little debate or published research in relation to their use in the regeneration of the local authority flats complexes. Given that these projects are pioneer test sites for what is a radical departure in public housing policy and urban development, and given their significant potential to impact on poverty in some of the communities experiencing the most severe inequalities in Irish society, close attention and detailed analysis from a community and public interest perspective is needed (Bissett, 2005; Dillon, 2004; Kelly and MacLaran, 2004, Tenants First,[2] 2005).

Some of the literature has pointed to the experience of the Fatima Mansions estate and identified a number of positive changes for communities brought about by PPP regeneration (Fatima Groups United, 2006; Government of Ireland, 2007; Norris, 2005). There has been, however, a growing body of literature that details from a community perspective the impacts and outcomes of PPP regeneration. *The Real Guide to Regeneration for Communities: Making the Right Decision about Urban Regeneration* (Tenants First, 2005), a community-produced document, identified significant conflict, stress, disruption and fear with many aspects of 'community' being lost in the process of de-tenanting,[3] demolition and redevelopment that was being experienced as part of other regeneration projects.

This chapter addresses these various themes through the presentation of a detailed analysis of the outcomes of the aforementioned PPP projects.

State rationale for PPPs in social housing regeneration

This radical change in housing policy reflected the government's strong support and rationale for PPPs in the delivery of public infrastructure and services at the time. The stated advantage of these projects was that they would provide additional funding and, therefore, greater value for money than traditional delivery mechanisms. This would be done by realising the market value of the land on the estates and would, therefore, according to the state, provide regeneration at 'zero financial cost' to the Exchequer:

> PPPs can capitalise in a cost effective and socially progressive manner on the escalation in the value of urban lands in public ownership ... The housing projects at Fatima Mansions, O'Devaney Gardens, Infirmary Road and St Michael's are particularly attractive because these projects are financially neutral for the Exchequer, as the private sector is providing public housing in return for development rights on the remainder of the sites. (Department of the Environment PPP Unit, interview, 2006)

By transferring the market value of the land on the estates over to developers, the state would receive, for 'free', a negotiated amount of social housing, community and other facilities:

> The Partnership model is based upon Dublin City Council optimising the use of its existing land holdings to leverage private finance. The developer in turn provides the local authority with an agreed number of social and/or affordable housing units and community facilities and funds the overall development in whole or in part from the sale of private housing units. (DCC, 2008)

DCC was very attracted to the model due to the potential synergies with private developers in relation to the redevelopment of local authority estates being planned as part of surrounding private developments – and, centrally, the finance that the private sector could provide:

> The PPP model was, given the strength of the economy and the strong demand for housing, considered the most appropriate mechanism to regenerate Dublin City Council's large mono-tenure flats complexes by utilising private expertise and capital. (DCC official, interview, 2007)

Given the totality of DCC's housing stock and its condition, it was apparent that regeneration was going to be a very lengthy process if it relied on Exchequer funding alone, which, as noted earlier, was being constrained as the government promoted private market-related options:

> We don't have the money to provide the housing ourselves. What are we going to do? Leave fifty-year old housing there and just do patch-up work? In an ideal world we would come out and deliver quality replacement housing ourselves but the PPP is a good way and the only way to deliver the quality housing we want for our tenants. (DCC official, interview, 2008)

Thus, the primary factor underlying DCC's decision to adopt the PPP model was that it believed PPP would be the only method by which it could fund the regeneration of its existing housing stock within a reasonable period of time:

> If we were to rely totally on funding from the government it would take many years to achieve what is going on in the city at present. Traditional funding does not deliver the regeneration at the same rate as PPPs. Funding is always an issue and PPP's have ensured the acceleration of delivery of redevelopments. (DCC Housing Project Management Unit, interview, 2007)

The PPP model would also address social exclusion and poverty by providing development gain to fund social regeneration and community facilities that traditional, state-funded, regeneration does not provide. It would achieve the government policy of a social mix of housing types and use (social, affordable, private and commercial development etc.) in areas of high concentration of local authority housing.

The mix, however, prioritised attracting financially beneficial uses over the uses that could contribute to addressing the poverty issues affecting existing tenants. For example, the Dolphin House feasibility study provided for a 'vibrant mix of uses' biased toward income-generating uses, such as private residential, commercial retail, offices, recreation (leisure, hotels) education (private third-level college), all aimed at maximising the development potential of the site 'to provide a very attractive and dense mixed-use new city quarter' (DCC, 2006).

A successful PPP project: Fatima Mansions/Herberton?

> The Fatima Mansions PPP project proved a major success with 150 high-quality social and seventy affordable homes completed in 2008 as part of a new mixed-tenure, sustainable community, at no cost to the Exchequer. (Department of the Environment, interview, 2010)

Fatima Groups United, the local community representative organisation for Fatima Mansions and DCC agreed a masterplan for the regeneration of the estate in October 2001. A Regeneration Board was set up to implement the plan and included representatives of DCC, statutory agencies, public representatives, residents and community groups. In 2003, DCC informed the Board that the plan could only be implemented if it was done through a PPP. The community, aware of the broader context of government spending restraints, consented to the PPP, but only on agreement of a number of essential principles. These included that the state would have to deliver the contents of the agreed master-plan, or better, and any changes would have to be negotiated and agreed at the Board. The Fatima PPP contract was then signed between DCC and the developer Elliot Maple Woods in 2004. It included, for the developer, 395 private apartments and 3,400 square metres of commercial retail space that he could sell or rent and, for DCC and the community, 150 units of public rented housing, 70 affordable units, a 3,500 square metre neighbourhood centre (costing €8.5 million), a crèche, 500 square metres of community enterprise space and €6.2 million towards a social development plan.

This significant community gain was achieved largely as a result of the strong action, vision and participation by Fatima Groups United in the regeneration process, in partnership with DCC. Within the affordable and social housing allocation Fatima Groups United argued for, and achieved, was the provision of a Super Affordable tenant purchase scheme where Fatima residents could buy their houses at a super affordable rate of between €100,000 and €130,000 when houses in the area at the time were valued between €400,000 and €500,000. This scheme became an incentive for residents to engage in training for employment so they could purchase their new home (Fatima Groups United, 2006). As of 2008, twelve tenants had bought their new public housing unit under the arrangement and twelve locals had put their names down to buy an affordable unit. Fatima Groups United believed that this was a vital element to sustaining the community, as the residents were buying with a view to staying in the area, so it was expected to have a positive stabilising effect on the estate.

Physical design and social housing

Speaking at the opening of the new neighbourhood centre in November 2009, the Irish President, Mary McAleese, accurately described the newly regenerated Fatima Mansions:

> The run-down old flats are gone. Instead, there are 600 smart and comfortable new homes in a mix of private and local authority housing. The LUAS just across the road has made it so much easier to access the services, facilities and opportunities of the wider city and suburbs. These things we can see and admire, but alongside all that changed physical infrastructure there have been other changes too, just as important and in the long term even more important – for you didn't just want the housing to change, you wanted people's hearts and hopes to change too, so that life would be fuller, safer, happier, more fulfilling.

The physical layout and design of the new development is very impressive, indeed it was short-listed for the Public Choice Award of the 2010 Irish Architecture Awards. It is an open-flow layout, in contrast to the 'island' nature of the pre-regeneration estate, with new streets providing a corridor between Rialto and the LUAS line, which has led to a through-flow of pedestrian traffic serving to integrate the redeveloped estate with the surrounding area.

The existence of a mixture of housing tenures that are more integrated than previously with the surrounding area has, in the first few years of the project, meant an end to the Fatima 'ghetto'. The landmark neighbourhood centre is located in the middle of the development, to promote integration between private and social units on the new estate, and has a play area and an all-weather football pitch in front of it, which provides an essential facility for the local youth.

At the start of the process, it was proposed to mix the public and private dwellings together in the style of 'pepper-potting' similar to the Part V provision of a small number of social units provided as part of private developments, but the local authority tenants requested to be clustered together for community and social support networks and the plan was designed to reflect their wishes.

Design aspects that promoted integration included the external facades and forms of the buildings, so that it is difficult to clearly identify which are social and which private. This was achieved to a certain extent, as the new low-rise social housing is similar to the private low-rise housing on a nearby street and there is a strong similarity in design between the social and private apartments. Although, there is a clear contrast between the low-rise social houses and the apartments and the private apartments, which appear to be designed to a higher specification than the social apartments, with more expensive features, such as glass frontages and wood panelling and the balconies are inset with a roof above them, it should be said that these differences are only noticeable on close and detailed inspection.

While concerns have been expressed in the literature about the reduction in the number of public units from the original 394, the reality for residents and community organisations at the time of the decision on PPP regeneration was that there were only 220 units occupied during the negotiations and this number had reduced further before the final deal was signed due to DCC's de-tenanting policy and the desire of residents to leave the deteriorating conditions. This meant residents demanded a deal to be delivered as soon as possible and the issue of the loss of public-sector units and land could not be taken on. The level of social issues affecting the 220 remaining tenants meant there was a need to reduce that number further or else the newly regenerated estate would face little chance of success because of the intensity and extent of problems. Furthermore, Fatima Groups United believed that if they had become embroiled in a prolonged argument against PPPs around the principles of social housing numbers, regeneration would not have been achieved. The loss of social housing was outweighed by the importance of ensuring a sustainable community:

> The loss of public land and housing was a bigger issue and when you are on the ground there are lots of other issues ... We only lost two and a half acres of land- when you look at our big neighbourhood centre and the football pitch, the crèche, the park area, and then what the residents gained. (Fatima resident, interview, 2008)

Social regeneration and sustainability

The redevelopment has resulted in a positive and hopeful atmosphere in the community associated with the new homes, community facilities and the impact of the social regeneration plan, which addresses eight themes, including: community enterprise, employment and training, community safety, sports and recreation, estate management, education, health and well-being, and arts and culture. It also increased employment opportunities, such as apprenticeships for young people. This, along with the support given to a number of particularly disadvantaged families, has played an important role in breaking the cycle of disadvantage.

The approach to estate management radically improved problems associated with drug-dealing and anti-social behaviour in the initial stages. Particularly important in this has been the partnership approach with the key stakeholders: DCC and the Garda Siochana. However, such issues around estate management have re-emerged as a central challenge that could jeopardise the success of the project.

The social enterprise plan strives to make the community self-reliant in generating its own economic base through the operation and management, by the community, of the impressive, purpose-built, neighbourhood centre and the letting and management of some of the newly built commercial units. The community and DCC are also investigating the potential of the community taking over the management and letting of some of the private apartments in order to provide an ongoing rental income to fund the social and enterprise plan.

There can be no doubt that the conditions and living standards for the Fatima tenants (now residents of the Herberton estate) have radically improved and are incomparable with what existed before. Given that the Fatima project is at an early stage, it is difficult to ascertain what role the new social mix has had. However, as referred to earlier, the success of the regenerated estate, particularly the social housing aspects, is dependent on a number of factors, including the quality of estate management and the on-going funding of the social and enterprise plans. Furthermore, the housing market crash of 2008 affected the sale of the private units and it appeared that a sizeable proportion of units were still vacant in 2010. The developer was offering some of the units to rent and an arrangement was made with a third-level college to rent a block of them for student use. It also appeared that a number of investors had bought some of the private apartments. This could provide a significant challenge to the integration and sustainability of the new community, as often those renting in the private market, such as students, are transient and do not engage in local community issues and events etc. If the situation of a high number of unsold private units continues into the future, it could also threaten the success of the entire regeneration project.

PPP negotiations and outcomes in the other estates

Unlike Fatima Mansions, the communities in the other estates were much less satisfied. While community influence was relatively strong within some aspects of the PPP procurement process in the other estates, the demands and requirements of the developer were foremost. For example, community representatives were initially to be excluded from key decision-making processes, including the assessment of the short-listed bidders and direct contract negotiations with the preferred bidder. DCC cited PPP 'confidentiality clauses' as the rationale. Community input was restricted to regeneration boards where DCC provided the details on direct discussions that it was holding with the developer. This meant the communities were excluded from some of the most critical parts of the process, leaving them quite disempowered in relation to the overall outcomes of the projects:

> It is PPP without the C [community]. What we did not win and what other communities should do is to get to that stage, get into that room where they are negotiating with the developer, because that is where all the decisions are made. (PPP project community worker, interview, 2008)

After exerting considerable pressure on DCC, the St Michael's Estate Regeneration Team did manage to get community representation on the Assessment Panel. Furthermore, the level of community and social housing gain and resources provided to the community to participate did not follow a uniform pattern or framework and actually varied considerably from project to project. They were not provided on a uniform basis across the areas by DCC as one might expect in agreements made between the same local authority and various developers. For example, only one estate, Dolphin House, obtained resources from DCC to develop a community feasibility study before PPP regeneration was agreed to. Also Fatima Mansions was the only one to succeed in convincing DCC to agree to the regeneration board becoming a limited company, and it was also provided considerable resources to participate within the negotiations process, including administrative support, capacity-building and architectural support, a development worker and on-site premises.

Of the projects that had reached contract closure and/or signing as of July 2008, at which stage the community gain was apparent, St Michael's estate was promised a €6 million dividend, while there was no clear social dividend allocated in the O'Devaney Gardens or Dominick Street projects. It is clear, therefore, that the level of community gain was dependent, to a certain degree, on the extent to which the community on an individual estate was organised and had the structural capacity to articulate its demands. For example, the communities of Fatima Mansions, St Michael's Estate and Dolphin House had strong locally based community and youth organisations that had worked with residents on the estates for a number of decades. The residents and their representatives in these communities, with varying levels of intensity, took a position to assert a community perspective within the PPP as much as possible and only to make agreements once community gain was maximised. It can be deduced that it was as a result of these factors that they achieved the highest levels of community influence and gain. DCC provided these resources because it recognised (after considerable pressure and cogent arguments made by the community sector) the importance and value for the success of the project of the community being able to participate in a genuinely equal manner.

The PPP mechanism also meant that funding could be provided up-front for these aspects by DCC and then reclaimed from the development gain provided by the PPP on completion of the project. The Fatima community in all likelihood achieved its ground-breaking level of resources because DCC wanted to guarantee community buy-in and avoid delays to its flagship social housing PPP. Fatima Mansions was to be used as a positive example that would encourage other communities to consent to the PPP model. Dominick Street, St Theresa's Gardens and O'Devaney Gardens, which did not have the same history and extent of community development organisation, did not receive such a level of support, but did obtain capacity-building training, consultation and technical support.

It is important to note that the local estate-based regeneration boards (that included independent chairpersons, community workers, local community representation, local residents, Gardai, DCC officials, elected politicians, other statutory bodies and, in the case of Fatima Mansions and St Michael's, had the support of a full-time Chief Executive Officer and administrative support) provided the opportunity for genuine resident participation in the planning and development of regeneration proposals. They also provided a space for the community to work with DCC to ensure day-to-day issues that affected residents, such as childcare, anti-social behaviour and estate management, were addressed. This ensured an improved level of accountability of service provision and estate management by DCC and other state agencies and a greater level of community involvement than would have been the case if these boards had not existed.

Historically, working-class communities have been disempowered within such planning and redevelopment processes because they are at a severe disadvantage in terms of their unfamiliarity with very complex contract and planning negotiations processes (McLaran *et al.*, 2007). On the other hand, DCC and developers have professional architects, surveyors and solicitors working for them and are, therefore, in a better position to maximise outcomes from the processes in their favour. In a visionary approach, the Regeneration Boards provided communities with such resources (such as regeneration community workers, architectural and planning expertise support, negotiation training etc.) to enable them to participate on a more equal basis with respect to the professional resources used by the other partners.

Absence of real choice

The framework or model which would deliver the projects was predetermined and effectively, non-negotiable. Therefore, what real choice or community input existed in the PPP processes? DCC informed residents and their representatives that PPP was the only option available for regeneration, and, if they did not consent to a PPP approach, then the only alternative would be to wait for funding from the traditional mechanisms through the Department of the Environment, which would, according to DCC, take much longer than that offered by the PPP process:

> Residents were saying: 'can you not just build a housing scheme for everyone in O'Devaney? There is enough room.' DCC said they don't have the money for that and what you have to understand is if we don't go down this road (PPP), there is no money for O'Devaney. So it meant we had no choice – it was a case of the estate gets worse or go for a PPP. (O'Devaney Gardens resident, interview, 2008)

Dolphin House

The history of the regeneration consultation process in Dolphin House also provides a clear example of this logic. In 2003, consultation revealed that residents' principal concerns were the maintenance of the flats and dealing with anti-social behaviour, and they were strongly against demolition and redevelopment. Reflecting this, a company brought in by DCC to design regeneration options recommended refurbishment. However, these proposals were dismissed by DCC, apparently because they did not suit the PPP regeneration policy that necessitated complete demolition and the rebuilding of private and public units in order for the project to be financially viable. The community also took a cautious approach toward PPP because of the negative effects on social housing numbers, insufficient guarantees that the local community would benefit from the resources generated out of the deal and private-sector profit rules that would inevitably mean higher density (Dolphin House Community Development Association, 2006).

DCC officially informed the community in September 2006 of its intention to commission a PPP feasibility study and stated that, if residents opposed the PPP, there would not be a major regeneration project for Dolphin as PPP was 'the only game in town' and Dolphin would 'miss the boat' in terms of opportunities for regeneration because of the lack of finance for any other model. The community was also told that, if it did not agree to a PPP, there would be no funding available to enable the residents to partici-pate adequately within the process or for community requirements, such as social regeneration.

Despite this pressure, the community requested the resources from 2006 onwards for independent expertise (architectural, planning and financial) from DCC to identify community regeneration options which would not necessarily be PPPs. Eventually, in 2008, DCC showed vision and commit-ment to the principal of genuine resident participation by granting the resources to the community to undertake an independent, innovative, consultation process to develop a number of community regeneration options. Both the time and effort taken clearly demonstrate the extent to which it was a struggle for the communities to assert their perspectives within the negotiations process.

Overall then, while DCC did resource participation, it persistently made the case for the minimisation of the other aspects of community gain (public units, social regeneration fund and community facilities) in order to ensure the regeneration projects would be economically viable enough for a developer to undertake them:

> The whole regeneration process has been based on the prospective sale of private apartments over the next few years. The state is exploiting the current economic situation. They are hugely lucrative sites. The whole process is market driven as everything is funded on the profit from the sale of private apartments. There is no state funding. This means the PPP mechanism is very restrictive, constraining and so tightly wound you cannot move once inside it. It is claustrophobic within the boundary; every proposal put forward from the community has to be based on the basis of 'no state investment'. They say no to a suggestion if it brings the project into deficit. (PPP project resident representative, interview, 2008)

The negotiations process organised by DCC minimised real community influence as they were excluded from the principal arena of contract negotiations. The evidence demonstrated that various community demands were excluded from realisation because they were not 'financially viable'. It revealed clearly how the PPP model enforced a minimisation of community gain and social housing within the regeneration redevelopments and how the Irish state planned and ensured on behalf of private developers such outcomes.

Increase in density and height

The increase in density in the new estates demonstrated how the commercial imperatives of the PPP model resulted in outcomes that went against the communities' preferences. The projects required a substantial increase in density from what existed originally on the estates in order to provide a large quantity of private and commercial units to provide a return to the private investors and finance the social housing and community facilities. The increase in density was also in line with DCC and government planning policy. Most of the estates originally contained low-rise buildings, ranging from two to four storeys in height and generous open public spaces.

The regeneration plans almost doubled the density in some instances, with average density increasing from 35.5 to 66.8 units per acre. Fatima Mansions, for example, increased from 33 units per acre to 56 units per acre, St Michael's Estate was to increase from 25 to 51 and St Theresa's Gardens, from 36 to 63 units per acre. The increased densities were accompanied by an increase in the heights of planned buildings in the projects. The Fatima Mansions, St Michael's Estate and O'Devaney Gardens projects entailed an increase in height to a maximum of eight storeys. The Dominick Street project included buildings of eight to fourteen storeys and St Theresa's Gardens, eight to ten storeys; Chamber Street/Weaver Court, a sixteen storey building and Dolphin House, twelve storeys. The communities expressed fears about the impact of the plans in terms of the community/public housing areas being 'squashed' into the least-attractive corners of the estates, a reduced potential for traditional houses with front and back gardens and other forms of low-rise housing, the loss of highly valued community spaces, particularly for children's play areas, and concerns about shadowing due to high-rise buildings. They expressed a wish for low-density and low-rise developments.

The increase in heights also made the feasibility of some of the regeneration projects much more dependent on a relatively high-risk planning process that could be subject to public appeals, decisions by An Bord Pleanala etc. compared to traditional low-rise regeneration projects. In the case of St Theresa's Gardens, delays were experienced in the project because DCC linked the height requirement and number and location of social units with the two nearby redevelopments of the old factory sites of Players Wills and Bailey Gibson. This meant delaying the regeneration process to await the outcome of the An Bord Pleanala hearing into planned development of the two aforementioned sites.

The privatisation of social housing estates

> What will the people get out of it? What land will be given to them? You won't see the City Council tenants like ourselves put in the part of the estate that runs along the canal. That will be prime land. How much land are we going to get back out of this? (Dolphin House resident, interview, 2008)

The majority of the proposed redevelopment in the PPP projects entailed private residential and commercial uses, while existing social housing numbers were to be considerably reduced (Table 5.3). A total of 2,795 private units were planned for the case-study estates, while the number of social units was to be reduced by almost half (45 per cent) from 2,033 to 1,121 units. This would result in a process of gentrification, as private ownership, in all likelihood composed of higher-income professionals and owner occupiers, would become the majority tenure (71 per cent) of the residential units in the regenerated estates. Meanwhile almost half of the working-class community was to be displaced through de-tenanting.

For example, the private residential units (including affordable dwellings) comprised almost 75 per cent of the total new residential units in the completed Fatima Mansions project. Private units were planned to comprise 77 per cent of all final units on completion of the new St Michael's Estate, 65.8 per cent in O'Devaney Gardens, 66.7 per cent of Dominick Street and 75 per cent in St Theresa's Gardens. In Fatima Mansions, for example, there are only 150 social units provided in the new estate, comprising a mere 38 per cent of the original 394 units. Similarly, in St Michael's Estate, only 165 new public units were planned, comprising just under half (48 per cent) of the original 346 public units, while in St Theresa's Gardens only 150 units (43 per cent) were planned in comparison to 346 originally.

Table 5.3 Planned private and social units in selected PPP projects as of May 2008

Estate	New private units (% of new PPP estate)	New social units (% of new PPP estate, % of original estate)
South city		
Fatima Mansions	615 (75%)	150 (24.5%, 38%)
St Michael's Estate	720 (77%)	165 (23%, 48%)
St Theresa's Gardens	450 (75%)	150 (25%, 43%)
North city		
O'Devaney Gardens	542 (65.8%)	281 (34.2%, 100%)
Dominick Street	240 (66.7%)	120 (33.3%, 60%)
Total for the 9 projects	2,795 (71%)	1,121 (29%, 55%)

Overall, the PPP regeneration projects were planned to facilitate the transfer to private developers, for private and commercial use (privatisation), of over two-thirds of public land on the estates that had previously been used for social housing for low-income families. This again demonstrated that the requirement of the regeneration projects to be economically 'self-financing' resulted in the individual component outcomes of the regeneration projects being determined by their financial attractiveness to private developers.

The scale of the planned privatisation of the estates also suggested that the social mix composition was determined primarily by the extent of private development required to make the projects 'economically viable' rather than what would address the social exclusion and poverty of existing residents, the majority of whom were being dispersed permanently as result of the reduction in social housing units.

De-tenanting

Once an estate became designated as an official regeneration project, DCC actively de-tenanted it. As explained earlier, this involved encouraging existing tenants to transfer off the estate by offering them better-quality dwellings elsewhere, and not re-allocating the vacant flat. This was done, according to DCC, in order to prepare for demolition. However, the extent of de-tenanting indicates that DCC were encouraging the maximum de-tenanting possible in order to reduce the requirement of social housing units in the PPP plans. This would provide a greater potential for private development within the plans and, therefore, increased the financial attractiveness of the projects to any potential developer. For example, during negotiations with the communities, DCC actively tried to convince them to accept a reduction in the original number of social units on the estates, and stated that the plans would only provide for the quantity of social housing that equalled the number of occupied units on the estate.

Community representatives felt that DCC was, therefore, promoting the greatest de-tenanting possible on the basis that it would reduce the requirement for new social units and increase the chances of a developer undertaking the project and, therefore, de-prioritised the impact of the de-tenanting process on the existing communities.

DCC also made it clear that it desired a reduction in the number of occupied units in order to provide a smaller, more 'manageable', sized estate post-regeneration. This was in line with DCC's expressed desire to move away from housing maintenance and management and transfer its housing stock to the private and voluntary sector (Kenny, 2003; Fitzgerald, 2004):

> The community break up is not an issue. The people who left wanted to leave. This gives DCC an opportunity to manage a complex more effectively instead of having high numbers and isolation now we are going to integrate and become part of the wider community. We are keeping the numbers of social housing in the clusters to an absolute minimum to suit our project. (DCC official, interview, 2008)

Government policy also promoted this as outlined in the *National Development Plan, 2007–2013*, which stated that PPPs would be introduced in order to allow social housing to be provided by private companies and these would be 'responsible for the design, construction and maintenance of units, often in co-operation with the voluntary and co-operative sector' (Government of Ireland, 2007, 212).

De-tenanting had the impact of making conditions worse on the estates, in particular due to anti-social behaviour, which reduced community morale, and the break-up of family and neighbour support networks, which further de-stabilised the communities and led to a decline in the level of community activities and of participation in the regeneration processes. While it was typical of local authority estates to have a certain transient population (Redmond and Russell, 2008), the scale of both voluntary- and DCC-encouraged de-tenanting that occurred over the period of the PPP process from 2000 to 2009 was unprecedented (see discussion on de-tenanting later in this chapter). A key factor in the deteriorating conditions was DCC's inadequate estate management, in particular the insufficient and ineffective maintenance (carrying out of repairs) of the flats complexes. The residents had been highlighting this problem to DCC for many years.

In Dolphin House, for example, as far back as 2002 residents' surveys revealed serious maintenance problems as 145 out of 165 surveyed flats had complaints covering sewerage, plumbing and dampness. The residents wrote to DCC at the time stating that 'there is a very serious problem with the maintenance of Dolphin House and the residents deserve a better service. The apparent lack of interest by DCC to seriously address the maintenance problem is evident.'

Four years later, in 2006, consultation with residents again found that there were significant problems with DCC's slow response to maintenance complaints from residents, particularly issues with sewerage clogging up baths, sinks and causing foul odours inside their homes. In order to proactively address the problems on a partnership basis, the community, in 2007, set up a formal 'maintenance' group with DCC to develop solutions. They also set up a community maintenance initiative where two workers, from the Dolphin House Community Employment scheme, supported residents in reporting their issues to DCC and documented whether they were addressed or not. DCC then used this information to follow up on complaints that had not been addressed.

In 2008, a DCC engineer's report accepted that 'the waste-water flowing back into baths (in Dolphin House) can have a disgusting odour. These types of problem usually happen where there is a choke or blockage in the system … And the choke car responded to sewage problems (in Dolphin) on average of four per week.' It is surprising that the state body responsible for ensuring adequate housing conditions in Dublin, DCC, explained that this was similar to the 'normal' attendance of a choke car in other flats complexes.

The maintenance group was working well at this time, with DCC improving its response time and carrying out repairs. However, in June 2009, DCC wrote to all residents stating it was no longer carrying out repairs that were the responsibility of tenants and any tenant over six weeks in rent arrears would no longer have routine repairs carried out unless an agreement on repayment was made with DCC. In that same month, the Dolphin House Community Development Association (DHCDA) wrote to DCC stating that 'there is considerable evidence that proves that there is a serious waste/wastewater/drainage/plumbing problem in a very substantial number of flats in Dolphin House ... These are a violation of national environmental health and safety regulations and need to be rectified on a satisfactory basis immediately.' It identified fifty-seven flats with some form of sewerage problem and stated, in response to DCC's comments on the level of attendance of the choke car, that: 'The residents of Dolphin House are not accepting the current situation as "normal" living conditions.' DCC's own figures reveal that in 2009 there were almost 1,000 maintenance repair requests logged for Dolphin House, and the choke car came out 115 times, which means that once every three days a resident in Dolphin suffered from serious sewerage problems in their flat.

The residents' representatives were concerned, that DCC, by neglecting estate management, exploited residents' need for immediately improved conditions and, therefore, were making it even more difficult for them to assert their perspectives in the negotiations:

> At the present time, if you were to ask residents, they would say 'pull these flats down now no matter what DCC offer us, as anything is better than what we have'. Social housing flat complexes are being run-down deliberately as DCC want the land to develop it. They need the land to feed the developer to provide the social housing number, but also it's a double edged sword. They know that the community is under pressure and if they offer any sort of attractive social housing units to this community, I believe they would bite and take it and I think DCC play on that ... At the moment, they could present hovels and people would accept them. (Dolphin House resident, interview, 2008)

The declining conditions on the estates undermined residents' hope for the future, leading many to request transfers off the estates:

> DCC are letting the place go to bits. If they don't do the maintenance and they don't do the antisocial – people are just going to say 'ah here knock the place down do what you like' – there is people like that already. People feel whatever DCC want they are going to get, that's the attitude around here; they don't think they have any power over the situation, they say just build me something new and give me a house away from here and then they don't care what you do. (PPP project resident, 2008)

Value for money
The data required to enable a full value-for-money analysis of the PPP projects were not made available for the research as 'the Public Sector Benchmark [PSB]is confidential and remains so until project close as it is

used on an ongoing basis as a benchmark for value for money' (Department of the Environment PPP Unit, interview, 2006).

In addition, requests made to DCC under the Freedom of Information Acts for records of the PSB reviews, and other assessments relating to the PPP projects, were denied to the author in June 2008. Despite an appeal, the requested records were withheld by DCC citing PPP legislation, which states that the PSB is exempt from disclosure, and various sections of the Freedom of Information Act. The commercial sensitivity clauses of the PPP records resulted in access to financial information being denied to not just to the researcher but also to the communities engaged in the regeneration projects and Dublin City councillors. This made it difficult to undertake a scientifically accurate cost–benefit analysis of the projects.

It appeared, though, that DCC itself did not undertake value-for-money analysis at the appropriate stages. The PSBs for St Theresa's Gardens and Charlemont Street, which had both already gone out to tender as PPPs, did not exist in 2008 despite the fact that a PSB is supposed to be carried out *before* a public authority enters the PPP route (Central PPP Unit, 2006b). It appears that, similar to the Fatima Mansions PPP, DCC had not undertaken a value-for-money appraisal or valuation of the land prior to the original decision to pursue a PPP for these projects. The fact that the suggested numbers of social housing units and community facilities for the sites were given to developers before a financial assessment had been undertaken demonstrates poor practice and a disregard for the value of the public land to residents and the taxpayer. Even after contract signing, DCC was unclear as to the extent to which the private developers were profiting from the deals and, ultimately, whether the deals, in fact, represented value for money or not. This quite extraordinary fact was revealed by this candid explanation of the assessment process by a DCC official:

> Questions remain unanswered at the completion of the PPP whether the state got a good deal or value for money from it. We could not estimate the profit margins that the developer got because the various developers who made bids, offered bids with very different components, which made comparison with the final bid difficult. It is a difficulty with PPPs that you can't compare the final bid to the different potential scenarios ... it is not accurate enough because you can't estimate what the PPP bidder is going to get from his part of the site. The state can't value what the developer is getting. The extra money earned in the project has tended to go to the developer and not to the state. (DCC housing official, interview, June 2008)

It is possible to undertake an estimated financial analysis of the PPP projects using some basic assumptions. These include the cost of provision per social unit of €200,000 and an estimated land value of €10 million per acre. These figures are based on average costs cited by construction sources in 2006. Using these assumptions, a financial comparison of the estimated value of the public land transferred to private developers with the cost of providing the social aspects (demolition, new social housing, dividend and community facilities) in six of the PPP regeneration projects demonstrated that, had the projects gone ahead as planned, the state would have provided an approximate gain of €330 million to the PPP developers from public land. In Fatima Mansions, the total estimated cost to the developer of providing the social aspects to the development was estimated at €40.5 million (comprising new public units (€23 million), the social dividend (€6.5 million), demolition (€3 million), neighbourhood centre (€8 million)). If you subtract those costs from the estimated value of the land there (€110 million), it suggests that the private developer was set to receive €69.5 million in land value, for free, from the state.[4]

In the case of St Michael's, the total social costs to the developer was estimated at €47 million (€33 million cost of providing new social housing units, social dividend of €6 million, demolition of €3 million and neighbourhood centre at €5 million), while the value of the land was estimated at €140 million, providing a net gain to the developer, and loss to the state, of €93 million.

This demonstrated that, on the six estates, public land worth €545 million was planned to be transferred to private PPP consortia in return for social housing and community facilities worth €214 million, leaving a net gain of approximately €330 million for the developers. These guided estimations[5] represent a startling level of transfer of public wealth to private developers through the process of local authority estate 'regeneration'. This level of transfer of highly valuable public land to private developers also contradicts government claims that the PPPs were at 'zero cost' to the Exchequer and would not involve asset transfer. Furthermore, it has been revealed that DCC spent €20 million of public finances on the Fatima Mansions project and €6.1 million on five other PPP projects, with €2.6 million spent on St Michael's Estate alone. A comparison of the state spend with the community gain in the Fatima project raises the question of whether the PPP provided any real additional financial gain to the state. It is unclear therefore whether it was the state, and not the developer, that financed the community gain.

These financial calculations also exclude the considerable cost to the taxpayer and to the tenants and communities of the state's decision not to carry out regeneration on the estates through the direct, exchequer, route as outlined in the original plans in 2001 and 2002. These included the expense of interim measures required to address the deteriorating living conditions on the estates when the PPP process was delayed or failed to provide projects.

Overall then, using the available data, the research cast doubt on the ability of these PPP projects to achieve value for money for the taxpayer and the local communities. This supports the critical literature which states that a clear evaluation of the financial rationale of the PPP model and comparisons with other options had not been carried out by the state (Bissett, 2005; Dillon, 2004; Fatima Groups United, 2006; Kelly and MacLaran, 2004; McGuirk and MacLaran, 2001).

This is a very significant finding given that this was, at the outset, the principle reason for introducing PPPs. It is quite worrying that a clear evaluation of the financial rationale of the PPP model and comparisons with other options were not carried out by the state and it has not detailed publicly how value for money was to be achieved.

Delays, contract difficulties and collapse

In late 2007 and through into 2008, Irish property prices decreased substantially on previous years as the overheated property market crashed due to domestic and international market factors. For example, the average price of houses nationally fell by almost 6% between the third quarter of 2007 and third quarter of 2008, from €319,000 to €301, 680 (DOEHLG, 2009a). As a result, the estimated profit margins for developers, from the future sale of the private residential and commercial units, upon which the economic viability of the PPP regeneration projects was based, narrowed dramatically. The regeneration projects that had reached contract award and signing stage in 2007 and early 2008 had, therefore, become very 'high-risk' investments for the private development consortia. The reality facing the affected communities, suffering some of the deepest social and economic inequalities in relation to income, health, education and well-being in Irish society, was that they were no longer living on high-value sites that had initiated the PPP model.

In late 2007, the private partners began to raise a number of problems with the financial composition of the projects. It appeared that they were looking for ways to transfer emerging costs (risk) in the projects on to the state. These included the cost of applying DCC's increased apartment size guidelines, increased construction costs, increased interest charges on loan repayments to the bank and soil decontamination costs. However, DCC was restricted by the PPP process in the extent to which it could alter the financial make up of the projects. The procurement rules meant that, if DCC contributed towards costs that were stipulated as belonging to the developer in the RFP, it could leave DCC open to a legal challenge from the other short-listed developers who had failed in their bids for the original PPP project – it would constitute a substantial change to the terms originally laid out in the tender documents and could lead to other developers arguing unfair competition.

Through the first few months of 2008, residents were extremely anxious about the future of their projects as they realised that the fate of their estate's regeneration had become intricately bound to conditions in the Irish property market and the global financial situation. It was very apparent that they were completely reliant on the developer for the survival of the project. As the contract negotiations reached their final stages in 2007 and 2008, the power and control of the developer to determine the projects' outcomes was revealed.

On 19 May 2008, despite attempts to achieve progress, DCC announced that negotiations with the developer McNamara & Co. in relation to the PPP regeneration projects, of St Michael's Estate, O'Devaney Gardens and Dominick Street and the affordable housing PPP projects in Infirmary Road and Convent Lands[6] had collapsed:

> The adversely changed circumstances of the current private housing market to that of 2005/6 when the bids were submitted, along with significant additional costs of increased apartment sizes and new energy regulations have rendered the whole concept of using the sale of private housing units to fund Social and Affordable housing and Community Services, along with a balancing site purchase figure, unsustainable in the current market, despite the best efforts of everyone involved. (Bernard McNamara, letter to DCC, 19 May 2008)

McNamara & Co. was only obliged to continue with the projects for which contracts had been signed (O'Devaney Gardens and Infirmary Road projects) as penalty clauses could apply if it withdrew and DCC could show that the terms of the deal had remained the same. The projects for which no contract had been signed, St Michael's Estate and Dominick Street were left unsure of their futures. The legalities of the PPP process, as referred to earlier, meant that DCC was restricted in what it could negotiate with the developer and it was, therefore, unsure what action to take. It was an unprecedented situation facing DCC and the Irish state. It revealed that neither DCC nor the Department of the Environment had contingency plans ready, nor had they considered what they would do in a situation where a developer withdrew from a project. It demonstrated the lack of safeguards built into the PPP model by the state to protect the interests of DCC and the communities.

Protests were held by the residents from the affected estates outside an emergency meeting of DCC, on 26 May, to address the collapse of the projects. No substantive progress was made to resolve the issues between that meeting and DCC's next meeting on 9 June. At that meeting, the residents walked from their estates into City Hall in a protest led by a black coffin to symbolise the death of their hopes and dreams. DCC then formally wrote to McNamara & Co. to ask the company to withdraw from the St Michael's Estate and Dominick Street projects so that it could enter negotiations with the second bidder. It also set up a dedicated multi-disciplinary team in the Housing Project Management Unit to examine new options for the regeneration of these areas. In September 2008, it was finally agreed that DCC and McNamara & Co. would mutually disengage from the three regeneration projects (St Michael's, O'Devaney Gardens and Dominick Street) and that the developer would release the sites back to DCC, provide it a licence to the designs for the proposed developments and pay a contribution of €1.5 million towards the costs incurred by DCC (Kelly, 2008b).

As the property market crisis intensified in late 2008, renegotiations with McNamara and Co. in relation to O'Devaney Gardens collapsed as did negotiations with the second bidder for St Michael's and Dominick Street. Negotiations between DCC and the preferred private bidder, Bennett Construction, for the Croke Villa project also collapsed due to the 'prevailing economic climate and global credit crunch' (DCC, 2008). It was reported that the developers were finding it very difficult to access finance to fund the projects through 2008. On 1 December 2008, DCC announced that 'the regeneration projects are no longer viable under the Public Private Partnership process that had been envisaged' because of the economic downturn and the communities would have to wait for regeneration when there was an 'upturn' in the market and PPP became viable again (DCC, 2009). In October 2009, negotiations were terminated with the three preferred bidders for the regeneration of St Theresa's Gardens.

At the time of the PPP negotiations in 2006, 2007 and 2008, financial institutions in Ireland were making unprecedented amounts of credit and liquidity available to large developers to finance development on the basis that the property market boom was going to continue for a long period of time. Developers such as Bernard McNamara had amassed borrowings of up to €1.5 billion from banks, such as the Anglo Irish Bank, secured on their extensive property portfolio. In McNamara's case that included the twenty-four-acre Irish Glass Bottle site in Ringsend, which a consortium led by McNamara acquired for €412 million in 2006 and the Burlington Hotel, for which €288 million was paid in 2007. The PPP projects were added to that list, as the government and DCC placed the regeneration of the flats complexes into that frenzied investment market, just like adding chips to the table at the casino, expecting that the wheel would bring up the right number.

The close relationship between DCC and private developers and financiers that was at the heart of this PPP model was also highlighted in the extent to which DCC undertook market soundings involving approaches to developers for the purpose of ascertaining interest in a particular location for regeneration. For example, DCC held a PPP 'information evening' in December 2006 for private organisations, such as developers, construction companies and financiers, that could bid on projects. By the end of 2008 and through 2009, the extent of the property crash became apparent by the massive drop in property values, for example in early 2010 the Glass Bottle site was valued at just over €160 million – a 60 per cent drop from its acquisition cost. An intricate web of governance, regulation and other institutional failures resulted in severe exposure to concentrations in lending on property, as well as high exposures to individual borrowers that culminated in a banking collapse in 2009. The PPP model had, therefore, become unfeasible because the financial institutions would no longer release funding for this type of development and the ratio of public to private units in the developments was unviable for developers.

Failure of risk transfer
The PPP model initiated by the Department of the Environment and implemented by DCC facilitated this outcome as it encouraged significant financial risk taking by developers and their financiers. For example, the decision-making process to choose the successful bidder involved a scoring of various criteria in each bid (including financial make up, design, experience etc.). The bid with the highest score was then chosen as the winning bid. The calculation, however, gave the highest score to the bid with the greatest amount of finance in a 'cash offer', over and above the investment in the design, provided by a developer (Bissett, 2009). It, therefore, favoured the developer that was prepared to gamble most and risk a financially large bid based on the expectation of earning sufficient income from the sale of a substantial amount of private apartments. The overall result was that when the property market was booming, the PPP model could financially cover the risk, but if the property market turned down, as it did, the developer's income was reduced and they decided it was no longer viable.

This demonstrates that one of the original justifications for the use of PPPs, the transfer of risk to the private sector, was, in fact, market-dependent, and, when the residential housing market collapsed, the private sector left the state, and ultimately the community, with the risk. The market principle central to PPP theory, the transfer of risk to the private sector, was demonstrated not to materialise in practice. McNamara & Co. was supposed to be taking the risk in its regeneration projects, and, in doing so, potentially gain over €300 million. PPP and market theory states that, if that €300 million did not materialise from the sale of private apartments and commercial development on the site, then the developer would take the loss. However, the state actually took the loss (€5 million) when the risk materialised and McNamara had to pay only €1.5 million when it withdrew from the projects (Kelly, 2008). The state, taxpayer and communities, took the risk when it materialised, not the developer.

The collapse of the projects starkly revealed the dependent relationship that the PPP model had engendered between the provision of vital social-protection infrastructure, in this case public housing, and the conditions of the private market. This form of PPP could be described as essentially a gamble with public assets. The projects were based on a developer's risk assessment of the potential value of the sale of private apartments built on land transferred to it from the state and, ultimately, the market forces that influenced that risk. The collapse revealed the power and responsibility handed over to the private sector in the provision of public-housing regeneration. It was the communities that suffered the most severe impacts of this market-led policy.

Communities bear the brunt of risk

Through 2007, 2008 and 2009, there was an intensification of the process of community break-up and dispersal as conditions deteriorated further on the estates and residents were de-tenanted by DCC. Increasing numbers of residents became disillusioned with the conditions and ever-lengthening time-scale for regeneration and they sought to transfer off the estates. This process has resulted in some cases in all the residents being relocated elsewhere, such as Chamber Street/Weaver Court and Bridgefoot Street. In St Michael's estate, there was a reduction from 270 occupied units in 1998 to 40 in 2004 and by August 2008, there were only 14 occupied (a mere 4 per cent of the original units). The residents explained that, despite their requests, DCC did not implement a strategy of estate management aimed at retaining residents. The living conditions for residents became unbearable:

> If you were living in an eight-storey block of 57 flats and you end up with maybe 15 flats left after de-tenanting, imagine what it was like to live in the block like that. It was very difficult. As soon as someone transferred out off your landing or your neighbour or someone you had a good relationship with left, it impacted on the people around. The less that lived in a block the tougher and tougher it got to look after it. If you are the only one on the landing, then anti-social people go into the landing and hang out as they know no-one is going to throw them off. It breaks the backs of the people who are willing to stick it out and so every tenant that leaves impacts on people. (St Michael's estate community worker, interview, 2008)

In O'Devaney Gardens, by mid 2007, sixty units (four blocks) were identified for de-tenanting and demolition under phase one of the regeneration and of the tenants in those sixty units twenty-five wanted to be housed off the site and only five wished to be housed on-site in the new development. The residents identified the lack of progress on regeneration plans, anti-social behaviour problems and the fact that over the years DCC had let conditions in the flats complex deteriorate as the cause of them leaving. They were concerned that this meant the break-up of the community:

> I am worried about the displacement of the community. By giving people who want to move off the site attractive housing elsewhere is having an effect like the surrender grant: the more stable, less vunerable, will move away and those left are the ones with most difficulties. (O'Devaney Gardens resident, interview, 2007)

The four boarded-up blocks that were de-tenanted in preparation for demolition caused considerable problems, as this became an area for people to engage in anti-social behaviour:

> When this started, there was not one empty flat in O'Devaney; there was actually a waiting list, and that in itself says it all. The more they let the flats run down the more you get disheartened. I met a block group member the other day and she was embarrassed to bring her cousins from the country up the stairs – she said I would love if they could close their eyes going up the stairs with the state of the place. She said they are judging us before they know the people ... 'You just have to be in here. It's torture to live in here with the dirt, the kids are running amok. Dublin City Council don't care about the place. A lot of people are just giving up. We don't have anything to offer people. We just don't know what's happening. (O'Devaney Gardens resident, interview, 2008)

A subgroup of the O'Devaney Regeneration Board that included DCC, residents and Garda representatives was set up to address the anti-social behaviour problems but residents felt 'really let down' over its lack of effectiveness. By August 2008, there were only 178 occupied flats (64 per cent of the original units) and serious violent anti-social behaviour reached the point where a riot took place within the complex.

In Dominick Street, one block of sixty flats was de-tenanted and demolished in summer 2006 in preparation for regeneration. That left only 120 flats occupied on the estate and in April 2008 only 108 flats were occupied (55 per cent of the original units). Overall, only 931 of the 2,033 original public units were occupied as of August 2008. By June 2010, Chamber Street/Weaver Court had been completely demolished and the site lay derelict, with wild grass the only development taking place. Bridgefoot Street was also demolished and the site vacant, while nearly all the residents had been de-tenanted off St Michael's Estate. O'Devaney Gardens was down to ninety eight tenants (35 per cent of original units), St Theresa's 180 (52 per cent), there were only 100 units left occupied in Charlemont Street, and seventy eight left in Dominick Street. Overall then, by June 2010, in the nine estates that had entered the PPP process, only 31 per cent (640 units) of the original 2,033 units were occupied (Table 5.4).

The outcomes of this process suggested that DCC was too heavily focused on reducing the number of public units, and sustaining a healthy and vibrant community was not given the priority it should have been. This was done in order to ensure the regeneration projects were financially attractive for redevelopment and reflected DCC's desire to obtain a much-reduced size of social housing in the estates. The process is resulting in the complete removal and dispersal of existing working-class communities, with an even more severe impact than the 'surrender grant' of the 1980s, thus irreversibly destroying the original communities. The residents that remain are left waiting in terrible conditions and are, generally, those suffering the most intense social and economic inequalities, such as levels of vulnerability, poverty and disadvantage (the elderly, lone parents, single men), and thus the cycle of decline and decay intensifies.

Table 5.4 Occupancy rates on PPP estates, June 2010

Estate	Original units	Units occupied June 2010 (% of original)
South city		
Croke Villas	87	30 (35%)
Fatima Mansions	394	150 (38%)
St Michael's Estate	346	4 (1%)
St Theresa's Gardens	346	180 (52%)
Charlemont Street	181	100 (55%)
Bridgefoot Street	143	0 (0%)
Chamber Street/ Weaver Court	60	0 (0%)
North city		
O'Devaney Gardens	278	98 (35%)
Dominick Street	198	78 (40%)
Total	**2,033**	**640 (31%)**

Life after PPPs: Dolphin House community uses human-rights-based approach
Given the collapse of the PPP regeneration model, the communities have had
to look at innovative ways to bring about improvements to their estates. It is
worth taking a more in-depth look at the experience of Dolphin House, a
community that provides such an approach. It is also a community that took
a more cautious approach to the PPP model.

A Regeneration Board was set up in November 2007 to oversee a process
of consultation with the residents and then plan the regeneration. The consultation process in 2008 and 2009 was uniquely community-led and organised,
and as a result of the innovative methods of resident participation and design
of regeneration options it won the Participatory Planning Award from the
Irish Planning Institute in 2010. The clear demand from the consultation was
for significant regeneration, and residents worked with independent architects to develop an exciting vision for a new Dolphin House that was
underpinned by a social, economic and environmental vision statement for:

> A safe, inclusive and active Dolphin community, with a broad range of local
> recreational facilities and activities designed for all ages. A Dolphin estate that
> allows for the evolution and growth of an integrated, healthy, and vibrant
> community. A diverse and buoyant local economy sustained by a locally
> educated and trained workforce and a regenerated Dolphin estate, that is safe,
> attractive, well maintained and environmentally friendly. A Dolphin estate that
> provides high-quality housing and community facilities for the residents that
> they serve. (Sheridan Woods, 2009, 3)

However, the collapse of the PPP model in 2009 left the community devas-
tated. The hope and determination that drove the participation in the
consultation process evaporated and the conditions deteriorated, with drug
dealing and anti-social behaviour worsening considerably. As a result, some
of the stronger residents and community leaders sought to transfer out.
However, the community did not surrender to despair.

A striking characteristic of Dolphin House is the solidarity and support
amongst residents for each other. They regularly call in on their neighbours
to see if they are alright or if elderly residents or those with babies need
anything; they hang out their clothes on the communal washing lines and talk
about their lives and the challenges they face. They are proud of their
community, many love their flats, they want to remain living on the estate
with their neighbours as there are often third or fourth generations of the
same families living there. Those who were committed to the community
gathered and decided they were not going to give in and give up hope. They
were provided key support from the workers from the Community
Development Project on the estate (the Dolphin House Community
Development Association) and a decision by the Barnardos Charity to fund

the community regeneration co-ordinator on the estate to keep up the momentum on the important issues.

In May 2009, Community Action Network[7] came on to the estate to work with residents in addressing the serious sewerage and dampness problems, using a human-rights-based approach. The human-rights-based approach is based on trying to realise the rights to a decent standard of housing and health that the government has signed up to providing in international human rights treaties. Because governments have signed up to such human rights treaties, they are obliged to respect, protect and fulfil these rights. The HRBA turns government and, therefore, public authorities/service providers into duty-bearers; they are obligated to demonstrate how they are working towards realising people's rights. The human-rights-based approach works to make powerful those most affected by human rights issues, enabling them to demand from the state adequate standards of housing and health (Participation and the Practice of Rights Project, 2007).

The application of the HRBA to Dolphin House aimed to affect lasting change in the relationships between DCC and the Department of the Environment (the duty bearers, that is state bodies responsible for housing) and the tenants (rights holders). A group of residents, local community workers and Community Action Network identified the duty bearers, gathered evidence, set indicators and organised a unique and ground-breaking human rights hearing on the housing conditions in Dolphin House in May 2010. The process of mapping the duty bearers led to the development of a 'ladder of power' that identified the state institutions that actually had the power and resources to change the housing conditions.

This led the residents to focus on the ultimate duty bearer responsible for housing provision and conditions, the Minister for the Environment. Up to that point they had been focused on working with, and trying to exert influence on, DCC officials, who, on analysis, were doing their best to try and find solutions, but in reality had little power or resources to provide funda-mental change. It also revealed the extent to which DCC was underfunded and disempowered by central government. For example, a quarter of DCC's funding came from the Department of the Environment in 2009, which was cut by 20 per cent on the previous year. As a result, DCC had to cut back its budget for housing maintenance by 12 per cent in 2009, from €73 milion to €64 million. Residents also discovered that there were minimum standards for rental accommodation prescribed in Irish law in the *Irish Housing (Standards for Rented Houses) Regulations, 2008* and *2009* (DOEHLG, 2008, 2009b). These apply to local authority and voluntary housing units, as well as private rented accommodation.

The Housing Acts state that all landlords have a legal obligation to ensure that their rented properties comply with the regulations, including that the property should have proper drainage, that the house will be kept by the landlord during the tenancy, in all respects reasonably fit for human habitation and 'shall be maintained in a proper state of structural repair which means sound, internally and externally ... and not defective due to dampness or otherwise' (DOEHLG, 2008, 2009b). At the Housing Hearing, the Irish Human Rights Commission condemned the deplorable substandard living conditions and asserted that these conditions clearly contravened the rights of residents under the United Nations Convention on Economic Social and Cultural Rights, to which Ireland is a signatory.

The residents are monitoring, over a twelve-month period, 'indicators' of what progress takes place in improving the issues of damp and sewerage towards the Human Rights Standards. The Minister for the Environment under the Housing Act 1966 could provide the resources to DCC and instruct them to take action as the Act states that 'whenever the Minister is of the opinion that a housing authority have failed to perform any of their functions under this Act, or have failed to perform any such function in a satisfactory manner, he may by order require the authority to perform the function'.

In Dolphin House some of the serious problems associated with crime, anti-social behaviour and drug dealing began to improve towards the latter half of 2009 due to pressure from the community for an increased Garda presence and DCC building walls to secure the estate, making it easier to police, and providing CCTV.

Through the human-rights-based approach, the residents have asserted their rights for housing conditions to be improved while waiting for regeneration so that the community can be sustained. Otherwise, it must be asked, who will the regeneration be for? They are aware that the community will not survive if the physical environment remains the same and there is no progress on social and physical regeneration.

Project status 2010

As explained earlier, DCC established a multi-disciplinary housing taskforce to develop alternative plans for the collapsed PPP projects with a focus on the priority regeneration projects of St Michael's Estate, O'Devaney Gardens and Dominick Street. The new plans include phased redevelopment with a much-reduced number of social units and very minimal allocation for social regeneration. Following Department of the Environment approval in 2009, construction on phase one of the St Michael's Estate project, based on two acres of the fourteen- acre site and providing thirty-two social and forty-four affordable units, a crèche, homework club and community centre, was expected to commence in September 2010.

Detailed proposals for the redevelopment of O'Devaney Gardens and Dominick Street are expected from DCC in 2010 or 2011 and it is continuing its strategy for the de-tenanting of these areas. Its proposal for O'Devaney Gardens included only sixty social units. A second task force was set up in early 2010 to examine options for Croke Villas, Dolphin House and St Teresa's Gardens.

Overall analysis of PPP outcomes

This PPP regeneration policy experiment can, after six years of implementation since the first contract was signed in Fatima Mansions, be most accurately described along the lines of that identified by Tenants First (2005) as a policy of de-generation, dislocation and devastation for the majority of the affected communities:

> Since 2003, we have been working in a PPP process that was not alone forced on us, but has to date not laid one brick. Now we have families at breaking point, not knowing what is going to happen with their homes and locals crying out for community amenities in an area which is hugely deprived. While the rest of the country enjoyed investment during the boom years, we have been struggling with PPP. We are exhausted and extremely angry with the whole PPP process. (St Michael's estate resident representative, interview, 2008)

By 2010, only one (Fatima Mansions) of the seven PPP projects that had entered the procurement phase had commenced construction. The PPP process in the other six (St Michael's Estate, O'Devaney Gardens, Croke Villas, Dominick Street, St Theresa's Gardens, Charlemont Street) had collapsed. The extent of this policy failure is emphasised by the claim of the DCC Assistant Manager for Housing, in 2006, that the PPP projects would provide almost €4 billion in investment, 8,500 new residential units (2,500 social and 6,000 private units). The reality was that, if DCC implemented its policy of providing social housing units only for those remaining on the estates, it would result in only 640 public units being provided in the regenerated estates, a mere 31 per cent of the original number and a loss of almost 1,400 public units.

For all the estates, except Fatima Mansions, the quality of life in the communities was much worse since the PPP regeneration process commenced. Dolphin House was the only studied estate that was still fully occupied. This is as a result of the community taking the decision to delay entering the PPP process and ensuring the continued re-allocation of vacant flats by DCC. However, conditions in that estate also deteriorated, particularly anti-social behaviour and illegal drug-related problems, because the collapse of the PPP process elsewhere meant a loss of community hope, as it became apparent that there would be no regeneration of the estate in the short term.

The very high level of private residential and commercial development combined with the reduction in social housing numbers and low levels of community gain demonstrate that the private partner's financial gain (profit requirement) from the PPP regeneration project was the key factor that determined the overall outcome of the regeneration projects. Furthermore, there was considerable evidence of uneven power relations, exclusion and disempowerment of local residents. While the community had representation at various regeneration boards and committees, they were excluded, without exception, from the negotiations between the developer and DCC.

PPPs were pursued by the state, both centrally and at a local authority level, in the regeneration of social housing estates because they offered an apparent solution to the 'problem' of large inner-city local authority flats complexes at no direct cost to the Exchequer by realising the increased market value of what it termed 'underutilised' public land. Therefore, significant regeneration could be undertaken while the government's neoliberal policy of reducing the funding for local government and public housing could continue.

The PPP model funded the regeneration of Fatima Mansions providing the remaining residents with high-quality new homes, a neighbourhood centre and a significant social regeneration budget. It also involved the privatisation of large parts of the estate, which reduced the amount of social housing available in the area and, overall, did not appear to provide value for money for the taxpayer. The Fatima project commenced principally because the residential property market was experiencing a boom of high land values and the reduction in social housing units as part of the regeneration project meant that the developers' prospective profits at the time were very high. So while PPP could provide regeneration when property values were inflated, as soon as the property market experienced severe retrenchment the attractiveness of the PPP projects to the private sector diminished, and, as they had no real commitment to the plans other than to try and achieve profitable returns, they withdrew from them. The crash in the property market also threatened the success and economic viability of the Fatima project as it neared completion in 2010, as many of the private apartments could not be sold due to the oversupply in the market.

The collapse and delays in the PPP regeneration projects revealed how the PPP process effectively transferred control and responsibility for the delivery of the projects to the private partners. It demonstrated the Irish state's vulnerability and reliance on developers and the private market. It reflected the wider government policy during the Celtic Tiger period that focused on achieving private economic growth through the promotion of the construction industry and developers who were encouraged to take risks, supported by government and financial institutions. These policies helped create a property bubble of extraordinary dimensions in the Irish property market, thus making the whole PPP process even more risky. The PPP projects were just one risk, amongst many, for developers and financial institutions. Generally, they took risks on private developments, but in this instance the state provided them with assets with which they could. This reliance on the private sector and the market to guarantee the provision of these key public infrastructure projects was a short-sighted policy and a naïve gamble that ignored, firstly, the reality that markets are inherently cyclical and unstable (Harvey, 2005) and, secondly, that the primary goal and interest of the private sector, in this case developers and their financiers, are providing profitable returns to shareholders with investors not being responsible for guaranteeing social outcomes.

The fact that the state, in this instance DCC financed by the Department of the Environment, had to intervene and provide the social and affordable units in the collapsed projects demonstrated the failure of this PPP model. Their collapse brings into question the viability and appropriateness of such a model for the regeneration of local authority estates, and indeed on a broader level for the delivery of essential public infrastructure and services that deliver social protection. The provision of this finance by the state, nine years after it refused to provide such finance to these very regeneration projects, raises the question of why did the state not provide the finance for these projects in the first instance and then it could have avoided the delays and catastrophe that resulted.

It also raises a question about the ability of PPPs to provide additional finance for investment in public services and infrastructure generally, a principal benefit outlined by the government. Furthermore, in contrast to the claim that it would be a 'speedier' process than traditional delivery, the PPP process actually led to considerable delays in the delivery of the projects.

The outcomes of this research into the regeneration of local authority housing estates by DCC lends strong support to the critical literature (Bissett, 2005, 2009; Dillon, 2004; Kelly and MacLaran, 2004; McGuirk and MacLaran 2001; Redmond and Russell, 2008; Tenants First, 2005) that questions the rationale of the state actors (namely DCC and the Department of the Environment) that underlay the introduction of PPPs in this sector. It questions the market-emphasis in the decision-making process, the dependency of the model on the logic of the market and revealed that the initial PPPs were going to result in a reduction in social housing units and, could, therefore, in the context of a declining local authority housing stock and increasing housing waiting lists, exacerbate the crisis of access to social housing (Bissett, 2009). It also questioned to what extent the PPP process was being used by the local authority sector to reduce its role in the provision and management of social housing.

This literature has analysed PPPs as a new form of neoliberal, entrepreneurial, local governance that aimed, not to meet the social needs of their populations, but to sell public assets to private developers and thus gain access to much-needed capital investment.

These outcomes in Dublin are similar to the large-scale residential displacement, loss of community-relevant functions, an exacerbated housing crisis and a deepening sense of disempowerment for inner-city communities that have resulted from neoliberal policy across the Western world (Brenner and Theodore, 2002; MacLaran and McGuirk, 2003; Punch, Redmond and Kelly, 2004; Smith, 1996).

This research supports the evidence presented in Dr John Bissett's groundbreaking work on the experience of St Michael's Estate, *Regeneration; Public Good or Private Profit* (Bissett, 2009), which identified regeneration as exacerbating the inequalities experienced by the already disadvantaged residents living on Dublin's inner-city local authority housing estates.

The research also demonstrates that this model of PPP clearly contradicts a number of central aims within the government's own housing policy, including the building of sustainable communities, the delivery of effective estate management and maintenance that would ensure social housing is not of an inferior quality to that of private housing and the promise of the delivery of regeneration of deprived areas.

Lessons for other regeneration projects

Below are outlined eleven lessons for policy makers, communities, local authorities and private-sector partners engaged in or planning social housing regeneration projects that were taken from the in-depth analysis of the completed, failed and planned regeneration projects of a number of Dublin's inner-city local authority flat complexes.

1 *Communities need to make their issues a public concern*
Residents and their allies in local community organisations should be organised, independent of local authorities and political parties, in order to create a public profile of the issues affecting them. Despite their vulnerability, poverty and neglect by the state, a number of these communities have already managed to organise successful campaigns. The human-rights-based approach adopted in Dolphin House is one example of this. The key features included: gathering evidence of the problems, preparing residents to speak to the media, engaging with the media and political parties and the local authority. Another example is where residents of the failed PPP project estates, through Tenants First, the local authority tenant-led organisation, campaigned for the development of the projects after the PPP collapse.

The persistent and high-profile campaigning by the residents and community workers in St Michael's Estate is an inspirational example of what is possible with clear messages, determination and persistence (see *www.stmichaelsestate.ie*). Despite their project appearing to be finished, their protest actions and media work achieved a commitment from the government to finance the first phase of the regeneration. While it is extremely difficult for local residents, community workers and representatives to find time and energy, while also addressing the daily demands from residents, to try and link with other areas and coordinate united actions, it is vital to gain the economy of scale of profile in order to exert political pressure that can provide the resources to implement the necessary estate and community improvements.

2 *Proper resident participation and consultation is essential for successful regeneration*

The success of regeneration cannot solely be based on the involvement of residents in the process. Success has been demonstrated only when they spearhead regeneration. This requires the greatest possible level of participation by residents in decision-making structures and their interaction in those structures on the basis of equality between all parties. DCC's Assistant City Manager stated in the Canal Communities Partnership document *'Regeneration Learnings and Insights'* which was adopted by DCC as policy practice, that 'real consultation, real participation and a real role in decision-making is vital for local communities and vital to achieving a successful outcome' (Canal Communities Partnership, 2007, 3). Similarly the Minister for Social Protection, Eamon O'Cuiv TD explained in the Dáil (June 2010), the government's acceptance of this principle:

> The regeneration of long-established communities requires sensitive management, and, for long-term success, a consensus approach to the development of proposals is important. In this regard, the City Council, in addition to addressing ongoing management and maintenance issues, is working with residents to develop regeneration solutions that are acceptable to the community and that can be implemented.

The local estate-based regeneration board structures provided a vital space for such genuine resident participation in the planning and development of regeneration plans. It also provided a space for the community to work with DCC to ensure day-to-day issues were addressed. This ensured an improved level of accountability of service provision and estate management by DCC and other state agencies and a greater level of community involvement than would have been the case if these boards did not exist. Proposals by City Councillors and DCC officials in 2009 and 2010, to downgrade the status of these boards and reduce the resident participation, appear short-sighted in the light of these findings. Future regeneration projects should have residents involved at the highest level of decision making and including contract negotiations.

This will ensure the projects are determined by the needs of the local community and will gain their support and will, therefore, achieve the ultimate goal of all stakeholders: the delivery of successful regeneration within the shortest possible timeframe. The experience of many communities has led them to adopt a position of extreme cynicism and caution toward state institutions, particularly given the collapse of the projects despite the communities' best efforts. Their inclusion at the highest level will provide some guarantees to address this. It is important to remember that the residents are the ones with the real-life experience and authentic expertise on what works and what does not in managing and designing estates and, therefore, their voice should be listened to very carefully, and continuously, through the process. Ensuring residents voices are heard is, however, not an easy task.

The regeneration process is structured in such a way that exacerbates the social, class, economic, education, health and family circumstance inequalities that exists between the residents and the other stakeholders. Because of society's educational inequalities, many residents in these areas do not have the professional language of experts in relation to the complex issues associated with regeneration, such as planning, architecture, design and organisation structures. They are also dealing with issues of poor literacy, lack of self-esteem, family and health difficulties and many other disadvantages associated with intense inequality, poverty and accumulated exclusion and disadvantage. Expecting such residents to be able to engage as an equal partner simply by inviting them to be present at the meeting where decisions are made is naïve, ineffective and unfair. Central to achieving equal and adequate participation, therefore, is for residents and their representatives to receive on-going support, training and education from independent expertise. They require this, in particular, to develop their own positions and views on such key aspects to physical and social masterplanning and regeneration. These include aspects such as what is good physical design for these estates in terms of height, density, mixing or clustering of public units, open spaces, the number of public and private units, defining what community facilities are required and what is the level of social need on the estate. The Assistant City Manager also accepted in 2007, 'That ordinary residents do require capacity building and local representation in order to allow them to positively engage and participate in a bottom-up approach and in partnership with DCC' (Canal Communities Partnership, 2007, 12).

The experience of the regeneration projects suggested that the most successful mechanisms for achieving participation are the provision of resources for estate-based community development projects that provide community and regeneration workers. These can work and interact on a daily basis with the residents, supporting them in on-going consultation with other residents on the estate and addressing the day-to-day estate, family and anti-social issues, while also engaging in a process of personal development, education and capacity building. Hiring local residents to train up in these roles and to act as champions of the regeneration project can be very success-ful. These estate-based services and workers, including Community Development Projects, Family Resource Centres, youth projects, homework clubs, community drug teams etc., are essential to ensure the direct access and uptake of services by vulnerable residents who are often unable to travel any distance and are generally reluctant to avail of services outside the area or from state bodies that they do not know personally, often fear and do not trust.

3 *Ensure the regeneration process sustains the existing communities and conditions do not deteriorate*
The destabilisation, decay and destruction of the existing communities would be a significant and irreplaceable loss to the individuals, these communities and the social and cultural fabric of Dublin. Therefore, alongside addressing the inequalities affecting residents, one of the key challenges is how can existing communities be made sustainable.

The delivery of high-quality and effective estate management both pre- and post- regeneration is essential. In particular, efficient and effective responses from DCC, the Gardai and the community to problems on the estate as they arise, such as serious anti-social behaviour of gangs, intimida-tion and drug-dealing, issues of allocations and operating from the principles of community development, providing family support services and continu-ing to work with the residents to try to improve living conditions. The procedures of allocating new tenants into the estates can play an important stabilising role in ensuring there is a social mix of family types, levels of vulnerability and income levels within the public units. There should also be a minimum of delay between the vacating and reallocating of the flats to sustain the communities and address the housing waiting lists. A potential solution would be for DCC to hire teams of maintenance workers, carpenters, electricians to do the work quickly, which would also provide much-needed employment locally.

During the PPP process, the possibility of stock transfer and the role of housing associations that would guarantee high-quality estate management and maintenance services was promoted. However, despite the issues with poor estate management, the residents in the estates opposed their transfer to another landlord and sought a commitment that DCC would remain. The residents explained they had concerns about rent increases, management charges and stricter estate management control. DCC was viewed as more accountable, as it was answerable to local political representatives to whom tenants had access. There was an evident fear of the unknown. Further investigations were taking place into the potential role of housing associations and other management companies in providing improved estate management.

4 *Ensure regeneration progresses in a timely manner*
Most of the communities living in these estates are in crisis and cannot afford to wait many years for regeneration to commence. There is, therefore, a clear need for the residents to be shown, as one resident described it, 'that there is a hope and light at the end of the tunnel'. They need a financial package urgently to facilitate the construction of new homes, even on a phased basis, that would provide hope to all the residents in the areas.

5 *The importance of social regeneration*
The Fatima project achieved very positive outcomes, particularly as a result of the significant social regeneration budget that addressed some of the inequalities affecting the residents in the areas of family support, health, education, training and employment. A key lesson, therefore, from the regeneration projects researched, is the requirement for, a social enterprise plan and estate management that has an adequate budget and is given equal importance as the physical plan. Ideally, the social aspects should be developed in parallel to the physical designs and the plan should have an economic sustainability strategy that puts jobs, enterprise and economic self-reliance at its core. For example, the range of social issues raised in consultation with residents in Dolphin House included:

- impacts of inequality;
- barriers to enjoying full social engagement;
- building resident leadership and capacity;
- the effects of anti-social behaviour and intimidation;
- the negative effects of poverty and unemployment;
- health impoverishment;
- poor literacy;
- the need for training; enterprise and employment
- the need for community and recreation facilities;
- mental health especially depression and stress;
- the need for family and child support;
- the desire to maintain and sustain the existing community.

The Department of the Environment acknowledge this:

> The scope and scale of the challenges faced for the regeneration of areas of large scale deprivation involves a comprehensive multi-agency approach to social inclusion and significant non-housing public investment in services and facilities to address the key issues underlying social, economic and educational disadvantage, and incentives to stimulate the balanced tenure mix required to deliver settled sustainable communities. (Department of the Environment, interview, 2010)

Similarly, DCC recognised its importance:

> social and economic regeneration is just as important as the physical regeneration. That, while strong architectural and planning solutions are necessary, a strong social solution must also be found for areas that have suffered serious deprivation and neglect for a long number of years. (DCC, 2007)

State agencies such as the Health Services Executive, Department of Education, FAS etc. should be required to participate at an estate level in regeneration structures, just as DCC and the Gardai, in order to make social regeneration a realistic possibility.

6 *The social and economic costs are higher to everyone if regeneration is delayed*
The economic and social cost of not undertaking regeneration will be a price that these communities should not have to pay. Dealing with the outcomes of these problems will cost the state and society much more in the short, medium and long term in health, constant maintenance of dilapidated housing, in spending on social issues such as drug-related problems, school drop-out etc. rather than if it provided the investment now. The labour intensive work in regeneration also would provide vital employment at this time of crisis to local people. This could also provide an alternative source of income away from the drug trade and, thus, could encourage local youth away from drug dealing and associated criminal activities. Furthermore, investing in the physical asset of local authority housing (through maintenance, repairing, painting etc.) on an ongoing basis would be much cheaper, over the long term, than allowing it to become run-down.

As explained already, the issue of poor estate management by DCC was a major factor in the requirement and demands from the communities for regeneration. Had there been sufficient investment in the estates to ensure that they were maintained to a good standard, there, perhaps, would not have been the requirement for regeneration. Future regeneration projects need a budget for sustaining the buildings and communities post-regeneration or else they will require regenerating again in a relatively short period of time.

7 Do not allow the absence of state funding to inhibit the possibility of regeneration

Communities need to actively argue for funding and to investigate and, if necessary, pursue other models. The PPP collapse has left a vacuum for funding models. This points to the need for a radical change in government policy relating to the regeneration of disadvantaged areas and social housing provision. The challenge is how to find a model of regeneration in a harsher economic climate that can deliver in the soonest possible timeframe for these communities. The fiscal retrenchment by the government means that the social housing budget to local authorities was savagely cut in the 2009 Budget. However, regeneration and remedial works were still allocated €195m in 2010, an increase of €30m on the 2009 provision. It is important that communities exert pressure on the government to ensure this allocation is spent wisely and efficiently where it is most needed.

It is also important for the state and private sector to note that there is an openness, enthusiasm and energy on the part of local communities to undertake regeneration and find innovative models of delivery. Through the 2000s, voluntary housing organisations (Respond, 2009), academics (Punch, 2009) and community campaigners (Tenants First, 2009) have pointed out alternative policy options to the current policy orientation. Tenants First have advocated that there are more cost effective and productive ways of delivering social housing than through the €391 million that was being given annually to private landlords in rent supplement and the many more millions in stamp duty loopholes and tax incentives. An alternative policy suggested was to make social housing an option of 'first choice' (Respond, 2009) by, for example, providing the finance currently allocated for private rent supplements instead to a nation-wide programme of social and physical regeneration of local authority estates. This would provide much-needed employment in these areas, a general economic stimulus, significant improvements to the local estates and provide secure high-quality accommodation for the 50,000 people on local authority housing waiting lists, the 60,000 depending on rent supplements and the 5,000 homeless individuals (Tenants First, 2009). There are other models internationally, such as community equity partnerships, Coin Street and the Eldonians in the UK that involve community-led redevelopment and management of estates.

Another potential model that could be beneficial is a National or Regional (Dublin) Regeneration Agency. This concept was put forward by Tenants First (2009) as a method for delivering community-based regeneration and addressing the social housing crisis. For example, in Dublin, despite work on a community level in Regeneration Boards and the publication of a number of policy documents, there is a lack of co-ordination and implementation of practice across the regeneration projects. No single agency or authority appears to have a solution for providing regeneration in the post-PPP era and new models require 'outside the box' thinking. The challenges of finding funding and implementing best-practice and community-appropriate models of regeneration appear too large, sensitive and complex to be left as the sole responsibility of a local authority such as DCC. John Fitzgerald, Chairman of the Limerick Regeneration Agency and former manager of DCC, highlighted similarly that the existing local authorities in Limerick are weak and may not have the capacity and the right skills to take ownership of the Limerick regeneration process when the Regeneration Agency reaches its stated completion date of 2013.

A Dublin Social Housing and Community Regeneration Agency could undertake, be responsible for and co-ordinate the regeneration of the various estates in Dublin (and across the country in the case of a National Agency). The Agency would be a partnership of people and organisations who could deliver regeneration on this scale, including potentially representatives of DCC, central government, tenants and community, housing associations and charities and statutory and voluntary organisations, with a focus on addressing social issues in the communities. The role of private funders could also be explored (this could investigate commercial and social, education uses and analyse the demand for private residential units given the over-supply that existed in 2009 and 2010). The Agency could be an effective mechanism to facilitate the cross-fertilisation and implementation of best-practice methods and creativity in relation to physical design, social regeneration and estate management by gathering the learnings from existing national and international regeneration projects. The Agency and its operation would need to be guaranteed the funding for regeneration, the resources for implementing its tasks, legally bind the agencies into delivering regeneration for these communities, and be underpinned by legislation within which the roles of various participating agencies are clearly defined and that makes local community involvement central.

It would place a focus on the regeneration of these areas, in particular as leverage with government and private funding to maximise economies of scale and possibilies. Also, politically, the estates together would have more weight combined than separately.

8 Learning from existing state-led non-PPP regeneration projects

The Regeneration of Ballymun in Dublin City's northern suburbs is one of the largest regeneration projects in Europe. It highlights that the successful regeneration of disadvantaged areas is expensive and can take a very long time. The project started in 1997 and was estimated to be completed by 2006 at a cost of €442 million. It is now expected to be completed in 2014, eight years longer than planned and the estimated budget has doubled in cost to €942 million. The Public Accounts Committee has stated that regeneration projects must be subject to greater certainty in the context of costs and time-frames as, up to this point, the risk analysis by the Department of the Environment has been weak and should have been built into the process from the outset (Public Accounts Committee, 2009). In the past decade, the state has invested more than €100 million in DCC inner-city flats regeneration programmes, including projects led by the state in Upper Bridgefoot Street and Ballybough/Poplar Row. These two exemplary redevelopments of public housing provide a successful example of new build and refurbishment schemes that are very attractively designed.

9 *Make the case for the implementation of the government's own best-practice policy guidance for regeneration projects*
Key documents to use in this regard include the Comptroller and Auditor General's Special Report No. 61 on Ballymun Regeneration (November 2007) and its recommendations on future Regeneration Programmes. Regeneration is also subject to a detailed policy framework set out in Chapter 8 of *Delivering Homes, Sustaining Communities* (DOEHLG, 2005). The Centre for Housing Research have published detailed good-practice guidelines entitled – Regenerating Estates, Rebuilding Vibrant Communities. The National Building Agency has a Regeneration unit that provides consultancy services to local authorities in the provision of social and affordable housing.

10 *Update the* National Development Plan, 2007–2013
The housing aspects of the plan are now outdated and inappropriate as the original plan is based on a PPP model that has failed in the delivery of social and affordable housing and regeneration.

11 *Implement Legislation underpinning these principles*
Legislation is required to ensure that local authorities and regeneration agencies implement these lessons on a coherent and uniform basis, regardless of a change of government or local authority personnel. The practice of regeneration is determined locally on the basis of the particular perspectives of the relevant local authority officials and the determination and organisa-tion of local community and resident organisations to articulate and assert their vision.

Notes

1 Some of the deeper causes of anti-social behaviour often lie in societal inequalities (Irish Penal Reform Trust, 2005).

2 Tenants First is a forum of tenants and community workers from Local Authority Estates across Dublin City who were formed in 2004 to share information and experiences and support each other on issues of common concern, particularly, in relation to regeneration.

3 Dublin City Council de-tenanted (de-populate the estates by moving residents elsewhere and not reallocating the vacant flat) the estates during the PPP process, in preparation for demolition.

4 These figures are based on an estimated cost of provision per social unit of €200,000 and an estimated land value of €10 million per acre (€24 million per hectare). These estimations and the associated demolition and social facilities costs were ascertained from interviews and secondary sources (Fatima Groups United, 2006; interview O'Devaney Gardens Residents' Representative 1, 2008; interview St Michaels Estate Community Worker, 2008; Kelly and MacLaran, 2004).

5 See note above for sources.

6 The Infirmary Road and Convent Lands were affordable housing PPP projects in Dublin City based on the transfer of public land to a private developer (in these instances McNamara). The private developer then builds affordable housing for sale on the land. These PPP projects are different from the social housing PPP projects that this chapter makes reference to.

7 Community Action Network is an Irish community development organisation that provides training, organisational development, facilitation, participative processes to organisations that work in communities. It is dedicated to creating a more equal society that has the well-being of its citizens at its heart.

6

Public Private Partnership outcomes in Ireland

There needs to be real clarity around what the obligations are on the private operator (in PPPs), who is responsible, who coughs up the money, because too often in my view it's the state that ends up picking up the tab, that's the difficulty. (Minister for the Environment, John Gormley TD, interview, 2010)

Delivery of private-sector finance

One of the principal reasons for the introduction of PPPs by the Irish government was that they would address the public infrastructure and services deficit through the provision of additional funding in the form of private-sector finance. However, PPPs failed to achieve the expected target objective to provide between 10 per cent and 15 per cent of capital investment over the period of the *National Development Plan, 2000–2006*. By 2008, PPPs involving additional private finance were completed only for the roads, education and housing sectors, despite also being planned for the waste and health sectors (Figure 6.1).

In order to address the poor level of PPP deal flow, the government decided to introduce a fourth piece of enabling legislation, the National Development Finance Agency (Amendment) Act, 2007, to extend the powers of the National Development Finance Agency (NDFA).[1] This includes the allocation of a new procurement function to the NDFA, giving it the power to enter into PPPs and then transfer them to a relevant state authority, or to act as agent for state authorities in PPP procurement. The Act also provides for representatives of the Social Partners (two extra private-sector representatives and a representative of the Irish Congress of Trade Unions) to become members of the Board of the NDFA. The Act aimed to allow the NDFA to support government departments rapidly to improve the level of funding, deal flow and rate of completion of projects. Its impact can be demonstrated by the expansion in 2007 and 2008 in the number of projects that were

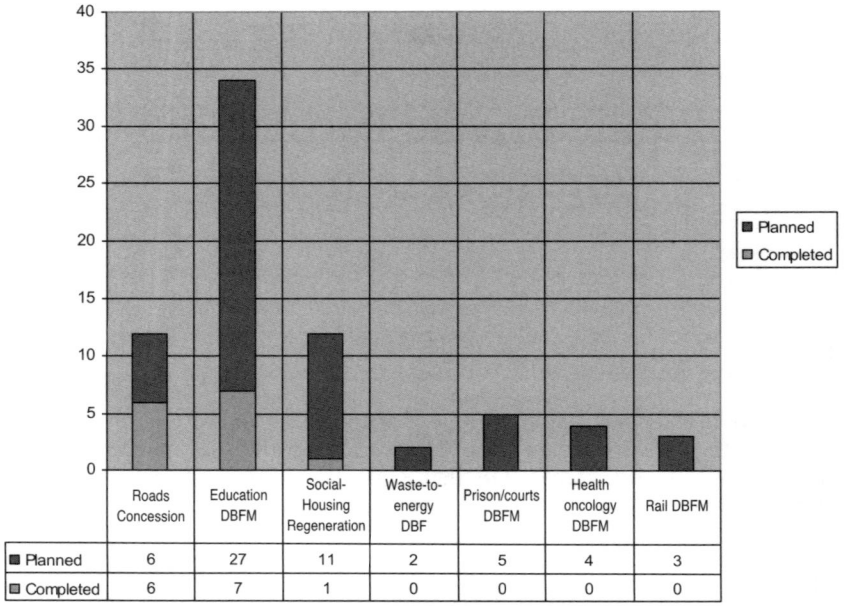

	Roads Concession	Education DBFM	Social-Housing Regeneration	Waste-to-energy DBF	Prison/courts DBFM	Health oncology DBFM	Rail DBFM
Planned	6	27	11	2	5	4	3
Completed	6	7	1	0	0	0	0

Figure 6.1 Number of completed and planned PPPs using private finance as of 2008

Source: Central PPP Unit (2005, 2006, 2007, 2008).

planned and reaching contract-award stage involving private finance, such as the extension of the LUAS line to the Docklands and Cherrywood and of public buildings, such as the Criminal Courts of Justice Project and the National Conference Centre (Figures 6.1 and 6.2). For example, up to 50 per cent of the projected cost for the extensions of the LUAS Green and Red Line PPPs was to be provided through private finance in the form of the sharing of development gain that was associated with the location of high-quality light rail as part of private developments.[2] As of 2008, the NDFA had advised on over sixty projects for which PPP procurement had been considered.

However, the collapse in 2007 and 2008 in the Irish property market, construction sector and banking system, combined with the international financial crisis and 'credit crunch' led to a severe contraction in economic growth. As a result, Ireland was the first Eurozone country to enter recession in 2008. As explained in the previous chapter, the banking and financial crisis resulted in the failure of DCC's social housing regeneration projects. The economic crisis also had a negative impact internationally on the volume and value of PPP projects that reached completion in 2008 and 2009 (European Commission, 2009).

Financial institutions were therefore less inclined towards PPPs. Some

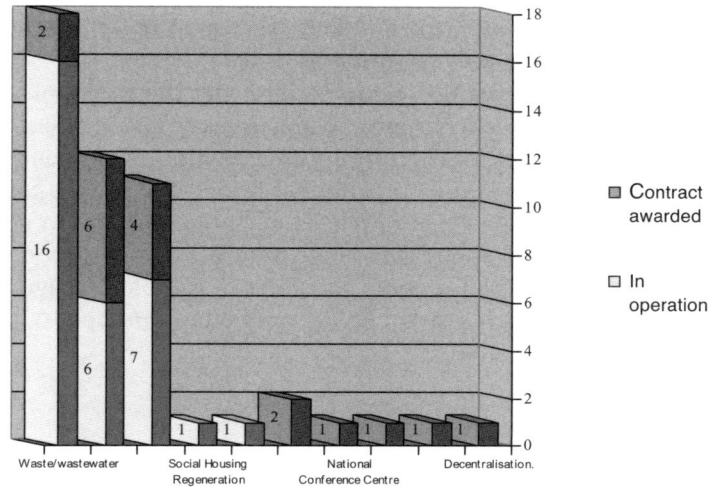

	Waste/ waste water	Roads	Schools	Social Housing	Rail	Prison/ Courts	National Con- ference	Urban redevel- opment	Waste- to- Energy	Decent- ralisa- tion
▣ Contract awarded	2	6	4			2	1	1	1	1
☐ In operation	16	6	7	1	1					

Figure 6.2 Number of PPP contracts awarded per sector up to 2008

Source: Central PPP Unit (2005, 2006, 2007, 2008).

were not prepared to provide credit to private consortia that were bidding on PPP projects because of a change in risk assessment associated with their development. In other cases, where they were prepared to lend to a PPP consortium, the financial conditions attached to the debt were very expensive. This led to a significant increase in the cost of debt for PPP projects and they therefore became increasingly unviable economically for private companies to undertake. Furthermore, the banks were unwilling to commit significant finance in advance of contract signature. This reduction in banking capacity to provide finance has resulted in less bidders being in a position to enter the procurement process, which has reduced the effectiveness and extent of competition, a key driver of value for money in the PPP process.

This has severely affected the viability of planned projects, particularly those that involved leveraging development gain through realising the value of property. These included land transfer PPPs planned to be used for the relocation and rebuilding of the third-level college, the Dublin Institute of Technology to Grangegorman, the redevelopment of public swimming pools in Dublin and the decentralisation programme (for which almost €1 billion was to be invested), which involved the sale and provision of new buildings for various government Departments. The collapse in the property market placed all these projects in serious jeopardy.

Overall, the Irish experience demonstrated that the provision of additional finance for investment in public infrastructure and services through PPPs, despite being a principal benefit outlined by the government, did not materialise to the extent planned initially. Moreover, the market collapse in 2008 and 2009 demonstrated that to rely on the private sector, in particular financial markets and private lenders, to guarantee the provision of finance for public infrastructure and services was a naïve gamble that ignored the reality that markets are inherently cyclical and, often, unstable (Callinicos, 2003; Harvey, 1989; Leys, 2001).

Speed of delivery of PPPs

The Irish government asserted that overall delivery times for the Grouped Schools Pilot PPP Project and PPPs in the water/waste-water, light rail and roads sectors have been faster than those achieved by traditional projects. However, the evidence from the Grouped Schools Pilot PPP Project is not as conclusive. The Comptroller and Auditor General (C & AG) found that the PPP route resulted in the provision of schools within the same timescale as the traditional route. More generally, the C & AG raised the methodological issue of comparing the relative speed of delivery of PPP projects with the conventional approach. While the government might state PPP projects were delivered systemically, or intrinsically, faster than traditional methods, this ignored the reality that once funding was provided for a PPP project, the legal contract with the private partner then ensured the project developed and progressed. This is not the case in traditional methods where the state sometimes decides to delay or halt the provision of funding for a project even when the project has already commenced and, as a result, the project's timescale of delivery is significantly lengthened. The availability of funding, therefore, in some instances, impacted on the timescale of delivery more than the actual method of delivery. This meant it was very difficult to compare the relative speed of completion of PPP projects with traditional projects in a balanced manner. The regeneration projects demonstrated that the PPP process could be subject to many delays and even termination resulting from complexities involved in the PPP contract and procurement negotiations. For example, PPP Assessments and a PSB must be prepared, the NDFA must then be contacted for financial advice and risk assessments and evaluations must be undertaken in a PPP process, but not in the traditional procurement process.

As of 2008, just over half of the Pilot PPP projects were developed, with the remainder either still at planning stage or, in one instance, being cancelled as a PPP project and procured instead through the traditional route (Table 6.1). In 2003, the Department of Health and Children announced the development of seventeen Community Nursing Units as a PPP project. It was to provide 850 beds in community units to reduce the requirements for acute beds in the major hospitals and provide a higher quality of care to older people. However, two years later, in 2005, the Health Services Executive (HSE) cancelled the project because of the delays, complexities over public and private staff hiring and greater expense in the PPP process. The delays associated with, and failure of, this PPP model, therefore, had a direct negative impact on the bed-capacity crisis within the health sector.

Table 6.1 Pilot PPP projects status

PPP project	Projected procurement Start date	Status
Post-Primary Schools Bundle	2000	2003 In operation
Cork School of Music	2000	2000 In operation
M50 Second Westlink Bridge	2000	2003 In operation
N4 Kilcock to Kinnegad	2000	2005 In operation
Dublin Light Rail	2000	2004 In operation
N25 Waterford Bypass	2001	2010 Projected
N7 Limerick S.Ring	2000	2010 Projected
Dublin Thermal Treatment Plant	2001	2010 Projected
Ballymore Eustace Water Works	2001	Cancelled

Source: DOEHLG (2001), Central PPP Unit (2008).

Examination of the available data from the Central PPP Unit reveal that there was a delay of at least one year for over half of all the PPP projects planned and/or completed in Ireland, between the projected date of commencement and/or construction of the projects in 2005 and the date projected in 2008. The delay applied to 50 per cent of PPPs in the roads sector, 61 per cent in education and, because of the withdrawal of private-sector interest, reached 91 per cent in the social housing regeneration projects (Figure 6.3). In addition, the planned PPP acquisition by the HSE of thirty-six new linear accelerator facilities to improve radiotherapy treatment for cancer patients was delayed by at least three years, in the main because of complexities associated with the PPP model of procurement and issues with staff transfer, with the projected completion date being moved from 2011 to 2014. A HSE report found that the facilities would be sourced more quickly outside the PPP model (Joan Burton TD, Dáil Éireann, 2007).

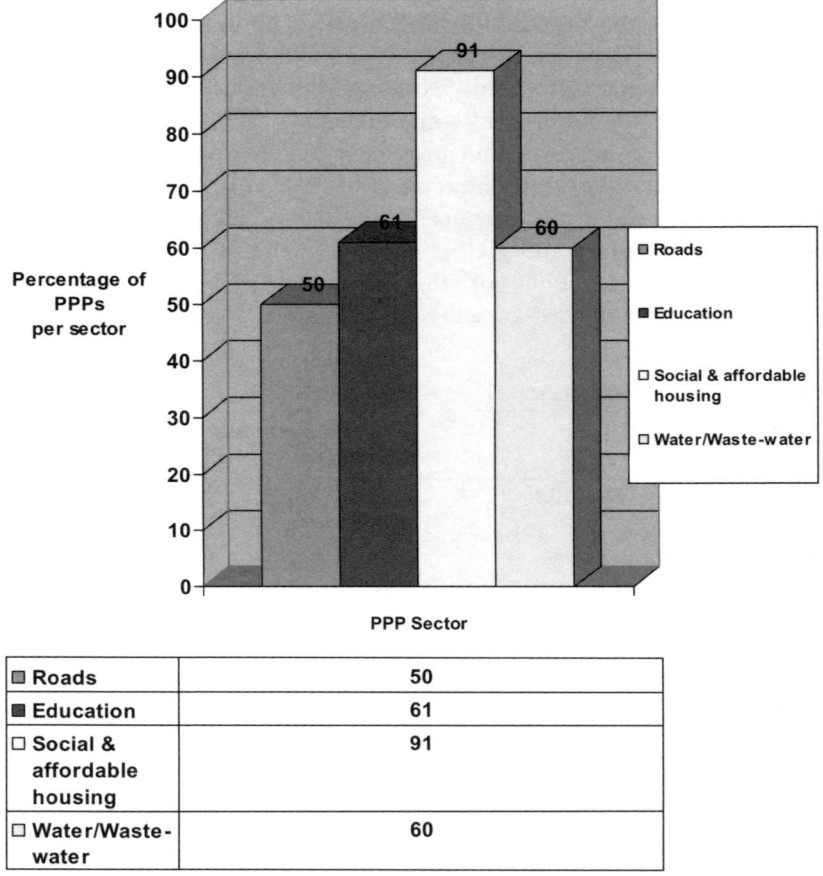

▨ Roads	50
▨ Education	61
▢ Social & affordable housing	91
▢ Water/Waste-water	60

Figure 6.3 Percentage of PPPs per sector in Ireland involving delays of at least one year

Source: Central PPP Unit (2005, 2006, 2007, 2008).

Value for money

> What sort of value are we getting from PPPs? In the short term and the long term – does it work out actually more costly in some cases in the long term? That's the question you have to ask yourself, and I don't think we have come to a definitive judgement on that as of yet. (Minister for the Environment, interview, 2010)

The C & AG undertook the only detailed assessment of the government's primary stated benefit of PPPs, the provision of greater value for money, available in the public domain. This includes analysis of the Beaumont Hospital Car Park PPP (2003), the Grouped Schools Pilot PPP Project (2004) and the Criminal Courts of Justice Project (2008).

The analysis of the PPP schools found that the PPP model was in fact *more* expensive, over the complete life-time of that project, than the conventional, direct, public-provision model and questions remained, therefore, about the ability of PPP projects to achieve value for money. As the C & AG (2004, 46) explained: 'it remained to be tested whether or not the final deal would deliver the required service to the school communities over twenty-five years at a cost that would be less than that incurred through direct state procurement and funding of the schools'. Similarly, the Audit Commission UK (2009, 12) explained its view on PFI projects: 'it is neither always good value for money, nor always poor value for money. It has the potential to deliver benefits but not at any price or in any circumstances. In practice, its value is contingent on a wide range of contract, sectoral and other factors.'

While the C & AG (2008) found in relation to the Criminal Courts of Justice Project that the PPP deal represented better value than procurement by conventional means, the extent to which value for money will be achieved in the project depends on the active management of various costs through periodic market testing and the extent of efficiencies achieved in the running of court business through this new public infrastructure.

It is difficult to independently ascertain whether or not PPPs achieve value for money because the information required to undertake such analysis has not been made publicly accessible. The PSB and the overall terms of the PPP contract are not accessible because of 'commercial confidentiality' clauses. This meant that the Irish citizens could not know, aside from C & AG Reports, or not till long after projects had been either commenced or completed, whether or not value for money was achieved. This is a radical reduction in the public and democratic accountability of public infrastructure and services projects, a vital aspect to providing quality and efficient public services and a central objective of a liberal democratic state.

The absence of accountability led Fine Gael, the largest political party in opposition at that time, to submit a motion to amend the NDFA (Amendment) Bill 2006 that would have obliged the government to publish the PSB calculations. However, the government opposed the motion. In addition, the refusal of state agencies, such as the NDFA and the NRA to report on their individual PPP projects at Oireachtas Committees, for example the Public Accounts Committee, further reduced accountability. This also left open the potential for conflict of interest as the NDFA both approved PPPs and had a very significant role in organising funding for them, having the authority to borrow up to €5 billion to do so. The confidentiality surrounding PSBs left open the possibility of their being altered if the outcomes were not favourable enough for PPP, identified in Chapter 2 as being the experience of other countries (Audit Commission UK, 2003; Murray, 2006; Pollock and Price, 2004). For example, if the value of risks transferred to the private partner is over-estimated, then the PSB could be biased in favour of the PPP option:

> It is about gamekeepers and poachers. The evaluation needs to be in the public domain so that we understand the basis on which we sign up to the project ... We in the Oireachtas receive no public monitoring of critical projects in the PPP cost–benefit process ... We must be careful about the PPP process because it has the capacity to go wrong if not properly managed. (Richard Bruton TD, Dáil Éireann, 2007)

Analysis of the Grouped Schools Pilot PPP Project, the water/waste-water and the Criminal Courts projects brings into question the accuracy and objectivity of the methods involved in the calculation of the PSB. It appeared that state agencies, in some cases, were exaggerating the risks associated with cost overruns in traditional provision in order to bias the PSBs in favour of PPPs. For instance, calculations undertaken by Services Industrial Professional and Technical Union (SIPTU) for the Ballymore Eustace water-treatment plant PPP found, in contradiction to a Department of the Environment analysis, that operation through the traditional public-sector model would provide better value for money than the PPP route. Supported by this analysis, SIPTU applied political pressure, including protest, and, as a result, the state accepted the analysis and decided to operate and procure the plant in the traditional manner by the local authority.

Further analysis undertaken by SIPTU, in conjunction with local authority management, found that PSB calculations undertaken by private consultants on behalf of the Department of the Environment were inaccurate. For example, their PSB, which projected savings of up to 28 per cent in a waste-water DBO PPP, had, according to SIPTU, involved '*massive speculation*' on the value of risk transfer that resulted in a bias towards the PPP option. Using more realistic assumptions in the PSB, SIPTU found that the PPP's projected saving was a mere 5 per cent. Similar calculations applied to other treatment schemes found that the planned PPPs would only be 7 per cent cheaper than that which could be undertaken through the traditional mechanism. The 7 per cent would have approximated to a €40,000 saving which, SIPTU asserted, was not significant enough to justify outsourcing the operation of the treatment plant to the private sector.

In addition, the Courts Service PSB for the Criminal Courts of Justice was criticised for not exploring the sensitivity of the results to different assumptions (C & AG, 2008). The PSB projected that it would cost €436 million to develop and operate the Criminal Courts over twenty-five years using a conventional procurement approach. The C & AG found that this was significantly greater than the cost projected in the original business case, and if some of the assumptions underlying the PSB were altered to accommodate more realistic circumstances, the results changed significantly. For example, if the recurrent costs were assumed to increase at the same rate as inflation (that is 2 per cent a year rather than the 4 per cent used in the PSB), the projected cost of conventional procurement would be €377 million, that is about €59 million (14 per cent) below the benchmark figure of €436 million. These outcomes corresponded to the international PPP experience, where government departments adjusted the PSB calculations, particularly the underlying assumptions, to favour adoption of the PPP option (Murray, 2006; Pollock and Price, 2004). Whitfield (2006) has pointed to the need to shift narrow PSB evaluation models away from a focus just on financial efficiency, risk transfer and value-for-money criteria to an integrated impact assessment covering social justice, economics, equalities, sustainable development and a community well-being assessment. These, he affirms, should be used for appraisal, selection and bid-evaluation stages of PPPs (Whitfield, 2006).

PPPs also included additional expenses to the traditional model, as detailed in Chapters 4 and 5, because of the extra costs that were central to the PPP form of procurement, including the large expenses related to the bidding process for both the private and public sectors, charges associated with risk transfer, increased scope of work to accommodate facilities management and to provide for third-party income generation. Because the public sector does not have the same level of expertise, skills or capacity to deliver and manage the highly complex and time-consuming bidding, procurement and negotiation processes, in comparison to the private sector, there is a need for a substantial public expenditure on professional, consultation, legal and financial fees associated with difficult and complex contractual issues, including appropriate risk allocation. Costs of bids have been as high as €5 million (C & AG, 2004, European Commission, 2009). The Audit Commission Scotland (2002) found that the combined set-up and advisers' cost in PPP projects ranged from £1 million to £12 million, comprising between 5 per cent and 15 per cent of core construction costs. As one DCC Official explained:

> A huge amount of professional services are outsourced by the public sector and as a result we are being fleeced by fees. In the multimillion PPP states it costs extraordinary amounts, e.g. it cost half a million euro in one regeneration project to draw up the legal document; it was daylight robbery. The bid costs are huge and the private sector has to get this back. The public sector ends up paying for it. (Dublin City Council Official, interview, 2006)

These are some of the 'inherent difficulties in setting up PPPs' (European Commission, 2009) which also include the fundamental requirement for PPPs to be designed in order to allow private partners the potential to generate a profitable return. These private-sector returns, which investment advisors estimate range between 10 per cent and 15 per cent of the cost of the projects, are an additional expense over and above that in traditional delivery. Speaking during the Seanaid debate on the introduction of the NDFA (Amendment) Bill 2006, independent Senator and businessman Fergal Quinn argued that this inescapable fact meant that PPPs are inevitably a more expensive way of funding a project because they must allow for an element of profit to cover the risk the private-sector partner is taking by getting involved.

The use of private finance further added to the cost of PPPs because it has been more expensive than exchequer-borrowed finance. Moreover, while private finance can provide access to large amounts of funding 'up-front' and can be placed 'off balance sheet', the annual payments required to pay for this more expensive form of finance are an, essentially, accountancy trick that obscures the true, full, cost of PPPs. Ultimately, over the long term, they will require additional *public* expenditure over and above that which would be required if public funding was provided up front. For example, the stated cost of the PPP DBFO Poolbeg incinerator is €350 million, but the total cost of repayments that the state will pay the private operator over the twenty-five year contract life will be €600 million. Meanwhile profits of €1 billion will be generated for the private companies involved (Irish Independent, 2010).

Furthermore, the Irish government's claim that involving private finance through concession-type PPPs that offer the ability to implement user charges, such as road tolls, would provide greater value for money through the reduction in the requirement for exchequer funding is questionable. This is due to the fact that the income generated from such user fees appears to have gone, in the main, to the private PPP consortia rather than reducing the annual payments required from the state. This can be seen in the significant profits made by National Toll Roads (NTR), the private operator of the M50 West-Link toll bridge PPP in Dublin when the state bought it out in 2008.

Growing traffic gridlock on the M50 motorway had reached crisis point in 2008 and the toll bridge was being blamed for adding significantly to the delays experienced by the users of the 100,000 vehicles that passed over it. It led to the point where Dublin's main daily newspaper the *Evening Herald* launched a campaign to 'Stop the M50 Toll Madness'.

The introduction of 'barrier free' tolling was proposed as a mechanism to reduce the traffic jams on the motorway, however the private operator was reluctant to make the necessary changes because of cost implications. The PPP contract meant that it would be another twelve years before ownership of the bridge could be transferred back to the state. As a result, the Irish government had to pay approximately €600 million (€50 million per annum to National Toll Roads between August 2008 and March 2020) to purchase the complete ownership of the project so that it could implement barrier-free tolling.

Ultimately, the assessment of the ability of PPPs to achieve value for money is difficult to accurately ascertain, because such an analysis can only be done when the contract of the PPP projects reach conclusion, which is in a period of between twenty and thirty years time, depending on the length and date of commencement of the contract. This means that PPPs could have a severe impact on future public finances if, at the end of the contract life of these projects, it is found that the projects undertaken and planned, do not provide value for money.

The economic crisis and resultant fiscal deficits that emerged from 2008 onwards raised an important aspect of PPPs that had, up to that date, been given insufficient recognition. That is the unaccounted economic and financial implications of PPP contracts and commitments that have been entered into for lengthy periods of time.

The Central PPP Unit accepted this, in response to questions from the author, when it stated that there are important considerations around the affordability and sustainability of payments allocated to PPPs into the future. For, at the simplest level, PPPs utilise private funds in the short term to finance infrastructure construction, and this debt must then be repaid by the Exchequer over the long term. It is, therefore, the Central PPP Unit (interview, 2010) noted, 'desirable that decisions about the use of PPPs will ensure that future unitary payments are kept at a sustainable level, taking account of other budgetary demands'. Similarly the Department of the Environment (interview, 2010) noted that the outstanding commitments of Departments and agencies in respect of contracted PPPs 'is a significant commitment to infrastructure projects given the current economic crisis'. Overall the Central PPP Unit (interview, 2010) noted that 'the PPP approach is demanding, and resourcing this complex form of procurement has proved to be a challenge across many jurisdictions'.

It can be argued then that PPPs have been used by governments as 'an accounting ruse to shift long-term financial commitments off the government's balance sheet, especially in times of fiscal difficulties' (OECD, 2008, 47). Thus, they conceal the real expenditure and liabilities from public balance sheets, loading up costs for the future, with unforeseen consequences, including the impact of the committed unitary cost obligations of these projects that must be paid regardless of the budgetary circumstances of government finances.

A form of privatisation and neoliberalism

The Irish government asserted that PPPs were not a form of privatisation as they would not involve any transfer of assets out of public ownership and that there would be no withdrawal from services, no impact of private shareholder interest, nor loss of control over public infrastructure and services to the private sector:

> PPPs are simply another procurement option to be pursued in certain cases ... PPPs do not diminish a public authority's role or abilities. Public authorities entering into PPP arrangements remain responsible and accountable for the delivery of public services. In this respect, PPPs are very different to privatisation. (DOEHLG PPP Unit, interview, 2006)

It was posited that PPPs would simply provide a more structured and co-ordinated approach for extending the areas of co-operation between the public and private sectors that had long existed in Ireland's mixed economy. PPPs were simply continuing the situation whereby the state did not own or maintain much of the public infrastructure and services such as hospitals and schools which, traditionally, had been built, maintained and managed by private religious organisations throughout most of the twentieth century. The Central PPP Unit (interview, 2006) explained that 'our schools were a PPP but it just wasn't a contract written down; it's been set up that way for 150 years. The British brought the private sector into what was a state-provided service – we never had that – it was state-financed provision rather than state-operated.'

The Irish Congress of Trade Unions (ICTU) agreed, in reflection of its acceptance of and agreement to the Social Partnership model, with the perspective that PPPs did not amount to outright privatisation and argued that the public project ultimately reverts back to public ownership and the standards, quality of service and charges are all factors in the equation that distinguish PPPs from privatisation. It believes that the state determines a lot more aspects in a PPP project than in outsourcing and privatisation as the state has a guiding role in setting standards. Therefore, ICTU consented to the introduction of PPPs as a preferable method, in terms of the impact on public-sector employees and public services, to privatisation.

There is considerable evidence, however, to support the contention that PPPs are indeed a form of privatisation and *neoliberalisation* of key aspects of the Irish state such as public policy, public infrastructure and services delivery and labour conditions. This supports the international literature, detailed in Chapter 2, which identifies similar trends in PPPs across the world (Allen, 2007; George, 2004; Monbiot, 2000; Sweeney, 2004; Whitfield, 2006). It contradicts the assertions made by both the government and ICTU.

The reality is that asset transfer did take place in PPP projects, such as the social housing regeneration projects, where public land was transferred into private-sector ownership. In addition, projects involved transferring aspects of the control and operation of key public infrastructure and services over to the commercial private sector in areas of the state that were, up to that point, purely the domain of the non-commercial public sector. For example, the operation and maintenance of public infrastructure and services in the water/waste-water, rail, waste collection and road sectors were transferred to private companies. While public schools and other public infrastructure and services traditionally had a high degree of private-sector involvement in the form of religious institutions, it was on a 'not-for-profit' basis as opposed to PPPs which involved 'for-profit' commercial companies. In these services, the control of the asset was transferred to the private operator for the duration of the contract, which was, in general, a significant length of time.

It appears then that the approach which proposed PPPs as a less severe form of privatisation, or as merely entailing the continuation of the religious-state provision model in another form, was promoted in order to minimise potential concerns and opposition. Had they been presented as 'privatisation' public-sector workers, trade unions, elected representatives and the public could have raised considerable objections. The descriptions and definitions of PPPs put forward by the state were about influencing the perception of PPPs and disguising the policy and practical reality. As a result, while some individual trade unions and citizen campaigns did oppose PPPs as a form or threat of further privatisation (for example, the protest at the 2001 Global PPP Summit held in Dublin by Ballymore Eustace water-treatment plant workers, trade unionists and anti-corporate globalisation protestors), among most trade unions, the public and political parties there has been very little opposition to the expansion and development of PPPs in Ireland.

The various components and impacts of the privatisation and *neoliberalisation* process, introduced into the public infrastructure and services delivery aspects of the Irish state, through PPP projects are now detailed. These include the significance and impact of the transfer of control of public services to the 'for-profit' private sector, the introduction of commercialisation, the increasing role of global multinationals and the impact on labour conditions.

Impact of private-sector involvement
This intensity of involvement of private businesses in the direct delivery of public infrastructure and services through PPPs could have very significant impacts on how and at what level and quality these public infrastructure and services are provided in Ireland. This is because, in PPPs, the private operator is given a considerable amount of control and power to define what the exact

day-to-day service and maintenance provision is over the lifetime of the PPP contract (Monbiot, 2000; Pollock and Price, 2004; Whitfield, 2006). In the transport sector, excellent service quality was achieved in the LUAS and motorway PPPs. The design and construction element for the Fatima regeneration project and water/waste-water treatment scheme PPPs in Cork, Limerick and Wexford were also successfully completed. The Grouped Schools Pilot PPP Project, however, did not prove conclusively to provide an improved service compared to that which existed in traditionally provided public schools. In some instances, the original private company refused to undertake the provision of services and equipment that were not clearly defined in the contract.

Furthermore, contrary to government claims, the public infrastructure and services provided through the PPPs was not an asset or service that was freely available to be altered or amended according to the requirements of the public sector. Any changes or flexibility required by the public sector, outside of contract definitions, in many instances entailed the private consortium charging large amounts for such changes. This was also found to be the experience in PFI schools in the UK (Partnerships UK, 2004). A SIPTU representative that had been involved in negotiating waste-water PPPs explained that the overall result of the PPP is that the facility is no longer in the full control of a public body. Generally, the public can have an input into public facilities through elected public representatives, but, if it is part private, then that is not as straightforward. He believed that PPPs are a form of privatisation, a way to restructure the work-force and, in the long-term, are a stepping stone to full privatisation.

An example of these issues that can arise is provided by the experience of the Dublin (Ringsend) waste-water treatment plant, the largest of such PPP plants in Ireland, with an estimated cost of €300 million. The residents of the areas in Dublin's south city in the vicinity of the plant, which include Ringsend, Sandymount and Irishtown, have suffered since 2003 from a persistent foul odour emanating from the plant (Kelly, 2008a). The extent of the impact on the local population from the odours led the Minister for the Environment to commission an investigation into the cause of the odours in 2008. The resultant Fehilly Report (2008) found that the odour problems were created to a significant extent by inadequate design and equipment failure in the plant. It also noted that there was constant conflict between DCC and the private operator, Celtic Anglian Water (CAW), in trying to deal with the problems.

Ultimately, it was the state, not the private operator, that had to pay for the changes required to address the problems. Of the €24.5 million allocated to the plant in 2006, €5 million was spent on odour-alleviation measures, which DCC asserted would be paid for by CAW. DCC, however, ended up paying €35.6 million to CAW to address the problem. This was despite DCC stating that it would not 'sign-off' on the project until the private operators had eliminated the problem and the Exchequer would not pay for the plant's inadequacies (Kelly, 2008).

This demonstrated that private-sector involvement did not automatically guarantee a better-quality service and additionally, in this instance, provided a service that had negative impacts on the local population and environment. This outcome resulted, arguably, from the private operator's profit maximisation requirements that meant it refused to invest the required finance to address the odours.

The Minister for the Environment (interview, 2010) stated that while he 'had no difficulty at all with PPPs in waste-water/water infrastructure, as the water quality has improved in many cases,' significantly he stated that the lesson from the Ringsend treatment plant is that 'there needs to be real clarity around what the obligations are on the private operator, who is responsible, who coughs up the money, because too often in my view it's the state that ends up picking up the tab, that's the difficulty'.

This scenario also highlights a potentially longer-term problem where, if environmental quality standards are changed and renegotiation of the PPP contracts is required, the private operator tends to charge significant amounts of money for any changes. The case of the West-Link toll road also demonstrates this point. When the public sector required changes to the service, it had to pay over half a billion euro to purchase the PPP contract from the private operator it could undertake the required changes.

These cases also demonstrate that when problems emerged in the PPP projects, and the private operators failed to take responsibility for these problems and did not adequately provide the necessary service, the state, because of its obligations and responsibilities had to remain involved in ensuring the public infrastructure and services were provided at the required standard and remained in operation. The 'risk' that had, officially, been passed to the private sector was actually taken on by the state when it materialised. Most significantly, this took place at a cost to the state and not, as PPP theory states it should, to the private sector:

> When the local authorities embark on something, if it doesn't work out, invariably, the state picks up the tab. I mean we were just talking about the banks there – if that doesn't work out the state will have to intervene in many cases and pick up the tab, unless you have a contract that states clearly what the private operator will do. But too often it doesn't work out like that, and that's my concern. You are talking about this phrase 'risk sharing', but who takes on the risk? And too often it's the state that takes on that risk. (Minister for the Environment, interview, 2010)

A senior official (interview, 2006) within DCC made a similar comment that criticised the reality that while, theoretically in PPPs, the private sector is meant to take the risk:

> when push comes to shove the private sector doesn't want to take the risk, e.g. in the odour/overcapacity of the Ringsend waste-water treatment plant PPP, the private sector didn't want to know about the problems; there were terrible rows and arguments over who would have to pay for alterations ... How many of these situations of risk allocation arguments will arrive down the road? It's just not true that the private sector takes on risk. The government sells the process with that terminology, but when the risk materialises, everyone runs away; the private sector doesn't want to know about it. (DCC, interview, 2006)

Therefore, it was the state, as proven in the Ringsend treatment plant PPP, West-Link toll bridge PPP and social housing PPP projects, despite the PPP proponents' claims, that was the partner left with the majority of risk because it, and not the private partner, was the partner that had to pay for the expense of a risk when it materialised. The successful transfer of risk over to the private sector was also supposed to ensure value for money was achieved in PPPs. It can be clearly seen then that the theoretical benefits of risk transfer assigned to PPPs were not evident to any great extent in completed Irish PPP projects. These important findings point to the requirement for a profound reassessment of the continued development and operation of this model of PPPs in Ireland. It is noteworthy that it reflects similar trends found in other countries, most notably the UK and Canada (Monbiot, 2000; Murray, 2006; Pollock and Price 2004; Whitfield, 2001, 2006).

Reduction in public-sector capacity

The PPP tendering process, which specified and packaged projects into suitable contract tenders facilitated the marketised restructuring of these public services and infrastructure. The formation of autonomous quasi-governmental institutions, such as the National Roads Authority, the Rail Procurement Agency and other agencies to promote and facilitate PPPs, increases the likelihood that these agencies and, therefore, services and assets, will be fully privatised in the future. For example Sweeney (2004) noted that the NRA could easily be commercialised to facilitate the privatisation of parts of major road networks in the future, particularly after the massive publicly funded investment programme already underway.

Over the extensive life time of the PPP contracts, it is also likely that experience and skills within the public sector will be lost within in these areas. This has been found to be the case in the UK, where there was a reduction in the extent to which public bodies retained ownership and control of the public sector's intellectual capital and institutional capacity. This includes the skills, experience, knowledge and information about the infrastructure, the rationale of services, how they work etc. that enables public bodies to respond effectively to changing circumstances and emergencies (Whitfield, 2006). This vital information, built up over decades, is being transferred to the private sector. This is a reversal of direct, 'in-house', public provision, which has built up skills and experience that enables public bodies to respond to changing demands, circumstances and emergencies. Critically, it also reduces the important ability of public bodies to examine from public service and local economy perspectives the potential impact of the policies of government, the EU and business. A likely result of this process is that the only option, at the end of a typical twenty-five year PPP contract, will be for the Irish state to re-contract the project to the existing, or another, private operator because the public sector, itself, will not have the skills or experience to undertake that area of operation or provision. Therefore, while a PPP might not entail immediate or direct asset transfer to the private sector; this is, in all likelihood, what ultimately will take place. The scale and extent of the increase in private-sector control and involvement in PPPs can be classed as nothing other than a form of creeping privatisation.

The involvement of the private sector combined with the unaccountable nature of PPP arrangements can also potentially lead to increased corruption. Questions were raised by Dublin City Councillors at the emergency meeting of DCC on 26 May 2008 about the awarding of the five PPP housing contracts and the contract for Thornton Hall Prison to Michael McNamara & Co.

Commercialisation of public services
The introduction of user fees for public services is central to the neoliberal policy agenda. PPPs have facilitated the introduction and intensification of this policy through the introduction of and increase in of user fees for toll roads and light rail. The necessity for such fees in PPPs was stated frankly by a PPP Unit representative (interview, 2008) when he explained that 'it has to be a quid pro-quo that the private sector gets profit, while it might cost more for the user. There has to be profit, otherwise it doesn't work.'

Indeed, the government promoted the *'unlimited'* potential for the development of PPPs funded by user fees. Assistant Secretary of the Department of the Taoiseach, Mary Doyle, speaking at the 3rd Annual PPP Policy Forum (2007) explained that, 'since Ireland is the home of the entrepreneur there is no limit on any projects that can be undertaken by PPP where they are funded entirely by using charges'. The roads, schools, waste and water/waste-water sectors demonstrate how, because the private sector required an income as the basis of its involvement, the use of PPPs necessitated, the commercialisation of, and private-capital control over, public resources and assets.

The experience of toll roads has also been contentious regarding the increased cost to road users as a result of the necessity to provide returns to the private operators. While the benefits for car users of the roads is considerable, concerns have been raised from sustainability and equality perspectives.

In 2005, there were only two toll roads in Ireland; the M50 and East-Link toll Bridges. Between 2005 and 2010, six new toll roads opened. For example, in 2005 the newly upgraded M1 Dundalk Western Bypass on the main Dublin to Belfast road and the M4 Kilcock–Enfield–Kinnegad Bypass (connects the Dublin commuter counties to the City and the main Dublin to Galway road) were opened. In 2006, the N8 Rathcormac–Fermoy Bypass in County Cork was opened and then in 2009 the Waterford Bypass, the Dublin Port Tunnel and Galway to Ballinasloe roads were opened. The tolls charged range between €1.70 and €2.90 for a motor car, but can be as high as €10 at peak hours for the Port Tunnel. Concerns began to hit the public spotlight in April 2006 when the Irish Road Hauliers Association protested at the East-Link toll bridge over the escalating costs of tolls. Later on that same year residents of Watergrashill in Cork protested at the opening of the N8 motorway. They wanted safeguards put in place to ensure that there would not be an increase in traffic through their village as a result of motorists trying to avoid the toll.

The private sector was also looking for user charges and PPPs in the water/waste-water sector: 'we'd be keen to see user charges for water treatment and water charges. We have apparently free water for domestic users – this can't be sustained into the future, it's maybe a good idea to do PPPs on water services' (Private Industry PPP Representative, interview, 2006).

Commercialisation of schools was evidenced in the case of the Grouped Schools Pilot PPP Project through raising prices charged to students (for example canteens and vending machines). Commercialism is likely to increase further in PPP schools in line with international PPPs experiences where it has extended to include exclusive agreements (like vending machines that only sell one company's products), private sponsorship of programs and activities, incentive programs, electronic marketing, for-profit management of schools, sponsored educational materials and appropriation of space (Whitfield, 2006).

This requirement to ensure profit maximisation and, therefore, adequate returns to the private partner's shareholders and equity providers led to the adoption of practices which de-prioritised, and in some instances were in direct contradiction to, public-service requirements. As explained by a senior SIPTU official (interview, 2006):

> If your income is dependent on your work, it's different; the nature of the public sector is 'not for profit': public services are not in the business of making

profit, but about delivering services at the best economic efficiency in the best manner ... The private part of the partnership is trying to get the most money, they will not have the interest of the public to the foremost of their mind; this is the bottom line.

Such practices and strategies pursued by private partners, both to cut costs and increase income, were identified in other PPPs in Ireland. These included providing cheap materials, design and outputs and the implementation of opportunities for income generation within the public services and/or infrastructure, for example through hiring out school facilities, the use of canteens and vending machines and cost reduction in many circumstances within the schools, resulting in some cases in compromised service quality and public education ethos. This has led to a commercialisation of the schools with a resultant loss of the school principal's and, therefore, public-sector control over the schools and, significantly, a reduction in community use of the schools. As one school principal explained:

There is an impact of the conflict of interest between the private operator's need to make a profit and schools as a public service. I don't believe schools should ever be used as a moneymaking enterprise. The school should be at the centre of the community. There is no finer facility in the town, but I'm not sure if having it privately owned and privately maintained ensures the community gets maximum use of it. The private operator uses the sports hall most nights from 6.00p.m. to 10 p.m. We have had a wedding reception in the sports hall and the cost of the use of the facilities is high for local clubs. The schools are owned by the people; but it's not theirs, it's the private operator's.

Related issues could arise in the Criminal Courts Complex as the private-sector partner provides a range of services, including building maintenance, helpdesk and reception services, security and traffic management, cleaning, portering, provision and operation of courtroom technology and utilities administration. It is important, therefore, to investigate what potential problems could arise from handing over such key aspects of the prison and courts service, and public services and infrastructure more generally, to a private commercial company.

A case study in commercialisation of public assets: the Poolbeg incinerator PPP

The case study of the Poolbeg incinerator provides an important insight into the impact of the involvement of a commercial company in the planning and delivery of public infrastructure and services through the PPP mechanism.

Significant public controversy and local opposition resulted from plans to locate one of the largest waste incinerators in Europe on the Poolbeg peninsula. This peninsula is located on the southern side of Dublin Bay. In September 2007, DCC (acting on behalf of the four Dublin Local Authorities) signed a twenty-five-year PPP contract to develop the incinerator with Dublin Waste to Energy Ltd, a joint venture of the American company Covanta Energy and Danish DONG Energy Generation. The private consortium is responsible for the financing, building and operation of the incinerator. DCC stated that the project will use 600,000 tonnes of waste per year – which would otherwise go to landfill – to generate electricity and district heating. It is part of the Dublin Regional Waste Management Plan, which, DCC claims, offers the best environmental solution to reduce waste, maximise recycling, minimise landfill and generate energy from waste.

The depth of opposition from residents in the areas of Ringsend, Irishtown and Sandymount that are adjacent to the proposed incinerator was revealed in 2006 when their campaign, the Combined Residents against the Incinerator, delivered over 3,000 individual appeals outlining their various health and traffic concerns to An Bord Pleanala, the planning authority that was deciding on planning permission for the incinerator. A public hearing was then held by the Bord into the project in May 2007.

Under the PPP contract, DCC guarantees to provide Dublin Waste to Energy 320,000 tonnes of residual waste (waste that can be burned by the incinerator) a year. DCC will suffer penalties, running into millions of euro, if it cannot supply that amount. Covanta, the private operator of the incinerator, will be able to charge a commercial rate to providers of the other 280,000 tonnes.

At the An Bord Pleanala hearing, the residents, concerned about traffic impacts, were assured by DCC that only waste arising from the Dublin Region could be used in the incinerator. However, after the hearing, Covanta, being a commercial company with shareholders that require returns, made it clear that it would source waste from wherever it required, including importing waste from outside Ireland.

Interestingly, the Bord's planning inspector recommended that the capacity of the incinerator be reduced to 400,000 tonnes due to a reduction in the estimates for the amount of waste that would be produced in the future in the Dublin Region, due to improved rates of recycling and minimisation. Despite this recommendation, and prior to receiving planning permission, DCC signed the contract for the 600,000 tonne incinerator with Dublin Waste to Energy in September 2007.

The Inspector, however, was overruled by the Board of An Bord Pleanala and, as a result, the project received planning approval in November 2007. Were the concerns of residents, their democratic participation in the planning process and the principle of waste minimisation overridden in favour of ensuring the incinerator had sufficient capacity to be financially attractive for the commercial operator?

Under this PPP model outlined in the contract for the incinerator, DCC, the local statutory authority that is responsible for promoting waste minimisation, reduction and recycling, is actually contractually bound to ensure the *production* of 320,000 tonnes of waste over a twenty-five year period. Could this result in DCC reducing the extent to which it advocates and develops recycling services and waste minimisation targets, in order to ensure there is enough waste produced for the incinerator and thus avoid the financial penalties if 320,000 tonnes is not produced?

The Minister for the Environment stated in 2010 that government waste policy is focused on ensuring that waste which can be recycled is not disposed of by methods in the lower tiers of the waste hierarchy, such as landfill and large-scale incineration. Will DCC, therefore, act in contravention of government Waste Policy? The Minister (interview, 2010) also asserted that there is not the requirement, in the Dublin region, for an incinerator with the capacity to burn 600,000 tonnes: 'it is my understanding that the quantities of residual waste currently being collected by the Dublin local authorities may not be sufficient to meet the volumetric contractual commitment which forms part of the public private partnership agreement'. It appears, therefore, that the principal reason the Poolbeg incinerator will be built with the enormous capacity to burn 600,000 tonnes is to facilitate the income-generating requirements of the private operator.

DCC indicated in 2009 that it would make it compulsory for private refuse collectors operating within its boundaries to provide their waste to the incinerator. However, the Irish Waste Management Association brought the issue to Court with the result that private waste contractors cannot be compelled by DCC to do this. This could make it extremely difficult for DCC to guarantee a waste stream to the operator. DCC has also made it clear that the incinerator will be paid for from user fees from householders and businesses through their waste charges. There have already been protests about the equity and financial impacts of waste charges since their introduction in 2004, as a form of double taxation that affects lower-income households most severely. These charges will, of necessity, have to increase beyond their existing amount when payments start to Dublin Waste to Energy. In 2010, DCC removed a waiver for those on social welfare so they would not have to pay waste charges. Was that removed in order to pave the way for future increases in waste charges that will be necessary to pay the returns to the American shareholders of Covanta?

These issues raise the question of who was this project really developed for? If it was to address waste management, then the changing policy environment and waste requirements would point to the need for greater investment in recycling and other approaches, and the suspension of the development of incineration, particularly in this sensitive residential and ecological area of Dublin Bay. It does not appear that it is being developed on a value for money basis, as explained earlier. €120 million has already been spent on the project before any construction has commenced, including DCC paying €70 million for the site and spending €50 million on private consultancy costs, legal bills, planning permission, environmental approval and other development costs (Burke, 2010).

The experience of this case study indicates that this PPP model of public infrastructure and services provision is largely about providing profitable investment opportunities in Ireland for foreign direct investment by large private companies. For example, Covanta Holding Corporation is the American-based owner of Covanta, the private operator of the planned Poolbeg incinerator. It is a world leader in the development and operation of large-scale 'Energy-from-Waste' and renewable energy projects. The company owns and operates over forty such facilities in the United States, dealing with more than 5 per cent of the United States' municipal solid waste. It views Ireland as one of many potential markets in its pursuit of profitable investment:

> This project is exactly the type of public-private partnership that we look for as we seek to grow our business in Europe ... Covanta's mission is to be the world's leading Energy-from-Waste company, with a complementary network of waste disposal and energy generation assets. We will build value for our shareholders by satisfying our clients' waste disposal and energy generation needs with safe, reliable and environmentally superior solutions. (Covanta, 2010)

The impact of this commercial logic (necessity for increasing share prices, returns to shareholders etc.) of the company is outlined in its, publicly expressed, frustration with delays that have resulted from the changing waste policy and governance environment, planning and consultation process in Ireland. Covanta's CEO, Tony Orlando, stated in a conference call to investors in April 2010 that the company is:

> routinely questioned by shareholders about the delays affecting our Ireland project (the Poolbeg Incinerator) ... We are at a loss to understand why the government appears unable, or unwilling, to ensure that its regulatory systems operate in a transparent and predictable manner so as to enable a project such as this, having national importance, to move ahead as speedily as possible.

The CEO added that the company was concerned about the potential financial implications of the delays:

> Additionally, the firm is battling political opposition overseas – particularly with the development of a facility in Dublin, which is forcing the firm to rethink

capital spending on this project because of potentially lower future returns. We think the Ireland situation is an isolated case and the firm's international operations will be the driver to future growth over time. (Covanta, 2010)

Covanta's expectation though was that the Irish government would ensure the right conditions existed for its project to proceed. Mr Orlando explained to Covanta shareholders that he believed 'that that atmosphere is going to change and that we are going to, at the end of the day, see the Irish government take steps because they do want to attract foreign direct investment'.

The danger of involving such companies, the main concern of which is ensuring profitable returns, in highly sensitive and potentially health hazardous sectors such as waste incineration is highlighted by that fact that Covanta has been fined by the US Department of Environmental Protection after it was found to have violated permitted limits for dioxin emissions at a number of its US operations in 2008 (The Irish Independent, 2010). There is steadily accumulating evidence of the health hazards arising from microscopic particles (dioxins) emitted by incineration. Local residents are, therefore, very concerned about the health impacts of emissions in the case of a violation from the Poolbeg incinerator. Their anxiety has been heightened by the experience of odour emissions from the nearby Waste Water Treatment Plant.

This project also raises the complexity of cases where a public-sector agency is bound in a PPP contract that is no longer suitable for public, policy or legal requirements. Cancellation of the contract could leave the agency open to penalty clauses and litigation from the private operator. The state agency must, therefore, weigh up the potential environmental, health and financial costs of proceeding with such a project versus the potential costs of withdrawal. The PPP regeneration projects demonstrated that, in some instances, the partner (in that instance the private developer) that withdraws only pays relatively small amounts of compensation.

Access to services

According to the Combat Poverty Agency (2005), access to public services and infrastructure was of most importance to low-income and vulnerable groups within Irish society. Access to such public infrastructure and services was, however, negatively impacted by the commercial logic of the private companies in Irish PPPs. For example, the location and extent of provision of key public infrastructure and services, such as social housing regeneration, transport and health services, were found to be dependent on the potential of returns on private-sector investment and the willingness of the private sector to participate in the project (i.e. financial viability considerations) rather than the identified public and social need or requirement. This followed the Irish government's *PPP Framework* (PPP Informal Advisory Group, 2001) which asserted that this very logic, private-sector viability and interest, should be amongst the key determining factors that influenced the adoption of a PPP approach for a particular project.

Overall, therefore, access to public infrastructure and services in these instances was made dependent by the Irish government, to a greater level than hitherto, on the '*bankability*' or '*commercial viability*' of that infrastructure or service as a PPP project (FGS, 1998). This introduced the requirements of private investment as just as important – indeed in the case of social housing regeneration even more important – a determining factor as the social needs of society within the planning and development of certain public services and infrastructure. The difficulty associated with that logic has long been identified in privatisation where the private sector has invested its own capital only in the development of public projects that have had the potential to generate a reasonable profit and offer future economic growth. They have also in some instances avoided responsibility for addressing the public sector's policies and priorities, and, therefore, selected the easiest and cheapest service to provide (European Commission, 2003; CUPE, 2007; Monbiot, 2000, Whitfield, 2006; Unison, 2003). This was demonstrated in the case of PPPs in Irish health services, public housing and unprofitable road or rail routes.

The Department of the Environment PPP Unit did not believe that this profit requirement, inherent to commercial private involvement, conflicted with providing the optimum service based on public requirements. It stated (interview, 2006) that it was, in fact, the marketisation policy practice of introducing 'competitive procurement processes' within PPPs, 'driven by the profit motive of a properly functioning and competitive market', that had the potential to optimise both value for money and public welfare outcomes in many areas of public provision, particularly where the output is readily measurable as in infrastructural-type projects.

This important statement revealed how the *modus operandi* of certain sections of the Irish state had become strongly influenced by the neoliberal belief that the market is the optimum provider of services and that public welfare outcomes would be optimised under the imperative of the competition 'for-profit' motive, rather than under the direction of the state. However, this dependent relationship between key aspects of the welfare state and the requirements of the private business sector instituted through PPPs has meant that essential public services and infrastructure that are not commercially viable, and for which the state is responsible for the provision, such as the provision and regeneration of social housing and public health facilities, have not been provided, despite their requirement by lower-income populations, or society generally. Meanwhile, public infrastructure and services projects that are profitable for the private sector that can generate income streams, such as motorways, urban light rail projects and Conference Centres, have been developed.

Multinational involvement

Analysis of the private consortia that were awarded PPP contracts in Ireland between 1999 and 2008, as detailed in the project Tracker data (Department of the Environment and Local Government, 2001; Central PPP Unit, 2005, 2006, 2007, 2008), discovered that, in reflection of international PPP trends, a very significant proportion (62 per cent, twenty-nine projects) of Irish PPP contracts were awarded either directly to major European and global financial, infrastructure and services multinational companies or to their Irish subsidiaries. These foreign-based multinational companies, such as Veolia, the largest private water company in the world, have been involved in bidding for PPP projects across Europe (Figure. 6.4).

The evidence for such market penetration in the education, water/wastewater and roads sectors is now presented.

Education sector

Hochtief Aktiengesellschaft (Hochtief) is a clear example of how PPPs represent an important and expanding new market for global multinationals. Hochtief is the fourth-largest provider of construction-related services in the

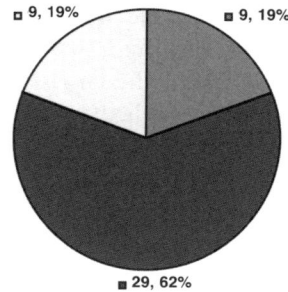

Figure 6.4 Number and per cent of PPP contracts in Ireland awarded to Irish, multinational and Irish subsidiary companies

Source: Central PPP Unit (2005, 2006, 2007, 2008).

world and market leader in Germany, with more than 52,000 employees and a sales volume of €16.45 billion in 2007. It is involved in thirty-two PPP projects around the globe, representing a total project cost of almost €13 billion. Hochtief now has 80 PPP schools in the UK, Ireland and Germany (Hochtief, 2008). It controls six out of the eleven (55 per cent) PPPs that are in operation and/or reached contract award stage in the Irish education sector (Figure 6.5). Hochtief (2008) itself explains the rationale for PPPs' importance:

> PPPs provide ... stable, long-term income stream and attractive returns. The promising market for concessions and operation assures attractive returns. Unlike traditional construction, it offers a guaranteed stream of income over the long-term, making it less vulnerable to cyclical fluctuations. By acquiring these new contracts, we are significantly strengthening our position in the educational field in the UK and Ireland and are well positioned for coming assignments in the strongly growing PPP markets of Great Britain and Ireland.

Furthermore, the successful consortium for the second Bundled Schools PPP Project in Ireland comprised Macquarie (lead sponsor and finance), Pierse Group (design and build) and Sodexho (facilities management). Macquarie is a global leader in the development, acquisition, funding and management of public infrastructure and essential services businesses. Through its Macquarie Capital Funds division, Macquarie manages almost €36 billion of equity invested in more than one hundred infrastructure and related businesses across twenty-five countries (Macquaire, 2008).

Its PPP experience encompassed equity and debt funding, capital markets, derivatives and financial structuring and it has closed more than forty PPP projects with a combined value exceeding €10.5 billion. Sodexho is a French multinational corporation and one of the largest *food services* and *facilities management* companies in the world. Sodexho will provide facilities management services. However, according to Corporate Watch (2007), Sodexho has a very poor record in other countries with regard to sanitation, food safety and labour relations. The commercial director for Sodexho Investments, part of the Macquaire consortium (Figure 6.5), similarly, referred to being awarded the contract for Facilities Management in the second bundle of PPP schools as providing the company 'with a great foundation to expand in this market' (Macquaire, 2008).

AECOM Technology Corp. is a US-based company, valued at US$4 billion, and is a global provider of professional technical and management support services. The CEO of the multinational further explained the important role that PPPs play in the global investment strategies of such companies. He stated, on AECOM's takeover of Earthtech, a company awarded PPPs in the Irish water/waste-water sector (see Figure 6.6 below),

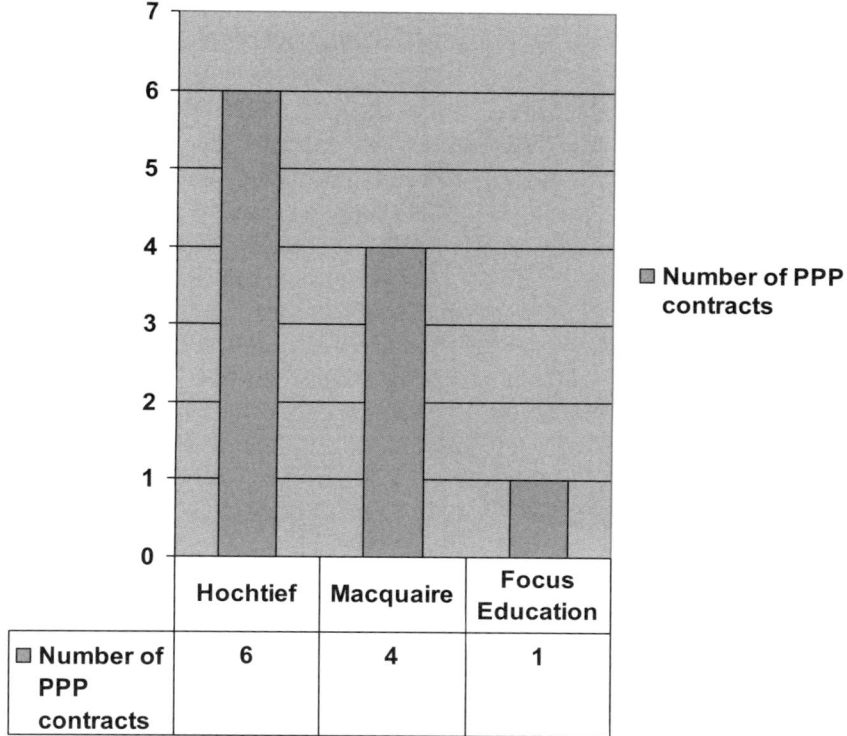

	Hochtief	Macquaire	Focus Education
Number of PPP contracts	6	4	1

Figure 6.5 Number of education PPP contracts awarded to Hochtief, Macquaire and Focus Education

Source: Central PPP Unit (2005, 2006, 2007, 2008); DOES (2007).

that 'clearly, the integration of Earthtech into AECOM strengthens our already strong service offerings and capabilities in the environmental, water/wastewater, transportation and facilities markets (Earth Tech, 2008).

Waste-water /water sector
Over three-quarters (76 per cent) of the companies awarded PPP contracts to date in the water/waste-water sector were foreign multinationals or Irish subsidiaries of foreign multinationals. These included the French multinational company, Veolia, whose Irish subsidiary Veolia Water Ireland was awarded 38 per cent (six of sixteen) of operating and construction phase plants in Ireland (five waste-water treatment plants and a water treatment plant, Figure 6.6). Veolia Water is the largest private water company in the world. Veolia's core activities include the provision of water, waste

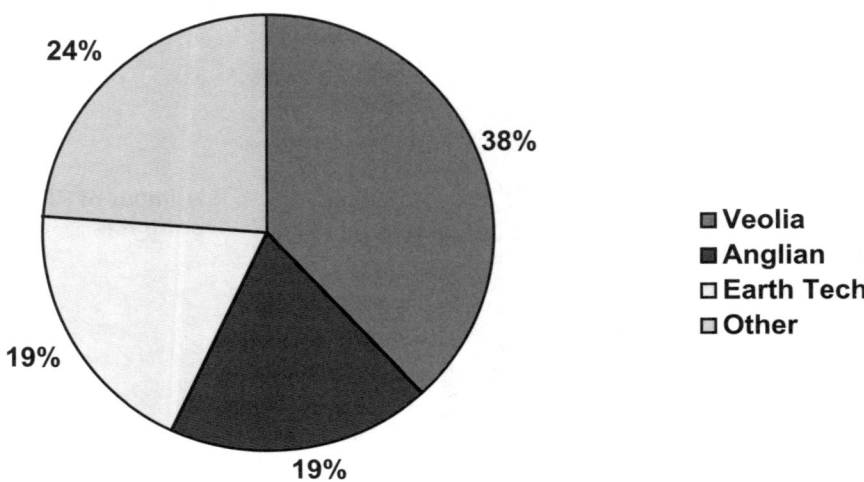

Figure 6.6 Per cent of PPP contracts awarded to foreign companies in the water/waste-water sector in Ireland

Notes: Number of contracts per company: Veolia 6, Anglian 3, Earth Tech 3, other 4. Total: 16.
Source: Central PPP Unit (2005, 2006, 2007, 2008).

management, energy and transport services. In 2008, it operated in twenty-seven countries, had revenues of US $47 billion and employed around 300,000 people (Veolia, 2008). The four divisions were active in Ireland, employing over 1,200 people in the water/waste-water PPPs, the operation of the LUAS light rail tram system (Veolia Transport) and waste services (Veolia Environmental Services).

The company with the next largest share of PPP contracts awarded in this sector was Anglian Water Group, which was the largest private water company within England and Wales. It operates the Dublin Bay treatment plant as CAW, a 50/50 joint venture with National Toll Roads. It also operated the Sligo and Waterford main drainage treatment plant PPPs (giving the company a 19 per cent share of water/waste-water PPPs in Ireland). Earthtech, which operated three waste-water treatment plants (19 per cent of the Irish water/waste-water PPP projects), as mentioned earlier, is owned by AECOM. These companies highlight the power and influence that global capital was being given through PPP projects in the water/waste-water infrastructure in Ireland.

Through PPPs, therefore, the Irish government had initiated a process of privatisation of a very significant proportion of the water and sewerage infrastructure of Ireland as the private sector controls the treatment plants while the public sector only controls the carriage and transport of water and sewage to and from those plants. The control over Ireland's water, sewerage and sewage infrastructure, therefore, has increasingly been transferred to global capital in the form of large, internationally based, private companies with all the challenges that might entail.

Roads sector

In the roads sector, foreign multinationals were part of the consortia in each of the twelve projects which had reached completion or for which the contract was awarded. For example, Direct Route (Fermoy) Ltd. operated the N8 Rathgormack Fermoy and won the contract for the N7 Limerick PPP toll roads (giving it a 16.6 per cent share of the total Irish PPP road projects; see Figure 6.7). Direct Route was a consortium involving, amongst other companies, Kellogg Brown and Root Ltd, Allied Irish Bank, the European Investment Bank and the Bank of Scotland. Kellogg Brown and Root is part of the Halliburton Corporation and headquartered in Houston US. It is a leading global engineering, construction and services company that has won many public infrastructure and services contracts across the world, most notably in Iraq (Klein, 2007). Eurolink Consortium, awarded the M3 and N4 Kilcock Kinnegad road contracts (16.6 per cent of the Irish road PPP market), involves Cintra (Concesiones de Infraestrucutras de Transporte S.A.) a major Spanish company with road PPPs in Spain, Portugal, Canada and Chile. Finally, ICON, comprising FCC Construction SA and Itinere Infraestructuras, both major companies from Spain, won the Galway-Ballinasloe and M50 upgrade PPPs (16.6 per cent of Irish road PPP contracts).

Financial capital and PPP re-financing

Global finance capital also views PPPs as considerable market opportunities. For example, KBC Infrastructure Finance is part of KBC, a large Belgian-based global finance institution, worth over €300 billion. KBC owns Irish Investment Bank (IIB), one of the leading providers of financial services in PPP projects in Ireland (City and Financial, 2007). Over the last decade, KBC

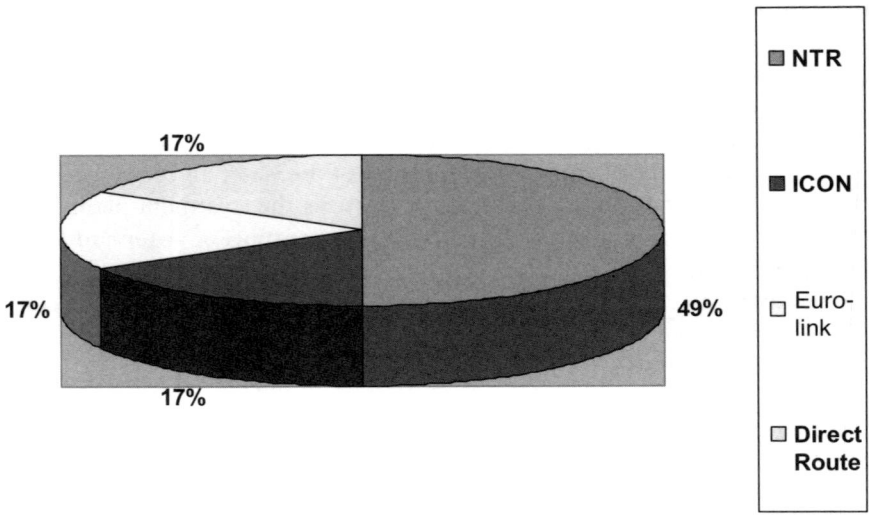

Figure 6.7 Per cent of PPP contracts awarded to private companies in the road
sector in Ireland

Notes: Number of contracts per company: NTR 6, ICON 2, Eurolink 2, Direct Route 2.
Total contracts: 12.

Source: Central PPP Unit (2005, 2006, 2007, 2008).

has been involved in PPP transactions in transport, health, education,
defence, water and prisons in numerous countries:

> Project Finance is a global business for KBC with dedicated units in Europe, the
> US and Asia. KBC and IIB Bank are a leader in the Irish Project Finance market,
> having been involved at a senior level in most of the significant project finance
> transactions in Ireland over the past number of years including, the Dublin
> Criminal Courts Complex, the milestone Tynagh Energy deal in Co. Galway,
> the M8 Fermoy Bypass and the 32MW wind farm at Sorne Hill in Co. Donegal.
> (City and Financial, 2007)

In addition, Barclays Capital, the investment banking division of Barclays
Bank Plc, which had a balance sheet of £1.4 trillion in 2008, was involved in
setting up dedicated secondary market investment funds in Ireland to acquire
PPP equity. Secondary financial markets have been set up in other countries
such as the UK that developed PPP projects to undertake re-financing and the

trading, sale and purchase of PPP projects. Under re-financing arrangements the ownership of PPP projects transfers from construction-led consortia to financial investment institutions. This, in turn, creates further new markets for private capital. For example, in the UK, the refinancing of twelve PFI projects between 1999 and 2005 resulted in a £142 million gain for the private consortia compared to just £27.3 million returned to the public sector. Refinancing enabled the private sector to increase profitability over and above the average 15–20 per cent return which was built into projects before re-financing. Laing sold a 50 per cent stake in UK highways in October 2004 for £26.3 million making a 33 per cent profit (Whitfield, 2006). While Ireland's PPP market is not yet at such a stage, it is inevitable that such secondary PPP market activity that attracts 'equity investors' will develop here:

> As the pipelines of primary deals reach financial close and go through their construction period, the secondary market will emerge. This is inevitable. Secondary market funds (such) as equity investors, are wholly interested in the long-term project performance. This is what is giving us our yield. (Finance Bank Official, speaking at City and Financial Conference 2007)

For example, the re-financing processes in the Grouped Schools Pilot PPP Project and the West-Link toll bridge demonstrate how PPPs facilitated public services and assets to be bought and sold as commodities by private capital with significant profits being made by private companies. The Irish taxpayers, public service users and workers paid for the private sector's profits in the form of the receipt of poorer conditions and services. The service quality is also reduced further through asset 'sweating,' as evidenced in UK PPPs, where the levels of service provision are cut after being subcontracted out to other private companies.

This reveals how PPPs have led to some of Ireland's key public infrastructure and services no longer being under the full control of the Irish government but rather subject to the considerable influence of foreign multinational construction, financial, infrastructure and service providing companies. Essentially then through PPPs the state is transferring a large segment of the control of these public services away from the nation state to global capital. The key goal of these global companies, as with businesses generally, is to increase their opportunities for profit accumulation and expand their business in order to provide ever-increasing returns to their shareholders. As detailed earlier, many of these companies have set up PPP Units within their business to submit bids for contracts to provide new markets and business opportunities for the company, build capacity to win more PPPs and diversify their range of assets to enhance profitability. Thus, Irish public services and infrastructure are being transformed, through PPPs, into new market opportunities for these global multinationals.

This reveals the important role of PPPs in the state-led conversion of public policy formation and decision making, infrastructure and services from being primarily a public function to now, in their PPP form, functioning as an important component of a global strategy for private investment capital to access new market opportunities. This raised a question of the wisdom of the PPP process from a 'public good' perspective as it involved transferring the control of key aspects of public infrastructure and services to private operators whose main interest in the Irish projects is how they can provide a return back to their global multinational parent companies. To what extent these global companies are interested in, or aware of, the concerns or the public service impacts of their Irish PPP subsidiaries is questionable.

Domestic market

It should be noted that domestic Irish businesses play a smaller, but still significant role in the Irish PPP market, for example a number of large Irish financial institutions and construction, service and infrastructure companies have been awarded, or are involved in, PPP projects. Allied Irish Banks Plc (AIB), one of Ireland's largest banks, through AIB Capital Markets has financed transportation (East and West-Link toll bridges, roads and light rail), hospital, accommodation and prison projects in PPPs in Ireland and across Europe. It identified considerable opportunities for private-sector infrastructure and services projects, particularly in areas such as transport and energy, and based on their Irish and International experience AIB advertised that it was well placed to partner industrial investors 'in availing of these opportunities' (AIB, 2008).

Treasury Holdings (Spencer Dock Consortium) was awarded the National Conference Centre PPP in 2007. The Treasury Holdings Group is based in Ireland, but operates globally. The Gross Development Value of the Treasury Holdings Group in 2008 was €24 billion. Furthermore, SIAC Construction Limited, one of Ireland's largest construction contractors is part of the Eurolink Consortium.

National Toll Roads (NTR) highlights clearly the importance of PPPs as a new market. NTR, with a turnover of €447m in 2007, is Ireland's leading private-sector developer, financier and operator of public infrastructure and services, with positions in toll roads, integrated waste management, water/waste-water treatment, renewable energy and broadband telecommunications. It pioneered the use of the PPP model in Irish road provision and operation. The company's first toll facility was the East-Link bridge, which opened in 1984. It developed the West-Link (1990), North-Link (2004) and, as part of the Celtic Roads Group, operates the Dundalk Motorway PPP, and successfully tendered for the Waterford by-pass scheme and the M7/M8

Portlaoise motorway (giving it a majority 50 per cent controlling proportion of the Irish road PPP projects). The Celtic Roads Ltd Group involves, amongst other companies, NTR and Dragados Concesiones de Infra-estructuras SA (a major Spanish firm). NTR's subsidiaries include NTR Roads, Greenstar, Celtic Anglian Water, Materials Recovery Limited (UK). NTR's PPP '*business*' was providing considerable profits to the company. For example, profits from the East and West-Link Tolls alone reached €18.2 million in 2005, a rise of 8 per cent on the previous year. Greenstar, despite only being seven years old, was the largest private company in the Irish waste market with a turnover of about €170 million per annum (NTR, 2008). NTR's Chairman, Tom Roche, received €118 million from NTR's realisation of €1.3 billion in shares in 2008, a large proportion of which came from the sale to the Irish government of its interest in the West-Link toll bridge in Dublin.

Labour conditions

The Irish government denied that PPPs would reduce workers' employment conditions and the role of trade unions in public services. The evidence demonstrates, however, that this did occur and indeed this was actually a motivating factor behind their introduction. In the Grouped Schools Pilot PPP Project, the only one which involved transfer of public-sector employees to the private sector, the original private operator delayed wage increases that the workers were due under National Wage Agreements and disputed the transfer of pension contributions. This indicated an ineffectiveness of the EU Directive on Transfer of Undertakings, Protection of Employment (TUPE) that was expected to provide protection in such circumstances.

Furthermore, in projects that involved new employees, such as waste/waste-water treatment plants, waste collection services and the LUAS light rail, significant problems arose, for example low levels of unionisation, trade union rights being curtailed, anti-union practices by employers and regressive employment conditions in comparison to public-sector employees in similar positions of employment (Table 6.2). For example, the private operators in the Grouped Schools Pilot PPP Project, waste collection PPP and LUAS light rail were all brought to the Labour Court[3] by SIPTU in an attempt to address industrial relation disputes that had arisen. A SIPTU Official (interview, 2006) explained that with PPP operators,

like the Jarvis's, Oxigens, Connexes etc. these companies, can come in and reduce labour conditions. They have made their major savings to date on the labour-cost side ... Its damn well difficult dealing with multinationals like these. Everything has to be fought for and secured in comparison to the public-sector.

The LUAS rail drivers had to sign a 'no strike' clause as part of their contracts. This was a historically unprecedented restriction of workers' rights in the Irish public sector. Poor pay and conditions, in comparison to public-sector drivers of the CIE-operated DART, have meant the LUAS drivers have taken unofficial strike action, despite the restriction. The Labour Court ruled in 2005 that the LUAS operator, Connex (operating since 2007 as Veolia Transport), had to pay compensation to a former Traffic Supervisor who was unfairly dismissed in December 2004 after the worker forwarded information to the Rail Procurement Agency (RPA) relating to the considerable difficulties in the LUAS operating system. Connex was also brought to the Labour Court in 2006 by SIPTU over its failure to pay National Wage Agreement increases. SIPTU criticised the lack of state-enforced protection for workers' conditions in these services that were, despite being privately operated, still the responsibility of the state: 'it is difficult to accept that the RPA, a government Body, can insert into a commercial contract to run a public transport operation a clause which ignores National Agreements' (Labour Court, 2006).

Table 6.2 The impact of PPPs on workers' conditions

PPP Workers' conditions and unionisation impact:	
LUAS	Right to strike removed Operator refused to pay National Wage Agreement Taken to Labour Court
Water/waste-water treatment plants	Lower levels of unionisation than local authority operated
Schools	Original Operator refused to pay National Wage Agreement Varying levels of unionisation Taken to Labour Court
Waste collection	Low levels of unionisation Lower pay and conditions than public sector Taken to Labour Court

Source: Labour Court (2005, 2006).

The challenge for trade unions and public-sector workers was that both the private *and* public sectors believed that public services would be more efficient if their influence was reduced:

County Councils are hamstrung by unions; just compare the M1 and the M4; compare the standard of road litter – which road is the council managing?

> Councils have limited budgets and the unions demand a certain number of guys per trucks (for maintenance); this means the councils don't have the flexibility we do. We can send out fewer guys per truck. This means we have the ability to manoeuvre and therefore private interests are more flexible than the established culture in the Councils. (PPP Road Operator, interview, 2006)

Similarly, a senior Official (interview, 2007) in DCC criticised the role of unions within the public sector:

> The private sector can do things we can't do. The unions always seem to be stronger in the public sector. Their approach is much more restrictive. Take a driver in a bin truck: one view is he's a driver or another view is his job is to drive and when they are out if two guys need a hand, he should help – it's a demarcation dispute. In the private sector, they muck in and help out. In the public sector, they can't and don't do that. The private sector has increased flexibility, reduced demarcation and increased productivity. The national agreements have brought this into the public sector and we are beginning to even out the scales.

The treatment by one PPP private operator of its employees illustrates the potential negative impact on workers' conditions. In 2003, a number of months' overtime had been unpaid to the PPP's employees and there were disputes over the payment of a monthly bonus. The workers claimed that their pay and conditions were significantly less in the PPP company than the public-sector equivalent, for example they were required to work significantly longer hours than equivalent public-sector workers. Workers who complained and tried to organise a union within the workplace suffered intimidation from management.

The workers were informed by the company that they would not be permitted to form, or be represented by, a trade union, and any worker joining a union would be dismissed. As a result, the workers felt they had no choice but to go on strike in an attempt to receive union recognition, adequate pay and conditions. During the strike, which lasted almost five months, the workers claimed that the management used a number of intimidatory tactics in an apparent attempt to persuade the employees to return to work:

> They used to drive trucks, at high speed, at us on the picket and they told us we were going to be visited in our houses and our lives were in danger; they threw empty bullet cartridges at us. The union caravan was put on fire. One union worker was sleeping in the caravan; if he had been in it at the time, what could have happened? During the strike at Christmas, the management threw 'Budget Travel' books at us to taunt us. (PPP Employee, interview, 2007)

The company refused to engage in the Irish industrial relations mechanisms such as the Labour Court (Labour Court, 2006). The local authority that awarded the company the PPP contract stated that, as the operator was a private company, it was not responsible for the conditions of the employees. However, in the face of a threatened solidarity strike by its own workers in other areas, the local authority agreed to request that the management of the private operator enter talks with its workers. Eventually, the employees were granted union recognition the following year. This case demonstrated that the trade union concerns that PPPs would result in such conditions were, unfortunately, realised:

> The outsourcing to private companies is being used to reduce workers conditions. The reason why the private sector is efficient is that it gets much more work out of us than the public workers. It's cheaper at the workers' expense ... The local authority workers fought hard for their conditions. Now in (the private company) we are back at the start of union demands, in terms of conditions, and that's why the local authority is outsourcing the service. It is outsourcing us as a way of undermining what local authority workers fought for. Outsourcing reverses all the conditions built up over years for and by workers. (PPP Employee, interview, 2007)

The reduced terms and conditions of PPP employees in comparison to their public-sector equivalents suggested that this was an important mechanism through which the private sector could achieve greater value for money over traditional state provision. A further example of this was provided by the exploitation of employees by the Turkish company, Gama, that was contracted by the Irish state to build roads.

This evidence highlights the requirement for an acceptance of responsibility on the part of state Agencies to monitor, and ensure the enforcement of, the conditions of employees of private companies in PPPs. Otherwise, this trend towards reducing labour conditions and the influence of workers and trade unions could be an indication of a state-facilitated imposition of neo-liberal policies in the area of worker's conditions and rights.

Government continues to promote PPPs

Despite these serious challenges and outcomes, the Irish government continued, in 2010, to implement, promote and expand intensely the PPP approach, as a small but significant component of overall public capital investment. The Central PPP Unit (interview, 2010) stated that, 'PPP procurement has the potential to provide value for money to the Exchequer and timely delivery of infrastructure when applied to projects of the right risk, scale and operational profile.' It set a target that 16 per cent of capital spending in the 2008–2012 period would be administered through PPPs. When measured as a proportion of national income, this would make Ireland's programme by far the largest in the OECD (OECD, 2008).

In 2006 alone, the value of the deal-flow of PPP projects closed was €2 billion, reflecting the key role they were expected to play in the roll out of the National Development Plan 2007–2013 (Table 6.3). For example PPPs comprised 11 per cent of the planned infrastructure spending in the school sector over the period of the plan. In the health sector, €415 million was planned to be spent through a complex DBFM PPP Project involving new cancer care treatment centres, including six sites for radiotherapy treatment (Table 6.3). In the transport sector, the Underground DART and Metro North, which are planned to run from the city centre to the Airport, described as the most important aspects of the governments public transport plan Transport 21, were being undertaken and financed through a PPP mechanism at a combined cost of around €5 billion, with an expected completion date of 2018. The planning application for the Underground DART, which will link with Metro North at St Stephen's Green, with the inter-city lines at Heuston and with the LUAS, was lodged to An Bord Pleanala in June 2010. There is also substantial public investment planned through the co-located hospitals via the direct granting of public land to private developers. Further spending was planned in PPPs in the environmental service, housing and sports and community infrastructure sectors. In addition, there was over one hundred projects, with a capital value of less than €20 million each, progressing as PPPs in the local government sector.

The fact that the government and state departments responsible for PPP development and promotion in Ireland, were not concerned with the problematic aspects in projects developed to date is very worrying in terms of delivering public services and infrastructure that provide value for money and, as important, are effective and suitable to meet the social and economic needs of the Irish People. This is also a further indication that the continued deployment of PPPs was being heavily influenced by the pursuit of a neo-liberal ideology rather than being evidentially based.

This policy direction was reflected in the continued belief in, and reliance upon, the private sector, at the highest government levels, to provide finance for major public infrastructure delivery such as the rail projects and the regeneration of disadvantaged areas:

> Clearly, the PPP model provided the best and fastest means for providing them (housing regeneration) rather than by their being exclusively Exchequer funded. It is not a question of whether something in Dublin or Limerick is not proceeding. It is a question of trying to ensure that we can get some private-sector buy-in in addition to the commitments that we are making, for example, in Limerick this year, a total of €25 million.(Irish Taoiseach, Brian Cowen TD, 2010)

Table 6.3 Planned PPP spending 2007–2013 in Irish social and economic infrastructure

Programme	Exchequer	PPP	Total
Economic infrastructure € million:			
Transport	19,858	7,035	32,914
Environmental Services	4,156	271	8,526
Govt. Infrastructure	1,222	191	1,413
Unallocated Capital Reserve	1,534	1,966	3,500
Social infrastructure € million:			
Justice	1,551	795	2,346
Health	4,555	415	4,970
Sports, Culture, Heritage and Community	3,312	288	3,631
Housing	15,455	255	21,214
Unallocated Capital Reserve	636	814	1,450

Source: Government of Ireland (2007).

Notes

1 Project development is the primary responsibility of the sponsoring department, with the assistance of advisers, including NDFA financial advice, as necessary. Procurement delivery is the responsibility of the centre of expertise. The centre of expertise undertakes the procurement after all policy issues are cleared by the sponsoring department or agency, output specifications are set and the PSB is signed off.

2 The RPA entered into agreements with developers, where in the case of the extension of the LUAS Red Line private developers will provide the land, at their own expense, and construct the rail and the civil works right up to the track level. When completed it is turned over to the ownership of the state, and in return for that the RPA will offer a frequent service in that area (RPA Representative, 3rd Annual Irish PPP forum, 2007).

3 The Labour Court was established to provide resolution of disputes about industrial relations, equality, organisation of working time, national minimum wage, part-time work and fixed-term work matters. Cases are only referred to the Court when all other efforts to resolve a dispute have failed. It operates as an industrial relations tribunal hearing both sides in a case and then issuing a Recommendation (Labour Court, 2008).

7

The twenty-first-century Irish state, services and infrastructure

The argument over PPPs is an argument over the direction in which the state is going. (Irish Trade Union Representative, Interview, 2006)

Theoretical understandings of the role of the state

So what has been the evolving nature and form of the Irish state in the first decade of the twenty-first century? Before entering that discussion, it is useful to provide a brief overview of a number of theoretical approaches on the changing role of the state (pluralism, managerialism and political economy) in an international context.

In the pluralist view, society consists of a collection of interest groups competing for control over government action through the electoral process. There is an assumption in pluralism that the state is a neutral institution, therefore it stresses the state's function to achieve consensus and maintain a rough balance of power between these different interest groups. State decision making and policy directions are determined by and effected in response to the relative strengths and balance of pressure between competing interests. The state acts as an arbiter between such groups supervising and regulating them so that none gains mastery and dominates state policy. Pluralism views state policy as a 'fair' and 'balanced' outcome of competition between different groups (Kirk, 1980). However, pluralism has been criticised for failing to recognise the enormous inequalities in resources between individuals, communities and classes in terms of economic power and the organisational skills upon which they can draw. While some are well funded, well informed and equipped to act effectively in their own interests, others are impoverished, fragmented and marginalised (MacLaran and McGuirk, 2003).

Managerialism stresses the power of public bureaucracy, particularly in the sphere of local authority decision making (Kirk, 1980). It recognises that bureaucracies may follow their own agendas, become 'social gatekeepers' allocating resources and prove difficult to influence. This perspective has the strength of acknowledging the power and complexity of central and local government bureaucracies, their domination by unelected, unaccountable bureaucrats and the fact that they are not necessarily responsive to pressure from below, such as from local residents in the case of local-authorities (Kirk, 1980).

Both the pluralist and managerialist perspectives, however, fail to question the relationship between central and local government and private business interests. The substantial inequalities in wealth and power in society, the fundamental role of private ownership of property and market forces, the power of business interests and assumptions about their validity and continuance are glossed over or ignored in these approaches.

Political economy, on the other hand, is founded on the notion that the economic and political spheres are inextricably linked. The structuralist political economy perspective provides a profound conceptualisation of the state's origins, its evolution and contemporary functions. It regards the state as a social institution, which arose historically in order to assuage the potentially inflammatory conflicts inherent in capitalist societies. Such conflicts include that between private businesses (capital) and workers (labour) over the division of the wealth and profit that is produced in the economy. The operations of the state ensure a sufficient degree of economic and political harmonisation and ideological control to enable the process of private wealth accumulation, the driving imperative of capital of which is to constantly search for more profitable forms and patterns of investment (Harvey, 1989), to continue. For example, the state intervenes in an attempt to regulate aspects of the economy (such as regulating financial markets) and plays an important indirect role in capital accumulation by taking responsibility for providing services which no individual capitalist is willing to supply on a universal basis (such as healthcare facilities, housing, schools, parks, education and training and so forth). This is because such collective means of consumption, though necessary to continued capital accumulation, are by their very nature 'opposed to the imperatives of profit':

> Due to the slow speed of rotation of capital in these sectors, to the risky and discontinuous nature of the progression of demand for them, public transport, schools, research centres, parks ... constitute so many domains foreign to capitalist profitability, while necessary to the overall reproduction of capitalist social formations. (Kirk, 1980, 81)

Thus the state, historically, has intervened in a welfare role to provide such collective means of consumption in order to maintain the cohesion of the capitalist economy and society (Kirk, 1980; MacLaran and McGuirk, 2003).

Under capitalism, however, there is a limit to the amount of state intervention that can take place before private profitability suffers (Harvey, 1989). First, state revenues – taxes – come from a pool of surplus value, and, hence, the higher the taxes, the less left over for capital accumulation. Second, state spending is not normally concerned with direct investment in the production of commodities. These are aspects of the inherent contradiction of the market-based capitalist system: that there is a need for state intervention, but this must not damage the driving principle of that system – private profit accumulation (Kirk, 1980).

The neoliberal state

Various political-economy approaches analyse that the state in Western Europe, and in most countries across the world, has undergone institutional restructuring at various scales in the period of neoliberalism, from the 1970s to the 2000s. This restructuring, as detailed in Chapter 2, provided new avenues for market growth, to ensure the on-going process of profitable capital accumulation (Bourdieu, 1998; Brenner and Theodore, 2002; Harvey 2005; Peck and Tickell, 2002).

The level of state intervention, revenue and spending associated with the development of the welfare state and the Keynesian approach was deemed by neoliberals to be a major factor in the crisis of declining profitability of global capital occurring during the neoliberal phase of capitalism. One of the foremost geo-political economists, David Harvey, identified that under the period of neoliberalism there has been a redistribution of wealth from the poor to the rich, through, a process of 'accumulation by dispossession' (Harvey, 2005, 154). The neoliberal state has done this through the reduction in the amount of surplus value that goes to the social wage (in the form of welfare state services and workers' wages and conditions) and an increase in the amount of surplus value that is returned to capital. It has facilitated global capital, in the form of large multinationals, developing new market opportunities for capital accumulation by the opening up to the private sector of areas of the welfare state, such as public services and infrastructure, through privatisation and commoditisation, for example PPPs. It has also been carried out in the *wage relation* through the systematic reduction in the power and influence of employees through trade union representation, and an increase in rates of productivity and a reduction in wages and employment conditions.

The shift from government (state power on its own) to governance (a broader configuration of state and key elements in civil society, such as private business representatives) is also marked under neoliberalism. It is the deeper integration of state decision making into the aforementioned dynamics of international capital accumulation (Harvey, 2005). The private sector, through domestic businesses and multinational corporations, not only collaborates intimately with state actors, but even acquires a strong role in writing legislation, determining public policies and setting regulatory frameworks that often specifically advantage private corporations. The traditional independence of the civil service is often undermined by the increased role of the corporate lobbyists (Allen, 2007; Harvey, 2005; Monbiot, 2000; Pollock and Price, 2004; Whitfield, 2006).

This influence of neoliberalism over the state can be attributed, in particular, to the role of powerful supranational institutions, such as the World Trade Organisation and its General Agreement on Trade and Services, the European Union and Commission, the International Monetary Fund, the Organisation for Economic Co-operation and Development (OECD), and the World Bank. Institutions such as these have placed intense pressure on national and local European governments to transform public services into tradable, market-based, services. They have achieved this through the liberalisation of trade and market rules that open up the public sector to competition in the private marketplace. In this way, public services have become a multi-trillion dollar market for the private sector. The importance of the public sector as a site for private businesses cannot be underestimated, for example the British government spend £120 billion per annum purchasing goods and services from the private sector (Whitfield, 2006), while the World Bank (2002) estimated that education had become a US$2 trillion global 'industry'. The size of the potential markets in public health and education are indicated by the proportion of total expenditure that is allocated to these sectors. For example, public expenditure on health accounted for between 65 per cent and 80 per cent of total health expenditure in most OECD countries; on education it was higher with a mean of 88 per cent. Ireland's total government spending in 2003 was €46.4 billion, while the waste market alone was worth about €1.5 billion (OECD, 2008).

Private businesses are looking for increased access to these public sectors and services. The services industry lobby, the European Services Forum, for example, lobbies on an ongoing basis in Brussels, the Headquarters of the EU, for such increased market penetration. PPPs can be situated as part of this process of opening up new markets for capital accumulation in domains previously unavailable to the private commercial sector.

The role of PPPs in the neoliberal transformation of the Irish state

The role of PPPs in this neoliberal process of transformation of the Irish state was captured succinctly in the candid explanation, given by the PPP Units in the Department of the Environment and Department of Finance (interview, 2006), that a key benefit of, and motivation for, introducing PPPs was the 'reduction in the role and responsibility of the Irish state' in the management of public assets and service delivery in order to allow state agencies to focus on their role as mere 'regulators and monitors'.

The development of Irish PPP policy and projects provide evidence of this neoliberal shift towards a deeper collaboration between the state and private capital. They reveal the emergence of a corporate-state complex of private actors that promote and implement this process of neoliberalisation within governance and public infrastructure and services provision in Ireland. This is being carried out on behalf of the interests of private business investment, both domestic and global. The corporate-state complex consists of private contractors, multinational corporations, financial institutions, consultants, business associations and politicians. Private firms, for example, were consulted about their preference on the size and scope of contracts via public-sector open days, workshops and informal meetings between government officials and the private sector.

The government produced PPP Guidelines encouraged state authorities to engage in market analysis and market soundings to determine the level of private-sector interest in entering PPP arrangements for the delivery of a project. This use of market consultation was encouraged in order to determine the 'market-interest' in a proposed project, to evaluate the risks that would be transferred and to assess the private sector's willingness to accept the required degree of risk transfer. For example, bidders were invited to extend the scope of the contract in the PPP process through the Request for Qualifications and Bidding process.

The PPP process introduced the requirements, discourse, logic and ethos of the private market into Irish governance, public services and infrastructure. For example, the government-commissioned report by PriceWaterHouseCoopers (2001b) into PPP potential within the local government sector consistently used the language and discourse of marketisation, referring to public services as 'markets' and 'products'. It also highlighted that departmental PPP Units had created and maintained private-sector interest in the PPP programme through marketing and communicating PPP opportunities to private interests within Ireland and abroad. This was being done through various consultation exercises with potential private-sector service providers, such as with IBEC and the Construction Industry Federation through the PPP Informal Advisory Group. The *Policy Framework 2001* also included the language and aim of marketisation in public services, outlining that the aim of the Central PPP Unit was to ensure PPPs became, 'a standard element of government procurement methods; and a stream of PPP projects is developed and a sustainable and dynamic PPP market is created in Ireland in the long term' (PPP Informal Advisory Group, 2001, 6).

The extent of private-sector involvement was demonstrated by the considerable amounts spent by state Agencies on hiring private consultant advisors. From 1998 to 2005, the government spent €174 million on reports by private consultants (Allen, 2007), while consultants involved in the roads network received more than €280 million in fees over a six-year period. Twelve consultant engineering firms received 4 per cent of the final building cost of those roads projects. In the 2006 government Budget estimates, almost €60 million was allocated to private consultancy services in a range of state agencies and departments (Dan Boyle TD, Dáil Éireann, 2007).

The practice of the Irish state hiring private consultants could be classed as a form of privatisation of decision making. The consultants commissioned to provide policy advice, such as Farrell Grant Sparks (1998) and PriceWaterHouseCoopers (2001a, 2001b) were renowned promoters of neoliberal perspectives, and, therefore, were biased in favour of advocating PPPs. For example, three of the firms hired to advise on PPPs (KPMG, PriceWaterHouseCoopers and Deloitte) were amongst the four largest global accountancy firms that had been aggressive promoters of neoliberalism and PPPs across the world (Table 7.1).

The legal, financial and consultation work associated with a PPP's complex contract and development presented these consultancy companies with considerable business opportunities. Farrell Grant Sparks (2007) stated that it provided a 'unique service to capitalise on PPP opportunities'. The Farrell Grant Sparks PPP team comprised business advisers, banking and financial consultants, taxation experts, cost planners, property and construction consultants and facilities management advisers. The research into PPP projects in Ireland revealed that many of the consultants were involved in advising both public-sector and private-sector clients, as well as financiers, on maximising the considerable 'opportunities' presented by PPPs (FGS, 2007; Table 7.1). This proliferation of private-sector advisors and consultants, from the late 1990 onwards marked a deepening involvement of the private sector within public-policy formation, as explained by a legal firm involved in PPPs: 'the past twelve months have been a particularly active and successful period for the firm's PPP Group, having had a key role in the delivery of all of the PPP projects that have reached completion in Ireland over the period, with an aggregate value in the region of €2.5 billion'. These private-sector advisors made it clear that their goal was to ensure PPPs would become a permanent feature of infrastructure and service provision:

> PPP will be here for the long term because no matter what difficulties exist with the procurement process, the DOES should get the school quicker through a PPP... The big accountancy firms are in this for the long-term – they are doing it internationally – people in London working on all types of projects – whether you like it or not PPP is here to stay. (Private PPP Advisor, Interview, 2006)

Table 7.1 Private advisors involved in Irish PPPs

Private advisor	Country of origin	PPP client Public	Private
FGS	UK	1 1998 Report 2 DOES 5 Pilot schools and Cork School of Music 3 National Conference Centre 4 Fatima Mansions 5 NDFA decentralised government offices 6 HSE co-located Private Hospital Programme	1 Bovis Lendlease, 2 National Maritime college
PriceWater-HouseCoopers	UK	1 2000 DOF Report 2 2001 DOEHLG Reports 3 DCC DBOF Incinerator	1 EuroLink Consortium, N4/N6 Kinnegad to Kilcock
KPMG	Swiss	1 NDFA, Criminal Courts Complex 2 National Roads Authority, N6 and N3	1 Spencer Dock consortium, National Conference Centre
Deloitte	UK	1 NDFA Thornton Hall 2 NDFA Schools bundle PPP	1 Macquire Ireland, schools bundle, 2 Private sector bidder, co-located hospital 3 Preferred bidder, Dublin Waste to Energy Incinerator
McCann FitzGerald	Ireland	1 OPW, National Conference Centre NRA, M3, N 6, 2 Irish Prison 3 Service Thornton Hall Local authorities, urban development	Short listed bidders for: 1 Schools 2nd Bundle, 2 Metro North, 3 Co-located hospitals 4 Urban development projects

Note: DOF: Department of Finance.
Source: City and Financial (2006, 2007, 2008); Deloitte (2007); FGS (2007); KPGM (2007); PriceWaterHouseCoopers (2007).

Adding to this trend was the fact that some of the new public agencies set up to develop PPP hired key staff that were previously employed in developing PPPs in the private sector. The aim was to bring the modus operandi of the private sector into the public sector. For example, Frank Allen, Chief Executive of the Railway Procurement Agency, since 2002, was previously Head of Infrastructure Finance at KBC Bank, where he was responsible for arranging finance for PPPs in road, rail and municipal services.

Case study: the Annual Irish PPP Forums

The Annual Irish PPP Policy Forums, organised by City and Financial, a British-based business conference company that specialised in corporate finance, government and policy and PPPs conferences, provide an insightful case study of the deepening alignment of the private and public sectors in relation to public services and infrastructure development. The stated purpose of the Forums was to examine the strategies of the Irish government PPP procurement agencies, review PPP policy developments and trends in PPP best practice and focus on PPP developments in a number of key sectors, including transport, courts, waste, education, housing and accommodation. City and Financial, the organisers of the forums also organised PPP summits across the world in close collaboration with national governments.

Evidence for close collaboration with, and support from, the Irish government was demonstrated in the Chairing of the 2007 and 2008 Irish Forums by the Assistant Secretary of the Department of the Taoiseach. In addition, the keynote speaker in 2006 was the then Minister for Finance, Brian Cowen TD. As explained in Chapter 3, the government agencies gave an update on PPP projects and policy developments in Ireland, while the private sector gave its perspective on the development of the Irish PPP market. Solicitors, bankers and consultants gave presentations on payment and performance mechanisms, as well as procurement and innovation in financing structures, such as debt finance and the secondary market. There was detailed analysis of developments in individual PPP sectors where the public-sector representatives and private-sector financiers and consultants presented papers together in various workshops (see Table 7.2).

The Irish Annual PPP Forums were closed to the media and the general public was effectively excluded by the very high attendance fee for the one-day conferences. This raised, once more, the question of the accountability of the PPP process when the only semi-public forum, where their development and outcomes were being discussed, was limited to those in the private sector who could pay the fee for attendance of €1,064.80 and those in the public sector who could pay the fee of €671.55.

Table 7.2 Public and private participants in the Annual Irish PPP Policy Forums (2006, 2007, 2008)

Speaker/agency	Year of forum
Speaking on behalf of the public sector government agencies:	
Minister for Finance, Brian Cowen TD	Keynote address, 2006
Assistant Secretary, Department of the Taoiseach Chair,	2006, 2007, 2008
Courts Service PPP Unit	2007, 2008
Assistant Principal Officer, Central PPP Unit	2007, 2008
Head of Central PPP Unit	2006, 2007, 2008
NDFA	2006, 2007, 2008
Head of Development, Cork Institute of Technology	2006, 2007
PPP Unit, DOES	2007
Head of PPP Unit, NRA	2007
Transaction Manager, Metro North	2007
Director, European Investment Bank	2007
Railway Procurement Agency	2007
Speakers from NHS (UK)	2008
Financial Partnerships Unit (Scottish government)	2007
Executive Manager for Housing DCC	2007
Assistant National Director of Contracts, HSE	2007
Speaking on behalf of the private sector were:	
Managing Director, Indaver Ireland	2006, 2007, 2008
Managing Director, Barclays Capital	2006, 2007, 2008
Partner, FGS	2006, 2007, 2008
Irish Business and Employers Confederation (IBEC)	2006, 2007, 2008
Director, Deloitte	2006, 2007, 2008
Partner, KPMG	2007, 2008
Chief Executive, Greenstar	2006, 2007
Associate Director, IIB Bank	2006, 2007
Partner, Arthur Cox	2006, 2008
KBC Project Finance	2007
McCann FitzGerald solicitors	2007
Spencer Dock Development Company	2008
Bank of Ireland	2008
AIB Bank	2008
Sponsors of the conference:	
FGS, Arthur Cox	2008
KPMG, McCann Fitzgerald, IIB, KBC	2007
Deloitte, FGS, Arthur Cox	2006

Source: City and Financial (2006, 2007, 2008).

PPPs have, through their development and practical outcomes, therefore, introduced and deepened the neoliberal trajectory of the Irish state in terms of embedding competition and marketisation and in increasing private-commercial ownership and corporatisation at the level of public governance, services and infrastructure and labour employment conditions. The outcomes of this process at central and local government levels are now summarised.

Impact on local government

> If we are serious about caring for people as people, everyone in the voluntary sector must reject the encroachment of privatisation in all its forms in the health and social services, and in the provision of accommodation for people who are homeless … We cannot expect the private sector, which is solely concerned with making profits, to protect people's rights to basic services. (Voluntary Housing Groups Statement following the collapse of Social Housing Regeneration PPP Projects (Carroll, 2008))

The potential danger in PPPs embedding aspects of neoliberalism within public services has been outlined internationally (Grubnic and Hodges, 2003; Harvey, 2005). If, in the future, local authorities and public bodies only commission services, and directly provide a limited number, this will have a significant impact on the organisation and purpose of local government and other public bodies. The market, with its cyclical characteristics, will determine public service levels, staffing levels, terms and conditions of employment, and public-sector trade unionism will be a thing of the past. Planning and needs assessment functions will be marginalised as the contract culture becomes pervasive and resources are sucked into managing contracts, co-ordinating contractors and arbitrating disputes (Whitfield, 2006).

The outcomes of Dublin City Council's social housing regeneration projects reflected this international experience, resulting in the privatisation of public land and services. In particular, it revealed clearly how the PPP process imposed the neoliberal logic of dependency of local government on the private sector and market. The resultant collapse of the PPP projects left individuals that were suffering from the deepest social and economic inequalities in Irish society dislocated and removed from their communities, while the remaining residents were left with no prospect of regeneration of their housing estates. It also led to a reduction in social housing units in local areas, at a time of considerable requirement for social housing. It is important to state that the underfunding by Central government of local government in Ireland meant that Dublin City Council (DCC) had little option but to introduce neoliberal policies, such as PPPs, in order to deliver the much-needed regeneration of inner-city estates.

These outcomes reflected the pattern for inner-city communities across the Western world, where the entrepreneurial approach to urban governance and planning, of which PPPs are a central policy, in many cases has contributed to large-scale residential displacement, the loss of community-relevant functions (for example, low-grade retailing, local social services), an exacerbated housing crisis and a deepening sense of disempowerment. Local government policy has concentrated, not on the needs of lower-income populations, but on attracting private investment back to previously unfashionable and unprofitable areas of the city. The outcomes of the research undertaken for this book into the regeneration of local-authority housing estates by DCC lends strong support to the writings of Brenner and Theodore (2002) that the focus of this new form of neoliberal, entrepreneurial, governance is not to meet the social needs of their populations, but to sell public assets to private developers in order to leverage investment.

It also supports the assertion made by Smith (2002) that neoliberal programs have been directly internalised into urban policy regimes as cities have become increasingly important geographical targets and institutional laboratories for a variety of neoliberal policy experiments, such as PPPs.

Impact on central government

> This is a fundamental change in the philosophy behind what we consider, or once did, an obligation of the government. We should be able to rely on it to put the essentials of life, water, power, transport, health and educational infra-structure and a few more basic requirements, in place without having to create a profit margin for private investors ... this kind of social change is fundamen-tal and has not been properly debated, let alone mandated. We should, before even one more tree is sold off, have the discussion to establish whose interests are being served and how the public's interests are best serve. (The Examiner, August 2008)

The private sector has been empowered by the Irish government, through the PPP mechanism and process, to develop and operate a significant propor-tion of new public (but privately controlled and operated) infrastructure and services. This is line with the global paradigm of neoliberalism, where the functions and role of the state at both local and central levels have been trans-formed since the 1970s. Governments and state agencies now concentrate on 'enabling' and 'promoting' the private sector to the detriment of state services by introducing market forces into the heart of public services and policy making (Brenner and Theodore, 2002; Castells, 2000; Cox *et al.*, 1982; George, 2004; Soros, 2000; Stiglitz, 2002). PPPs, therefore, are a key stage in the *neoliberalisation* process at the central and local welfare state levels. This has created more fragmented, commodified public services and infrastructure that allowed markets to penetrate within these areas.

Thus, PPPs added to the possibility of neoliberal actors within the Irish state, on behalf of capital, instituting a 'utopia of unlimited exploitation' (Bourdieu, 1998) through the creation of new avenues, such as neoliberal policy, forms of governance and services, in which capital accumulation can be undertaken (Harvey, 2005; Whitfield, 2001, 2006). This process of *neoliberalisation*, that could ultimately produce outright privatisation, has avoided political and other forms of public opposition because it is taking place through, apparently, an innocuous form in PPPs.

The private sector's profit-maximisation requirement, as played out through the private partners involved in PPPs, introduced fundamental conflicts of interest with social objectives in public service and infrastructure delivery. For example, Irish PPPs had negative impacts on inequality and poverty and compromised the governments' ability to fulfil commitments to tackle social inequalities, social exclusion and maximise the well-being of its citizens. These included reducing the quality, accessibility and availability of public services and infrastructure through focusing on profit-maximisation requirements rather than social outcomes. The profit motive at the heart of private involvement in PPPs conflicted with public service objectives, such as waste minimisation targets and equitable fares for road tolls and rail. The introduction of user fees, such as road tolls and increased rail fares also demonstrates how PPPs have facilitated the transformation of the payment for public infrastructure from direct state investment (from direct taxes) into the more favoured neoliberal mechanism of indirect 'stealth' taxes in the form of user fees. Stealth taxes are a term used for taxes levied in such a way that is not recognised overtly as a tax. They are contrasted with progressive forms of direct taxation that provide a sliding scale of increasing rates according to income levels. Stealth taxes, on the other hand, are regressive, in that low-income earners pay the exact same amount for public services and, therefore, a higher percentage of their income than high-income earners.

In addition, workers' conditions were negatively impacted and the public sector's long-term capacity to directly deliver services and infrastructure was reduced. For example, vital services such as social housing regeneration became dependent on the private market which meant they were not delivered at the point of great need for those services. Or, taking transport infrastructure as an example, it is clear that roads were being developed by the private sector at an unprecedented rate due to potential high returns from tolling. In contrast, the provision of new rail infrastructure across the country, which is not as financially attractive to the private sector, is left waiting, even though the logic of sustainable development suggests that more urgent investment is required in this area. This clearly demonstrates how

PPPs have introduced commercial values that resulted in the replacement of the central planning of social needs with market forces in public service and infrastructure projects. This is in line with negative impacts associated with such neoliberal policies internationally (Leys, 2001; Monbiot, 2000; Pollock and Price, 2004; Whitfield, 2006; Stiglitz, 2002).

The outcomes of PPPs in Ireland demonstrate that the process of neoliberalism in Ireland has entailed a continuation of the high level of involvement of private-sector actors in the provision of public services and infrastructure. The Irish government decided, over the period of the Celtic Tiger, that rather than use the budget surpluses that existed at the time, or undertake government borrowing, to address the public infrastructure and service deficits, it instead continued fiscally conservative economic and social policies at the welfare state level.

This policy trajectory has been pursued in various forms since the foundation of the state. It is being continued and intensified by opting for the neoliberal model of low taxation on wealth with a consequent under-funding of public services and a process of *neoliberalisation* and privatisation of public assets and services through PPPs.

The healthy budget surpluses of the late 1990s and through to 2007 could have been used for the direct-state funding of public services and infrastructure, but instead the government decided that the private 'for-profit' sector should be intimately involved in state governance and public services and infrastructure provision, maintenance and operation. Therefore, Ireland, in contrast to other countries, did not replace a public service, equity-oriented, welfare state with a neoliberal state. Instead the form of implementation of neoliberalism involved the supporting, and continued functioning, of a competition state, the priority of which has been primarily to promote private enterprise. This is visible in the manner in which PPPs are replacing the involvement of the not-for-profit religious institutions in the provision of key social infrastructure services with the commercial private sector. It also demonstrates that neoliberalism, as outlined elsewhere (Brenner and Theodore, 2002; Harvey, 2005), does not represent a reduction in state intervention, but rather a political, institutional and geographical reorganisation of the manner and methods by which the state intervenes (Castells, 2000; George, 2004; Stiglitz, 2002).

This analysis supports the classification of the Irish state as exhibiting strongly neoliberal characteristics. It concentrates on providing only basic levels of services and has a weak commitment to reducing inequalities. It is characterised by the low proportion of resources devoted to social spending and a lightly regulated labour market. Ireland's welfare state embodies low expectations and achieves low outcomes for a minority (NESC, 2005). Kirby (2002) and Allen (2007), applying such a political economy approach, note that what has evolved in Ireland is a neoliberal state with a pay-related welfare state in which minimal levels of universal entitlement to income and services are supplemented by market-based resources. Using this critical perspective, the Irish state can be classified as a 'competitive' state where a national industrial welfare state, under the pressure of economic globalisation, has expanded state intervention and regulation in the name of competitiveness and marketisation.

International market competitiveness of the economy, state and society has therefore been the Irish state's and successive governments' overriding objective and priority (O'Toole, 2003; Kirby, 2002). As a result, the role of the Irish state has concentrated on promoting enterprise and creating a competitive economy and to a much lesser degree than other Western European countries provided welfare state public services and infrastructure.

For example, the Irish welfare state has proved ineffective in modifying in any significant way the inequalities generated by market forces and, indeed, has exacerbated them (Kirby, 2002). One may contrast the trends in absolute poverty (steadily declining) and relative poverty (steadily rising) in Ireland that have taken place since the mid 1980s (Allen, 2007). As the NESC Report (2005) noted, significant minorities in Ireland's population were experiencing one or multiple forms of social disadvantage, while present strategies and policies are not proving adequate in helping them.

As taxes on wealth have been reduced in Ireland, the cost of running the welfare state and public services has increasingly shifted on to indirect taxes and stealth taxes. Indirect taxes make up 43 per cent of the overall tax burden in Ireland compared to 34 per cent in the EU. For example, in the six-year period between 1997 and 2003, waste refuse collection charges grew by an average of 37 per cent a year (Allen, 2007). Irish consumers pay 42 per cent more than the EU average for housing, water, electricity, gas and other fuels, 25 per cent more for education and 24 per cent more for health. Furthermore, Ireland's labour market still counts as one of the least regulated in the OECD, its employment protection legislation being the fifth least strict of twenty-eight countries examined by the OECD in 2003 (OECD, 2005). SIPTU, Ireland's largest trade union, expressed concern that workers' living standards had been considerably undermined in the decades of the 1990s and 2000s by the erosion of pension benefits for private-sector employees and the constant undermining of pay and employment conditions by the widespread use of lower-paid agency workers and migrant labour (SIPTU, 2008).

Failure and collapse of Celtic Tiger model

The collapse of the Celtic Tiger economy in 2008 revealed the lack of sustainability of that economic model, which significantly reduced taxes on income and capital and prioritised private-sector-driven economic growth. The model did provide unprecedented levels of growth, particularly in the construction sector, but also promoted the private delivery of public services through PPPs, and restricted public borrowing while private borrowing (personal, business and development) was extensively encouraged.

However, the economic growth was largely based on a property and credit 'bubble', which followed the classic 'free market' boom–bust scenario. As a result of the economic crash in 2008, the Irish citizens faced a situation whereby the Irish banks and the developers they had lent to, and who had significant shares in the banks, required €73 billion to stabilise the financial system. The state and its taxpayers were left to deal with the bad debt as the value of property plummeted. In 2009 alone, the Irish government invested €7 billion in the country's two main banks, the Bank of Ireland and Allied Irish Banks, in order to try and keep them in business.

Unemployment soared from just 4.6 per cent in 2007 to 13.4 per cent in June 2010. Between 2007 and 2010, over 140,000 jobs were lost in the construction sector alone. The rise in social welfare payments required for this massive increase in unemployment combined with the reduction in economic growth and the resultant collapse in tax receipts for the state meant the Country faced a fiscal crisis in 2009 and 2010, as the deficit between income and expenditure grew considerably. In order to address this fiscal deficit, the Irish government, in contrast to many of the major developed countries across the world, imposed policies of severe retrenchment in public spending. It decided, however, not to impose increases in tax on large corporations or high earners through measures such as increasing corporation tax rates, capital gains tax or wealth taxes etc. It thus continued in a neoliberal policy trajectory.

The extent of the fiscal retrenchment was apparent in government plans to reduce public expenditure by €12 billion over three years, from 2009 to 2012. It planned to achieve this through reducing current spending, facilitating a structural lowering of public service numbers through the introduction of a moratorium on the filling of vacancies by recruitment or promotion and early retirement in the public and civil service and severely cutting the capital investment programme. For example, in 2009 the Public Capital Programme, at €7.3 billion, was reduced by €1.7 billion, or almost 19 per cent on the 2008 figure. The Department of the Environment's capital expenditure housing allocation for 2009 was just over €1.1 billion, a €355 million decrease on 2008.

Interestingly, the capital allocation for PPPs in operation was not reduced as part of the retrenchment – because of contractual commitments. Therefore, in 2009, in the transport sector there was a reduction in the capital allocation for public transport, which would result in a delay in the implementation of a number of projects that were still in the planning stages. However, the €1.44 billion capital allocation for national roads was unaffected because it was already contractually committed to be spent through PPP projects.

Clearly, the government's ability to decide where it should prioritise spending reductions was reduced by its commitments in PPPs. Capital investment in necessary social infrastructure, which had not been committed through the PPP route, was severely reduced. For example, the healthcare capital budget was cut by 28 per cent in the 2008 and 2009 budgets.

Similarly, the retrenchment had a fundamental impact on the model of provision of social housing, evident in the Dáil exchange (22 April, 2010) between Joanna Tuffy, a TD from the opposition Labour Party, and the Minister for the Environment:

> Joanna Tuffy: The model of council housing whereby people rented at a low rent from the public authority with the option to buy over time has worked very well in this country over the years. What will the Minister do about frontloading actual county council houses?
>
> Minister Gormley: As the Deputy will know, the model has changed. Again, this comes down to the amount of money we have available. We are moving towards two models: first, social leasing and, second, the *rental accommodation scheme* or RAS system.
>
> Joanna Tuffy: Does that mean we are moving away from council housing?
>
> Minister Gormley: Of course it means that.
>
> Tuffy: *Why?*
>
> Minister Gormley: The money that was available before is no longer available. There is a thing called reality and the Deputy must get used to it.

During the economic boom it was claimed (as detailed in Chapter 3) that PPPs were necessary in order to keep public spending and borrowing at relatively low levels so as not to breach the EU budgetary debt guidelines. However, when the major banks and developers faced financial crisis in 2008 and 2009, these budgetary restrictions were dismissed by the government as it stated it was prepared to take on whatever level of borrowings and debt necessary to deal with the crisis. The original fiscal policy – that the government restricted public spending for over a decade during an unprecedented economic boom – was then discarded in order to borrow and spend the billions of euros required to support the banks and developers that faced financial collapse.

This demonstrates that the government's fiscal policy pursued throughout the decade of the Celtic Tiger was short-sighted and driven by their adherence to neoliberal ideology. The Irish state could have used the economic buoyancy of the period, adopted the present policy of borrow and spend, to develop key infrastructure and services, which would have provided a more sustainable level of growth and addressed the infrastructure and services deficits. This would also have eased the impact on the population of the recession that existed from 2008 to 2010 by avoiding the situation where, in the depths of the crisis, there remained considerable infrastructure and services deficits.

The case of the Irish National Pension Reserve Fund also demonstrates both the failure of the free-market model and the lack of vision of the government to use the funding it had available to it during the boom creatively, to provide sustainable development. The state invested €16.87 billion (almost €2 billion per annum) between 2000 and 2008 in the Fund. However, by December 2008 the market value of the Fund (at €16.1 billion) was less than that cumulative contribution, due to the fall in the value of equities on international financial markets. It could be argued that investing that €2 billion per annum on schools, hospitals and social housing would have produced a quantitatively better outcome for society and the economy.

While it appeared that Ireland became a wealthy country over the period of the Celtic Tiger, the reality was that 'it was never wealthy: those years of high income were largely wasted ... because years of high income must be invested wisely for a country to become wealthy' (Davy Stockbrokers, 2010). Over the period of 2000–2008, the net capital stock of the state doubled from €222 billion to €477 billion, but almost two-thirds of the increase was taken up by unproductive capital stock in the form of housing (increased in value by 156 per cent, from €118 billion to €302.5 billion). In 2000, the unproductive capital stock exceeded the productive stock by €14 billion. By 2008, that gap was €118 billion. Furthermore, it was the state and semi-state sectors that invested almost €50 billion in 'core' productive capital stock that included schools, hospitals and electricity and gas supplies. Roads, which increased from €13 billion to €27.5 billion, accounted for almost 30 per cent of this.

Over the same period, the private sector only invested €17 billion in 'core' productive capital (Davy Stockbrokers, 2009). The achievements of the Celtic Tiger period are visible, therefore, in the unprecedented investment in private housing and apartments, office and hotel developments, world-class motorways, convention centres and sports stadiums.

During this period, public-sector spending and employment growth did not keep up with this development and the high rates of population and economic growth. Ireland's real average annual growth rate in public expenditure between 1995 and 2005 was 5.1 per cent, significantly slower than real GDP growth of 7.5 per cent. Government policy actually decreased the total number of public-sector employees as a percentage of the labour force. The data from 2005 indicate that general government employment in Ireland represented around 14.6 per cent of the total labour force, which was relatively low among OECD countries and significantly less than the level of public employment in Norway, Sweden, France, Finland and Belgium (OECD, 2008).

Infrastructure deficit

The outcome of these investment priorities during the Celtic Tiger period meant that, as of 2010, there remained an urgent requirement for increased investment in public infrastructure and services, highlighted in the number of international competitiveness surveys that pointed to the significant deficits in Ireland. For example, in 2008 in terms of overall quality of infrastructure, Ireland ranked twenty-second out of twenty-five; in terms of transport infrastructure, twenty-seventh out of twenty-eight; and in terms of efficiency of energy infrastructure, twenty-sixth out of twenty-eight. Dublin City ranked twenty-eight out of thirty in terms of average peak-hour speed of cars (Engineers Ireland, 2010).

The deficit, as noted earlier, is causing considerable challenges to the successful social and economic development of Ireland. In the area of transport, infrastructure is urgently required in order to deal with the dramatic increase in car ownership, the sprawl of cities, the emergence of commuter belts associated with large urban centres and the routes between them that have seen massive increases in traffic, and inadequate public transport provision for both urban and rural communities (Engineers Ireland, 2010). Between 1991 and 2002, the total number of cars owned by private households increased from 445,226 to 1,601,619. By 2002, over 62 per cent of workers travelled to work by car compared to 47 per cent of a much smaller workforce in 1991. By contrast, the percentage usage of public transport (bus or train) decreased from 9.4 per cent in 1991 to 8.7 per cent in 2002, even though the actual number of users increased substantially by 31 per cent from 107,211 to 140,381 (Government of Ireland, 2007).

There was also a crisis in access to local authority social and affordable housing. There were almost 80,000 families and individuals on social housing waiting lists in 2010. The waiting list for social housing in the four Dublin local authorities jumped from 11,490 in 2005 to 13,535 in 2008 and 25,494 in 2010.

Another sector impacted by the government's fiscal policy has been the public health system. Healthcare is one of the most important priorities for many users of Irish public services and they rightfully expect high-quality service and treatment when needed. However, many patients were experiencing difficulties in accessing beds in hospitals and there were long waiting lists for treatments. On a near daily basis, there were media reports or discussions regarding difficulties within the health system. The number of acute care hospital beds in Ireland was 2.8 per 1,000 of the population in 2005, below the OECD average of 3.9 beds per 1,000. In contrast, Japan, Korea, Germany and Austria all achieve ratios of over six acute care beds per 1,000 (OECD 2008). As a result, 500 patients were treated on trolleys in Accident and Emergency units in hospitals in January 2010. The Irish Nurses and Midwives Organisation claimed, in response, that Accident and Emergency units had reached 'breaking point with corridors crammed with the sick and injured'. This was higher than the 2006 beds crisis, which Health Minister, Mary Harney, called 'a national emergency'. This is despite the annual budget for the health sector being over €16 billion in 2008. These experiences have been compounded by a series of scandals in the health services from issues in relation to blood transfusion stocks, superbugs in hospitals, the neglect of children in care of the public health system and clinical malpractice cases involving consultants that have challenged public faith in the governance of public health services.

Much of the population believe, therefore, they are not getting sufficient quality of care from the health system and that the only way to secure treatment is to have private medical insurance, and, as a result, some 51 per cent of Irish people hold private medical insurance. This is despite the fact that all members of the population, irrespective of income, are entitled to free treatment in public hospitals. Despite these problems, a significant majority of the Irish public has indicated high levels of satisfaction with the service they receive, once they are able to access hospitals for treatment. It has been argued that a system of health 'apartheid' is developing in Ireland, as those who cannot afford private healthcare or insurance are left dealing with a public health system that is bursting at the seams (Burke, 2009; Tussing & Wren, 2006). The OECD Public Service Review 2008 identified a need for investment in buildings, medical equipment, managerial tools and electronic health records in the Irish healthcare system, and, in some instances, urgent action is needed to upgrade existing acute or community care facilities, to provide appropriate isolation rooms and to acquire more modern diagnostic equipment.

In the public water system, the pressure of historic underfunding has impacted upon the quality of service provision. The Irish water network is some 44,000km long, has been installed for over 200 years and is in serious need of repair. The cryptosporidium outbreak and resultant health crisis in Galway City demonstrated the impact of the infrastructure deficit and challenges in this area. Engineers Ireland (2010) have also highlighted how the impacts of climate change will demand a very different approach to how we organise society and plan and develop all forms of infrastructure, particularly from increased sea levels, rainfall patterns and extreme weather events that will necessitate major adaptations for the protection of cities in coastal areas and river basins.

In 2008, in the area of education, at the height of the economic boom, Ireland had one of the lowest levels of investment in the developed world, spending only 4.4 per cent of GDP on education, in comparison to the internationally accepted benchmark of 6 per cent. Ireland came twenty-ninth out of thirty-four countries in a 2007 OECD education spending survey. Inadequate investment in schools has resulted in severe classroom overcrowding (average class sizes in Ireland are the second highest in the EU), teaching in temporary accommodation, leaking roofs and inadequate facilities. Many schools do not have sufficient funds to cover basic maintenance and running costs. For example, a 2007 survey of over 200 primary schools indicated that over 80 per cent of primary schools depended on cake sales and other fundraising by parents for basics like heating oil to meet the shortfall in government funding (Flynn, 2007). The survey also found that the schools received an average grant of just €25,000, even though their running costs averaged €48,000.

The extent of the investment deficit is also demonstrated by the unprecedented growth in commercial schemes run by supermarkets and other private companies, which involve the collection of tokens issued on the purchase of a certain value of product. The school receives much-needed school equipment such as PE gear, science equipment and computers, once it provides a sufficient quantity of tokens to the supermarket/private company (Allen, 2007).

The Irish National Teachers Organisation passed a motion at its 2006 Congress condemming the underfunding of the Irish education system, which has deprived schools of resources and public funding, and expressed its concern at the growing commercialisation of education, such as schemes that required teachers to promote products in classrooms (Carr, 2007). In 2008, the Public Accounts Committee expressed concern that some children spent their entire student life in temporary portacabins and that the Department continued to purchase and hire such 'prefab' buildings to meet accommodation needs in a reactive rather than in a planned way. The Department spent €35 million on such rented accommodation in 2007 and this figure rose to € 52 million in 2008.

Population changes will also have a major impact on the infrastructure deficit, particularly as public infrastructure takes a considerable period of time to develop. It is, therefore, important to plan for future demographic changes. After a period of negative population growth between 1986 and 1991, Ireland's population grew rapidly with the result that in 2006 the population was 4.24 million. That figure is projected to grow to between five and, possibly, seven million by 2041, a doubling of the population of 3.5 million that existed in 1986. The composition of Ireland's population will also undergo considerable change over the coming decades.

The OECD projects that Ireland will experience the largest expansion in the population range of the five- to fourteen-year age group (by 19 per cent) among all OECD countries over the 2005 to 2015 period. This is primarily the age group in primary school level. Based on these demographic developments, the Department of Education and Science is expecting a dramatic increase in the student population of 100,000 at primary school level by 2016. Based on the number of children in primary schools in 2008, approximately 50,000 extra pupils will enter second level by 2013 (Government of Ireland, 2007). This will place a further demand for new and improved school buildings, on top of the need for the refurbishment of substandard school buildings. Appropriate infrastructure and services will also need to be planned to address the urbanisation of the Irish population and the substantial increase in the number of senior citizens. By 2050, the proportion of the population aged 65 and over relative to the population aged fifteen to sixty-four (the elderly age dependency ratio) will be in the order of 45 per cent, nearly treble the 2004 figure of 16.4 per cent.

What future for the state and its role in public service provision?

The ability of existing public-sector service providers in Ireland to satisfy users and retain the confidence of the public has come under unprecedented strain from the significant deficit, underfunding, insufficient reform, PPPs and privatisation policies. There is a widespread public perception that the state on its own is no longer capable of providing quality public services and infrastructure, as there was clear evidence of a drift by the public away from using them where other options existed (NESC, 2005), and the use of many core public services was becoming increasingly associated with the poor and lower-income populations.

To these issues, one can add the on-going revelations of planning and political corruption, an historical distrust of the state, the proliferation of private-sector alternatives and intolerable delays in accessing many public services. These problems have been compounded by the political culture in Ireland, which permeates state institutions, including elected political representatives and public and civil servants.

In its 2006 report, the Taskforce on Active Citizenship described a cynicism and a lack of confidence on the part of the Irish public in democratic and consultative structures, with individuals and organisations not feeling that they are genuinely listened to. This is exacerbated, the Taskforce noted, by the focus in public services on customers rather than on citizens and the fact that Ireland has very centralised policy-making and service-delivery systems.

Adding to this general lack of confidence in public services is the long-held view and experience of the public that politicians and the state operate according to the principles of clientelism, nepotism, political patronage and corruption. It is believed, and experienced, often that it is those who are in some way connected to individuals and groups in power (such as individuals in central and local government and public and civil servants), or those who have such people advocating on their behalf, that are the ones who can access much-needed public services rather than the services being available and accessed according to a priority of those who require and qualify for the service.

This clientelist, or personal, culture has promoted practices that reflect patterns of social and political relationships similar to village life in southern Italy (Coakley and Gallagher, 1999). It has also fostered consensus-based public dialogue, and an anti-intellectualism, that is characterised by a repression of different opinions on religious and political values that continues virtually unchallenged.

This social and political culture has led to state institutions allocating their spending according to electoral cycles, reacting to crises and problems as they emerge, particularly on an individualised or localised level, allocating funds according to the local constituency requirements of the relevant Minister of a Department (Suiter, 2010) and planning decisions being made according to the wishes of private developers. Ultimately it has led to an absence of long-term planning that would prioritise the requirements of society and the economy on a strategic and sustainable basis. Large-scale investment in infrastructure projects and social services, which require long periods of planning and development, has, therefore, not been prioritised by the Irish political system because it does not provide short-term outcomes that facilitate the gaining of electoral support within the timeframe of local and national elections.

Overall then, the Irish state is held in low regard by the Irish population. The Irish public service, state institutions and political class are rapidly losing the confidence of the Irish public. This collapse of trust in the Irish state and public service delivery is taking place in parallel to the failures and collapse of the private developer and market-led models. A debate is emerging, therefore, about how the state, civil society, the citizen and private organisations can interact and engage to provide a sustainable model of economic growth and development, while also addressing the infrastructure and service deficit in an efficient and effective manner, taking into consideration value for money.

Public-sector reform
In the first instance, there is a requirement for the urgent reform of the existing direct, traditional, provision of public services and infrastructure.

Citizens rightfully expect higher standards of delivery, expect more flexible and responsive services, and want governments to develop and implement policies that provide solutions to new and more-complex problems. Instead, many experience delays in response times or a lack of any response from the civil and public services, and they regularly see anecdotal evidence – usually through media reports – of service breakdowns and failures in the delivery of housing, health, education, transportation and justice services. In the context of this requirement for radical reform of public services, we need to figure out how we can get public services to meet the needs of society and to work to optimum effectiveness. Indeed, an important justification for the decision to roll out PPPs was the requirement to reform the delivery and provision of public services. The agenda and context for this reform is explained in the OECD's (2008) review of the Irish public service. It highlighted a number of practical problems associated with traditional public-sector delivery, including the inflexibility in redeployment within and between the Civil Service and non-commercial state bodies and local authority workers, the need to ensure that the numbers employed in the public service are no greater than are necessary to deliver public services and the need for a significant improvement in professionalisation of employees.

The OECD review also asserted that there is a requirement for a culture of evaluation within individual public-sector organisations. Public services need to become more focused on performance and delivery and must be made more accountable to the public for what they achieve through the measurement of that performance. It noted that underperformance must be challenged and there is a need for a clear link between the performance ratings given to individuals and actual achievements in delivering services and improved outcomes for the public. Many public servants themselves feel that the system inhibits rather than challenges them, that it does not reward innovation and is quick to penalise failure. The public service, it stated, could be characterised as a system that focused largely on controlling inputs, such as funds and personnel, rather than focusing on performance and results. There is an identified need for a modern, responsive and citizen-focused public service in Ireland that can translate increased wealth and prosperity into better services.

In May 2008, a Task Force on the Public Service was established by the Taoiseach, Mr Brian Cowen, to develop an action plan drawing on the analysis and recommendations of the OECD (2008). It outlined the importance of reform, as the public service is 'of vital national interest. How well it performs and how efficiently it operates are of critical importance to the lives of every citizen and the well being of the community as a whole'. As further indication of the necessity for reform a report carried out by Ernst and Young on behalf of the Department of the Environment in October 2009 investigated 143 capital projects valued at €330 million. The report covered nine programme areas, including housing, water, waste, fire and emergency, libraries, local services and urban regeneration and investigated whether or not there was compliance with the relevant Department guidelines, reviews of project processes and an assessment of compliance in areas such as procurement, budgetary control and reporting arrangements. It found, significantly, that over 30 per cent of projects were over budget and 24 per cent went beyond the planned completion date.

Public services and infrastructure need to be efficient, effective, accessible and responsive to society's needs. Therefore, considerable reform is urgently required. The manner, in which that reform takes place, and its fundamental aim, is essential to what the outcome will be.

Pushing the 'pause button' on PPP development
The neoliberal period from 1980 to 2009 has been an attempt to role back state intervention by Keynesian governments that imposed limits to capital expansion and the free market. As the neoliberal period enters a crisis, its catastrophic results are being experienced across the world. The Irish PPP experiment was, and in 2010 still remained, part of that neoliberal paradigm. The results of the initial phase of PPP development in Ireland demonstrate that, as a policy, it had insufficient practical foundation and was based on an ideological pursuit by government and the private sector with the aim of providing new markets and business opportunities for private enterprise. It was also planned to play a part in the rolling back of the limited Keynesian welfare state and labour protections that existed in Ireland. The full extent of the long-term impacts on the Irish welfare state of these policies more generally are just beginning to be experienced and understood.

Therefore, along side the requirement for public sector reform, there is a need to pause the existing model of PPP development. Further research is required to complement this research and determine whether these disquieting trends intensify or ameliorate over the contract lifetime of the PPPs and whether the broader governance transformations materialise further in the workings of the Irish state. The most appropriate course of action for government may be to temporarily halt the development of new PPP projects until further informed analysis is undertaken of the effectiveness and appropriateness, from both a 'value for money' and social perspective, of PPPs in the delivery and management of public infrastructure and services.

The need to develop alternative models

Models of best practice, from the public, private and not-for-profit voluntary, charity and community sectors should be analysed and, if appropriate, their implementation extended to public services and infrastructure delivery.

There are many examples of efficient and high-quality traditional delivery of public services such as the DART rail system, Dublin City Council-led housing projects such as Ballybough and Bridgefoot Street, public schools, some hospitals, waste collection services etc. The OECD (2008) highlighted that public services have played a key role in Ireland's economic growth and there are many instances where public services are efficient, accessible and effective. The Irish Public Service – and in particular the Civil Service – is providing a bigger service with less resources relative to the size of the overall economy and workforce compared with other countries (OECD, 2008). Even when factoring in the major investment that took place over the Celtic Tiger period, public expenditure only reached 35 per cent of GDP in the ten years prior to the economic crash, which was the lowest in the European Union and OECD.

There is also high-quality service delivery in the not-for-profit sector, such as the social housing provided and managed by the Respond Housing Association, the child and family services provided by the Barnardos charity, Focus Ireland homeless charity, youth projects, Community Development Projects, Family Resource Centres, local community drug support projects to name but a few. In order to develop the highest possible standards of public service and infrastructure provision in Ireland, these models, and other successful ones from Ireland and other European countries, should be researched. In particular, it would be useful to identify how they provide such high-quality services and what differentiates them from poorly performing public services and infrastructure.

The Institute for Public Policy Research in the UK has put forward an interesting model of public service reform that involves citizens themselves, whether as individuals or communities, participating much more than has been the case in the past on delivery of public services. It argues that citizens and communities have been the missing link in public service reform and, therefore, key societal challenges, such as chronic health conditions associated with lifestyle, aging populations, climate change and anti-social behaviour, require a shifting in the relationship between the citizen and the state. Developing effective service solutions require an exploration of citizen and community empowerment and the role communities and citizens can play in directly producing services. This would involve moving from the passive consumption of services, which is often neither sustainable nor desirable, to services which work best when consumers and recipients are involved in producing them, ensuring citizens are engaged as active partners in the process. Suggestions include allocating personal budgets, communities coming together to run schools and changing models of ownership to co-production between service provider and service user in partnerships and cooperatives.

These could include self-care skills training in health, youth courts for young people engaging in non-violent offences, and also involving citizens in building social capital and empowerment (Institute for Public Policy Research, 2009). While there are many challenges to ensure real participation, particularly in terms of the impacts of class, income, education etc., as the regeneration projects have demonstrated, if citizens are given support, it can be achieved. There are experimental examples in Ireland of this model, such as Educate Together Schools, Community Development Projects and local community-based organisations that provide some very successful outcomes, although their funding was targeted for reduction in government budgets in 2009 and 2010.

Another alternative model would be to invest in public infrastructure as part of a Keynesian-type stimulus plan that would reinvigorate the economy by providing much-needed employment and would address service deficits. This could include regenerating local authority estates and communities suffering most from Ireland's considerable social and economic inequalities, providing schools, hospitals, green energy projects, swimming pools and community centres. The state could develop plans with local communities for the key infrastructure that is needed in their areas and then contract in Irish construction companies to build them according to those plans. Local people from the surrounding communities could be then employed by State Agencies or not-for-profit organisations with proven track records in delivery, to operate them. High levels of value for money could be achieved as construction prices have fallen considerably since the height of the economic boom in 2007. For example, tender prices fell by 30 per cent between 2007 and 2010.

Sources of funding for this stimulus could include re-directing the annual allocation of 1 per cent of GNP to the National Pension Reserve Fund (€1.7 billion in 2009). Another source could be requiring private industry to invest, say 2 per cent of its annual revenue, in a national social and productive capital infrastructure fund that could then be used for public infrastructure and service provision. This could also address the low levels of investment by the private sector in core productive capital. The government could also launch an infrastructure bond that would help fund major capital projects (Engineers Ireland, 2010). The management of Irish pension funds, for example, informed the government in 2010 they were willing to invest up to €6 billion in a range of state infrastructure projects.

Think Tank for Action on Social Change, an independent think-tank, has put forward a number of methods of raising such funding. For example, the government could also change the tax system that has favoured higher-income earners. For example, tax breaks for various private investments cost around €7.4 billion to the exchequer in 2009. One tax rebate available to landlords, alone, cost around about the same in 2010 as the saving to the Exchequer made from cutting Social Welfare rates in the Budget (TASC, 2010).

Such investment in public infrastructure and services could provide tens of thousands of new jobs which would reduce the state's social welfare bill that it pays to the unemployed and provide an increase in income taxes. For example, providing 70,000 new jobs would reduce the state's social welfare costs by €1.3 billion (ICTU, 2010). In 2009 and 2010, other European countries and the United States were implementing such ambitious recovery plans in order to limit the impacts of the recession on citizens and the economy. According to the European Commission (2009, 2), 'investment in infrastructure projects is an important means to maintain economic activity during the crisis and support a rapid return to sustained economic growth'.

If Ireland is to learn the lessons of the past, it should avoid what happened in the 1980s when public expenditure was drastically reduced. Those cuts in spending led to the deficits in public infrastructure and services that were still affecting Irish society and its economy three decades later. Moreover, we should look to when the state undertook some of its largest investment in social infrastructure in the 1950s, when it developed a very large programme of social housing construction. The state, at the time, did not have the anything approaching the wealth that existed even during the recession at the end of the 2000s. As Joan Burton, Labour Party economic spokesperson explained to that party's 2010 Annual Conference:

> To get a depressed economy moving, you must have a stimulus...When demand slumps, when deflation is a greater menace than inflation, when consumer and corporate confidence has collapsed, fiscal conservatism makes little sense. Instead it makes sense to reflate (sic) through a carefully managed programme of public investment. It's smart economics to invest in education and infrastructure like public transport.

Such alternative approaches will require academics, community activists, citizens and politicians making their case, advocating it publicly, transforming the public mindset from inhibitions and limitations into imagining what could be possible in terms of delivering adequate, effective and accessible public services and infrastructure that would underpin the redevelopment of Ireland as a more equitable, sustainable and better place for its citizens. To do this will require a debate about the need for equitable taxes, and for services to be provided on the basis of universalism according to people's needs and not just their ability to pay.

The question for those in power, in government, in state and private institutions, indeed for Irish society is: will the clear legacy of the decade at the end of the twentieth century and that of the start of the twenty-first century be that Irish society, its government and its people gave the highest priority to ensuring the survival of its banks and financial institutions, while the health, housing and other social infrastructure that are key to providing a decent quality of life for all citizens was relegated in importance and given no such support?

Bibliography

A&L Goodbody Consulting (2005) *Ireland's Strategic Infrastructure Investment 2020*, Dublin: A&L Goodbody.

Ahern, B. (2006) *Statement of An Taoiseach at the Launch of the Dominick Street Flats Complex Regeneration PPP*, Dublin: Department of An Taoiseach.

Allen, K. (2007) *The Corporate Takeover of Ireland*, Dublin: Irish Academic Press Ltd.

Allied Irish Banks (2008) *Public Private Partnerships*, www.aib.ie.

Association of Teachers and Lecturers (ATL) (2006) Northern Ireland Assembly Sub-Group on School Admissions, www.atl.org.uk.

Audit Commission Scotland (2002) *Taking the Initiative – Using PFI Contracts to Renew Council Schools*, www.Audit-Scotland.Gov.uk.

Audit Commission UK (2003) *PFI in Schools*, London: Belmont Press.

Audit Commission UK (2009) *Private Finance Projects*, London: Belmont Press.

Babcock & Brown (2008) *Company History*, www.babcockbrown.com.

Bacon, P. & Associates (1998) *An Economic Assessment of Recent House Price Developments*, Dublin: Stationary Office.

Bartley, B. and Kitchen, R. (eds.) (2007) *Understanding Contemporary Ireland*, Dublin: Pluto Press.

Bissett, J. (2005) 'PPP and the politics of regenerating St Michael's estate', paper presented to the Centre for Urban and Regional Studies Seminar, Trinity College, Dublin, 13 December 2005.

Bissett, J. (2008) *Regeneration, Public Good or Private Profit?* Dublin: New Island Press.

Blackwell, J. (1988) *A Review of Housing Policy*, Dublin: National Economic Social Council Office.

Blair, T. (2006) 'Our nation's future', speech by the Prime Minister www.number-10.gov.uk.

Bourdieu, P. (1998) *Acts of Resistance: Against the New Myths of Our Time*, Cambridge: Polity Press.

Bradley, F. and Allen, F. (2001) 'Value for money in Public Private Partnerships: myth and reality', *Administration*, 49(1) 46–58.

Brenner, N. and Theodore, N. (2002) 'Cities and the geographies of actually existing neo-liberalism', *Antipode*, 34(3) 349–79.

Brenner, N., Theodore, N. and Peck, J. (2005) *Neoliberal Urbanism: Cities and the Rule of Markets*, www.geography.wisc.edu/faculty/peck.

Burke, J. (2010) 'Losses likely on Poolbeg Incinerator', *The Sunday Business Post*, 17 January 2006.

Burke, S. (2009) Irish Apartheid: Healthcare Inequality in Ireland, Dublin: New Island Books.

Callinicos, A. (2003) *An Anti-Capitalist Manifesto*, London: Polity.

Campaign against the EU Constitution (2008) *Why You Should Vote No*, www.caeuc.org.

Canadian Union of Public Employees (CUPE) (2006) *P3s for Alberta Schools Don't Add Up*, www.cupe.ca.

Canadian Union of Public Employees (CUPE) (2007) *P3 Schools: A Disaster Waiting to Happen*, www.cupe.ca.

Canal Communities Partnership (2007) *Regeneration Learnings and Insights*, Dublin: Canal Communities Partnership.

Carroll, S. (2008) 'Resisting PPPs "Critical"', *The Irish Times*, 29 May 2008.

Castells, M. (1993) 'European cities, the informational society, and the global economy', *Tijdschrift voor Econ. En Soc. Geographie*, 84(4) 247–57.

Castells, M. (2000) *The Rise of the Network Society: Economy, Society and Culture*, Oxford: Blackwell Publishers.

Centre for Public Services (2004) *How to Exclude Support Services from BSF and PFI/PPP Projects*, Sheffield: Centre for Public Services.

Central PPP Unit (2002) *PPP Communications Strategy*, www.ppp.gov.ie.

Central PPP Unit (2004) 'Briefing on PPPs prepared by Central PPP Unit at Department of Finance for the Dáil Public Accounts Committee', www.ppp.gov.ie.

Central PPP Unit (2005) *PPP Project Tracker Update*, www.ppp.gov.ie.

Central PPP Unit (2006a) *PPP Project Tracker Update*, www.ppp.gov.ie.

Central PPP Unit (2006b) *Guidelines for the Provision of Infrastructure and Capital Investments through Public Private Partnerships: Procedures for the Assessment, Approval, Audit and Procurement of Projects*, www.ppp.gov.ie.

Central PPP Unit (2006c) *Assessment of Projects for Procurement as Public Private Partnership*, www.ppp.gov.ie.

Central PPP Unit (2007) *PPP Project Tracker Update*, www.ppp.gov.ie.

Central PPP Unit (2008) *PPP Project Tracker Update*, www.ppp.gov.ie.

Central PPP Unit (2010) *PPP Project Tracker Update*, www.ppp.gov.ie.

City and Financial (2006) 'The 2nd Annual Irish Public Private Partnerships Policy Forum', City and Financial, London.

City and Financial (2007) 'The 3rd Annual Irish Public Private Partnerships Policy Forum', City and Financial, London.

City and Financial (2008) 'The 4th Annual Irish Public Private Partnerships Policy Forum', City and Financial, London.

Coakley, J. and Gallagher, M. (eds.) (1999) *Politics in the Republic of Ireland*, London: Routledge.

Combat Poverty Agency (2002) *Combating Poverty in a Changing Ireland: Combat Poverty Agency Strategic Plan*, Dublin: Combat Poverty Agency.

Combat Poverty Agency (2005) *Working for a Poverty-Free Ireland: Strategic Plan 2005, 2007*, Dublin: Combat Poverty Agency.

Combat Poverty Agency (2006) *Submission to the Department of Finance on the National Development Plan 2007–2013*, Dublin: Combat Poverty Agency.

Combat Poverty Agency (2007) *Combat Poverty's Submission to the OECD Review of the Irish Public Service*, Dublin: Combat Poverty Agency.

Commission for Architecture and the Built Environment (CABE) (2005) *Design Quality and the Private Finance Initiative*, www.cabe.org.uk.

Community Technical Aid (2008), *Community Technical Aid*, www.cta.ie.

Comptroller and Auditor General (C & AG) Northern Ireland (2004) *Building for the Future: A Review of PFI Education Pathfinder Projects*, Belfast: Northern Ireland Audit Office.

Comptroller and Auditor General (C & AG) (2003) *Value for Money Report No. 42 Car Parking at Beaumount Hospital*, www.audgen.gov.ie.

Comptroller and Auditor General (C & AG) (2004) *The Grouped Schools Pilot Partnership Project: Report on Value for Money Examination*, www.audgen.gov.ie.

Comptroller and Auditor General (C & AG) (2008) *Annual Report 2008*, www.audgen.gov.ie.

Corporate Watch (2007) *Privatisation and Public Private Partnerships*, www.corpwatch.org.

Cowen, B. (2006) Address by the Minister for Finance, Brian Cowen, TD, The Second Irish Public Private Partnerships Policy Forum, Gresham Hotel, Wednesday, 5 April 2006.

Covanta (2010) Holding Corporation First Quarter Earnings Conference Call held on 22 April 2010, www.covantaholding.com.

Cox, K. R. and Johnston, R. J. (eds.) (1982) *Conflict, Politics and the Urban Scene*, London: Longman.

Crawford, C. (2001) 'Gardai hold 14 after protest at hotel', *The Irish Times*, 11 October 2001.

Davy Stockbrokers (2010) *Years of High Income Largely Wasted*, Dublin, www.davy.ie.

Defend Council Housing Campaign (2007) *The Case for Council Housing in 21st Century Britain*, www.defendcouncilhousing.org.uk.

Deloitte (2006) *Building Flexibility: New Delivery Models for Public Infrastructure Projects*, London: Deloitte.

Deloitte (2007) *Public Private Partnerships: Building With the Best Team*, London: Deloitte.

Dempsey, N. (2002) Speech by Minister for Education, Dáil Éireann, 2002, www.debates.oireachtas.ie.

Department of Education and Science (DOES) (2006a) *School Building Programme: Key Achievements 2000–2005*, Dublin: Stationary Office.

Department of Education and Science (DOES) (2006b) *Whole School Evaluation Report for Ballincollig Community School*, Dublin: Stationary Office.

Department of Education and Skills (2007) *Schools Private Finance Initiative*, www.teachernet.gov.uk.

Department of the Environment, Heritage and Local Government (DOEHLG) (2001) *Circular HS 13/01 Framework for Public Private Partnerships in Housing*, Dublin: Stationary Office.

Department of the Environment, Heritage and Local Government (DOEHLG) (2005) *Building Sustainable Communities*, Dublin: Stationary Office.

Department of the Environment, Heritage and Local Government (DOEHLG) (2008) *Irish Housing (Standards for Rented Houses) Regulations, 2008*, Dublin, www.environ.ie.

Department of the Environment, Heritage and Local Government (DOEHLG) (2009a) *Social and Affordable Housing Statistics*, Dublin, www.environ.ie.

Department of the Environment, Heritage and Local Government (DOEHLG) (2009b) *Irish Housing (Standards for Rented Houses) Regulations, 2009*, Dublin, www.environ.ie.

Department of Social, Community and Family Affairs (1997) *The National Anti-Poverty Strategy*, Dublin: Government of Ireland.

Department of the Taoiseach (1996) *Delivering Better Government*, Dublin: Department of the Taoiseach.

Dillon, B. (2004) *Changing Partners: How PPP has Replaced Community Partnership in Urban Regeneration*, Dublin: Combat Poverty Agency.

Dolphin House Community Development Association (2006) 'Future development of Dolphin House', Draft Position Paper.

Drudy, P.J. and Punch, M. (2005) *Out of Reach, Inequalities in the Irish Housing System*, Dublin: New Island Press.

Dublin City Council (DCC) (2002) *Regeneration, Next Generation*, Dublin: Dublin City Council.

Dublin City Council (DCC) (2006) 'Guidelines for Dolphin House Regeneration Feasibility Study', Dublin City Council.

Dublin City Council (DCC) (2008) 'Regeneration projects to be delivered', Dublin City Council, www.dublincity.ie.

Earth Tech (2008) *Public Private Partnerships*, www.earthtech.com.

Economist Intelligence Unit (EIU) (1999) *Vision 2010: Forging Tomorrow's PPPs*, New York: Economist Intelligence Unit.

Engineers Ireland (2010) *Infrastructure for an Island Population of 8 Million*, www.engineersireland.ie.

Esping-Andersen, G. (1999) *Social Foundations of Postindustrial Economies*, Oxford: Oxford University Press.

European Commission (2003) *Guidelines for Successful Public Private Partnerships*, www.ec.europa.eu.

European Commission (2009) *Mobilising Private and Public Investment for Recovery and Long Term Structural Change: Developing Public Private Partnerships*, Brussels: European Commission.

Fahey, T. (ed.) (1999) *Social Housing in Ireland: A Study of Success, Failure and Lessons Learned*, Dublin: Oak Tree Press.

Farrell Grant Sparks (FGS) (1998) 'A report submitted to the Inter-departmental Group in Relation to Public Private Partnerships', Farrell Grant Sparks, Dublin.

Farrell Grant Sparks (FGS) (2007) *Solid Support and Underlying Strength*, Dublin: Farrell Grant Sparks.

Fatima Groups United (FGU) (2004) *The Value of a Promise, the Promise of Value: Delivering and Improving on the All-Party Agreed Essentials for Fatima's Regeneration*, Dublin: Fatima Groups United.

Fatima Groups United (FGU) (2006) *8 Great Expectations: A Landmark and Unique Social Regeneration Plan for Fatima Mansions*, Dublin: Fatima Regeneration Board.

Fatima Regeneration Board (2005) *The Fatima Regeneration Board*, www.frb.ie.

Fehilly, B. (2008) *A Review of and Report on Certain Matters Relating to Dublin City Council's Ringsend Wastewater Treatment Plant*, Dublin: Department of the Environment.

Fitzgerald, F. (2004) 'Dublin City Council's social housing: time to take stock, time to transfer stock?', *Cornerstone*, 20, 8–10.

Finlay, F. (1998) *Snakes and Ladders*, Dublin: New Island.

Florio, M. (2004) *The Great Divesture: Evaluating the Impact of British Privatisations, 1979–1997*, London: MIT.

Flynn, S. (2007) 'Parents help fund 80 per cent of primary schools', *The Irish Times*, 27 January 2007.

George, S. (2004) *Another World is Possible If*, London: Verso.

Gill, S. (1995) 'Globalisation, market civilisation and disciplinary neo-liberalism', *Millennium*, 24(3) 399–423.

Giddens, A. (1993) *Sociology*, London: Polity.

Government of Ireland (2000a) *National Development Plan, 2000–2006*, Dublin: Department of the Taoiseach.

Government of Ireland (2000b) *Programme for Prosperity and Fairness, 2000–2003*, Dublin: Department of the Taoiseach.

Government of Ireland (2001) *Policy Framework for Public Private Partnerships: Working Together for Quality Public Services*, Dublin: Department of Finance.

Government of Ireland (2002) *Irish State Authorities (Public Private Partnerships) Act 2002*, Dublin: Department of the Taoiseach.

Government of Ireland (2004) *Sixth Progress Report of the Cross-Departmental Team on Infrastructure and PPPs*, Dublin: Department of the Taoiseach.

Government of Ireland (2007) *National Development Plan, 2007–2013*, Dublin: Department of the Taoiseach, www.ndp.ie.

Government of Ireland (2008) *Building Ireland's Smart Economy: A Framework for Sustainable Economic Renewal*: Dublin, Department of the Taoiseach.

Grubnic, S. and Hodges, R. (2003) 'Information, trust and the private finance initiative in social housing', *Public Money and Management*, 23(3) 177–84.

Hall, P. and Pfeiffer, U. (2000) 'Urban Future 21 – a global agenda for 21st century cities', The Federal Ministry of Transport, Building and Housing of the Republic of Germany.

Harvey, D. (1982) *The Limits to Capital*, Chicago: University of Chicago Press.

Harvey, D. (1985) *Consciousness and the Urban Experience*, Oxford: Blackwell.

Harvey, D. (1989) *The Urban Experience*, Maryland: John Hopkins University Press.

Harvey, D. (2000) *Spaces of Hope*, Edinburgh: Edinburgh University Press.

Harvey, D. (2005) *A Brief History of Neo-liberalism*, London: Oxford.

Hearne, R. (2006) 'Neoliberalism, public services and PPPs in Ireland', *Progress in Irish Urban Studies*, 2, 1–14.

Hearne, R. (2007) 'Public Private Partnerships in Irish schools: an appraisal', *Journal of Irish Urban Studies*, 4–6, 55–72.

Hochtief (2008) *Hochtief Opens up its PPP School Portfolio to Investors*, www.hochtief.com.

International Monetary Fund (IMF) (2004) *Public-Private Partnerships*, www.imf.org.

Institute for Public Policy Research (IPPR) (2001) *Building Better Partnerships: The Final Report of the Commission on Public Private Partnerships*, London: IPPR.

Institute for Public Policy Research (IPPR) (2009) *Who's Accountable: The Challenge of Giving Power Away in a Centralised Political Culture*, London: IPPR.

Irish Business Employers' Confederation and the Construction Industry Federation (1998) *Report to government on Public–Private Partnerships*, www.ibec.ie.

Irish Business Employers' Confederation and the Construction Industry Federation (1999) 'A further submission by IBEC and CIF on Public Private Partnerships to government', www.ibec.ie.

Irish Congress of Trade Unions (ICTU) (2005) *Guidelines for Unions on Consultations with State Agencies and Public Authorities in the Republic of Ireland Concerning Public Private Partnerships*, Dublin: Irish Congress of Trade Unions.

Irish Independent (2010) 'Poolbeg firm repeatedly fined in US for flouting pollution laws', *The Irish Independent*, Monday, 25 January 2010.

Irish Penal Reform Trust (2005) 'Anti Social Behaviour Orders (ASBOs)', a briefing paper prepared by the Irish Youth Justice Alliance, www.iprt.ie.

Kay, M. (2002) 'Ireland's Public Private Partnerships: unaccountable procurement in an excluded landscape', paper presented to Regional Studies Association, Bunratty, Co. Clare, 25–26 April 2002.

Kay, M. and Reeves, E. (2004) 'Making PPPs accountable: the case of Ireland', in A. Ghobadian, D. Gallear, N. O'Regan and H. Viney (eds.), *Public Private Partnerships: Policy and Experience*, London: Palgrave Macmillan, pp. 71–81.

Kelly, O. (2008a) 'Inquiry into €35.6m Ringsend sewage plant payment', *The Irish Times*, 1 July 2008.

Kelly, O. (2008b) 'Partnership projects not viable, builders claim', *The Irish Times*, 27 December 2008.

Kelly, S. and MacLaran, A. (2004) 'The residential transformation of inner Dublin in Drudy', *Dublin: Economic and Social Trends*, 4, 36–59.

Kenny, B. (2003) 'Discussion report on possible transfer of ownership of city council rented housing stock', Dublin City Council, Dublin.

Kirby, A. (1982) *The Politics of Location: An Introduction*, London: Methuen.

Kirby, A. Knox, P. and Pinch, S. (eds.) (1984) *Public Service Provision and Urban Development*, Beckenham: Croom Helm.

Kirby, P. (2002) *The Celtic Tiger in Distress*, Basingstoke: Palgrave.

Kirby, P. and O'Broin, D. (eds.) *Power, Dissent and Democracy: Civil Society and the State in Ireland*, Dublin, A. & A. Farmar.

Kirk, G. (1980) *Urban Planning in a Capitalist Society*, London: Croom Helm.

Klein, N. (2000) *No Logo*, London: Flamingo.

Klein, N. (2007) *The Shock Doctrine: The Rise of Disaster Capitalism*, London: Penguin.

KPMG (2007) *National Governments Lean Towards Private-Sector Financing*, www.kpmg.com.

Labour Court (2004) Recommendation Number 17735, Dublin City Council and Services Industrial Professional Technical Union, www.labourcourt.ie.

Labour Court (2005) Recommendation Number 18432, Jarvis Facilities Management and Services Industrial Professional Technical Union, www.labourcourt.ie.

Labour Court (2006) Recommendation Number 18506, Connex Transport and Services Industrial Professional Technical Union, www.labourcourt.ie.

Labour Court (2008) The Labour Court, www.labourcourt.ie.

Leys, C. (2001) *Market-Driven Politics: Neo-Liberal Democracy and the Public Interest*, London: Verso.

MacLaran, A. (1993) *Dublin: The Shaping of a Capital*, London and New York: Belhaven Press.

MacLaran, A. and McGuirk, P. (2003) 'Planning the city', in A. MacLaran (ed.), *Making Space: Property Development and Urban Planning*, London: Arnold, pp. 63–94.

MacLaran, A., Clayton, V. and Brudell, P. (2007) *Empowering Communities in Disadvantaged Urban Areas: towards greater community participation in urban planning*, Dublin: Combat Poverty Agency.

Macquarie (2008), *Macquarie Partnerships*, www.macquarie.com.

McFadyean, M. and Rowland, D. (2002) *PFI Versus Democracy? School Governors and the Haringey Schools PFI Scheme*, London: The Menard Press.

McGuirk, P. and MacLaran, A. (2001) 'Changing approaches to urban planning in an "entrepreneurial city": the case of Dublin', *European Planning Studies*, 9(4) 437–57.

McNamara, B. (2008) Letter to Ciaran McNamara re. Dublin City Council Regeneration Projects, 19 May, 2008.

MCO Architects (2007) 'Dolphin House feasibility study report', MCO Architects, Dublin.

Minister for Education and Science (2010) *New PPP Schools Bundle Announced*, www.education.ie.

Monbiot, G. (2000) *Captive State: The Corporate Takeover of Britain*, London: Macmillan.

Monbiot, G. (2003) *The Age of Consent: A Manifesto for a New World Order*, London: Flamingo.

Murray, S. (2006) *Value for Money? Cautionary Lessons about P3s From British Columbia*, Ontario: Canadian Centre for Policy Alternatives.

National Economic and Social Council (NESC) (1999) 'Opportunities, challenges and capacities for choice', Report No. 104, National Economic and Social Council, Dublin.

National Economic and Social Council (NESC) (2005) *The Developmental Welfare State*, Dublin: National Economic and Social Council Office.

National Toll Roads (NTR) (2004) 'NTR Plc preliminary results for year ended 31 December 2003', www.ntr.ie.

National Union of Teachers (2003) *The Privatisation of Education: An Overview*, www.teachers.org.uk.

Norris, M. (2001) 'Regenerating run down public housing estates: a review of the operation of the Remedial Works Scheme since 1985', *Administration*, 49(1) 25–45.

Norris, M. (2005) *Mixed Tenure Housing Estates: Development, Design, Management and Socio-economic Impacts*, Dublin: Housing Unit.

Northern Ireland Assoociation of Secondary Teachers and Lecturers (2006) *Private Finance Iniative*, www.atl.org,uk.

Nurture (2007) *Growing our Future Together: A Regeneration Plan for St Theresa's Gardens*, Dublin: Nurture Development.

OECD (2005) *Growth in Services*, London: OECD.

OECD (2008) *Towards an Integrated Public Service*, London: OECD, www.oecd.org.

O'Hearn, D. (2001) *The Atlantic Economy: Britain, the US and Ireland*, Manchester: Manchester University Press.

O'Gorman, A. (2000) *Eleven Acres Ten Steps*, Dublin: Fatima Groups United.

O'Riain, S. and O'Connell, P. J. (2000) 'The role of the state in growth and welfare', B. Nolan, P. J. Connell and C. Whelan (eds.) *Bust to Boom? The Irish Experience of Growth and Inequality*, Dublin: Institute of Public Administration, pp. 310–39.

O'Toole F. (2003) *After the Ball*, Dublin: New Island.

O'Toole, F. (2009) *Ship of Fools*, Dublin: Faber & Faber.

Osborne, S. P. (ed.) (2000) *Public-Private Partnerships*, London: Routledge.

Oxigen (2003) *Partnerships Working for a Cleaner Environment*, www.oxigen.ie.

Pacione, M. (1990) *Urban Problems: An Applied Urban Analysis*, London: Routledge.

Pacione, M. (1997) *Britain's Cities: Geographies of Division in Urban Britain*, London: Routledge.

Parker, D. (1997) *The Impact of Privatisation: Ownership and Corporate Performance in the UK*, London: Routledge.

Participation and Practice of Rights Project (2007) *First Housing Hearing – Findings of the International Panel*, Belfast, www.pprproject.org.

Partnerships UK (2004) *Partnerships UK Report 2004*, www.partnershipsuk.org.uk.

Payne, G. (ed.) (1999) *Making Common Ground: Public Private Partnerships in Land for Housing*, London: Intermediate Technology Publications.

Peck, J. and Tickell, A. (2002) 'Neoliberalizing space', *Antipode*, 34(3) 380–404.

Pierre, J. and Guy Peters, B. (2000) *Governance, Politics and the State*, London: Macmillan.

Pinch, S. (1985) *Cities and Services: The Geography of Collective Consumption*, London: Routledge & Kegan Paul.

Pollock, A. and Price, D. (2004) 'We are left footing the PFI bill: the public pays the price when contractors pull out of projects', *The Guardian*, 27 July 2004.

PriceWaterhouseCoopers (2001a) *Review of PPP Structures Report*, Dublin: Stationary Office.

PriceWaterhouseCoopers (2001b) *A Policy Framework for Public Private Partnerships for the Department of Environment Heritage and Local Government*, Dublin: Stationary Office.

PriceWaterhouseCoopers (2005) *Delivering the PPP Promise: A Review of PPP Issues and Activity*, London: PriceWaterhouseCoopers.

PriceWaterHouseCoopers (2007) *PriceWaterHouseCoopers Public Private Partnership Expertise*, London: PriceWaterHouseCoopers.

Public Accounts Committee (2006) *Eighth Interim Report on the 2003 Report of the Comptroller and Auditor General (Committee Hearings October 2004 to July 2005)*, Dublin, www.debates.oireachtas.ie.

Public Accounts Committee (2006) *Annual Report of the Comptroller and Auditor General and Appropriation Accounts*, Dublin, www.debates .oireachtas.ie/committees.

PPP Informal Advisory Group (2001) *Policy Framework for Public Private Partnerships: Working Together for Quality Public Services*, www.ppp.gov.ie.

Punch, M. (2001) 'Inner-city transformation and renewal: the view from the grassroots', in P.J. Drudy and A. MacLaran (eds.) *Dublin: Economic and Social Trends*, Dublin: Centre for Urban and Regional Studies, Trinity College Dublin.

Punch, M. and Kelly, S. (2005) 'The regeneration game: Public–Private Partnerships, community participation and social housing redevelopment – a case study of O'Devaney Gardens', Combat Poverty Agency.

Punch, M., Redmond, R. and Kelly, S. (2004) 'Uneven development, city governance and urban change', paper presented to City Futures: An International Conference on Globalism and Urban Change, Chicago, 8–10 July 2004.

Redmond, D. (2001) 'Social housing policy in Ireland: under new management?', *European Journal of Housing Policy*, 1(2) 291–306.

Redmond, D. (2002) 'Policy and practice in tenant participation: empowering tenants?', *Journal of Irish Urban Studies*, 1(2) 1–18.

Redmond, D. and Russell, P. (2008) 'Social housing regeneration and the creation of sustainable communities in Dublin', *Local Economy*, 23(3), 168–79.

Reeves, E. and O'Sullivan, E. (2001) 'Can Public Private Partnerships deliver? The case of Ireland', paper presented to Workshop in Evaluation of Public and Social Policies, University of Limerick, Limerick.

Reeves, E. (2001) 'Examining the case for Public Private Partnerships in Ireland', paper presented to the Public Policy Seminar Series, University of Limerick, Limerick.

Reeves, E. (2003) 'Public–Private Partnerships in Ireland: policy and practice', *Public Money and Management*, 23(3) 163–70.

Reeves, E. (2005) *Expansion of PPP Programme is Premature*, www.tascnet.ie.

Reeves, E. (2006) *Public Private Partnerships in the Water and Wastewater Sector: An Economic Analysis*, Dublin: Services, Industrial, Professional and Technical Union.

Respond Housing Association (2009) *Building Communities*, Dublin, www.respond.ie.

Rose, K. (2006) 'Principles of development for Dolphin regeneration', Dublin City Council.

St Michael's Estate Task Force (2002) *Past, Present and Future: A Community Vision for the Regeneration of St Michael's Estate*, Dublin: St Michael's Estate Regeneration Team.

St Michael's Estate Regeneration Team (2008), *Regeneration Section*, www.stmichaelsestate.ie.

Services, Industrial, Professional and Technical Union (SIPTU) (2008) *Lisbon Vote Shows Government Must Address Workers' Concerns*, www.siptu.ie.

Shaoul, J., Pollock, A. and Vickers, N. (2002) 'Private finance and value for money in NHS hospitals: a policy in search of a rationale?', *British Medical Journal*, 324, 1205–9.

Sheridan Woods (2009) 'Dolphin House regeneration community masterplan', Sheridan Woods.

SIAC (2008) *Company Businesses*, www.siac.ie.

Skidelsky, R. (2009) *Keynes: The Return of the Master*, London: Penguin.

Smith, N. (1996) *The New Urban Frontier: Gentrification and the Revanchist City*, London: Routledge.

Smith, N. (2002) 'New globalism, new urbanism: gentrification as global urban strategy', *Antipode*, 34(3) 427–50.

Soros, G. (2000) *Open Society (Reforming Global Capitalism)*, London: Little, Brown & Company.

Srinivasen, T. N. (2000) 'The Washington consensus a decade later: ideology and the art and science of policy advice', *The World Bank Research Observer*, 15(2) 265–70.

Stiglitz, J. (2002) *Globalisation and its Discontents*, London: Penguin Press.

Sweeney, P. (1999) *The Celtic Tiger*, Dublin: Oak Tree Press.

Sweeney, P. (2004) *Selling Out? Privatisation in Ireland*, Dublin: New Island Press.

Suiter, J. (2010) 'Political patronage still controls the purse strings', *The Irish Times* Tuesday, 4 May, 2010.

Teachers Union of Ireland (TUI) (2004) 'PPP: a new approach', *TUI News*, 27(1) 6–7.

Tenants First (2005) *The Real Guide to Regeneration for Communities: Making the Right Decision about Urban Regeneration*, Dublin: Tenants First.

Tenants First (2009) *Housing for Need not for Greed: Tenants First Action Plan for Sustaining Homes and Communities*, Dublin: Tenants First.

The Examiner (2008) 'Creeping privatisation – who benefits most from toll roads?', *The Examiner*, 27 August 2008.

The Irish Times (2004) 'EU relaxes investment rules', *The Irish Times*, 12 February 2004.

The Observer (2009) Interview with Shadow Chancellor, George Osborne, *The Observer*, Sunday, 15 November 2009.

The Sunday Tribune (2008) 'State slashes PPP target by a quarter amid funding chaos', *The Sunday Tribune*, 19 October 2008.

Think Tank for Action on Social Change (TASC) (2010) *The Solidarity Factor: Public Perceptions of Unequal Ireland*, www.tascnet.ie.

Tussing, A. and Wren, M. (2006) *How Ireland Cares: The Case for Health Care Reform*, Dublin: New Island Press.

Unison (2003) *What is Wrong with PFI in Schools*, www.unison.org.uk.

Urban Design (2004) 'Redevelopment scenarios for Dolphin House', Urban Design Architects.

Veolia (2008) *Veolia's Public Private Partnerships*, www.veoliawater.com.

Village (2007) 'Just one large commuter belt', *Village*, 4 January 2007.

Whelan, K. and Masterson, E. (1998) *Bertie Ahern: Taoiseach and Peacemaker*, Edinburgh: Mainstream.

Whitfield, D. (2001) *Public Services or Corporate Welfare*, London: Pluto Press.

Whitfield, D. (2006) *New Labour's Attack on Public Services*, London: Russell Press.

Wilkinson, R. and Picket, K. (2009) *The Spirit Level*, London: Penguin.

Williamson, J. (2000) 'What should the world bank think about the Washington Consensus?', *The World Bank Research Observer*, 15(2) 251–64.

World Bank (2000) *World Development Report 2000/01: Attacking Poverty*, Oxford: Oxford University Press.

World Bank (2002) *Promoting Access to Postsecondary Education: Meeting the Global Demand*, www.oecd.org.

Index

THE LARK
IN THE
MORNING

SUSANNA M. NEWSTEAD

PASTMASTERY PRESS

Published by PastMastery Press
Medlar House
Hanover Drive
Brackley Northants. NN13 6JS UK
sue@pastmastery.com

ISBN 978-1-9162444-0-5

THE LARK IN THE MORNING

Lie still my fond shepherd and don't you rise yet
It's a fine dewy morning and besides, my love, it is wet
Oh let it be wet my love and ever so cold
I will rise my fond Floro and away to my fold.
Oh no, my bright Floro, it is no such thing
It's a bright sun a-shining and the lark is on the wing.
Oh the lark in the morning she rises from her nest
And she rises in the air with the dew on her breast
And like the pretty little ploughboy she'll whistle and sing
And at night she will return to her own nest again.
When the ploughboy has done all he's going for to do
He trips down to the meadows where the grass is all cut down
Oh the lark in the morning she rises from her nest
And she climbs in the air with the dew on her breast
And like the pretty little ploughboy she'll whistle and sing
And at night she will return to her own nest again.

ENGLISH FOLK SONG.

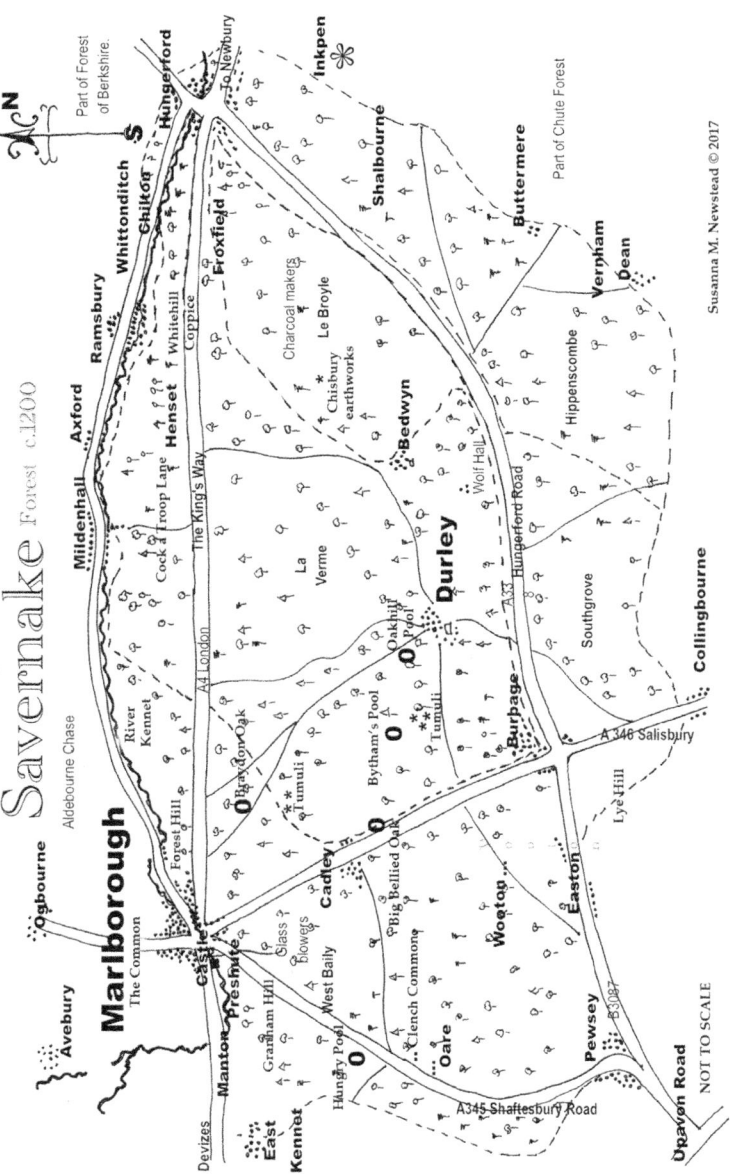

Savernake Forest c.1200

Susanna M. Newstead © 2017

NOT TO SCALE

Durley Village c. 1200

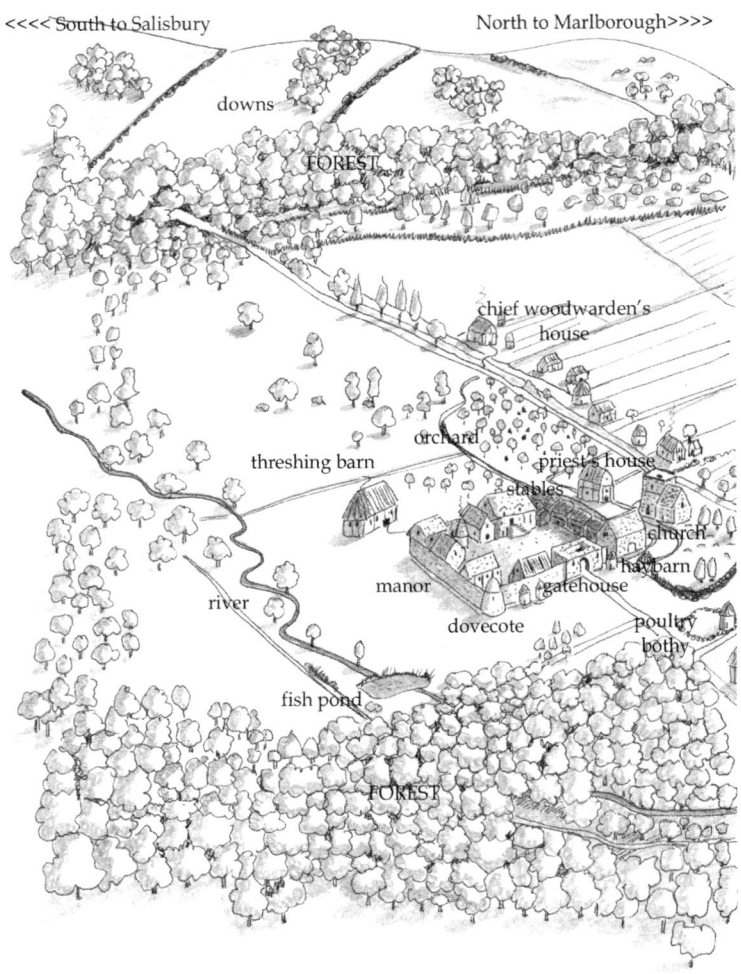

<<<< South to Salisbury

North to Marlborough >>>>

downs

FOREST

chief woodwarden's house

orchard

threshing barn

priest's house

stables

manor

church

hay barn

gatehouse

dovecote

poultry bothy

river

fish pond

FOREST

Susanna M. Newstead © 2017

Durley Village c. 1200

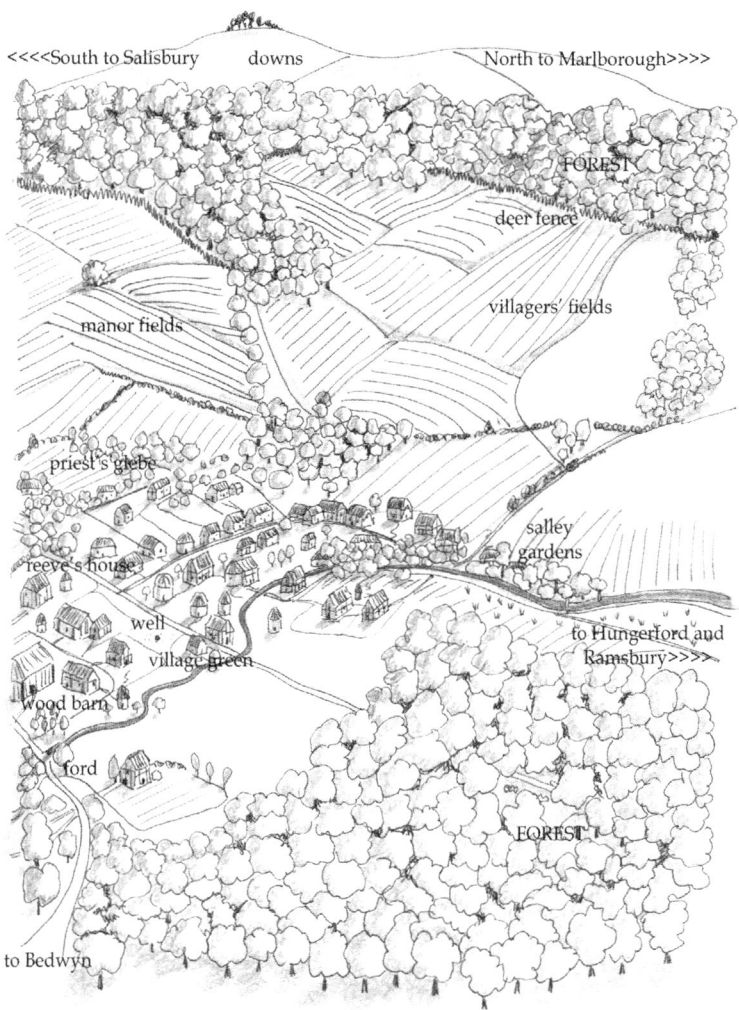

<<<<South to Salisbury   downs   North to Marlborough>>>>

FOREST

deer fence

villagers' fields

manor fields

priest's glebe

salley gardens

reeve's house

well

village green   to Hungerford and Ramsbury>>>>

wood barn

ford

FOREST

to Bedwyn

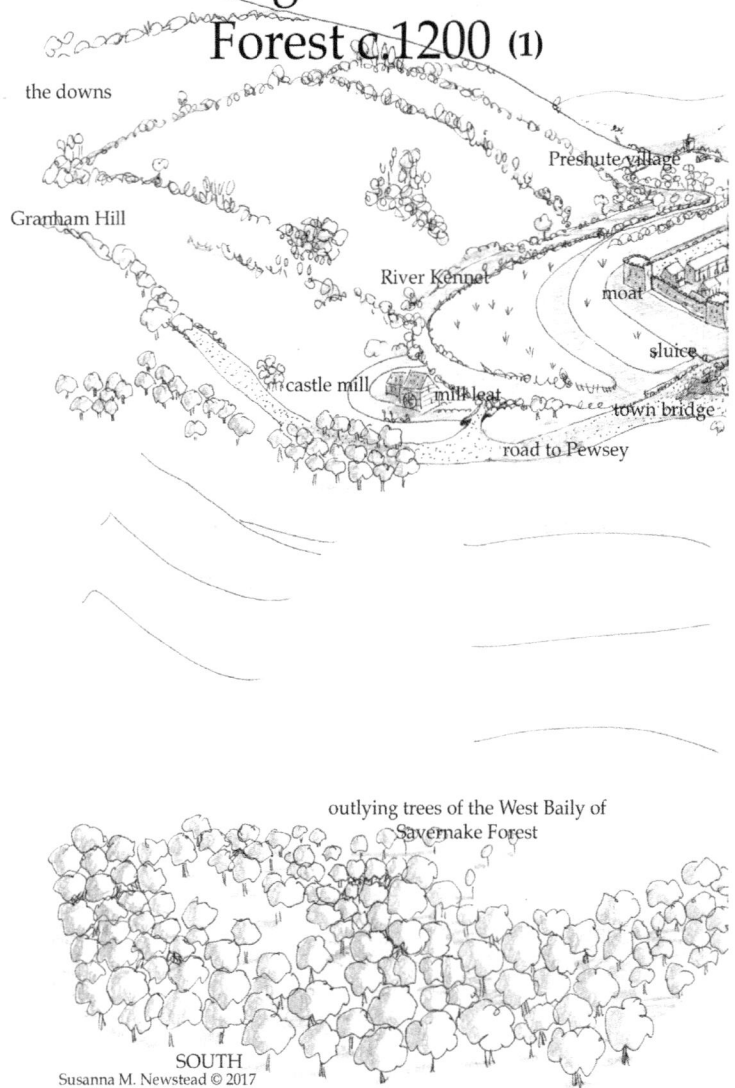

Marlborough and Savernake Forest c.1200 (1)

the downs

Granham Hill

Preshute village

River Kennet

moat

sluice

castle mill

mill leat

town bridge

road to Pewsey

outlying trees of the West Baily of Savernake Forest

SOUTH

Susanna M. Newstead © 2017

Marlborough Town and the forest c.1200 (2)

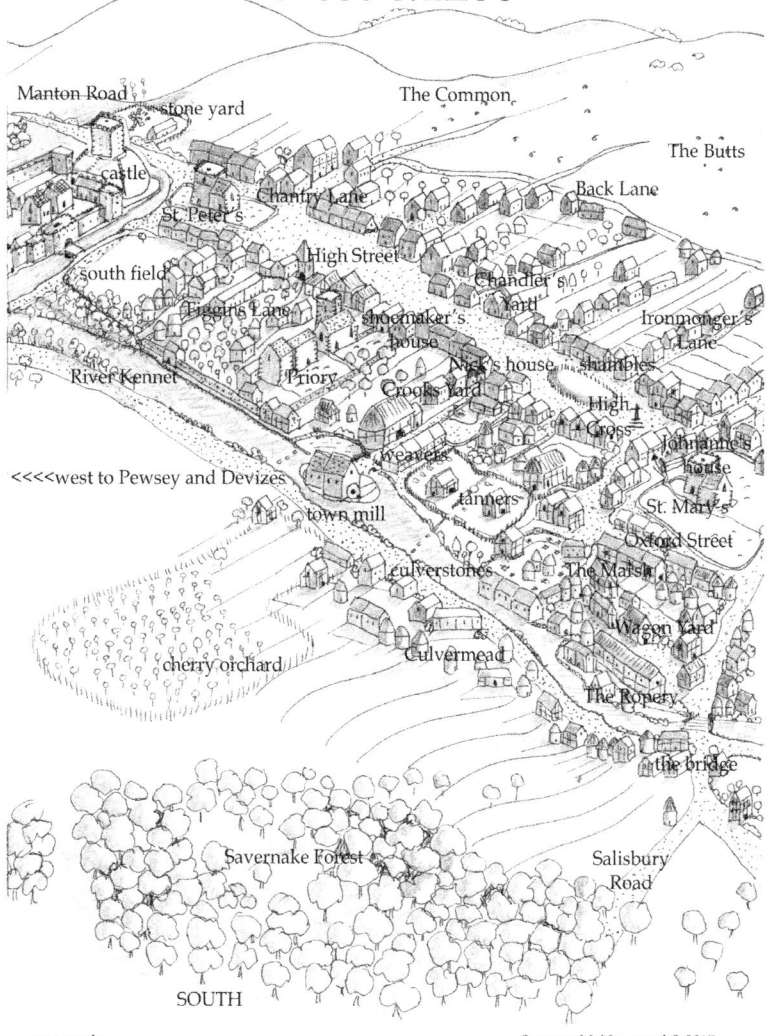

Manton Road — stone yard — The Common — The Butts

castle — Chantry Lane — Back Lane

St. Peter's

High Street — Chandler's Yard — Ironmonger's Lane

south field

Tiggin's Lane — shoemaker's house — Nick's house — shambles

River Kennet — Priory — Crooks Yard — High Cross — Johnanne's house

<<<<west to Pewsey and Devizes — weavers — St. Mary's

town mill — tanners — Oxford Street

culverstones — The Marsh

cherry orchard — Culvermead — Wagon Yard

The Ropery

the bridge

Savernake Forest — Salisbury Road

SOUTH

not to scale

Susanna M. Newstead © 2017

Marlborough and the forest c. 1200 (3)

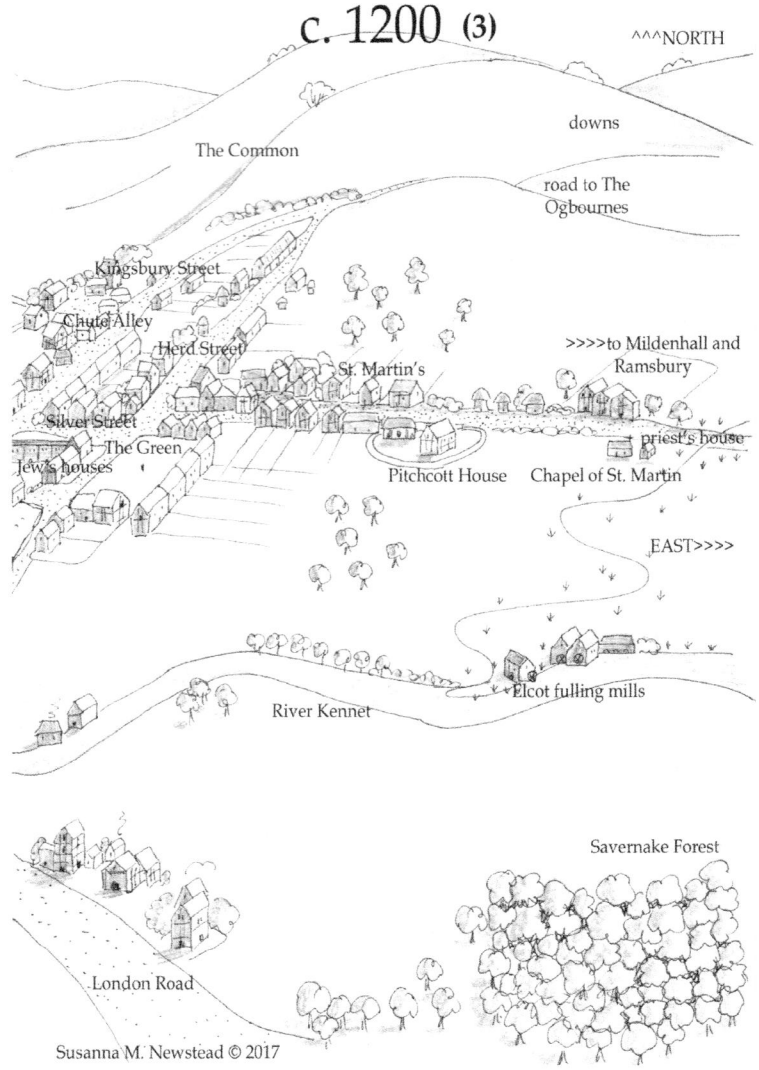

^^^NORTH

downs

The Common

road to The Ogbournes

Kingsbury Street

Chute Alley

Herd Street

St. Martin's

>>>>to Mildenhall and Ramsbury

Silver Street

The Green

Jew's houses

Pitchcott House

Chapel of St. Martin

priest's house

EAST>>>>

Elcot fulling mills

River Kennet

Savernake Forest

London Road

Susanna M. Newstead © 2017

Cha[

CW01502059

"We'd like permission to enter..."

It was a blustery day in late January 1207 when my shepherd, who lived on the outskirts of the forest, came to me to ask if he might enter the Marlborough Flitch contest.

Every four years, in the little town of Marlborough, which was close by the Forest of Savernake, in the county of Wiltshire, the forest of which I was warden, a competition was held to find the happiest married couple in the area.

For one year and a day, they must have lived together in marital bliss and must never have had a cross word between them.

How was this to be achieved? Neighbours must vouch for them, friends and family must speak up for them and the prize was a large ham...a flitch of bacon so huge, it would keep them going almost all year!

For a year and a day from the time they entered their names, they must speak to each other with nothing but loving words; must be seen to be kind to and caring of each other or they would be disqualified and the title of Flitch King and Queen be given to another.

"Are you sure, William?" I asked, "that you can manage a whole year with never a cross word to Elswith and she to you?"

He laughed then. "We go on as we always have, sir. From the very first day we were married."

"Twenty years ago?"

"Aye, sir..."

"Well, I have no objection, none at all."

I thought surely that this couple would be the favourites to win.

William Larkworthy had to come to me for permission, for this couple were my tied serfs, not freemen, and were feudal tenants entirely subject to me as their lord, to whom they paid dues and services in return for land. The man worked my sheep up on the downs and his wife tilled their own small plot and worked as a spinster for my thread business.

William would need permission to go to Marlborough to enrol.

The Marlborough Flitch contest had been an event which had been instigated about eighty years ago by a wealthy man of the town who could not believe that it was possible to live with one's spouse in total harmony all year. His equally rich neighbour had wagered that he could find a couple who would prove him wrong and so the fun was begun.

Good harmless fun, resulting in a day's junketings and feasting, every four years in January.

Six other couples entered the fray; three from Marlborough town and one from the little village of Cadley which was situated on the road from Marlborough to Salisbury and which traversed the forest. The last couple were Marlborough people. Not so many couples, then, were all that confident of success.

That evening I spoke to my wife Lydia and told her that one pair of our serfs from the downs were entering the competition and a pair from Cadley village.

She laughed. "You don't mean for us to enter do you, Aumary?"

I was sitting on a chair in the solar and I put my feet up on a stool and chuckled.

"I'm sure we could."

"I have no doubt of it," she said, "but I just don't like the fact that people would be spying on us, watching, prying, waiting for us to fail..."

"We would have to be watched by our neighbours and staff, all the villagers of Durley. No, we'd have no privacy," I said.

"Others can live for a year and a day in that way, should they wish," said my wife, biting off the thread of linen she had used to mend a rent in one of our seven year old daughter Hawise's, dresses, "just not you or I."

"I think it would be very difficult for the likes of us to prove that we'd lived in harmony."

"How so?"

"The life we lead. I am Lord of Durley, Warden of the Forest and as such carry a deal of authority. I have a role at Marlborough castle as under-castellan and what's more I'm Constable of the county, with the authority to search out and confine felons, and investigate murders and wrong-doings. How could I do all this and still retain my dignitas and authority and at the same time have folk poking into my personal affairs? No. We could never do it. And anyway, folk might feel they could not speak ill of us and that would not be fair."

Lydia came up and threw her arms around my neck. "We do not need a contest to show us, or anyone else, that we are a devoted couple, Aumary. We are and there's an end to it."

I lifted my chin and she kissed me.

The next few days were also blustery. The clouds scurried across the sky like streams of white sheep. The odd black cloud followed like the rangy pied dogs the shepherds used to keep the flocks in order.

Four days later I was out in the forest, with my right hand man John Brenthall and his son and apprentice Peter, checking the woods and glades. At the end of last year we'd had some fierce gales which had stripped some trees bare of branches and blown over the more vulnerable specimens.

We would need to make a detailed inventory of where damage had occurred.

I left my two men busily chatting about work to be done and rode over to the closest forest trees across the Shaftesbury Road to the lane leading to East Kennet. Here I stopped and looked across the downs to the next stand of forest trees. The wind ruffled my curly black hair and my cloak streamed out behind me.

These downs were close turfed chalk hills which reared and dipped into steep coombes and valleys, falling away and rising up as far as the eye could see. Here few trees blocked the magnificent views and on a day like this, when the white flat bottomed and billowing clouds ran before the wind, showing their undersides of sunlit gold and pink, it was wonderful to sit on my roan gelding Bayard, and watch them. I watched too the wraithlike ever changing shadows they made as they flitted across the grassy surface of the downs.

I gentled his soft ears. "We are lucky Bayard, you and I," I said to him, "to have all this spread out before us knowing that almost as far as we can see, it is ours and all is right and well with our world."

Three or four larks were rising on the wind, their song spiralling and falling with them. How they managed to keep their course in the fierce breeze I do not know. These birds were one of nature's best musicians, singing all year, though obviously longer and better in the breeding season.

I located some sheep cropping the grass halfway down the hill. My sheep; the fleeces of which would go to be carded, spun, made up into cloth, fulled and dyed in Marlborough town and sent to market wherever we could obtain the highest price, for our good English wool was prized all over.

I surveyed a complete circle of downland, standing in my stirrups. Sheep everywhere. As far as the eye could see. Towards Clench in the south, the slopes of the Kennet valley in the north, this side of the river. East Kennet in the west and, pictured in my mind's eye, the boundary of the forest in the east.

I narrowed my eyes.

The huge forest of Savernake rolled before me. One hundred and fifty square miles of trees, glades, meadows and thickets. A small cottage nestled in the bottom of the nearest coombe. Of course, William and Elswith's cottage. Smoke was lifting from the fire-hole in the roof and was streaming southeast with the stiff wind.

I spurred Bayard on and we gently trotted down the hill. Another cottage came into view and another. Yes, here were three cottages belonging to my shepherds. One occupant was out in the garden plot behind the house, sweeping late blown forest leaves from the chalk path with a besom. A forlorn task in this weather.

The second cottage seemed empty but the third and nearest, where the smoke exited the hole in the roof, looked inviting. I threw my leg over Bayard's ears and jumped down.

"Ho! William, Elswith?" I shouted. "Anyone home?"

"Here m'lord," came a voice. I peered around the gable end of the cottage.

William Larkworthy was up a ladder filling in a hole in the chalk and flint built wall.

"I saw you over the roof, m'lord, riding down the hill."

"Problem, William?" I asked.

"Oh no sir, just a bit of a fall with the end wall. Gets all the weather it does, facing north east."

"I'm sure."

William patted the last chalk block into place and came down his ladder.

"Mug of ale, sir?" he asked as he stored the ladder at the back of the house. "Bit of a chilly wind that, when the sun goes in." He wiped his hands on his jerkin.

I chuckled. "Don't mind if I do, William." I ducked my head under the low lintel for I'm a full six feet tall and my shepherd and his wife topped only five foot five and three.

The cottage was warm and smoky and as tidy and clean as a hound's tooth.

I looked round. "Good to see you keep everything in such good order, Larkworthy," I said. The house of course belonged to me. Not all my tenants were as scrupulous in mending and maintaining their cottages.

This was the typical two roomed house. One part the living place and kitchen and a loft above the animal pen for a sleeping place, accessed by a ladder.

A wooden mug was set before me.

"So we are five days into the contest, William. How are we faring?" I took a sip of the sweet ale.

Larkworthy gave a gentle chuckle. "Never a cross word, sir. Elswith and I are as happy as a pig in a muck heap."

"I'm glad to hear it. I hope you can keep it up for a year and a day."

"We can. We haven't had a quarrel in all our married life." William took a deep swig of ale.

"The Lady Belvoir and I don't argue either," I said. " We spar a little but it's not truly arguing or crossness," I said.

William smiled. He was a small man with a square jaw, which ended in a spade-like grey beard. His fingers were gnarled and misshapen. His face was tanned with wind and sun and his eyes were sunken into creased sockets where he had habitually narrowed them in order to battle the wind and weather and search for the sheep on the hills.

I looked round the cottage. "Elswith away today?"

"Aye, sir. She's away to take her spinning to town. Master Steward said she could go once a week."

I noticed a distaff placed on the plain elm trestle table.

"She spins the findings for herself, I suppose?"

"Aye sir, she does. The bits of wool from the creatures which catch on briar and bramble, or shed on the bark of trees and suchlike."

The whole fleeces were destined for the town and all my wool went there eventually. Some of my tenants would spin the fleeces in their own homes and be paid accordingly.

Those women who could, found bits of wool caught on hurdles and hedges and kept this for themselves to spin. Sometimes they wove themselves a small garment. Sometimes they sold the spun thread for coin or bartered it for goods in the town. It was allowed by me. Not all lords allowed it, I know.

We chatted a little more and I finished my ale. "Well, I'll be off back into my forest."

I stood. "Give my regards to your good wife when she returns and good luck for the contest."

"We do hope to win, sir."

"Aye I've no doubt..." I ducked under the lintel. The wind flicked my cloak sideways. "Who are you up against? Do you know?"

"Oh aye, sir. A couple from Cadley. We meet them at church for we go there sir, it being close."

"Who are they?"

"Osmund and Godgifu Hart, sir."

I nodded. "I know them. In their thirties with three children. Alan Hart, my deerman, is Osmund's brother."

"Then two couples from the town, Edwig and Godiva Crosscastle. He's the forge master from the mint."

"Yes, I know him too, to nod at."

"He's Elswith's cousin sir. And Thomas and Enid Ash. He's a wheelwright in the town."

"No, I don't know them."

"Neither do we, sir." And the others I don't recall."

I reached for Bayard's reins and was about to hoist myself into the saddle when there was an almighty scream.

A woman came running out from the next cottage about fifty yards down the valley.

She stood in her garden and screamed loudly into the wind.

William turned quickly and yelled, "Floro! What's the matter?"

This was the wife of another of my tied people, another shepherd, a taciturn man called Dunstan Weard whom I had never managed to get to know well.

The woman who had been sweeping her yard looked over her shoulder. She threw her besom over to the cottage wall, picked up her skirts and ran up the hill.

I left Bayard where he was and both Larkworthy and I ran down the valley to the screaming woman. She was hysterical and kept pointing into her house.

"Stay with her," I shouted and pushed back the ill fitting wattle panel door which was the only entrance to the little cottage.

The inside was dark and I had great difficulty seeing anything after the relative brightness of the outside. I strode back and wedged open the door then opened the one shutter. The cottage was of the same sort as that in which the Larkworthys lived. A beam of light fell on the beaten earth of the floor.

There lay a woman. Her head cloth was partly across her face and neck, her knees were drawn up, her arms slightly flung out.

I stepped up and scanned the area in case I might disturb any evidence. Nothing to see. I lifted the cloth from her face.

As I did so, William ducked under the lintel. "She's better now and Hilda is...."

His eyes fixed on the body on the floor. The colour left his face. His shoulders sagged. He reached out for support and found the door frame.

"Elswith," he whispered and fell to his knees.

"Aye, William. Elswith. I'm sorry to say, she has been strangled."

*****

Well, here we are again Paul, my scribe. Here you are once more writing, another of my tales of murder for me. One which I investigated as Constable of Wiltshire back in 1207, the eighth year of the reign of John the King. Forty years ago now. Now I can't even hold a pen and I certainly can't write with it. Then I was a young man of thirty-one and fit as a firkin of fleas.

What, Paul? Oh yes, it was very sad indeed to have to discover the body of William's wife Elswith. She was a comely woman of about forty three, with dark brown hair and hazel eyes which were always kind and smiling. To see her so bruised and battered, her tongue poking from her mouth, her eyes bloodshot and staring and the marks of hands disfiguring her neck, was awful. Imagine how much worse it was for her poor husband of twenty years. He never really fully recovered, you know.

Well, shall we carry on and write the history of this foul murder? How Johannes of Salerno, my friend and the doctor of the town, Hal of Potterne, my man at arms and I, investigated this terrible deed and how we tried to bring the perpetrator to the gallows?

Are you ready? Do you have enough ink and paper? Then we shall carry on.

Chapter Two

I rose quickly from my knees and grabbed hold of William Larkworthy before he toppled over and pulled him outside to sit on a convenient log by the wall of the house.

The woman Hilda had pacified the living occupant of the house and was taking her down the hill to her own cottage. She looked back once over her shoulder as if to reassure me that she would take care of her.

I found the outside water barrel and slopped some water into the dipper.

"Here William, take a drink, slowly now."

"Elswith..." he moaned.

"Yes, William. I'm sorry you had to see it but, yes, she is dead."

He drank then shook his head over and over repeating her name.

"Let's walk the few yards to your house and sit you down." I said.

I walked up the hill with my arm over the distraught man and pushed open the door with my foot.

He collapsed onto the bench in their cottage, folded his arms, leaned his head on them, bent to the table and wept.

His neighbour Hilda came in shortly afterwards.

"I have managed to calm Floro, m'lord," she said. "She's at my house with my childer. Her man is coming back home. I can see him from the hill. Will you catch him sir, before he goes into.... He will care for her. Can I help you with William?"

"Aye, Hilda, you can. I'll ride for someone to help and send a rider for the doctor and the coroner. No one must go into the cottage, do you understand that?"

"Yessir."

She sat down beside William and put her arms around him. He turned his tear stained face up to her, cried out and she embraced him like a child.

I leapt up onto Bayard and rode a short way up the hill. I intercepted the man Dunstan Weard.

"Weard, the body of Elswith Larkworthy lies in your cott. Your wife is at Hilda's house. Go there and stay with Floro until we come again."

He stared up at me, sitting on my horse, the wind ruffling my hair and the horse's mane, my cloak streaming wide. He narrowed his eyes against the brightness.

"Aye m'lord" he answered. "Where's Will?"

"Hilda is with him. Do not go into your house. Is that clear?"

A little while later I entered the forest and rode quickly down the Shaftesbury road. John and Peter were still close by and I yelled at them long before I reached them.

I explained as quickly as I could and Peter rode off to ride the few miles to Marlborough to fetch Johannes of Salerno, the town doctor. He would also report this murder to the coroner.

John jumped up on Fire and rode to Durley, a scant mile away, to fetch his wife Agnes back to the little cluster of cottages.

My shepherds were a quiet, self contained group of people, much as the charcoal burners of the forest were. They kept to their own kind and only strayed from the hills to go to church and now and again to the town. They were not well known individually, either in Durley village or the forest. They came to the local court when needed but they dealt with their own tragedies and upheavals in their own ways. However, these three houses were the closest to the forest and to one or two of the villages in it and so perhaps had more contact with folk in them than some of the others. Most of the sheep men lived scattered up on the further downs. It was a lonely place. There were few roads, only paths and sheep tracks.

How had someone managed to get unseen into Floro's cottage to murder Elswith?

What had Elswith been doing there in Floro's house?

I rode back at a hazardous speed to the small cottage at the top of the hill. Hilda had managed to get William to take some ale and she had put a blanket around him for the shock had made him shiver. She had built up the fire and was now on her hands and knees feeding it with twigs.

I smiled and nodded as I ducked under the lintel.

"He went and puked sir, just after you left. I got him outside for that, praise be."

"Aye, it's the shock, Hilda," I said.

William sat at the plain table staring at the farther wall. He neither blinked nor moved. I watched him carefully. It was almost as if he didn't breathe but his chest rose and fell.

I told her I had asked Agnes Brenthall to come and that the doctor was on his way.

She looked at me strangely then.

"What can the doctor do sir? Poor Elswith is beyond his help and Will here has no money for doctors."

"Let me worry about that, Hilda," I said. "The doctor helps me to look into unexpected deaths in the area. The King, in his wisdom, has made me the constable. It's my job to investigate and try to find the culprit."

"Oh!" Hilda looked quickly at William "I didn't know that, sir."

She smiled uneasily up at me. "You won't be taking Will away for the murder of his wife will you, sir?"

I sat down on the bench at the other end to Will.

"Now, why should you think that, Hilda?"

She shrugged. Her scanty tunic fell off her shoulder. It was covered by a blanket shawl and she pulled them all closer to her again.

"Just that the priest at Cadley was saying that most murders are committed by the person that the victim knows best. A wife or a husband, a brother or a daughter."

"Now why would he be talking about that?" I asked "it's an odd subject for a priest."

She shrugged again. "Dunno sir. 'Spose 'cause he was telling us the story of Cain and Abel."

"Well, he is right...mostly. It is often someone the victim knew well. Like a neighbour for example."

Hilda closed her lips with a frown and was quiet after that.

Until I asked..."Where's the dog, Hilda?"

She looked round the cottage as if the beast was hiding there.

"I 'in't seen Beval, sir," she answered.

*****

I went back the twenty yards or so to the middle cottage and opened the door.

I stood looking down at the sad body of Elswith Larkworthy. I was still there when Johannes' shadow fell over me and grew large on the further wall.

I propped open the door once more and opened the shutter wider.

"I was just coming up the Cadley hill when I met Peter riding like a fury."

"I wondered how you managed such a quick journey here," I nodded.

"So what can we learn, Johannes?" I asked.

As was his custom, Johannes stood over the body and stared at it for a while.

He was a big man, over six foot tall and forty three years of age. He had shoulder length brown hair, scrupulously clean and shining, with just a hint of grey at the temples, which was tied back in a queue. He was clean shaven, contrary to current fashion, which dictated that men wore beards, as I did myself. His eyes were an amber brown, clear and direct of gaze.

Johannes of Salerno and I had been friends since 1195. He had been called then to look to my first wife Cecily when she had received a mysterious wound to her temple and was near to death.

He lived in a small house which doubled as his workplace at the top of the High Street in Marlborough, directly behind the High Cross and in front of the church of St. Mary. All in the town, wealthy and poor, knew that he would open his doors to them and would do his utmost to help them. He was a wealthy man, having made his fortune in The Holy Lands where he had accompanied our previous king Richard, on crusade.

That fortune he now deployed for the good of the poor and sick of

Marlborough.

We had a history of looking at dead bodies, Johannes and I. I knew we were gaining quite a reputation for the solving of mysterious deaths in our area of Wiltshire.

He hunkered down.

"Strangled by someone with strong, large hands."

"That might be any man around here then, for they are all workers with their hands and all strong. Some women too."

"The body's stiffening is establishing. I would say she has been dead four to six hours."

"Why are her legs raised? Surely they would slump as she died."

"Hmmm." Johannes gently lifted Elswith's skirt and carefully peered underneath. I looked away.

"No sign of rape, God be praised."

I crossed myself. A small winter fly came buzzing in through the open door and I chased it out.

When I returned Johannes had managed to roll the body aside and was supporting it with his hand.

"Lividity… hmmm… odd."

"Why?"

"The blood has pooled in the lower back, thighs and buttocks." Johannes rearranged her dress again. He stood and Elswith returned to her almost supine position.

I stood for a while staring down at Elswith's corpse.

"I would say that she has been moved, Aumary."

"Moved? Because the blood has pooled at a lower place, she must have been seated and left there for rigor to begin?"

"And her arms are partly out to her side where perhaps she has tried to fight off her attacker and then when she died, they fell over the edge of the arms of a chair. Hence the position she is in - arms slightly out, knees raised."

"A chair? They are unusual amongst the folks of the lower sort," I said.

"Undoubtedly."

"In order to straighten the limbs you'd have to break the muscle hold, wouldn't you?"

"Yes. Why would someone want to move the body?"

I looked into Johannes' amber brown eyes, "Because it was in a place which would throw suspicion onto someone," he answered.

"Or because you want to throw suspicion onto someone else, somewhere else."

He nodded.

"Why wait until the body was stiff, to move it? That must have been a difficult job."

I looked around the sparse cottage. "No chair with arms here."

There were only three cottages in this part of the downs. No body could be carried in a cart from another area for the occupants of these cotts possessed no cart. Therefore Elswith died in one of these houses.

I looked around for something with which to cover the body and found a blanket cloak hanging on a peg driven into a wall. Johannes closed the woman's eyes for the last time.

"Let's go and check the other cottages. Also two people are in need of your help, perhaps, Johannes."

He nodded and picked up his medical bag, without which he never travelled.

We strode up the hill with the wind at our backs and entered William and Elswith's cottage.

"Thank you Hilda. You might go home to your children now. We shall see you in a moment."

Johannes sat down on the bench opposite William, who continued to stare into space.

"He has been weeping and staring by turns ever since he saw the corpse." I said.

"Did he find her?"

"No, Floro Weard is the first finder, it was her cottage we have just left."

I told Johannes how William came to see the dead body of his wife.

"It's shock," he said. "There will be anger and disbelief later."

"Aye, I know."

Johannes looked up quickly. "Of course, I know you know," he smiled.

My first wife, Cecily and my five year old son, Geoffrey, had both been murdered within a short time of each other, some years ago. Johannes knew what the grief had done to me.

He undid the buckles of his pack.

"It's a lonely old place this. Just these three houses. No one else for a mile or so."

"Cadley lies in the forest about a mile away and Shaw a mile or so in the other direction. Six adult folk in three houses here. Yes, very isolated. Nothing but sheep for company."

"And hundreds of those," he smiled sadly.

He took out a small blue glass bottle and dropped a few dribbles into a wooden cup. He then filled it with ale, leaned over and put it to William's lips. As he spoke gently to the man, I looked around the cottage.

As I've said, everything was clean and tidy. I looked about for a chair. Yes, there was one chair with arms here, at the head of the table. A rustic, rough thing which looked homemade. All other seats were triangular stools and there was one three seater bench. No doubt, William had made them all.

Under the table I found a shoe. A woman's simple, brown leather shoe, scuffed on the heel and tied with leather thongs. One of the thongs had snapped.

"Wait here..." I ran to the door, "I shall be but a moment."

I pelted down to the Weard's cottage. I lifted the cloak and the hem of Elswith's light brown dress. It was a little torn at the hem. Yes. She had but one shoe. I looked round. I checked. No chair with a back and arms.

"She was killed here, in her own home, I think, Johannes," I said as I returned.

"Oh?"

"A chair here. And the shoe she wore torn off and lying under the table," I pointed.

I got down on my hands and knees. "Scuff marks on the beaten earth floor," I said.

Johannes came to stand beside me. "When a person is throttled, often with other manners of death too, the feet can drum on the ground."

"Here I think Elswith scuffled her feet, lost a shoe and died sitting up."

"She knew her attacker then?"

"Aye, I think she did."

William was helped to his bed and he lay down quietly, like an exhausted child.

A few hours rest would give him the energy he needed to get through the rest of the day.

"I will need to ask him some questions later but before this, let's tackle the first finder."

Floro Weard was sitting on a bench in Hilda Sceap's house chatting with her neighbours. She had recovered her poise and they all leapt up when Johannes and I entered the house.

The women curtsied, the man nodded a bow.

"Please, all be seated. This is Doctor Johannes of Salerno from the town."

The three looked at each other.

"He is here to help me identify how Elswith came by her death."

"I can tell you that, sir," said Floro shivering, "Mortal great handprints on her neck. She were wurried."

"Yes, Floro, she was strangled."

I sat down on another bench very similar to the one in William's house. There was no chair here with a back and arms.

"Tell me everything."

The woman took a shaky breath. "I was out to the forest edge to get in some twigs, 'cause the wind had blown a load down. I comes back to me cott and leaves' em at the door..."

I'd seen the pile of twigs she had left on the stump upon which I had seated William outside.

"And in I came and then I saw 'er." Her eyes glazed with tears.

"How long were you out?"

"The sun was over the south east forest when I got back. I went out just a mite after dawn."

"And you ranged all along the forest edge? You were out of sight of your cott for a while?"

Floro squirmed, "I dinna go into the forest, sir. I know it 'int allowed to pick up wood from there."

The fallen wood of the forest all belonged to me, though I turned a blind eye to the odd piece ending up on my villeins' fires. Wood found on the downs was free to all. It was not my law, it was Forest Law.

"So you couldn't see your home?"

"Er, no, sir. Not all the time."

"You, Hilda?"

"I was in the garden at the back. Sweeping up leaves to dry for kindling."

"All the time? No, I don't think so."

"No, not all the time, just when I saw you on the chalk, m'lord, and I heard you come down the hill on your great horse and when I heard Floro screaming."

"Before that?"

"I was in the house, skinning a coney for the supper pot." She pointed to the table where, sure enough, a rabbit carcass lay jointed and diced for the crock. She grimaced. It was forbidden to take rabbits from the forest. I trusted this beast had been taken as a runaway from the warrens up on the downs.

"You too could not see anything?"

"No sir, facing the wrong way when I was out, to see aught at Elswith's or Floro's, see 'cos..."

"Yes, your cottage gable end was in the way."

"Just so, sir."

"And you, Dunstan?" I asked.

The man straightened up a little. "I was up at Shaw Down, by the copse. The weather is fine and I thought to go up and see how many had lambs. They'm coming fast now."

I smiled. It was a surprisingly mild January and my sheep were multiplying nicely.

"Alone?"

"No m'lord, Hilda's man Esmund was with me. He's there still."

I nodded. "Why did you come home, Dunstan?"

"Got a few lame sheep, sir, I came home to get me remedy for it."

"Thank you. All of you. I may wish to speak to you again." I cut the questioning short for I'd heard the drumming of two horses' hooves on the hard chalk.

"Sir...?" said Hilda, "Wher'll you take poor Elswith?"

"To Cadley church I expect. She was a worshipper there, wasn't she?"

"Yessir."

"And Will, sir?" asked Floro. I had the feeling they had all been discussing the matter of William's guilt - or no - as we had entered the house.

"He is at home. For the moment two of my village folk will look to him."

"Sir, couldn't we...?

"Hush woman" said Dunstan to his wife. She stopped and looked at me with wide open eyes.

"He din't do it sir."

"No, Floro, I'm sure he didn't."

Chapter Three

The coroner with his clerk lagging behind on a slow mule was just dismounting in the space before William's cottage.

John Brenthall, with his wife riding pillion, had just ridden up beside him. The clerk puffed his way up the hill.

"Sir Hugo." I called as I exited the small cottage at the bottom of the incline. I waved my arm.

John waved back and turned to help Agnes down. She rearranged the folds of her dress.

We all met by the door of the Larkworthy cottage.

"The body lies in the middle cottage, Sir Hugo. You'll have a difficulty getting enough people in this lonely place for a jury."

He looked round with disdain. "Then where am I to..."

"Cadley is near enough" Johannes smiled. "Would you like me to call in on my way home and send some men to you from there?"

"Thank you, Dr Johannes, that would be kind. Sir Aumary, the woman is one of yours, I hear?"

"Yes, the poor woman is one of my spinners...." I stopped, for I'd suddenly had a thought which I must investigate immediately.

"Excuse me..." I ducked once again into the small cottage.

Where was the work, the spun thread which Elswith had been taking to the town? I looked round. It was not in the house. Perhaps she had been to Marlborough and had come back; no, surely not. She hadn't had the time.

I met the coroner outside the house again.

"What the devil am I doing investigating the death of a villein? The woman has no rights...."

"Sir Hugo, all my people have rights."

The man looked at me as if I was mad.

"I will investigate her murder as if she was a free woman… I'd hoped that you would help me… I am sure the King…."

Hugo of Ramsbury stuck his finger in his ear and wiggled it about. "Ah, yes, well…"

"Let us take you to the house, Hugo. John, Agnes, can you go and look after William please? I will be back."

Johannes explained what he could about the body to the coroner and then was on his way to collect together twelve men over fourteen to act as a jury.

I hung about wishing I could go home, but it would be poor form to leave the coroner on his own. After all, my job was to find the culprit.

For something to fill the time, I said, "The first finder was a woman called Floro Weard, also a serf of mine. The murdered woman's husband is asleep, sedated by Dr Johannes, for he took the news badly and the woman who helped, Hilda Sceap and her husband, are looking to both Floro and Dunstan her husband, until the body is removed and they can return home. Her own husband is still on the hill."

Hugo of Ramsbury nodded. "In situations like this we usually find it is the husband who has murdered the wife."

"I think you'll find this not to be the case here, sir. They are…were…a devoted couple. They had just recently entered the Marlborough Flitch Contest and were the favourites to win."

"Even devoted couples can fall out, Sir Aumary."

"Perhaps, but I know these people and I really do not think…"

"One bad word, one raised fist and…"

"But this was not a raised fist, Hugo, this was a sustained pressure on the throat. You heard Dr Johannes. Enough prolonged pressure to break the little bone in the front of the neck. If William had taken his wife by the throat in a moment of anger, then he would've let go pretty quickly."

"No, it was no accident. But nevertheless."

"I saw the man when we found the body, Sir Hugo. No man can fake such grief, such shock," I said louder than I needed.

Hugo sniffed. "Come. Whilst we are waiting, let us go and talk to these serfs of yours."

The clerk followed us at a short distance.

Hilda was chopping up something for the pot, when we scratched on the door and entered. She looked up, a little startled.

The other two rose to their feet. A black and white dog slunk under the table.

"Sit, Dunstan, Floro." I saw the coroner give me a strange look.

"This is the coroner, Sir Hugo of Ramsbury. He would like to ask you some questions and his scribe will write it all down."

They curtsied and bowed.

"Tell him exactly what he wants to know."

The coroner started with the account of Floro and how she had found the body of Elswith Larkworthy. Her story did not deviate from that which she'd told me.

I leaned against the wall, out of the way, and listened. It wasn't the coroner's job to investigate too fully; his job was to pronounce upon the manner of death, but I let him have his say.

"Larkworthy. Where was he?"

"I din't see him m'lord," said Floro. "He was up at the far side of his cott mending the wall, I think."

"I can add to that, Hugo," I said, "for when I arrived he was there and had been working on his house for a while, by the look of the chalk blocks he'd replaced."

Hugo turned to me, "He might have replaced those blocks yesterday… or another day. Only a few might have been today's work. He might have had time to dispose of his wife."

I flinched and nodded slowly.

The coroner turned to Hilda Sceap. "And you woman?"

"I saw Floro come out of her house. I didn't see Will for the same reason Floro couldn't. It's the top cottage and higher up."

"No other man came to the place?"

"Only the Lord Belvoir, sir," said Hilda.

"You heard nothing?"

I saw Floro Weard stiffen… she looked sideways at Hilda.

A look passed between them and was gone. "No sir."

*****

The clerk scribbled on. We waited. At last the jury arrived and the coroner took them all up to the Weards' house to view the body. I left the cottage at the bottom of the dip and ran up the hillside to the Larkworthy house.

Agnes had boiled a pannikin of water to make some soup and John was building up the central fire, feeding it with twigs as Hilda had done. Lastly a dry branch went on and the flames licked at it greedily.

"Well done you two," I said, "it will get really cold later, I feel."

"Sir, what do you want us to do?" asked Agnes, "when William wakes?"

"Send for me. I want to ask him some questions. I'm glad he's not awake for the coroner to quiz him."

"But sir," said John. "It's not the coroner's place to ask too many questions about the murderer only to find out how a man died and when. That is your job."

I laughed. "Let him have his way. He's harmless enough."

How wrong I was.

Johannes could not find twelve men over fourteen in the tiny village of Cadley. Most of the people were out working in the trees, for many of them were my verderers and foresters. Sir Hugo had to command Dunstan Weard to make up the twelfth man. Reluctantly he strode up the hill into the cottage.

I heard later from Agnes Brenthall what had happened.

When asked by the coroner, tales were told about the Larkworthys. How devoted they were. How they lived quietly at the top of the hill and kept themselves to themselves. No one had heard any noise and it was thought that somehow a murderer, a masterless man from the forest perhaps, (though there were none for I had cleared them all out many years ago and did not allow wolfsheads or miscreants to hide out there for long), had killed Elswith.

All was going well until Dunstan was asked if he had heard anything.

"I heard them arguing," he said. "This morning afore I went out. Loud voices came from the cott."

"What were they saying?" asked the coroner.

"I couldn't tell."

"C'mon man. It's not that far that you can't hear what raised voices are saying from your cottage, through your piddling little walls!"

"Just voices, sir."

"First time ever, m'lord," put in Floro. "Since ever we knowed them. They never argued… ever, but this morning… Dunstan did say he'd heard them."

"So, William was angry?"

"It was an angry voice, yes, sir," said Dunstan.

"I do know…," said Floro, "that William wanted to go in for this flitch thing but that Elswith was a little shy of it. She did tell me she wasn't happy about it at first."

"So they argued about that, did they?"

No one confirmed this.

But the jury had heard it and they argued amongst themselves for a while and gave a verdict of murder.

William Larkworthy had murdered his wife Elswith in a fit of temper, they said, over the flitch contest.

*****

John and Agnes came haring back to Durley at past dinner time.

Agnes flew into the hall.

"Sir, m'lord." She put a hand to her breast and coughed and wheezed. "William has been taken for the murder of his wife, sir. We were powerless to stop them."

"Now, now, Agnes. Sit down and get your breath. Tell me what happened."

John was now striding through the hall and up to the dais where we were all at meat.

"Hilda came running up before the verdict was made to tell us that it was likely that William was to be taken," said John.

"Was he awake then?" I asked.

"Only just."

"They roped him behind the coroner's horse and set off for the castle, sir," said Agnes with a catch in her voice. "Poor Will was so confused and tired. He could hardly walk, m'lord."

"All right, Agnes. Thank you. Thank you both for all you did. Now tell me how this came about."

And so they told me the tale.

As I've told you, Paul, my scribe.

"So on the word of Dunstan Weard, they arrested him?"

"Yes, sir, and his wife backed him up, though I know she can't be sworn in. She said that her man had told her that morning he'd heard cross words coming from their cott and it was not right for they were now to be disqualified from the flitch contest, sir."

"And then... murder, sir," said John.

"Hmmm." I took up my belt and buckled it on. "I'll be off to the castle to have a word with William. There's nothing I can do at present about his arrest but I may get the truth from him."

"You don't think...?" began Agnes.

I reached for my cloak and Lydia put it into my hand. "No, I don't believe it. I don't believe that Will murdered Elswith. As I told the coroner, no man could fake such shock and horror."

It was mid-afternoon by the time I reached the castle and stood in the gaol under the keep.

Peterkin Gayle, the part time gaoler and guardian of the royal treasury situated in the castle, stood behind me. He was a short, smart, middle aged man with a ring of fluffy white hair and a wide smile.

"He's done nothing but sleep, sir."

"Johannes gave him a potion before I left him, to help him through the night. He was sorely affected by seeing his wife's body, Pete. I have never seen such grief."

"You don't think it was false then, Sir Aumary?"

"No, I don't. The coroner has the wrong man, of that I'm sure."

I stepped up to the man who was huddled on the stone bench which served as bed and seat, running round the outside of the gaol. I gently shook his shoulder and hunkered down.

William tried to rise and make an obeisance but I pushed him down. His eyes were half closed; he couldn't focus properly. There was a graze on his cheek I presumed where he had fallen when dragged behind the coroner's horse. His hair was tousled and his clothes dirtied.

"Sir. M'lord Belvoir," he managed to say.

"Aye, Will."

I looked back at the gaoler. "Have you any further prisoners at the moment?"

"None."

"Can we strike off his gyves and manacles? I'll take responsibility. He'll go nowhere. And make him comfortable... blankets, a pillow perhaps? See to his hurts?"

"Yessir." said Gayle, grinning. He leaned forward to undo the restrainers. "Anything to discomfort old...."

"What's that?" I chuckled, "Old Hugo of Ramsbury?"

Gayle looked a bit self-conscious. "I can't stand the pompous ar...." He sighed, "Now, the last coroner:... he was a great man."

"Yes, I knew him. He was a friend of my uncle William. He was getting too long in the tooth to gad about the county, he said. So he retired."

"Aye, and we got this podgy apology for a horsefly. Have the old one back in a flash, sir," said Peterkin Gayle.

I smiled.

I sat by the semi-conscious Larkworthy. "William, I'm sorry that you have to be so treated but… someone said they heard you arguing with Elswith this morning. Is it true?"

Larkworthy's face crumpled into a hideous grin of grief.

"No sir. No. Never a cross word!"

"Someone said you might have argued about entering the contest for the Flitch."

Larkworthy wiped his hand over his eyes. "We spoke about it but did not argue. I was all for it but Elswith was not sure," he slurred.

"Did you shout at her that you must enter, for the flitch was a prize worth having."

William hiccoughed. "Shout sir?" Tears streamed down his cheeks. "I never shouted at her in twenty years."

"You discussed the contest then?"

"Aye, we did. I explained that it was an honour and that the ham would keep us alive through the lean time, for it's a prize, as you say sir, worth having."

"In the end she was convinced?"

"Aye sir, she was, for we had nothing to do but go on the way we had always done," said William, sobbing.

"So what were the harsh words that this person heard this morning?"

"It was not us, sir," and William began to sob again in earnest.

I sat on the bench, leaned forward and waited for him to stop crying.

"Why should Dunstan Weard say it was so if it wasn't?" I asked.

William wiped his eyes and nose on his sleeve. "He's a good man. He wouldn't lie but I can't understand why he should say such a thing."

"Might it have been Hilda and her husband…?"

"Esmund. No, he had been on the hill all night with the lambers, sir. It was my turn tonight."

"Have you quarrelled with Dunstan or Floro that he should be revenged on you at all, Will?"

"I ain't a quarrelsome man sir."

"No, Will, you aren't."

I fingered my short cropped black beard.

"Where were you before you started to mend your wall? Might someone have crept into the house?"

William held his head in his hands. "I was at the end of the house. I could see up the hill, that's how I saw you...I wouldn't see anyone coming up the hill from down. Besides, sir... Elswith was in Floro's house, wasn't she?"

His face registered real puzzlement.

I told him what we thought had happened.

"Elswith was in the cottage for quite a while before she was moved to the Weards' house. Why I have no idea."

William took a shuddering breath. "Really early I was out cutting bricks at the chalk pit at Wooton, sir. I brought them back in a sack and started work."

"Ah, I see."

"But sir... Elswith went out. She went to Marlborough to take her threads to the weavers there."

"Yes, you told me and I have looked for her spinnings: they aren't in the cottage."

"Then she must have...."

"No time. She had been dead a few hours when Dr Johannes saw her. She didn't have time to walk to the town and back," I said.

Larkworthy's face took on a semblance of the William of old.

"Then where's the fruits of her labours, sir? Where's her work?"

*****

I asked Peterkin Gayle to look after Will and mounted Bayard, setting his head for home.

The last question I'd asked was, 'to whom did Elswith's spinning go?'

Before I went home I would ask at the weavers.

I clattered through the arch made by the close touching houses of Crooks Lane in the centre of town and told Bayard to stay put. He was an obedient horse. I knew he would.

I counted the cotts lining the lane and came to the fourth house along. Master Teller.

He opened the door and tucked his hair over his ears and back into his coif. I introduced myself and he bowed and went into the small house.

The weavers of this part of town had houses which pressed close together in a row. Each house was a two roomed affair with a sleeping space above and another room above this as a work place. The top floor had large window spaces to let in light and went almost the whole height of each house loft. This was so that they could accommodate the large looms which wove the cloth for which Marlborough was famed.

Master Teller had several men and women working at the looms and I could hear the chattering as they carried on their work above us.

"Master Teller, I know that my wool, spun by some of the women who are married to my shepherds, comes to you to be woven into cloth. Tom Herder, my wool factor, tells me you buy the spun fleeces from us and pay the factor accordingly."

"This is correct sir. Your whole fleeces come into the town too and some are spun here."

"And the rest go to Collingbourne to the spinsters there?"

"Correct, sir."

"Can you tell me if Elswith Larkworthy came to bring you some threads today?"

"Aye, she was due to come."

"You did not see her?"

"My wife came to me at dinner time and said that Elswith had not come. We hoped she was not ill but that no doubt we should see her soon."

"Ah."

"Is there a problem, sir?"

"You didn't see her at all and no one you know mentioned seeing her anywhere in town?"

The weaving master then opened the door at the back of the house, shouted, and his wife came clattering into the house in her wooden pattens.

No, she said, no one had seen her and they had looked for her because from the top of their weaving loft they could watch the edge of the forest and she could usually be seen coming down the nearest part of Granham Hill to the Newbury Road. She would then cross the bridge and come up the High and into Crooks Lane.

Elswith had not come to Marlborough that day.

I told them nothing. They would know soon enough why she would never again be seen coming down the Granham Hill.

*****

I went home, reaching the manor courtyard just as the light was fading.

Naturally, I had to tell all concerned about my visit to William and what was said. Agnes then took John off to their own house for supper and I sat at the table in the solar and demolished one of my cook Matthew's excellent meat pies.

Lydia leaned over and peeled me an apple. Unlike many of my class, I was partial to fruit.

"So William cannot account for his movements and has no one to vouch for him, and Elswith wasn't seen in the town, forest or hamlet?"

I cut up the apple with my eating knife and gave it back to her on the plate. I wasn't in the mood for apples.

"No, it's a mystery. And her body was moved and no one saw it happen."

Lydia shook her head and the waves of black hair cascading down her back from her barbette and crown, rippled in the firelight. I noticed she had removed the net holding her hair in place, in the privacy of the solar.

"Will wouldn't kill Elswith any more than I'd kill you."

I laughed. "No, I do not believe it. In order though, to save William's neck from the noose, I must find the man who did."

"But Aumary, it's the word of one man. One man only says they heard him arguing."

"I have a feeling that Hilda Sceap too heard the voices but she will not speak and anyway...."

"Her word cannot be taken in evidence as she is a woman. Pah!"

"I know my love. It's the law but... I cannot do anything about it."

"I know." Lydia sighed. "So who might want to murder Elswith Larkworthy?"

I leaned back in my chair. "She was, I think, well liked. Twenty years married and no problem. They enter the contest and she is killed. Is it anything to do with the flitch or is it a coincidence?"

"You mean rivals. Oh surely not, Aumary. No one would kill for a side of bacon!"

I raised my eyebrows. "People have killed for a halfpenny, dearest one."

"No, I cannot believe it."

"Well, tomorrow I must find the other folk entered in the contest and quiz them. One pair in Cadley, one at the castle, one in the town and who knows else."

"Did Elswith know any of them?"

"One of them is her cousin. Another pair they know from church: my deerman Hart's brother and one of the others is an unknown from the town, a wheelwright."

"Then you must get your rest. Tomorrow you'll be dancing around the forest like a midge over water!"

I yawned. "Will I sleep? It will all go round and round in my head."

And I was right.

*****

The village of Cadley, a small hamlet of about twenty houses, was on the road to Marlborough from Salisbury. Some of them were buried deeper in the forest. Most strung out on the lane which eventually left the woods and headed for the downs. The old wooden Saxon church however, was on the eastern side of the road with few houses close by.

I was up early and wanted to catch the forest folk before they went out to work, for the day.

And so I ambled down the Marlborough road and clopped gently up the lane to the house where, I had been told, the entrants to the flitch contest lived.

It was Godgifu who answered the door. Her husband was still breaking his fast. She invited me in with a sweeping curtsey. The three children were hurried out of the back door.

Osmund stood and bowed to me, touching his forelock.

"M'lord. This is an honour."

I smiled. "Just a fleeting visit, Osmund. You will know by now, won't you, that William Larkworthy has been taken for the murder of his wife and languishes at the castle. Elswith was killed yesterday."

"Yes, I did hear...," began Osmund.

His wife Godgifu sat down with a shocked cry. "No, the poor woman!"

She turned stricken eyes up to her husband's face. "You didn't tell me." Then she bounced up again, aware she should not sit in the presence of her lord.

Osmund went to her and took her shoulders. "I didn't know how to put it to you. I know you were fond of the woman. Aye and I like the man too...but...."

"He didn't do it, of that I am sure," I said. "It is my duty as constable to bring to law the man who did."

Godgifu's face lost all colour then. "If not Will then...who?"

"I am talking to those folk who knew the couple and who have entered the flitch contest."

Osmund jumped. "You cannot mean to lay the blame...."

"No, not at all. I am merely gathering information. You have entered and I would like to know if you know anything about the Larkworthys which might throw some light upon the death of Elswith."

Osmund knelt with one knee on his bench beside his wife, his hand on her shoulder. "We know them only from church. We meet now and again on the road to and from town, sir. Elswith spins, as does Godgifu. You meet now and again don't you?"

"Aye, we do."

Godgifu swallowed.

"When my mother in the town, was dying and Osmund was working, Elswith came to look to the children for me one afternoon. She was a nice woman. Kind and quiet."

"And the favourite to win the contest, I hear."

The two exchanged a glance. "You cannot believe because she and William was favourite that someone would kill her to clear the way for... no that is... it can't be. No one would kill for...," said Osmund.

"Where were you Osmund yesterday, between dawn and the fourth hour of the day?"

"At dawn? Here breaking my fast with the children. And Godgifu of course. Then I went to work in La Verme close by Big Bellied Oak. The gang will vouch for me. Wilfrid Frithson was there, sir."

I nodded. La Verme was far enough away from the cotts on the downs. It would not have been possible to be missing for too long. Absence would be noticed in the tree felling gang.

"Thank you." I looked at Godgifu's capable hands. "And you, Godgifu?"

I wondered if hands as large and strong as hers could inflict damage on such a small woman as Elswith, for Godgifu was tall and large boned.

"Here with the children sir. Then my neighbour came in and I went and helped to dress and wash her old mother who is bedridden, sir, and she needs help to manage her. I was next door till dinner time."

"Thank you both." I put on my gloves as I reached for the door, "Do you know the other contestants?"

"We exchange pleasantries with the wheelwright if he comes to the village but no, we know none well."

"Ah…. Good luck in the contest, then. For now there is now one less couple with whom to compete."

I found Bayard being held by a small child of about ten years.

"He's a lovely horse," said the cheeky young boy, smiling.

"Like horses do you?"

"Oh aye. I do."

I saw his father come out of the cottage to find him. "Well, when you are older, perhaps you can come to Durley and be a groom. That is if you don't want to be a forester," I said.

The young boy jumped up and down grinning and his father cuffed him gently around the ears.

"Horse mad he is."

I laughed.

"Watches all the beasts going to and fro, he does. Knows them all. All along the Marlborough road and Cadley road to Mud Lane. Rather do that than his chores."

I laughed again. "Thank you Osmund. God keep you all."

From there I rode into town. I left Bayard at Johannes' house. Of course he had heard that William had been taken for Elswith's murder and like me, he did not believe it.

"Murder by person or persons unknown it should have been. That verdict would never have been given under the old coroner."

"No, indeed it would not. Not on the say so of one man."

"Why might this fellow lie, Aumary?"

"I do not think he does."

"But, from what I hear, William would not kill his wife," he said in a pleading tone. "Would he?"

I shook my head. "I cannot see why he would lie about this, but no, I'm sure he didn't."

I wrapped my cloak tighter around me for the day was cold. "I'm off to see a wheelwright and a moneyer. I'll be back with news as soon as I can."

The wheelwright worked in the yard at the top of Crooks Lane, where I had talked to the weavers yesterday the day before. Thomas Ash was a Master Wright and he was busy supervising his apprentices sorting wood and giving them a lecture on which wood was best for what.

"... And ash is the best timber for a wheel and is measured in fellowes length...."

I called to him. He turned.

He was a rather rotund man in his middle forties with a receding hairline and a scanty beard.

His leather apron strained over his belly as his arms came up akimbo and he shouted, "Who wants me?"

I nodded and introduced myself. "Go!" he shouted to his three apprentices and they fled into the workshop.

I followed into his office.

There was a very pleasant smell of wood shavings and glue.

"Master Thomas. Good day. I am making inquiries about poor William Larkworthy, whom you will know, has been taken up for the killing of his wife Elswith in their house yesterday."

"If you have the man, why ask me questions, m'lord?" said Master Ash.

"You do not know him?"

"No... no I don't. He's a man of the downs they tell me. I am a man of the town."

"He is a fellow competitor for the title of Flitch King."

"So I have been told. But now... well eh... has rather cooked his goose hasn't he, hmm?"

"Master Ash, what would you say if I told you that William did not kill his wife?"

"I would ask, sir...," he said, "why, with all respect due to you and the coroner, is the man still locked up? If he did not do it and you can prove it, then he must be released."

"This is why I am making inquiries. I want to find the man responsible."

The wheelwright put his thumbs into the waist of his leather apron. "I have told you sir, I know neither the man nor the woman."

"By reputation perhaps?"

"Only that it has been said that they will win for you cannot get a breath of fresh air between them. Two peas squashed in a pod, sir." He shrugged. "Now.. they will not win."

"Do you think perhaps that someone has killed Elswith Larkworthy so as to remove the favourites from the race, Master Ash?"

"Nonsense, sir. No one would kill for a flitch of bacon."

"Just harmless fun, eh?"

"Just that, sir." His eye strayed to the door of his workroom. "Hubert Smith, take your eyes and ears elsewhere and keep your fingers to your work or I'll have them shaved with a spokeshave, so I will."

The head disappeared.

"So you can tell me nothing about the people involved, Ash?"

"I know of the moneyer who works at the castle and who lives, I believe, on Chantry Lane, but I do not know the forest folk at Cadley. I have never met any of them, to speak to... I believe. There is a man out at St. Martin's, I heard, who was going to enter the contest but I am not sure if he did."

"Thank you." I turned to leave. "By the way, where were you between dawn and the fourth hour yesterday, Ash?"

"Where all good folk should be. At church. In my bed to dawn, in church till the second hour, at the breaking of my fast with my wife of a year sir, at home on Oxford Street, then here with my apprentices till we broke for dinner at the sixth hour."

"Someone to vouch for you the whole time?"

"Aye sir. The whole while."

I backed away and nodded "Good day, Ash."

He watched me go all the way up the lane and onto the High, then as I turned to look, he ducked into his yard again.

Chapter Four

My next visit was to the castle; to the mint.

William the First, known often as the Conqueror, had established mints and treasuries at various places around the country. One of them was at the castle at Marlborough and this was one of the reasons there had been so much re-building and extending there. There had to be a secure place for the coins to be minted and there had to be rooms in the castle for the silver coins and the treasure to be stored.

Our friend Peterkin Gayle was, amongst other things, in charge of the security of the treasury and I sought him out now, in his office in the castle wall. He had another smaller room close by the gatehouse, where he lived.

"I want to talk to Edwig Crosscastle, Pete," I said. "About the death of Larkworthy's wife."

Gayle looked surprised as he rose from his table and shrugged on his gambeson. "You think he may have something to do with it?"

"No, not really, but I'm asking everyone who has entered the flitch contest and he and his wife are contestants. He is also the murdered woman's cousin. He may have known her quite well and maybe knows something which can help us."

Peterkin made a moue, "You might be lucky. He's a quiet type, doesn't socialise much with the rest of the castle men. Wealthy man you know. Has a good stone house on Chantry Lane. Good luck."

Gayle took me through a door at the back of the office and we travelled out over the bailey. The forge seemed to be sunk up against the outer wall of the castle which was eight to twelve feet thick.

The forge was a building of twelve feet square, made of stone on three sides with a wood shingle roof and one open side, covered with linseed oiled canvas which might be lowered in inclement weather. These were now open for the weather though cold, was clear. Light streamed in, enough for the solitary moneyer to ply his trade. Smoke billowed up from the fire and pooled in the apex of the roof.

Crosscastle worked the mint here. He was a master moneyer and I'd learned from Peterkin that every man was his own master, owned his own silver and paid a fee to the crown to produce the coins he made. He also received a percentage of the value of the coins he struck, giving him a goodly income.

Gayle told me that goldsmiths often aspired to be moneyers, so affluent were these men.

The silver, some of it in the form of old coin, was set in crucibles amongst hard wood charcoal and heated to red hot. I watched as Crosscastle filled a crucible with old finger rings and a brooch or two, some small coins and snippets of silver, small pieces from the snippings from the blank coins. Then he lifted his bellows and pumped. There was a roar as the bellows drew up and down and the charcoal crackled and snapped. Red sparks flew from the forge and I stepped back hastily so as not to be singed. I asked if I could be shown how the coins were made.

The moneyer was watching his crucible carefully and told me that he thought, if he wasn't watchful, it might crack and spill the silver. No matter; it could be recovered, he told me. Nothing was wasted.

I must admit I was fascinated by this artistry. I had been at the castle some years and had never been to the forge to watch this man. I had passed him by, heard him of course, for moneying is a noisy business and it was impossible not to hear the banging and thumping from anywhere in the castle. I watched in fascination as the man told me how all the silver was weighed into the forge and all the coins were weighed out. In this way they would be able to know, to within a small amount, that all the silver had been accounted for. All the while the man chatted, he weighed the silver on his scales with great precision. It was almost as if he could do it in his sleep.

I was told that after the silver ingot had been made it would be beaten to a required thickness to take the coin dies. Small silver ingots, which had been made by pouring the molten silver into formers, were first quenched in water then laid on an anvil and beaten out. This operation was known as sheet making.

The resultant flat silver sheet was then punched out with sharp round tools called planchet cutters and the blank coins were then ready to be placed on the die and hit hard with a hammer. These were also known as flans. The moneyer would place the dies onto the metal and make the coins by hammering with a heavy hammer to produce the design of the coin.

I watched as Crosscastle, now in a different role, known as a hammer man, took a blank coin and set it to the top of a patterned die, which was set into a section of tree stump I looked around: this was the only stump in the forge. One for each moneyer and only one die per man. Gayle had told me that the dies came from London and were specially made by skilled engravers. Once the die was finished with, it must go back to London to be disposed of and another was sent to replace it. In this way, dies were kept sharp and the resultant coins were perfect, (or as perfect as the moneyer could make them,) and the new ones took their place in the tree stump. If the dies did not arrive, no coins could be made.

The flan lay on the bottom die, known as a pile. The top, the trussel, was laid over the blank and the resultant column produced was hit hard with a hammer. The man showed me a coin he'd made. Shining and new; the King's head, John's father's head if truth were known; John didn't bother having a new image made, was staring out at me upon this silver penny. I turned it over. On the reverse was a short cross with small pellets at the ends and the superscription showing where and by whom the coin was minted. We take these for granted, I thought, these small silver pieces. We use them every day and never give a thought to the men who strike them; the men whose names appear on the coins of the realm. I stared hard at the letters. I thought I could make out the name Edwi and the word, or part of the word, Marl.

I nodded to two soldiers who stood just outside the forge. These men would accompany the coin to the place of storage at the end of the day. I knew them both for I had seen them about the bailey now and again.

Crosscastle looked up from his work and wiped his forehead with his sleeve. We retired to a corner. The noise of the manufacture was loud but I had been told with several moneyers in larger mints it could be deafening; the banging of the silver sheets; the thump of the dies and the chink of the coin as it was tossed into the bag in which it would be transported, was noisy enough but suddenly, because the moneyer had ceased to work, all was strangely silent.

I introduced myself. The man bowed low. He was of medium build with a thin, tight face, a nose which had been broken at some time and a thatch of dingy brown hair like old straw. His clothes were good and he wore a woollen tunic of silver grey, to match the coins he made and chausses of dark blue wool. Over it was a half leather apron.

"Crosscastle, I hear that you and your wife have entered the flitch contest."

The man looked most perplexed. "Yes m'lord, we have."

The look he gave me said, 'and you have come here especially to talk to me about that?'

"You know that your cousin Elswith and her husband have also entered the contest?"

Crosscastle chuckled. "Aye, sir, I do. She is likely to run off with the flitch, her and her Will but my Godiva and I might get the second prize of some gammon."

"I wasn't aware that there was a second prize." I said, my eyebrow raised.

"Oh aye... worth having just the same."

I grimaced "Crosscastle... you haven't heard?"

"Heard what? Have they cancelled the contest, sir?" he laughed.

"No, the favourites are no longer in the running."

The smile left his face.

"Elswith was murdered yesterday," I added as gently as I could.

Crosscastle slumped onto a stool.

"Dead?"

"Yes. She was strangled."

"Jesus' wounds!"

"You really haven't heard. I was sure it must be all around the town by now that WIlliam has been taken for her murder."

He jumped up! "No! That could never be."

"Why do you think that?"

"Because William loved Elsie more than he loved his own life, that's why. He could never harm her."

"How come you haven't heard? The whole town seems to know. None told you? You are after all family?"

"I stayed late last night, after dark… ask Gayle here. I went home late and went straight to my meat and bread. The wife was up with the littl'un- she's been poorly and I fell into my bed and was asleep in a trice. My servants said not a word this morning."

"Your wife didn't tell you? Surely she knew?" I asked.

"If she did, she didn't wake me to tell me and then I was up this morning and out before she had come back from the kitchen with the morning's water. I broke my fast at the castle, in the refectory. One of the perks sir. None of them told me. I didn't sit with anyone. That's why they were giving me strange looks."

I looked over to Gayle. I would ask him about this later.

"Can you think of anyone who might want to kill Elswith, Crosscastle?"

He shook his head. "She was well liked was our Elsie. No, I can't believe it. William didn't do it, sir."

"No, I don't believe he did." I scratched my head.

"Can you tell me where you were between dawn and the fourth hour of the day yesterday?"

"I can sir, I was up before dawn and took bread with Godiva. Then I walked about a bit in the town. You don't know what it's like being holed up here all day, sir. It was a lovely day if a bit windy and I thought I'd take a turn about the town, by the river and such, before I went to work to get a bit of fresh air, peace and space, if you see what I mean. This place is dirty, noisy and smelly. Why do you want to know?"

"I'm asking everyone that question."

I looked around the forge in which the moneyer worked. The four window spaces, were quite small for, as I say the place was built onto the wall of the castle. The nearest to Crosscastle's place of work faced due south. Air and light came in as well as the noise from the eastern side of the bailey and moat. The moneyer's work place was situated by one of these windows in the light. His words bore out what Gayle had told me - it seemed they were out here all the day in the cold and noise. I stepped out and rounded the forge and by looking up I could just see the strip of sky above the moat, and by cricking my neck I could see through an arrow slit in the back wall, the south field and the river and bridge a few hundred yards along the Granham road.

"Did you see anyone on your walk?" I asked, returning to the forge.

"Oh aye… lots of folk were out and about on my way back." His face assumed a dolorous stare. "Poor Elsie. Poor Will. He'll be lost without her."

"Names of the folk you saw please, Crosscastle."

Four or five names tripped from his tongue. One of which was my good friend the shoemaker, Gilbert Cordwainer. I wrote them down in my small waxed tablet, my aide memoire which I carried with me in which to make notes.

He stood up and sighed. "I suppose it must have been some masterless man from the forest." He looked up quickly.... "She wasn't.... you know.... interfered with, sir?"

"No, she wasn't, I'm pleased to say. That notion had crossed my mind when I saw her but no. Doctor Johannes had a look at her and she hadn't been assaulted in that way."

"Always horrible to tell the womenfolk that... well... that sort of thing has happened to a woman they know, sir."

"Yes, it must be."

I turned to leave. "Will she be buried in Cadley, sir?"

"Yes, she will."

"Then I'll have some time off to go. I can find out when it will be. I'll get me a horse from the castle and ride out there."

I smiled. "Thank you for your help," and I left him.

As I exited the door, Gayle came up and I smiled. The noise of the banging began again.

"How many coins might the moneyer strike, Pete, in, let's say, a week?"

"Oh about ten pounds."

"That's a lot of coins for one man."

"In the bigger mints, there are several moneyers, but we are only a small mint. Just Crosscastle. So he does the lot from the beginning."

"Melts the silver, makes the ingots, beats the sheet, makes the flans and strikes the coins?"

"Everything."

"Where does the silver come from?"

"He buys it in himself, from whoever has it to sell. The Jews on Silver Street sometimes have some for him."

"And I take it he pays for the silver with the coins he strikes and some will go into storage?" I said.

"That's right."

"Does he work every day, all day on coins?"

"It depends. He works when there's silver to make coins. He doesn't just make coins. He's a very skilled jeweller too. He works when he needs to."

I smiled again. This moneying fascinated me, I must admit.

I exited the castle bailey and waved to my friend Andrew Merriman, officer of the watch, who was at the gatehouse talking to a man who had come in with a large basket of cheeses.

I walked down the High Street, past the church of St. Peter, on past the priory and ducked into a tiny square where lay the priory gates. To the side here my good friend Gilbert had his workshop and home.

Master Cordwainer was an avuncular man with a large round red face, thick brown hair and a permanent grin.

I knew him well for he had made my boots and shoes firstly as a journeyman, then as his own master, since I was a lad and could first walk in them, His house, workplace and shop were right next to the priory entrance and there is no doubt he benefitted from being in such a spot. No pilgrim, visitor, secular or clerical could pass by into the priory without first casting their eyes over his wares.

He was a mine of information about the town, a town councillor and a church reeve at the newly built St. Peter's. He'd often helped me solve the murders which had occurred in the town and he was a very good friend.

I scratched at the door and made to step in. His apprentice Felix Castleman forestalled me and opened the door bowing me in.

Gilbert was in the back room tapping on... whatever it is that shoemakers tap on.

His mouth was full of tacks.

"Ar... er Emmeryee, neece to see you. Oo stip in. Eelix, sum rine er ah gist."

I chuckled. "Hello Gil, don't want to stop you working."

"Not at orl. Iyal ree done in a rorent."

He dropped a tack and tutted, as best he could.

"Eelix inish dis er mee il you." He spat the tacks out into his hand.

"One of these days I'll swallow a mouthful of those you know," he said in his normal speech.

"I got my rine... Gil...," I said laughing, showing him the little leather cup Felix had given me.

"Can we go up?"

Sitting comfortably in his little parlour on the long bench at the side of his table, I took a swig of the Bordeaux wine which his brother in law imported from France.

"Ah... as good as ever."

Gilbert smacked his lips and ruffled his dark brown hair. I noticed there was a little more silver at the temples than there had been.

"Heard the news?"

"Now, what news would that be?" He leaned back on the bench. "News that would bring the Constable into town. That would have to be the death of poor Elswith Larkworthy and the arrest of her husband."

I chuckled "Hit it with one arrow Gil. Or should I say tack!"

He smiled. "Wrong man, definitely the wrong man," he said, taking another swig. "But what do I know, I hardly know the man. It's just what I hear."

"Not my doing. It was the coroner."

"Does he have powers of arrest?"

"He does if he involves the sheriff and he has. He is empowered to take into custody anyone he feels guilty of a crime."

"Oh dear. How come?" He put up a finger, "Ah, I think I know. He's related you know."

"Hugo... to the sheriff?"

"Sadly, yes, to his wife Mabel de Swain. How do you think he got the job?"

I put my head in my hands. "Oh...and there was me thinking John chose him...."

"The King chose him because he paid the highest fee," said Gilbert.

"No, not the King, the justiciar I think, or some other lackey," I countered.

"Well, we are stuck with him."

"I have to find the real culprit to save William, Gil."

"How can I help?"

"What do you know about the Larkworthys? Why would someone want to kill Elswith? I'm turning up flans with everyone I speak to...."

"What?"

"Oh sorry Gil, I have just been to the mint to talk to Elswith's cousin. He's the moneyer at the castle. A flan is the blank they make the coins from."

"Ah, I see." Gilbert filled the small leather cups again.

"Well, let me see. I know she spins and brings her stuff to...."

"Yes, I know that too. She works for me. She didn't turn up yesterday when she was due at the weavers."

"I know they haven't got any children."

"None grown up?"

"No, none."

"Where are the girls and Grace then?" I asked. These were Gilbert's own two children and his wife.

"Market day - you mean you walked the half the length of the High and didn't notice it was market day?"

I laughed out loud. "No, I had my wits in my purse, obviously." I shook my black curls,. "I was out so early this morning, I left my wits behind."

It was Gilbert's turn to laugh then. He returned to our conversation. "There's just the two of them up on that hill. They go to Cadley now and again."

"Yes, I know that too. I've spoken to one of the other contestants for the flitch."

"Ah yes. The flitch. Favourites they were."

"And I've spoken to the wheelwright - he's a prickly fellow."

"Ash? Oh, he's all right. Just a bit self-important."

"You think he might feel himself important enough to think he must win the title of Flitch King and so get rid of the competition..?"

"No, no, not Tom. He's too much of a coward."

I sighed. "And then as I said, the cousin Crosscastle. Spoke to him just now."

"Hmmm. Lives on Chantry Lane. I see him about," said Gilbert.

"He tells me he hadn't heard that his cousin had been murdered. He was working hard and...."

"It was all about the town today."

"He says he was out too early and off to his work. And he is busy most of the day. He likes to walk about early he says."

"Aye I saw him. Yesterday morning walking about with a long face."

"Where was this?"

"High Street. He was just passing the house," said Gilbert.

"He told me he'd walked about early yesterday and that there were few people about. He said he'd seen you."

"Aye, that was right."

"Was he coming down or going up?"

"Down, towards the castle," said Gilbert, "I asked him where he'd been so early. He said he'd been walking about taking in the air."

"Hmmm... it's very noisy and smoky where the forge lies, you know, Gil. Not a nice place to work."

"Security is high, I suppose?"

"They keep an eye on their silver and on the finished coin."

I finished my wine. "Anyway, can you keep your eyes and ears open Gil?

Anything might be useful."

"I will," he said.

Before I left, Gilbert had gone down into the back room, taken the pins back into his mouth and was singing joyfully about a "raiden an her rad in readows green, rull o lowers."

I hummed the tune all the way back to Johannes' house then took Bayard from the stables, looked in and spoke to Little Agnes, Johannes' housekeeper, and trotted out of town and up the hill on the Salisbury Road.

I wanted to follow the path which I thought Elswith might take through the forest and over the hills to town.

I reached the cottages on the hill and could see Dunstan out on the downs with his dog. I hailed him and he came running. The sheep scattered but with a whistle, the dog gathered them in again.

"Dunstan, I am going to try to follow the route Elswith might have taken into town when she took her spinning to the weavers."

"They came for her body sir. It's gone to Cadley church. It will be interred day after tomorrow, late on."

"Can you go and ask them to hold onto Elswith for a little while longer please, Dunstan, on my order. I want to delay the funeral." The weather was cold, it would not be a problem.

Dunstan looked at me strangely but acquiesced.

"You have gone home, to your own place?"

"Floro has scrubbed the place from top to bottom, sir. She thought about asking the priest to come and bless the place."

"I am afrighted, sir that Elswith's ghost...."

I turned. Floro had come silently up the hill from her house behind me. No, Will was right. You could not be heard walking up the hill.

"Floro, would Elswith have hurt you in life?" I asked.

"Oh bless you, sir, no."

"Then why do you think she would hurt you in death?" I shook my head. "She didn't die in your house, Floro, she died in her own home."

Floro looked at the grass. "See what you mean, sir."

I walked Bayard to the Larkworthy house door. "I am leaving my beast here whilst I walk down the hill to see if I can find anything on the way to town. Keep an eye on him."

I set off down the hill at quite a pace for just here it was quite steep. The forest sent fingers of trees out into the downs here and there and they strayed from the main forest in little copses and groves. I crossed the Wansdyke, an old earthworks, more of a track and ditch and reached the hill above the town. I could see the church of Preshute below me.

Here the forest spread out further and I must scramble through a few trees before I reached the scarp out in the open.

I found nothing.

I descended the hill and met the road to Shaftesbury. I passed the castle mill, crossed the bridge and made my way into town.

No, I had found nothing, not a glimmer of Elswith. Neither her pack nor a twig bearing a lock of her hair, nor a print of her foot in the mud.

I sighed angrily and then looked back up the hill.

The weavers had said she could be seen coming down the hill. Where else might she have come from?

I recrossed the bridge, turned off left onto Newbury Road and just as the houses began, I left the road and started to climb the hill again. This was slightly easier going. I stopped and looked back. I could see the houses on Crooks Lane with their long windows in the weaving lofts.

I struggled up the hill. Now, there was more forest to walk through. I was quite close to the glassblowers camp. They had made their own new track through the trees from their camp to the River Kennet, where they gathered the gravel from the bed to make glass. Their carts trundled up the hill and they had made quite a good road. Perhaps Elswith had taken advantage of this.

A little way up the hill, I found the snippet of Elswith's dress. The dress she had worn when she had been murdered. It was a dark saffron colour, almost light brown and a tiny torn piece of it was hanging from a briar just to the side where the lane disappeared into a side track. I teased it from its restraining branch and put it in my purse.

Now I knew she used to come this way.

I walked very carefully now looking for the pack in which the woman would have put her spinning.

I reached the glassblowers clearing and passed on by. I now needed to veer west to come out on the downs where my sheep grazed. A quarter of a mile further on and quite close to the cottages where my shepherds lived, I found her pack.

It was sitting in the lee of a small bare hawthorn bush a few hundred yards from the forest trees.

What was it doing there?

Did Elswith take it to this spot and for some reason abandon it? Not likely. It was full of her work... her hard work and that was worth money to her.

Did she go so far and turn back home, leaving the pack for later collection? Perhaps.

Maybe she had forgotten something, went back to the house and someone was waiting there to kill her. Her pack then stayed uncollected.

Or did someone else collect it and carry it there? I looked back up the hill. Or, I suddenly thought, did someone offer to carry it to the town for her?

I sat down to collect my thoughts and my breath.

The wind of yesterday had died down and a gentle breeze now blew over the downs, ruffling the longer grasses and sparse bushes. It was still however quite a cold day for it was still only January.

I looked down the hill. There were a few furze and hawthorn bushes dotted about here. The furze would give a lovely yellow show in the early spring. Now they were dark green and spiny. I narrowed my eyes. Under one of them I could swear I saw something move. It was not a sheep, of that I was sure.

I ran at full pelt down the slope.

A brown and white dog whimpered as I came close.

Poor creature. It had a rope halter around its neck and this had been wound and wound around the bush so that the dog couldn't extricate itself. It tried to stand when it saw me and wagged its tail in joy.

I took out my knife and broke the hold of the halter. The dog leapt up to me and wriggled and wagged its tail for all it was worth, if a little weakly.

What had I heard the dog was called?

"Beval...there's a good dog."

I scooped up William's dog and trudged up the hill towards the cottages.

"Did you not bark and howl, Beval, didn't you call for help?"

But I knew as soon as I'd said it; I knew that the wind would have taken the bark away for it was blowing fiercely to the north east yesterday.

When the wind had died as it had done in the past few hours or so, its cries may have been heard but by then, it was a weak dog. Weak with thirst and hunger, no doubt, and tired with struggling.

The further I trudged the more angry I became for it was obvious to me that the poor dog had been tied there and had not tangled itself in the bush. I took the rope from my cotte where I had absentmindedly stuffed it. There were knots, complicated knots in it and no dog I knew could tie knots. This was the work of a man. A man who wanted to separate a woman from her loyal canine companion. A man who did not want the dog to attack him or defend his mistress when he put his hands around her throat to choke her to death.

This can only have been done when William was out at the chalk pit and Elswith was about to begin her downhill journey to Marlborough.

I took the dog home to William's cott and fed him some scraps I found in the house. He drank a whole bowl of water and asked for more.

Then I took him to Hilda's cottage and asked her to feed and water him until I could secure the release of his master.

I gathered up Bayard, flung myself in the saddle and trotted down the hill where I recovered Elswith's pack.

I made a mental note of exactly where I had discovered it. I did not need it and it was worth money to poor William. I rode for the town and the weavers. They could have the results of Elswith's hard work and they could pay William instead of my wool factor. I vowed to write a note to that effect as soon as I returned home.

I quickly came back to the castle and asked Gayle to open Will's cell for me. The confined man jumped up quickly as I entered.

"Nah, Will... you are not free yet... but I hope it will not be long."

I then told him about the pack and the dog.

"Tell me, where was the dog when you set off for the chalk pit?"

"At home sir by the fire. I left him there."

I nodded.

"Before Elswith rose that morning to go off to town?"

"I set off in the almost dark sir. Elswith would travel to town when it was just light. Beval would go with her."

"It's as I thought. This murderer is someone who knows your movements William, who knows what you do."

I ruffled my hair.

"Is this the first time you have mended your wall?"

"I have a barrow, sir. I take that to the chalk pit...you know where it is...?"

"Just past Starling's Roost and the old burial mound?"

"Aye sir. Well, for three mornings I've been collecting a barrow full and been working on that wall."

"So someone knew you were doing it and were away early?"

I suddenly stopped and replayed in my head what William had said.

"Tell me again how you get the chalk blocks to the house from the pit?"

"I barrow them, sir. I put them in a sack and I leaves the empty barrow at the gable end."

"That facing Floro's house?

"Yes, sir."

"Then William, we know how the body of your much beloved wife was moved from your house to Floro's."

William paled. "In my barrow, sir?"

"Yes, William," I said.

I sat down on the stone bench. "Someone took the opportunity to move

Elswith when you were engaged at the other end of the house and Floro was at the forest edge gathering sticks."

"I wouldn't have heard the barrow sir, the wind was so blustery."

"No, you wouldn't."

But I still didn't know why.

I slapped William on the back. "We are getting there Will...."

I saw him smile feebly.

Then I set off for home and supper. On the way home a thought came to me. William came back from the chalk pit and immediately began his restoration work. He didn't go into the cottage where lay his dead wife and possibly her killer. Had he done so, might he too have been killed?

I sagged in the saddle as I saw the gate house of Durley Manor approaching. Home at last. Hal was coming in the gate from the village, his thumbs thrust through his belt.

"Ah, Sir Aumary, we expected you back earlier."

"Yes, Hal, I was detained - again."

I threw myself off Bayard's back. "I'm very weary." Cedric my groom with a cheeky grin, came and took the horse from me.

Hal scratched his long forked grey beard which he wore in imitation of his Viking forefathers. "Well they do say that brain work is 'arder than physical, don't they?"

"Do they...? Well, today I have had a surfeit of both."

I plodded up the steps. "What's for supper? I've had no dinner?"

"Ah, you'll have to ask the Lady Belvoir that, sir," replied Hal.

And talking of the Lady Belvoir, here she was striding down the hall, with a determined expression on her face.

"Aumary, thank Heavens you are back." Her face softened and she reached out for me.

"Ah, just the sort of homecoming I love, Hal," I said jokingly over my shoulder and reached for her hand.

"You won't think so when I tell you this...."

"Oh?"

Her eyes met mine and there was worry in them. "It's Hawise, she has gone missing."

Chapter Five

My heart leapt into my mouth. "Missing?"

I sat down heavily on a bench. "What do you mean, missing?"

"She went out for a ride on Felix her pony with Tostig. Neither of them have been seen anywhere about the nearer forest where she usually rides," said Lydia.

"And they haven't returned, m'lord, when they said they would," said Cedric. "It'll be dark soon."

"You've sent folk out to look?"

"Just after dinner. Hawise should've been back for dinner," answered Lydia. "No sign of them," added Cedric.

"Is John back from work yet? Send him, he'll track them" My chief wood warden, John Brenthall was the best tracker in the village, nay, in the forest.

"He went out a while ago," said Lydia, sitting beside me.

"Well... he'll find them," I said with a confidence I didn't feel. "Tostig knows his way around. They won't be lost."

Hal stared at Lydia and Cedric with an open mouth. "Why didn't you come an' tell me? I'da gone out with John to 'elp look." He subsided into mutterings.

"I came looking for you Hal," said Lydia "But I couldn't find you either and time was pressing."

"I was at the Widow Giffard's testin' 'er new ale, mistress. I was... out in 'er back yard."

"A few villagers have gone out with John," added Lydia, speaking to me.

I stood up and stretched. "Right, Hal and I will go out now."

My daughter had been told not to go too far from the village and she never did, unless she was visiting her grandparents. She always had a groom to accompany her and it was always one who knew the forest well. Tostig had been born in the forest and could navigate around. He also knew not to let Hawise stray too far.

In moments, I was back in the saddle and with Hal riding the big grey, Grafton, his favoured mount, we clattered across the chalk path.

Lydia told us that Hawise sometimes liked to ride towards Bedwyn for she would often stop there to see her grandparents who lived at Bedwyn Manor.

So towards Bedwyn we went.

It wasn't long before we met John quartering the ground, with Jonathan Reeve on foot.

They told us where they had been. I suggested we make for the track called Hatchet Lane and thence to Bedwyn.

"She's not at Bedwyn, sir, nor has she been," said John. "I've asked."

"Then we try Chisbury," I said.

There were several small villages dotted about in the forest, simple hamlets really. Chisbury was one of them. This was an old circular earthworks where one of my farm houses was situated. It was only a couple of miles away as the crow flies but the forest paths were circuitous.

We set off calling Hawise's name.

Eventually we were answered.

Hal turned quickly to me and yelled "It's Tostig!"

We turned towards Chisbury Copse and Hal shouted back, "Keep calling, Tostig!"

Eventually we found him, wandering around leading his horse and Hawise's pony.

I dismounted, thunder in my heart but I hid my anger and approached the young man with a smile.

"Well, you led us a merry dance."

"Sorry sir. I've been going round and round for ages, looking for the young Lady Hawise."

Hal offered him a drink from his water bottle. The water in his own was long gone.

"Thanks, but I've been to Bewley pond to water Damsel, so we aren't thirsty," he said.

"Good man."

"What happened Tostig?" I asked.

"We were going towards Bedwyn sir, when suddenly the Lady Hawise's Felix was startled by a deal of shouting and screaming coming from somewhere close by."

"He bolted?"

"Aye, he did. I caught 'em up pretty quickly but... there was no sign of Lady Hawise, sir."

"Just Felix?"

"That pony doesn't run off like that, he doesn't. He's a good lad," said Tostig. "My horse was spooked, sir but I managed to get his feet back on the ground."

"Must 'ave been some shoutin' n' screamin' then," said Hal.

"Aye, it was, Master Hal. Swearin' and cursin' and then a long drawn out squeal as made your blood freeze followed by a frightened whinny of a scream."

"A scream?"

"Like a pig stuck with a knife, sir."

I digested this. "So let's go back to where you last saw Hawise."

"'Twas up by Faggoty Copse, sir. I was on my way home to get more folk."

"Then let us ride for Faggoty copse. John, lead the way." It was getting quite dark now.

*****

Faggoty copse was a dense woodland of oak and ash, holly and birch. We dismounted and leading the horses, continued to call Hawise's name.

A cock pheasant, disturbed by my foot fall, rose up clacking and whirred over the branches of an ancient oak. A robin sang a winter song somewhere above me and was stilled as we passed.

"Here sir," called John, hunkering down. "I think she came this way." It was getting too gloomy now for tracking carefully.

He stood and frowned. "And so did another horse, sir."

"One of ours I suppose, already been out looking here."

John pursed his lips, "I don't think so. I don't think any have come this far out."

"Right," I said. Fan out and turn up the floor and what's left of the undergrowth...."

"Sir!" called Hal, "Look at this."

I crunched through the dry leaves on the forest floor.

"Blood, sir."

My heart clenched.

The ground here was spotted with blood; drips of it had collected on leaves and the branches of a spreading holly.

We fanned out.

Jonathan Reeve found the source of the blood at last; a horse, wild eyed and trembling, had become enmeshed in the bushes of the under-storey.

Tostig came up and took the dangling and tangled reins. "There now girl... you're all right now. We got you."

Hal came up behind him and looked round. "No sign of the rider?"

"Yes, there is, Hal" said John from a little further on. "Here."

Several yards away from the little brown rouncey was a body. A man, or what had been a man, for his face was smashed to pulp. Scratches and bruises disfigured him; his limbs were broken and twisted awry, his left leg was almost pulled from the socket; his clothes were torn and tattered; ripped by briars and brambles; sharp holly leaves and broken branches.

I leaned over the body. "Not long dead." The horses' saddle and back was coated in blood. So was this man.

Something made me fill my lungs with air and shout "Hawise" as loud as I was able.

A weak answering cry came from somewhere up ahead.

I blundered through the crispy brush, "Hawise?"

There was a rustling and shaking of a large holly tree to my left. Two dingy white hosed legs, one quite torn, appeared from the lowest branch.

"Ouch!"

My daughter dropped down in front of me and staggered.

"Oh Dada!" cried Hawise "I am so glad to see you." Then she burst into tears.

*****

We slung the body on its rouncey. We found that the horse had bled from a wound to its flank. Someone had taken a knife to it and slashed a line, not deep but long across its sleek brown coat. It had other wounds too, scratches where it had bolted along the forest floor. It limped along slowly. Edward stopped it, lifted and looked at the left leg.

"Aw poor girl. She's hurt a muscle in her upper leg I think. Tostig or Rich will be able to doctor it."

We walked on slowly.

Hawise was up before me on Bayard, nodding. "I'll ride on ahead and take the Lady Hawise home. I'll see you there."

I made for the road to Bedwyn and thence to Durley.

Lydia came clucking down the manor steps when she saw Hawise and Felice, Hawise's devoted nurse, shrieked and followed her down. Together they got the child up to the solar.

I would follow once I had settled the horse in the stable and the dead man in our mortuary.

The body was laid out and something about him was familiar.

He was a large man with broad shoulders. Short cropped brown hair, almost shaved, was just visible under what was left of a light coif. His clothes were dull but serviceable, or they had been for they were tattered and ripped and some parts were entirely missing. No doubt we should find the pieces if we quartered the ground along his passage through the forest floor.

At last, I went to the stable and watched Tostig doctor the poor rouncey.

"Sir," Tostig led me to the right flank of the horse. "We know this brand, don't we sir?"

"Aye Tostig, we do."

"I found it when I took off the saddle cloth."

The horse bore the royal brand of Marlborough castle.

"A horse from the castle? Hmm. What's she doing in my forest?"

Tostig said. "Someone passing through on a borrowed horse? A messenger? One of their grooms?"

I tossed my head up. "I can't say, Tostig, but I'll think on it. I don't think the man is a messenger, for they usually wear livery. Do your best for the poor horse."

"I will sir," he said.

I took the solar steps two at a time and quietly went through the door. Five or six steps brought me to the door of Hawise's sleeping place.

Lydia was with her, speaking quietly, but when Hawise saw me, she took her hand from the capturing linen sheets of her bed and stretched it out to me.

I smiled. "Now my girl. Tell me what you were doing up a tree. Why did you leave Tostig?"

Hawise struggled up and I could see a few bruises on her cheek and some scratches.

Her stepmother arranged the pillows for her.

"Felix heard a noise and he bolted."

"Yes, Tostig said he'd heard it too. He had a hard job keeping hold of his own horse. By the time he'd managed it, you were gone."

"I...," Hawise looked away. "Tell him I'm sorry."

"He's only happy you were found in one piece."

"I shouldn't have run away but I was following the horse you see."

"Start from the beginning sweeting," I said sitting on the edge of Hawise's bed.

Hawise sniffed, "Well, the first thing was the noise."

"Tostig says it was a scream."

"Yes, it was. A horrible scream. Felix bolted and I fell off a little way into the ferns and bracken. Then I heard a thundering of hooves. It wasn't Felix, he'd gone galloping on ahead. It was another horse. A brown one. Not Tostig's."

"We found this horse. Yes."

"She was so frightened, I could see her eyes. She didn't have a rider on her back but when she'd gone past me, I could see that he was still attached to the stirrup."

"Ah, that's what happened."

"I ran after them thinking I could catch her and stop the man from being hurt."

"That was very brave."

Hawise smiled. "No, I didn't think to be brave, I just ran." She wriggled up a little more in her bed.

"Then the horse stopped and I had gone quite a way ahead and I couldn't see Tostig or Felix."

"What did you do then?"

"I wasn't really *lost...*," she said, her chin jutting. "Just a bit lost."

"Hmm."

"I went carefully up to the horse. She was shivering and her eyes were awful. Her nose was quivering and her ears were flat. Tostig once told me this is a sign a horse is scared, dada."

"Yes, he's right."

"So I tried to get near but she kept backing away and she pulled the man who was caught by the stirrup, with her. In the end I didn't have enough time to do anything because I heard another person coming through the bushes and bracken. I was scared then."

"And you jumped up the holly tree?"

"Well, it was the only one that had any leaves to hide me," said Hawise. "It was really hard to climb and prickly and I hurt my hands."

She stretched them out to me. I caught one and looked at the scratches and punctures.

"But there was a bit where there were leaves that weren't so spiny."

"Yes, further up the tree?" The holly leaves further up the tree are younger and are not likely to be grazed by animals and so do not bear so many spines.

"So I climbed and hid."

"And what did you see?"

She turned her head away. "I could see the man with the horse. He was all mashed up and his leg was broken and his neck funny... so... so... I thought...."

Lydia moved to the head of the bed and took Hawise around the shoulder.

"You thought he was dead?" she asked.

"Yes." Hawise swallowed, "I did. So I stayed quiet while this other man came up...."

"On a horse?"

"Leading his horse. And he laughed. He laughed horribly. He cut the man's stirrup and left him there then he slapped the poor horse on the bottom and off it went again a few yards and he turned and went. I stayed in case he came back."

"My brave girl. That is just what I would have done."

She smiled, "It is?"

"Yes, indeed."

I stood up. "Get some rest now, Hawise. Felice will stay with you. We shall leave the door open.

"Can Hal come and see me, dada?"

I smiled, "Of course he can. And you can tell him your exciting tale."

My man at arms and my daughter were as close as uncle and niece, a relationship I encouraged, for they loved each other dearly.

"He will think you are brave too."

Hawise beamed.

*****

Hal stood up as I reached the floor of the hall.

"Hawise will tell you her own story Hal. She'd like to see you. Go on up."

Hal grinned. "All ended 'appily then?"

"Not for the poor fellow in the mortuary."

"Ah no. Not for 'im."

"Do you recognise him?"

" 'Ard to do that sir with all the damage and the bashin' and the swellin', but no, I don't."

"I think he is one of the blacksmiths at the castle, a man called Beecroft."

"A castle farrier, sir?"

"Yes. Now why would someone want to lure such a man into the forest and set his horse bolting?"

Hal screwed up his lips. "Beats me, sir," he said.

*****

Very early the next morning I sent a messenger to Johannes in Marlborough. We had a body for him to look at. However Johannes was away from home and was not expected back until the following day, Friday.

I had Old Joan take off the fellow's clothes. I searched through them but found nothing.

However, Joan did draw my attention to the knife wound the man had sustained low in the belly.

"Wouldn't kill him outright, sir," said Joan, who had seen more knife wounds in her long life than I'd tasted Matthew's pies, "but he would die of it eventually. Always do."

"But the fall from the horse killed him I think. Let's wait and see what Dr Johannes thinks," I said, escorting her from the mortuary.

Johannes came to Durley on the Saturday. The doctor did indeed think the man had broken his neck for the head was floppy and could be turned at a most unnatural angle. It reminded me of the forest owls and their strange ability to turn their heads.

"Wounds sustained before death. Dislocation of the leg at the hip; fracture of the ribs, many scratches and bruises, poor man. His neck was broken and the left femur cracked as well. The bone is protruding through the skin. He was dragged some way I think."

"And the knife wound?"

"To the lower guts. Inch wide blade thrust straight in and up."

Our assailant was placed lower than our dead man, then?"

"He was. The man was probably on his horse, the other was on foot, came up and sliced him."

"The castle man fell off but his foot caught in the stirrup: he broke his leg. The horse was then sent on its way with a vicious knife jab to the flank but the rest of the injuries killed him."

"The broken neck killed him."

"Was this meant to look like an accident, Johannes?"

The doctor shrugged. "I suppose it might, to anyone who didn't examine the body properly."

"Hmmm." I put my hand to my head. "Now I suppose we must inform the coroner."

We exited the mortuary.

"Hawise was there you know. She saw it all."

"I hope the killer didn't see her."

"She had the forethought to climb a tree and stay quiet."

"That's my girl! Is she all right?"

"As far as we can tell, yes," I said.

"Oh dear, this is becoming a habit," said Johannes with a serious expression, "Hawise finding bodies."

My daughter had discovered a murdered man, packed into the ice bound water of our little river, two Twelfth Nights ago. This finding had worried her: so much so that she'd had nightmares but she had seemed fine this morning after her latest ordeal.

"Can she identify the killer, do you think?" asked Johannes as we crossed the courtyard.

"She saw him quite clearly but didn't know him. Who knows where he comes from. A medium man with no beard, a red face and brown hair with a dark supertunic. Not a lot to go on. She thought he was a bit ugly," I chuckled.

Johannes joined my chuckle. "Did I hear you say that our murdered man is one of the castle blacksmiths?"

"Yes, even in that state I recognised him. His name is Beecroft. Are you riding back to town? I'll ride with you if so, for I want to ask around at the castle, see what manner of man he was."

"Aye, I am. It's market day yet again... I get so many patients on market days. I swear they save up their ailments all week and only crawl out of bed for market days."

We rode together to Marlborough side by side through the winter forest, chatting about this and that and comparing this winter to the winter of 1205 which locked up the land for a whole four months into late March.

We parted at the top of the High Street and I negotiated the market stalls beginning to be laid out higgle-piggle along the road. Here could be found everything from caged birds to birds for supper, from hogs to hams, hides to hairpins.

I waved at a few people I knew.

At last, after much dodging about, I reached the castle gate and clattered into the bailey. An ostler came to take my horse.

"Bates, might your master be somewhere about? I'd like a word."

"Aye sir... he's just up there talking to Master Gayle." He pointed behind me to the western wall walk.

I turned about and made for the wall steps taking them two at a time.

Gayle was just about to finish his business with the master of horse but I delayed him with a "Ho! Pete, good morning!"

"Good morning, M'lord Belvoir" he answered. "You know Master Chevalier of course."

"Indeed I do, and it was with him I wanted a word... no, don't go Peterkin, you may be able to help."

We moved a few paces closer to the wall. I leaned on the parapet.

Master Chevalier bowed. "How can I be of help, sir?"

"The blacksmith Beecroft. He didn't turn up for work this morning, did he?"

"No sir. He should have been here just after dawn when the castle gates were opened and he didn't come."

"Is he ill, Aumary?" asked Gayle.

"Aye he is. Ill unto death Pete, for he was found last evening mangled by a fall from his horse and a dragging across my forest floor. I have him in my mortuary at Durley."

Both men crossed themselves.

"His horse, you say?" asked Chevalier with surprise.

"Aye, one of the rounceys you keep here for general work around and about and for the royal couriers to change mounts. I have her in my stables. When she is fit, I'll get one of my grooms to bring her back."

The man nodded absently. Then he said, "Dead you say?"

"Aye, his neck broken but he had been stabbed first - so this is murder."

"No!" said the two men together.

Chevalier said "Why would anyone want to murder him?"

"When did you last see him, Chevalier?"

The man's eyes wandered around a little as he thought. "Just before noon I think. Here in the stable."

"What manner of man was he?"

"Lively, popular, never ever had any money...spent it soon as he got it. Good joker, liked a game or two of merrels. Bit of a fool really."

"He was out in the forest at dinner time, so after the fifth or sixth hour."

"With one of the castle rounceys?"

"Aye. She has the castle brand on her flank."

"What was he doing in the forest? Had he a need to go there?" asked Gayle

I turned to the master of horse with a raised and inquiring eyebrow.

"No, none that I can think of," he said.

"He wasn't missed at work?"

"I would need to ask the men. I wasn't here all day yesterday as I was out at the Manton grange discussing fodder with...."

"It would not be difficult for Beecroft to take a horse out of the castle ward, would it?"

"No sir, he would just say to the gate guards that he was going out with it. They know him. He need not give a reason but it is customary to say something."

"I'll speak to...who was on duty at dinner time yesterday, Pete?"

"Our new man FitzAlan and his crew."

We had at last been able to replace one of the officers of the guard who had been found wanting earlier in my career as a crime solver. As a consequence poor Andrew Merriman had been performing double shifts for so long it was getting difficult and dangerous and so we needed another man to share the job with him. At my request, one of de Neville, the castellan's, men had been promoted into the post. I'd heard good things of this young man and was happy that he had at last arrived.

Sir Maurice FitzAlan was a rangy man in his late twenties with a small moustache and a close cropped beard like my own. However he was as fair as I was dark.

He had alert blue eyes and an intelligent face which was one of those able to hide his true thoughts and feelings. I took his arm and welcomed him to our castle. He thanked me for speaking up for him.

"So in your first week here, we have a murderer to discover. Aren't you the lucky one?" I joked.

Sir Maurice FitzAlan smiled, "I'd heard you were constable now of both castle and county."

"Well, my small bit of it. I have too much to do to be going all the way down to the south of it. But the King knows that and is happy with his appointment."

"I hear you have quite a reputation now, Sir Aumary, for solving riddles."

"Let's hope I can solve the latest, Maurice, and you may be able to help."

"Ask your questions, m'lord."

"Yesterday an ostler took out a horse from the stables and went outside the castle. The man's name was Beecroft. Now, I know you won't have got your memory fixed yet for everyone in the castle... it takes me all my time... do you remember him?"

FitzAlan called to his soldier in the gate house.

"Beecroft, Bunce, did he go out yesterday with a beast?"

The guard was chewing on a piece of black bread.

"Yesterday about the hour past noon, took out ol' Dorling saying she was to go to the town farrier sir, 'cos ours were too busy to see to her 'oof."

I nodded. "Thank you."

" 'Corse I thought it a bit odd he had her saddled but.." he shrugged, "thinks I, maybe he don't wanna walk. And… then...," he scratched his head. "Since when 'ave the farriers 'ere bin too busy to…?"

"Anyone else go out then?"

Bunce thought a moment. "No, sir. Everyone was present and correct," and he stuffed the rest of the bread into his face.

"Except the courier, sir," he added with a full mouth.

"I turned back. "Courier?"

"Aye sir, them that have fancy clothes and bags with sewing on. Messengers they are aren't they?"

"Yes, heralds. One went out yesterday?"

"Several, sir... all day long," answered Bunce. "On and off."

"Ah."

"They comes in, they goes out. Never usually here long."

I smiled. "No, I know what couriers are like, Bunce," I said.

"They got burrs on their bums they 'ave. Can't sit down for long," he chuckled.

"Never a truer word," I answered.

"Feet on fire," continued Bunce. "One went out after Beecroft did."

The couriers were the royal messengers and took government documents all over the realm. Proclamations, legal papers, letters from the King to his subjects and his government left behind here in England. I'd had a few of these myself and had been party to the opening of many of them.

"Well, thank you anyway."

I wandered back on foot through the market day crowds.

So Beecroft had a castle rouncey. Where had the other man obtained his horse? Did he own it?

An inquiry at the bottom end of Herd Street, where lay the only livery stable in town, gave me the news that no man answering Hawise's description had been seen hiring a horse and going in the direction of the forest on Thursday, nor had any stabled their horse there.

On my way back, I dropped in at Simon Smith's, one of the farriers in town, and the first smith you would come to, if you'd walked from the castle. No, Beecroft had taken him no horse to shoe on the day in question. The other farrier was out by the wagon yard. I would check that one on my way home. Perhaps the second man did own a horse.

Damn. I was fast running out of options.

When that happened there was only one place to go. Gilbert Cordwainer's.

Gilbert was in his yard when I called and the apprentice Felix led me out the back.

"Ho Gilbert!"

Master Cordwainer was sitting on the doorstep of one of his store rooms looking at pieces of hide.

"M'lord Belvoir. Welcome."

He struggled to his feet and plodded along to me. "Drop of the red, sir?" he asked.

"Do you know, Gil," I said, "I think I fancy some of Mistress Brewster's good ale if you have any?"

"Fresh this morning sir, it being market day."

We went up to his parlour and I stood for a while looking out of the window at the marketplace, on the High Street below.

"I suppose you've heard about Beecroft being found in the forest?"

"Aye, that I have. What was he doing there, then?" said Gilbert as he filled a horn cup with ale.

"I have no idea."

"I didn't know him, seen him 'a corse, but Grace knows his older sister, who he lived with. She dwells out the top of Kingsbury Hill. Grace says the man was no trouble at all, a bit of a prankster, worked hard, liked fishing in the Kennet, where allowed. No one can imagine why he's been singled out for murder, sir."

"The same as Elswith? Why her?"

"Yes, I suppose so."

We lapsed into a solemn silence for a moment.

I came from the window to sit down. "I must bring you up to date, Gilbert," and I told him about the dog, the pack and how Elswith's body had been moved by barrow.

He shivered. "You mean to say that the killer was sitting in the cottage with the body whilst poor William was working outside? As cool as a cat with cream."

"Looks like it. I can't see how else it was done unless he had time to move it immediately, but then, the barrow wasn't available to him at that point, was it? And Elswith's body would not have stiffened in a sitting position."

"William must have come back when he was still there. Thing is - why move it at all? Why not leave it in Will's cott and be off down the hill and into the forest like a fleeing fly?" said Gil.

I looked at Gilbert. "I've been puzzling that one. Either to divert suspicion from William or to incriminate his neighbour Dunstan Weard."

"But...," Gilbert shook his brown curls. "It didn't work, did it? And anyway, you murder a man's beloved wife and then you say, 'sorry, didn't want you to suffer for it.' Don't seem right to me."

"No... nor me." I drank some ale. It was sweet and light. As it went down I remembered one of my previous conundrums, where a head had been found in a barrel of ale.

You remember it Paul, don't you? Particularly nasty vicious murderer. Blame was to be cast onto someone else there, though the whole scheme turned upside down when the head was found, didn't it? Was this the sort of thing that we had here?

"So... our blacksmith, why might he be a threat to someone?" I asked Gilbert. "So that he must be killed?"

"It really wasn't an accident?"

"No, it was meant to look like one but there was a stab wound to the belly before the man fell from his horse."

"Hmmm... Revenge?" offered Gilbert.

"Something he knew which might have hurt our murderer?" I said.

"Greed... something he was party to and the killer didn't want to share?"

"One or both of those."

"You don't think that it's connected to Elswith's death, do you?" asked Gilbert.

"No, I don't think so. Well, maybe. They didn't know each other, did they?"

"Not as far as I know."

"And they weren't related?"

"You'll have to ask Grace for that sort of thing... she knows all the ins and outs of Marlbury families."

Gilbert tipped back on his stool.

"Grace!" he shouted and his wife came in with floury hands through the door of the room at the back."

She bobbed a perfunctory curtsey. "Oh, Sir Aumary, I didn't know it was you, I wouldn't have started the bread had I known."

I smiled. "Not to worry Grace, Gil has been looking after me." I tipped her my ale cup.

"The Lord Belvoir wants to know if there's any gossip around town about the murder of Beecroft the blacksmith."

She wiped her hands on her coarse linen apron and sat down.

"Gossip?"

"Amongst the women maybe?"

Grace pursed her lips and shook her head. "No, not that I know, poor man."

"Aye, he did suffer I'm afraid, before he died," I said, "He wasn't a pretty sight."

"Oh Lord!" exclaimed Grace. "Was the poor man murdered? I thought he fell from a horse. That's what's being said, sir."

"He was stabbed first, Grace."

She crossed herself. "Your forest is a dangerous place, sir."

I smiled and sipped my ale. "Were Elswith and he related in any way, do you know? I'm trying to piece all the facts together. Trying to see if there's a connection between the two murders."

"No, not Beecroft, he wasn't related, but Thomas Ash, the wheelwright, he's married to his second sister... Eva Beecroft as was."

"Ah, that's interesting," I said, "Maybe I'll have a word with him."

"And Elswith's cousin is a moneyer and works at the castle."

"Yes, I know that, though they don't get about much so they don't know too many folk," I said.

"Surely he'd know the blacksmiths and farriers," said Grace, "Being as they all work with metal".

"Perhaps. He's a very wealthy man. Does he consider himself above the ordinary?"

'Not as far as I know," said Gilbert.

"Anyway why, sir, do you want to know all this?" asked Grace.

"I can't see a connection and I want as much information about the people involved as I can. But you know what it's like..."

"Are your famous thumbs pricking, sir?" asked Gilbert.

"Aye, Gil, they are."

"Well, you have to go with the pricking of your thumbs sir," he replied. "Don't you?"

I laughed. He'd got that from Hal of Potterne.

*****

On my way home I stopped at the top of Crooks Lane and dashed into the wheelwright's.

I found the man hammering the metal of a wheel rim. This must be for some wealthy man, for most wheels for carts were solid wood and consequently cheaper.

"Ah, Master Ash. I have a question for you. The blacksmith Beecroft, how well did you know him."

Ash put down his hammer slowly.

"I know... knew him. He is... was my brother-in-law."

"Know why anyone would want to murder him?"

"But I thought he fell from...."

"After he'd been stuck with a knife, Ash."

"Mary and Jesu...," he crossed himself. "No, no, I don't."

He wiped his brow with a cloth. I noticed he was sweating even in the chilliness of the day.

"We didn't always see eye to eye, I know, but..."

"Why's that?"

"Well, he was a joker, a fool. Life could never be serious with him. Everything was a joke. Try to have a serious conversation and you'd end up wanting to strangle...."

"I tipped my head to one side. "Yes, Ash?"

He stuttered then, "Irritating, he was damn irritating, but you don't kill someone because they're irritating, do you?"

"So, he wasn't serious enough for you?"

"He was not a Godly fellow. Mocked holy mother church and all it stands for. Always joking, always carping," said Ash with some venom behind the words, "Poking fun, imitating folks."

"Did he imitate you?"

"Not to my face, he didn't," said Ash taking up the wooden hammer again. He gave the rim a mighty thwack.

"So you aren't all that sad that your brother-in-law is no longer with us?"

"Not really, though Eva is very sad. My wife sir. His little sister. She loved him. Can't say why, he was a waste of...."

"And his elder sister, at the top of Kingsbury hill? She will miss him, for they lived together."

The wheelwright roared with laughter at that. "Miss him?" he roared again. "She'll miss him like a belly full 'o' stones!"

"Why's that?"

"No love lost there," he said. "He supped on her as good as a suckling pig does its dam."

"He didn't pay his way?"

He shook his head, "Like I say, when his wife left him...."

"Ah, that's it, is it?"

"Aye, got out with the two children. Off with a tinker from Malmesbury they said. He went to live with her, his sister, and he used her like a skivvy."

"And her name is...?"

"Widow, sir, Mistress Scarlett, Milly, Milisende Scarlett. Her man was a dyer."

*****

Before I went home, I stopped off at the second blacksmith in the town. This one was used by folk at the eastern end and by people travelling down or up the hill from out of town and either using the Salisbury or the London roads. It was furthest from the castle at the top of the Wagon Yard.

Master Farrier lifted his round head from the horse's flank upon which he was working. "Don't get no work from the castle. They got their own smiths. Don't need me, sir."

"And if they're too busy, the castle farriers, I mean?"

"Never too busy. There are eight of them. Works day and into the night if they have to. Like the coin men. I know that 'cos my boy Alfred is one of them."

"A moneyer?"

"No, a castle farrier," he said as if I was simple. "They keeps up with the works there."

"Thank you," I said as I mounted Bayard again.

So no help there. Beecroft had definitely intended to go into the forest on a saddled castle rouncey. He had not thought he was going to his death.

Whom was he going to meet and why?

Chapter Six

I reached home just on dinner time and when the repast was over I locked myself in my office and scribbled.

I had not written a list of suspects since one of the first murders I'd investigated, that of Father Swithun, my village priest here at Durley, some three years ago.

But a list I did write.

William Larkworthy, shepherd, husband of the deceased.

Dunstan Weard, shepherd, neighbour of the deceased.

Osmund Hart, acquaintance, forester, fellow church goer and flitch contestant.

Thomas Ash, wheelwright and fellow flitch contestant. Unknown to the deceased.

Edwig Crosscastle, cousin to the deceased and fellow flitch contestant.

I added the other two contestants in the flitch competition, whom Hal had questioned. A man from Elcott who was a fuller and another from St. Martin's, in the northern part of Marlborough, a worker at the goldsmiths. Both had stone hard alibis.

Beecroft, blacksmith, dead.

Master Ash, wheelwright, related.

He was our link to Elswith - but the only one.

The words swam in front of my eyes. What possible motive could any man have for killing Elswith and the blacksmith Beecroft? Or, were they two completely separate crimes?

I saw Hawise skipping out in a corner of the manor yard and decided to try once more and see if there was anything else she could tell me. Enough time had elapsed, I thought, for her to feel a little less worried by her ordeal.

I took myself down to the yard and between Felice and I, we turned the rope a few times so that Hawise could jump.

Then I sent Felice off to the solar and Hawise and I wandered over to the stables.

We looked in on Fitzroy, my beautiful Arab stallion who had been a gift from a grateful father for the solving of the murder of his son.

"You say this other man, the one who laughed, was leading a horse, Hawise?" I asked, tying my daughter's hair in a blue band which had worked loose.

"Yes. It was just like the one that got hurt."

"A rouncey. Like Tansy there and Coro?" I pointed to two of our own service horses. They were stocky brown beasts used for servants and workmen and as beasts of burden in the forest and were not as finely bred as my other horses.

"It had a star on its head."

"What else can you remember?"

"About the horse?"

"Anything."

"It had a mark on it."

"No, that was the horse that got hurt, Hawise," I said.

"This one did too. It looked like a...." She screwed up her face, "Like a ball with a house on top. It was on its bottom." She giggled.

Yes, that was the castle brand. A hill with a tower on top. So, two castle rounceys were out that day.

"Did the man who laughed say anything at all?"

"He called the dead one a...." She looked over her shoulder to make sure no one was listening. "Bastard," she whispered. "And he kicked him... hard. Even though he was dead."

"Could you hear the voice... how did he sound?"

"Like he was cross."

"Hmm. Was his voice... deep... like this...." I imitated the man in a bass voice, " 'Bastard', or was it higher, like this 'bastard?'" I asked in a tenor voice.

Hawise giggled and fell about laughing.

"He was lower than you, dada," she said.

So a man with a deep voice.

"And you said he was ugly."

"Well, I didn't see his face very much, I only really saw his hood 'cause I was up high. But he had a big nose."

"What colour was his hood?" I asked.

"Oooh, brown," said Hawise. She sounded unsure.

We started to walk back to the hall.

She added, "When the horse with the man had gone, he said, 'No more jokes...' or it sounded like it,".

"Ah... yes, the dead man was a bit of a fool. Used to play jokes."

"Aw that's sad, dada," said Hawise. "It's good to make people laugh."

Her head came up and she said. "Hal makes me laugh!" and she skipped off to be with my senior man at arms as he came down the hall steps.

I turned back to the stable to find Tostig gently massaging the castle rouncey's forearm.

"How is she doing?"

"Well, sir. That was a nasty rent in her hide but we managed to close it up. Good as gold she is."

"She seems a placid beast," I said. "Tostig, do you know any of the castle ostlers or blacksmiths?"

"No sir, I speak to the occasional one when we go there together but no, not really, just to hand over our beasts and chat about the weather or exchange information about horses."

"Any of them...," I fingered my ear lobe. "Perhaps accepting bribes or not doing their jobs properly, turning a blind eye maybe, do you think?"

"How do you mean, sir?"

"The Lady Hawise has just confirmed that the man who killed the blacksmith also had a castle rouncey. How did two horses legitimately get past the guards eh?"

Tostig's brow furrowed. "Aye, I see what you mean. Want me to make inquiries?"

"Come with me next time I go to the castle. Get in amongst them. Ask about. We want to know who got the horse ready, or let them be got ready and who took the second one out. We know Beecroft had one... who had the other?"

"Aye sir... I can try that."

I slapped him on the back. "Ah, Tostig,"I said turning back. "How long till your nuptials now?"

My groom beamed. "Five days sir...Wednesday next."

Tostig and a woman from Wootton were to be married soon and Alysoun Dexter was to come to live in a newly refurbished house in Durley.

"I'll be there my good man!" I laughed.

*****

I went back to Marlborough the next day, taking Tostig and Hal with me.

I sent Hal up to the Widow Scarlett to ask about her impecunious brother and his fooling. Tostig went to the castle stable and I went to talk to William in his prison cell.

As usual the dapper Peterkin Gayle let me in.

"Will, how are you?"

He rose slowly and nodded. "Good morning, m'lord. I am..." he looked over the room in which he sat, "Well, sir."

"I hope to have you out soon."

"That is good news, my lord. Does this mean, dare I ask, that you have found the man who killed my Elswith?"

"I am on my way to it, Will," I said. "I just want to ask you a few questions now we are...ahem...a little further on from the dreadful day." I smiled reassuringly. "Do you know if Elswith knew a man called Beecroft, a blacksmith from the castle?"

"I don't believe she had ever been here, sir. I hadn't until...."

"No, of course."

"Why, sir... is he the man who might have ...?"

"No, he is dead himself, William. Killed in Savernake."

William sat with a bump on the stone bench. "Dead? By the same hand?"

"Ah, now that I don't know. You didn't know the man?"

"Not at all. I have no cause to come to the castle. You know that sir. If I need to come to town I will always ask you, my lord and Master Steward, and the only time I came recently was to enrol in the flitch contest."

"See anyone that day?"

"I saw Master Cordwainer. He waved. I saw Master Fletschier, the arrrowsmith on the High Street. We spoke about the weather and then I went into the town mill where I made my mark on the book to enter the contest."

"Ah yes... kept by Master Bullard, the town reeve's scribe."

"Just so, sir."

"The other contestants?"

"Most had already declared, sir. We were almost the last, I believe," he said sadly.

"Hmm. You do not know the wheelwright Ash, you say."

"No sir, nor did Elswith."

"He is the brother-in-law of the murdered man."

"Ah I see... do you think that the two deaths are connected, sir?"

I laughed. "I have not the slightest bit of evidence to say that they are but... truthfully I don't know, Will…. It's a coincidence and I don't like coincidences." I sat by him on the bench. "I am sure they are in some way related. But how?"

I saw William raise his eyes to the whitewashed barrel roof. "Do you know, sir, I have been puzzling and puzzling, with nothing else to do, why Elswith should have been killed? And why she should be in Floro's house."

"Aye that puzzles me too," I said. "The man Dunstan. I'll ask you again, Will. You and Dunstan get on all right?"

"Aye, we are neighbours. No harsh words between us. He's a good man to know, sir. A steady man. A friend."

"You say you cannot understand why he would lie about hearing you arguing with Elswith. You say you did not. Might Dunstan be mistaken? You set off early to the chalk pit. What if he heard another man in the cottage, arguing with your wife?"

William Larkworthy looked at me as if I was mad. "Another man?"

"It was still quite dark. Off you go as the sun is just coming up. Your wife readies her pack and calls up your dog. A man comes in...."

"One she knows sir, for Beval would allow no stranger into the house."

"Oh yes, it would have to be one she knows. They talk... loud enough for Dunstan to hear. Elswith is killed. The man takes the pack and the dog...."

"No, no, sir," interrupted Will, "It won't do. Beval would have defended his mistress with his life, I'm sure."

"Ah yes, you're right." I caught at my lip.

"So somehow they all leave the cottage and go down the hill. Do you think this person might have said, 'I'll take your pack into town to the weavers?'"

"He might, sir. But I can't think who."

"We still have the problem of the dog." I rubbed my cropped beard. "Ah well... it's close I think. By the way we found Beval and he is alright."

"That is good news. I'll think on it for you, sir. I have nothing else to do," said Will with a weak smile.

Hal came back into the castle office first.

He had a taste in clothes as bright as a May day. He readjusted his red tunic, tightened his green leather belt and gave me his report.

"Woman about forty, 'elpful sort. 'As a loom and weaves at 'ome, works for Master Flacsman. 'Er brother was, as the others say, always short o' money. Lived with 'er two years. She 'ardly ever saw a penny, sir. 'Er being the soft sort wouldn't turn 'im out. Apart from that, 'e was a good soul."

I sat back on my chair.

"She showed me the room he slept in, sir."

"Did she, by Jove?"

"Untidy. Nothin' much there. Did find a coupl'a silver pennies. Good coin of John's realm. Not new ones like they make at the mint but good all the same."

"Where were they?"

"Lyin' on the table with some other stuff. Bits' o string an' some round wooden blocks with holes in. 'Ee had what looked like a fishin' net too, propped up in the corner."

"Hmm."

"The widow were weepin' a bit but I think she'll fare better without 'im," said Hal. "I think he tried her sorely, sir, sorely, 'e did. She'll rent the room out soon."

"They tell me he was a bit of a joker. Know what these jokes amounted to Hal?" I asked.

Hal smirked. "Just the usual stuff a lad does to his sisters, sir."

"Now I know you had sisters and you know I didn't, so tell me, what might he do?"

"Oh burrs in 'er clothes, 'iding 'er shoes and so she 'as to go out in the yard to find 'em... and imitatin' folks voices so she thinks it's a neighbour at the door and it 'int. And...," Hal chuckled, "Lettin' next door's cockerel get into her 'ens. Devil of a job gettin' 'im out, I 'eard. Oh yeah, and callin' 'er ol' dog to 'eel when she 'int asked it, in her own voice."

"Thanks Hal. Well done...." I said, then I stopped. "Say that again, Hal... about the dog."

" 'Ee was such a good mimic see, 'e could call 'er old dog, a mangy looking brown thing, to 'im in this Mistress Scarlett's voice an' it'd come runnin'." Hal chuckled.

I looked at the rafters, "Thank you Lord!"

"Whasat?"

"Hal, we have just found a connection between the man Beecroft and Elswith Larkworthy."

"We 'ave?"

Hal's face grew puzzled. "No sir... you'll 'ave to tell me." Then I saw light dawn in his expression. "Ah... yes... so we jolly well 'ave. Well, I'll be buried in Burbage!"

*****

I sent Hal home, saying that Tostig and I would follow. I had a mind to visit Johannes at the top of town before we left Marlborough but I might send Tostig on sooner. I might be invited to dinner at the doctor's house. I often was.

I waited for Tostig to appear. He came scratching at the door a while after Hal left.

"Ah Tostig. Was that like getting a drink out of Hal of Potterne?"

These two had a friendly rivalry and a joke or two about one or the other always went down well.

"Aye sir," chuckled my groom, "They were all interested of course in Fitzroy, but I still had a devil of a time getting anything out of them. They're a suspicious, close lipped lot."

Today I'd purposefully ridden my beautiful stallion Fitzroy, who was bred for horse racing, to the castle.

"What did you learn?"

"That Beecroft hung about quite a bit around the castle moat. Sitting there and dangling his feet in the water in the summer months, staring into space, in the times they were slack and were taking breaks."

"No harm in that, Tostig. I heard he liked fishing. The moat is full of fish..I've seen them myself."

"Aye, sir. Also that he was quite a joker...."

"That we know, Tostig and we have now discovered it was his liking for jokes which put him in the way of Elswith and William Larkworthy's dog."

Tostig frowned. I would tell him more later.

"He worked mainly with shoeing the rounceys...."

"What a surprise."

"Yes."

"I questioned them about betting and the racing crowd, like you asked. Well, it was easy with Fitz being with me. They went a bit quiet then. Almost as if they thought they'd say too much. One man did say that Beecroft was often seen at the Green Man, the new ale house in town, with the racing crowd, but he was always on the fringes. Had no special friends amongst them."

"Friends here at the castle?"

"Only the lads at the stables, and a couple of the soldiers."

"As one might expect... one socialises, as do you at home, with those we work with and with whom we live in proximity."

"No one said anything about the rounceys; just that a man was responsible for them. No one would care if they were sent out. People just came to this man and asked for a horse."

"Right. Go on home and will you tell the Lady Belvoir I will be home later as I shall stop at Dr Johannes before I leave the town, Tostig?"

"Yessir."

He turned back.

"I'll probably think of something else they said later, I'm sure I'll remember more of their gossip. Oh yes sir, one of Beecroft's friends was called Luke. They seemed to find that funny. They sniggered as they told me."

"Hmm.Think on it then, as you go home."

"Aye, I will, sir."

*****

As I said, I stopped at Johannes' house and ate a bit of bread and smoked ham with the doctor and his housekeeper, Little Agnes. I brought Johannes up to date with all the news.

"So if you can prove that there's a connection between the blacksmith and Elswith's dog, William must go free for he cannot have murdered Beecroft."

"I can prove that the dog was lured away and tied."

"By Beecroft."

"Yes. I don't know for, or with whom he was 'working'."

"The man who killed him."

"Might the man who killed Elswith and Beecroft, not have Larkworthy in his sights?"

"That would depend on why they, or particularly Elswith, was killed."

"I think for the time being William is safer where he is."

I'd stayed longer than I'd wanted at Johannes'. I'd have to clip along if I was to reach Durley before the dark came in. It was after all only the end of January. Day length was short.

I made my goodbyes and rode down the winding track to the bridge, through Oxford Street.

It was growing colder. I stopped by the bridge and shrugged on my woollen supertunic. Then Fitzroy and I set off up the hill on the Salisbury road.

Just past the upward hill at Cadley, Fitzroy shied and stopped.

"Whoa boy... what's the matter?" I looked around but could see nothing untoward. I tried to make the horse go on but he stood his ground and whinnied. I loosened the knife in its scabbard at my hip.

Fitz whinnied again.

There was an answering call; another horse close by.

"Come then... you take me...." I turned the horse and let go of the reins. Fitz tossed his head a couple of times and made for the side of the road. Not long ago I'd had the sides cleared of vegetation for masterless men could ambush merchants or those about their legitimate business on the road and I'd continued the practice so there was nowhere to hide here. Fitz plunged into the dead bracken and fern further in.

I slid from the saddle. A few yards in, hidden by the great bole of the Big Bellied oak, was a horse. Fitz went up to her and nuzzled her ear. He was particularly fond of this horse and they were stabled close together at Durley. Athena was a fine boned grey, no Arab but a pretty horse and Tostig had been riding her home.

I called out then – quickly, "Tostig!"

Fitz lifted his head and forced himself through the undergrowth. I followed hollering for all I was worth.

Tostig was a good rider. There was no way on earth that Athena would have thrown him.

I reached the place where Fitz nuzzled the ground.

There lay Tostig, an arrow in his back.

*****

He'd been dragged off the road and the horse pulled away and encouraged to stand in the forest trees. Fitz was particularly used to Tostig and was nuzzling him as if to try to get him to stand up.

I bent over the man. He moaned.

"Praise God, you live."

I gritted my teeth and I took out my knife and broke the arrow a way down the shaft, not an easy task. The man wore his Belvoir gambeson and it had saved him from too much damage. I lifted the semi-conscious Tostig to Fitz, roped Athena to Fitz' saddle and mounted behind him. Thank Heavens he was a small man. I had to avoid the stub of the arrow and it was hard-going to navigate but Fitz seemed to know what to do.

I turned once more to the road and carefully plodded back to Marlborough and Doctor Johannes' house.

*****

"He lives still?" was the first thing I asked as Johannes lifted Tostig from the back of Fitz. I heard Tostig groan again so was reassured that he did.

We got him into the house and up the ground floor passage into Johannes' work room, where there was a large table upon which to lie patients. Little Agnes followed us with a candle.

We gently lifted Tostig to the table and Agnes went to light more candles and fetch a lamp.

Johannes rolled up his sleeves.

"I am glad that your men wear their gambesons when they are out in the forest, Aumary, many a life has been saved by these padded garments."

"I insist on it when we are travelling though obviously, the foresters don't wear them when working. They are warmer too in winter."

I sat down wearily. "I shall not get home now. Poor Lydia, she will be worried."

Johannes cut the woollen gambeson from Tostig's back and the shirt underneath it.

"Tsk... this is a very lucky young man. I think we shall be able to save him."

"You better had Johannes, he is getting married in a few days' time," I said.

Johannes dug out the arrow. I have never helped anyone do anything like that but I gritted my teeth and prayed that Tostig would not feel the probing and cutting. He didn't for Johannes had given him some dwale and he fell into a sleep so deep, nothing could rouse him. It seemed the fall from his horse had driven the barbed bodkin arrow further in and poor Tostig had probably struck his head too upon hitting the ground. Johannes was expert in making the soporific which he used to keep his patients asleep. Many people, I know, had been killed by ingesting a fatal dose. We spoke of the recipe as we worked upon Tostig.

At last, we washed our hands once more, for Johannes was adamant that everything had to be clean when working on his patients and we moved Tostig to the bed in the corner of the workroom.

Little Agnes sat with him whilst we went for something to eat and a rest by the kitchen fire. I stood and warmed my hands.

"So now you can tell me why someone was trying to kill your groom," said Johannes after a long draught of ale and a contented sigh.

"He was at the castle this morning asking questions of the ostlers, farriers and blacksmiths about the death of Beecroft and the rouncey which was found in the forest."

"What did he learn that someone didn't want him to know or didn't want him to report?"

I scratched my head and yawned. "He told me all he knew and there was nothing there worth killing him for. I think the man who killed Elswith and

Beecroft is panicking now."

"Hmm. And you still have no motive for either death?"

I told Johannes that I had managed to connect Elswith's dog with Beecroft's ability to mimic voices and so the murders were likely to have been perpetrated by the same man.

"Well, that is progress I suppose. William is definitely vindicated now."

"Yes, yes he is and we know that it's someone in the castle."

"Ah, but do we?"

"What do you mean?" I asked, rubbing my tired eyes.

"Just that people are coming and going all the time through the castle. Tradesmen of Marlborough, couriers, wives of the men who work there, masons and other town artisans, even me. I have been called once or twice when the castle doctor has needed help or he isn't there."

"Ah, I see what you mean. It could still be anyone in the town." I sat down with a bump on the nearest stool. "And it's a man who can draw a bow and has access to one."

"Hmm. The wheelwright, has he reason to be at the castle? The butcher, the baker, the chandler, the fletcher?" All of them maybe have a reason to be there."

"Without a motive for the killing I am half way up a birch tree, aren't I, Johannes?"

The doctor pursed his lips and shook his head.

"Why, why, why was Elswith Larkworthy killed? When you know that, then you'll have a motive."

I sat with Tostig until the darkest part of the night when Johannes relieved me and I curled up in my cloak and slept till past dawn.

That morning, I was not much refreshed as I splashed my face with cold water and rubbed my teeth with salt. I managed to tease out the tangles in my hair. My clothes were crumpled and I smoothed out the creases as best I could. Then I swung my winter cloak over it all and shrugged it tightly round me for a walk down the High to the castle. Tostig slept on peacefully in the corner. Johannes told me he would wake soon and then he would look at the wound again.

I opened the door of the workroom.

"Wait!" said my brain. I looked down at my cloak, wrapped as it was, around my other clothes. Who would know what I had on underneath? My boots were visible poking out of the bottom of my cloak, my hood worn over my gambeson was up against the biting east wind which had now settled in to blow down the High Street.

I turned to Johannes. "Getting out of the castle as a courier is not such a difficult thing Johannes," I said, as I came back into the room.

"All you need is a pannier with the royal cipher on it and there are plenty of those lying around at the castle. Wrapped as I am now, perhaps with a hood on, anyone could play at being a courier, demand a horse and be off out of the gate. The only thing someone would be sure of is that couriers carry bags with the royal cipher on. Couriers come and go all the time."

"Aye, it would be easy. Harder in better weather when their livery would be visible."

"I think that is how our killer got the rouncey from the castle."

Now I walked down to that castle and entered the warm fug of the stable. I sought out Master Chevalier and took him aside.

I explained that I thought that a rouncey had been taken by someone posing as a courier and asked for him to find out, if he was able, who it was who had saddled up the horse and led him out to the supposed member of the royal staff. I wanted a word with them.

"I'll make inquiries sir. Someone will have taken on the job and complained about the task I've no doubt."

"Good man."

I came out of the stables and made for the office close by the gatehouse when Hal of Potterne clattered through the gate.

He saw me at once and rode up to me, dismounting and giving Grafton to an ostler.

"I bin sent, m'lord."

"I have no doubt you have, Hal."

"To find out why you and Tostig haven't been 'ome like you should'a bin."

"Lady Belvoir sent you I suppose?"

"She were right worried what with all that's bin goin' on in the forest."

I took hold of Hal's arm and led him to my office. "I was half way home, Hal, when…I found Tostig in the scrub, wounded by an arrow." I closed the door.

Hals' eyes narrowed. "Wounded, you say?"

"Aye."

"That means, praise be, that 'e still lives."

"He's at Johannes' house. The doctor took the arrow from him," I said.

"The doctor got the arrer?"

"He has the head and shaft, I have the fletching in my pannier. It's a standard castle arrow."

"Or one of Master Fletschier's?"

"It will tell us nothing Hal, almost everyone who uses a bow legally around here, has his arrows in this town, if they don't make them themselves"

"Aye we have some don't we, in our Durley armoury?"

I kept some weapons at the manor under lock and key in case of trouble in the countryside or the forest. Master Fletschier made our arrows.

"Damn...!" I thought.

"I know. It would have been lucky for us if the arrow used had been a special one made by the person who loosed it. And it was known to folk."

"So what did Tostig tell you that was so important that 'e 'ad to be killed for it?"

"That's the question Johannes asked me. I don't know. Nothing he was able to impart before he went on his way was important enough to close his mouth forever. He did say that there was more but that he would think on it and tell me when we got home, which of course neither of us did."

"What do you want me to do, sir?"

I sat at de Neville's table and thought, rubbing my face with my hands and knuckling my tired eyes.

"I'd say go and talk to the shepherding folk again but it's apparent that the person who has killed Elswith, Beecroft and made an attempt on Tostig Frithson's life is able to ride a horse. None of the shepherds, as far as I know, are able to do that."

"No sir, they 'ave no need do they?"

"I don't think that Master Ash has a need either for he has a cart and a draught pony, too small for him to ride. Master Crosscastle has no need either. He is a townsman and lives so close to the castle, he walks everywhere he needs. He's a wealthy man but I doubt he has a need to ride or keeps a horse."

"So we are looking for a man who can ride and who can draw a bow."

"Looks like it."

"And we have no suspects now, do we?" asked Hal with a blank face.

"Just a man, as Hawise said, a medium sized man with no beard, a red face and brown hair, wearing a dark green cloak, with a large nose and a deep voice."

"Fit 'alf the fellas in Marlborough that would," laughed Hal.

"Aye, it would."

"So, again sir, what do you want me to do?"

"Go home Hal, and tell the Lady Belvoir the news and I suppose you'll have to tell poor Alysoun that Tostig is sore hurt and won't be able to marry her on Wednesday. Can you let Father Crispin know too. He was to perform the ceremony which will now not take place. If Alysoun wants to come back, can you bring her? She can't ride either."

"Alysoun is at John's 'ouse in't she, not at 'er own 'ome in Wooton."

"Yes, she is staying with Agnes for the time being."

"Poor girl. This is twice in a few months she's had a scare over Tostig...what with 'im being bashed on the 'ead a while back."

Poor Tostig has been brained with a branch last autumn in the forest and he almost lost his life by being tipped into a bog.

"Anything else I might do?"

"Yes, Hal, on the way home you can go to Gilbert's and tell him the news. See if he can throw any light onto anything. He knows things he doesn't know he knows." I chuckled.

"Right you are sir," said Hal with a smile.

*****

Castle business claimed me for the rest of the forenoon. There had been some sort of trouble with the building works. The master mason came and told me that the old block wall at the southwestern edge of the castle was collapsing and we must shore it up before the whole lot came tumbling down. Well, some of it was a hundred years old and showing its age. It was due to be rebuilt anyway.

I gave permission for the wall to be looked at and the masons to send a team up there to work out if the wall walk could still be used by the soldiers patrolling the outer limits of the castle bailey. I'd been up there with Gayle and Chevalier the other day. It looked fine to me but I wasn't a mason. They would know what to look for.

Master Chevalier came to me a little while later saying that he'd found the man who had made the rouncey ready for the couriers. He remembered one of them being muffled up tight against the cold of the day.

"Good. Send him to me."

"Ah sir...," Chevalier said rubbing his nose. "He won't come. He's too afraid, he says."

"Afraid of what?"

"Well, Beecroft has already been sent to meet his maker. He's afraid that if he's seen speaking to you, he'll be dispatched too."

"So he can tell me something important can he?"

"He looked mightily afraid to me when he heard that you wanted to know who'd taken Beecroft's job."

"Tell him we can't be overheard here."

"No sir, he won't come."

"Then make him. Tell him his job will be forfeit if..." I stopped. I sighed. "No. Don't. I will meet him when and where he wants. Where he thinks he'll be safe."

"I'll let him know. His name is Carrier sir, John Carrier."

*****

John Carrier wanted to meet me when it was going dark up on the wall walk, where I that day, had sent the masons to check the stonework.

I felt a little nervous I must admit, but as I said, I'd been up there in the past few days and it seemed sturdy enough to me. I'd leaned, for Heaven's sake, on the parapet and wasn't sent tumbling down into the moat. Masons were naturally cautious men. They had to be. They were at risk from so much in their job.

The sun was going down when I climbed the steps at the back of the stables. I walked along the wall walk for a while. No one was walking up here with a lit flare which the guards often carried on their perambulations. I always kept a candle stub in my scrip and thought, if it was going to get darker before our business was done, I would need to fish it out and light it.

One of the soldiers came racing up the stairs behind me. "Sorry sir. Come to light your way with a flare," and he lifted the rush light above him. Instantly a rusty, yellow glow pervaded the walls. I looked back.

"It's all right Hardcastle, I'll be fine." I did not want another man to drive away the nervous Carrier.

"You can go." I took the light from him and he disappeared into the gloom.

The corners where the wall turned were still in darkness and I remember my friend Andrew Merriman, one of the officers at the castle, telling me how dark it was in the middle of the night here when he made his patrol.

I carefully leaned out and watched the last rays of the sun dip over the horizon along the downs to Avebury and beyond to Devizes.

I waited. It grew darker.

The lights in the bailey flickered as the guards walked to and fro finishing their tasks.

I heard someone calling out and laughing down in the castle yard and another clattering over the wooden bridge to the road to town. Doors banged, horses snorted, children laughed somewhere in a house across the moat. The gates of the castle banged shut and I heard the bar going into place.Then all was silent. Into this I heard the church bell of St. Mary tolling for vespers, followed by our own chapel here; and then St. Peter. It went quiet again and I stood and mused a little.

The flapping of a heron on the river bank brought me back to life and I turned to face into the castle yard. I heard footsteps running up the bailey stair at the back of the stable, the way I'd come up to the wall walk.

Softly spoken I said, "Carrier?"

"Here, sir."

I could make out a shape just beyond the end of the wall walk.

"Come closer, then we needn't shout," I said.

Into my view came a man of small stature, with curly hair which sat like a mop on a round head. His legs were short and bowed. I'd seen him about the castle.

Cautiously the man came closer.

"Come on man, I'm not going to leap on you."

He moved just two paces nearer. "What have you to tell me about the man who took the rouncey from you last week, the one you made ready after Beecroft went out of the bailey?"

"He weren't no courier," he said.

"How do you know that?"

"He didn't have the livery."

"You saw his clothes? Then why did you allow him the horse?"

"Not my job to tell people they can't have horses. Only my job to get 'em ready."

I sighed. "So did you know this man?"

"Aye, I did."

"One of your fellow grooms?"

"No, he ain't no 'orse man."

I saw this was going to be a difficult conversation so I decided to play for time and let the man give his information in his own way.

I turned away from him and folded my arms once more carefully on the stones of the parapet.

"Tell me what you know," I said, looking out into the dark.

"He's a dangerous man. He's been a soldier. I can't be seen talking. That's why I wanted to come up here, now, in the dark. I di'n't know what he was about when I give him the horse but I know he knew Beecroft and I know now what he did to him. I don't mind saying I don't wanna end up the same way."

"You tell me his name and I will make it my job to see that you are protected from him."

"Not sure you can do that, sir."

"I can have him brought in for questioning and..."

"He's a lyin' toad. There ain't nothing to connect him with the stable. You'd soon have to let him go. He's a slippery fish and as sharp as a pike."

"Perhaps I'll be the judge of that, Carrier," I said.

The man dithered, moving from foot to foot.

"If I tell you sir, can you put me in the gaol and keep him out o' there and don't let him near?"

"Why ever would you want to be locked up in the gaol, man?"

"He can't get me in there. It's safe. Master Gayle's got the key."

"If you tell me his name I'll have him under lock and key in a trice, man, there'll be no need to lock you up."

"Promise!" he shouted and then looked down into the bailey in case anyone had heard him.

I shook my head and looked him up and down, what I could see of him, for he'd moved a little further away and was just visible now in the light of the flare I carried.

I turned back to stare out over the wall. Carrier was really terrified of this man.

"All right... as long as you feel it's needed for your safety, you can stay in the gaol. Now what's his name?"

I heard a rustling sound and an 'oomph' and looked back to where the man had been standing. Two figures now grappled on the wall walk.

I heard a scream and what sounded like the word, 'look.'

I threw away the flare; it only hampered me; and I grabbed my knife from my hip and made for the grappling pair, along the wall walk.

They'd backed into the darkest corner now, where the wall turned and marched round the bailey close by the keep mound. There was a double moat here. One to the outside of the keep and one which travelled around the bailey wall and was traversed by a wooden bridge.

I heard a grating sound and a scream, and then a dull thwack as a body hit the ground at the base of the wall. Then running footsteps went down the stairs.

My man Carrier had gone over the parapet.

I followed the other man carefully down the steps shouting "Harrow harrow!"

This was supposed to bring people to my aid but it was a while before anyone could locate me. Then Sir Andrew Merriman came tumbling out of the gatehouse. I could just see him below, by the light of his lantern, looking up at the site of my cry. It was so dark, it was impossible to see clearly. Few people were about and some came out to look with their supper in their hands.

"Felon off the wall walk, Andrew, now down in the bailey by the stables."

I saw him lift his arm in acknowledgement.

"Sir Aumary, is it you?"

"Yes. Head him off, he's making for the east wall. He's armed. Knife." I'd seen this flash in the flare light as he'd made to stab the poor unfortunate Carrier.

"Pincer, Aumary. I've got the right."

"I've the left."

The gate guards came out of the recess and joined us. Two stable hands finishing their tasks for the day and bedding down ready for sleep in the stable came running into the bailey and I saw them stare up to the northern end where the keep was situated.

"Felon, catch him as he comes across the open yard."

"Aye sir," they yelled.

My eyes had their night sight now I'd come away from the flares held by some of the soldiers and I could see two men had been talking quietly at the base of the mint wall. Now they turned in my direction.

"Gayle! Felon off the western wall walk!" I saw him release his sword and he and the other man came forward into the lightest part of the bailey.

"With you, m'lord Belvoir."

Another man joined them from the shadows of the forge wall. I could see he had been carrying a tray of food from the kitchen. He put it on the step of Gayle's office.

I came down the final steps at a dangerous run.

When we all met in the middle of the bailey there was no sign of our man. He'd simply melted away.

"Where did he go?" shouted Gayle in frustration.

"Thought I saw someone going up the keep steps, sir," said the man who had been taking the tray from the kitchen to Gayle's office.

I looked up towards the keep. All was in darkness up there, except for the flares carried by soldiers on the walk which ran around the eaves of the roof. Four soldiers were positioned there at all times. When questioned later that evening, they had seen nothing.

"Andrew, rouse some of the garrison. We shall corner him there. Oh, and send someone to recover the body of Carrier - it will be somewhere outside the northwest corner."

I ran to the bridge and waited. He could not escape now, unless he swam the moat.

I'd had experience of this before and so I sent some soldiers out of the main gate round to the northernmost moat to make sure no one exited there. Then I began a systematic search of the keep.

There was no one there.

Chapter Seven

It was going to be a long night.

I spent some of it in the office and some trying to sleep in the guest house of the castle.

Carrier's horrified face, reflected in the torch I'd held as the knife entered his back and he was tipped over the parapet, kept looming up at me as I dozed. I just could not get there quick enough. I followed the villain as nimbly as I could but again was just not fleet enough to waylay him. I hadn't seen enough of the killer to give a good description. All I could do was reiterate what Hawise had said. A man of middle height in a brown hood. In fact, I had noticed it was a capuchon, one of those garments which go over the head and fall about the shoulders like a small cape. The rest of him was shrouded in darkness. The hood concealed his face.

No one else had seen him except Master Crosscastle, who was about to go home. He had been coming from the kitchen where, as a favour, he had collected some food for Peterkin. The tray of food in his hands, had seen the man, he thought, cross the bridge and go up the steps to the keep, two at a time.

The other man was one of the guards and Peterkin Gayle had been in his office too, working late.

"We have had a deal to do lately, with the King's demands for coin and the new tax being collected, Sir Aumary," said Gayle the next morning, "that Crosscastle told me he has had a greater amount of silver to process and there must always be a guard on hand to accompany it to the treasury, when that is happening. Three of us were still about when we heard you cry harrow."

He sniffed. "Hamelin the guard and I had stepped out for a short while to take the air and Edwig kindly went for some food for us."

I nodded. "I cannot think where our miscreant went but that he is a member of the castle staff and he just blended in with the rest as if he had never left the comfort of the fire inside."

"Save questioning every man in the place, we cannot hope to know who was not with his fellows for supper."

"Who in the castle wears a brown capuchon, Pete?" I asked.

Gayle scratched his head.

"I do, now and again when it's very cold," he chuckled. "Some of the men in the stable I think, but I don't remember the colours."

"I've seen a few of the guards wear them round the castle," I said, "Bunce for one."

"Aye, useful garments they are for the cold weather."

"A forlorn hope then that we'd find the man who wore a brown capuchon and who struck poor Carrier in the back."

Gayle shrugged.

At last I gave up and went to collect Fitz from the stables. I was going home. I stopped at Johannes' house to look in on Tostig. He was awake and though he looked grey, he didn't look as bad as I thought he might. He was more worried about his impending nuptials and the effect the news of his injury might have on Alysoun, than his wound.

"Hal has gone ahead to tell everyone. It will be postponed, that's all. We shall arrange it for another day. I expect he'll bring your beloved back with him soon."

"Yes, sir."

"Tostig," I sat down beside the bed. "I am so sorry that you had to be attacked like this. The second time in a few months... I...."

"Oh no sir. It doesn't matt...."

"It does matter. You aren't a soldier, you are a groom and I have no right to ask you to perform tasks for me that might get you injured or killed."

Tostig laughed then and it pained him. "I might be kicked by a horse sir, in the course of my work...."

"Aye, well you might. But it seems that the role I've taken on can become dangerous to me and mine. I don't want to be responsible for the death of one of my workers just because some felon I'm chasing takes a bow to him. Many I ask to help me are young men with their lives ahead of them."

Tostig raised himself carefully in the bed.

"Sir, I am honoured to work with you. I think I can say this for all of us who are your men, we are proud of what you do and wouldn't think twice about helping you out." His eyes held mine and in them I saw the truth. "Truly sir, we are your men, use us how you will."

I took his good shoulder. "Rest and mend. I will call in again when I am next in town. It won't be long."

I was almost tearful as I mounted Fitz again and turned his nose for the forest. What amazing loyalty.

As I rode home, I thought about how I had used my foresters and grooms, my men at arms, farm workers and artisans to form a sort of militia of my own, with the King's permission of course. It was, as I'd said, a dangerous occupation being the Constable. Naturally I would like to pay them to put their lives under my instruction and arm them against attack but that wasn't going to be possible. They earned only the wage as a groom or a miller; a blacksmith or a forester. Naturally my tied peasants were not paid but worked land and gained protection from me, but I knew I could not recompense them for their aid as much as I'd like to. I had no doubt this would not be a popular action. Some of my neighbours and folk hereabouts might think that an odd thing to do.

As I was thinking upon it and as Fitz was plodding back to Durley, for I had kept him at a steady but slower pace, half way through the village of Cadley, he shied at a small boy running out in the road in front of him.

"God's teeth boy!" I shouted, "Don't you know not to run out in front of a travelling horse?"

The boy stood stock still. I recognised him. It was Osmund Hart's lad.

I looked round. There was no one else about.

"You were lucky not to be trampled and that's a fact. Fitzroy is a feisty beast!"

"Sorry m'lord," came an answer then. "I didn't think."

"Well, if you are to work with horses, boy, that's the first thing you must learn. To think."

He hung his head then and shuffled his feet.

"What were you doing anyway?"

"Just watchin' "

"What's your name?"

"Aelfnod, sir."

I chuckled, "Well named then," for his name meant bold elf.

"Folk call me Nod, sir."

"Well, Nod. This is Fitzroy and he is a racing stallion." I dismounted and held the reins.

Nod reached up: he could only just manage to touch Fitz' nose. Fitzroy ducked his head. I fished in my pannier and gave the lad an apple to give to him. "Hold it in the flat of your hand and he will take it."

Fearlessly the boy gave Fitz the apple which he crunched with delight.

"He is a really beautiful horse, sir."

"He is beautiful I grant you, and clever too. The horse you saw the other day is called Bayard and he is also clever. More than once he's saved my life."

Nod's eyes grew round and almost started from their sockets. "Saved your life, sir? A horse?"

"I have taught them both tricks, Nod, which allow them to look after me should I be in danger."

"Cor," said Nod, gentling the stallion's nose.

"He's a lot prettier than most of the horses what comes along here."

"He prefers to be called handsome, Nod," I said. "You watch all the horses do you?"

"I sometimes go up to the glassmen and hold horses for folk while they are there."

"Ah, do you. And do folk give you a fee for holding them, Nod?"

"Most of 'em do. There are some old skinflints but most people are kind. I hold the carts too, the ponies what draws them. Sometimes I get a ride in the back of a cart. That means though that I gotta walk back home from wherever they leave me."

"You must be careful of doing that, lad," I said.

"Oh no, I don't go with strangers. Folk what I know. Like Master Thatcher and his pony Gem."

"Yes, I know them," I said, slowly starting Fitz, leading him on the road home again. "Master Thatcher is a good man,"

"And Master Turner up the road and old Godly Ash and his pony Angel."

"The wheelwright?"

"Aye. He delivered a wheel the other day to Master Turner in the village up there. She's a nice pony she is."

"Did he?"

"I held the pony for him whilst he walked out onto the downs."

"Once he'd delivered the wheel?"

"Oh no, it were right early. I was up see, 'cos my sister was coughin' all night and I got up in the dark. I saw Master Ash clatterin' past on his wagon. I jumped up and went with him and held the horse till he came back and then he delivered the wheel and went home."

"And you were with him all the time, except when he walked out onto the downs?"

"Aye, I were. Till I got home again. And he didn't give me nothing. He sometimes gives me a wafer or a bit'o cheese and bannock."

"That was very bad of him."

"Well, he's mean, is Master Ash, and I ain't holdin' for him ever again. He's boring too, cos all he talks about is God and sinning and going to church."

"That's why you call him Godly?"

Nod giggled. "Aye, da does."

"Your father knows him, does he?"

"Only a little bit, m'lord."

"How long was Master Ash away from you, Nod?"

"Aw crikes, sir. I dunno. A while. That's why I was so cross, cos I had to get back and do me chores and he was makin' me late. But I thought, it'll be worth it because I'll get summat, but I di'n't, sir."

"Thank you Nod, you have been very helpful. And here is the coin Master

Ash should have given you. If ever I need a horse holder, I'll come to you."

He watched me ride away until the road dipped and I could no longer be seen.

*****

So, Ash had lied to me. He did know the Harts. He certainly knew Aelfnod and he had said that he didn't know Elswith but if I was a betting man, I'd bet a pound to a penny, he'd met her too.

He had been out on the downs early, left his cart on the Cadley road into the forest and had Aelfnod hold it for him. He was not, as he had said, in bed with his wife of a year and in church.

Which church, I wondered? He was closest to St. Mary's, the elder church in the town. All those at the top end of the High Street would worship there and those at the western end, like Gilbert Cordwainer, would go to the newly built St. Peter's.

A visit then, to St. Mary's and the priest there, Father Torold. Then a word with the errant wheelwright. But first, home.

I met Hal as I ambled through the gate.

"Ah Hal, what did you learn from Gilbert, anything?" I gestured that we might walk up to the hall together as Cedric took Fitz away.

"Aye sir, I did. After the murder of that fella Beecroft, word about town is that 'im and one of the guards were quite pally. Then somehow they fell out and it was black looks from then on."

"I wonder why? Did Gil have any idea?"

"No sir. Except that it might'a bin over money."

"Money... Beecroft never had any it's said."

"He didn't gamble it away did he sir? At the Green Man maybe?"

The Green Man was a relatively new alehouse in town. The only alehouse in town. The man who owned the building had obtained a licence to brew beer every day, instead of the usual now and again as some alewives did. These alewives made the beer and sold it for consumption at home. People would come to their homes when they saw a green branch had been positioned in the eaves of the roof. This told them that a new batch was due that day. They brought pots, jugs, pails and filled their own vessels and went home again.

Master Green, the landlord of the ale house, served beer all day on the premises to those who came and paid to drink it in his own home. It had become the place for the horse racing crowd to collect and conduct business.

"We need to find out about the gambling, Hal, and we need to know who this guard is too. You tackle the Green Man and I'll ask about the guards at the castle."

"Aye... might 'e 'ave bin the man you saw up on the wall walk sir?" asked Hal.

"What business would a friend of Beecroft have with Carrier... unless…?"

"I dunno sir," said Hal, "But the 'ole lot stinks 'igher than a 'erring with 'oles it does!"

*****

I pottered about the manor and the village all the rest of the day and fell into bed that night absolutely exhausted. I didn't even hear my son Simon yelling at the top of his lungs in the middle of the night.

Hal took Alysoun riding pillion to town to see to Tostig. He returned before dark.

The next morning saw me back on Bayard and Hal and I clopping down the hill into town. I met Father Torold coming out of the church after the morning mass.

"Good day to you, Father."

"Ah, Sir Aumary. It's good to see you again. Please don't tell me you have yet another body for me to inter in my churchyard." In the autumn poor Father Torold had to bury, in his cemetery, many victims of a particularly nasty murderer.

"No father. My latest body will lie at St. Peter's."

The priest crossed himself. "Another death? Ah, yes, I heard about the poor unfortunate man who fell from the castle wall."

"The very man, though his fall was helped on a little."

"I hope you are not looking in my direction for the culprit, sir?" he laughed.

I chuckled. "No, sir priest, but one of your flock has lied to me and I need to understand where he was last week when Elswith Larkworthy was being strangled in her house."

Father Torold crossed himself again. "Who is this miscreant?"

"The master wheelwright, Ash."

Father Torold's face was a picture of disbelief.

"No sir, you must be mistaken. He is a most upright Christian, a church reeve, a benefactor of our little church."

I saw Hal fold his arms over his chest and look unconvinced.

"Nevertheless he was seen up on the downs very early, close to the time when Elswith was being strangled. He tells me that he was at home with his wife till dawn and then here at church. Can you confirm the latter, Torold?"

The priest ran his hand over his forehead. "Please let us go and sit down... follow me to my house, sir."

Once seated in his little cottage which was close to the alleyway leading to Johannes' house and to the church of St. Mary.

""Every day, sir, every morning, he comes to church for the first worship of the day. Every night he brings his apprentices to vespers."

"But that day?" asked Hal.

"I will admit he was missing at the morning mass."

"Hmmm."

"But I cannot believe that he was up on the downs killing poor Elswith Larkworthy. Why? What reason does he have?"

"I have no motive for her killing at all, father. I cannot say why anyone would do so."

"He was there the very next morning as usual. I quizzed him why he had been missing the previous day. He was ill, he said, feeling a little poorly and so chose to stay abed."

"He delivered a wheel to the turner in Cadley later in the morning. No, he wasn't ill."

"Ah. Then you must ask him and be happy with his answer. I'm sure there will be a perfectly innocent explanation for his journey."

*****

Johannes and I went down together to the wheelwright's workshop. We met him as he was opening the gate and ushering his apprentices inside. Hal had gone to the Green Man.

"Again, Sir Aumary, you wish to speak to me *again*?" he said, his eyes wide with incredulity.

"Aye, Ash, I do. You have lied to me, sir, and I don't take kindly to being lied to."

Ash threw a quick look at his apprentices. "Go to your places, now!" he shouted. They scurried off without a backward glance.

"I can assure you, my Lord that I...."

"You told me you didn't know the Harts."

Ash sat down on his bench and then bounced up again, realising that he should stay upright in the presence of an officer of the crown.

"No sir... I don't know them," he blustered.

"They know you."

"I may have exchanged a good day with them when I am out and about with my cart delivering but I do not *know* them, sir."

"Ah yes, and you were out delivering a cart wheel the morning that Elswith Larkworthy was killed, were you not?"

"I… I... I cannot recall."

"I'm sure that your books will record, Ash, that you made a wheel for the turner at Cadley and delivered it that morning. If we might just have a look at your records? You do have records don't you? You are, I think, at least a semiliterate man?"

"A record… yes, I have a book."

"Then perhaps we can see it."

Ash stared at me and did not offer to fetch the book. "Shall I ask one of your apprentices, Ash?"

This time the wheelwright sat down with a bump on the stool and stayed down. He groaned.

"Yes, I did deliver a wheel to Cadley."

"And you were out before dawn that day, you were seen as you trundled in your cart to the Cadley road. You left that cart and incidentally the wheel, later destined for the turner, and went out onto the downs on foot. You were not, as you claimed, in bed till after dawn, not at church shortly after. Father Torold missed you, my man."

Ash dropped his head into his hands. "Oh, I shouldn't have done it. I knew I should not have done it."

Johannes and I looked at each other.

"What *did* you do, Ash?" asked Johannes.

I closed the door of the workshop office and perched on the table.

Ash shook his head.

"I went out early, it's true. I went to speak to Elswith Larkworthy."

"So you did know her."

"No, no, I'd never met her before. It was the one and only time I ever met her."

"It was still dark when you turned the cart into the forest and just coming light when you went on foot to the cottage?"

"Aye, it was."

"Why did you go there?"

"I went… I went…." He covered his face with his hands. "My wife, my wife Aeva, I wanted to please her. I wanted her to be recognised as a good wife and a wonderful woman. So I entered us in the Flitch contest. I'm sure you understand m'lord about making your wife happy, especially one as pretty and young as my Aeva, sir."

"Go on Ash," I said.

"Then I realised that we wouldn't stand a chance, when William and Elswith entered. I knew... I just knew that they would win and my Aeva would not be Flitch Queen."

"When did you learn they had entered? They were, I think, one of the last people to put their names down."

"That morning, the day that William came into town and his name was entered in the book. I saw Master Bullard coming up the lane and greeted him and asked him who else had entered the contest. He told me."

"You saw your chance slipping away then, at least for another four years?"

"Aye I did. I didn't know the couple, you understand, but I had heard that they were favourite. Head and shoulders above the rest of us, sir. Master Bulllard knew them and he told me that they would win without doubt."

"You murdered Elswith all because of a damned contest, Ash?" said Johannes quietly. "You didn't think for a heartbeat that you might not win because there were four other couples who might?"

"No, sir, NO! She was alive when I left her. She was alive I tell you! And I know that there were other folk entered but I thought Aeva and I could gather together more witnesses to vouch for us."

I looked towards Johannes, "So you went to talk to Elswith about withdrawing from the contest?"

"I did sir."

"What did you say?"

I told her that my Aeva and me, we hadn't been married but a year and that I worship the ground on which she walks sir, for so I do... yes I do. I wanted my girl to be Flitch Queen for she deserves it...."

"And incidentally you would be Flitch King, eh?" said Johannes. "Of course you didn't think anything about that did you? That fact didn't enter into it." It was clear Johannes felt Ash was a pompous ass.

"No sir. It was for Aeva I did it and Aeva alone." He wetted his lips and went on. "I'd heard that the shepherd's wife was a little reluctant about entering in the first place. I asked her if she would consider backing out. I would make it worth her while. I'd taken some money with me... enough, I thought, to make her think about it."

"But she refused?"

"She didn't refuse, no sir. Not outright. She said that it was her husband's choice too. She could do nothing without him. He too would have to be asked and he was out on the hill. Well, when I heard this, I knew that it was hopeless for I didn't think the man would back down."

"Did you at any time raise your voice? Did you argue with her?"

"I might have got a little warm with her, sir but she was such a mild woman, I felt bad at trying to browbeat her, so I left."

"She didn't argue with you, she didn't raise her voice?"

"No sir, as I say she was a mild, quiet woman. I think it would be something for her to raise her voice to anyone."

"Aye... that's the Elswith I knew," I said sadly.

"It is the truth, sir. I swear it." Again he hid his face in his hands. "Oh, I am so ashamed."

"Where were you last night at dusk, Ash? The truth this time please. First time."

"Dusk sir? Why here. I locked up and my apprentices and I went home. We were in the house the rest of the evening, after a last visit to church and supper, sir."

"Vespers?"

"Aye sir. I always take my apprentices to vespers before we go home."

"Right." I stood up. "You do not ride, do you, Ash?" I asked.

"Ride, sir? No sir." I never learned. I've no need."

"Do you own a bow?"

"A bow? No sir."

I nodded. "As I thought."

We turned, Johannes and I, to leave the workshop's office.

The stern, self-important apprentice master I had seen on the day of my first inquiry was reduced to an almost blubbering mouse of a man.

"You got your wish anyway, Ash," I said, " Elswith was removed from the contest."

"But not by me, sir. Oh no, I would never have harmed the woman."

"I believe you Master wheelwright," I said. "You are still in the running for the title of Flitch King and Queen."

"Thank you, sir," said Master Ash quivering and bowing low. "Thank you."

"Good luck," said Johannes sarcastically as we closed the door.

We walked back to Johannes' house.

"What a pompous, bumptious, conceited man," said the doctor.

"My guess is he is well under the thumb of that wife of his. I do know she is a good many years his junior. A very pretty piece by all accounts. What's the betting this talking to Elswith was her idea and not the wheelwright's?"

Johannes laughed. "That would not surprise me in the least."

*****

"How many guards do you have, Gayle?" I asked when I had found the man responsible for security at the castle.

"Thirty in all, though they aren't all deployed at once of course, Sir Aumary."

"They are on duty in the rest of the castle at other times aren't they?"

"Yes, and some go out with the carts when they take the finished coin wherever the King wills it."

"So there are always two when the coin is deposited in the treasury?"

"Yes, that's right. Sometimes just one if the amount of coin isn't so significant or Edwig needs the forge watched. "

"Might I talk to the ones who were at the forge this week, Pete?"

He gave me a searching look but took hold of his keys and we marched across the bailey to the western wall.

Outside the forge building were two guards. These were the two who had accompanied the silver to the treasury that week. Neither of them admitted to knowing Beecroft well.

It was likewise with the two who had worked for Crosscastle the previous week.

Two others were sought out and came shambling across the bailey.

"Names?"

"This is Henry Pygge and this Roger Canard," said Peterkin Gayle.

Pygge, as his name suggested, was a barrel chested, if not rather portly individual with several chins. He smiled and showed me a mouth full of black teeth. He was well named.

"Sir," he nodded.

Roger Canard was a well-built man in his late thirties, with short cropped black hair and small beard and moustache. I looked him over, "Sir," he said as he looked just over my right shoulder at the far wall.

"I'd like to ask either of you if you knew the blacksmith Beecroft?"

"The fella what got murdered in the forest, sir?" asked Pygge.

"One of the guards of the mint has been seen going about town with him, especially into the Green Man." I invented this for as yet I hadn't seen Hal to confirm it.

"Aw no… twern't me. I don't go there. Ale's like horse piss." His eyes shifted to his companion.

"I have to agree with you there, Pygge," I said. I'd had cause once or twice, to taste the small ale and the stronger stuff and wasn't impressed myself.

"And you, Canard?"

The man folded his arms over his chest. "I knew him. He was a friend… once. What of it, sir?"

"Ah. Pete, might we step away a moment?"

"Certainly. Are you going to your office, sir?"

"Aye, it will be private."

We walked down the long stone wall of the gatehouse and Gayle accompanied us into my office.

I unlocked the room. "Step in please, Canard." I sat on the table edge.

"You admit to knowing Beecroft?"

"Aye sir, there's no denying it. Many will tell you we were friends."

"Were friends, Canard?"

"We been friends for years and then well, he starts cheating me."

"How did he do that?"

"We'd go to the Green Man like you said. We like a spot o' the horse racing up on the downs. We placed money on a few o' them now and again."

"Is this why it's said that Beecroft never had any money? He was poor at choosing his winning horses?"

"Not always. He were a bit of a fonkin when it came to money. It just seemed to trickle away. Mind you, he pissed a lot of it into the gutter of an evening."

"So how did he cheat you?"

"I'd give him the money; when I was working I couldn't always get to the ale house to place the bets so he'd do it and he'd collect the winnings. His smithing job was a bit freer than mine as a soldier."

"And you didn't get your dues?" I asked.

"No sir. He started to keep some back. Oh, he denied it 'a corse, said the odds weren't so favourable but I know what's what and I was always a few pence short."

"Do you know why he might've been keeping some back?"

"Except that he was greedy you mean, sir?"

"Was he having to pay another perhaps?"

"Blackmail you think, sir?"

"It's a possibility."

"I dunno anything about that." The man suddenly looked decidedly shifty. I watched him carefully.

"So you fell out with him."

"I bloodied his nose for him, called him a thief and that were that."

"You didn't go into the forest on a borrowed castle rouncey and deal with him permanently?"

"I was here at my work when Beecroft went out. Ask anyone."

"I shall, Canard." I kept him waiting a little.

"So, you know what time he went out?"

"Common gossip now, sir."

Through the door I heard Hal's voice exchanging a few laughing words with the gate guards.

"Where were you that day?"

"On duty up on the wall walk, sir."

I heard Hal shout for FitzAlan. I moved to stand behind the table.

Canard was sweating and his eyes were all over the room as if he was searching for an escape route.

"You could have got another to take your place. Taken a castle mount, gone out and disposed of your erstwhile friend."

"It wasn't me what done it."

"Do you have any idea who it was and why?"

"Perhaps it were another man he'd swindled."

"Maybe, but right now I have you and you don't look very comfortable to me, Canard."

"I don't know, I tell you. It weren't me. That's all."

"You know that I will ask Master Gayle where you were on that day. If you were missing or weren't where you said you were, it will not go well for you."

"I were outside on the walls doing my job."

"Did you see Beecroft that day, go to the stable or from it?" I asked.

"No, I didn't. I weren't speaking to him or looking at him." The man licked his lips again.

"Did you know this man Carrier, Canard?"

"The fella what fell from the wall? No, I seen him but I di'n't know him well. There's a mortal lot of men work here at the castle. I can't know'em all."

"So you can't tell me why Carrier was killed or what he knew about your friend Beecroft which got him stabbed in the back?"

The man had had enough. He was sweating profusely now and was very agitated. He began… "I don't know… I…," then he turned on his heel, flung open the door behind him and ran at a pace for the open castle gate.

I jumped over the table and pulled myself through the office door. I swung round into the path of a horse clattering under the gatehouse roof. I could see Canard crossing the drawbridge.

I shouted "Harrow… harrow!" as I'd done last evening.

This time FitzAlan came out of the gate guard's room almost opposite me. He shouted into the room at his back. "Out here!"

"Felon exited the castle!" I shouted, "Catch him," moving off into the darkness of the gate.

Hal came running out of the guard room. "Felon sir?"

I pointed. "Aye, Canard - he knows something. STOP HIM!" I yelled.

Hal and I began to run out across the drawbridge.

There was a twang behind me and then a thud. I stopped and looked back. Bunce had a crossbow in his hand. He lowered it.

"Stopped sir," he said and gave me a gap toothed grin.

Hal had almost reached the man Canard, who was writhing and screaming on the roadway. As Hal reached him, he lay suddenly still.

Hal of Potterne looked down, turned the man over, looked up once more and shook his head at me.

"Christ's Bones, Bunce! I said stop him, not kill him," I yelled.

Bunce's grin left his face. "You said he was a felon, sir."

I grabbed a lock of my curly black hair in frustration. "Aye… but catch him and stop him doesn't mean kill him, Bunce!"

"My fault, Sir Aumary," said FitzAlan, coming over the path to me. "Andrew told me last night about the man on the wall walk. When you said 'felon' I imagined it was the same man and that we were about to lose him again. I told Bunce to stop him. Though I had thought he'd aim for the leg." He turned about and glared at the man at arms.

"You know I aint a good shot with these damn things," said Bunce. "Sir," he added pointedly, for good measure, "Give me a proper bow any day."

I rubbed my forehead where a headache was beginning, a legacy of being thumped on the head a year ago by a mad woman in the forest.

"You were too good a shot, Bunce," I said angrily.

Hal came up to my elbow. "Dead sir. Bolt right through."

In 1139 the Pope had banned these weapons but the prohibition was very ineffectual and they were still used at the castle. De Neville thought crossbows worth keeping.

"Aye ... thank you, Hal. Get someone to recover the body and take it to the chapel. Tell Father Columba that he has a soul to save."

"Yessir."

I was very angry but also saddened and frustrated. Now I'd never know what Canard could have told me about Carrier or Beecroft. I suspected he knew who the murderer might be.

I sat in my office and stared at the wall. Hal came back and planted himself in front of me.

"Sir?"

"Yes, Hal?"

"Is this the right time to let you know what I found out at The Green Man?"

I sighed. "No, but I'll hear it all the same. Christ's Bones, every man I speak to about this damned affair ends up dead."

"Nah... sir, only three and you've only spoken to two of 'em!"

Trust Hal to put it all in perspective. "So, what's the news Hal? Sit down for goodness sake." I poured us two mugs of ale.

"I 'spect it was this Canard fella then with Beecroft that were often in the Green Man, sir."

"Yes, he told me that."

Hal looked crestfallen. "Oh... ah... well. They were best of friends until about a month ago."

"He told me that too. He said Beecroft had swindled him out of some money."

"They 'ad a big bust up in the ale'ouse. A fight. Landlord threw them out but they continued fightin' in the road, till they was taken up by the watch."

"Did they go in the lockup?"

"Beecroft did, Canard was locked up at the castle for a bit. Andrew's orders."

"He swore it was not he who killed Beecroft, Hal."

"Master Barbflet fined the blacksmith, cos 'a corse 'e's a townsman."

"Yes, lived on Kingsbury Hill. I remember."

"Master Barbflet fined 'im quite a bit, sir."

"Don't tell me, he had no money, he couldn't pay."

"Oh no sir. Paid up quicker than a drunk pisses up a wall," said Hal. "Strangely."

What's that Paul? Oh yes. Old Hal of Potterne was a most extraordinary man. Very, shall we say, colourful with his language. I still have a titter now and again at some of his sayings. In fact, I find myself using them, so I do.

"Hmm. That's interesting. Gives credence perhaps to the tale that Canard told about Beecroft stealing his winnings."

"Word in the Green Man, sir, is that Beecroft came into quite a bit o' cash, lately."

"More success on the horses than hitherto perhaps."

"Maybe. But word is sir, that 'e'd been bragging about how much 'e was going to get."

"Had he now?"

"More where that came from 'e said."

"Hmmm."

" 'An' I did find them two coins on 'is table in 'is room didn't I?"

"You did, Hal and I think a man like him would not leave them lying around. If he didn't have many pennies, he'd want every chink, as I've heard the folk call it, with him, wouldn't he?"

"So, sir," asked Hal screwing up his face. "Why did 'e leave it lyin' around? Eh?"

Chapter Seven

"I don't know about you Hal, but I could eat a horse!" I said a little while later.

"Ah no, sir," said Hal, "You'd 'ave to be pretty desperate to do that."

I chuckled.

"Nah sir, 'orses are what makes a knight, a knight. He takes more care of 'is 'orse than 'e does his wife, sir."

"What are you saying, Hal of Potterne?" I joked.

Hal guffawed, " 'Orses are worth money, sir. 'Orses are what sets you aside from us common sergeants and foot soldiers. You'd never eat Bayard!"

"It has been known, Hal, for a knight to eat his faithful steed."

"Aye, aye, I know it has." Hal's face grew wistful. I knew very little about the man's early life as a foot soldier and felt it best to keep it that way.

"So what say you we find ourselves something to eat, eh?"

"Shall I go to the kitchen sir, and see what I can get them to sling together?"

"Aye, we are a way past dinner time Hal, it probably will be slung together."

Hal exited the office chuckling into his beard.

I shouted after him, "Hal, if you see Master Gayle, get him to release William Larkworthy; he is totally innocent for it could not have been he who murdered Carrier."

"Right you are, sir," came Hal's voice from the castle bailey.

I searched the room for two clean cups, a jug of wine and a new flagon of ale. Fresh ale had been delivered that morning to the office, as it was every day. De Neville had stocks of Burgundy and Bordeaux in the castle cellars specifically for his use and had told me to avail myself of them when I was working. Someone had topped up the jug and placed a soft cloth over it. I poured myself a measure and Hal, a cup of ale. Hal wasn't really a wine drinker.

My man at arms returned in a short while.

"Well, that was 'andy," he said, opening the door with his elbow and pushing backwards through it, "A fella was just coming with our dinner and I met 'im outside the kitchen. They said they knew we hadn't had anything, so 'ere it is."

On the tray, under a cloth there was fresh bread and a stew of some kind, nice and hot. On a separate dish was some goats' cheese and some dried fruit.

"Aw no... said Hal as he uncovered it all. "Not goats'. I can't eat goats'."

"Oh yes, that's right, brings you out in a rash, doesn't it?" I remembered him telling me this when we were offered goats' cheese by the monks of Avebury Priory.

"Ah well... more for me." I broke off a piece of the white crumbly cheese and smeared it on the bread.

Hal attacked the stew with gusto.

We did justice to the stew, though I had only a little of that; I let Hal have most of it for I could eat the goats' cheese and was partial to it. This one was sharp and crumbly. I left half for later.

As we ate, we mused on the people involved in this series of murders.

"Ah, but sir," said Hal, waving his spoon at me. "We 'ave quite a few people who 'ave no alibi or at the very least, questionable ones."

"You mean like wives vouching for husbands and people being alone on the hills with the sheep?"

"And men walking about town and men going up on the downs and not seeing no one, nor bein' seen."

"Not to mention our murderous horseman standing below Hawise's holly tree and my man on the wall walk." I bit into the bread and cheese.

"Folk have been under our noses, sir, but we just 'aven't seen'em well enough."

"Then this afternoon, we must go about and ask a few more questions. The stables, the forge, the shepherds, Beecroft's sister again. "

"What do you reckon that guard skewered this morning was involved in then, Sir Aumary?"

"He became very nervous when I asked about Beecroft and Carrier. He bolted when I asked about the death of Carrier."

"But he's a guard, sir. Sometimes works for the forge."

"He was simply a guard, Hal; he has no contact with the actual coins nor the metal involved in making it. Nor the treasure contained in the lockup."

"Do we know that's true, sir?"

"True Hal? Well, as I see it, the treasury is tied up tighter than a miser's purse. Gayle does his job very well. No one can smuggle anything out. He's wise to all the tricks. There are soldiers everywhere and too many of them to bribe or suborn. Only Gayle and his trusted men get into the treasury building."

Hal shifted on his seat, "Sir... erm, I know that you are friendly with Master Gayle but... are we absolutely sure that 'e is completely trustworthy?"

"Gayle has been in charge of security at the treasury since he came to the castle. There has never been a whisper of anything improper about him. He came from the King's own household."

"Ah, no sir, I suppose not."

"If he was stealing money, someone would have noticed by now, or he would have been off long ago - suddenly a rich man - fled abroad somewhere."

"No, you're right. 'E takes 'is job very seriously don't 'e?"

"He does, and he has hand-picked the guards who guard the treasury and who accompany the minted coins there. Maybe we'll have another word with him about the guard Canard though. Why did he run away?"

"Why did Bunce kill'im, sir?"

"It seemed at the time as if it was an accident. You and I watched it happen. A case of mistaking Canard for the felon who killed Carrier. A moment to make a decision."

"We don't know for certain it was the wrong one, sir," said Hal.

"No, he might indeed have been the man who killed Beecroft and Carrier. I doubt it, his build was not that of the man I saw on the wall walk that night."

"Hmmm. But if he was killed to keep 'im quiet... like the rest, then..."

"Bunce is our murderer. Yes, Hal, I had thought of that."

"Shall we 'ave a word with 'im then?"

"Another one on the list, Hal."

"And yet another one sir...."

"Yes?"

"Sir Maurice FitzAlan?"

"FitzAlan? You mean he was the one to give the order to shoot?"

"Well, I didn't actually hear 'im say, 'shoot'im down,' did you, sir?"

I thought back to the moment. It was all over with so quickly.

"No, I don't think he did, Hal. Mind you, you were running out of the gate, I followed you. We might not have heard everything FitzAlan said to Bunce."

"And if he said shoot 'im, well, we didn't hear."

"No, you're right."

I swilled down the last of my half cheese with a swig of the Bordeaux.

"So this afternoon, let us start with Bunce."

*****

"I think I told you di'n't I, my Lord Belvoir? I just followed me order. "Stop 'im," you shouted and I stopped 'im."

"Did FitzAlan ask you to shoot?"

Bunce took off his arming coif and scratched his head. "Now I ain't sure about that and I don't wanna put no blame on no one. I shot 'im and for that I'm sorry. I'll do some big penance for it no doubt, when Father Columba gets to know. I didn't mean to kill'im, just like you said - stop him - but these gert machines are a devil to control in a hurry and me aim wasn't as good as it mighta' bin had I had a bow. I'd a got'im in the arm with a bow I would."

"It's done now Bunce, but next time, please don't be so ready to act without asking first."

"Asking sir, is the difference, if you don't mind me sayin', between a man being killed and me being killed. Ain't that right Hal?"

Hal looked a bit discomforted. "I see what you're sayin' Ol' Bunce. Sometimes you just gotta act. You move first and ask questions after."

"That's the nub of it, Hal. I knew you'd understand."

I sighed. "Next time Bunce, wait for an order."

The man turned from me grumbling, "I 'ad an order, stop 'im, and I stopped 'im"

Hal looked at me and shrugged. "It's a tough one, sir."

"I know, it's often kill or be killed but in this case, the man hadn't even drawn a weapon."

Hal's face puckered and his lips became a fine line. "But 'e 'ad a sword and a knife sir. 'E mighta used 'em."

"He was running away man. He'd no intention of fighting."

"Ah but sir, if I'd caught 'im - 'e'd a fought then, I'll be bound."

I cleared my throat. I wasn't going to win.

"So in conclusion we can say that Bunce may have killed him purposefully, knowing he'd been in with us and spilling whatever he knew, or it might have been nothing but an accident."

"All we can say at the moment," said Hal.

We passed on to the stables. We got nothing further from the ostlers and stable lads. A couple of the men there said that they knew that Beecroft had been boasting about having more money; just the news Hal had heard at the Green Man.

We left the stables and headed for Gayle's room. He was sitting at his desk and rose when he saw me.

"Sir Aumary. Back again. I hope you haven't come to take another of my guards away to execute."

"No, Peterkin. I'm truly sorry about that. It wasn't my intention to have him killed. He bolted from the office in some distress. I asked that someone catch him and the message was... misinterpreted. I...."

"If he ran then there must have been something to run for," said Gayle, the usual smile missing from his jovial face. "What do you think he was trying to avoid?"

"A question about Carrier."

"The man who was stabbed and fell from the wall?"

"The same. It seemed to me that he knew who had done it... I can't be sure, mind, but he might have been going to tell me and suddenly thought better of it."

"Canard worked for us for five years with never a murmur of trouble," said Gayle. "He worked both outside the treasury room and accompanying the coins which Master Crosscastle makes."

"Are the soldiers who accompany the minted coins paid for the job, Pete?"

"They are," said Gayle, lifting his chin. "Two of them walk with Master Crosscastle from the forge to the treasury when money is deposited."

I ran my finger along the inside of the collar of my shirt; my, it was hot in here.

"Do the men vary, day to day?"

"Yes, it depends who Master Crosscastle calls upon that day," answered Gayle. "Are you alright, Sir Aumary, you have gone very pink?"

I staggered forward. "I do feel very odd. I'll just sit a moment."

A terrible griping pain attacked me in the guts. I doubled over.

I was feeling very dizzy and hot. I saw Hal look at me strangely and the next I knew, I had pitched forward and I saw the floor coming up to meet me.

*****

The next few hours were the strangest I think I have ever experienced. They tell me I went down like a mined castle tower.

I don't remember. What I do remember were the very odd dreams I had.

See Paul, I can remember them to this day. Forty years later. But I shan't bore you with them.

I don't remember them getting me to a chair. They say I became delirious quickly and started to fight them. I remember some monsters trying to grab me and hug me to death. I suppose that was Hal and Pete getting hold of me and putting me into the seat.

Apparently, they told me afterwards, Hal yelled for one of the lads who were always about in the bailey to fetch Johannes. The doctor came running quickly from his house at the other end of the High Street.

It was decided not to move me too far but to get me to Pete's room where he had a bed.

It was next door to the castellan's office and so not far away. Nevertheless, I fought them every inch of the way; these monsters who were trying to help me. Johannes didn't want to give me anything to calm me for he was unsure of the problem and didn't want to mask any symptoms.

I was sick. I was fevered. I was cold. When lucid my vision was impaired; I saw everything doubled and wavering. I babbled. I garbled. Then at last, I fell into a sleep and Johannes feared that my heart was failing.

It was only a little while or so later when, after much consultation with Hal, Johannes came up with the answer. Some sort of poison had been mixed in with the food I'd eaten or the wine I'd drunk.

Hal ran next door for the remainder of the cheese and the dregs of the wine.

It could not have been anything but the cheese or the wine because Hal was unharmed. He had not eaten either. Johannes sniffed it.

"I can't do anything here. I shall have to take it back to my workroom and ask Gabriel Gallipot to help me," he'd said, "And I'm loath to leave Aumary in case his situation worsens."

Hal convinced him in the end that it would be best to try and find out what it was that I'd ingested, so that he might know what the poison was and then I could be treated accordingly.

Before Johannes left he fed me salt water and I vomited some more but it was not enough.

Hal and Pete, waited with me, they told me, for some time, whilst I writhed in agony and raved about huge trees with legs wrapping their branches like arms around my middle and squeezing.

Johannes had come in a little while later, breathless and agitated.

In his hand he'd had a bottle which he'd tipped down my throat. By the middle of the night, I had lapsed into a torpor with a fever so hot, I ran with sweat and shivered with cold by turns.

As I grew calmer, Johannes fed me yet another potion. This one, he'd said, was to protect, the stomach from the long term effects of the poison. He described it to me later as charcoal and something called tannic acid which is made from oak bark. I like to think that the trees of my forest saved my life that night.

Gradually I returned to something near normal and dropped into a better form of sleep.

The next day, very early, in the dark and before too many folk were up and about, they lifted me carefully onto a cart bed and drove me the length of the High Street to Johannes' house. There he could observe me more closely, for there was a possibility of the poison resurfacing and harming me again.

Hal set off for Durley to inform Lydia. He'd no doubt she'd return with him as soon as she could.

I remember waking some time the next day with the most terrible pain in my guts. I know, to my shame, I'd voided my bowels like a baby - it could not be helped. Johannes was pleased for he said this meant that the poison was being driven out of the body by the remedies and that my system was working well and hadn't been damaged by the action of the antimony - for this was the poison I'd taken in.

It's very like arsenic - and both Johannes and I had had experience of this poison for my beloved first wife Cecily had been murdered by being given doses of arsenic over a length of time by a vicious killer and then one fatal, higher dose.

Johannes knew what to look for. Antimony, he told me afterwards, does the same sort of thing to the body. Now I knew the agony my poor wife had been through and in my weakened state cried for her pain all over again.

What was this antimony? Johannes said it was easily obtained for it was used as a cosmetic by women, when it was known as stibium or kohl. Master Gallipot, the apothecary on Chute Alley, was known to keep this in his shop.

I was indebted to Master Gallipot for his knowledge had enabled he and Johannes to prepare just the right counteragent to combat the damage done.

I slept again, after Johannes had told me what had poisoned me and how, and when at last I awoke, Lydia was sitting by my bed in Johannes' workroom. I looked up and my eyes filled with tears.

"I am glad to see you," I said weakly.

"And I you... alive...," and she burst into tears.

*****

It was four days before I could toddle about on legs which felt like one of Matthew Cook's jellied confections. I staggered from piece of furniture to wall and back again with Lydia helping me. I was as weak as a day old kitten and my vision was still impaired, but gradually I regained my strength, though I slept much still. Johannes said this was the natural defence of the body for this was how we mended ourselves.

On the fourth day, I sent Hal to Gilbert Cordwainer and to the castle to let my friends there know I had recovered. Word would no doubt reach our killer and poisoner. He would be more afraid now, for as I'd said to Hal, we must have been getting close to him for him to react in such a way. To attempt to kill the person investigating his deeds.

Lydia had gone with Little Agnes out into the town. They were out to market day for we had eaten poor Johannes' stores down to a crumb.

Johannes had been called out - a case of croup down in the area known as The Marsh, the boggy area down by the river, a little up the hill from the rope yards. I was alone.

I lay on the bed looking up at the ceiling of the workroom trying to fathom, other than at Master Gallipot's, where our murderer might have obtained the antimony.

Gallipot would need to be quizzed about that.

The sounds of the day receded. I dozed.

Few people passed the workshop for they all took the shorter route across the road by Mistress Juliana Glazer's house, to pass up or down the Kingsbury hill. The men who had been working on the new High Cross had gone for their dinner. The old cross had been damaged beyond repair last autumn by a felon who, leaping from it onto Andrew Merriman, had hurt his leg. Poor Andrew, grappling with him, got himself a broken head and had lain in this very bed for a couple of days, whilst he mended.

I'd heard the workers cutting stone and fixing the cross upright in the morning. I'd closed the shutters against their chatter and lay down to think.

All was quiet now. Again the noises fell away. I heard a dog bark; ah yes, the attached neighbour had a small yappy hound. I heard through the wall someone dip something metallic into the water butt at the house side, at the end of the alley way. Then all was silent save for the distant hum of the market.

I have no idea what roused me to attentiveness. Then, I was sure I'd heard a measured tread; footsteps coming up the alleyway beside the wall of the room in which I lay. Why should I be worried by that? The alley-way served two houses and the church; Johannes' and the widow who lived next door with her two girls, all spinsters. Why shouldn't people walk the alley-way to the church which was just beyond the yards of both houses?

I strained my ears. The tread was purposeful and slow, almost secretive. I sat bolt upright. My head swam. I swung my legs over the edge of the bed. Where had Johannes left my knife and sword?

I searched the room.

Damn - they weren't there.

I stepped quietly to the workroom door and opened it. I looked left up the short, dark passageway. The front door was closed but not bolted. I spent an agonising moment wondering if the back door too was closed and bolted and whether I had time to reach the kitchen and find my weapons before whoever it was in the alleyway gained the kitchen door.

I opened the inner kitchen door. My sword and knife lay on the table. I picked up the sword. The shutters were all open. I risked a quick glance out into the yard. No one had entered yet. I quickly slammed the shutters fast and bolted them and made sure the door was locked and bolted.

Then I backtracked to lock the front door.

As I approached the front door I heard the footsteps crossing the roadway outside the house. No time. I ducked back into the workroom and was able to lock the door, for Johannes had left the key here. He often left his front door unlocked so that patients could come and wait for him in his passageway but he always locked the workroom, for there was valuable equipment and expensive compounds and remedies in this room.

I waited behind the door.

The front door opened slowly. If this was a genuine patient, they would have called out Johannes' name. They said nothing.

I hardly dared to breathe.

The footsteps came closer and rang on the flag-stoned floor. I heard the hard leather of his heel hit the hard surface of the stone. They stopped outside the workroom door. Nothing happened.

I breathed again.

Perhaps this was a patient and they were waiting outside. Should I open the door?

Something in me said, 'No. Wait.'

I waited.

Then, the door latch was tried. I leaned my weight against the board as if I'd not just the moment before locked it with a key. The door rattled. I heard an oath whispered.

The man waited again.

I listened for any clue. Who was this man? Should I open the door quickly and confront him?

No, I was still weak. I would be no match for him, I thought, in this state. If I had to I would defend myself but I could not take the fight to him.

I waited still.

The footsteps faded back along the passageway and I heard the front door close. Then the two shutters at the front of the house were rattled. First one, then the other. Thank God I had bolted them.

No, this was no patient of Johannes'.

The steps receded and faded away.

I risked a look through the shutter which I opened a crack.

I saw the town cross to my left slightly. I could see down the High Street to the slaughter pens. People were milling around there.

By shifting my line of vision I could see down the hill towards Simon Smith's forge. I could just make him out at work through his opened gates. A few people walked to and fro on the road between us. I saw one man disappear into the beginning of Oxford Street, three houses away to the left. He seemed to be carrying two empty baskets. Of course, I knew him, the cheese man who visited the castle. He'd come no doubt, from up the High on the southern side of the street.

I wondered what time of day it was.

It seemed an age before I felt strong enough to open the front door again. I stepped out onto the road. I noticed it had begun to rain. Here the road was wide as it swept round the corner and came from Kingsbury Hill to the High Street. Johannes lived almost exactly behind the High Cross and so there was a large piece of road which was rarely walked unless folk were going to his front door.

I looked left and right.

There was no one.

I turned to enter the door again.

Suddenly, from the alley-way only a few paces from the front door, a man appeared, swathed in a cloak and hooded. He lunged forward but slipped on the rain dampened and pocked ground and the knife he held missed me by a foot or more. I backed quickly in the door and slammed it in his face.

Fumbling with the key I locked it and pulled the locking bar down with a thump.

The man rattled the door ineffectually. I put my back to it and breathed hard.

The whole episode had left me weak and so I once more went into the workroom, locked the door and lay down. The front shutters rattled. Again, I was glad I had fixed them.

This time I could not doze. Every little noise was my attacker returning.

The men working on the High Cross came back to work and began their chatter and scraping, sawing and banging again.

This time I was glad of their noisy company.

A little while later there was a furious thumping on the back door. I got up and listened, standing in the passage.

"Aumary... the door's locked. Let me in!"

It was Johannes.

I staggered to the back door and undid the lock and bar. I know I was shaking.

Johannes came through the door and caught me as I fell forward, losing my balance. The world was spinning around me. I was eased onto a kitchen stool.

A mug of water was put into my hand.

"What happened?" asked Johannes.

I told him about our would-be attacker.

"You didn't see him at all?"

"He had his hood up and a cloak was wrapped tightly around him, except when he lunged at me, then I was turning so quickly out of his way, I didn't see anything."

"Pity."

"Who *did* you see as you walked up from the Marsh?"

"The world and his wife, been to market," said the doctor.

I leaned forward and put my head in my hands. "I have never felt so vulnerable in my life Johannes." I was still shaking.

Johannes sat down opposite me.

"I have been so used to knowing that at least I can defend myself with sword and knife, against an enemy. This poison has robbed me of all my strength and confidence."

"It will return. You know it will."

"Aye I suppose so. I felt so much at his mercy, you know."

"He wants you to feel afraid. He's playing a game. Don't give in to him," said

Johannes firmly.

I smiled. "No, no I shan't." I looked up at my friend. "I will catch him. I will catch him and he shall hang."

"The girls will be back soon. I saw them coming from Master Philbert Fleshmonger. We shall have some good meat this evening I think. That will do you good. Build up your strength once more."

It was true I had lost weight this past few days.

I laughed. "Lydia will enjoy doing some cooking. She rarely gets the chance at home."

Hal came through the back door then, smiling and with a sack slung over his shoulder.

"The compliments of the treasury guard master, sir...." He threw the sack down on the kitchen table.

Johannes rose, "Ho, ho, what have we here?" he said, rubbing his hands together.

"Fish sir, from Master Gayle, caught in the moat, this morning."

"Then we shall have a veritable feast at supper," said Johannes, chuckling.

"Ah...?" I began.

"Did Master Gayle himself catch the fish, Hal?" asked Johannes, knowing what I was about to say.

"No Doctor, but he saw it caught and it was handed to him immediately."

"No fadoodling around with it?"

"Oh no, Johannes."

"Then we shall eat well tonight."

The thought of food made me nauseous and tired.

"I am off to lie down for a moment." I reeled my way to the door.

I saw Hal cock his head in my direction with a quizzing look at the doctor.

I heard Johannes begin to tell the tale of our would-be intruder. As I lay down once more I heard Hal say, "I'll not leave 'im alone again. This killer is a chitty faced killcow. I'll not 'ave 'im afeart like this."

*****

Two days after this event, I managed to hoist myself onto Bayard and ride gently for home, my wife beside me on her horse, Penelope. No physical wound I had ever sustained had made me feel so weak and lacking in stamina.

Johannes said this was because the whole body of systems had come to grief. It would take some time to fully recover, he said.

It did. I was not back to normal for another week, even then I was still weak.

In that time I did a lot of thinking and list making. I scribbled my thoughts down on parchment and then scrubbed them out again to write them once more.

On a grey day when rain was threatening and the black clouds scurried over the forest like old maids with their heads down against the wind, I rode with Hal at my side to Larkworthy's cottage.

Hilda Sceap told me that William was up on the hills near Furze Copse.

We rode through the sheep and came out on a windy scarp at the edge of West Woods.

William was on his knees looking at a Wiltshire horned ewe's feet. He rose, let her go and ruffled her fleece as she passed him. I saw him look up as he heard us riding towards him.

"My Lord. It's good to see you."

I dismounted. "And I you, William." I reached out my hand and took his shoulder, giving it a small shake.

"I heard m'lord that the murderer tried you, sir... that you were poisoned."

"Aye man, 'e were," said Hal, dismounting. "It were a close thing. I reckon 'e was ready to try on some wings I do, before Doctor Johannes pulled him away from 'eaven."

I laughed. "Oh Hal... it might have been the other place... it certainly felt like it. I have never been so hot in all my life."

William Larkworthy allowed a smile to flicker across his face.

"Sir, the barn's up yonder, shall we get out of the rain?"

I had several barns scattered about on my sheep lands. Here was stored fodder for the animals in ill winters and they were also a refuge for my sheep and shepherds caught out on the hills in bad weather. The Wiltshire horned variety needed no such shelter but the other breeds were not so suited to the terrain.

We led the horses into the small barn and stood at the door looking out at the rain blowing across in sheets.

"William, I wanted to ask you if you had had any further thoughts on who Elswith might have been talking to that day?"

"No sir... none, I'm afraid."

"It now appears that the Master Wheelwright came up to speak to her, very early in the day."

William's head came up. "But she didn't know him, sir."

"I know that Will. It was the first and only time they met, he said. He wanted you both to give up your place in the Flitch contest. He was willing to pay you to withdraw but Elswith would not make a decision without asking you first and you weren't there to ask."

"Aye, it was always our way to discuss together what we were going to do." He looked into my eyes. "Was he then the man who...?"

"No, I don't believe it was, Ash," I said. "He went away again, a little shamefaced I think."

"Thank you sir for delaying the buryin'. I just made it. Father Justin said you had asked that Elswith be kept above ground a little longer. I know why you did that. That was kind."

I nodded. "I had intended for you to be let loose earlier but things rather overtook me."

"Aye sir. I'm right glad you recovered."

"Will, who came to the burying? Anyone who you might have thought it strange to see?"

Will pursed his lips. "Some of the Cadley folk, Dunstan and Floro and Hilda and Esmund 'a corse. A few other shepherds from further afield. It was good of them to walk so far."

"She was well liked, Will."

He looked at the beaten earth of the floor. "Her cousin."

"Crosscastle. Aye he told me he was going to try to come." Something tickled at my brain as I said his name but it was gone as quickly as the scudding clouds above us.

"Some people from the weaving community. I really didn't think they'd come but they did."

"That was kind. As I say, she was well liked."

"And it was kind of you to ask your good lady wife to come too, sir. I really appreciated..."

"Lady Lydia?"

"Aye sir, Lady Belvoir was there. She said you were too busy but that someone from the Belvoir's ought to be there since Elswith was one of the larger 'Belvoir family,' as she put it."

"I didn't ask her, Will, and she hasn't said she was there, but she is right. I would have been there but...."

"Aye sir, it were the day you were poisoned."

"So no one odd turned up?"

William looked up at the sky. "No sir, save an old friend from the town. I didn't know him but he said he knew Elswith before she married me." He gave a dry chuckle. "I imagined by the way he spoke of her, that he had had a thing for her when they were young. Still had a bit. You know that Elswith was a town girl before me, sir."

"I do."

Elswith had come from Marlborough and was born a free woman. By marrying William she put herself into servitude and became an unfree peasant. Not many women would do that, even for love. This was one of the reasons I knew that the Larkworthys were a devoted couple.

"Do you know who this man was, Will?"

He shook his head. "He didn't give his name to me, maybe one of the others might have remembered him speaking it, but I don't."

"Who else did he speak to?"

"Hilda, she knew about him too, I think, and Father Justin."

"Thank you Will. I'm not saying this man was the killer but he might know something if we can find him."

We rode back down to Hilda and Esmund's cottage. Esmund was out the back on the little plot hoeing the bone hard ground and he tugged his forelock when he saw me.

Hilda was in the warmth of the cottage setting some bread to prove beside her fire.

She rose from her knees as we entered and curtsied. "M'lord. Didn't you find him?"

"Aye, Hilda, we did. Please don't let me stop you. Do whatever it is you have to do. I just want a word."

"Aye sir," she said, but didn't move.

"On the day of Elswith's burying, William says that there was a man there whom he didn't know."

She busied herself then and scurried across the room, putting the work trestle between us.

"Oh?"

"He thought maybe you might recall who he was."

She started to knead more dough.

"Aye that were an old flame. I heard her speak about him before but I never met him till that day."

"What did she say about him?" I asked, sitting down slowly on a stool. Hal stood at the door.

"Just that they grew up together in the town and that this man thought that she were more fond of him than she were. This were 'a course, afore she met Will."

"Twenty years ago. So this man perhaps thought that she would have married him?"

"Oh I dunno. She didn't exactly say that."

"What's his name?"

Hilda lifted her eyes to the rafters and sighed. She stopped her kneading for a moment. "Now... I'll have to think about that, I only heard it once, at the burying, you see, sir."

I ran my hands through my hair.

"Try, Hilda."

"Elswith called him Harry."

" 'Arry? As in 'Arold?" asked Hal.

The woman shrugged. "Harry... just Harry."

I put my elbows on the table and leaned towards her. "Hilda, the day that Elswith was killed, I had a feeling that you and Floro were... well... not telling me something which you perhaps should have said?"

She stopped kneading again.

"Oh, sir?"

"About the shouting and arguing that you heard coming from Will's cottage."

Hilda wiped her hands on her apron.

"Will tells me that you said, sir, that there was another man there that day."

"There was."

"Then it must've been him what we heard."

"You saw no one."

"It weren't quite light and it's...."

"At the wrong angle to see anyway, yes, I know." I looked her in the eye. "Hilda, the visitor was Master Ash the wheelwright in Marlborough. He has confessed to being there but tells me that Elswith was alive and well when he left her."

Hilda sighed. "Ah, well then, sir."

"But he also said they didn't argue. They didn't raise their voices."

Hilda's expression took on a puzzled look. "But I heard them."

"Dunstan Weard said he heard them too, but he couldn't make out what was being said."

Hilda scoffed. "Aye well. Dunstan is as deaf as a heathen to the Christian word, sir. He wouldn't hear nowt."

"But you?"

Hilda banged the bread dough on the table one last time and then put it in an earthenware dish, covered it with a cloth and set it to the side of the central hearth to prove.

"I thought it were Will. That's why I di'n't say anything. I di'n't want him taken up for the killing."

"You should have had more faith in your neighbour, Hilda." I smiled.

"Aye, aye, I should."

"So what was being said...as far as you could tell?" I asked.

Hilda looked straight at me for a short while. I gestured for her to sit.

"I couldn't hear it all. But what I could hear, I didn't really understand." She sat down on her bench.

"You tell us, gel, and then we'll see if we can understand it," said Hal.

Hilda wiped her hands on her apron again and pushed her hair back into her head cloth.

"It were something like, 'I tell you it wasn't.' Then Elswith said 'it was you, I saw you.' Then the man said 'if you tell anyone...' or something like that. 'it's a good thing I got... something,' he said. 'You were giving him... something...,' she said."

"So Elswith had seen something this man didn't want generally known?"

"I dunno sir. Then he said 'where's the 'arm in it?' And she answered, 'it's against the law it is.'"

"Looks like she were killed for something she knew then, sir," said Hal.

"Go on, Hilda."

"He said, 'You won't tell anyone.' Then she answered. 'I'll have to think about that.' Then there were a few murmurs what I couldn't hear and finally he said 'You do that, my girl and I'll.....'"

"Yes?"

Hilda pulled her face into a strange grin. "Well, I thought he said, 'marry you.' But he couldn't could he, sir, 'cos she were already married?"

"Hmm."

Hal stroked his long grey beard. "Sir, might he have said 'wurry'? You know that's local for throttle."

I looked up. "Of course, Hal. Thank you. Yes, that is no doubt what was said."

Hilda's hand flew to her mouth, "Oh no. That's awful."

Hal reached over and patted her hand.

"He did, didn't he? He throttled her," she added.

"Yes, Hilda. For something she was going to say to someone."

I stood up. "Oh, Hilda, I wish you'd spoken up before. I'm not saying we are any nearer a reckoning but it might have helped to know all this earlier."

"Oh your lordship, I'm right sorry. It's just I wanted to protect Will. We all did."

"I know." I patted her shoulder and made for the door. We had taken up our reins and were turning away when Hilda flung open the door again and came out.

"Sir! M'lord!"

I wheeled Bayard round.

"The name of the fella what was sweet on Elswith. I remembered...It were Pygge, sir, Pygge. The man at the buryin'. It were Pygge."

Chapter Nine

H al looked up at me. "So it 'in't 'Arold, it's 'Enry."

"Yes, some people called Henry are also known as Harry."

"He's one of the guards at the treasury i'n't he?"

"He is."

"And a companion to the fella who got shot by Bunce."

"Canard, yes."

"It's a trip to the castle again, is it sir?"

I sighed. "As much as I'd like to avoid the place for a while...."

Hal chuckled "An' I don't blame you...."

"Yes, it's there we must seek an answer to this puzzle."

We rambled down the slope from the cottages and rode along the Shaftesbury road for a while, eventually descending the Granham Hill. We veered off north to the town bridge across the River Kennet and not long after entered the bailey of the castle.

A few people raised their arms to me, wishing me well.

"Word's out then," said Hal with a chortle.

"I think word had been out some considerable length of time, Hal. It's impossible to keep secrets in this place."

"Someone manages it though, don't they, sir?" he said.

Peterkin Gayle came jogging across the bailey to meet me.

"Oh, Sir Aumary, I am so glad to see you."

"Thank you Pete," I said dismounting.

"Are you sure you are well enough to be gadding about? That was a terrible scare you gave us all, you know."

I remembered then, in one of my lucid moments that late afternoon, poor Peterkin praying out loud hard for my recovery for all he was worth.

"Thank you for your prayers, Pete," I said as I gripped his shoulder.

"God heard this humble sinner," he said with a shy smile.

"And protected this one," I added at a whisper.

"Sir Aumary, for all the world I do not want to have to break in another constable. I am getting too long in the tooth for such doings."

I heard Hal laugh at that. "Better the devil you know, eh Pete?" he said.

Gayle chuckled "You could say that, Hal. Sir Aumary here is approved of by everyone. Now, where are we likely to find his like, eh?"

I squirmed a little at the praise.

"God forbid they made that little weasel Hugo of Ramsbury constable," he said.

"Oh? Has that been mooted then?" I asked.

Pete shook his head. "Only by the idiot coroner himself. Heard you were... ahem, under the weather and in two shakes of a lamb's tail, was offering his services. Well...," Gayle sniffed. "I gave him short shrift I can tell you."

I grinned, "I ain't dead yet."

Peterkin crossed himself. "No, praise be to God. Though that night... I really did think...." He sighed heavily. "Ah no, let's not dwell on it."

We repaired to his office. I glanced at his little bed in the corner.

"Doctor Johannes tells me it was antimony," said Gayle.

"Yes, Pete, it was. And that same doctor says I am on water for a while I'm afraid so no wine for me - thanks."

He nodded and took a long draught himself. Hal was offered ale.

"Where had it come from?"

"Hal's been up to the apothecary, Gallipot. He sells antimony to many of the ladies of the town to make themselves more beautiful."

Pete raised his eyes to Heaven. "They poison themselves to make themselves attractive?"

Hal and I laughed. "It's pretty harmless as a cosmetic, I hear. Ladies draw their eyebrows with it."

"Oh." Peterkin lived in a completely male world and as far as I know had never been married.

"So this means it is readily available in many of the wealthier houses in the town," I said.

"Oh dear."

"Yes, not easy to trace."

"It was in the cheese, Johannes said."

"It was, powdered. The sharp taste disguised it."

"And I don't eat it," said Hal, "so I escaped."

Gayle's open expression changed to one of absolute horror. "But...but..." he stammered, "You could *both* have been killed by it. This killer doesn't care who he murders, does he?"

"I can understand him wanting to be rid of me...." I said.

"But Hal too, just because he was with you?"

I shrugged. "No one knows that Hal can't take goat's cheese because it brings him out in a rash."

"Only you sir," said Hal. "And the little Lady 'Awise." Hal always gave Hawise his portion of goats' cheese at supper, if it was served up at Durley.

"And you now, Pete," said Hal.

"Saints protect us," said Gayle, crossing himself again. "Where had the cheese come from?"

"I can answer that Pete," said Hal. "I met a man coming from the kitchen, 'e 'ad a tray for us covered with a cloth. 'E was coming out of the kitchen as I walked in. I took it from 'im and the rest you know."

"Do we know the man?" asked Gayle.

"Hal made inquiries," I said. "The tray was made up for us and sat on the side for a while. Then stew was ladled into the two bowls. When they got to us they were still hot. When that was done it was covered over and a servant - you found him, didn't you, Hal?"

"Aye I did."

"...brought it out of the kitchen and bumped into Hal."

" 'E says, when the cook made up the bowls and bread with some dried fruit and covered it up there was no cheese there," said my man at arms firmly.

"The cheese was added somehow, later."

Gayle nodded. "Food is often left hanging around like that waiting. It's so often cold when it gets to us."

"Plenty of opportunity to tamper with it."

"So it was known that this tray was the one destined for you?"

"Oh yes, it was no accident."

Pete sat down heavily at his table.

"We have to catch this monster, Sir Aumary."

"I'll say we do," said Hal "So I can tear out his livin'..."

"And we have today heard some news which might help us," I said smiling at my grim man at arms."

"Tell me...," said Gayle

Once we had explained the story about Pygge and the burial of Elswith Larkworthy, Peterkin narrowed his eyes and said, "You think this guard too has something to hide. Jesu! I hand-picked these men, sir. They have been loyal and good soldiers most of them this past twelve years or so, as long as I have been here. Never so much as a breath of scandal."

"I know Pete. It's hard to fathom."

"I'll get the man to come down and talk to you."

"Thank you. And can you ask Peter and Stephen to step down here too please?". Stephen Dunn and Peter Devizes were my two men at arms. I kept these two at the castle at my own expense, for a time when I might need them; if we were called, for example, to fight for our King. They were both seasoned warriors and their loyalty was to the Belvoirs.

They came in a little before Pygge arrived.

Peter was a local man, from the small town of Devizes about fourteen miles west, as his name suggested; Stephen was a jovial Durley man with a shock of dark hair, hence his name.

They nodded a bow and stood by the door and grinned and Hal slapped both on the shoulder.

Pygge came in flanked by Gayle and another guard who retired when the door closed.

Gayle came forward. "This is the constable, Pygge. You remember him."

"Aye, sir, I do." He stood as tall as he could make his portly frame. "Glad to see you've recovered, sir."

"Thank you, Pygge."

I stood behind Gayle's table.

"I hear that you attended the burial of poor Elswith Larkworthy the other day, Pygge."

I saw his eyes widen.

"Why was that?"

Pygge licked his lips. "It's no secret, sir. I knew her. Years ago before she married her shepherd. We were friends."

"Both of you being Marlborough folk?"

"Aye sir, that's right. We both lived on The Green. Our families were neighbours."

"And so you went up to Cadley and attended her interment because of old times, eh?"

"Yes sir. That's the nub of it. I did."

"Were you off duty when you did this?"

Pygge glanced at Gayle "It were in the late afternoon, the burying. Yes, I was off duty."

I looked at Peterkin, he nodded.

"How did you get there?"

"I walked, sir."

"And walked back?"

"I got a lift on a cart tail, sir, on the way back."

"He came back into the castle shortly after dusk, Sir Aumary," said Gayle. "The gate guard confirms it."

"Was this the only time you went up the hill to meet up with Elswith, Pygge?"

"Meet up, sir... but she was dead?"

"Did you perhaps go up to see her on the morning of her death and remonstrate....argue with her, Pygge?"

"I never argued with Elswith. We hadn't seen each other in years. I saw her a couple of times about town when she came to deliver her spinning but the last time was oh...two years ago, maybe."

"What might you argue about?"

"I didn't argue with her. Why should I?"

"So it wasn't you who said that you would throttle her."

Pygge swallowed hard.

"No sir. I couldn't do that. She was a very mild woman, sir. No man could argue with her."

"Someone did, Pygge. And throttled her."

"I know, sir. It wasn't me. I loved Elswith ever since we were young. I couldn't hurt her."

"People who love, Pygge, can often be moved to hurt the thing they love. Even destroy it."

Pygge turned his head to look out of the window to his right. "No sir. I will admit she hurt me sorely when she married that shepherd. Her a free woman and him one of your serfs, but it was her choice and I reckon she never regretted it."

"No, I don't think she did, Pygge." I stood and walked round the table to face him.

"How do you know she didn't regret it?"

"I asked her. About four years ago. We met by the priory. I was coming from visiting me old mam up town, going back to the castle and she was coming into town with her pack of spinnings."

"You chatted there, did you?"

"Aye, we did, sir. I asked her if she was happy and she said she had never been more happy in her life. She loved it up on the downs, she loved her spinning and she loved her husband."

"Hmmm."

"Made me feel...sad and happy at the same time. I knew there was no hope for me then. And I was glad she was happy."

The man's gaze never wavered.

"Tell me Pygge," I said, changing the subject. "You must have known Canard quite well. What was it he was hiding? Why did he bolt?"

"Did he, sir?"

"Aw c'mon! You know he did. The news was all over the castle. He fled across the moat and was brought down by a crossbow bolt fired by the gate guard Bunce."

Pygge sighed. "He was friends with that blacksmith Beecroft."

"Beecroft?"

"He told me that the smith swindled him out of some money."

"That's what I heard too," I said. "You know that Carrier was killed when he was about to talk to me on the wall walk. He knew the name of the man who had killed Beecroft the smith and incidentally the man who killed Elswith and was about to tell me. Know anything about that?"

Pygge shifted his feet and crossed his arms. "Sir, do you think if I knew anything about the man who killed Elswith, I wouldn't take that knowledge to the authorities? To you, sir? Before I did, mind you, I'd beat him black and blue. You'd be hanging a corpse, you would sir. If I knew who it was, he'd be a dead man."

I looked carefully at the man before me. I believed him.

"Thank you, Pygge. If there is anything you can remember, come and let me know. If you see or hear anything odd, come to me."

"I will sir."

The guard nodded a bow and Hal opened the door for him.

He stood in the doorway. "It might've been different sir, if Elswith had married me. I wouldn't have been a soldier. I had an apprenticeship lined up for me but, when Elswith went …. I couldn't settle."

"No, Pygge?"

"No, sir."

"What might you have been then?"

"I was going to be a wheelwright, sir. Mind you, you can't ask a girl to wait seven years, can you, before you can marry? Till you finish your apprenticeship."

I nodded. "No. Not really. And there's nothing wrong with being a soldier."

"No sir. Thank you, sir."

I sighed loudly as Hal shut the door.

"Believe 'im sir?"

"Aye Hal, I do."

"Me too, for what it's worth."

"Pete, what do you think? You know the man?"

Gayle took off his coif and scratched his head. "He's never been in any trouble. Yes, I think I believe him and if he does know who the killer is, I believe he'd tell us."

"After, as he said, beating the man to a pulp?"

Gayle smiled. "No more than the felon deserves."

*****

Our last task of the day was to ride up to the Kingsbury Hill and speak with Beecroft's sister again.

Mistress Millisende Scarlett.

The woman answered the door holding a bare shuttle in her hand. I introduced myself. She curtsied low and bade us enter.

"We are sorry to take you from your work, mistress." I nodded to a piece of cloth she had been weaving on an upright loom next to the back wall of the house.

"I was just about to set on another lot of thread, m'lord," she said. "I can spare you some time. Have you come about my brother?" She threw a cautious glance at Hal.

"We have, Mistress Scarlett. Might we see his room again?"

The room was as Hal had described it. Untidy, although the remains of the plates of food left here and reported by Hal, had been cleared away by the widow Scarlett.

"I am sorry for the state of it, sir. It's just as he left it. I don't feel I can do anything with it just yet. I...."

"No, mistress, no need to apologise. This is just what we want for if you had tidied it, we might not have been able to find anything which may be lying around."

"Lyin' around?"

"Things which might give us a clue as to why he had to die."

"Clues, sir?"

"Things which might help us work out who might have killed your brother."

"Oh," she said absently. "You mean like who came up here to see him and that sort of thing."

"That sort of thing precisely. So who did come up to see him?"

"A couple of his friends."

"Do you know who they were?" I asked as I picked up a wooden cup from the floor and a blanket which had slipped from the bed. I sniffed the cup. No smell.

"He had some fella he used to go fishing with."

"He was a Marlborough man, was he? Do you happen to know his name?"

She shook her head. "No, he just called him Luke."

"Just Luke?"

"Yes."

"What did the man look like?" I folded the blanket and put it on the bed.

"Look like? Oh, I don't know sir... erm... he weren't as tall as you. He had a good head of hair. He was always jolly he was. Always smiling. He had lovely teeth. None of them missing nor cracked nor black nor nothing. And his clothes were nice."

"Fat, thin?"

"Oh he weren't neither of those sir, just middling."

"Anything special you can tell me about him, mistress?"

"No, sir. Not really."

"Nothing?"

"He liked nice clothes. He told me he'd just bought a lovely new blue cotte from Mistress Wyndcraft."

"He was quite wealthy then, to buy such things?"

"I dunno, sir."

"Do you know where he lived?"

"No sir. Up the other end of town, I think," she said. "He said it were long walk up here in the rain."

"Nice clothes? What were his clothes like, mistress?" I asked.

"Ooh, sir, I don't remember that. I just let the man in and he came up to this room. He never had no fancy clothes when he was here nor nothing. Just a brown cloak. They were good cloth though."

"Good?"

"Aye. I used to tell my brother, 'why can't you look after your clothes like what your friend Luke does?' He kept 'em really nice." She stooped to pick up one of a pair of very worn boots from the floor. I took it from her.

Just old worn boots, with a hole in the sole and cracked leather uppers.

"No holes in his boots, like those. Ever so clean and nice they was. And I always knew when he was coming down the stairs 'cos his soles used to clip on the wood. Clip, clop, clip clop."

"How long did your brother know this man?" I fished through more detritus of the man Beecroft's life, which was lying on the small table.

"I'd say it was ever since he came to live here."

"Two years ago? How often did the man come?"

"He'd come to collect him when they were going fishing. Not too often."

"And they'd go out immediately?"

"Not always. Sometimes they'd sit up here laughing and joking," she said, "And making a devil of noise."

"Noise?"

"Aye, sounded like that man with the noisy feet was dancing on the floor."

"Dancing?" said Hal with a puzzled expression.

"Well, it were more of a banging."

Hal and I looked at each other.

"I asked them what they was doing to make such a noise and they said that if it disturbed me, they'd go down in the cellar and play."

"Play? Play what?"

"Some game they said they like to play. Men and their games, sir. Us women we don't have time for such frivolleries do we?"

"And did they?"

"Oh aye, they did. It were quieter down there."

I rubbed my close cropped beard.

"You said there was another friend?"

"Aye sir. I know him because his family lives close by. His ma and pa and his sister."

"Who is that then, Mistress?"

"It were that poor soul what fell off the wall at the castle. John Carrier, sir. He's an ostler from the castle stable."

"Yes, I know."

"It ain't right, he should'na be up there on them high walls at night and so unsafe, sir. I blame the man who let him go up there when it's in such a dangerous state. Why it crumbled under his feet, so it did."

"He was stabbed, Mistress Scarlett and was pushed over," I said.

The widow was now in full flow. "Wicked, unkind thing to do to let him go up there in the dark. That man should be horsewhipped, I say."

"Ah madam... then I'm afraid you would have to horsewhip me, for I was the man Carrier had made an appointment to meet. His choice of meeting place, not mine."

Mistress Scarlett blanched.

"Oh sir... I didn't mean...."

"No. I'm sure you didn't."

I saw Hal smirk.

"You know of no other friends?" I said quickly to cover the woman's embarrassment.

"No... sir, none what came here."

"No, ahem... women?"

"My Lord Belvoir!" said Mistress Scarlett, affronted. "I would never allow...!"

"No, I'm sure you wouldn't."

"Besides, Martin had had enough of women to last him a lifetime after his wife. He weren't interested."

I heard Hal laugh quietly.

"Thank you Mistress Scarlett. By the way, where are the coins which were lying here on the table when my man here came to make his first visit?"

"Coins, sir?"

"Two silver pennies here on the table.... That right Hal?"

"Aye sir. Two pennies with that esteemed monarch, father of the King, Henry the second, on them."

"No sir. I haven't seen any pennies. Not here sir."

Hal's eyebrow rose.

"Can we see your cellar, mistress?" I asked.

"Aye you can, but it won't do you no good."

"Why's that?"

"Because I swept it the day afore yesterday. There's nothing in it save an old stool and a brush. It's all clean and tidy, sir."

She was right. Swept completely clean and not a clue to be seen.

There was one odd thing though. In the corner we found a section of tree trunk with the bark still upon it; the rings of the tree radiating out like ripples on a pond.

"Used like a table sir?" asked Hal.

"Maybe," I said.

*****

Hal and I stood outside the small house and looked at each other.

"So what was they doin' in that cellar, sir?"

"A game of some kind?"

"I don't know no game where you have a lot of bangin'. Leapin' about maybe and stampin' on the floor but I doubt they was playin' 'opsctoch.'"

Hal was often called upon to play hopscotch with my daughter Hawise.

I shrugged. "I have no idea."

"And where's that money then?" said my man at arms. "I definitely saw two pennies sittin' on that table." He held up two fingers.

"I expect the woman has found them and kept them, in lieu of all the rent her brother owed her. Spent them, I don't wonder."

"Aye, that'll be it I 'spect."

"No doubt everything he owned...," I began.

"And that weren't a lot sir, were it?"

"No, Hal, not by what was left in that room. Everything will be hers now anyway. She can spend those two pennies if she wishes."

"Aye she can do what she likes with the stuff now."

"I wish we knew who was the friend who went fishing with him."

"Well, sir, we know a man as might help us there." said Hal, thrusting his thumbs into his jerkin.

"We do?"

"Walt Fisher."

Walt Fisher lived with his son Peterkin in a bothy by the River Kennet on Southfield. Several times before they had helped me in my investigations. These two were the fisherfolk of the town and fished the river and other pools hereabouts to provide food for fish Friday, and other fasting days in the town. Hal and I walked down Figgins Lane and scraped at the door of their little house.

"Anyone home?"

Walt's head appeared over the river bank.

"Here, m'lord."

We stepped to the river's edge. Walt was sitting in his boat mending a rent in the side.

He stood and stepped up onto the bank. Hal extended a hand to help him up.

"Good day to you, Walt." I said, "I wonder if you might be able to help us."

"If I can, m'lord."

"I know that you fish for a living, Walt. There are some who fish just to pass the time and catch a trout for the dinner table. Know any locals who sit around the riverside or the castle moat?"

"What, them as fish for pleasure you mean?"

"That's exactly what I mean, Walt."

Walt Fisher sucked his teeth. "Well, you know that blacksmith what was murdered, 'e liked to fish in the moat. This past two years or so."

"It's about this man we are inquiring, Walt. He had a friend who used to go with him. We'd like to find him if we can."

"A friend eh?"

"We're told," said Hal, "they used to go out fishin' together."

"Well, that fella Beecroft, 'e was always sat on his own when I saw 'im."

"Mostly at the moat was that?"

"Aye, there are some gurt fish in that moat. When they open the sluices they get in there an' 'a corse, the moat's mostly deeper than the river."

"Plenty to feed them?"

"There's pike. They feed on the smaller fish."

Pike was not a fish I enjoyed eating. Too many bones.

"He was mostly to be found under the southern windows."

"At the southern side eh?"

"Yessir. I 'as to say, I never seen 'im with anyone else. It's a bit of a lonely job, fishin' like that. But then fishin' is a lonely job."

"Anyone else, Walt?"

The fisherman hitched up his belt and reached for a long pole which was lying propped up on the hut.

"Gilbert sometimes goes out the back of the priory."

"I didn't know he was a fisherman."

"Likes the peace he says. Away from his womenfolk."

"Isn't that why they all do it?" said Hal, laughing.

"There's a couple of the tanners. They fish the pool up by the rope works."

"Ah yes, I've seen them."

"An a couple o' fellas go out towards Preshute beyond the moat. I don't know their names. Can find out if you like. I see them now and again."

"That would be kind, Walt." I said, getting a little disheartened.

"Corse, recently I seen a castle bloke out by the moat where Beecroft used to do his fishin'."

"Who, Walt?"

"Ah... I don't know his name. Just know he works in the castle."

"How do you know he works there?"

"Seen 'im in the castle when I bin deliverin' to the kitchen."

"Ah. Not the guard who was killed the other day? Canard."

"Haha. That's a good'un. Canard. Was that 'is name? That's French for duck 'in't it?"

"Yes, yes it is."

"What'd 'e done to get himself spitted like a chicken then?"

"It was a misunderstandin'," said Hal, fingering his beard. "He got in the way of a crossbow bolt."

"Nasty."

"Hmmm."

"No, I don't say it were 'im."

"Can you describe him, Walt? This man."

Walt's eyes rose up to Heaven. "Oh now that i'n't easy. 'Es one of them folk what looks well... like everyone else. He's not tall, not short. Got mousey hair... I think. Not a good lookin' man. A bit sorta' cocky like he's got summat he knows you want."

"Clothes?"

"Good but not flashy. He don't seem to like wearing colours much." Walt's eyes strayed back down to Hal's bright kingfisher blue cotte.

"Was the man still fishing there, now Beecroft has vacated the spot?" asked Hal.

"No, he were just sittin' there admirin' the view, his back to the wall and his feet out."

"Not the fishing friend of the dead blacksmith then?"

"Seems not."

Walt leaned on his pole. "You know sir. It seems odd but I never saw Beecroft catch nothing."

"He must have done."

"Aye. I suppose, I just didn't see him."

"Well, if there's anything you notice, do come and tell me."

"Aye sir, I will."

"And thank you for the fish, Walt. The other day. I presume it was you who sent the gift through Gayle?"

"Aye sir. Thought you might enjoy a bit o' trout bein' as 'ow yer stomach was turned up like a ton o' tripe."

"Very thoughtful, Walt. Give my regards to your son Peterkin."

Hal saluted him and we went on our way.

As we found the horses again and mounted ready to ride home for Durley before it became too dark, Hal turned to me.

"Might pay us to watch the moat, sir. We don't know who this fella is but we might recognise him."

"Have we the time to sit around waiting, Hal, for some man to come and plonk himself by the moat side?"

"Ah yes. Well...."

"We need to find someone who has the time," I said, "to do it for us."

I turned back to the path. "And we need to see just how many men there are in the castle who fit our description."

"God's Cods, sir, that's gotta be over a dozen."

*****

The sky was tinged with purple as we rode up the hill and into the forest. I was beginning to feel rather tired. Johannes had warned me that my stamina was going to be a long time returning.

We chatted about this and that: the weather and we reminisced about the terrible winter of 1204/5. We talked about those who had not made it through that winter and how their loss was keenly felt in the village.

We had just begun on what might be on offer for dinner when Hal turned in the saddle and peered down the road.

"You got your gambeson on under that cotte, 'en't you sir?"

"Aye Hal... what is it?"

"We're bein' follered."

I looked carefully over my right shoulder.

"Did you see him?"

"Just a flash."

"Mounted?"

"Aye."

"Hal, we are getting foolish about our unknown felon, don't you think? It's probably some Cadley man coming home from town."

But as we approached the Cadley turn and started up the steep hill, Hal said, " 'E's still with us."

 I can hear his hooves now," I said. "Shall we speed up?"

We spurred Bayard and Grafton to a faster trot and at Big Bellied Oak we veered right, around the slight bend in the track there.

"He follows us still," I said.

"Do we get in the undergrowth and wait for 'im to pass, then pounce?" asked Hal, "or do we git goin' fer 'ome like a sparhawk fer a spadger, sir?"

"Neither Hal. We veer off onto Charcoal Burner's track and home that way. If he is following us, he'll follow into the trees: if not we'll lose him."

"Might lose him anyway. He likely don't know the tracks like we do, sir."

"Much as I'd like to ride quickly for home, I really want to know who this man is and why he is following us, Hal. If he is."

A little while later we moved off left into a dry, narrow fern and bracken bordered track.

Hal risked a look behind.

"Still there, sir."

No sooner had he spoken than there was the thwang of a released bowstring and an arrow came humming past my ear. I ducked. Another followed and fell harmlessly into the brush.

"I think we confront him, Hal," I said. "He's no friend."

I threw my legs over Bayard's ears and drew my sword.

Hal followed my lead and we led the horses into the trees.

The man came clopping along on a brown rouncey and had almost passed us when we ran out of the brush and made a lunge for him and his horse's reins.

He was too quick. I think he'd seen Hal's blue tunic amongst the dull greens and browns of the forest.

He spurred on his beast and he disappeared through the trees.

"Follow, Hal!" I shouted and I sprang into Bayard's saddle again and turned the horse's nose in the direction of the deeper forest. We travelled some way, when suddenly all grew quiet and we could hear nothing but the soughing of the wind in the treetops. The rooks, who had been calling raucously, fell silent. We stopped to listen.

I dismounted and began to search for hoofprints and clues to the man's passage through the forest.

Hal narrowed his eyes and carefully scanned the trees.

"We better watch it," he hissed quietly. "We'd not see an arrow in this light and tangle of trees till it was too late."

No sooner had he spoken than an arrow came speeding out of a holly thicket, narrowly missing Grafton. Hal slapped her backside and she ran off in disgust, whinnying. Another arrow followed and arched over Bayard's back.

"Go Bayard! Go!" I shouted and Bayard took off in the same direction as Grafton, out of bow range. I knew we would be able to recover them again quickly. I would not have my horses disabled or killed for that is what our pursuer seemed to want to do.

"Come out and show yourself!" I shouted to the holly bush as we made for the substantial trunk of an old ash tree.

Just to the right of the prickly holly there was a flash of brown and I saw the man, hooded and wearing a short brown tunic, dash into the undergrowth and disappear. His clothes were the same colour as the decaying bracken.

"He might have a bow...," whispered Hal in my ear. " But he 'in't got an ever lasting supply of arrers, has he?"

"He's used three already."

"If we can get 'im to use' em up...."

I stooped and found one of the flints which litter the forest floor here and there. I tossed it a way to my right.

Sure enough, an arrow followed it and was lost in the trees.

I threw another. Another arrow hit an ash tree and vibrated there for a while.

Hal stooped and threw one further on.

We heard the man laugh. No, he was not going to take the bait.

"Damn," said Hal at a whisper.

One more arrow hit our tree and Hal dashed out and fetched it back. "Castle issue, sir."

"Like the last one we saw."

"Aye, the one in Tostig's back."

"What say you, Hal? One of us tries to get behind him?"

Hal ground his teeth. "The other draws the fire, eh?"

I nodded.

"I'll go. With yer poisonin' you're still not as fleet as you were."

"I'll have you know, I'm nearly fifteen years younge...."

But Hal had gone with a quiet chuckle.

I scanned the trees in front of me. Nothing. No movement save that which was made by the breeze in the few dessicated leaves left on the trees.

There was a dry rustle ahead and I shouted in that direction, "Come on you coward - make a move. I haven't got all day!"

Nothing stirred and no arrow followed the direction of my voice.

I couldn't see where Hal had gone, even with his bright blue tunic.

"We're waiting."

To my left the brush shook a little. I moved to the right of my tree. An arrow came out of nowhere and grazed the trunk upon which I lay my cheek. Too close. I moved back.

I put my back to the trunk and scanned the further trees. Here there were some large ash trunks and a couple of holm oaks. These trees were not common in the forest but were evergreen affording cover in winter. I looked back once and sprinted to the trees, lurching round their trunks and into the understorey like a pursued deer.

My attacker now followed. He'd seen me.

He was now behind the tree I had just left.

'Where are you, Hal?' I said to myself and as if in answer, I heard the call of the nightjar or goatsucker, a bird of the forest and downs.

This was Hal's special call but it could also just be the bird itself. It was active in the fading light but the birds did not appear here until April. I looked over to where I thought the cry had come from. I couldn't see Hal.

I hooted like an owl. I was answered immediately. Hal was now behind the man.

It was really beginning to go dark now and the forest was shrinking before our eyes to a few dozen feet all around.

I scanned the distant trees; dark shapes in a grey light.

I heard a scrabbling and Hal came rearing out of the undergrowth just to the left of the man.

There was a tussle behind the tree.

I leapt over the bracken and fern and chased round the trunk. Hal had the man by the throat.

I reached for him and received a vicious kick in the cods followed by one to the stomach. Being vulnerable there still, I doubled up on the ground, retching.

Hal was sliced with a knife but it bounced harmlessly from the padded wool of the gambeson he wore beneath, tearing his favourite supertunic. He roared in anger.

Our attacker threw away the bow and with the edge of his hand gave Hal a blow to the front of his neck.

I saw all this through a pink cloud as I attempted to stand feeling very dizzy. I reached at last for my knife but the man was running at top speed through the trees.

It was a couple of heartbeats before I could follow.

It was even longer before Hal had recovered enough to follow me.

We pounded along the tracks and in and out of the darkening trees. Birds roosting for the night in the larger bushes flew up squawking as we disturbed them. A pheasant lying low in the brush flew up with a startled 'carkcarkcark'.

Ahead of me I heard a splash.

Stopping to allow Hal to catch up and to catch my breath, I listened carefully. Our man was swimming the pool which lay ahead. It was longer than it was wide and he wasn't going to take the time to go around it.

Many people think that a forest is nothing but trees but it is so much more. Savernake is an area made up of dense woodland, glades, meadows, small streams, commons and ponds.

We were approaching one of the biggest now, Oakhill Pool. Here alders and birches sank their feet into the boggy ground at the edge of a reed banked stretch of water. It glistened black in the crepuscular light.

I saw the man striking out for the furthest bank.

Hal had picked up the man's bow. He had but one arrow, which he'd rescued from the tree. He fitted it to the bow and aimed.

The string twanged. The arrow sped into the water. The man convulsed. He dived with a spume of white spray into the water, in the middle of the pool.

We waited for him to surface.

The breeze lifted the small wavelets of the pond; the ripples created by his swimming had fanned out to the bank and disappeared.

The man did not come to the surface.

"Damn," said Hal.

We waited.

Our felon had disappeared.

Chapter Ten

H al and I stared at the water for a long time. The man didn't surface.

"It's dark now, I know but I in't seen 'im come out, have you lad?"

"No, Hal. Nor heard him splashing."

"He's drowned then. Me arrer must've got 'im," he said.

"I would like to have known who he was."

"Aye. Sorry about that. I didn't expect to get 'im so well. I only meant to wing 'im. Bit like Bunce eh?"

"Can't be helped in this light, Hal."

"Still, if someone's missing in town, we'll know who it was," he said as he turned away.

"As we were chasing him, did you get a glimpse of who it might have been?"

Hal shook his head, "No, nothin'."

"Me neither."

"It stinks. The whole thing stinks," said Hal putting his fingers to his lips and whistling for Grafton. "Stinks worse than a rotting leech in a log!"

I called loudly for Bayard and received an answering neigh.

We both began to trudge back to the path where our horses stood.

On the way back we found the horse the man had ridden. It was a castle rouncey.

A while later we clopped into Durley and dropped from our horses' backs. Hal clapped me on the shoulder.

"I'll see you at supper. I gotta go and see about sewing up the rent in this," and he took hold of a fold of his cotte. Hal was a pretty good seamstress and he went off to his room which was on the south wall of the courtyard.

I heard him chunnering as he stomped off. "Bloody man! Making a hole like that. Deserved to bloody drown."

I chuckled and went in to supper. I knew Hal and I knew that he was upset about more than a ruined item of clothing.

*****

Two days later we made the return journey to the town. We went by the Oakhill pool, in case the man's body had surfaced but there was no sign of him. Over two days and his body hadn't floated to the top.

Hal and I rode gently down the High Street and stopped by the priory gates. We tethered the horses to the wooden pegs driven into the wall for just such a purpose, scratched on Gilbert Cordwainer's door and stepped over the threshold. The rouncey was to be returned to the castle stable in a little while.

Harry Glazer, one of Gilbert's apprentices, was behind the door and he turned as we entered. His face split in a grin.

"My Lord Belvoir, good day to you, sir."

"And to you Harry. How goes it with you, lad?"

"Fine sir. Fine. I will be entering my journeymanship in May, sir."

"Well deserved, Harry. You are a fine shoemaker," I said.

"I had a good teacher."

"Speaking of that teacher, is he about?"

"Upstairs sir, just shout up the stairway and go on up."

I did as I was bid and Gilbert stood up as we gained the top of the stairs.

"Well, well," said Gilbert. "My favourite constable alive and well and looking, if I might say so sir, as pink as a new baby."

"Thanks to Johannes and Gabriel Gallipot, Gilbert," I chuckled.

Gil crossed himself. "I got a prayer said for you by Father Columba at St. Peter's when we knew you were as dire as demon's dinner, sir."

"That was kind, thank you, Gil."

"And here you are as... sit down, sit down. Wine?"

"No thank you, Gilbert, the stomach can't yet take such stuff."

"Ah yes... I see. Hal, a spot o' ale for you?"

We sat and the ale was poured.

"Gilbert, do you know if there's anyone reported missing in the town over the past two days? Especially anyone from the castle?"

"Missing?"

"As in hasn't come home or back to his quarters."

Gilbert made a moue, "I haven't seen Nick today and he would be the one to know, for it should be reported to him, being as how he's town reeve."

"Ah yes... but you know most things going on in the town before it's known by Nick."

"Do I?"

Gilbert smiled into his ale cup. "I don't know why that should but yes, folk pop in and tell me stuff." He shrugged, "An' Grace is a good gleaner of gossip. I haven't heard though."

"Not to mention your two lads."

"Aye. Felix's dad would know about the castle situation, wouldn't he, being one of the guard."

Gilbert walked into the back room, opened a shutter and yelled down into the yard.

"Felix! Can you come up here a moment lad?"

A heartbeat or two later Felix Castleman came galloping up the stairs. "Yes master?" he said as he bobbed his head at me.

"Yer dad, you seen him yesterday or today, lad?"

Felix's father was a resident of the castle and Felix lived with his master Gilbert in the cordwainer's house. His mother had died when he was fourteen and he had then been apprenticed to Gilbert, but he saw his father often.

"Aye, last night. Dad weren't on duty then, why?"

"Did he say anything about anyone being missing from the castle - not turned up for work, missing from their billet; that sort'a thing?"

"He didn't tell me specially but I did hear a few things."

"Anyone not around when they're meant to be, Felix?" I asked.

"Dad did say that Bunce was meant to be in night before last but he sent his mate to say he was ill."

"Ill...? I wonder what's wrong with him?"

"A case of water poisoning, sir?" said Hal with irony.

"No man could stay underwater that long, Hal and not drown."

"No, 'e didn't come up not even for a breath, did 'e?"

I shook my head. We then told Gilbert and Felix the story of our evening at Oakhill Pool.

"Anyone else, do you know, Felix?"

He too shook his head. "Master Philbert across the road...his missus said he was out late and she feared for him but he did come home and said his cart pony had cast a shoe, making him late. After curfew."

"Hmm. He's far too portly to be our man," I chuckled.

Gilbert slapped his own growing paunch. "Us prosperous men eh?"

"I'd be grateful Felix, if you can get your dad to ask around. Better than me doing it. I'd just have people keeping their mouths shut."

"Yes, sir. I can do that. I shall see him this evening."

"Good man." I nodded and Felix clomped back down the stairs.

"And Gil... we have a description of sorts of the man seen in the forest. Do you recall a middling man, with a shock of mousey hair, good teeth, big nose, a bit full of himself perhaps?"

"Sounds like Taske?"

"Your old journeyman, up on Kingsbury Hill?"

"Yes! Taske is more a cobbler than a cordwainer 'a corse. He mends more than he makes."

"Ah yes, I remember you telling me," I said.

I saw Gilbert frown.

"I'm sorry I can't be more precise about the man. The descriptions I am getting are very varied and a bit vague. He wears good but not generally colourful clothing. Mistress Melisande says the wool was good cloth."

"New?"

"If not, worn. He keeps his clothes well, so maybe new."

"Hmmm. I'll have to think."

Gilbert rubbed his chin. "You know that Master Webber made some beautiful cloth for Nick about four months ago. A lovely ankle length...." He stopped. "Ah no. It wouldn't be Nick would it?"

I smiled.

"He also made a new cotte for FitzAlan when he first came. Master Pitkin has a fine new cloak, a blue'un. Now who else likes to dress really well?"

He rubbed his chin again more vigorously. "Leave it with me, I'll ask around and send a message."

"Thanks."

"Where will you be?"

"Today about town and the castle. We shall go home tonight," I said.

"Harry comes out of apprenticeship in May and he'll be needing a new set o'clothes. I'll ask him to go and ask too."

Gilbert followed us down the stairs and opened the front door. Harry had gone into the workshop at the back.

We were met by a screeching and yelling echoing along the street.

Diagonally across the wide street a few people had gathered and there seemed to be an argument going on.

I watched for a while.

"I tell you they in't right... summat funny about 'em."

"There can't be nothing wrong, I tell you." It was a woman's voice.

Gilbert looked at me and shrugged his shoulders. Hal stepped out into the road and craned his neck.

"Master Mercer, sir," he said to me.

A couple of town urchins sidled up to the group and pressed between the knees of the onlookers.

I heard, "Theymz wrong way round fer a start."

"Don't be ridiculous," said the woman with a screech to the voice.

A few more townsfolk joined the crowd.

"C'mon ol' Mercer, what's the matter with it?" shouted one man.

"Wrong way round," the shopkeeper replied. "Just not the right way round like the others."

"Aw c'mon man, you can't tell...."

"They ain't all perfect you know," said another woman.

I saw the shopkeeper make a grab for the woman at the centre of the row.

"You're coming along with me. Master Barbflet'll sort you, you thief!"

"Who are you calling a thief?"

A basket was tugged to and fro. A couple of men tried to grab the mercer.

"Leave it Alfred," I heard one say, "it's only a few...."

Another woman picked up her empty basket and took a swipe at the angry merchant.

Her husband tried to restrain her and got a buffet on the head from one of the other men for his pains. He turned and swung at the man behind him, who had simply been staring at the fracas, grinning.

I ran across the road, Hal following.

"Let the constable through!" I shouted. They took no notice. Someone turned and took a swipe at me before they realised who I was. I stuck out my foot and he fell headlong into the dust of the road.

"Stop this now!" I looked over the heads of the crowd, for I was taller than any of them. I could see the town watch, two burly men employed by the town reeve, running as fast as they could from the town cross end of Marlborough High Street.

One of the urchins cried, "Town watch!" and legged it up the alley by the side of the old chandler's house.

One or two of the protagonists had come to their senses and had backed off. Two slaughterhouse men, their aprons gory and fouled, each grabbed one of the two men who had started the fighting.

I pushed my way into the centre of the mêlée. "Stop this now. Quiet!" I bellowed.

One or two folk carried on but strangely the two original combatants fell silent.

I glared at the rest. They backed off. The town watch arrived and stood at a respectful distance.

"Stand apart, I say!"

At last the groups parted to stand in two distinct camps. One for the woman and one for the mercer.

I faced the mercer. "What seems to be your problem, Alfred?"

He pointed a shaking finger at the woman now tearfully being assisted by a woman friend, the one with the flailing basket.

"She sir, is a thief and I'll tell anyone who cares to argue with me that it's so."

I spun round.

"Mistress Scarlett?"

She bobbed a perfunctory curtsey. "My Lord Belvoir."

"What is it you are accused of stealing?"

Several voices started up at once and I was forced to bellow again. "Are you all called Mistress Scarlett, then?"

Voices tailed off and someone giggled. I saw Hal, his arms folded across his chest, trying hard not to laugh.

"Mistress, what is this about?"

"I am buying some trimming with coin, sir. I'm not stealing anything."

"Coin! Pah!" shouted the merchant. "Might as well be rabbit droppings."

"How dare you!" screamed Mistress Scarlett.

"I dare. They ain't right, I tell you."

"Mercer, what isn't right?"

"Show the constable, I dare you... go on, show him!" screamed the merchant.

Mistress Scarlett drew her basket close to her bosom with two hands.

"I'll take my money elsewhere Alfred Mercer. As if I haven't been buying from you this twenty years or more."

"Aye... and I wasn't so clever then maybe? So watchful."

"Alfred," I said quietly. "What has Mistress Scarlett to show me?"

"The mercer drew himself up to his full height. "Money sir," he said. "Coins."

Suddenly an idea flitted across my brain. An unpleasant feeling hit me in the guts. I reeled.

Hal was there at my elbow.

"All right, sir?"

"Yes, Hal… a moment only." I swallowed.

"Please can I see the coins, Mistress Scarlett?"

The woman sniffed and then unclenched her hand.

She stretched out her arm and on the flat of her palm were two silver pennies.

I reached for them. They were warm from her grasp.

Turning from both the mercer and the woman, I stared at them on my own palm.

Hal steered himself through the crowd which had gathered at my back and looked over my shoulder, standing on tiptoe.

"Watch!"

"Yessir."

"All but Mistress Scarlet and Alfred Mercer are to go about their business."

"Yessir." They set about moving folk along quickly.

I saw the two urchins peer round the corner of Chandler's Lane.

"Mistress - come with me," I said as I took her arm. "Master Mercer, stay here. I will speak to you in a moment."

I steered the woman across the road and met Gilbert at his shop front again.

"Gil, might we step in a moment, for some peace and privacy?"

"Surely." He opened the door wide and nodded to the Widow Scarlett.

"Milly."

"Gilbert."

Some folk had bypassed the watch and had scurried after us across the road. Gilbert shut the door on them and barred it.

A couple cheekily went to the window. Gilbert pulled up the flap and secured the window shutter.

"Please sit, mistress," I said.

She had lost quite a bit of her bluster now and was sitting shocked and rather tearful with a trembling lip.

I asked Gil to see if Grace might step down a moment. It wasn't fair: the woman was all alone with three men.

Grace came tripping down the steps a moment later and Millisende dissolved into tears as soon as she saw her.

"I've never been so embarrassed in all my life," she wailed, "me called a thief."

"No, no I'm sure that's not so" said Gilbert, looking at me quizzically.

I put the two coins down on Gilbert's table with a click.

Without the light from the lowered front panel of the window it was quite gloomy in the little shop.

"Gil, can we have some light, do you think?"

"Aye...," he fetched a couple of candles from the back room. Felix poked his head from the workroom, tutted and then disappeared again.

I sat down on the stool and faced the little woman.

"Mistress Scarlett. I asked you when I last saw you, where the two silver pennies had gone which my man Hal here, saw in your brother's room."

"Aye sir," she sniffed.

"Are these the two coins?"

"Yes, sir. The very same."

"Ahhh...." I heard Hal exhale.

"Why did you keep them back from us?"

She looked at me coyly from under her lashes.

"I wanted them, sir. I thought, why shouldn't I have them? They was my brother's and what's his is mine now and...," she started to snivel again. "They are mine, sir."

I looked carefully at the coins in the light of the candles.

"Were there any others?"

"No sir. I 'in't found any others."

Grace put her arms tightly around her.

"Good," I sighed. "Because if you had, and you'd spent them, I would have had no alternative but to arrest you."

The woman screeched and put her hands to her face, dropping her empty basket to the floor. Hal picked it up and put it on the table.

Gilbert coughed. "That's a bit harsh, i'n't it, Sir Aumary?"

Grace looked daggers at me.

"No, Gil. Come look."

Gilbert came round the table. "See here." I added.

I pulled open my purse and from it took a silver penny. This was the currency we were all used to, the only coin we handled, day in, day out.

I put it by the two pennies on the table.

Gilbert bent to look at all three. I turned the second of Milly Scarlett's pennies to the obverse.

"Look carefully, Gil."

Hal leaned in also.

Mistress Scarlett ceased to snivel and with a hiccough now and again stretched her neck to look at the coins sitting on the table.

I watched her face.

"Well, I'll be... bugg... buried in Burbage!" said Hal.

Gilbert's eyes grew round. "Can I?" he asked, picking up a coin. He brought it up to his eyes and stared at the image on the face.

"Aye Hal, I think I'll be joining you in that churchyard!" he said.

The widow's eyes grew huge, her face was the colour of uncooked pastry.

Grace took in a sharp breath "Oh!"

"They'm in't real," said Hal at last.

"Fakeries," added Gilbert.

"Nooo," whispered the Widow Scarlett.

"Well, I never," said Grace letting go of the woman she had been comforting just a breath before.

"They are," I said. I looked sternly at the widow. "You didn't know, did you, Mistress Scarlett?"

She had now gone very white in the face. Her brown eyes rose to meet mine. "Nooo," she whispered and slumped in a faint on Grace's breast.

*****

With a vinegar potion from Gallipot the apothecary, which Grace kept for emergencies, wafted under her nose, the Widow Scarlett regained her wits quite quickly.

A cup of water was put into her hand and she sipped it gratefully.

The silver coin of the realm bore the head of a crowned king inside a small circle. On the coin which I had taken from my purse, the right hand lay just outside the ring and in its grasp the sceptre crossed the border of the coin on his right hand side, looking at the coin, on the left. On the coin which Mistress Scarlett had in her possession, the King grasped the sceptre in his other hand and it passed to the left, the right as we looked at it.

"So, I'll ask you again, Millisende. This is the first coin you have tried to spend which belonged to your brother?"

"Aye sir, it is. I had no idea it weren't right money, sir."

"And you have found no further coins?"

"I 'in't searched his room, like I told you the other day."

"Hal, that's something we shall need to do now."

"Aye sir."

"Take the room apart, floorboards, bed, everything."

"Aye sir. Now, sir?

"Yes, now. Get Peter and Stephen from the castle."

Hal turned to leave "And Hal... anything you can find which looks strange. Stuff you don't understand."

"Right you are, sir."

"Bring it to my office or Gayle's in the castle. Or tell me and I'll come up to the house."

"Gilbert, can you go down to Nick's house and tell him we might have a pile of money circulating in the town which is false. Anyone can have it and not have noticed."

"Yes, sir. Does this mean that...?"

"Yes, Gil, it does. It can be anywhere. Absolutely anywhere. You, me, Nick, Gabriel. Anywhere. It's an offence to pass it on but we might not know... we must keep our eyes open."

"Aye, sir." Poor Gilbert looked shocked. I knew the first thing he would do when out of sight was check his own purse for coins.

"Mistress Scarlett, stay here with Grace whilst I go and placate the enemy."

I saw Gilbert smile at that but I thought my comment passed over the head of the Widow Scarlett.

As I followed Gilbert out of the door, I heard the widow say, "That Alfred Mercer, I shall never speak to him again." Perhaps she had understood me after all.

Across the street I went, noticing that a few folk out and about lifted their heads but no one asked me any questions.

I walked into Master Mercer's small shop, now empty of customers.

"Now Master Mercer. It's like this. We have a problem in the town."

His belligerent face rose up to meet me as he stepped to his feet from a tall step stool.

"Oh?"

"Someone has been making false coins and well done for spotting that."

"Aye well... it was obvious it was the wrong way round. I see coins all the time...."

"Ah, but not everyone would notice such a small difference."

"I got good eyes, I have."

"Indeed you have. Whoever made these coins has used a die which has been reversed."

"I don't know about that. I just know it weren't right."

"Mistress Scarlett wasn't as observant as you, Mercer. She had no idea what she was trying to give you was a forgery."

"It's a crime, sir."

"Indeed it is. Please, Master Mercer, might I look at your own coin... those in your purse and those in your money box here. To make sure I'm right about it being a false one. You see, I don't carry money around with me. I leave that to my men. I've nothing with which to compare it."

The mercer gave me a hard stare then slipped his purse from his belt and emptied it.

He went to the counter beside the window and pulled out a box secreted under some bolts of cloth.

"Here sir."

I searched through both piles.

"Ah... see here Master Mercer. Even you missed this one."

The mercer's face suffused with blood.

"No! I...."

"Yes - look here. I took out one of the coins which Mistress Scarlett had been trying to pass and compared the two.

"Identical."

The mercer stared at it, then sagged onto his stool again. "You'd better take it with you then, Sir Aumary," he said. "I can't be accused of passin' it along then, can I?"

"Check all your coin, Mercer and let me know if you find any others. They can be handed in at the castle."

"Mistress Scarlett, sir...."

"Yes, Alfred?"

"Can you tell her...," the mercer squirmed. "I can't... apologise... like...."

"Yes, I know... I'll tell her."

*****

I smiled and I left.

As I shut the door, I reached into my purse for the other false coin. I jingled the two in my hand. Master Mercer's 'false' coin had never existed, of course. It was a ruse to get him from Mistress Scarlett's back.

Gilbert Cordwainer came jogging along the road. Ahead of him, Nicholas Barbflet, the town reeve, was striding along purposefully.

"Aumary!"

"Nick." We clasped arms.

Nicholas Barbflet was the master miller here in the town, a prosperous man; a man with a good business head and he was a fine friend. This was his second term of office and he was a popular choice. He led the town council, as it was becoming known, and was responsible for law and order and the smooth running of the town of Marlborough. Gilbert Cordwainer was also a councillor, as was Gabriel Gallipot.

"Gil tells me we have false coin being circulated in the town," said Nick.

I took his hand and tipped the two coins into it.

He stared at them. "They look like old coins, maybe from Henry's reign."

"Well, neither Richard nor John have seen fit to alter the design of coin on the heads side, and it's the obverse which tells you they aren't what they seem."

Nicholas Barbflet flipped one over. "Stern ol' Henry's head on the one side...."

"Just the personification of the strong ruler...," I said.

"And a short cross on the other."

He lifted one up to his eyes, just as Gilbert had done. "What's wrong with it? I can't see…."

"It's back to front, Nick. The die has been made in reverse. I wouldn't be surprised if the silver is short weight and too much copper has been added."

" Well! I'll be….! Still says 'Henricus' though" said Nick.

"Surely there are some old ones still in circulation?" said Gilbert.

"John hasn't changed the coins. Neither did Richard. They're still his father's design," I said.

"There must be several at the mint…."

"That's where we must go. Speak to Gayle," said Nick. "At the treasury. He'll know what we have here."

We turned about and walked up to the castle. Gilbert followed.

As we wandered along, Nick told me he was glad I'd recovered from my poisoning and I asked after his broken leg and crushed knee. From the way he strode about, it looked to me that it was all mended perfectly. He'd been involved in an accident at the mill in 1206 and we had all been worried that he would not walk properly again.

"We both have Johannes to thank for our lives, Aumary," said Nick. "He's such an asset to the town."

"Amen to that," I said as we passed under the portcullis.

Gayle stood as we scratched on the door and entered at his call. He was in his office with a parchment under his nose.

"Well, well. This is an honour," said Peterkin Gayle with a titter. "The Lord of the Forest and the Lord of the town, all in one moment."

I chuckled. "You won't think it such an honour, when you hear what we have come about, Pete."

Gayle ruffled his sparse hair and set it straight again with his fingers.

"Don't tell me... you want to have another look at one of my guards. Since you started your inquiry my workforce has been shrinking, you know."

"Oh?"

"First Beecroft, then Carrier, Canard...."

"Surely no one else has...?"

"Now Pygge's gone missing."

Under my breath I said to myself, 'He's not our man in the forest. Too portly and not fleet enough of foot He's not our drowned man.'

Peterkin Gayle heard me. "Drowned?"

I had to tell the tale of our trip to Oakhill Pool again, for Nick Barbflet and Peterkin Gayle.

"Oh dear," said Gayle. "Your life is still threatened, Sir Aumary."

"So where has Pygge gone?"

"I've no idea. He just didn't turn up for duty this morning."

Gayle flicked the edge of the parchment lying on his table, "You have no idea how difficult it is to organise the rotas for the treasury and the guards when people keep disappearing."

"He lived in the castle?"

"Aye, he did. Does. We mustn't speak of him as if...."

"No, we mustn't," I replied. "I hear that Bunce too has been ill."

"Him too. Good job I have enough soldiers for the garrison. Of course, FitzAlan brought some with him."

"What's wrong with Bunce?"

"Ha, ha, slipped on a step in the wet and hurt his arm badly. All strapped up it is. What's the good of a guard who can't guard, eh?"

"Hmmm."

"Anyone else missing?"

"'That not enough for you, sir?"

I smiled.

"Bunce in his billet, Pete?"

"As far as I know, sir."

"Then I'll have a word with him too in a while. Anyway, Pete, what do you make of these?"

I dropped the two forged coins onto his table.

He picked them up and firstly weighed them in his hand.

His eyes rose to meet mine before he'd ever looked at the silver.

"God's Cods! Are they what I think they are?"

"Aye Pete. False coin."

"Where did they come from?"

"Beecroft's sister tried to pass them in town today. She had no idea they were forgeries."

"Beecroft? Mistress Scarlett then?"

I nodded. "She found them amongst the blacksmith's effects. I have Hal at her house now searching for more and for anything which might tell us why he had them."

"Are these old coins, Pete?" asked Nicholas.

Gayle tutted. "Not my field. I just organise the guarding. You need to speak to Master Crosscastle."

"Then might we do that? Here?" I asked.

"Aye, I'll have him fetched."

*****

Hal came back into the room as we were waiting for Crosscastle to be brought to us.

He fished in a cloth bag. " 'Ere sir, no idea what they are but...."

I took the tubular wooden blocks from him and turned them around in my fingers.

"And this, sir, under the mattress."

The small wooden box contained a rather degraded die with a crowned head on it. The sceptre was held on the opposite side.

"Then under a loose floorboard, we found these."

Hal tipped out a dozen or more coins onto the table. They settled with a tinny rattle.

Crosscastle entered, took in at a glance the number of people in the room and his eyes strayed to the table where lay the coins. His brow furrowed.

"Crosscastle. Good day. We need your help," I said.

He bowed and smiled cheerfully at us. "I'd be delighted to help, sir, if I can."

"These were found at the dead man Beecroft's house. Might you tell us what you think of them?"

Crosscastle picked up a handful.

He went over to the window and peered at them.

He kept one in his fingers, leaned over and dropped the rest onto the table. He felt the remaining coin with his finger and thumb.

"Sorry to say it, sir, but these aren't the real thing."

"Might they be old coins from the King's father's reign?" asked Nick.

The moneyer shook his head. "No sir...and even if they are, they would still be legal. These are coins which have been struck back to front."

"And?"

"I wouldn't be at all surprised if they contained only a fraction of the silver which they should contain."

We joined him in the light. "How would you know?"

"I'd have to melt them and see how much copper was in them."

"Crosscastle, can you take a look at this and tell me what you think?"

I handed him the die. His eyebrows rose.

"Ah... this is a new punch, sir. One which has been made with the image reversed... these were found at Beecroft's too?"

"Aye."

Crosscastle shook his head. Then someone has maybe been copying stuff…."

"What happens to the old punches?"

"We send them back to London and there they are defaced."

"What's that?"

"Defaced, sir? Strike off the pattern on it, so it can't be reused."

"This die is a little degraded, isn't it?"

"Yes, it's probably done 10,000 strikes. That's when we get rid of them. The top die doesn't last as long."

"How long?"

"100 to 300 strikes."

"So Beecroft was striking coins..."

"The noise in 'is room and cellar, sir," said Hal.

I nodded. "And the turned up tree stump."

"Beg your pardon, sir?" said Crosscastle.

"We found a tree stump just like your own from the forge in the cellar at Beecroft's lodging and I wager if we upended it we'd find a hole for a die bored into it. Where do you think his silver might come from?"

Crosscastle shook his head.

"It can't be the castle. Nothing escapes from my forge."

"Hmm. "And these pieces of wood?"

Crosscastle took one of the blocks from me. "See here, sir. The bottom die, the pile is inserted into a hole and the flan is placed on the top. It helps to keep it secure, so it doesn't move. Then the top, the trussel, is put on... did you find the pile, sir?"

"Did we, Hal?"

"No, sir."

"And the whole thing is struck with a hammer. You saw that happening when you visited the forge, m'lord."

"And a very noisy process it was too."

Crosscastle grinned a gleaming smile. "We get used to it, sir."

"So you say that no silver escapes the forge. Where did Beecroft and his fishing friend get it from? Any ideas?"

"Another source, sir. Maybe the silversmith on Silver Street?"

"Surely not." I replied. "It would be too expensive for a blacksmith. It must have been stolen."

"Stolen from there, sir?" asked Hal. "You know what those Jew's houses are like. They're worse than the castle. Trussed up tighter than a nun's... chin."

"Has anyone reported a theft of silver, Nicholas?" I said, chuckling at Hal's levity.

The town reeve shook his head.

"You know as well as I do, Aumary, that it would not be reported even if it were stolen. The Jews keep themselves to themselves."

"I would like to think they'd report it to you... or me."

Nick just shook his head sadly.

I turned back to Crosscastle who was absently staring at the coin in his hand.

"You say, Crosscastle, that a guard must have smuggled this die out of the mint?"

"No, it won't have got out from there," he said. "I take my dies with me at night. The new ones are guarded in and out."

"We have two guards, one missing and the other dead...."

"Pygge and Canard, sir." He shrugged. "I heard that Pygge didn't turn up for duty today."

"I'll speak to Andrew Merriman. I'll see if I can get some men out looking for him."

I saw Hal nod and disappear through the slightly open door. It closed silently behind him.

"I need to know how the die was able to be made. And where did the metal come from which was used to make it." I clenched my jaw in frustration. "You say the legitimate dies are made in London?"

"They are. We only have one at a time and as I say, we return the old ones. I look after mine with my life."

"Then where would the die for these come from?" I asked, pointing to the coins.

The moneyer shook his head. "No one here has the skill to make such a die, m'lord. It's a very skilled job, engraving the design, for it has to be done in reverse and the metal must be scratched away so the design stands proud. That's how this mistake was made. The man who made it forgot that as he turned the die up, the design would be the other way round."

"As a man's image is in a polished piece of steel?" I had such a piece in my office for when I trimmed my beard. Looking into it, the image was reversed as it is when you look at your reflection in a pool of water.

"And I can be absolutely certain that the silver did not come from my supplies."

"How, Crosscastle?"

He folded his arms across his chest. "I know how many coins I have fabricated that day and I know what we have left. The remaining silver is weighed. I know exactly how much we've used and what's left over, sir."

"Who weighs it?"

"I do. And I record it in a ledger."

I nodded. "And the leavings?"

"The same, sir. All returned to the crucible to be melted down."

"Where is it stored?"

I suddenly realised how ignorant I had been all this time about the process of the minting of coins in the castle. I'd left the whole thing to others, without questioning. Somewhere there must be a depository for the silver. There was no special place in the forge.

Crosscastle answered. "The finished coin is either taken by me, for it's my silver, sir, home to my house and I have a strong box for it, or the coin is deposited in the treasury."

"Where does the silver come from?"

"I buy in silver as I need it. Sometimes the Jews, sometimes Master Metier the goldsmith has some. Old coins, old jewellery," he replied. "Depends how much we can get as to how much we can make."

"Thank you - all of you."

I turned to the window. "Please keep your eyes and ears open."

Now I understood the significance of the tree trunk in the cellar at Beecroft's lodging. Gayle sat down at his table and picked up a forged coin as Crosscastle backed out and, I presumed, went back to the forge.

"I'll follow in a moment," said Gayle.

Gilbert nodded and left with a smile at me; Nicholas followed him with, "I'll make inquiries amongst the Jews, Aumary."

"Thank you Nick."

Hal and I looked at the paraphernalia found in Beecroft's room.

"We need to find out who this second man is."

"The fisherman friend?" asked Gayle.

"Can you spare me a lad, Pete? One to sit around and watch the moat-side?"

"Aye, I reckon I can do that."

"Set him to watch on the southern edge of the walls."

"The newly built section?"

"The piece of moat at the back of the wall where the forge is situated, for that is where Beecroft has been seen. I hope his friend will carry on where he left off."

*****

Hal and I marched around the northern wall and entered a large room partitioned off into sleeping cubicles, four beds to a section. Here the garrison soldiers who didn't live in the town slept, (there were only a few of those), amused themselves when not on duty and kept their belongings.

Bunce was lying on his bed with his ankles crossed and a large floppy rush sun hat over his face.

"Bunce!" I yelled.

The man started like a hare from a hedge and sat up spluttering. The hat skidded over the flagstone floor. Hal picked it up.

"Sir?" said the soldier rubbing his face with his good hand. The other arm was bandaged from the hand to the elbow.

He peered through piggy, sleep filled eyes. "Oh, M'Lord Belvoir, it's you." He struggled up.

"Bunce, you haven't been at your post today, they tell me."

"Ah, no sir. On account of this." He lifted the bad arm and grimaced at the action.

I perched on a trestle in the middle of this section of the room.

"How did you get that then, Bunce?"

The soldier chuckled. "Bein' stoopid, I was."

"Nah. I can't believe a seasoned soldier like you can be stupid," I laughed.

"It were damp. Well, wet really, yesterday mornin' 'afore I was due on duty."

"Yes?"

"I slipped on the steps and fell. I hit my arm so I did, summat awful and gashed it on the stone. Black and blue and pourin' a blood."

"Hal, can you look around please. We're looking for some clothes."

"You mean like these, sir?" Once again Hal had anticipated my instruction and had been foraging under the bed.

"Just like that Hal." I turned to the soldier.

"These look, Bunce, like they have been wet. Very wet."

"Aye... well it was into the moat I fell after I missed me footing."

"Did you now?"

"You have a bow don't you, Bunce?"

"Aye sir, I do. But I don't have no sharp arrows…."

I looked around, "I don't see it."

"That's a 'cos it 'in't 'ere, sir."

"Where is it then, Bunce?" I asked.

"In the moat where I fell in, sir."

"What were you doing 'Ol Bunce, so that you fell in the moat?" asked Hal, grinning

"I can answer that, sir," said a voice.

I turned around. Another of the gate guards had just come in the door.

"What do you know about it, Hereward?"

"Well," the man wiped his nose with the back of his hand. "I was with 'im wa'n't I, sir?"

"What were you two doing?"

Bunce chuckled. "Taking a pot-shot at a goose what had landed on the moat. I would'a had him, if I hadn't slipped."

Hereward handed Bunce his bow. "I fished it out for yer." He leaned a dripping net up against the dormitory wall.

"Youm'z a true friend Hairy," said Bunce. "I owe you."

"I fished you out too, you old trout turd, so that's two you owe me!"

The castle doctor then appeared in the doorway. He hesitated. Then he opened his mouth to speak. I forestalled him.

"Here to minister to your patient, doctor?"

"I am, if I can have some space and peace and quiet, my lord."

"We shan't disturb you," I said, smiling my sweetest smile. "In fact I'd like to see this terrible wound of yours, Bunce. Just to satisfy myself that you aren't about to die of some nasty infection, you understand."

"Sir!" said the doctor, affronted that I had called his skill into question.

"Unwrap away, doctor," I said, stepping back out of the way.

It was as Bunce had said, a nasty bruised gash to the elbow and a swollen wrist.

Hal and I turned away.

"Well, sir, he weren't our man in the pool. That i'n't no arrer wound."

I sighed. "No Hal. We must keep looking."

Chapter Eleven

W e stepped up to Johannes' house, through the busy town, for again it was market day.

"The doctor'll be busy won't 'e?' said Hal, "Folk coming in for market day."

"So he says," I answered, but Johannes was dealing with his last patient of the afternoon as we arrived.

"Two drops in a cup of water. Water do you hear me William. Not ale."

"Aye, aye, I hear you."

"Just you be sure to remember."

An old man came pushing past us out of the workroom and along the passage. It was Will Chasier, the cheese-man, or rather it was the current cheese-man's father, also Will. The other was known as Young Will, though he was in his forties.

The whole family was involved in the trade and lived on Herd Street the main road through the town, on the hill.

"Good day Will," I said.

Chasier hobbled round on his stick.

"Ah it's… erm.... Sir… erm…."

"Aumary, Will, Aumary Belvoir."

"Thats'im," he said, smiling and showing terrible red gums. He tugged his forelock, well he would have done if he'd had any hair there.

"How are you?"

"Well, I can't lie can I?" said the old man, "Or I wouldn't be seen 'ere would I now, m'lord?"

I smiled. The man was over seventy.

Yes, Paul, he was the same age as I am now.

"You look well," I said.

"Don't be deceived m'lord. I could die tomorrer, so I could."

Johannes came out of his workroom drying his hands on a piece of linen. "Nonsense Chasier, you'll live till you're ninety."

The cheeseman looked chastened.

"Not if that son of mine has anything to do with it."

"Why? What's wrong with Young Will then?" I asked, amused.

Chasier sniffed and then gave a terrible cough which rattled his old lungs like a barrel full of pebbles. "Him! Nowt' wrong with 'im. He's stone lazy, that's all."

"Aw, I don't think that's fair, Will," I said, "I often see him out and about in town with his baskets and he's a regular at the castle."

"We supply the kitchens there, my lord. Have done since my dad were a pup," said Chasier proudly.

A thought suddenly jumped into my head and I leaned on the wall beside the old man.

"Will, is it cow's cheese, sheep or goat's you supply the castle?"

"All of 'em when we can make it.... Why?"

"Does Will take it straight to the kitchen?"

"No, it goes to Ansell the victualler first to be recorded."

"Of course. He will write down what you've brought that day?"

"Aye, otherwise, how will we get paid?"

I nodded.

"Then we takes it to the kitchens, to the stores."

"Anyone else ever buy some from you, at the castle I mean, say for their own dinner or supper?"

"Now and again. We make sure we have enough."

"Regularly or not?"

"Well, there's always someone stops us and asks."

"Who stopped and asked two weeks ago last Wednesday?"

"How should I know, sir? I don't deal with the sellin' nowadays."

"No, of course not."

I rubbed my nose. "Well, thank you William. I might call in and buy something for my dinner. I have a mind for some nice strong yellow cheese."

"Ah yessir. We'll have that all right," He gave me his gummy grin again.

"And maybe Young Will might be around so I can ask a few questions, eh?"

The old man turned for the door. "Aye, he'll be around, makin' eyes at that new churn girl, I'll be bound. Later in the day mind."

"I might catch him if I see him about town."

"You might. My grandson Hambidge comes and sells at the market Wednesday and Saturday. Young Will brings the cart into market with him."

"Thank you for that information, Will," I said.

The door opened.

"Two drops in a pint o' ale you say, doctor," said Will with a grin.

"You know darn well...," said Johannes sternly and the rest dissolved into a chuckle.

*****

Johannes was still chuckling as we went through to the kitchen. "You know what, the old bugger *will* take the medicine in ale, you know."

"Will it affect the usefulness of the potion?"

"Not a jot. I'm just trying to stop him drinking so much. He doesn't need to know that though does he? At his age he gets too unsteady. He'll fall and it'll be the death of him."

"At 'is age doctor, he i'n't got a lot of pleasures left," muttered Hal.

We all laughed.

"Hal, can you step out to the market and see if Hambidge is still there? It's a long shot, but there might have been someone from the castle who bought from him the day I was poisoned."

"He isn't the only cheesemonger in the town, Aumary," said Johannes.

"No, but it's the biggest cheese business and the Chasiers buy from other dairy folk."

Johannes shrugged. Hal left.

"How are you feeling now?"

I sat down at the table. "Tired in fits and starts and the stomach is still sore."

"Aye, it will be for a while. You realise that amount would have killed an older, less fit man?"

"Yes. Yes I do."

"Thank God you didn't eat all the cheese."

I looked up and smiled at my best friend. "I owe you and Gallipot my life."

"Think nothing of it," said Johannes. "So how is the hunt for the killer coming along?"

"It's slow. Our murderer is extremely elusive. Both Hal and I have been within inches of the man and still we don't know him."

"Hmm." Johannes sat at the table. "Do be careful, Aumary. This man seems to want to stop you finding him at all costs."

"I'm travelling with Hal and Stephen and Peter now. I shall be protected: I always wear my gambeson and my mail over it now. And as you say, I'm tough."

"I didn't say that," he chuckled. "By the way, I dropped in on Tostig the other day."

"He's doing well," I said. "We have re-organised the wedding for St. Juliana's day; the 16th day of February so not long now. Can you come?"

"Try to keep me away!"

Johannes searched the larder for a large onion and egg pie and we sat chewing on it until Hal returned. Johannes cut him a slice.

"The cheese man says that the only person from the castle what bought goats' cheese the day you was got at, sir...."

"Yes, Hal...?" Hal took a bite of the pie. "Was Maurice FitzAlan, sir."

I sat stock still and stopped chewing.

Johannes looked at me from under lowered brows.

"Well! Our new captain of the guard."

" 'E didn't know Beecroft, did 'e?" asked Hal. "What I mean is, 'e i'n't bin 'ere long enough...."

"More to the point, Hal, what is his connection to Elswith?"

"Where did he come from, Aumary?" asked the doctor.

"De Neville land out in Lincolnshire but he has been here before. Before he was appointed to the castle. That's how I met him...." I rubbed my face with my hand. "I recommended him, for Christ's sake."

"Ah yes, he was part of the de Neville retinue which came in with Matilda for her wedding, wasn't he?" said Johannes "in 1204?" De Neville's daughter had come to Marlborough to be married to Guy de Saye and FitzAlan was in her retinue of soldiers.

"So what might 'e 'ave against Elswith, Beecroft and Carrier?" asked Hal

"And Canard... remember, he gave the order to shoot Canard," Johannes added.

"I haven't the faintest idea," I said.

*****

Hal, Peter, Stephen and I rode for home later that afternoon. I made sure it was before dusk and there was still enough light by which to ride safely.

Hal sidled up to me on Grafton and told me that he'd seen Peterkin Fisher when he'd been in the town.

" 'E found me at the cheesemonger, sir, in the High Street. The message is that the fella what was seen at the moat-side hasn't been there since Beecroft died."

"Damn."

"Aye sir."

Hal tutted. "Looks like it were a case of innocent fishin' and the mate hasn't the 'eart to go there without 'is pal."

"I don't know about that, Hal," I said.

"I said... looks like it... didn't I, eh?" grinned Hal.

I chuckled at my man at arms.

"Owever, I reckon as 'ow the bugger is lyin' low 'cos 'e knows we rumbled 'im, sir."

"That is a great possibility, Hal. He'll be much more careful from now on, I think."

Hal guffawed. "Or he'll panic like a swarm o' nuns at a Viking raid," he said.

*****

Henry Pierson, my steward, met me at the door. "Sir, a message from Gilbert Cordwainer."

"Ah yes, Henry."

"It's about the...," Henry read from a small scrap of birchbark paper, "clothes on the villain, sir?"

"Ah yes, Henry. Shall I read it or shall you?"

"I think it'd make more sense to you, sir," smiled my steward.

I took the small piece of paper from him. It was a list of folk that had new clothes made for them this past month. Five names were listed. I recognised them all. I thrust the paper in my cotte.

"And Lady Belvoir would like to see you, sir, it's about the Lady Hawise."

My heart thumped. "Is she all right, Henry?"

"Oh quite, sir. It's something she'd like you to know."

"Who?"

"The Lady Hawise, sir."

My heart beat returned to normal.

"Thank you, Henry." He bowed and jogged up the steps.

"Hal, get the lads settled. I'll see you in the hall at supper."

"Right you are, sir."

Hawise and Lydia were sitting close together in the solar.

Hawise was reading from a small waxed block and now and again she would scribble furiously with her bone tool.

I watched them for a moment from the open door. After a while Hawise asked,

"So, how do you spell... sil-ent-ly, mama?"

"S-I-L-.... Come in, Aumary, don't loiter in the doorway," said Lydia, " E-N-T-..."

"L-Y," I said as I poked my head around the door jamb.

Hawise dropped her writing on the stool in front of her and jumped up.

"Dada!" she cried.

I walked into the room, picked her up and kissed her.

"So... what was being said or done silently that you must write it down, my sweet?" I put her down and went over and kissed my wife. "Hello my angel," I said.

"Mama and I are writing a story."

"Oh that is very exciting."

Lydia chuckled. "It's a true story, Aumary," she said, signalling for me to sit down. "Ale?"

"No, thank you. I've just come from Johannes' house and ale."

Yes, Paul, even a while later, my stomach was not ready for too much ale. Water and milk were the two preferred drinks. I felt a little bit like my son Simon, just ten months old.

I looked over to the nurse Felice where she bounced my son on her knee. I went to her and lifted him up. "My, you are growing into a big lad!" He cackled an almost toothless laugh.

Hawise beamed. "He's crawling all over. We have to watch he doesn't pull stuff off the table. And he's getting more teeth, dada."

I sat down with my son on my knee and jiggled him up and down. Simon giggled and reached into the neck of my shirt which was just visible inside my gambeson, pulled it out and began happily chewing.

"So what is this story about?"

"Well, now you are here, dada," said Hawise, looking over at her mother, I won't need to write it down."

"We were writing it because we wanted to remember it, Aumary, and make sure we had all the details right. And it's a good exercise in writing."

"Now we'll just tell you," said Hawise, sitting on her hands and leaning forward.

"I'm listening," I said.

Hawise took a deep breath.

"I was out with the dogs, yesterday."

"Time, Hawise?" said her mother.

"About vespers."

"Going dark then?" I said. "And this is a story about you, Hawise?"

"Yes. Mama told you, it's a true story."

"Right...."

"I was out in the stables with the dogs. Well, some of the dogs. I'd been playing in one of the empty stalls which still had some hay in it, with Mildred and Ben. The end one."

"Rough and tumble," said her mother, looking rather disparagingly at her daughter. "You should have seen the state of her when she came in! Straw, cobwebs... muddy paw prints...."

"Aw Mama, you promised not to say!" Hawise tossed her copper curls.

"Ah well... I don't suppose it matters. You hadn't torn anything... this time!"

Hawise tutted. "Anyway, I saw that the bats in the top of the stable roof were wriggling about."

"Ah yes, they live there all winter don't they?"

"Yes."

"They wake up when it's warmer."

"They are so sweet and I like to watch them. They dance about and change places and stretch their wings and then they go back to sleep."

"I've seen them. Richard complains about the mess they make," I laughed.

Hawise laughed too. "Yes I know. But we aren't going to get rid of them. I told him they were my bats."

"Belvoir bats...," I joked.

Hawise giggled again. My son Simon reached for my nose and tweaked it. Then he grabbed for my close cropped beard. I turned him round to face his mother and sister; the neck of my shirt was soggy.

"So I climbed up to the hayloft at the end...."

"How?"

"Well, the roof comes down at the back and it's easy to squeeze up there and wriggle between the thatch and the wall."

"Is it by Jove? I'll have to tell Bevis Joiner about that." Bevis was one of the village woodworkers.

I didn't tell my daughter that I'd done the very same thing as a youngster.

"Aw no dada, don't...."

"Go on...."

"If you are careful you can swing up into the top of the roof."

"How many feet above the floor, Hawise?"

"That's what I asked," piped up Lydia. Felice the nurse, behind me, tutted.

"This is a bit that wasn't repaired a while ago, you remember, dada? It's full of old straw and bundles of this and that, forgotten stuff. Stuck up there."

"I'll get it cleared out."

Hawise looked at me sidelong. "Right by the big beam."

"The king rafter?"

"...Was a group of bats. I could reach out and almost touch them."

"I hope you didn't, they can bite, you know," I said.

"I lay down flat on the beam nearest and watched them."

"Sounds like fun," I said yawning.

Hawise pouted... "I shan't tell you if you are going to..."

"No, no, go on." I joggled Simon some more. Lydia came forward and took him from me.

"The smell of the droppings was quite strong. I was going to move and get myself out of the smelly bit when...."

"Yes."

"I didn't because I heard a voice below."

"Someone you knew?"

"No, Aumary, but someone she had seen before." Lydia's face was earnest and a little worried.

"Go on, Hawise," I said, suddenly serious.

"I didn't move. I stayed there. I could see through the rafters even though the man had his back to me. Then someone else came into the stable."

"Who, Hawise?"

"One of the men who works with the cows."

"She means the cattleman, Kineman."

"He works out in the fields. He has a house in Braydon Wood. What was he doing here?"

"Talking to this other man, dada."

"To be fair, Aumary, he had a good reason to be here yesterday. He'd come to ask about taking some of the cattle to the town. Time for some of them to go to the leather workers I believe."

"He came to speak to Master Henry Steward but it wasn't Master Henry he was speaking to in the end stable, dada. It was the man I saw in the forest. The man with the big nose and the brown hood. The one who was horrible to the poor pony."

I was silent as I took in this tale. Then I said, "But he doesn't work here surely?"

My girls didn't answer. What was our murderer doing here in Durley? He must have ridden here. Where had his horse been hidden?

I sat shocked as Hawise continued. "I heard them talking but I didn't really know what it was all about at first."

"What did they speak about?"

"The man in the hood said, 'He's alive then?' and the other one said, 'Yes, he recovered.'"

"Hawise thought they were talking about you, my love," said Lydia.

"But they weren't, dada, they were talking about Tostig."

"Ah...."

"The hood man said, 'He's guilty of knowing too much.' Then the other one said, 'He doesn't know. He has no idea we know.' They walked around a bit and I couldn't hear what they said when they went to the bit by the wall, but then they walked back and I heard the hood man say 'he must be dealt with before he can realise that we know.'"

"The man Kineman, Aumary, wasn't convinced that killing Tostig was the answer," said my wife.

" 'I won't be part of any killing,' he said, dada. Then the hood man said, 'Too late for that,'" said Hawise.

"The hooded man said that Kineman would be well rewarded," continued Lydia.

"Then the cow man got very cross. He wasn't going to kill anyone. He said he wouldn't."

"This hooded man asked Kineman to kill Tostig, Hawise?"

My daughter shrugged. "I think so. The cow man belonged in the forest and it would be easy for him. The hood man didn't and it was more difficult to get there. He would be... erm...what did he say...? He would be suspected if he was found where he didn't belong. Like today, he said."

"Did you see any more of this man, Hawise, than you did last time you saw him?"

"No dada, he had his back to me still and I was up in the roof. He had his hood up too."

Hawise sighed. "They talked a bit more and argued quietly. Then the cowman left. The other one kicked the big post. He was angry. That made me jump because I was right above it. The bats fluttered... and... and...."

"Oh no. Don't tell me. The man looked up." I shielded my eyes with my hand in concern.

"Yes, he did."

"Did he see you?" I asked, my heart in my mouth.

"No, because I'd ducked back behind the stuff balanced on the beam and it was going quite dark by then."

"Thank God for that."

"The bats wriggled about a bit more and flew about then and then came back and then the man swore at them. I just managed to stop giggling at that."

"Good old Belvoir bats!" I said. "We must, tomorrow at first light, get hold of this Kineman and question him."

"There's more, Aumary," said Lydia, looking worried.

"Yes dada. I was just wriggling back down when I heard another voice. So I stopped where I was."

"And that was?"

"In the bit by the hay loft."

"Yes, I know it. Go on."

"It was Tostig. He came into the stable from the outside, carefully, on a stick as he still isn't quite better, and he looked back out of the door and shouted 'What are you doing here?'"

"So Tostig knew the man?"

"I think he only knew him a bit," said Hawise. "He didn't know his name or he would've shouted it wouldn't he? He would've said, 'What are you doing here, Alfred or Henry?' "

"Hawise, if ever I give up my job, I will just tell the King that you'll take over. You are very good at this sort of thing."

"I am?"

"You use your brains, my girl. That is very clever and just the sort of thing he would've said."

I saw Lydia smile.

"No dada, I don't think the King will let me. I am a girl and girls can't...."

"I'll have a word with him, Hawise...." I joked, winking at her.

Her eyes grew large, then, "Oh no...," she said, as she realised I was teasing her and she grinned and carried on.

"So Tostig asked him what he was doing. And the man said he had come to see you. That he had information for you."

"Did he now?"

"And Tostig said that he could tell him. But he wouldn't."

"Hawise, this man, he made no attempt to hurt Tostig then?"

"Cedric came into the stable and Ed was outside, I think. He couldn't touch him. There were too many people about and Tostig was standing a long way from the man."

"They all saw him?"

"Ah... today I asked Cedric and Edward if they'd seen him. They said they hadn't seen all of him in the dark," added my wife. "And they weren't really looking."

"Did you ask Tostig?"

Lydia and Hawise exchanged glances.

"We went looking for Tostig, Aumary," began Lydia.

"We couldn't find him, dada," finished Hawise. "We couldn't find him. Anywhere. No one could."

*****

I sat down, worried by this news.

"Have you found Alysoun and asked her if she's seen Tostig today?"

Again my girls exchanged a look. "Yes, dada. I ran up to Agnes' house. Alysoun was there doing some spinning and... Tostig wasn't there."

"She hadn't seen him since last night, Aumary," said Lydia.

"He's not back yet?"

"We haven't asked but no one has told us he's back and we left messages everywhere."

"And...," said Hawise. "There are no horses missing. Wherever he is, he was walking."

"Walking. But he isn't fully recovered. Right. We don't know that he is missing... really. He might just have decided to go -somewhere…."

"Like where, dada?"

"Well...." I hoped that Tostig had not had a night to sleep on his accidental meeting with the killer and had come to realise who he was and had gone to look for him... in town.

"Maybe he's gone to town."

"He didn't tell anyone. He would tell Richard. He's his master," said Hawise in such a grown up way I wondered if my daughter was eighteen and not coming up eight.

"He'd take a horse to town surely, Aumary? said Lydia.

"You know Tostig," I said lightly. "You know what he's like. Tomorrow at first light, we'll go out and look. I need to speak to Kineman too."

"Oh yes, dada... I forgot. Tostig asked the man his name as he left. So that he could say that he had been here and was asking after you."

"And did he give his name...?" I asked in desperate hope that it was this simple.

"Yes. I heard him say it, just his given name," said Hawise. "He's called Luke."

*****

I lay awake that night wondering who Luke was.

The only Luke I'd known in the town had been Luc Mason and he had been murdered last year. There was one other, I knew that, but he was a child of seven.

I worried about Tostig. I wondered about Pygge. Should I have gone out immediately to look for Tostig? What might we have achieved in the dark when we didn't know in which direction he'd gone?

As you can imagine, I got very little sleep that night and was up early and in my office consulting my maps of the forest before anyone had stirred.

Hal came into the office, yawning and ruffling his hair. His long beard had been washed and combed to perfection.

"So what's for today, sir?"

"I take it Tostig hasn't returned in the night?"

"No sir. I bin over to the stable. He's not there."

"Then we search," I said. "I'll draw up a list of people and we shall divide the forest into sections and quarter it."

"Before we do that sir, hadn't we better make sure Tostig isn't in the town? He might'a followed that fella back."

"I've thought of that, Hal. I've just sent Bill on Fitzroy to see if he's at the castle or at Gilbert's maybe or Johannes'."

I'd told him at supper about the cow man from Braydon Wood. I mentioned him again.

"'E's one of your tied men, 'in't 'e?"

I knuckled my tired eyes. "Yes he is. I cannot imagine how he's involved. He would need permission to leave the forest and he hasn't been to me to ask to go into town."

"The mistress says 'e came yesterday looking to see Henry or you for permission to take some cattle to the slaughter houses."

"Yes, and that's something else. That normally happens before Christmas. Why should they want to do it now?"

"An excuse?"

"We need to get Kineman in here."

"Right you are sir. I'll send Peter and Stephen shall I?"

"No, Hal. I have a better idea. We shall go to him. We'll divide the forest as I say and we shall take Braydon Wood and Thornhill, then Cadley and go as far as Kingstones. The others can do the rest."

The four of us rode out a little while later.

I've explained that the Forest of Savernake is an area of woods and glades with some meadows and commons between. On these grassy areas, we kept cattle. These were beasts raised for their beef, but mostly for their hides. The prosperity of Marlborough was predominantly based on the produce of the sheep. Wool was spun, woven, fulled and dyed in the town. There was also a thriving business in hides and our farms contributed to this wealth. As time marched on, the tanning industry would grow to become one of the most important trades in the town.

Kineman had a small cottage on the edge of the forest which looked out onto Braydon meadow. Here in summer my red cattle were scattered happily over the lush grass. Now they were confined until the spring, to the barn which sat close by the houses.

I hollered startling some starlings which had been sitting on the cottage roof. Two large black birds rose cawing from the space behind the barn. Ravens.

"Ho, Kineman!"

There was no answer.

"You know, sir," said Hal, "My Viking ancestors thought that ravens were the messengers of the Gods."

"Did they, Hal?"

Stephen crossed himself.

I dismounted and looked round. I yelled again. Kineman lived alone here but there were other cattle workers quite close by. Perhaps one of them would hear me.

"They are just large black carrion birds to me, Hal," I said.

I caught Hal's eye. Oh dear!

We raced for the back of the barn where we'd seen the birds.

"There, sir" said Hal. He pointed to a wattle fence which projected from the back of the building. We could see two legs sticking out.

There lay Kineman on his front, a knife protruding from his back. I looked at his knife sheath. Empty.

"Killed with 'is own knife," said Hal. "What an insult!"

I asked Peter and Stephen to look around for anything which might help us work out what had happened.

"Hal, am I right... did it rain in the night?"

"Aye sir, it did."

"Then our man here was killed before the rains came down for the ground is dry beneath him."

"It was raining when I made my last rounds of the manor." Hal always walked around the courtyard before retiring and he locked the sally port at the back of the kitchen and made sure that Wyot Gatekeeper had closed and locked the main gate.

"Yes. I went to the stable, as you know, to ask if Tostig had returned, before I went up to the solar. That was late. It wasn't raining then."

"It rained about the sixth hour of night, it did."

Hal looked round. Peter came out of the cottage and shrugged his shoulders. "Nothing."

Stephen came around the corner of the barn. "Can't find nothing what shouldn't be here. And no Tostig neither."

I nodded. "Stephen, can you ride to Red Vein Bottom and ask Bouvery to come up and look to these beasts? Peter, can you ride to the coroner and report the murder? Then come back to the forest and help to look for Tostig? After that you can go back to the castle."

My two men at arms rode off in opposite directions.

"Dead last night then, sir," said Hal.

"My guess is that he walked home in the semi-dark and he was surprised before he got into the house. His knife was grabbed and he was stuck before he'd time to turn."

"This Luke fella then?"

"Why would someone kill a lowly cattle man?"

"No, he was 'armless."

"We can't help him now, Hal. Let's continue looking for Tostig."

We rode through the forest on one of the straighter tracks, past the earthworks, to Cadley village.

People were just arriving for church, it being a Sunday.

Father Justin, the priest, was standing in the doorway of the tiny wooden building, greeting his parishioners. There were only a few, not above fifteen adults.

I raised my hand to him as I passed. "Good morrow, Father Justin."

He bowed. "God keep you, Sir Aumary. What brings you out on a Sunday morning? Is Father Crispin not preaching in Durley today, sir?"

"Father, might you travel out to Kineman's cottage and deal with his soul? He was murdered last night."

"Murdered?" he crossed himself, his face horror stuck. "Such wickedness!

Indeed I will."

"And yes, indeed, Father Crispin is preaching today. Sadly we have to be missing, for we are out looking for one of my men whom we think might also be in some danger."

His black eyebrow flew up into his hair. He put out a hand to the last one of his flock and chivvied them into entering the church.

"Who is missing, sir?"

"Tostig Frithson, one of my grooms."

" 'E in't bin seen since last evenin'," added Hal.

"And this danger?"

"His life has been attempted and he is still, it seems, at risk."

"This was the man whom you found near Cadley some while ago. Shot with an arrow?"

"The same. You haven't seen him, father?"

"Come into the church and I'll ask my flock," offered the priest.

We stood at the back by the door. It was not a large church: we could see everyone.

"My friends," said Father Justin, lifting his arms. "The Lord Belvoir is here looking for a man whom he says may be in danger of his life, but he is not a felon. This man was last seen I believe, in Durley village... is this correct, sir?"

I nodded. The whole congregation turned to the back with one movement. I couldn't see William Larkworthy but I recognised many faces. I raised my voice.

"The man is about thirty eight, small and well made, with blue eyes and fair hair. He will have been on foot and he was wearing a brown red tunic to the calf with a blue hood, leggings of brown, and short black boots. He had no coif. His name is Tostig Frithson."

There was an intake of breath. People stared at each other.

Suddenly a small voice piped up.

"I know Tostig."

I craned my neck.

"Yes, Nod, I expect you do."

"He's one of the horse men. I see him coming and going sometimes."

"Have you seen him recently, Nod?"

Aelfnod's mother shushed him and drew him to her side but he broke free. "Aye, I have, sir."

"Come up here, Nod, and tell me what you know."

People began to chatter and Father Justin quietened them with, "Does anyone else have anything to say?"

Most people shook their heads. Some looked vaguely around them.

"Then we shall begin our worship."

Nod came confidently up the nave and, taking him by the shoulder, we stepped out into the path before the little church. Hal closed the door quietly.

We heard the priest begin to intone the Latin mass, almost at a whisper, for many priests preferred it this way.

"Now, Nod, when did you last see Tostig?" I asked.

Nod wiped his nose on the back of his hand. "It was just after dark yesterday."

"What were you doin' out after dark, lad?" asked Hal.

"I was late with me chores and it was dark 'fore I finished, sir."

'Where did you see him?"

"It were just across the road. He were skulkin' around in the bushes."

"Was he indeed? Did it seem to you, Nod, that he was following someone?"

"He told me he was when I spoke to 'im."

"You spoke to him? What more did he say?" I asked gently.

"That the man he was follerin' was a murderer, sir and that I was to go 'ome."

"He had no horse?"

"No. He usually does du'n't he? That's why I went up to him, to pat the 'orse. But it weren't there."

"Where did he go?"

"Sorry sir?"

"After you spoke to him. Where did he go? Tostig ?"

"I di'n't go 'ome."

"No lad, I don't expect you did," said Hal with a chuckle.

"I watched him and follered 'im, sir. Well, it were eggcitin'. He were follerin' a murderer, sir." His voice was filled with the awe only the young can give such a terrible statement. His eyes glittered.

"Where did he go, Nod?"

"He crossed the road from there and came up here." He pointed past the church.

"Did you see the man he was following?" I asked.

"No, sir. But somethin' 'appened."

"What happened, Nod?"

"Like I told me Dad, Tostig went across the road and disappeared behind the church. Then I heard a sort 'a shuffling sound."

"And...."

"Tostig had gone, sir."

"And what did you do?"

The lad sniffed. "I ran 'ome an' told me Dad. He di'n't believe me. Said I was makin' it up an' sent me to bed."

I rubbed my forehead in frustration. "Your father didn't believe you?"

"No, sir. He said, 'What would this man be doing follerin' a killer,' sir. That was your job. 'He were just a groom', he said."

I shook my head. "Thank you, Nod."

I gripped his shoulder and he winced but never moved. "Now, show me where Tostig was when he disappeared."

He took us to the other side of the church. "About 'ere, sir."

We searched the ground. There were footprints in the damp ground but they were too scuffed to be of any use.

"A scuffle here, sir," said Hal bending, his hands on his knees. "No blood, praise be."

"The other fella, he had a 'orse," said Nod suddenly.

I fixed Nod with a stern stare.

"Do you know the horse?"

"It were a castle 'orse sir. One 'o them what has a mark on its flank."

"You could see this? In the dark?"

"Aye sir. I gotted up to it."

"And still, Nod, you didn't see the rider?" I said in exasperation.

"No sir. He'd gone by then."

"Where?"

"He were like one 'o them wraiths what Father Justin talks about. Just...."
Here the boy wriggled his fingers to simulate a disappearance. "Just disappeared
like smoke," he whispered.

Hal looked up at me. " 'E can't a' just disappeared, sir."

"No, Hal."

"Did you hear the horse being ridden off?" I asked Aelfnod.

"No sir, I ran home to tell me Dad an' he...."

"Sent you to bed without supper."

"Aye sir, 'cept me ma came in later and she'd kept some back fer me, she did."

I smiled indulgently.

"We must search the area thoroughly," I said, peering around into the
encroaching brush. "It seems Tostig didn't get further than this."

"Shall I go up to John at Furze Coppice? E's got the nearest group o' men
there. We'll need more folk to search," said Hal.

"Yes, Hal, good idea. I'll begin here."

Hal vaulted onto Grafton's back and was away, through the forest along the
lane known as Church Road.

"Can I help you, m'lord? asked Nod with bright eyes.

"No. Thank you Nod. You go back into the church. You have been a great
help already."

"What if the killer is still here, sir? I could...."

"That is very brave of you, Aelfnod, but I think he's long gone now. I just
hope he hasn't killed Tostig."

Nod's eyes grew wide and wild. "Nooo… I like Tostig!"

"So do I, Nod. So do I."

I searched, as best I could, the whole vicinity of the church, from the main road to the little lane along which Hal had disappeared. Right around in a circle. There was nothing more than the signs of the scuffle which we had already noted.

Inside the church the voice of Father Justin rose and fell and the liturgy carried over to me on the breeze with a familiarity born of the repetition of years. It seemed I was alone for an age.

Then there was silence.

It was a short while before everyone filed out of the church and made their way home. I saw Father Justin, divested of his robes, looking around.

I hailed him. "Here father."

He puffed up to me. "Was Aelfnod any help?"

"Indeed he was. Thank you."

"He's a bright lad. I've been teaching him to read, you know."

I nodded. "That's good. He's not only bright but observant."

"Aye," chuckled the priest, "that he is. Some might say nosey."

I shook my head, "Not me."

I turned to face him. "Father, might I come into the church to look?"

"Erm... By all means... step in."

I hadn't set foot in the nave of this church for many years; the last time being when I was in my early teens and had accompanied my father, Geoffrey Belvoir, to the funeral of one of his old friends. It had not changed a jot.

I looked up to the altar at the eastern end and nodded to it. I searched for a stoup and crossed myself with holy water.

"Might I search father? There may be something... I don't know what."

Father Justin grimaced. "The tower is a little rickety. I don't advise you go there but the rest of the place...."

"I must, sir priest. I will be careful."

Father Justin stood in front of me suddenly. "No sir, I cannot be responsible."

"Have you been up there lately?" I asked

"No, no... I... it's too unsafe. It's a very old building. Before the Conquest you know... I..."

"You seem very reluctant to let me see the tower, sir. I promise you I will tread carefully."

"I cannot allow it, sir."

I stared at him. He was very nervous, licking his lips and fiddling with the neck of his robe.

"What have you hidden away up there, sir, that you will not let me up to see?"

"Nothing, m'lord," said Father Justin weakly.

"Indeed Father. I am the lord of this place and I say, I will go up there."

I pushed past him and began to ascend the wobbly wooden stairs. I heard him sigh and then a few heartbeats later, follow me.

I reached to my hip and loosened the knife in its scabbard.

Reaching the bell tower I opened the door carefully.

There was a scuffling which was made by no rat or mouse I knew of. It was quite gloomy but there was enough light to see by. I looked past the single bell.

"Well, Pygge. This is a fine place to find you," I said.

The priest followed me into the room. I kept the wooden wall at my back.

"Sir Aumary," acknowledged Pygge, bowing.

"I'm sorry Henry. I couldn't stop him."

"It's all right Justin," said Pygge. "It doesn't matter. He's a good man."

I looked from one to the other.

"So, would someone like to tell me what is happening here?"

They looked at each other warily. "Come let's go to my house," said the priest. "We can tell the tale there."

*****

We sat together in the little house next to the church which belonged to the incumbent priest of Cadley.

"Refuge? You have taken refuge but not sanctuary?"

"I have no need of sanctuary, sir. I've done nothing wrong," said Henry Pygge.

"So tell me why are you here and not doing your duty at the castle?"

Pygge shifted his feet and looked at the floor. "I'm sorry for... for running away."

"Is that what you've done? Run away? Why?" I asked.

Father Justin put a cup of ale in front of me. I pushed it towards Henry. "You have it. It seems you are more in need of it than I."

The priest sat down at the head of his table. "Henry came to me a few days ago. He was...."

Pygge shook his head. "I don't mind saying it. I was... deranged, sir. Not in my right wits."

"Gone mad?" I asked.

"No sir. He was in deep despair and raving with unhappiness and anger."

I looked at them both and then I saw the resemblance.

"Henry is your brother, Justin?"

"Aye, sir, he is. My younger brother."

I smiled. "So the death of Elswith affected you more than you could know, Henry?" I was sure this was at the root of it.

Henry Pygge shrunk into his seat. "I couldn't accept that she was dead sir, even though I'd been to her burying. Even though she wasn't mine to grieve over."

"It's often the case, sir," said the priest of Cadley. "Folk often can't understand...."

"Yes, I know." I said. "You don't have to tell me."

There was a silence as the two men thought back to my own bereavements. Father Justin spoke first. "Aye, I remember."

"So you came here? Where Elswith is buried and where your brother could...."

"Give me comfort, sir?"

"Is there such a thing, Henry?"

He smiled weakly. "I don't know what I was doing, nor where I was going. My feet just took me. She wasn't my wife, sir. But I loved her. As long as she was in the world, it was a good place."

"I found him m'lord, outside at dusk, staring at the humped plot of Elswith

Larkworthy, blubbering and disorientated."

"You did what any priest would do. You took him in. Let alone a beloved brother."

"I did not want it to be known, in case those at the castle got wind and charged him with desertion, sir," answered the priest. "I know it was probably wrong."

"You think I would charge you with desertion of your duty, Pygge?" I said looking at him with what I'd hoped was sympathy.

He looked at me then with sad brown eyes. "I didn't know, sir."

I sighed. "I would have commanded you to take as long as you wished to be fully recovered and to decide what you wished to do."

The two men looked at each other. Pygge's mouth opened but no sound emerged. Then he swallowed some ale.

"I've had a few days to think, sir."

I heard Hal returning with the men in John Brenthall's group of searchers.

"And, Henry?"

The two brothers looked at each other. There was genuine love here.

"Henry would like to be released from his oath, sir. He no longer wishes to be a soldier."

I looked at Pygge carefully. I saw resolve in his face at last.

Hal entered the little room with a scrape on the open door.

"I found.... Well, well, Pygge?"

Henry Pygge smiled at Hal.

"I'll tell you the story in a while, Hal. Henry, I can release you. I know you never wanted to be a soldier. A wheelwright you said?"

"Nah sir... too late for that." He laughed. "I want...."

He took a deep breath. "I've been talking to my brother, sir."

"We have discussed this at length, Sir Aumary," said Father Justin with a serious tone to his voice.

"And I want to take the cowl, sir. I want to go to the Gilbertine Canons in town. If they'll have me."

Hal looked from one to the other.

"Brother...? Father? Cowl...? Well! I'll be bugg... buried in Burbage!"

Chapter Twelve

We emerged into the grey of the day and I acknowledged the group of people who had been searching Furze Copse.

"The last sighting of Tostig is here so can we fan out please and search the forest around about. All the brush. Everywhere."

I turned to Father Justin and to Henry Pygge. I squeezed his shoulder. "Good luck Henry. Oh...."

I took out the waxed tablet which I always carried and scribbled a note into it and gave it to Henry.

"No doubt your brother will read it to you when we have done."

It simply said that I released him from his place at the castle. He was, as of the date he left the place, no longer a soldier there.

"Take it into town with you and present it to Andrew Merriman. He knows my seal." I took off my seal ring and pressed it as hard as I could into the soft wax.

"He will give you the necessary papers to go to the priory and enrol as a free man. Tell them you come with my blessing. They know me there."

We shook hands to seal our bargain and shyly Henry Pygge thanked me.

My men were spreading out around the church. I took hold of Bayard's reins and ran him into the road.

John was sitting on Fire, his favourite mount, supervising the men at the far side of the road.

"Tostig was last seen here by the church. We can find no blood, thank Heaven, so this time he hasn't been injured and been dragged or crawled off the road."

"Aye, sir."

"Can you look at the tracks and see what you can find, John?"

John Brenthall was the finest tracker in the forest. He dismounted. "Hal will show you where he was last seen. And there's a horse to track too, John."

"One of ours, sir?"

"No, John. Tostig was on foot. Our murderer had a castle rouncey... again."

John ran off to find Hal who was in the coppice at the back of the church.

The men fanned out further and further. Henry and Justin went back into their house and the door closed. It went quiet save the crunching of the brushwood as folk systematically searched.

I went back to the church and pushed open the door. I stood looking at this ancient and holy place in which Savernake folk had worshipped for nigh on seven hundred years.

I walked up to the altar. The church was wooden and faced on the inside with plaster but the altar was stone, as was the font.

I looked up through the windows.

My own church at Durley now had glass in the windows but this ancient church had shutters folded back to the wall.

The plaster was painted with pictures and patterns. I noticed a representation of John the Baptist and another of Christ in Majesty. I turned. Above the wall to the bell tower was a picture of a very crude Adam and Eve in the garden with Eve's apple and serpent. I smiled. The serpent was a forest adder with a woman's head.

I took in a breath to chuckle at some more at the paintings and smelled smoke.

I tilted my head. Father Justin was cooking, I thought. I looked out of the window. Smoke trickled out of the little cottage's smoke hole.

I exited the church again and walked down the road to find Bayard where I'd left him.

John ran up. "Nothing sir, as yet."

"The horse?"

"Stood in the trees at the back of the church and then was ridden off down Church Lane."

"Not the main road?"

"No sir."

"Keep looking."

I leaned against Bayard's side and he turned to nuzzle my shoulder. I reached in my scrip and brought out an apple for him; one of last autumn's picking and a trifle wizened but he crunched it happily enough.

I smelled the smoke again and I realised how hungry I was, for I'd had nothing to eat or drink but had just come straight out at dawn.

To this day I have no idea what made me take one more perambulation of the church, but I left Bayard with a tap to his rump and told him to stay put and walked back up the little path.

I began at the church door and walked round the western end first. I'd reached the eastern side when once again I smelled the smoke. Only this time it was much stronger.

The churchyard here was overgrown. The congregation was so small in Cadley that any burials were made at the western and southern sides, nearest the road. There was a small but serviceable path right round the church but beyond a few feet there was nothing but brush and scrub.

I struggled to the southern side. The smoke here was visible, coming from the base of the southern wall of the church.

Batting the smoke from my eyes I peered down.

Nothing. Just a wooden wall which was built on a stone plinth. The split oak logs were laid in vertical lines and were filled in between with a lime mixture. As I'd seen, the inside was plastered.

Smoke was now pouring from the plinth of the little church.

I ran round the building up to the priest's house, hammered on the door and pushed it open. "Justin... what is under the church?"

"Under it, sir?"

"Yes, under it man!"

"Why... nothing, sir. There is no crypt. Never has been. Why do you want to know?"

"Are there any doorways inside which have perhaps been blocked up?"

"No sir. There is but one door. The one you came through. There isn't even a door to the tower at the western end."

"Well, there's a fire somewhere at the base of the church and smoke is pouring from the plinth. There must be a space under the floor."

"No sir. There are no trap doors or stairs…"

"Come man, I'll show you."

Father Justin, Pygge and I ran back to the church and I took them to the southern side. I saw Father Justin cross himself.

"No, sir. It's just not possible. There's nothing. I've been here seventeen years and I have never known there to be a crypt."

"The previous man didn't say anything?"

"No sir… Oh… Oh…." We all started to cough.

I took out my sword and made to slash at the plants growing up the wall. The ivy and briars, the dead plants and stalks. There was one very old yew tree here which was practically growing from the wall. I slashed at it.

Pygge pulled the vegetation away with his bare hands.

"Mercy me!" shouted Father Justin, coughing, "There's a tiny door."

It was indeed a small silver grey oaken door with rusting iron hinges and it was set into the plinth and part of the wooden wall of the church. There were three small steps down, filled in with vegetation. I kicked at the door and there was a hollow bang. Both Pygge and I kicked hard at it.

The central stave of the door buckled. We kicked it again. And again.

The ancient door fell into itself with a splintering sound.

Smoke poured out at a great rate now. I pulled my shirt up over my nose and mouth and tied the neck, which yesterday my son Simon had been sucking, in a knot. It was a little stiffened but it held. I plunged my head into the space.

Pygge followed.

I yelled at the priest. "Fetch help… my men are round about."

It was dark in the hole beneath the church. The only light came from the now ruined doorway.

I narrowed my eyes against the smoke. To enter the place one had to step down three inner steps and then jump down about four feet.

I felt Pygge at my back taking in the sight before him with the same smoke filled eyes as myself. He coughed.

"Put something over your mouth Pygge," I yelled. The man obeyed and fetched his tunic above his chin and pulled it over his mouth and nose.

"There sir!" he pointed.

Ours eyes were becoming adjusted to the complete darkness of the furthest wall, no more than twelve feet away.

There a man lay bound hand and foot. There was a stool in the room but it was tipped over. I jumped down. Pygge followed.

Reaching out I was burned by the flames licking around the debris on the floor.

I snatched my hand back and tried to stamp on the flames. Pygge too reached forward to the prostrate man and pulled him by a free end of the rope binding him, away from the flames licking around the floor.

I leapt back as a flame, hungry for a new victim, flickered up to the ceiling and took hold. A pile of rubbish in a corner was well alight and most of the smoke came from this.

I pulled my cotte over my head and used it to beat back the flames which licked around the man on the floor. He was unconscious for he neither spoke, coughed nor moved. Please God, I thought, if this is Tostig, let him be alive.

Pygge had more confidence now and leapt forward to grab the man I thought was Tostig and pulled him free of the flames.

He stood upright and as he did, a beam from above slid inexorably into the void beneath.

"Watch out," I cried and made a grab for Pygge's clothing. The beam hit him on the shoulder and he staggered and fell to his knees with a scream. I tried to catch him under the armpits but was unable to reach him.

In the next moment, accompanied by much shouting from outside, the rest of the ceiling began to crumble slowly into the subterranean room.

I felt heat at my back and turned to see the doorway aflame as the dry and ancient wooden planking of the wall of the church began to burn in earnest.

Phil Wheelwright the younger was suddenly at my elbow and was dragging the man on the floor up the steps and out through the burning doorway. He handed the man up to our brawny farrier and blacksmith, Hubert Alder.

I turned back to see Pygge struggling with the huge beam which had pinned him by the leg and which was burning fiercely.

"Go sir... get out!" he screamed.

"Hubert!" I yelled to the doorway... in here."

Someone fanned the doorway flames and they receded enough for Hubert, who was very tall, to bend double and duck under the lintel or what was left of it.

He reached the stricken Pygge, lifted the fiery beam as if it were made of parchment and took him up under one arm as I threw the beam away from us, burning my hands. The man was large and heavy and Hubert struggled to the door. I pushed them along, holding Pygge's legs.

More shifting and collapsing ensued and the whole of the room now growled in an inferno as the floor of the church above at last dissolved into the space beneath and air was sucked into the room. There was a deafening roar and as Pygge's legs receded through the doorhole, I raced for the gaps the whole lot went 'whoosh' in flame.

I vaulted the step, leapt through the door and turned a somersault, much as my father had taught me to do when falling from a moving horse.

Next I knew I was retching and coughing and looking up at the trees.

Hal came up and got me under the arms and pulled me further away from the inferno into the old dried bracken and bush, where I lay panting and coughing by turns.

"Tostig?"

"Aye lad."

"Alive?"

"Just"

"Pygge?"

"Burned but alive."

"Hubert?"

"Coughin' and cursin'. His lovely black locks are singed, sir," he said with mock sympathy.

I laughed then, till I dissolved into more coughing and had no breath left.

*****

It was a while before I could get up and see what was happening.

The church was ablaze. Folk from the village were chucking water on it but it made very little difference. The thatch slid down in a wall of flame and I heard a 'Ware!' shouted by someone as it landed on the northern side with a thump and crackle.

The flames hissed and steamed as the water hit them. The timbers cracked and bowed. All this was overlaid with shouting and the sound of running to and fro to the pond across the main road.

John came and found me. "Sir, come and look at this."

As I passed one of the village tithing men I grabbed him. "Alfred, can you get a cart and put Tostig and Pygge and anyone else hurt into it, and get someone to take it to Dr Johannes of Salerno's house... quickly."

He tugged his forelock, "Aye, sir."

I bowled after John into the undergrowth at the back of the church.

John stood looking down at what seemed like a hole in the ground only twenty or so feet from the church.

Men were clearing the brush from around what looked like stone steps.

"Been used recently, sir," said John. "Mud here on the first step and broken stems where something has passed."

I leaned into the hole. "Clear it and then we'll go down."

"It's very finely built in stone, sir. I doubt it has anything to do with the church."

"We'll look," I said.

I turned back to stare at the church. The fire was beginning to take hold of the walls good and proper; I could feel the heat generated from here. There would be nothing left above ground. All those lovely paintings gone. The cleverly constructed wooden paling of the walls was burning with gusto. Dried ancient timbers were going up like a Beltane bonfire. I watched as the tower began to topple.

"Watch out... the tower!" I yelled to a group of workers feverishly throwing water at the western end.

They all moved back as a man. Down came the construction in almost one piece. Timbers and sparks flew everywhere. The bell clanged. The bracken where the tower had fallen was damp from the overnight rain or we might have had a forest fire to contain too.

"Quick! I yelled, "Soak the thatch of the priest's house!"

Several flickering sparks had fanned out on the air and were heading for the priest's thatch.

The group took their buckets and brushes and disappeared round the side of the cottage.

John had finished clearing the steps. "Three small steps down, sir, the rest is covered by soil. I think the whole flight is about twelve steps and five feet wide. It's so overgrown with moss and soil."

I furrowed my brow in puzzlement. Whatever could this be?

"I'll go first. You follow, John."

I stepped gingerly onto the first step. It rocked and I balanced myself carefully. Three steps down and I found a flight of twelve wide steps descending into a passage with stone walls.

It was a beautifully constructed barrel vaulted passage of cut stone about ten feet wide.

I backed to where John was coming in.

"We shall need a few lights, John... there's not a chink coming in beyond the three feet of the outside."

John carried a candle and I gave him mine from my scrip which he lit from his own. I always carried a stub for emergencies. Together we walked down the passageway.

Soil and roots had done their damage to the roof and there had been a few falls here and there. We walked around the debris littering the floor. John ducked under a stone which was teetering and threatening to fall.

His eye caught something. "See here, sir." He hunkered down.

"Footmarks in the dust. Lots of them," I said, walking back and bending to look. "This has been used regularly, unlike the little door in the church."

"Well laid flagstone floor, sir, even though some are broken and disturbed."

"Listen. Can you hear the fire?"

We stood silently for a heartbeat.

"I can sir, a little, I think," said John.

We could hear the timbers of the roof still falling into the nave of the little church with a thud, almost above us.

"Go on as far as we can."

We walked on a few more paces, the gentle yellow light of our candles steady for there was no breeze here to waver them.

"No further," I said.

There had been a fall of the roof here and blocks were piled up one on another.

"I have a feeling that if we clamber over we shall be in the crypt of the church and I have no desire to be roasted like a boar."

John again bent over, wonder in his voice. "Look at this."

On the floor, inset into the flagstones, was a picture made in tiny pieces of stone fitted together. I could just make out in the poor light, a hooked dagger and a torch set at angles to each other. I dusted off the stone picture.

"A dagger, a torch and what looks like a cup or bowl."

"What is it, do you think, sir?"

I shook my head. "I don't know. Obviously this building was here before the church was built and it was accessed by those steps and this corridor."

Another beam fell into the nave with a thud. "C'mon. We will have to wait for the fire to die down before we can truly see what we have."

We turned about and made our way out again. My candle stub was almost burned down and wax was dripping onto my fingers. I blew it out and dropped it.

Some of the villagers were using hay forks to pull down the burning thatch and wood, spreading it out on the ground and eliminating the fire.

"It will be tomorrow before we can go in there and look," I said.

"We need it to rain," said Hal's voice behind me.

"Hal, have the injured been taken to Johannes?"

"They 'ave, sir."

"Was Tostig...."

"No sir, still sleepin' in his own 'ead. Not a word."

"Then I'll ride down to town and have a word with him if I can." I said. "He knows who the murderer is and I want his name."

"You 'ave his name sir... Luke...."

"No, Hal...I think that was just to put us off the scent."

Father Justin came bustling up. His eyes were red with smoke and his face black with soot.

"Gone m'lord. All gone... nothing left."

I put my arm over his shoulder. "We can rebuild and build in stone, Father. Like the phoenix, the church will rise again bigger and better."

"But that costs money, sir," he sniffed.

"We'll find it somehow."

"How is this tiny place to afford such lucrum, m'lord? We have no surplus money to...."

I patted his back. "Let me worry about that, Father Justin."

I strode down the path and recovered Bayard who was cropping the meagre grasses of the road verge at the far side, away from the fire.

I had my foot in the stirrup before I realised what the priest had said.

I did not need to ask Tostig what he knew about our killer.

I knew who it was.

*****

I rode into Marlborough; my head full of unspoken thoughts.

Johannes was in his workshop bending over the leg of poor Pygge. The man was moaning and grimacing and gritting his teeth.

"How is it, Johannes?" I asked.

"The leg is badly burned. The beam was alight when it hit him and it has burned through a deal of the poor man's flesh. I doubt he will ever walk properly again." He turned away.

"That is if I can save the leg," he whispered.

"And Tostig?"

He nodded to the corner where stood his small infirmary bed. Tostig lay, his head swathed in a bandage.

"Oh no, not his head again."

"The back this time, not the side like last time."

"Small consolation."

I hunkered down by the bed. "Tostig, can you hear me?"

My groom stirred and his eyes opened.

His speech was slurred. "Sir Aumary?"

"The doctor tells me you have a hard head, Tostig."

The man managed a smile, then closed his eyes again.

"Can I just say a name to you and I want you to tell me if this is the man who hit you and whom you think might have killed Elswith?"

Tostig didn't risk a nod of his head but lifted his hand.

I leaned to his ear and mouthed the name. Tostig's eyes flashed open.

"Yes, sir."

"Thank you. I think I know what has been happening now."

I squeezed his hand. "Sleep, and we shall see about getting you home to Alysoun."

He smiled again.

Johannes turned back to me. "Are you sure you know who it is now?"

"Oh yes. I've pieced it together and Tostig has just confirmed it. We have been led a merry dance. The man has been going by his nickname. That is one of the reasons why we haven't been able to unmask him. He's played with us. Teased us."

"I told you he was playing a game," said Johannes.

"All the time we thought him a friend when he was a vicious foe."

Johannes dipped his hand into a sticky substance and gently slathered it onto Pygge's burnt leg. Pygge grimaced then winced but lay still.

I sniffed. "Ah! That brings back memories."

Johannes turned to me with a puzzled expression.

"The day Lydia and I met when I burnt my hand and you made me spread that foul concoction on it."

Light dawned and Johannes chuckled. "Saved your skin though didn't it."

"I hope you can do the same for Henry." I leaned over. "Tsooo, that looks terrible."

"It is," said the doctor.

*****

I walked down the High Street in the direction of Gilbert's house. I found him in his yard at a trestle table cutting up skins and I brought him up to date with the latest developments.

"Thanks for your note, Gil."

"It was no hardship to speak to my mates. I thought you'd need to know who had bought clothes." He carried on cutting.

"Gil, tell me; the day of Elswith's murder, you remember telling me who you saw that morning. Tell me again, in detail."

Gilbert paused in his cutting, then wrinkled his brow and reiterated his tale. I nodded, "Thanks."

"So why do you think this Luke fella has been going round disposing of folk then, sir?"

"The first murder was to cover his tracks. Elswith knew about his illegal trade and told him she was going to the authorities. The thing I don't know is exactly what she knew and how she knew it."

"Beecroft was in on it and what... got greedy?"

"I think so. Beecroft wasn't the brains. He was just the errand boy. Carrier knew who the murderer was because he saw him take a rouncey out of the stable once or twice and put two and two together and...."

"Canard?"

"Ah. That threw us for a while but sadly, that was nothing to do with our murderer. Oh yes, Canard knew what had been going on; he was one of the soldiers who often worked at the mint and perhaps the killer would have disposed of him later but Bunce did it for him."

"An accident then."

"I'm sorry to say, yes, it was."

"And you sir?"

"I was getting too close. The killer panicked. I had to be eliminated."

"Ah. And poor Tostig?"

"He'd been in the stables asking questions. Our killer thought he was safe. Tostig had learned something which, he didn't really piece together until he'd thought about it recently. The murderer came to Durley yesterday... an audacious move. Like I say, he's panicking now. He'd hoped to do away with my groom quietly and carefully that evening but then a thought struck him. What if Tostig had already told me?"

"Ah." Gilbert waved his sharp shears about. "The killer wasn't to know you hadn't spoken to him about what he'd remembered and thought, was he?"

"He made sure that Tostig saw him and made sure he followed. He locked him up, I think, until he could return and torture him to find out what he'd told me."

"But he never got the chance because you found him."

"Thank Heaven we did. If he'd had the chance to find out, Tostig would be dead and our murderer either long gone or bluffing it out with me, inventing excuses, having had time to think. He's a very sharp man."

"But you worked it out without Tostig's help?"

"Just something which Father Justin said. Oh yes, and something both Hawise and Mistress Scarlett misheard."

"Clever that. Not many folks know Latin."

"Like I say, our killer is a clever man."

"Ah but m'lord, you'm cleverer," said Gilbert, grinning.

*****

There was one other person I needed to confide in then I'd confront our killer. Why had I not asked Gayle before?

Because I had taken the word of a respected man without demur. I hadn't even thought to question what the culprit had told me. I felt a fool for that but then in the next breath was telling myself, if you didn't believe what people told you, you'd be forever questioning and checking. Life isn't like that. It cannot be.

When someone tells you they are called Henry, you never think, for example, that they might also be called Harry, or Luke, or have a nickname like Hairy, Bunce's soldier friend, Hereward.

When someone says that they are worked off their feet when actually, they aren't, who are you to disbelieve them?

If you are told that their day is a busy one and that person's word seems beyond reproach, who are you to question it? Why would they lie to you, you'd think?

I was crossing the drawbridge of the castle when I heard my name called. I looked back over my shoulder.

Coming at a pace up the road from the town bridge was Davie, the young lad from the castle kitchen. His father was one of the cooks there. I'd used Davie before as an errand boy and he was reliable. Gayle had put him in charge of watching the moatside, as I'd asked.

I waited for him to catch up.

"Sir Aumary!"

"Davie. Catch your breath."

Davie had been watching for the moatside fishermen today, since it was a Sunday and a day off.

"Come with me."

Davie followed me into the castle and I turned to the right and unlocked the office door. The boy was reluctant to follow me in but I reached for his arm and he gave in.

"I don't want us to be overheard and I don't want you seen with me, Davie." I looked out of the door, right and left and then shut and locked it again.

"So where did you hide?"

"By the sluice, sir."

"Good place. Quiet and secret."

"And no one comes by it much but I had a good view from there," said Davie.

"And how many days did you give it, Davie?"

"Three sir. Like Master Gayle said."

"Did he now? And how long did he ask you to watch?"

"In four hour watches, sir."

"From dawn?"

"No sir, the times the men takes breaks and have their dinner and that...."

I rubbed my forehead in frustration. I'd been such a fool.

"So what happened?"

"No one came, sir."

"No one at all?"

"No sir." Davie stood tall. "I didn't leave till it was dark and I only went to have something to eat when I knew they was all at work busy and wouldn't come out."

"Thank you Davie. It wasn't what I wanted to hear but you did well."

"I didn't even leave for...." He giggled then whispered, "I even peed in the moat, Sir Aumary."

"You're a good lad... here." I tossed him a coin.

"There's some huge fish in that moat sir. I saw 'em." He bit the coins as he'd seen his elders do.

I chuckled. "I'm sure."

"That fella from the mint he feeds 'em he does. Perhaps that's why they'm'z so big."

I laughed. "Bits of food thrown out of the window into the moat eh?"

"Yes sir. Sometimes the bits of bread and that land on the grass and the ducks come to gobble it up. And the geese."

I chortled. "Bunce the gate guard was trying to get an arrow into one of those geese for his supper when he slipped on the wet stone and fell in the moat."

Davie laughed. "They're always there now, cos they knows theym'z going to get fed."

I stopped and sat down.

I stared into space.

"Sir? You all right, sir? Shall I call for the doctor? Youm'z gone a very funny colour, sir."

I blinked. "No Davie, it's fine."

I unlocked the door and made sure the lad wasn't seen scurrying away back to the kitchens.

'Idiot! Idiot!' I said to myself. Not only did I now know who our murderer was. I knew also why he had killed and what it was poor Elswith Larkworthy had seen which had cost her, her life.

*****

I found Gayle in his small office next to mine, sitting with his feet up on his table and a mug of ale clasped to his bosom. Well, it was Sunday.

"Ah, Sir Aumary. How are you now?" He stood up.

"As well as can be expected Pete. You know... how long have we known each other now?"

Gayle put down his mug.

"Must be, nigh on four years now, sir."

"And still you give me my title each time we meet and call me, sir."

Gayle blinked. "Aye, I do. Seems right and proper to me. You being a knight and a lord and that."

"Pete, please call me by my name. I think it's time now. And there is no need either, to bob up and down like a... like a strutting pigeon when I walk in, you know."

Pete laughed at that. "Well, if you insist." He sat down.

"Has my kitchen lad come back to you?"

"He has and there is no action at the side of the moat."

Gayle sighed. "Then our fishermen were just that, fishing and the one won't go there without the other."

"I think one will... now... but probably after dark."

I told Gayle what I suspected.

He jumped upright. "The conniving...."

"Just to be sure, Pete. Tell me, what is the routine for the staffing of the stable?"

"The stable?" Gayle was seated again and I perched on the edge of the table.

"The men are detailed by rota."

"You do that don't you?"

"Aye, I do."

"So it's not the same people each day?"

"Oh yes, but they work at different times. Even though the castle opens at dawn and closes at dusk, the stable has to be open to all, all the time."

"In case a courier or a traveller or a visitor should come in after dusk and before dawn?"

"You know what these couriers are like. Any hour of the day or night."

"John my forester called them 'driven men,' once."

Gayle chuckled. "They seem like it."

"So there's always someone on duty. Day and night?"

"Yes, and we have a rota. They work from dawn till the eighth hour and then another lot take over and work till dusk or another eight hours and so on."

He counted on his fingers.

"Everyone contributes. The King has been known to descend on us with his retinue well into the night so we need people on duty."

"Ah yes. John also is driven, I think," I said, smiling.

"Whatever we might think of him Si... Aumary, he's a hard worker and he expects the same hard work from all his men."

"Don't we know that?" I roared. "You're doing the job of three men and I'm split four ways!"

"Why do you want to know?"

"I'm checking my facts. I heard someone say that there was also a rota for the farriers."

"Again to make sure there's always one on duty."

"And the forge and treasury?"

"The soldiers who guard the treasury, as you know, are also those who patrol the walls. In bad weather it's not so good to have them standing about in wind, rain and cold."

"The gate guards have their warm little cubby hole. The soldiers patrolling the walls do so every so often and can get into the warmth every circuit. Why not treasury guards eh?"

"Of course."

"And the moneyer?"

"He's his own man but he can go out should he wish."

"He'd need not go from the forge to the latrines?"

Gayle's head tilted. "Yes, and the forge is guarded if he goes off by one of the treasury men."

"Who suggested this, anyone in particular?"

"Oh... it's been in operation so long... I can't remember."

"So if someone wanted some time off to go out of the castle?"

"If they want to be absent it's up to them. They'd have to make sure that they made up time by exchanging with one of their fellows." Pete looked bemused. "Why?"

"Think about it, Pete. Our killer is able to come and go at will. He is often out at dusk, when everyone is going home, yes, but he has been out and about in the middle of the day too."

"...and he knows the staff at the stable, when they'll be on duty," he said wide eyed.

"When Beecroft would be on duty. He could take a rouncey out then, with no problem at all and be off up into the forest quickly and return quickly, though why he needs to be in the forest I don't know. He doesn't have to walk. When Beecroft became a problem to him, he got rid of him. Then he had to pretend to be a courier for he had no helping hand in the stable. Carrier knew this and was killed for it."

"Who is it Aumary... who's the killer?" By his face I think he already knew, for he was thinking back to how many times he'd seen this man missing from his work.

I told him.

"He's a respected man. No one is going to gainsay him," I said. "Both you and I have been taken in by him because he's a figure of authority. What he tells us will be believed. And what he's told us is not always the truth. Thinking about it I only recently concluded that you and I have been separated more often than not when this man has been speaking to us. Unless I repeated to you what he told me, he could not be contradicted."

"Lord have mercy!" said Gayle. "So what do we do?"

I sat down and drummed my fingers on his table. "I think we watch him. It's the only way."

"Catch him at it eh, Aumary?"

"Yes, my friend... and watch him try to squirm his way out of it."

Chapter Thirteen

I found Stephen and Peter in their lodgings in the garrison dormitory. They looked at me with a sigh and a grimace when I asked them to go out into the cold of the night and watch the moatside under the mint wall windows, but they donned their warm thick cloaks and prepared for a night in the open.

"The watch will patrol the walls, as they do every hour. Andrew Merriman is on tonight. I'll tell him you are out and about and that he's not to worry about what you are up to," I smiled.

"Aye," said Stephen, sniffing. "I don't want to be skewered by a friendly arrow fer just doin' me job, like Canard."

"I'll make sure they know. Take your knives but no swords. I think you'll be safe enough if you just watch and follow. No heroics now."

"Where will you be, sir?"

"Here in my office. Come at any time and knock on the door three times. I'll open it and take a report."

"Yessir."

They clomped their way down the steps and out into the bailey. I went to find my friend Andrew Merriman, told him what I had planned, then lay down on a pallet to sleep a few hours.

My men came in just on dawn, wet and disgruntled. Nothing had happened that night.

Later that morning I made my way to the wooden drawbridge and jumped down from the platform, landing with a squish on the muddy ground by the castle wall. It had been raining much of the night. The verge here was about three to four feet wide; it was kept free of vegetation so that no one could swim the moat without being seen and no plant offered them a hand hold. The moat was usually full of water right to the wall but in times of peace we didn't top it up by opening the sluice, so leaving more water in the river. I rounded the southerly turret and gingerly made my way towards the south wall. I looked up. The narrow squint of a window was quite a few feet above my head.

I looked down at my feet.

Well, well, just as I had thought. Amongst the muddy grass were some dull pellets. I picked one up and rolled it between my fingers. It was a small ingot of iron. Someone had thrown it out of the window.

I stuffed the ingot in my purse and walked back into the castle.

There was no point in wasting my day waiting, so I wandered up to Johannes house in the hope of some decent food for dinner. I was not disappointed. Little Agnes, Johannes' housekeeper had managed to buy a pastry roll and was busy filling it with diced meat and vegetables.

Her face gleamed when she saw me poke my head around the door and she beckoned me to enter.

I embraced her with one arm around her shoulder and then told her I must go and see Tostig and Henry Pygge. She told me Johannes was out, he'd be back later. He'd only gone up Kingsbury Hill to Gabriel Gallipot's apothecary for the week's supplies as he always did on a Monday.

I opened the door to the infirmary, as I had begun to call it, even if only in my own head.

Tostig was sitting up chatting to Henry who was lying with his leg on a contraption which was a sling of light material, roped to the beam above his head.

I frowned. "What on earth is this thing?" I asked, coming in and shutting the door.

Tostig chuckled. "One of the doctor's inventions." His eyes raised up to Heaven.

Henry was looking pained but better than I'd seen him yesterday.

"It's to keep my leg from contact with the bed and to drain the fluids, says the doctor. I must say, it's more comfortable than having the bedclothes pressing on it, sir," said Pygge.

"Johannes hates to have anything covered you know," I laughed. "Air is good he says."

We all chuckled. "So, how are my two brave lads coping, eh?" I asked, reaching for a wooden item on Johannes' table and examining it. I had no idea what it was. I put it down.

Tostig answered first, "Better, thank you, sir. Master Hal is coming back later and we shall go home."

"Good."

"I'll feel better though, sir, when you get that bastard who hit me."

"Tell me what happened."

Tostig shifted on the edge of his bed. "I saw the man in the stable... or rather coming out of it...."

"At Durley?"

"Yessir. Suddenly I thought about what had been said in the stable in the castle. You remember when you sent me to talk to the grooms."

"I do."

"I told you, I think, that they were very tight lipped about the comings and goings."

"You did."

"I was talking to one fella with his friends looking on and in comes a man. They all went silent like a charm of goldfinches at a sparhawk, sir. They'd already told me that one man who shouldn't have been there and who could ride had ridden out a couple of times when Beecroft was alive."

"So it was obvious they knew something."

"Oh they were afraid of him, sir. No doubt."

"Why didn't you tell me before?"

Tostig smiled sheepishly. "I wanted to find out the man's name but... all I could get out of them was sniggers at first."

I saw Pygge blink and look up at the ceiling. Leave him be for the time being, I thought. He's enough to deal with.

"He swaggered around a bit, saw me - and then he went, just like that."

"That's when you asked directly who it was."

"Yes, and they told me it was, what I thought was Luke, sir."

"Hmm."

"It was this man I saw at Durley and I wondered what the devil he was doing there. He'd no need to be there."

"So you challenged him."

"How did you know, sir?" asked Tostig, sitting up as straight as he could.

"You have the Lady Hawise to thank for that, Tostig. She heard the conversation between the mint man and one of our cattlemen... I still don't know his involvement... but I will... soon. She knew they were up to no good."

Tostig frowned. "I didn't see her, sir."

I laughed. "No... she was... erm...." I rubbed the side of my nose, "up in the rafters watching the bats."

"Bats, sir?" chuckled Tostig.

"Hmmm."

"Most young ladies of her standing would be frightened of bats, sir."

"Not our Hawise."

"Well, you can thank her from me...," began Tostig. "Sir... the man didn't see her, did he?" His face was worried.

"No Tostig. Have no fear."

He gave a small nod. "I wasn't satisfied with the man's answer sir. He was off on his horse and I thought to follow."

"You didn't take a horse?"

"No sir, he'd hear that. I went on foot. Running. It wasn't easy with my wound paining me but... he dawdled a bit, I'll give him that."

"You reached Cadley?"

"Aye, sir. He tethered his horse behind the church. It was really dark then."

"And you met young Nod."

Tostig's eyes widened. "You've spoken to him, sir?"

"Aye, I have. Thanks to him we knew you'd not left the vicinity of the church."

"Seems I have a couple of children to thank for my safety, sir," said Tostig, grinning.

"So what happened then?"

"I followed. He just disappeared."

I wriggled my fingers like Nod had done. "Like a wraith... or so Nod said."

"I'd told Nod to go home. I was worried for his safety."

"And he for yours."

Tostig touched his bandaged head. "Then the man just reared up out of the ground and hit me."

"It was an underground chamber beneath the church. The steps are some feet away in the undergrowth. We've yet to investigate it; we shall when the fire has cooled."

Tostig looked a little sheepishly at me. "Ah, yes, sir. I'm sorry, that was my doing."

"Hmmm?"

"I woke once to find I'd been tied to a stool. I wriggled. It was fiendishly dark in there except for one small stub of a candle which the killer had left. I tried to get free and knocked over the stool... and then...."

"The candle?" I asked.

"Yes. I blacked out again as I fell, hitting my bad head again."

"The church is burned to a cinder."

Tostig put his hands to his face. "Mother of God, whatever can I do to put that right?"

I shook my head. "So the candle ignited the rubbish and the whole place went up in smoke with you at the centre of it."

"I suppose so, sir. I felt Pygge here grab me and pull me free and then... nothing until I woke up here bandaged and trussed up like a parcel of washing, sir."

I stood up and gripped his shoulder. "You were exceedingly lucky. Nothing to be done. You are both alive and for that I give thanks to God."

Pygge's gaze came down from the rafters. "Sir, I knew that Canard was edgy and worried but I couldn't tell what was happening."

"Oh, I know, Pygge. It's a very clever deception. Canard suspected who the murderer was but was probably unable to prove it. I don't wonder you weren't sure what was happening. Why, I myself have only just worked it out and I'm on